Double TROUBLE

by **Joyce Carol Oates**

WRITING AS 'ROSAMOND SMITH'

CRIME NOVEL

A HARD CASE CRIME BOOK
(HCC-168)
First Hard Case Crime edition: February 2026

Published by
Titan Books
A division of Titan Publishing Group Ltd
144 Southwark Street
London SE1 0UP

in collaboration with Winterfall LLC

Hardcover ISBN 978-1-83541-721-8
Paperback ISBN 978-1-83541-544-3
E-book ISBN 978-1-83541-545-0

Design direction by Max Phillips
www.signalfoundry.com

Typeset by Swordsmith Productions

The name "Hard Case Crime" and the Hard Case Crime logo are trademarks of Winterfall LLC. Hard Case Crime books are selected and edited by Charles Ardai.

Printed and bound by CPI (UK) Ltd, Croydon CR0 4YY

EU RP (FOR AUTHORITIES ONLY):
eucomply OÜ, Pärnu mnt. 139b-14, 11317 Tallinn, Estonia
hello@eucompliancepartner.com,+3375690241

Visit us on the web at www.HardCaseCrime.com

CONTENTS

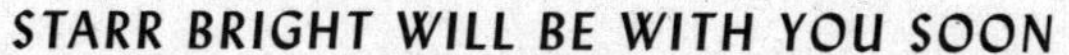

STARR BRIGHT WILL BE WITH YOU SOON

For John Hawkins, long a secret sharer

I resolved in my future conduct to redeem the past.
—Robert Louis Stevenson, *Dr. Jekyll and Mr. Hyde*

How many of you pigs. Emissaries of Satan. Adulterers in your hearts & fornicators. How many rapists & despoilers of the innocent, how many creatures groveling in lust. How many of you deserving of God's wrath STARR BRIGHT might have killed & chastised had I not been run to earth before my time I cannot know for such knowledge is withheld from us in the wisdom & comfort of the LORD GOD. AMEN

I
At the Paradise Motel, Sparks, Nevada

In the desert, through shimmering planes of light, the hazy mauve mountains of the Sierra Nevada in the distance, autumn sunshine fell vertical, sharp as a razorblade. The sky was a hard ceramic blue that looked painted and without depth as a stage backdrop. "Starr Bright" woke startled from her druggy reverie of the past several hours wondering where she was, and with whom. A familiar-unfamiliar succession of motels, restaurants, gas stations, enormous billboards in Day-Glo colors advertising casinos in Reno and Las Vegas—but it was CITY LIMITS SPARKS, NEVADA they were entering, Billy Ray Cobb behind the wheel of his classy rented platinum-gray Infiniti with the red leather interior smelling of newness. "Starr Bright" removed her smoke-tinted designer sunglasses with the dazzling white frames to see more clearly, but the glare was blinding. Her eyes felt naked, exposed. She wasn't a girl for the harsh overexposed hours of morning or afternoon in the desert, her nocturnal soul best roused at twilight when neon lights flashed and pulsed into life. *But why am I here, why now? And with whom?*

Not knowing she was awaiting God's sign.

Proud and perky behind the wheel of the Infiniti like an upright bulldog was Mr. Cobb of Elton, California, an electrical supplies manufacturer's representative—as he'd introduced himself the previous evening at the Kings Club. A sporty fun-loving loud-laughing man of any age between forty-five and fifty-five who perspired easily, with a thick neck, heavy-lidded bulldog eyes and wattles and a damp, hungry smile punctuated by chunky teeth. He wore casual vacation clothes—this *was* his vacation, after all—an electric-blue crinkled-cotton shirt monogrammed *B.R.C.* on the pocket (so maybe "Billy Ray Cobb" was his name?), checked polyester trousers creased tightly at the thighs, a "Navajo" hand-tooled leather belt with a flashy brass buckle into which his soft, prominent belly pressed. A black onyx fraternity ring on his right hand and a gold wedding band on his left hand, both rings embedded in fatty flesh. Almost shyly he asked, "Had a little nap, Sherrill, eh?" Or, his breath quickened as if he'd run up a brief flight of stairs, he sounded shy. Then boasting, "Well, we made good time. Two hundred twenty miles in under three hours."

"Starr Bright" perceived that Billy Ray Cobb was one to crave praise from a woman like a dog craving tidbits at the table—no matter what tidbits, however dried out or tasteless or not even food at all, rolled-up paper napkin pellets would suffice. In her sexy throaty voice she murmured, "Hmmm, yes. Fan-tastic."

Seeing how Mr. Cobb was peering eagerly at her she quickly replaced the dark glasses. *Don't stare at me God damn you don't you stare at me.* But of course she was poised, at ease, gave no sign of annoyance. "Starr Bright" was always elaborately made up; her heart-shaped face a flawless cosmetic mask like something hardened to a single substance, a single texture. She knew she looked good, and more than good, but in this damned white-glaring desert sun she might look, if not her age precisely, for "Starr Bright" never looked her age, but maybe thirty-one or -two, not twenty-eight as she'd led credulous Mr. Cobb of Elton, California, to believe.

So far as he knew she was "Starr Bright"—an "exotic interpretive" dancer at the Kings Club, Kings Lake, Nevada. An independent young woman with a flair for the performance arts—not just dancing but singing as well (she had a lovely trained mezzo-soprano voice). Before Kings Lake she'd worked in Lake Tahoe, California, and before that in Los Angeles, San Diego and Fresno; before that, Miami and West Palm Beach, Florida. And there'd been an interlude in Houston, Texas.

Before that, memory faded. Like once-colorful travel posters on a wall frayed and weatherworn with time until one place looked very like another.

It was not yet 6 P.M. And bright as noon. Yet Billy Ray Cobb was eager to check into a motel. Pawing and squeezing "Starr Bright" as he drove the Infiniti, now slowed to forty miles an hour, along the crowded two-lane highway; he was panting and florid-cheeked. *Stop staring at me God damn you.* His sporty-macho smell was mixed up with the aggressive smell of the red-leather interior; the air-conditioning hummed like a third presence. "Starr Bright" was flattered by her new admirer's sexual attraction to her, his look of awe commingled with frank doggy desire, or should have been; but it was a bummer his wanting to stop so soon. "Just that I'm crazy about you, baby," Mr. Cobb said, a whining edge to his voice as if he suspected that "Starr Bright" might not believe him. "Like last night, you'll see."

"Hmmm."

Did she remember last night, no she didn't remember last night.

Wouldn't remember tonight tomorrow night, or so she hoped.

Her father's long-ago voice gentle in wisdom *You won't remember tomorrow what seemed so important today.* But he'd meant worldly vanity, tinsel hopes. Not being fucked like a dog in heat.

So: Billy Ray Cobb did not drive on to Reno as "Starr Bright" had been led to believe they would; and from Reno to Las Vegas.

Might it have made a difference if they'd driven on to Reno?

Only a half-hour drive, more desert but it would have flashed by glittering like mica.

God damn you: no. But her face betrayed no unease, not even annoyance as, impulsively, Billy Ray Cobb swung the Infiniti into a motel that was one of dozens or possibly hundreds of "bargain-rate" motels along the Sparks–Reno strip, just inside the Sparks city limits. PARADISE MOTEL BARGAIN ROOMS & HONEYMOON SUITES! VACANCY! HAPPY HOUR 4-8 P.M. EVERY NITE! "Starr

Bright" narrowed her aching eyes trying to recall if she had been here before. Maybe yes, maybe no. It was all vague. Billy Ray Cobb was chattering excitedly and she was murmuring "Hmmm, hmmm—" in her throaty just-mildly-bored exotic-performer's voice.

If "Starr Bright" was bitterly disappointed in the Paradise Motel, in Sparks, Nevada, having envisioned a first-rate casino-hotel in Reno for the night, smelling beforehand the insecticide-odor of the shabby room, she gave not the slightest clue. She was not that kind of girl.

With her ashy-blond hair cascading to her shoulders and her strong-boned classic face and her long dancer's torso and legs, certainly "Starr Bright" was accustomed to the close scrutiny of men; and knew to keep her most mutinous thoughts to herself. Never to bare her teeth in a quick incandescent flash of anger; never to frown, or grimace, bringing the near-invisible white lines of her forehead into sharp visibility. Never to raise her carefully polished thumbnail to her teeth like an unhappy adolescent girl and gnaw at the cuticle until she tasted blood. *Never never never so long as you are "Starr Bright."*

While Mr. Cobb checked the two of them into the Paradise Motel, "Starr Bright" strolled restlessly about the poolside area, an interior courtyard flanked by thin drooping palm trees that looked brittle as papier-mâché. A six-foot concrete wall painted Day-Glo orange blocked the view of an adjacent motel and cars, buses, motorcycles and campers moving relentlessly along Route 80, but could not keep out the steady noise of traffic. The kidney-shaped pool, in which several near-naked swimmers splashed, smelled sharply of chlorine. And there was the familiar odor of insecticide pervading all. "Starr Bright" glanced quickly about to see if she recognized anyone at poolside—if anyone recognized her—for, having been acquainted with so many men, over a period of years, she must always be vigilant.

In fact, eyes had drifted casually onto her. Strangers' eyes both male and female. But that was to be expected: "Starr Bright" was used to the attention of strangers and would have been discomfited if no one noticed her, so leggy and glamorous in this third-rate Paradise Motel.

No one seemed to recognize her, however. Nor did "Starr Bright" recognize anyone.

Thank you, God!

Uttered quickly and shyly in her inward voice, her head bowed. As one might murmur words of gratitude to an elder, not wanting to be heard, exactly. Not wanting to call attention to oneself.

Of the ten or twelve guests in the courtyard, most had positioned themselves luxuriously in the waning sun: visitors to the Southwest, obviously. "Starr Bright" heard a foreign language being spoken—German, she guessed. Why would anyone come so many thousands of miles to spend even a single night *here*? And others were midwesterners, oily gleaming bodies in scanty bathing suits, bathing suits straining against flesh, young firm flesh and aging raddled flesh, dreamily shut eyes reckless in the sun's killer rays. Of course, they'd smeared on "suntan lotion"—"sun block"—in childlike trust that such flimsy protections could shield them from cancer. There were pastel-bright drinks with melting ice cubes in tall glasses, empty beer, Coke and Perrier bottles accumulated on the wrought-iron tables. From overhead amplifiers, rock-Muzak made the air vibrate; the pulse quicken. "Starr Bright" felt a wild impulse to dance. She was worn out from the drive, she'd taken her meds for a placid low-voltage buzz, yet the music excited her; that heavy erotic beat, the slamming percussive rhythm. After the initial attention she'd received she was now not being noticed: why? *Look at me, here I am, why are none of you looking at me? Here is "Starr Bright"!* She was wearing a tight silky-black miniskirt that came barely to midthigh, and a gold lamé halter top that fitted her good-sized breasts tightly; her long blond smooth-shaven legs were bare; her feet bare in cork platform heels. A thin gold chain around her left ankle, a tiny gold heart dangling. Pierced earrings that fell in glittering silvery cascades nearly to her shoulders, a half-dozen rainbow-metallic bracelets tinkling on each arm. Crimson lips moist as if she were quick-breathing, feverish. And the glamorous designer sunglasses that hid bruises, or the shadow of bruises, beneath her eyes. *Why will you not look at me? I am more beautiful than any of you.*

"Starr Bright's" first celebrity came early, at the age of thirteen, when she'd won first prize in a children's talent competition in Buffalo, New York, singing "I'm Always Chasing Rainbows." She'd been dazed by the sudden applause, a cascade of applause, strangers' faces beaming and their lifted, clapping hands and the blinding heat of the spotlight on her so she'd felt naked, yet blessed.

They love me. These people I don't know—they love me.

How long ago? Don't ask.

When they stop staring, and their eyes go through you, one of the older dancers at the Kings Club had told "Starr Bright," you're in deep trouble. You're on your way to being dead meat. So be thankful for the rude stares. Those pigs are money in the bank.

"Starr Bright" didn't want to think they were pigs exclusively. She'd had many admirers, and many of these were gentlemen—almost. Billy Ray Cobb for example. The kind of well-intentioned guy, if you got to know him when he was sober, gave him half a chance, he wouldn't be half bad.

Strange how, after their initial interest, the poolside loungers at the Paradise Motel didn't seem to notice "Starr Bright." Even a fattish man sprawled in a canvas chair had returned to his copy of *USA Today.* Which was God's sign, too, as "Starr Bright" would afterward realize. Not knowing at the time the import of such signs just as she did not know but would subsequently learn from newspapers and TV that Billy Ray Cobb was signing them into the Paradise Motel as *Mr. & Mrs. Elton Flynn of Los Angeles, CA.*

In the pool there was an outburst of noisy-splashy activity. A voluptuous young woman in a tiny yellow bikini was squealing and kicking, hugging an inflated air mattress striped like an American flag to her breasts, as a tanned muscled young man tickled her; their cries and laughter pierced the air. What exhibitionists! Both were good-looking, with well-developed bodies; youthful, *young* —in their late twenties perhaps. "Starr Bright" stared at them covertly, in envy. But she was disapproving. So close to naked, their bodies gleaming and squirming and thrashing, so vulgar!—the girl and her boyfriend were almost making love in the pool, in plain sight. Bright water heaved and rippled about them. Others at poolside stared openly, gaping and grinning; the lovers behaved as if they took no heed, though obviously delighting in being watched. *Yes, look at us, how happy we are, how beautiful we are, how we deserve happiness because we're beautiful, young and beautiful, what pleasure our bodies take in one another, aren't you all jealous? jealous? jealous?* The girl's shapely arms flailed in a pose of helpless alarm, her heavy breasts nearly exploded out of the skimpy bikini bra, her strong legs thrashed and the young man pushed himself boldly between them, aiming a biting kiss at her throat, as the striped air mattress slipped from them and they began, wildly squealing, to sink beneath the surface of the water. Amid the splashing, paddling, squealing "Starr Bright" pursed her lips and looked quickly away.

It was at this point that Billy Ray Cobb caught up with her. He'd been lugging suitcases, and set them down on the puddled concrete; he was panting, and a vexed little frown gave his face a pouty, petulant cast. He closed his fingers around "Starr Bright's" left wrist. Saying two things to her in a lowered jocular voice and afterward she wouldn't be able to recall which he'd said first. One was, "Wondered where you'd got to, sweetheart," and the other was, with a smirk, "Looks like the fun's already started, eh?"

Not in her slightly scratched leather Gucci bag, a Neiman-Marcus gift from an admirer now forgotten, but in her midnight-blue sequined purse crammed with wallet, cosmetics, amphetamine and Valium tablets, did Starr Bright carry what she called *protection.* A pearl-handled stainless steel carving knife with a slender five-inch blade. Very lightweight, very trim. Kept wrapped in tissue at the bottom of the purse, its razor-sharp blade not yet put to the test.

Protection she thought it, not a *weapon;* still less a *concealed weapon.* So far as she knew, without making inquiries ("Starr Bright" was not one to make inquiries about such things), carrying such a knife on one's person was not illegal, in the states in which she'd been traveling; this was after all a carving knife, a kitchen knife, readily enough purchased in any household supplies store. A knife for preventative purposes, not for any act of aggression.

Protection after she'd been accosted and arrested in a cocktail lounge of a luxurious Hyatt Regency in Houston, Texas, by two plainclothes vice squad detectives who'd detained her in "custody" in a squad car for hours during which time they'd forced her to commit upon their pig-persons sex acts of a repulsive nature, under threat of charging her with "public soliciting" and "resisting arrest." *Never again will "Starr Bright" be humiliated, never again will "Starr Bright" service pigs on any terms but my own.*

That night "Starr Bright" dreamt so strangely!—obsessively, in anguish, of the motel pool, and the air mattress floating in the pool.

She'd scarcely seen the mattress, had little impression of it except it was made of plastic, red, white and blue stripes, about five feet long, not a child's but a grown-up's plaything; a mattress to float on, basking in the sun; an object of salvation if you were in water over your head and couldn't swim.

No death worse than drowning, a slow choking agonizing death and your life flashing before you like a crazed film reel.

"Starr Bright" wasn't much of a swimmer, water frightened her. The transparency, the eerie buoyancy that can't be depended upon; the disequilibrium when you tried to walk in shallow water, or in the surf; the loss of control. Though, of course, she'd always liked to lounge beside pools and on attractive beaches: "Starr Bright" in eye-catching swimwear; "Starr Bright" lavishly oiled against the sun's rays; a wide-brimmed straw hat on her head, dark sunglasses protecting her sensitive eyes. She was a beautiful shapely blonde of the type seen at such places, or in advertisements of such places: luxury suited her, she was a luxury item herself. But water frightened her, the thought of trying to swim, having to swim to save her life, gave her a taste of panic cold and metallic in her mouth.

In her druggy dreams that night how cruel to find herself naked in the tacky motel pool, not a glamorous sexy figure in her sleek black bikini but a helpless flailing naked figure, an object of male derision, crude teasing. She was clutching at the air mattress sobbing, gasping for breath, heart pounding as someone (a man, a stranger, faceless, squat-bodied) tried to pull her from it and into the water to drown. Like the girl in the yellow bikini she'd kicked, thrashed, flailed about, screamed; but this wasn't play, this was deadly earnest. It seemed that her assailant might be Billy Ray Cobb (except she couldn't remember his name), then he was a stranger, then there were two men—or more?—jeering at her terror, which was a female's laughable, contemptible terror, their fingers hard and pitiless as steel tugging at her ankles, her bare vulnerable legs, arms, gripping the nape of her neck to force her face into the water as cruel children do to one another. "Starr Bright" was naked, defenseless as a child, the water lapped darkly about her and was no longer the synthetic bright turquoise of the motel pool. If only she could pull herself up onto the air mattress she could save herself!—but her arm muscles were weak and flaccid, her feeble strength was rapidly fading, her mouth filled with poisonous water it would be death to swallow. And the jeering, the laughing!—the hard hurting male fingers!

Help me! Please help me! O God!

I will be your servant forever, if You save me O God!

So "Starr Bright" thrashed about wildly, flailing her arms, kicking, fighting for her life—yet she was paralyzed, and could not move. Waking bathed in perspiration, cold clammy sweat; her muscles rigid, face contorted. Waking—where? In an unknown bed, a bed of damp rumpled smelly sheets, in an unknown room that hummed loudly with cheap air-conditioning that could not dispel odors of whiskey, cigarette smoke, human sweat and semen and insecticide. "Starr Bright" was not alone but beside a stranger, a fattish naked man who lay sprawled on his back in the center of the bed, a sheet pulled to midchest, head flung back and mouth gaping, wetly snoring.

Mr. Cobb it was. Who'd been unexpectedly rough and impatient with her. The first time, at Kings Lake, he'd been shy, boyish and fumbling like a new husband; last night, reddish-veined pig's eyes contracting and his vision going inward as *Uh! uh! uh!* he'd grunted grinding himself stubbornly and then desperately and at last furiously into "Starr Bright." *But I thought you admired me, my dancing; I though you were "crazy" about me…* Twenty pitiless minutes she'd clocked this copulation as she'd clocked their earlier episodes, eight minutes, twelve minutes, sixteen; a part of her brain detached and clinical despite the line of coke she'd snorted with her bulldog-jowled friend whose name, or names, kept eluding her. She hadn't even pretended to respond, her usual low throaty sexual moaning as if she were being tortured but loving it, loving it but tortured, why bother, Cobb wasn't paying attention. They'd checked in early at the Paradise Motel for this purpose, were naked in bed trying to *make love* as Cobb called it; thrashing about on top of the bed for a while; then rose to go out hurriedly not taking shower and cleanse their sticky bodies as "Starr Bright" badly wanted; yes, and to shampoo her hair; it had been two days since she had cleaned herself thoroughly and how badly she wanted to wash between her legs, her chafed tender thighs, run the shower in the bathroom as hot as she could bear it but Cobb grown suddenly bossy insisted upon going out to buy a bottle of Jack Daniel's and several grams of cocaine innocently white and powdery-granular as confectioner's sugar and so the night had shut abruptly about her like walls pushing inward, threatening suffocation. *C'mon baby! What'd they call you—"Starr Bright"? Loosen up.*

Though the man was a stranger to her, "Starr Bright" seemed to know beforehand that it might be a wise move to anesthetize herself. So she'd only pretended to inhale a second and a third line of coke held on a shaky spoon-mirror to her nostrils; in fact in the secrecy of the ill-smelling bathroom, the only place she could go to hide from Mr. Cobb, she'd quickly swallowed not one, not even two, but a risky three tablets of Valium, the most she ever allowed herself in even the worst emergency situations, or when alcohol was involved. (Trying not to think of women she'd known, dancers like herself, "exotic" or otherwise, who'd overdosed on drugs and alcohol, overdosed and died and their names forgotten.) So she'd been more or less dulled against Mr. Cobb's grinding, grunting and panting; his semi-flaccid penis like a hunk of blood sausage that though limp yet has substance, and can be made to hurt, jammed into her; his hard grasping hands like tentacles; his red-rimmed frog's eyes, his escalating demands. How quickly the man had changed: as if they'd run through a twenty-year marriage in twenty hours, Mr. Cobb aging and coarsening before her eyes. How many minutes, how many hours, precisely where they were, and why she, "Starr Bright," a top "exotic interpretive dancer" admired by other dancers for her Ice Princess glamor and her evident intelligence and sensitivity, more than once compared to the French film actress Catherine Deneuve—why she was here, in this despicable bed, in a despicable man's arms, she could not know, could not comprehend. But the Valium had kicked in, the Valium was precious as any savior, she was sinking to sleep again, shivering, cold with sweat like congealed oil, trying discreetly to keep as far as possible from the snoring man in the center of the bed. She knew from experience *You don't want to offend them, don't want to make them angrier than they are*. And sinking into sleep again, "Starr Bright" found herself another time in a swimming pool—in a distant city, in a distant time, she was a child again, nine years old, and she'd been brought to a park by an older girl cousin who lived in town, what a treat for little Rose of Sharon Donner visiting for the day, excited as always when visiting her relatives in Yewville, which seemed to her a large city of mystery and adventure. (And it pleased her, too, that for some reason her sister hadn't been included. How much more fun without Lily, who was so shy and hanging-back!) But something seemed to have gone wrong: her cousin Beverly wasn't watching her as she was supposed to, Beverly had gone off with her own friends and so Rose of Sharon in her pink swimsuit found herself surrounded in the pool by children she didn't know. *Hey who're you? Where're you from?* Older boys of eleven or twelve, skinny strangers with hair wetly rat-slick and narrowed curious eyes that Rose of Sharon believed were friendly eyes, she was a child accustomed to being admired, being liked, of the Donner girls it was Rose of Sharon and never Lily of the Valley people fussed over, poor Lily was so shy, and Sharon was so bright and bold and outgoing and pretty, naturally boys paid attention to *her*. So she told them her name, and they laughed at such a name—but nice-laughing teasing-laughing. She told them she was from Shaheen, and they laughed saying *Where?* for Shaheen was miles away in the country, not even a town just a place. She told them proudly that her daddy was Ephraim Donner, Minister of the First Church of Christ of Shaheen, and that impressed them she thought, that made them listen! So they invited her for a ride in their big inner tube, which was a truck inner tube, the biggest in the pool. Rose of Sharon had seen other children riding in the tube, so big, shiny-black and floppy, the center of much splashing and hilarity; it seemed to her that only privileged, favored girls were allowed to ride in this tube, head and arms thrust through the opening, legs kicking behind, so of course Rose of Sharon said yes, she hadn't even glanced around to look for Beverly, in her excitement she'd forgotten entirely about Beverly. The Yewville boys were so friendly, grinning at her so of course she trusted them, she was nine years old and a country child and the favorite of her daddy, so Rose of Sharon Donner trusted these boys though they were strangers and her mother had warned her not to play with children she didn't know unless Beverly was with her but in the giddy excitement of the pool this was forgotten. *Hey c'mon little girl! Blondie Blue-Eyes. Don't be scared!* So she let the boys push her through the inner-tube opening, she was squealing, giggling and kicking as the boys tugged the tube across the pool, and toward the farther end of the pool where the water was five feet deep and Rose of Sharon began to be frightened but the boys doggy-paddling and splashing beside her said not to be scared, not to be scared she was O.K. because the inner tube couldn't sink. The boys were ducking beneath her and jostling her, pulling at her feet, tickling at first and then pinching; poking their hard fingers into her ribs, between her legs as she began to thrash her arms and legs, panicked, helpless and sobbing. She tried to cry *No! no! let me go!* but she swallowed water, there was so much noise in the pool no one could hear her, the boys wouldn't let their pretty little blond captive go, a gang of them now was hooting and chortling tugging her across the pool into the deep water where only older children and teenagers were allowed to swim, and at last a lifeguard intervened, a teenaged girl blowing her whistle and shouting so the boys quickly shoved Rose of Sharon out of their tube and into the water and escaped, and Rose of Sharon sank swallowing water, flailing about and would surely have drowned except for the lifeguard rescuing her, carrying her out of the pool and onto the puddled concrete where she lay sobbing and coughing up water, stricken as a wounded animal. And so ashamed! so humiliated! When she'd thought the boys had liked her so much! Her cousin Beverly was squatting over her, guilty, frightened, saying how sorry she was, how sorry she was please not to tell on her, begging Rose of Sharon not to tell either of their mothers ever, and so the nightmare was ended, and Rose of Sharon never told. For to tell would be to admit how she'd been tricked, made a fool and humbled bawling like a baby among staring strangers.

Except: the nightmares of childhood never end but continue forever beneath the surface of memory as beneath the surface of choppy murky water. So long as memory and life endure.

So it was that "Starr Bright" woke agitated and confused, half-choking out of her drugged sleep another time. She was not "Rose of Sharon Donner" now and had not been "Rose of Sharon Donner" for a long time. Luminous red numerals floating in the dark beside the bed indicated 4:46 A.M. There would be no more sleep for "Starr Bright" that night.

* * *

Through discolored Venetian blind slats a fluorescent-crimson neon sign flashed in rumba rhythm, PARADISE MOTEL. PARADISE MOTEL. Quietly "Starr Bright" slipped from the damp smelly pigsty of a bed and discovered herself naked. Naked! Shivering in the drafty refrigerated air though her body was covered in sticky sweat and there was a burning sensation between her legs. Dared not waken the man, what was his name, Cobb. Had to escape from him, a dangerous man, cruel, surprising how he'd changed after a few drinks, snorting coke and he'd become a real bulldog, he'd hurt her, bruised her breasts he'd said were so God-damned beautiful they drove him crazy with wanting to suck suck suck the first time she'd undressed before him in the privacy of his Kings Lake motel room, but this time he'd been a different man, squeezing and pinching her breasts, bruising the insides of her creamy-pale thighs, grinding his only part-erect penis into her grunting *Uh! uh! uh!* as if he'd wanted to kill her, eyes bulging and pink-flushed face swelling like a balloon about to burst. Drunk, and high on cocaine, not a man accustomed to cocaine, he'd turned into a bully, a pig, and he'd lied to her, too, promising she could bathe herself, wash her sticky hair, like all of them he'd lied to her, he had no pity for her suffering.

Must change my life. Help me O God. I'm run to earth.

For God had sent her the miracle-dream, a dream of her lost, repudiated childhood. She had not had the drowning-dream, as she called it, for eight years or more. Since West Palm Beach. Or had it been Miami. *A sign of Your terrible love.*

Quickly, fumblingly, "Starr Bright" dressed herself in the dark palely raddled by flashing crimson neon from PARADISE MOTEL PARADISE MOTEL outside the window. Stepping into the torn black lace panties Cobb had ripped from her, struggling into the absurdly tight skirt, the phony-gold lamé halter. And where were her shoes? and her Gucci bag? and the blue-sequined purse?

One day they would ask why hadn't she fled Billy Ray Cobb and the Paradise Motel. Why not run out of the room, why not run for help into the motel office, bright-lit and open for business at 4:46 A.M. as at 4:46 P.M. For indeed "Starr Bright" might have done so, seeking refuge on foot in Sparks, Nevada, a police station perhaps, except she feared and loathed the police, above all you can't trust the police. Nowhere to go, *run to earth*.

When God sends His sign, it's after you are run to earth. And beaten, broken utterly. So you cast your eyes upward to Him, there is no one but Him.

There stood "Starr Bright" hastily clothed now pausing to look through Cobb's clothes flung onto a chair. The fake-Navajo belt with the brass medallion buckle. The monogrammed shirt smelling of sweat and deodorant, the polyester trousers. By the rhythmically flashing light she could see only well enough to go through the trouser pockets, remove the wallet thick with bills and credit cards, the keys for the rental car. Hands shaking but determined. And there on a table the almost-empty whiskey bottle, somehow she'd taken hold of it, and she raised it to her mouth and drank impulsively, regretted it immediately as she began to cough and Billy Ray Cobb's snoring ceased and he woke and sat up muttering, "Eh? What? Who's that?"

There followed then an episode distended and distorted as in a dream never to be recalled precisely by "Starr Bright" except in quick-jumping flashes, images.

She told the groggy suspicious man it was just her, it was just "Starr Bright" and he should go back to sleep, but Billy Ray Cobb had flared up in anger swinging his bare legs out of bed, demanding to know, "Baby, why're you *up*? It's fucking *night*." And she'd tried to hide the wallet and car keys inside her clothes, turned from Cobb, saying she needed to use the bathroom. But by now Cobb was on his feet. You wouldn't have believed a man his age, his size and fattish condition could wake up so quickly, must have been adrenaline charging him, swaying but belligerent demanding to know what the hell was going on. He was just a little taller than Starr Bright in his bare feet, no more than five feet nine but he outweighed her by one hundred pounds. Saying, advancing upon her, "Yeah? Happens the bathroom's in this direction, sweetheart. Or were you gonna take a leak on the floor?" And "Starr Bright" was stammering trying to explain she wanted to take a shower, needed to take a hot shower, wash her hair, couldn't sleep smelly and dirty as she was and Cobb interrupted, "Shower in the middle of the fucking *night?* You expect me to believe that?" She was about to make a run for the door though knowing the door was chain-bolted and double-locked and she wouldn't have had a chance to escape and by this time he'd seen the wallet and car keys in her hand, and grabbed her, limp and weak as a rag doll she was as he shook her, slapped her. "What the fuck, bitch? Caught you, eh?" getting a hammerlock on her and grunting dragging her toward the bathroom. "You say you want a shower, eh?—dirty hair washed? Dirty cunt washed? How's about in the toilet bowl? Think you can put something over on *me*! Make an asshole out of *me*! You're messing with the wrong man, bitch!"

"Starr Bright" was on her knees. Cobb was slapping, punching her furiously, an undertone of shame in his voice, "—Telling me all that shit last night and I fell for it! What a sucker! Shoulda known you whores are all alike, don't deserve to live! Going into my wallet! Can't wait till morning to be paid!" and he'd picked up his wallet where it had fallen to the floor and extracted a handful of bills tossing them into the air in derision and pushing "Starr Bright" down on hands and knees where they fell, saying, "Crawl for it, bitch, pick 'em up, bitch, pick 'em up with your cunt," and when she refused to move he pushed her down and straddled her, heavy sweating naked body on her back, penis and testicles flopping against her back, "Hey, you like it, babe! You know you like it! 'Starr Bright'—what a crock of shit! Phony bitch, all of you phony bitches, whores! Don't deserve to live, you contaminate the world for decent women." He snatched up his belt and began to strike her with it, the brass buckle against her legs, thighs, buttocks, he was laughing, "Giddyup, horsey! Giddyup, horsey! You like it, eh?—cunt? Sure you do," and when "Starr Bright" collapsed beneath his weight Cobb ground himself into her, penis like a steel rod now, hardened with fury, loathing, the wish to hurt, and the rattling air-conditioning muffled their cries if anyone had been listening, if anyone had cared to listen here at the Paradise Motel, Sparks, Nevada, but of course no one did, as Billy Ray Cobb hooted and laughed and collapsed onto her, and lay heavily panting, unmoving for several seconds. When he rose from her, "Starr Bright" lay limp on the floor.

Cobb was immensely pleased with himself, you could hear it in his voice. Not just he'd punished a thief but he was right to do so, it was a good deed he'd done, her punishment deserved. And more: "Now get out of here, 'Starr Bright.' Before I get mad." He prodded her with his foot, he grabbed her by the hair, teasing, "Before I do something can't be undone," teasing, "Don't play no more games with me, cunt, like you're hurt or something. Like you're so sensitive or something. This room *I'm* paying for, get *out.*" Forcing her to crawl in the direction of the door, through the scattered bills, his fingers gripping the back of her neck. How triumphant he was, how triumphant other men had been at such moments, waves of animal heat rippling from his body that was covered in coarse graying hair like wires. Saying again she didn't deserve to live among decent women, lucky he hadn't broken her jaw, "Starr Bright" fumbled for her sequined purse lying on the floor and he said, "Yeah! Right! Take your trash with you! Stinking up the room." He unbolted and unlatched the door, opened it as "Starr Bright" managed to stand, her clothes torn, her nose bloodied, Cobb sighted her cork-heeled shoes on the floor and snatched them up and tossed them out the door, "Trash! Stinking! Get out!" and when "Starr Bright" failed to move quickly enough he gripped her again by the back of the neck about to fling her through the doorway after her shoes but in that instant no longer dazed and fumbling *for God gave me strength, guided my hand according to His desire* "Starr Bright" had the knife out of her purse, held it with desperate tightness and drew its razor-sharp blade swiftly across Cobb's throat and he cried out more in astonishment than in pain as at once he began to bleed profusely, a virtual fountain of blood springing from his throat, he clutched at it trying to stem the flow, his clumsy sausage-fingers trying to repair the terrible damage in his flesh, and "Starr Bright" leapt free of him as he fell, sinking to his knees, murmuring with what remained of his voice, "Hey, what—? My God, help—help me—"

No help. None. No pity, and no mercy for she'd been bled dry of such herself. Run to earth, and broken utterly. And suffused with God's will. *God gave me strength, guided my hand* and so it was, and so it would be. So "Starr Bright" calmly watched Billy Ray Cobb die as you would see a task through to its necessary and inevitable completion. As you would not even wish to hurry such a task, surrendered to a greater will. *Thank you God. Thank you God. Thank you God.* The quivering pig-body amid a gathering pool of pig-blood dark as oil staining the cheap nubbed carpet in the flickering crimson-neon winking from the window.

Why "Starr Bright" dipped her forefinger into the pig-blood, to test its heat perhaps, to test its viscosity, she would not know and would not afterward recall. Whispering aloud, in wonder great as the dying man's before God's wrathful throne, "Now you see! Now you see! Pigs and fornicators!"

* * *

In the light of early morning, not yet dawn, an eerie calm prevailed. It was the silence of the West, the vast empty desert, the vast empty Western sky, the silence of unclocked time. In the courtyard of the Paradise Motel the kidney-shaped swimming pool was deserted, looking smaller even than it had looked the night before. And there floated the inflated air mattress, not striped like the American flag as "Starr Bright" had thought, but only red and blue stripes. A toy for adults, something demeaning and sad about it floating on top of the insect-stippled turquoise water that was like a skin stretched out over something living, invisible and inviolable and unknowable.

At 5:47 A.M. and in no apparent haste, "Starr Bright" quietly departed room 22 of the Paradise Motel; shut the door behind her, and crossed the empty courtyard to the parking lot at the rear of the motel; unlocked the platinum-silver Infiniti sedan with the Nevada rental license plates; placed her Gucci bag on the passenger's seat, and her midnight-blue sequined purse on top of the bag. Had there been an observer he would have noted a tall, poised, coolly attractive blond woman in white linen trousers, a pale blue silk shirt, practical flat-heeled sandals. Oddly, she was wearing gloves; and though the sun had not yet risen, her eyes were hidden behind dark, smoke-tinted glasses. Her ashy-blond hair, still damp from the shower, had been brushed back neatly from her face and fastened into a chignon. She was stylishly attractive but not glamorous; her flawless cosmetic mask was subdued in tone, her lipstick beige-pink; she might have been an executive's assistant, or a professional woman herself, alone on holiday. Certainly she appeared utterly natural departing the Paradise Motel at this early hour, showing no sign of agitation, nor even of unease. *As if Starr Bright had been here before. In His sign. And all has passed in a whirlwind in His terrible justice and mercy.*

In the eastern sky, beyond the fake-Spanish facade of a neighboring Holiday Inn, dawn was emerging out of an opalescent darkness of massed clouds. A fiery all-seeing eye. Beneath the scrutiny of this eye "Starr Bright" drove the Infiniti out of the parking lot and on Route 80 turned left and steadily east and south she would drive on that road and on Route 95 curving through the desert planes arriving later that morning in Las Vegas where amid a vast sea of sun-glittering vehicles parked at the Mirage she would abandon the Infiniti. She meant, for as long as she could, to keep that fiery eye before her.

2
At the Golden Sands, Las Vegas, Nevada

She was here, somewhere. He'd know when he saw her and maybe, even, she'd know him.

He carried himself through the crowds with the cocky air of a man bearing a secret too good to keep for long. Sucking a cigarette, licking his upper lip with his tongue as if savoring it, eyes roving, searching. He wore $150 cowhide boots with a substantial heel, designer jeans, a sporty wide-shouldered Italian-style gunmetal-gray silk-cotton-and-polyester jacket and a black silk shirt open at the throat. He was, with the heels, almost five foot ten; muscular through the chest and shoulders (a former athlete, maybe? high school football?); his flesh just slightly soft, going flaccid at the waist (but the stylish jacket hid that); his hair, receding sharply at the temples, was brush-colored and wiry and had been combed at artful angles to minimize hair loss. With his close-set watchful eyes and sharp-boned western-looking face he resembled a hawk ever vigilant for prey. Here in Vegas for the weekend he was thinking he deserved a good time, deserved some God-damned happiness like anybody else and he meant to get it.

In the Barbary Coast casino into which he'd stepped out of a sun-glaring temperature of 97°F a blast of refrigerated air caressed his forehead like a woman's soothing fingers. *Mmmmm* he liked the sensation, he believed it was his due.

Back home in Sumner County, Nebraska, he had a life known to many: a "career"; an identity linked primarily to the career. He was proud enough of this without being blind to the fact that probably he'd never be promoted much beyond his present rank. When thinking along these familiar lines he was in the habit, when alone, of shrugging and muttering aloud, "So? What the hell." Smiling a quick pained smile as if some asshole had told a joke meant to be hilarious and, sure, Ernie Fenke was a good sport, he'd laugh.

It wasn't the first time he'd flown to Vegas for a weekend. And this time a three-day weekend, end of October. Leaving the Omaha airport late on Thursday, taking a single suitcase containing his Vegas clothes which were not clothes he wore in Sumner County, Nebraska. They were not clothes his wife knew about, nor anyone in his family; he kept them in a locker at headquarters. Going to Vegas once or twice a year was his own business, nobody else's. None of his colleagues knew, either. In dreams he saw himself illuminated and virile as on a video screen. In dreams he had the power to gamble away all the cash in his pocket, reaching deep into his pockets and drawing out more, more, more, no end to the cash he had, he'd live forever. At craps, at blackjack, at poker betting ever higher stakes and winning as strangers watched in awe; beautiful women watched in awe. He worried he might be a binge gambler, maybe a binge drinker, he knew from professional experience what a deadly combination this was, what it did to even intelligent, decent people but he was too smart to allow any such weakness to overcome him. *It's just I deserve a good time, shit a man deserves some happiness doesn't he!*

His wife Lynette, poor sweet dumb girl he'd married, already pregnant, out of high school, the best-looking of the varsity cheerleaders but he'd always known how to keep her in line. Not scared of him exactly but never fully at ease, not her or the kids, never taking Ernie Fenke for granted the way the wives of most of his friends took them for granted. Why couldn't I come with you just once, Lynette would ask, and he'd tell her bluntly no, these were professional trips, not vacations; these were "conferences" and "seminars" he had to attend, not in Vegas but, for instance, Salt Lake City, another time Albuquerque, this time Des Moines—hardly places a man would choose to spend a three-day weekend.

And maybe Lynette believed him, and maybe she didn't; looking sometimes as if she had more to say but hesitated to say it.

Though never once in eighteen years of marriage had he hit her, and vowed he never would, Ernie Fenke wasn't that kind of man. Not in Sumner County, Nebraska.

In Vegas he rented a car and checked in, not at one of the big hotels, but at the Golden Sands Motor Lodge on the strip, a motel of no distinction, moderate-priced with a pool he wouldn't use and where each room opened out directly onto the parking lot. Which was what you required when you required privacy. Not like the high-rise hotel, the Sahara, he'd made the mistake of staying in on his first Vegas visit six or seven years ago, bringing a girl back to his room and when things got too rough the girl had lost it and started screaming and within minutes a house dick had pounded on the door and he'd had no choice but to open it, disheveled and sweating and wearing only trousers he'd hastily yanked on, but managing to say in an offended voice, "Officer, there's nothing wrong here, just my girlfriend and me," and the detective said pleasantly, "I'll need to look around, it's just routine." And so the man had come in and looked around, sniffing like he smelled a bad odor, and the girl was in the bathroom hurriedly fixing herself up, and Ernie said, "My girlfriend is a screamer, that's all it is. Somebody called down to the desk?" and the detective said, pausing outside the bathroom door upon which, too, he knocked, "Oh, yeah? Is your girlfriend a screamer?" and Ernie said, managing to laugh, laughter like clearing his throat of clotted mucus, "Yeah, but I don't hold it against her." The girl then emerged from the bathroom, in a kimono wrapped tight about her short-legged, chesty body; she'd slapped on makeup to disguise the welts on the underside of her jaw, and she was wearing bright lipstick, and she was smiling; stiff-bleached hair falling over half her face, and her eyes glassy as marbles. "Tell this officer there's no problem, Sonya," Ernie said, and Sonya said, "Officer, no problem," with a twitchy smirk. Ernie was wondering if he should offer the detective a bill or two, fifty dollars maybe; or would that be a mistake of offering him money which was a God-damned insult—as if he, Ernie Fenke, was looking for bribes; as if he, Ernie Fenke, was in fact bribable!—which maybe in another set of circumstances he might be, but these days sting operations were so common, in the papers and on TV, so anyone who imagined Ernie Fenke was stupid enough or desperate enough to be tempted to take a bribe had insulted him doubly. So he decided no; and the girl was convincing enough; and the detective seemed to want to believe them, backing off and saying in a bored voice, "O.K., kids, but take it easy from now on." So it was O.K. but Christ he'd resented having to deal with it. He resented his privacy invaded and scrutinized by some s.o.b. private cop near enough to him in age, size, disposition and possibly income to be his twin brother. So he'd never returned to any big hotel again, much preferring the small two-story motels along the strip like the Golden Sands which was about two miles from the center of Vegas.

At Caesars Palace, at Pleasure Island and the Mirage and the Hilton and the Sahara. At craps, at poker, at blackjack and at craps again. He'd won a few bucks, and lost; lost, and won; drew on his American Express card taking a chance he'd win enough to keep going, and so he did; for five hours of strain coming out a lousy $238 ahead. And he hadn't yet hooked up with a girl, he'd been so anxious waiting to get hot, really hot; but it wasn't happening.

I need one, I need a woman. For luck.

He had a habit, not nervous exactly but half-conscious, of slipping his hand inside his jacket and rubbing his chest; touching the .32-caliber pistol he carried close beneath his heart everywhere he went as if to check yes it's there, he's O.K.

In Barbary Coast cruising the slots hawklike and alert for prey. A man handsome and stylishly dressed as Ernie Fenke with his macho swagger *Yeah, I think pretty well of myself and you would, too, in my place* shouldn't have trouble attracting desirable women, right? His hair oiled and combed to hide the balding spots, a gold chain glinting at his throat, and chest hair just visible at his opened collar. Of course there were always hookers, high-priced whorehouses outside the city limits (with shuttle service provided, he'd tried it once) but Ernie Fenke wanted something better. And deserved something better. The cowhide boots giving him a full inch or more in height, so he moved through crowds catching sight of himself in mirrors and reflective surfaces and admiring what he saw. But he was disdainful of the many homely, frankly ugly and overweight women in the casino; so many middle-aged, old and even elderly men and women playing the slots, dozens, hundreds, acres of them in Vegas, everywhere in Vegas, their clawed arthritic hands covered with liver spots and visibly trembling as if with palsy or Parkinson's and some of them blind or in wheelchairs, or both, Ernie was shocked to see such behavior among his elders, people his parents' age, damned depressing sights, and most of them smoking, too. The slots were, generally, depressing. Rigged for the house to win, for penny-ante suckers to play, lowest level of gambler. Not like the more manly games poker, blackjack and craps where intelligence and gambling ingenuity might prevail.

It was late, he was getting anxious, his eye snagged on two young women in jeans and designer blouses and too much makeup squealing with excitement as a small jackpot of silver dollars spilled out of a machine to the accompaniment of flashing red lights and hurdy-gurdy music. Ernie saw it was just a $277 jackpot, chump change but the girls were making a show of catching the coins in paper cups, exclaiming to each other. "Hey girls, congratulations!" Ernie said, and the plumper of the two actually whirled about and hugged him, a total stranger, smearing lipstick on his cheek like it was New Year's Eve or Mardi Gras. So Ernie fell to talking with them, and bought them drinks at one of the bars, Irma and Janice who were "executive assistants" as they called themselves, meaning probably secretaries, from Topeka, Kansas, here in Vegas for the weekend. Their first time in Vegas, their first jackpot ever, oh they loved Vegas it was even more exciting than they'd hoped, there was surely nothing like Vegas back in Kansas! Breathless and giggling displaying their young bodies for Ernie

Fenke and, yes, he was moderately turned on, bought them another round of drinks and listened to their chatter, then suddenly bored he said, "Hey, you gals are terrific but I gotta run. Have a great weekend," tossing bills down for the waiter and walking off knowing Irma and Janice would be hurt, disappointed. The tall homely one with the buck teeth and the shorter plumper one with the brown cow-eyes like Lynette's gazing after him wistfully as he strode off brushing his oiled hair back with deft motions of both hands.

Eat your hearts out, girls.

Enough of Barbary Coast, where his luck wasn't with him. He left, crossing the street, surprised to see it was dusk already, almost night. In the casinos, which were windowless and clockless, you were led to forget there was such a thing as time. Or, glancing at your watch, you saw it was 10:48 not knowing was this morning or night. And there's a satisfaction in that. Like the time he'd poked a girl with the .32, teasing, tickling, nudging her breasts and belly and between the legs, not rough, really just playful and even affectionate, and she'd been laughing, high and laughing and suddenly she'd stopped laughing and got scared and it came to him in a flash *You could, you know—just do it.* And there'd be a satisfaction in that, for sure. Ending everything, not just her, whoever she was, but him, too. But in the next moment he'd forgotten, of course—Ernie Fenke could think of better things to do with a woman than blow her away.

He was headed for the Century, a tall golden-glimmering tower of lights against the murky sky. Grateful the sun had gone down though it was still muggy, hot; temperature in the high 80s; and the hazy-gritty air hard to breathe. He was excited, edgy; he recognized the symptoms; another drink helped, but not enough. Knowing his luck wasn't with him yet but, God damn, he was too restless to keep from trying it; found himself at a blackjack table where he dropped $370 in four minutes. To prove what? When he already knew? Not lonely but keenly feeling the absence of a woman, a good-looking sexually charged woman at his side. A woman to bring Ernie Fenke the luck he deserved, a woman to explore that king-sized bed at the Golden Sands Motor Lodge with him. Not a screamer if he could help it but how'd he know beforehand? He never did.

Wandering through the crowded noisy smoke-filled casino with rainbow spotlights overhead, crisscrossing one another like the tails of random comets. What a place, Vegas: a dream, but not a dream you had to sustain, yourself: an easy dream, a pure-pleasure dream, like a fold-out 3-D children's storybook. His pockets were stuffed with coupons, everyone trying to give away something, or give that illusion to bring the suckers in. He had coupons for a half-dozen meals but hadn't sat down to one yet; too much excitement, too much electricity in the air. It was like being a teenaged kid again, in Vegas; horny as hell, charged up ready to explode. In his cowhide boots, in his sexy Italian-style jacket, his black silk shirt open at the throat he was a predator uncertain of the specifics of his prey but knowing it was in his vicinity, he'd locate it soon; knowing he had to eat, and soon. Following a woman then abruptly losing interest when he saw she was his age, at least—late thirties; following another, fantastic ass in almost-translucent purple shorts and a tiny halter top, punk-style dyed green hair meaning she'd be wild as hell in bed and wouldn't need to be respected, but, God damn, he lost her to a guy. Mostly the Century was packed with couples, all ages, all sizes and races; Vegas had changed in just the six or seven years he'd been coming here, more ordinary people every season, more families with kids; there were couples who reminded him of his parents and in-laws; couples who reminded him of himself and Lynette as they'd been ten years ago, or would be twenty years in the future, God! No wonder he hadn't any appetite to eat.

At last at a crowded roulette table he sighted a good-looking redhead in an eye-catching costume: sexy gold lamé minidress and high-heeled cork shoes, she appeared to be alone, though plenty of guys were noticing her; numerous rings on her fingers so he couldn't tell if she wore a wedding band, but in the case of a woman like this, what would a wedding band signify if the husband wasn't within a hundred feet of her? A divorcee, Ernie supposed; maybe spending a few days in Vegas to clear out her head; looking for a pickup, too—maybe. It was Saturday night, after all. (In Vegas it was always Saturday night except for a few depressing hours on Sunday morning.) He saw her pushing chips out, and not getting chips back; pushing chips out, and not getting chips back. He saw a hurt, stung, scared look in her face that's the look of a woman losing a bet; he couldn't see how much she'd lost, but he was glad she'd lost; when a woman wins, she isn't likely to need a man. He followed her when she left the table abruptly, walking quickly in her high-heeled shoes, her pale face slightly flushed, a breathless look to her, hoped to hell she wasn't meeting up with some guy. Red-haired and sexy and not too old for him, in her late twenties possibly; reminded him of Sharon Stone, that tough-sexy look. Like her legs would wrap around you and practically break your back and you'd love it. He didn't like it that she was tall, preferred shorter women, of course the heels added inches to her height and when she kicked them off she'd be more to his taste. A creamy-pale face smooth as a mask, not much expression, a bright red mouth like something gouged into flesh. He followed her through the casino, in and out of crowds, possibly she was aware of him by now and not minding it that he, a good-looking guy, was following her; you don't dress like that, wear your hair tousled like that, unless you want men to look seriously at you, and think serious thoughts about you. Jesus!—that gold lamé dress that fitted her slender but voluptuous body as if she'd been poured into it! The sight turned him on, shiny gold fabric tight as a tourniquet especially at her belly, pelvis. Her legs were long as a dancer's legs, maybe she was a showgirl, or had been; long, bare, smooth legs; a thin gold chain around her left ankle. *Honey look at me: Ernie Fenke's your man.* He was disappointed, though, she'd gone to the slot machines; losing at roulette and back to playing slots, both of them sheer blind chance and slots the lowest form of casino gambling. And she wasn't having luck here, either. Slots was a sucker's game, took no brains at all, still there's always the flutter of hope you *might* win; rigged to favor the house ninety-nine times out of one hundred but you *might* win; there were wins timed regularly in a row of machines to keep the credulous hopeful; to keep the suckers going, going and gone.

Until the last quarter is gone. And the good-looking redhead was losing; playing with an air of expectation tinged with hurt; a childlike look to her glamor-face; she was playing and losing, playing and losing so Ernie felt sorry for her; it was an emotion he enjoyed, feeling sorry for women. As long as it wasn't expected of him. This woman was looking anxious now, and she was looking more and more like someone in need of company. She paused in her playing to open a blue-sequined purse to look for, Ernie guessed, a pack of cigarettes she couldn't seem to find. "Here y'are," Ernie said, his own pack in his hand, there he was smiling and available and ready to assist; the woman lifted her eyes to him in mild surprise, pleasantly, as if she hadn't been aware of him watching her intensely for the past ten minutes or more. She smiled in return, and accepted the cigarette, and said in a throaty, husky voice so soft Ernie Fenke had to lean close, inhaling her perfume, to hear, "Why, thank *you*."

So they met in the Century, in the midst of numerous strangers avidly playing slots, and became acquainted; very quickly acquainted, for in Vegas there isn't time to spare. "What's your name?" he asked, and in her soft-sweet-sexy voice she said, "Sherrill," and he said, "'Sherrill'—I like that name. Sherrill what?" and she said, "Sherrill Dwyer," so easily and looking him full in the face so he believed absolutely she was telling the truth. He grabbed her hand and shook it, squeezing the soft, rather cold fingers hard, "I'm Earl Tunley," which was the name of a right-wing state congressman from Sumner County, Nebraska, and she said, "'Earl'—I like it, I've never known any 'Earl' close up," and he said, "There's always a first time, Sherrill, right?" and they laughed together as if this was quite a joke. And he saw that Sherrill Dwyer's eyes were a cool bluish-gray, like pebbles washed by rain; he saw without exactly noting that he saw, in the excitement of the moment, white near-invisible lines radiating outward from the corners of her eyes. He smelled something metallic and ashy beneath the ripe-peaches scent of her perfume. He liked what he saw, and what he smelled, and the effect she was having on him, a sexual stirring he understood to be the stirring of his luck, returning to him. He asked would she like a drink, and she said yes; and later he asked would she like something to eat, and she said yes; it was clear they got along, Earl and Sherrill, they liked each other a lot, understood each other it seemed; maybe even, as Sherrill speculated, they'd somehow met before, in another lifetime. Wasn't that possible? So Earl Tunley laughed indulgently and said, "Sweetheart, in Vegas anything's possible."

It was 2 A.M., a giddy crazy hour in Vegas and not really a time for serious eating. So they left most of their food on their plates and retired to the Golden Sands, to room 19, to become better acquainted. Ernie who was Earl bought a bottle of Jim Beam en route and two packs of Camels and they were feeling good, keyed up and amorous and grateful to have found each other. Their first time in bed, to be specific on top of the king-sized bed, was so great so terrific so fantastic it truly did seem, as Sherry insisted, they'd known each other in another lifetime. And Earl sighed yes, could be. Lying then naked and luxuriant smoking cigarettes, sipping whiskey out of tumblers, still too excited to sleep. In Vegas, who wants to sleep? Earl Tunley was saying he was from Council Bluffs, Iowa; owned a TV and video store; Sherrill who'd become Sherry in his arms, blowing in his ear and moaning in sexual heat, described herself as a PR girl from Fresno, California, between jobs. She was staying in a motel farther out on the strip, not liking the congestion of the big hotels—"And all these crude guys hitting on you." Earl wasn't a married man any longer, he'd been married for almost ten years and lucky he and his wife hadn't had any children so he was spared child support and his ex-wife was remarried so she was out of his hair permanently; and what about her, Sherry? —and glamorous red-haired Sherry said, sighing, for a fleeting moment sad, that she'd been married, too, at the age of eighteen; but it had ended a few years later, and she tried never to think about it. She said, "I was just a child, back in—this small town in Pennsylvania no one's ever heard of. I thought it was true, deep love Michael and I felt for each other but it was a delusion, oh I was flattered this rich man's son, who'd been a football hero at our high school a few years ahead of me, was crazy about *me.*" And she wiped carefully at her eyes, not wanting the silvery-blue eye shadow and the inky black mascara to run; perhaps the makeup was waterproof, since it didn't run.

In a playful growling voice Earl who was Ernie, unless he was Ernie who was Earl, said, "Sweetheart, anybody'd be crazy about *you.*" And it was time to make love again. Jesus, he was feeling good!—feeling his old luck return, coursing through his veins, into his cock, like molten gold. Whoever he was, Earl, Ernie. Tunley, Fenke or somebody not yet known he was grateful to this terrific woman, and he was the kind of good-sport good-hearted basically generous guy to show it. Only watch.

* * *

Am I afraid?—I am not.

Am I despairing?—I am not.

For You have given me a sign, & Your blessing. & I am patient, I have learned to bide my time.

The next man, maybe. Always there was the promise of the next man. When she danced, always there was the promise of being singled out, raised above the others, a photo-feature in a newspaper, or in *Nevada by Night*: "Starr Bright." Always the promise of a really serious male admirer who would love her for herself alone and wish to marry her.

Now, no longer dancing, lacking that arena for display, "Starr Bright" was temporarily disadvantaged. And her money was rapidly running out.

Not just money for food, for necessities and a decent place to stay, but money sufficient to maintain "Starr Bright's" cultured-classy appearance; the crucial "Starr Bright" appearance that made all the difference. For you can't attract the attention of a worthwhile man unless you look good; and looking good, even if you're a beautiful woman, doesn't come cheaply.

Where had the money gone?—*her* money she'd earned. She'd counted $692 from the man's wallet before tossing the wallet away in a developer's landfill off Route 80 where no one would ever find it; $692 which should have been enough to stake her for a while, staying at the cheapest motel in Vegas she could tolerate, and mainly playing the slots which was minimal risk with the possibility of a big jackpot; in fact she'd won a $444 jackpot at Vegas World on her second night but hadn't been able to repeat the win; believing that her luck was building up, gradually building up like steam pressure that had to explode eventually. When the slot machines disappointed, she'd tried blackjack, roulette, keno and the Nevada State lottery, praying *Just this once, O Lord, and I will never ask another favor of you.* And perhaps she believed this, and meant it. As years ago, when they were little girls, she'd cajoled her sister Lily into praying with her, reasoning that double prayers had double power.

One of "Starr Bright's" problems was that if she'd been drinking she was susceptible to wild mood swings. She was susceptible to behaving impulsively. Bursting into tears—tears of happiness?—when she'd won the $444 in silver coins. And later that night meeting up with a sobbing fat woman who'd lost all her money in the casinos and said she had nowhere to go and the woman's name was Lilia (which could not have been a coincidence, could it?) and "Starr Bright" had peeled off three crisp $50 bills to press into the woman's hand. And the woman had stared at her in disbelief, and stammered thanks, and blessed "Starr Bright" as an angel of mercy sent direct from God.

Just this once, O Lord. And I will never sin again.

Though knowing that God disapproved of gambling. Disapproved of these sinful cities of the plain, Sodom and Gomorrah. As in her innermost heart she disapproved. For hadn't she been brought up in a devout Christian household to love God and her savior Jesus Christ above all earthly vanities; brought up to know that the wages of sin are death. But: there are times of upheaval when you have no choice except to gamble, gamble your very life, you're desperate and run to earth and this was one of those times, He would understand, surely He would understand. A God of wrath but also a God of mercy and forgiveness.

For this was the one true fact: He was always guiding her hand.

"Starr Bright's" trembling hand gripping the razor-sharp carving knife that was her secret protection.

For if He had not guided her hand, how could she have acted? How could she have defended herself against her violator?

As, that morning in October, she'd driven in the rental Infiniti from Sparks to Reno, from Reno to Vegas, how many solitary hours in the desert singing hymns at the top of her lungs she hadn't sung in more than twenty years, singing a tune of her childhood:

"Starr Bright will be with you soon!
Starr Bright will be with you soon!
Starr Bright, Starr Bright!
Starr Bright will be with you soon!"

And laughing, and talking to herself, and already she'd begun to forget; what had happened in the Paradise Motel she'd begun to forget; for forgetting is part of healing, and God's grace is to heal. At dawn as the fiery eye emerged from the dark side of the earth she'd known that she would be guided, she would not come to harm. A wind rose out of the desert blowing dust and tumbleweed across the highway and she'd arrived in a gritty cloud obscuring the sun. Calmly locking the Infiniti with a gloved hand and tossing the keys beneath the car and walking away unobserved carrying her Gucci bag and other items, traveler's items, through the sea of vehicles parked at the Mirage. *And I saw a sea of glass mingled with fire and knew I had come to the right place.* In this Sodom and Gomorrah of the desert "Starr Bright" stepped into a dream, but it was not a dream of her own, it was not a dream that depended upon her to sustain it, it was a dream already existing, in which she could hide, as a hunted creature can hide in the wilderness; she'd been in such cities before, and knew the solace of such anonymity. And in a women's rest room at the Mirage she'd changed certain of her outer garments and fitted her beautiful red wig exactingly to her head, it was a finely woven $300 human-hair wig she'd purchased for professional reasons in Miami that had the power to change her appearance, and her personality, utterly. And so if pigs' eyes moved onto her snagging onto her they were not eyes to capture *her*.

Thank you O God for this safe passage.

Strange then the next morning to read in the tabloid *Las Vegas Post* the banner headline

BLOODY RITUAL EXECUTION
"PIG DEATH" IN SPARKS MOTEL ROOM

because already she'd forgotten so much. Because already she'd begun to heal. Like the ugly welts on her breasts and her belly and between her legs that were beginning to heal, with God's grace. Like the bruises at the nape of her neck and at the small of her back where he'd straddled her. It was an ugly, lurid but fascinating story the *Post* had featured on its cover and inside front pages. How many times such had happened, and would happen. In the desert, beneath the vast empty sky into which you might fall, fall forever. A DO NOT DISTURB sign had hung outside the door of a motel room for a full day, the blinds of the room had been closed tight and the customer's car was gone from the lot and there appeared to be no activity and at last a maid unlocked the door to discover to her horror what waited inside to be discovered. *A forty-seven-year-old California man lying in a pool of congealed blood. A corpse bloodied, mutilated, naked. His throat slashed so he'd bled to death and there were multiple stab wounds in the genital area and there was blood splattered everywhere, even on the ceiling. And on the wall beside the bed in eight-inch bloody letters*

DIE PIG FILTH
DIE SATAN

The murdered man had been identified as "William Raymond Cobb of Elton, California." His wallet and rented car, a new-model Infiniti, were missing, and Nevada State police were searching for a female companion with whom he'd registered in the motel as "Mr. & Mrs. Elton Flynn of Los Angeles." A photograph of Cobb reprinted in the paper had not resembled anyone "Starr Bright" could recall. She was certain she'd never seen this man; she'd never seen any bloodied wall. *The maid must have written those words on the wall, & the star-sign to cast suspicion onto "Starr Bright."* As in a vague, shifting dream she could remember a swimming pool filled with bright turquoise water that stank of chlorine, and she could remember a child's plastic toy or inner tube floating in the pool; but she couldn't remember any "William Raymond Cobb" and doubted that she had ever been in such a man's proximity. At Kings Lake, as elsewhere, so many men had introduced themselves to "Starr Bright," how could she remember them all? And why should she remember them all? She studied the face squinting up at her out of the cheap tabloid paper, a jowly middle-aged face, a coarse male face, a face "Starr Bright" might pity as one might pity the face of a victim of any brutal or humiliating misfortune. *God, have mercy on this sinner. If You deem such a sinner worthy of Your mercy.* "Starr Bright" was skeptical that, as the article claimed, Cobb had been married for twenty-two years; and was "survived by" a wife and children, a brother and a sister.

The desk clerk at the Paradise Motel told police that it had been obvious to him that "Mr. & Mrs. Flynn" hadn't been married. As if it mattered! The man had behaved nervously and guiltily, making awkward jokes; must've been twenty years older than the woman; the woman was beautiful, glamorous; looked like a supermodel, or an actress, or a hooker—"but a high-class hooker." Another witness, staying at the motel, claimed she'd seen the woman swimming in the pool, wearing a tiny yellow bikini; the woman and Cobb were swimming and splashing in the pool, drunk; later, in the cocktail lounge, the couple had been observed quarreling by several persons, including the bartender. The desk clerk described the missing woman suspect as platinum blond, approximately twenty-three years old, stylishly dressed; about five foot five, weighing maybe one hundred pounds; the bartender, who was a woman, described her as dishwater blond with a "coarse skin," thirty-five at the youngest, heavily made up, five feet eight or nine and weighing possibly one hundred twenty pounds. Other witnesses recalled her seeming drugged, or drunk; as friendly and smiling; as not friendly at all but stiff, icy-cold—"Looking at you like she'd like to slit your throat."

"Starr Bright" laughed angrily. A tower of Babel, a crowd of false witnesses, she would pay them no further heed.

But for curiosity's sake, and as memento of her Nevada visit, she tore out the pages from the *Post* containing the account of William Raymond Cobb's murder. And carefully folded them, and placed them inside the slightly tattered silk lining of her Gucci bag; with a bulky brass belt buckle wrapped in toilet paper. And she counted the cash in her possession that bright-glaring October morning: $692.

Next day, the *Post* published a police artist's drawing of the "female suspect" who'd shared a room and a bed with Mr. Cobb of Elton, California, and who was now missing. An ugly picture, "Starr Bright" thought: a stark, staring hungry face, oversized lips and tousled showgirl hair, of any age between twenty-five and forty. *This is not me, nor anyone known to me.* What relief in such knowledge!

The dead man's rented car had been discovered in the parking lot at the Mirage; a Reno woman, a psychic who'd worked with Nevada State police in the past, claimed she'd had a vision of the suspect dead herself at the bottom of a ravine in Red Rock Canyon, but a search in that desolate area had turned up nothing; there had been, and would be, numerous scattered sightings of the suspect through the Southwest, as far away as Nogales, Arizona, and San Diego, California; but nothing came of these leads; police were reported "continuing with their investigation" but no arrest had been made.

Not me, nor anyone known to me.

In her red wig, her miracle-wig that altered her appearance and her personality entirely. "Sherrill" she was now, or "Sherry." And "Starr Bright" in hiding secret as the dark side of the moon.

Except most of the money was gone. Not only the fat woman sobbing her heart out in a women's rest room but waitresses, waiters, the motel maid who was a Hispanic girl of about sixteen, and pregnant—these parties "Starr Bright" couldn't resist tipping, sometimes with $5 bills. So the money was going, down to $37 the night she met up with the man who introduced himself as Earl Tunley.

Trying not to be scared, living as she was from day to day, hour to hour. The slots, blackjack, roulette and keno and the lottery and again the slots. Waiting for her luck to change. Waiting for a man, the right man. Waiting for a sign. And there was Earl Tunley so powerfully attracted to her, she saw desire shining in the man's eyes suffusing her like flame. Hadn't she reason to believe her life might be changed for the better. Hadn't she reason to believe her bad-luck streak had ended.

Wanting to believe that Earl Tunley in his cowhide boots, black silk shirt and Armani-style jacket, Earl Tunley with his hot, quick hands and mouth was truly from Council Bluffs, Iowa; for she had the idea that a man who sold TV and video equipment in Council Bluffs, Iowa, was a man you could trust. And he'd promised to stake her "as much as required" and this, too, she wanted to believe.

Except hadn't there been, from the start, something swaggering and authoritarian in his manner? As if, somehow, she'd met this man before?

After their fantastic lovemaking, there she lay naked and content in Earl Tunley's king-sized bed in the Golden Sands Motor Lodge lazily stroking Earl Tunley's chest, running her long polished fingernails through his steely-gray chest hairs and stroking the glittering gold chain he wore around his neck which looked like the real thing, 24-carat, and she'd thought with girlish naivete *This one, this one maybe I could love, maybe* seeing in her mind's eye dimmed and confused by alcohol and by the late hour something looming chalky white, a dreamy image of Council Bluffs, Iowa. And her new lover was smiling saying, "You want it, sweetheart? Take it." And for an instant she thought he was serious, then she realized he was being sarcastic; and she said quickly, "Why no, Earl," and he said, "Sure, sweetheart, it's yours." He tumbled to undo the clasp and she stopped his fingers and said in a husky, earnest voice, "Earl, no. I don't want a single thing from you, ever—except a little more loving." So he shrugged and said, "Well, O.K.," staring at her smirking *Sure you want my gold chain, sweetheart. You know and I know you want all you can get from me, right?* But she'd pretended not to know, and kissed him, and ran her hands rapidly over his muscular body, stroking his clammy-cool penis reverently until he groaned forgetting any sarcasm, any doubt of her motives, and it was all right between them again. Or seemed so.

"Oh, lover. Oh my God—"

Later in the bathroom, readying herself for another stint of casino gambling (though in fact she'd rather have soaked in a hot tub and gone to bed to sleep, alone) she realized that ugly moment between "Sherry" and her new lover had been her own damned fault. She'd made the guy anxious alluding to a former husband—a "boyfriend"—God knows, men are worried about their sexual performances, this one had tensed up at even the hint she might have been comparing him to some teenaged "football hero" stud. That was it!

An error "Starr Bright" vowed never to make again with Earl Tunley, or another.

* * *

JACKPOT!

$1000 SILVER DOLLARS JACKPOT!

"Oh, Earl! Look!"—as the slot machine released a cascade of silver dollars like madness.

Laughing, incredulous, cigarettes clenched between their lips, they held CASINO AMERICANA buckets to the machine's opening, to catch the miraculous coins. "Baby, you've got the touch. Congratulations!" Earl said, kissing her as a small crowd of onlookers cheered and applauded. Envy shining in their eyes, "Starr Bright" could see even in the midst of her exhilaration. Envy not just that "Starr Bright" had won a $1000 SILVER DOLLARS JACKPOT—the machine lighted up red, white, and blue like a berserk American flag, hurdy-gurdy music playing loudly—but that she was a beautiful glamorous sexy redhead in a gold lamé dress tight as a tourniquet across her breasts and pelvis and she had a lover, good-looking, manly, a gold chain glinting around his neck, clearly crazy for her. *Thank you God thank you God thank you God.*

"Now, let's play craps. Slots is small-time."

"Oh, but Earl, honey—"

"Baby, don't worry, I'll stake you—five hundred dollars. The one thousand is all yours."

"But, Earl, craps scares me; you can lose too much too fast. I trust the slots."

"Baby, I told you: slots is small-time. Craps is the real thing."

Earl had staked "Starr Bright" for the slots; she'd played as many machines simultaneously as she could manage, while he looked on indulgently, supplying them both with drinks, cigarettes. Now it was 3:43 A.M. in the casino at the Americana amid lavish neon-flashing red-white-and-blue American flags, eagles, replicas of Uncle Sam and Abraham Lincoln, George Washington, John F. Kennedy gazing out over the swarming sea of gamblers. "Starr Bright" had been playing the slots only twenty minutes when she'd won the jackpot and she owed her good luck to Earl Tunley, leaning now against the man, twining herself around him inhaling his rich ripe manly odor liking it that people were watching them, sad-faced fattish women with too much makeup who hadn't ever won a jackpot and hadn't any man to love them like Earl Tunley. "All right, lover," she said, sighing, hugging the bucket of gleaming new-minted silver coins, "—you know best."

So they left the slots, and went to play craps; "Starr Bright" dazed with excitement, exhaustion; smiling upon everyone she saw; in a state of bliss. Her lover Earl was excited, too; edgy, positioning himself at the craps table with "Starr Bright" beside him, at his left elbow—"Now don't budge. You're my good luck, baby." Calling her "baby" so frequently now she guessed he'd maybe forgotten her name.

Earl pushed out $300 worth of chips and got into the game immediately. And when "Starr Bright" opened her eyes again he'd won: chips were being pushed in his direction. "Starr Bright" kissed him, crying, "Terrific, lover!" But Earl scarcely paid attention, gathering in his new chips and mingling them with the old. He counted out $500 worth of chips for "Starr Bright" and told her to do what he said; they'd both be betting, and he intended to win, big. "Starr Bright" pretended enthusiasm; she'd been drinking whiskey sours, on a near-empty stomach; she smiled, smiled and looked gorgeous which was what a gambling man required, a great-looking redhead beside him at the craps table. "O.K., baby," Earl said, drawing in a deep, exhilarated breath, like a man on a high diving board, "—bet *pass.*" When "Starr Bright" hesitated, Earl closed his hand over hers and pushed out a pile of chips. The principal player at the table was a fattish flush-faced man with startling blue eyes; he was the one who wielded the dice, and all eyes avidly fastened upon him as he shook, and rolled—and whatever it was, half the players at the table seemed to have won, along with him; and half the players seemed to have lost. Earl grunted with satisfaction, squeezing "Starr Bright's" hand so hard he nearly crushed the bones, so she figured they'd won. How much? It looked like a lot.

At 4:10 A.M. it was Earl Tunley's turn to shake the dice. "Starr

Bright" had been drifting off, woozy and blissful in her private space thinking *My jackpot! My 1000 silver dollars!* She hated craps, a fast cruel confusing game involving numerous players, side bets on bets, "points" that were made, or lost; the rapid motion of dice, chips, dice, chips was too much for her eye to follow; the pattern of numerals and figures on the tabletop, the calm expressionless manner with which the uniformed casino girl (beautiful, years younger than "Starr Bright") raked in piles of chips with a little Plexiglas rake, taking hundreds or even thousands of dollars from losing players without a blink of an eye—God, what a cruel game! "Starr Bright" followed Earl's directions betting he'd make his point, she wasn't aware of how much she was betting only that he'd staked her and she couldn't lose, could she?—the bucket of silver dollars was at her feet. She wanted him to love her, she'd experienced, almost, a glimmer of emotion, and of sexual excitation, in his arms, in his king-sized bed at the Golden Sands Motor Lodge. There was something consoling about Council Bluffs, Iowa—wasn't there? *A pig like any of them, a mask of Satan. You know.* Earl was nudging her impatiently to place a bet, "Everything you have, baby," and "Starr Bright" said in a pleading little-girl voice, "Oh, Earl honey—*everything*? I'm scared to go all the way." Earl's face shone with an oily perspiration and the gold chain glittered around his neck like a living thing. His eyes were red-veined, but sharp. He was saying, boasting, "Redheads are my good luck," loud enough for other players, men, to hear. "Starr Bright" saw both her hands, trembling just visibly, push out a messy pile of chips onto the pass line. How much? How much was she risking? Grandly, Earl shook the dice, shook and rolled and all stared as the dice turned up four and three.

"Seven! Won!"

Earl was grinning, excited as a kid. The casino girl scarcely gave him a glance as she pushed a large pile of chips in his direction. Cool as swabbing down an emergency room splattered with blood, "Starr Bright" thought. That was the kind of professional hauteur you needed to be an exotic dancer, too.

Thank God, they'd won. Five thousand? Or more? Earl gulped down the remainder of his drink, sex-moaned in "Starr Bright's" ear, "Oh baby, baby—" but didn't otherwise pause. No time to rest, no time to catch his breath, Earl wanted to stay in the game now he was hot. "Starr Bright" was beginning to feel faint. Not long ago she'd been a terrified passenger in a Porsche being driven at one hundred miles an hour along a rain-slick highway and it was the identical sensation—exciting, exhilarating, but crazy and dangerous. Too much too fast.

By 4:35 A.M. they'd won—what? Thirteen thousand, Earl was saying. He was counting his chips, muttering to himself, grinning and wiping his damp face; his eyes were glassy and bright and his lips slack, loose. There was something about him "Starr Bright" could almost identify, some characteristic, trait—but what? As if she'd met him before this night, or someone very like him. He was looking flushed with success. He hadn't wanted to take time to shower or even wash himself after they'd made love, eager to get back to the casinos, and now a powerful odor wafted from him, "Starr Bright" hoped no one else at the table could smell it—male sex, male heat, male passion. *A filthy pig like any other. You know.* She had to admit, winning made a man sexy; winning made a man desirable; this was a man she could love, maybe. Except he'd developed a habit of nudging her in the breast saying, irritated, "Stand still, right here, don't be moving around, I told you. You're my good-luck piece of ass." And he laughed loudly, and "Starr Bright" tried to smile. He was shaking dice again, he'd pushed out half his enormous pile of chips and wanted "Starr Bright" to bet he'd make his point, so vaguely, blindly she pushed out half her pile of chips, too.

Thinking *God, don't let us lose. Let him love me.* A dazed-groggy prayer that was the same prayer mouthed everywhere in Vegas by hundreds, thousands of anxious gamblers every second of every hour of every day.

Another time, Earl Tunley rolled and won.

Following this things became even more confused. A roller

coaster going faster, faster, faster. They'd won $12,000? 15, 20? Her lover from Council Bluffs, Iowa, and glamorous sexy red-haired "Sherrill Dwyer" from—somewhere in California. Earl was saying, gloating, "Jesus, I'm hot. Back home they can kiss my ass. A man needs respect and this is *it*." He'd been squeezing "Starr Bright's" upper arm, there were red welts in the flesh. Now that she had money again, she could repay the loan from her sister—what had it been? $500, not much—she'd had the feeling that her sister's husband, whose name she couldn't remember, resented the loan, or loans; well, fuck him! Lily's sister Sharon always repaid her loans and with interest, too.

"Starr Bright" must have been easing away, her feet aching in the ridiculous high-heeled shoes that pinched her toes forcing the weight of her body into a tiny pointed space, for Earl Tunley gripped her arm again and smiled hard at her and repositioned her at his side. "Now stay still, baby. We're going for broke." "Starr Bright" winced, "Please, Eddy—that hurts," and Earl said, his voice slurred, "'Ernie' you mean—no: 'Earl.' You mean 'Earl.'" And "Starr Bright" said quickly, "'Earl'—that's what I said, honey. 'Earl' is your name," and Earl laughed harshly saying, "Fucking 'Earl' is my fucking name, not fucking 'Eddy,'" his laughter explosive as a sneeze. He took up the dice again exuberantly and "Starr Bright" murmured, "Here we gooo! Sky's the limit!" and planted a kiss on his burning cheek; but instead of rolling the dice as everyone expected, Earl turned to her, his lips drawn back from his teeth in a savage grin, and said, "Watch it, cunt. I'm warning you." So "Starr Bright" went very still, and contrite. And Earl rolled the dice, and came up with a number that wasn't good, muttered, "Shit," so "Starr Bright" thought in a panic they'd lost, but, as it turned out, he had another roll and another chance, and this time he rolled—two sixes. And this wasn't good, either. "Starr Bright" said in a giggly-drunken little-girl voice, a voice meant to dispel the sickening sensation in the pit of her belly, "Oh, damn! You'd think a twelve would be better than an eleven, wouldn't you?"

But no one laughed. Glazed-eyed Earl didn't hear.

No pause in the game. Not a heartbeat. A few of the players avoided Earl's eyes out of brotherly sympathy perhaps. "Starr Bright" stared as the casino girl coolly raked in Earl's big pile of chips—and "Starr Bright's" without an eyeblink. How much had they lost? "Starr Bright" was whispering, "Oh, lover. Ohhhh." She meant to console him slipping her arm through his but he shook her off, uttered something she didn't catch, stooped to take up the bucket of silver dollars from the floor and as "Starr Bright" stared uncomprehending after him he went to a nearby cashier's counter to cash the silver dollars into chips. And came back, grim, determined, sweat gleaming on his face like congealed grease, and the look in his eyes warning her not to fuck with him. "Starr Bright" tried to protest faintly, "Earl, honey, those silver dollars were mine, you said—you promised," and Earl repositioned her at his side and said, "Just stand still, baby. And shut the mouth."

So Earl bet one thousand dollars' worth of chips on a single roll and "Starr Bright" hid her eyes behind her trembling fingers praying *God oh God!* though seeming to know the prayer was helpless to intervene. And even as Earl threw the dice, sent them flying and bouncing across the table, "Starr Bright" must have suffered a moment's weakness, a mini-blackout—falling against him, so that, even as he lost the roll, he'd turned to her and slapped her across the mouth, the movement of his hand so swift that no one at the table saw, or seemed to see; and "Starr Bright" herself could not comprehend what had happened, except her lower lip throbbed with pain and began to bleed. Earl's face had gone the color of bread dough and his bloodshot eyes glared. "Cunt, I told you not to fuck me up," he said, advancing upon her as others at the table scrambled to get out of the way, leaving "Starr Bright" to her boyfriend's mercy, "—didn't I tell you *not to fuck me up*."

"Earl, I'm sorry—"

"Y'know what you cost me, cunt?—*twenty-seven thousand dollars*!"

Abruptly as if he'd emerged from out of a trapdoor a casino

security guard appeared, a hefty black man of few words, "That's enough, mister, come this way please," and before they knew what was happening they were being escorted politely but unerringly out of the casino. "Starr Bright" supposed that the girl at the craps table had summoned the guard with a secret buzzer. Earl was sullen, blustering and intimidated, his words slurred, "Butt out, asshole, this is a private discourse, this cunt cost me a bundle," and "Starr Bright" was trying earnestly to explain, "Sir, he doesn't mean it, he's my friend, he didn't hurt me, he's excited 'cause he just took a big loss," and Earl said angrily, "Shut it!" and "Starr Bright" said, "Really, sir, he's the sweetest man, he never meant—" But the robotlike guard who was six foot five, two hundred fifty pounds and dark-skinned as a polished hickory nut seemed scarcely to hear as if this, his task, was too familiar and too boring to require from him more than a few clipped words mechanical as a recitation, "Thank you for patronizing the Casino Americana and perhaps another time you will revisit us under more favorable circumstances." When Earl hesitated at the exit, the guard hoisted him into the revolving door and gave the door a fierce spin and a moment later Earl and "Starr Bright" were out in the warm, faintly sulphurous night.

Earl said, aggrieved as a lost child, wiping his face on the sleeve of his Italian-style jacket, "Craps is my *game.* I was *w-winning.*"

"Starr Bright" slipped her arm around his waist (which was warm and rumpled as damp laundry) and said, soothingly, "That's right, Earl, you *were* winning. You *were.* You can win again. You can draw on your American Express card, can't you, lover? Sure you can."

Because I had hope, still, that he would love me. I would love him.

Because I was afraid to be alone that terrible night.

Because I wanted the $1000 he owed me.

Because I knew that my heavenly father would watch over me in time of peril.

* * *

And at first it had not seemed an unwise decision. She had not seemed in immediate danger.

Taking a cab back to the Golden Sands Motor Lodge because the man who'd introduced himself to her as Earl Tunley wasn't in any condition to drive. Stumbling into the dim-lit room that smelled still of their bodies, and stained bedclothes; fecund odors of sweat, semen, damp wadded towels and insecticide. Always the odor of insecticide. And Earl was amorous in his misery, wishing not to think of the many thousands of dollars he'd lost which seemed to him in his confusion to have been his money from the start, stolen from him by the cruelty of chance and a woman's blundering. Kissing "Starr Bright" roughly with his tongue, burying his hot face in her neck and between her breasts and moving his hands swiftly and hungrily over her. Like a drowning man he groaned, "Oh baby, baby—"

"Starr Bright" eased her neck and head away from her lover's fumbling caresses, cautious he might dislodge her wig; the human-hair miracle-wig that fitted her head snug as a bathing cap. He'd slapped her pretty hard there in the casino and her lip was swelling but in the urgency of the moment she wasn't thinking of it; anyway, other men had struck her and she'd survived; and maybe deserved being struck now and then for *you're a cunt, you know it* and she guessed she knew and accepted this judgment for hadn't she abandoned her own baby years and years ago, wished even to drown her own baby years and years ago and the very memory by now vague and faded like a Polaroid snapshot too long exposed to light. But, oh God: if he would let her alone and she could shower and cleanse herself and fall into bed and sleep, sleep. The sweet sleep of dreamless sinless oblivion. The sweet druggy-alcohol sleep like dying. And next day he could withdraw cash with his credit card and they would hit another casino, another craps table, and just maybe win, and win big. Because it did seem plausible to her that Earl Tunley deserved to win back the $27,000 he'd lost; he'd been winning, he'd been on a roll, and it had been taken from him unfairly. For this was gambler's logic and it was

"Starr Bright's" logic in her innermost heart. *That which you sow, you shall reap.*

And when her lover got back the $27,000 that was rightfully his, she would share in it, too.

It seemed to be dawn. Hazy tendrils of flame in the eastern sky. The Venetian blinds of room 19, at the far end of the long graceless concrete-block Golden Sands Motor Lodge, were tightly drawn. On top of the TV was a nearly empty bottle of Jim Beam, and greedy Earl Tunley snatched it up and gulped its contents like a thirsty man. And "Starr Bright" sighed, and was going to make a practical suggestion about a little sleep, and suddenly Earl turned on her, cursed her, "—told you not to fuck me up, didn't I?" and when she protested he grabbed her, and they struggled, and he said, grunting, "—could smash your face, cunt—make you ugly like you deserve! Strangle you—" and she was too terrified to scream for help, knowing that no one would hear, no one would wish to hear, and she was too weak suddenly to defend herself as the man pushed her backward, threw her onto the rumpled bed, and reached with grasping fingers up inside the tight lamé skirt to take possession.

God help me.

Waking with difficulty, her head aching, pounding where he'd struck it repeatedly against a wall. Slowly she disentangled herself from the snoring man, cautious of waking him. His hairy sweaty limbs had been flung over her, pressing her to the bed; his heavy torso, slack belly. And how heavy his head, his eyes shut upon a thin crescent of white like mucus. Eddy? Earl? Though knowing he had surely lied to her she saw again a fleeting vision of chalk-white cliffs—Council Bluffs, Iowa? Her mouth throbbed with pain, the lower lip was grotesquely swollen. Like a bee sting she'd had as a child, and her sister Lily had said *Oh I wish the nasty bee would sting me, too!* Her left eye, too, was swollen—he must have punched her there. And the nipples of both breasts had been pinched, hard. He hadn't removed her dress but had pushed it up to nearly her armpits. He'd threatened to kill her if she screamed and perhaps he had killed her, it was not "Starr Bright" but her child-spirit Rose of Sharon who awakened in her now. *Because the spirit cannot be extinguished, the spirit liveth and abideth forever.*

The man stirred, groaned as if in pain—but didn't wake. A wet whistling snore issued from his slack mouth. Except for black silk socks on his feet, the lower half of his body was stark naked; his shin was unbuttoned and open upon a fattish-muscular chest covered in isolated wirelike hairs. The skin was creased, the color of rancid lard. No beauty here. Only the glittering gold chain around his neck.

Recalling with shame how he'd jeeringly offered her that gold chain. As if he'd thought her a prostitute. Why hadn't she fled him, then!

Pig, fornicator and despiser of women.

Emissary of Satan.

"Starr Bright" extricated herself from the man who'd raped her, beaten her, threatened death. It was just 7 A.M. She'd been unconscious for more than an hour. A fierce fiery light penetrated the slats of the window blind and the crack beneath the door. "Starr Bright" tried to smooth down her dress, which was badly stained, torn at the shoulder. In the bureau mirror she saw her wavering, cringing reflection. Yet the red wig was still in place. Her makeup had been rubbed virtually off, her face was white, pinched-looking, sickly; her left eye blackened, her lower lip swollen to twice its normal size. *Is that me? Is that who I've become? God, have mercy…*

"Starr Bright" would have slipped from the room and left behind the snoring man except: headed for the door, she stumbled upon the man's jacket on the floor, and stubbed her toe against something heavy in an inside pocket.

She investigated, and discovered—a pistol.

A pistol! It shone like blue steel, with a short barrel of about four inches; compact, and deadly. "Starr Bright" stared at it in astonishment. She knew little about guns, she'd held a gun in her hand upon occasion but had never fired one and could not have identified this except to know that it was a revolver, each bullet in its chamber in the revolving cylinder. What a good clean metallic smell.

Its make was Ruger. Of this, she'd never heard.

As soon as the pistol was in her hand, "Starr Bright" felt a deep suffusion of relief. Though her hand visibly trembled, and her head and body were encased in pain. She understood that the child Rose of Sharon would be protected now, inviolate. "Starr Bright" knew that the man could not hurt her now. God had gifted her with unexpected power over the man.

"Thank you, God! Praise God!"

In other pockets of the jacket she discovered the man's wallet, and a badge, and a law officer's ID, with a photo: ERNEST D. FENKE DEPUTY SHERIFF SUMNER CO. NEBRASKA.

"Deputy sheriff—!"

And now she began to laugh. "Starr Bright" hooked up with a cop! An off-duty cop, one of the enemy.

You never could predict God's designs. For the God of wrath was also a God of jokes, tricks. You had to have a sense of humor to comprehend Him.

Playful as a mischievous child "Starr Bright" affixed the shiny brass badge to the gold lamé fabric above her left breast, it snagged in the material, but held. Wild! She stood very tall in her bare feet, tall enough it seemed to brush the ceiling of the room with her head. She was suffused with strength and joy like a sudden fountain of clear, pure water; almost, she could stand on her tiptoes, a graceful ballerina.

"Wake up."

She was standing above the snoring man, gripping the pistol in both hands to steady it. She'd released the trigger guard and cocked the hammer. She'd spoken calmly, with assurance, though very excited; when the snoring man failed to wake, she prodded his shoulder with the gun barrel. His eyes flew open, at first unfocused. Then he saw her. Saw the gun. The badge above her left breast.

She said, smiling, "'Deputy Sheriff Ernest D. Fenke, of Sumner County, Nebraska.' You are under immediate arrest."

Fenke blinked rapidly as if a bright light was being beamed into his bloodshot eyes. A look of incredulity tightened his features, a stab of quick fear. The worst thing that could happen to a cop had happened to him: his gun had been taken from him. He said, "H-hey! Honey! Don't kid around with that—"

"Deputy Fenke, get up."

"Jesus, look—honey? Give that gun to me, it might go off and—you wouldn't want—"

"So you're a cop? That's your secret? 'Deputy Fenke of Nebraska'? Why'd you lie to me?"

"Please, honey—"

"You get to carry a gun, eh? Deputy Fenke? Persecute people? How many people has this gun killed, Deputy Fenke?"

"N-nobody."

"You're a liar." "Starr Bright" spoke with a strange sort of authority. Her voice serene, glistening. As if the deep soothing peace coursing through her had brought with it an eloquence not her own; the purity of the child Rose of Sharon, that sweet clear delicate soprano voice.

"Out of bed, and on your knees. Now."

And he obeyed her. Groveling, cowardly like all such craven men—he obeyed her. It was fitting that the man, part-naked, should tremble before the woman, his pig-eyes shining with fear, awe, trepidation; his limp fleshy genitalia like a skinned baby creature prominent between pale trembling thighs. "Starr Bright" saw the logic of it, how God had once again guided her hand in His shrewd wisdom. A man, kneeling before a woman of such power, has become, by mock-miracle, *a woman.*

"Starr Bright" said, "You raped me, and you defiled me, and you stole my money from me, Deputy Fenke—my jackpot, my one thousand silver dollars. And now you must repay me."

Fenke pleaded, "Honey, I—I didn't mean to hurt you! Ever! I thought we were—just—" He gestured toward the bed as if to say just *fooling around, screwing around—nothing serious.*

It wasn't clear whether "Starr Bright" meant to arouse such fear in the man or whether, barefoot, her gold lamé dress riding up to her thighs, the glinting badge on her left breast, she was being playful, seductive in a new way. In almost an incantatory voice she said, "Rapist. Filthy pig. And thief—common thief, Deputy! Taking my jackpot from me when you'd promised it was mine to keep."

"Honey, I'll pay you back—I was going to pay you back—"

"You were, Deputy?"

"—I was going to draw five thousand dollars on my credit card tomorrow. Get back into action, the two of us—"

"That's the truth? You lied to me once, Deputy Fenke, why should I believe you now?"

"Baby, I didn't lie to you. I was maybe drinking too much—I got carried away. I'm crazy about you."

"Yes? That's why you raped me?"

On his knees, trembling before her, the man tried to smile. A sick guilty feeble smile. Staring at "Starr Bright" with his bloodshot eyes as if trying not to see the pistol in her hands, aimed at his face; trying not to acknowledge that he saw it. He was saying, "I—didn't r-rape you, honey. That's a terrible thing to say. I would never force a w-woman—"

"No?" "Starr Bright" indicated her swollen lip, her throbbing eye. Lifting her skirt to show bruises, welts. Torn black-lace panties.

And the man gaped at her miserably. Could only shake his head as if in honest befuddlement. *I did such a thing? No!*

"Starr Bright" began an interrogation. Asking the man did he love her and he said quickly sure, oh sure he was crazy about her! She asked was she beautiful in his eyes and he said eagerly oh yes, yes she was beautiful—"Baby, you know it! You're terrific." And she said coyly, redheads were his good luck, yes? Was she his good luck? and Fenke was nodding yes, emphatically yes when in a gesture of triumph "Starr Bright" yanked off the red human-hair wig, revealing her ashy-blond hair flattened and matted, pinned in unflattering clumps around her head. And Deputy Fenke's slack pale hungover face showed yet more astonishment, incredulity.

Slyly "Starr Bright" asked, "*Am* I beautiful, Deputy?"

He'd swallowed hard, and was stammering, "Y-yes…"

"Starr Bright" laughed in delight. Like the cruelly prankish girl she'd been long ago. Rose of Sharon who was the unpredictable Donner sister but of course you forgave little Sharon, she was so vivacious, so beautiful. Taunting the man now, "Crazy about me, eh?"

"Yes…"

Laughing heartily at the look on his face. Sick sinking flailing look of a man who's trapped. It was cruel, it was heartless, such taunting, but she could not resist. "Say, Deputy, a law officer is supposed to be observant. How old d'you think I am?"

"I—don't know—"

"When you picked me up last night, put your moves on me, what age were you estimating?"

"I—don't know—"

"Starr Bright" laughed even more loudly, thoroughly enjoying this interrogation. "I'll be thirty-seven, my next birthday."

Fenke laughed nervously. "That's—not old. I'm thirty-nine…"

"Would you have picked me up, if you'd known my age, Deputy Fenke?"

"Yes!"

"You *do* think I'm a beautiful woman?—desirable?"

"Baby, I'm crazy about you—I said. Only please—maybe you should give me the gun now? So nobody gets hurt? And we can get dressed, and go out, and I'll get some cash, and—"

Fenke was reaching out toward her, hesitantly, in appeal; but "Starr Bright" stepped away, frowning. She waved the pistol at him.

"No! Stay right where you are, mister. Or I swear I will shoot you right in the face."

"Jesus, Cheryl—"

"'Sherrill.'"

"—Sh-Sherrill. I meant to say."

"My name is 'Starr Bright.'"

"'Starr'—?"

"You never saw 'Starr Bright' dance. You aren't the one—that was another one—did you know him? 'Cobb.'" For a moment she was confused in time; the men were confused, interchangeable; perhaps in fact they were the same man. It seemed to "Starr Bright" that in some mysterious way the men, or the man, knew her; and knew his ineluctable fate. So they might discuss it together calmly, as if reminiscing. "They said in the papers, on TV—'Starr Bright' slashed a man's throat and danced barefoot in his blood. Drew the sign of the star in pig's blood on a wall. I don't know if it's truth or falsehood, it was something that happened in Sparks, Nevada, at a certain hour and it was not a choice." The memory of what had happened in that other motel room in the desert was blurred as tissue in water; this man's lightened dough-face was a barrier between her and the memory. Or perhaps it was no memory at all, perhaps she'd only read about it in the *Las Vegas Post* and studied the photographs of Cobb and the blood-smeared wall. She said, smiling, "Oh, that one bled like a stuck pig, he *was* a stuck pig. All of you—*pigs*."

"W-what are you saying, Sherrill?"

"Cobb. You know 'Pig Death.' It was written up in all the papers, it was on TV."

Fenke stared at her, his eyes glazing over in horror. In a hoarse voice he said, "You're kidding, aren't you? My God."

"Starr Bright" laughed in girlish delight. How like performing before an audience this was. She'd known, at age thirteen, this would be her life.

She told Fenke how, immediately, she'd liked him; he'd stepped forward to offer her a cigarette in a moment of need, a weak moment of hers, and she'd been grateful to him. She had a hopeful heart, she was a professional singer-dancer and yet a woman who craved love; a woman who wanted to be respected, treated right. And she'd thought, at first, for a while last night, that he was the man for her. "But then you spoiled it, Deputy. You raped me, and you defiled me. And you stole my thousand dollars."

"I—I—I'm sorry—oh God, Sherrill, I'll make it up to you, I promise—"

"You *are* sorry? That's the truth? You won't do it again?—hurt me again?"

"Honey, I promise."

"You apologize? On your knees? To me? And to all the women you've defiled in your life?" As Fenke nodded with pathetic eagerness, "Starr Bright" continued to point the pistol at his head. She said, "Your wife?—do you have a wife? Yes? Back in Sumner County, Nebraska?" Fenke nodded, his eyes snatching at hers guiltily. "You apologize to her, too? You, an adulterer? Fornicator? How many times, Deputy? You apologize on your knees to all the women you've defiled? You beg forgiveness from them, and from God?"

"Y-yes…"

"And you'll pay me back my thousand-dollar jackpot?"

"Yes. I'll withdraw five thousand from my account right now, Sherrill. Let me get dressed, and we can go out and find a bank—"

"*Stay on your knees.* Why should I trust you, Deputy?"

"Please, you can trust me…"

"Why should I believe you? Any word out of your mouth? You say you're sorry? But men are never sorry."

"Sherrill, baby, I *am* sorry…"

"Starr Bright" was speaking more rapidly, in her high sharp soprano voice like flashing shears.

"Men are masks of Satan, never sorry. They can't get it up unless they hurt women."

"No, no! I'm not like that," Fenke said desperately. "Jesus, I got a daughter—I'm the father of a daughter. I'm not like that."

"Father of a daughter?—*you*?"

"Please, honey, let me make it up to you? Give me the gun, and nobody will get hurt…"

"Starr Bright" stood staring at the man. This part-naked man on his knees. But his shoulders were straighter now, his head higher. He seemed less afraid. *Father of a daughter—him?* A terrible clarity was opening in her brain, a tiny pinprick of light like a distant star rushing closer. Almost softly she said, "You won't be angry with me, if I give you back your gun?"

"No! I promise, Sherrill."

Fenke reached out hesitantly to accept the gun from "Starr Bright" and for a moment it almost seemed that she would surrender it to him. But there was a tawny light in her eyes, her smile slipped sideways like grease. Nimbly she sidestepped him, and raised the pistol higher to take aim between his eyes. She laughed. "And if I do? You won't change your mind and be cruel again? And hurt me again? And say you'll kill me?"

"Jesus, no. Honey, I was drunk. I didn't mean it."

"Because it's in your power, Deputy. You're a man, and a man's got the power. And 'Starr Bright' has no power. Only just this." She indicated the gun, smiling. "And if I surrender my power, what will stop you from hurting me again?"

"Sherrill, honey—no. I promise."

"Starr Bright" backed away to the air-conditioning unit near the window, and turned the fan to high. She switched on the TV, loud. A morning talk show dissolved in peals of laughter switching abruptly to a jingly cartoon-bright advertisement for Sani-Flush.

Fenke blinked as if she'd slapped him. "W-what are you doing?"

"Deputy, tell me: are you in a state of sin?"

"S-sin?"

"Have you been washed in the blood of the lamb?"

"I—I was baptized—"

"Baptized what?"

"Catholic."

"Catholic! You! So—you believe?"

"I…I believe."

"In God, and in Jesus Christ?"

"Yes…"

"In Satan, and in sin?"

"Y-yes…"

"You believe God is watching over you? At this moment?"

"Yes…"

"God would not allow harm to come to you, then. Unless it was his wish."

"Sherrill, please, honey. I said I was sorry…"

"Starr Bright" spoke rapidly, and clearly, to be heard over the noises of the fan and the TV. "A man is a mask of Satan, Deputy, and maybe can't help himself. Like a scorpion. Born in sin and travail and lust and wickedness and a love of inflicting hurt on weaker creatures, Jesus saw, and didn't judge. He said, 'Forgive, and love thy enemies as thyself.' But God says, 'I am a God of wrath, and none shall hide from my vengeance.'"

Now she was wrapping a towel carefully around the pistol, and around her hand that held the pistol. Until the tip of the barrel was only just visible.

Fenke said, in a quavering voice, "Why are you doing that, Sherrill? Baby, please—"

"'This is the Father's will which hath sent me.'"

"Sherrill—"

"One thing about Vegas, people mind their own business. You might hear women screaming—you might hear firecrackers—might even hear guns sometimes. But people respect each other's privacy." She was advancing upon the kneeling man dancerlike, knowing how, in his terror, she grew ever taller, more radiant. The light from her face alone was enough to blind him! He tried to shield the naked part of himself with his arms, and by cringing, hunching over; bringing his thighs closer together. As if ashamed of the fleshy thing between his legs, shrunken now, of the hue and texture of a slug. "My first boyfriend. the first boy I loved, I told you his name was Michael but that was not his name. He raped me, took my love for him and defiled it. And shared me with his buddies. I was fifteen; never told a soul. Too ashamed. You count on us being shamed." She paused, breathing quickly. "A cop raped me once—more than once. In Miami, and in Houston. Cops prey on the weak because they have the power. All this fallen world is, Deputy, is those with power preying on those without. You made a mistake, Deputy. You stole 'Starr Bright's' thousand-dollar jackpot."

A sickly jaundice-light shone in the man's eyes. He was begging, shivering. "Please, don't. Don't shoot me..."

"Look, I'm a sinner, too. I am 'Starr Bright' and I am a fallen angel. My daddy warned me as a headstrong child and I failed to heed. My daddy was a man of God, a shining man of God and he spoke to his flock who adored him of the dark heart of mankind. He spoke of Jesus as his brother, and of Satan the fallen angel as his brother. The one walking at his right hand and the other walking at his left hand. I broke his heart, I betrayed my daddy's love. All the days of my life I am accursed. I have not seen that man in fifteen years. Wishing to drown my own baby girl in sickness and despair and lashing out at those who would forgive me, and love me." She wiped her tearful stinging eyes on her forearm. Her vision wavered as if about to be extinguished, then came into sharp, painful focus again. She saw the kneeling man cringe before her, yet saw his eyes ratlike and alert, waiting for an advantage. She said, slyly, "Well, Deputy—all I need is your credit card."

"Sherrill, no. I'm begging you..."

"For what?"

"My life..."

"Then down. *Down*." She was moving, dancerlike, closer to him. The high-humming air conditioner and the noise of the TV made the air jangle. If she stumbled, if she weakened he would know. By instinct he would know. He was cringing, craven and terrified yet ratlike he would know. The fact excited her, like sex. Like sex as it had once been. In her ecstasy, in her exultation, she was drawing dangerously near to him. Whispering, "Pray for forgiveness from the Lord, and 'Starr Bright' will forgive you, too."

Fenke clasped his hands together clumsily, in an eager display of piety. His chest gleamed with sweat and his face was a mask of sweat, the creases in his forehead shining like metal.

In a stammering voice, a tremulously sincere-sounding voice, he began to pray, "Our F-Father who art in heaven—" then seemed to lose his breath, and needed encouragement, so "Starr Bright" said, "hallowed be thy name—" and quickly he continued. "—h-hallowed be thy thy name—Thy k-kingdom—" and again he paused as if his throat had closed, and "Starr Bright" was obliged to lead him, as, as small children, years ago in Shaheen, New York, she and her sister Lily had been led tenderly and firmly in prayer by their parents, "—thy kingdom come, thy will—" and the man eagerly repeated, "—thy w-will be done—on earth as it is in—in—"

Suddenly then making his move. Lunging at her, trying to grab the gun. But "Starr Bright" was prepared for this. Oh yes: "Starr Bright" was prepared for this. As if she'd been watching the kneeling man from a far corner of the room, or from a distant prospect of time. Noting how, his head bowed, chin creased against his chest, he'd been watching her covertly, desperately, in an attempt to deceive. "Starr Bright" gracefully sidestepped him, and pulled the trigger, sending a bullet into her enemy's face.

Point-blank.

"Didn't I warn you, Deputy! Deputy-pig!"

A single deadly shot aimed at the bridge of her enemy's nose. A bullet piercing the man's flesh, his bone, plowing into his brain in an instant. He had no time to cry out, to turn away or duck. He deserved no time to prepare himself. The towel wrapped around the gun had only partly muffled the sharp, cracking sound, but "Starr Bright" believed she was in no danger, no one would hear; God would protect her as He'd protected her all along. She stood over her fallen enemy, panting in triumph, "Didn't I warn you, Pig-Deputy! Mask of Satan! All of you!"

But Deputy Fenke had collapsed, was dying, or dead. So swiftly, it had to be a miracle. His eyes were opened in astonishment and his lustrous-glassy gaze was fixed to hers—then fading, failing like a dimming light. "Starr Bright" bent to peer closely. Where was the man's soul?—had it departed his body? Was it already gone? Gone—where?

Soft now and spineless as a creature pried out of its shell to die on dry land the man lay at her feet. Her bare feet. She stepped back, out of the flow of blood. Blood flowing darkly from the single wound to his broken face and soaking into the cheap nylon carpet of what unknown room he'd brought her to, to rape her; what unknown cheap hotel in this Sodom and Gomorrah of the desert that God might strike with lightning to annihilate should He wish at any time. "Starr Bright" was trembling, panting. Her thoughts blasted clean. *For these are the days of vengeance, that all things which are written may be fulfilled.*

3
Days of Vengeance

In Joshua Tree, California. In Tempe, Arizona. In a Malibu beach house at Thanksgiving. Things got complicated.

I don't want to kill. Not a one of them. I am not one who kills. I am Rose of Sharon, I am not one who kills.

Knowing not to travel by plane. Passing through any metal detector, sending her new suitcase through any X ray. For she could not leave her protection behind.

Angry words in blood on bloodied walls. Dancing in blood. POLICE OF FOUR STATES SEEK VENGEFUL FEMALE KILLER. "STAR" KILLER SOUGHT IN SLAYINGS. A lie, most of it. Trash to sell cheap newspapers. Dancing in blood, barefoot!

Never.

Sticky warm pig's blood, infected blood: never!

In Tempe, Arizona, purchasing at a discount mall a $6.99 Holy Bible. She was a brunette with soft-doe eyes. She was Sylvia, she was Durelle. But things got complicated. Once you toss the dice you have to play the game out.

"Starr Bright" yearned to dance again! "Starr Bright" was too young to retire! Audiences loved her, roused to cheers, whistles, applause, lust. "Exotic interpretive dance." Oh she was lonely, she grew resentful. Things got complicated.

One night swallowing painkiller capsules a man (youthful middle-aged, good-looking, TV producer separated from his family) gave her to quiet her but she vomited up, sick as a dog, the chalky clotted mess.

And laughed in bitterness, resignation. *God has His plans for "Starr Bright." No sinner can intercede.*

Their names were newsprint. Their names were syllables pronounced on TV news broadcasts. Their photo-faces which were not faces she recognized.

Masks of Satan. Not true faces.

How can you tell?—the pig-eyes.

From X in Joshua Tree, $588 which probably wasn't worth it. And the Land Rover she'd driven in a trance from Bishop, California, to Salt Lake City. A vision in the salt flats, God had drawn her. From Y, $1800. He'd given her not knowing how his life was spared. But Z, in San Diego, New Year's Eve. Things got complicated.

Eastward then by Greyhound. Not daring to board any airplane.

In the papers and TV they maligned her. "PIG DEATH" KILLER SOUGHT.

In the papers and TV they celebrated her. "STAR" KILLER SOUGHT.

Threw away her clothes, the bloodstained gold lamé dress scissored into pieces, burnt. The Gucci bag, stained shoes and lovely red human-hair wig. Designer sunglasses. Purchased Kmart clothes, a foam rubber pillow for her belly. Eight months' pregnancy. Dark circles beneath her eyes, graying-brown hair the hue of dishwater. Flat shoes, nylon stretch slacks, no rings except a cheap wedding band on her third finger, left hand. And her nails needing a manicure.

Oldish to be pregnant, maybe in her forties. A blotched face, pale pulpy mouth. Favoring her right leg, a limp.

Men's eyes drifted past her, through her. Even cops'.

Always you can rely on pig-eyes *not-seeing* what doesn't turn them on.

In a diner near Denver, Colorado. Seeing the TV news, a flash of the "STAR" KILLER's heavily made-up glamorous face. Sitting round-shouldered in shapeless clothes, slack face, belly and dishwater hair. In a row of Greyhound passengers that would have looked to a neutral observer companionable. Though no one knew anyone else. More coffee ma'am? the bored teenaged waitress asked and the oldish pregnant woman lifted her cup daring a small almost-shy smile *Hey I've been a pouty pretty kid like you, not so long ago,* yes she said, thanks, but the bored waitress didn't catch the smile, why bother. On the TV now the cruel likeness of beautiful "Starr Bright" had vanished, a grinning man in a checked suit held a pointer to a U.S. weather map across which eerie tendrils of vapor-smoke swirled.

On the Greyhound things were smooth and clear and dull and not complicated. But you can't ride a Greyhound bus forever.

I am not one who kills, I am Rose of Sharon who sings in the choir.

I am "Starr Bright." I am an exotic interpretive dancer. I am gifted, beautiful, glamorous, singled out for a special destiny.

How can you tell?—the pig eyes.

At the shadowy rear of a tavern parking lot in Council Bluffs, Iowa. In the guy's new-model Caddy, in the plush backseat. Things got complicated. You end up fighting for your life, defending your life. Struck, stabbed, pierced the enemy pig-flesh to defend your life. Things got complicated and went their own way not like on TV.

She took pig-money to protect herself. It was too complicated to explain and no one to whom she might explain, for God required no explanation, God guided her hand. As He had directed her not to destroy her baby rock-hard and swelling like a bulb in the earth in her belly *For through this baby you will be reborn.* And not to destroy her baby after its birth as her hands had urged, seeking to hold its small head under water *For through this baby you will be reborn.*

In Council Bluffs, Iowa. She'd wanted to see the "bluffs."

Things got complicated. Can't ride a fucking Greyhound forever.

A purchase of a second Bible. A smaller one, with tissue-paper pages. Why?—"Starr Bright" hadn't yet said.

Thirty-five knife wounds to the chest, belly, "genital area" as the newscasters fastidiously reported.

Wild! How in Malibu she'd tossed the disgusting flesh-clumps into the ocean after using them to smear, stain, spell out "Starr Bright's" curse DIE PIG on the bedroom wall. Wearing rubber kitchen-gloves of course. Learning afterward from a tabloid how the "genital parts" had washed up on a private beach close by owned by a Hollywood celebrity.

An innocent memento: platinum gold cuff links inset with pearls. No initial.

Enter into the rock, and hide thee in the dust. For fear of the Lord.

I
The Nightmare

You have to do what I say! You have to! You're my slave!

Lily Merrick shook herself awake, terrified, from a nightmare. She was dry-mouthed as if she'd been running, panting; for a confused moment she couldn't comprehend where she was.

Pleading, "No. No. No."

Heart pounding erratically. Her body, tense, tight as a fist and covered in sweat, in that state of suspension in which the muscles seem paralyzed as if under a spell. The childish demanding voice rang in her ears: an old nightmare, at one time a familiar nightmare but one she'd believed she had outgrown since marrying the man who was her husband, and moving to a house of her own. Lily opened her eyes in the dark of a room that should have consoled her with its comforting dimensions and whispered aloud, "I—am Lily Merrick. My husband is Wesley Merrick. We have a daughter Deirdre—Deedee. I am not—"

But what was it Lily Merrick was *not*?

She couldn't think. Didn't want to think.

She was a woman so upset by violence and the mere reportage of violence that she could not bear to watch much of the evening television news; nor could she force herself to read of atrocities in Bosnia, Nigeria, Iraq; the vicious racial beating of a young black college student by a gang of whites on Long Island last week; a rape-murder case currently being tried in Westchester County. Virtually any details of the Holocaust. Torture and mass murder in the killing fields of Cambodia. The terrifying devastation after the bombing in Oklahoma City at which all of America had watched appalled—Lily had turned away, crying. To see that heartrending photograph of a dying baby held in a fireman's arms—she was wounded, sickened. As a citizen of the world, as a responsible adult and the mother of a fifteen-year-old daughter she understood that she had an obligation to know; to know the worst; she was married to a man who didn't flinch from the worst, or so she believed of Wes; yet evidence of man's—and woman's—cruelty filled her with dismay and horror. Exhausted her, she might have said, spiritually. *If I can't intervene, it seems wrong to know.*

Of course she wasn't that unusual, she had numerous women friends and acquaintances who felt as she did; who stayed away from violent movies, never watched offensive television programs. Lily's was just a more extreme reaction, visceral, immediate as if her own being, her very nerves, were abraded. She'd been brought up to feel sympathy for others, not detachment; she'd been brought up to abhor destructive gossip; she had no natural prurient interest in celebrities' heartbreak or scandal, of which there was, in America, an inexhaustible supply marketed by the media; she had no interest in "gory details" of any kind; never watched TV tabloid programs; a kind of glaze came over her eyes, a willful yet genuine blindness, if she happened to see, by accident, atrocity photographs in the paper; yet another bloodied body lying on a dusty road somewhere in Middle Europe; in Africa, bodies heaped like kindling; the aftermath of an IRA bombing in London. She most shrank from reports of violence against children, of which there seemed, in recent years, so much. And she was particularly sickened by individual acts of systematic, apparently purposeful violence: serial killings, serial killers. This most recent serial killer, a woman, who'd murdered as many as eight—or was it nine, ten?—men in the Southwest and California; leaving behind mutilated corpses, bloodied walls and Satanic symbols. What Lily knew, she'd picked up from Deedee; she hadn't cared to watch a TV news segment on the case, or read about it in the paper; she'd happened to pass by the recreation room where she'd overheard her daughter and girlfriend talking, one of them saying, "Wow. About time there's a *woman*...Always some damn *man*..." and the other murmuring agreement, and both girls giggling. Lily passed by calling out, "H'lo, girls!" cheery and unobtrusive as always. Never meddled in her daughter's business, tried not to impose her sensibility on others, yes and frankly she was grateful that Deedee had a few girlfriends to invite to the house.

Waking from the nightmare, yet lying, still, in that state of muscular paralysis. She was thinking of Deedee, and of the guilt she felt about Deedee; that Deedee could not *know*...certain facts of her parentage. One day, but not yet.

You promised. Remember! Always.

It was a gusty sleet-driven February night, somewhere past midnight. Wes hadn't yet come upstairs; wasn't in bed beside her; must have been working in his office. The man was naturally restless, insomniac; even before going into the Marines, he said, and enduring boot camp, he'd never required more than four or five hours sleep a night.

"Wes! Where *are* you!"

So Lily would give the nightmare, the experience of the nightmare, a wifely-playful tone. That was best. As she did with most problems, hurts, disappointments, household and professional matters of a trivial nature. Make them into entertaining anecdotes, or jokes. She was Lily Merrick of 183 Washington Street, Yewville, New York, an attractive small city of thirty-five thousand people twenty miles south of Lake Ontario; resident of an old, handsomely restored colonial-style house in Yewville's oldest residential neighborhood. She was an amateur potter, she taught an evening class at the local community college once a week, she was the wife of...the mother of...She knew who she was!

You have to do what I say! You have to! You're my slave!

Well, it was Wes's fault. Not coming to bed at a reasonable time. His side of the bed empty. His warm weight beside her missing. The sound of his breathing, his snoring. The sagging of the mattress in his direction.

She would go downstairs to get Wes. She'd kiss him, and chide him. "Honey, come to bed! Please." No, better for her simply to go back to sleep, stop making such a fuss. It wasn't like Lily to make a fuss.

Lying in an odd position on her side, cramped, uncomfortable. Her forearm was pressed awkwardly against her breastbone and she could feel her heart still beating hard. *You have to. My slave!* These dreams she'd been having sporadically since—when?—sometime last fall. Remnants of old childhood nightmares. Like picking through the cluttered attic and cellar of her parents' old house in Shaheen after her father's death. Never know what you might find.

Lily of the Valley: her name. A silly, lovely, extravagant name, on her birth certificate.

And her sister—*Rose of Sharon.*

Since their father had died five years before, two years after their mother's death, Lily had lost all practical connection with her past, rural life as the daughter of a minister of an obscure Protestant sect; she sometimes seemed, in certain of her dreams, to have lost her way in time. In a flurry of wonder and mounting panic not knowing how old she was, in which house she was, in which bed. Or whether Sharon was close by—her blond curls on the very pillow beside Lily's. And hadn't she a husband, and—*who was her husband?*

Lily supposed that, in the human brain, deep in the cortex of memory, there is no such thing as "time"—"chronology." Everything is present tense; nothing is "past." We may be numerous selves simultaneously. Adult, adolescent, child, infant. Was she six years old, sixteen years old, thirty-six years old? Shrewdly she guessed that no one was ever *older* than his or her actual age, in dreams. Because you can't yet remember.

Lily's flannel nightgown was damp with perspiration, and her hair was heavy and warm at the nape of her neck. Her heart was still beating quickly as if in the presence of invisible danger. Outside, the wind blew, blew! A northerly wind, down from Lake Ontario, and Canada. A sound like rage, jeering. *I can get into that house of yours, that house you're so proud of. I can come through the windows that have been caulked, I can come through the walls that have been insulated.*

"No. No. *No.*"

* * *

Lily switched on a light, saw it was 2:10 A.M.

She was standing in front of the bedroom closet looking for—what? Her robe, slippers. She couldn't seem to locate her slippers. As if someone, a mischievous child, had kicked them into the shadowy rear of the closet.

You're my slave, Lily.

Do what I say: inside. I command you.

Like bile in Lily's mouth it came to her, then: the dream, the nightmare, had been a memory of her twin sister Sharon tormenting her, more than thirty years ago.

The dreams she'd been having intermittently for weeks, that left her so dazed and exhausted in the morning—all were remnants of memories. The sweet clear cruel relentless child's soprano voice was the voice of her sister Sharon. "Sherrill." Whom Lily hadn't seen for fifteen years and hadn't spoken with since their father's death and the funeral Sharon had been so terribly, terribly sorry she couldn't attend—she'd had a "professional commitment" she couldn't break.

The sisters were twins, though not identical. "Fraternal."

I am Rose of Sharon Donner, you are Lily of the Valley Donner! We can't ever be lonely like other people. We have each other.

But that wasn't true, once they started school. Already in junior high Sharon had been eager to detach herself from Lily. She wore her hair differently, "glamorously." She spoke, laughed, moved her body differently. On the sly, she wore bright lipstick. The sisters weren't mirror-twins and didn't in fact closely resemble each other. Sharon's hair was ashy-blond, Lily's a darker blond; Sharon was an inch taller than Lily, though always more slender; Sharon was the "pretty one"—the "one with the boyfriends." It came to seem by the time they were in high school that Sharon was an older sister of Lily's and this was an assumption Sharon was keen to promote. *Just say we're sisters if anybody asks, I'm older and that's a fact. We don't look anything alike!*

Never caring how she hurt Lily's feelings, never much aware of others' feelings. Disappearing into Manhattan to pursue her "career" and no looking back except when she wanted favors from the family. Pursuing the kind of people, powerful, well-to-do, exclusively male, she believed could advance her in her career. Falling in love with the wrong men again, and again.

Sharon had returned home only a single time, since leaving to become a model. And then only for a reason. *Lily, promise me. You are the only person in the world I can trust. The only person I love.*

Then she'd gone away again, of course. She'd been out of touch with Lily at the time of their mother's sickness and death; hadn't come to their father's funeral; when Lily got married to Wesley Merrick, Sharon hadn't even sent a card. It bewildered and exasperated Lily that her own sister had no interest in, not the slightest curiosity about, the man Lily had fallen in love with and married.

And Deedee. How bizarre, Sharon's attitude toward Deedee. As if she'd forgotten the child altogether. When she called home, which was infrequently, hardly remembering to ask about her. *Oh, yes—and how's my little niece? With the exotic name—"Deirdre"?*

Lily had learned not to be hurt by her sister. Which is to say, Lily had learned long ago not to expect anything other than hurt from her sister. She would have thought that she'd eased Sharon out of her mind entirely. She would have thought that she was free of their shared past.

Except, what to make of these disturbing dreams? Beginning last October and continuing through the winter, until this very night. Riddlesome dreams, prankish dreams. Dreams that left a brackish taste at the back of her mouth. Lily knew the Goya engraving, "The Nightmare": an ugly creature squatting on a sleeper's chest. So were her nightmares ugly creatures burrowing their way up out of her body, squatting on her chest and gloating. *You have to, you're my slave! I command you.* The creature was her sister Sharon as a young child. As if somehow she and Sharon were still children, somewhat lonely children, no sisters or brothers except themselves living with their parents in a ramshackle farmhouse in Shaheen, less than one hundred feet from their father's church and the hilly cemetery of plain stone markers and crosses behind it. *You know what that is?—a boneyard. You know who's there?—dead people. That's a nasty place.*

Before they'd been bused to town schools, Sharon hadn't any outlet for her energy, her amazing vivacity. So she'd "teased" Lily as their mother called it, unwilling to concede that one of her girls was tormenting the other with the relentlessness of a pilgrim. The nightmare that had wakened Lily this night was a confused, heightened memory of the cemetery; the wooden storage shed behind the church where groundskeeping equipment was kept; a dank shadowy ill-smelling place into which Sharon had forced Lily upon more than one occasion when they were playing together. *Inside! Go inside! On your hands and knees like a puppy-dog!* And there was the yet more dank and ill-smelling cellar of the church, a virtual tomb of oozing rocks, cobwebs and rot where of course the girls were forbidden to "play." *Slave, I command you!* It was meant to be a game, it was meant to be fun—wasn't it? Lily often laughed, giggled shrilly; wet her pants with squealing; scrambled on her hands and knees, wanting only to please her sister, who had an unpredictable temper—the more readily Lily gave in to Sharon's whims, the more likely Sharon was to relent, sometimes even to join her. For the test seemed to be the act of command and the response of obedience in themselves. Like the unpredictable God of the Hebrew Bible (as Reverend Donner called the Old Testament out of deference, he said, for his brethren the Jewish people), the scourge of Judah and Jerusalem and the sinful cities of the plains, little Rose of Sharon needed to know she was master.

There were times in fact when Sharon had taken the lead. Boldly and recklessly scrambling up onto the steep roof of the church, for instance, and commanding Lily to follow; making her way across a rock dam in the creek, to the opposite shore; venturing out onto the frozen creek in winter; crawling on hands and knees through a tunnel of wild rosebushes alive and buzzing with honeybees. *You have to follow me, Lily. I command you.* And Lily followed, or tried to. She'd been like one entranced, hypnotized. Frightened to obey, yet more frightened not to obey. She remembered one time when they were a little older, perhaps nine, in the presence of other children, country neighbors, and in a clearing on the creek bank, at the bottom of the cemetery, Sharon had lighted a small brush fire and intoned over it "magic" words—ZEKIL-HOSEA-OBADIAH-HABAKKUK-ZEPHANIAH-ZECHARIAH—and commanded Lily to put her hand in the flames, and Lily had hesitated, and Sharon commanded her more forcibly, and still Lily hesitated, for she wasn't such a silly fool she didn't know what fire was, and how it hurt to be burnt; and, conscious of the other children's eyes upon her, she'd shaken her head, no. Sharon cried *You have to do what I say, slave!* and pushed Lily toward the fire, pushing her head down, her hair dangerously close to the flames, and Lily screamed and wrenched away and said *No! No I don't!* and ran back up to the house.

Lily quickly put on her robe, struggling with the sleeves as if, behind her back, a prankish child were twisting them.

She was barefoot, in the hall outside the bedroom. Shivering and clammy with perspiration and her heart still beating disconcertingly fast. *Wes, just hold me. I've had the most upsetting nightmare.*

There was Deedee's room: thank God no light shone beneath the door. Sometimes Deedee stayed up late, studying, or reading, or writing in her journal; experimenting with her computer. She wasn't Wes's child biologically but she often seemed his child temperamentally: restless, twitchy in her sleep. As an infant she'd had bouts of severe colic and as a toddler she'd been high-strung, a dynamo of energy and impatience with fixed routines, bed-, bath-, nap-, mealtimes. Her cries had been lusty, ear-shattering and protracted. Yet she'd been a happy child, anyway. Husky, bold, inquisitive.

Until the age of twelve or thirteen when she'd begun to change, her personality becoming more tentative, uncertain. Entering ninth grade had been sobering for Deedee; entering high school this past fall had been traumatic. All of life that had meaning was a popularity contest which only a very few pretty, self-assured "popular" girls could win. And only boys were to judge.

It angered Lily, as it angered the mothers of other teenaged girls of her acquaintance. What can you do, it's adolescence! Adolescence in America!

Deedee was Wes's adopted daughter; it was difficult to know if he loved her "as if she were his own" for how could Lily judge? She'd entered Wes's life as a twenty-two-year-old "unwed mother" with an eighteen-month daughter; a young woman with a confused and never very explicable past, who'd moved away from overly protective, God-besotted parents in the remote countryside south of Yewville. Lily sometimes thought, I am a figure in a fairy tale whose origins and whose ending I don't know.

Lily, promise! Never never go back on your word.

Someday, she would. But not yet.

Downstairs, Lily made her way to Wes's office on the far side of the house. By night, the house seemed unfamiliar; it might have been a stranger's house; and she an intruder. She stubbed her toe against something sharp-edged. "Oh—!"

The house was a woodframe and brick colonial originally built in 1919 and several times remodeled; the first house in which Lily had lived as an adult, and as Wesley Merrick's wife. When she'd moved away from Shaheen, where her parents had assumed she'd remain, as the mother of Deirdre, she'd lived in a small apartment in downtown Yewville, and worked at a succession of modestly paying part-time jobs, and taken courses at Yewville Community College. She'd met Wes Merrick almost immediately and had been astonished by his interest in her, his kindness and generosity. Yet somehow Lily had had faith that things would turn out well for her; if she didn't believe passionately in Jesus Christ as her parents had taught her to believe, she did seem to believe in a benign providence.

When Lily had been introduced to Wes, by a woman in an office in which she'd worked as a part-time secretary, he'd been presented to her as a quiet, difficult-to-know man; never married, an ex-Marine who'd had trouble readjusting to civilian life after being discharged from the service; though born and raised in Yewville, something of a mystery. He was thirty-one at the time, nine years older than Lily, but he'd looked older; not a handsome man, yet, to Lily's eye, an attractive man; with a slightly coarse, creased skin, thick dark hair sharply receding at his temples, broad sloping shoulders. He was a self-employed carpenter and builder: his forearms were dense and wiry with muscle. His eyes were of the color of stone and appeared lashless, stark with melancholy knowledge. *What I've seen, I've seen. What I know, I know. Just don't ask.* Yet Wesley Merrick wasn't cynical, didn't seem pessimistic. If he liked you, and he'd liked Lily Donner from the start, he trusted you. If not, not. No way he could be coaxed into smiling if he didn't want to smile; he shook hands sometimes in silence, which made other men, accustomed to the exchange of glib, meaningless but assuaging banalities, uncomfortable. Lily noted Wes's habit of frowning at individuals as they spoke as if trying to decode what they were saying beneath their chatter, and this made people yet more uncomfortable. A woman who'd gone out with Wes a few times before giving up on him had warned Lily that he didn't care to be questioned about his Vietnam years, which set well with Lily, who didn't care to be questioned about Deedee and her own past.

When people inquired about Deedee, hoping to pry out of Lily one or another illuminating detail, Lily would feel her face burn, not exactly unpleasantly, and say quietly that her daughter's father was not involved in their lives, by choice. Implying that the choice wasn't hers, of course; still less was it Deedee's; but they would make the best of it, here in Yewville in a "new" life.

Wes had been charmed by Deedee, as by Deedee's spunky young mother. It must have surprised and impressed him that Lily was so cheerful, so optimistic and outgoing; no moping about, no reproachful remarks about men. Why, Lily seemed to like men as—people. She'd never been a girl to arouse violent romantic passion in boys and had thus been spared emotional turmoil herself. (That province belonged to Sharon.) But she'd had a few friends who were boys in high school, and she related to men in a frank, sisterly fashion. When she took time to style her hair and wear makeup, she could be "pretty"; when she smiled, she was "prettier" still; but "prettiness" seemed hardly the point of Lily Donner, as you knew within a few minutes of meeting her. Wes had said afterward that Lily had been the only woman he'd met in years who seemed to know who she was. "You don't just invent yourself for any guy who comes along." Lily was flattered but thought. *Invent? I wouldn't know how.*

Wes had a small office downtown and an office in the house, in a long narrow first-floor room formerly a sunporch. There he sat, past 2 A.M., at his aluminum desk, illuminated as if on a screen by a single lamp. Lily was going to call out to him but hesitated. *No. You might regret it.* He was frowning at a computer screen, and at a swath of papers and documents spread across his desktop. His stiff, thinning steely-brown hair was disheveled as if he'd been running his hands through it, his jaws were unshaven, stubbled; he looked older than forty-five, clearly tired, in an irritable mood. Wes was a physically direct, blunt man who loved to work with "materials"—with his hands; who disliked the financial side of his business, the continuous and relentless task of trying to extract money from clients who owed him so that he could pay his own creditors on time. (This side of his life Wes rarely discussed with Lily, who wished she might be of more help to him.) Yet he was ambitious, as a contractor; he specialized in the restoration and renovation of old, solidly built family houses like the one they owned, not because there was money in such work (the money was in new "luxury" houses on two-acre lots in the suburban countryside) but because it was work he could respect, work with a purpose.

Lily saw then, suddenly, with a stab of disappointment and hurt, that Wes was smoking. He picked up a cigarette burning in an ashtray and inhaled with a savage sort of intensity. A pocket calculator in one hand, the cigarette in the other. *He hasn't quit after all. Or he's begun again.* In fact, Wes had quit smoking a dozen times since Lily knew him: quit, and began again; and again quit, and began again; he hated the habit but couldn't seem to overcome it. He'd smoked heavily in Vietnam, he said, and had "done some drugs," too. He was a man who disapproved of weakness in himself and others but particularly in himself; he smoked when he was angry with himself and he was angry with himself when he smoked. But only last week he'd declared to Lily and Deedee that, this time, it was permanent. He hadn't touched a cigarette in nineteen days, twelve hours.

So sheepish, so boyish and proud, Lily and Deedee had laughed and broken into spontaneous applause.

And now. *Not only smoking: drinking. Look!* Lily saw to her dismay that Wes was lifting a glass to his mouth even as he continued to stare at the papers on his desk. Whiskey? Somehow, Lily doubted it was a soda drink or fruit juice. Wes was a man who enjoyed drinking, beer, ale, wine, hard liquor, he'd acknowledged a drinking problem before their marriage but so far as Lily knew he had no problem now, he drank only moderately she was sure. *Yes but can you be sure? Do you really know that man, at all?* She was frightened, suddenly; she shrank back into the shadows, and did not dare call attention to herself. How angry Wes would be, to discover her spying on him. He had his pride, his sense of privacy. Though Lily would never have admonished him for smoking—and drinking—he would not have accepted her silence, either.

You're alone, you see? Like me.

Slave!

Lily stumbled away from Wes's office, not knowing where to go except back upstairs. What a poor, misguided idea it had been, to rush downstairs with her fear carried like precious crystal to present to Wes, her protector. What a fool she was. She groped her way half-blind through the downstairs, unsteady as if she'd been struck a blow to the head.

The wind, the wind! Roaring overhead like a freight train with endless rattling cars. And in every car windows framing faces of the dead, the damned and dead! Lily was shivering, her heart pounding absurdly. She saw herself as a woman in a medieval woodcut possessed by spirits, devils; running mad tearing at her hair, her face, her clothing until there came Jesus Christ in a white robe to calmly cast out devils except Lily didn't believe in devils. She was a civilized woman, she didn't believe seriously in evil.

On her way back upstairs she realized that it was the eve of her (and her twin sister's) thirty-seventh birthday.

2
The Birthday

The door at the rear of the house opened, and closed. And there came Deedee's uplifted voice in the kitchen, "Hi, Mom."

A voice that was bright and animated and girlish. Or meant to give that impression.

It was 4:55 P.M. A darkening winter afternoon, mid-February. Deedee was just home from school, later than usual; Lily, who'd been feeling apprehensive through much of the day—not because it was her thirty-seventh birthday, she hoped—heard with relief her daughter enter the house by the rear door, stamp her boots clear of snow and ice, and enter the kitchen. In her cluttered workroom next to the kitchen, at her potter's bench where she was modeling a clay vase, her fingers quick, deft, practiced in their instinctive motions, Lily could picture Deedee, flush-faced from the cold, dismantling her clumsy bookbag which she wore strapped to her back like a beast of burden, letting it fall onto the kitchen counter. As if in the girl's familiar greeting Lily hadn't detected a subtle note of adolescent sadness, hurt, resignation, and sensed it in the hurried, graceless tread of Deedee's walk, Lily called out with equal brightness, "Hi, honey! Welcome home."

It was a familiar and reassuring exchange. Every afternoon when Deedee arrived home from school, when Lily was herself home. An exchange that had continued for years. And would continue for years. (Deedee was only a sophomore in high school.)

Though long ago, in another lifetime it seemed, Lily had driven to pick up Deedee at school every afternoon, preschool and kindergarten; and the two of them stopped at a neighborhood dairy for their ritual of "afternoon tea."

In Deedee's young, foreshortened memory, those days would

seem very remote, indeed. "Afternoon tea" at Ewald's Dairy—the kind of small islanded memory a mother vividly recalls. Her own happiness as a young mother.

When Lily came into the kitchen, smiling, Deedee had already shrugged off her bulky sheepskin jacket and was peering critically into the refrigerator. Lily caught the jacket as it was about to slide from a chair onto the floor. "Hi, Mom, happy birthday," Deedee said, humming to herself as she deliberated what, if anything, to eat. Deedee wore jeans, a loose-fitting sweater; she was a solid, compact girl, not fat, nor even plump, but rosy-fleshed, like, Lily thought, a girl Renoir might have painted. Deedee was a pretty girl but couldn't bear being told so, at least not by her mother. A few weeks before, in her car, Lily had happened to see Deedee walking near the high school, a figure that appeared at first glance to be neither female nor male, in jeans, boots, the bulky khaki-colored jacket; the girl strode along with her head bowed, eyes downcast as if she were searching the snowy sidewalk for something precious. Deedee was resolutely alone and took no notice of a noisy group of boys and girls crossing the street near her, as they took no notice of her.

Lily washed her hands at the sink and resisted touching Deedee where she stood slouched and sighing, leaning on the refrigerator door. Lily would have liked to smooth down the girl's disheveled ashy-blond hair that looked as if it hadn't been combed for days, but she knew better. She said, "You've already wished me a happy birthday, honey, and I love the card"—a large red construction-paper HAPPY BIRTHDAY MOM! in the shape of a heart, which Deedee had made in obvious haste, now prominently positioned on a windowsill. Deedee said, taking out a can of diet Coke and a container of blueberry yogurt from the refrigerator, "Well, it's a big day all day. And more to come." There was something sweetly forced about these words as if Deedee's mind were on other things and she was going through the motions of speaking to her mother.

Even as Lily herself was distracted, edgy. Not knowing why.

The ridiculous dream of the night before—she'd all but forgotten. She'd decided it had been the wind that caused it. But you can obliterate such trivial memories the way, with a few quick swipes of a kitchen sponge, you can clean a Formica-topped counter.

Lily said, lightly, since these were dull-motherly, damning and familiar words, "Now, sweetie, don't spoil your appetite, please. Your dad's taking us all out to dinner." Deedee sighed and rolled her eyes like a boy of twelve. Saying, "You kidding, Mom? Spoil *my* appetite?" She laughed as if the idea was preposterous. As if her appetite was deep and trackless as the Grand Canyon.

"Now, honey."

How a teenaged girl hurts her mother: by speaking crudely and disparagingly of herself.

Deedee was an intelligent, sharp-witted girl; prone to irony, but also childlike, hopeful and sweet; an A student, well liked by her teachers; physically mature for her age yet in crucial ways immature. Her face was round, moon-shaped as her grandmother's had been, with a small nose, rather small close-set eyes; inclined to plumpness; her pebble-blue eyes were shyly watchful, and to Lily beautiful. If only…Lily understood that Deedee ate compulsively to assuage her hurt feelings (mysterious hurts! high-school hurts! don't inquire into them), and her compulsive eating, her ten pounds or so of extra flesh, intensified her susceptibility to hurt. Lily touched Deedee after all, drawing a hand along the girl's arm as Deedee, with an impatient gesture, pried open the lid of the yogurt container. Deedee laughed and said, "Mom, your hand smells like *clay.*" Lily said, trying not to sound concerned, "You're home from school a little late today, aren't you? It's almost five." Deedee said, shrugging, "There was a yearbook staff meeting and half the kids were late and some didn't show up at all, I was the only sophomore." Deedee spoke with both resentment and pride. Lily said, "Try not to let them take advantage of you this year, sweetie," recalling how in ninth grade, Deedee had been one to volunteer for class committees, editing the school newspaper, spending an entire day decorating the gym for the graduation dance to which she hadn't gone. Defensively, Deedee said, "No one takes advantage of me, I do what I want. Anyway, Mom, you should talk—everybody in Yewville takes advantage of *you*."

Lily considered: was it true? She could always be counted upon to canvass for the local Red Cross chapter, and for the wildlife sanctuary; she was a perennially elected officer in the PTA; her numerous women friends were always calling her for favors, and rarely had time to reciprocate. For the past six years she'd been teaching pottery at Yewville Community College, for a small salary, working with her students many more hours than the course required; yet when there'd been an opening for a permanent instructor, at a higher salary, the director of the program, an affable longtime acquaintance of both Lily's and Wes's, had passed over Lily to hire a man. Wes and Deedee had been outraged on Lily's behalf but Lily insisted she didn't mind, truly. *I love to teach, I love working with beginners but I'm just an amateur as a teacher and a potter. Truly, I wouldn't have wanted the extra responsibility.*

Deedee had brought the day's mail in with her, and was sitting at the kitchen table sorting through it. This, too, was a weekday ritual. "Doesn't look like much," Deedee said, pushing aside bills, flyers, advertisements; handing Lily several envelopes which Lily opened with childlike anticipation—birthday cards, from women friends and relatives mainly.

Deedee said, "What's this? We-ird." She was squinting at a postcard.

Lily's heart leapt. Yet she asked calmly, "For me?"

"For 'Lily Donner.' Like whoever sent it doesn't know you're married, even."

Yet whoever sent it, Lily saw, knew she lived at 183 Washington Street, Yewville, New York.

Lily leaned over Deedee to examine the mysterious card with her. Neither could make out the signature which was in red ink, shaky as if it had been scrawled in a speeding vehicle or by a drunken person. Deedee said, "'Far'—'Farrer'?—no, that's an S—'Starer'? The last name looks like 'Dwight.'"

Lily said, "I don't know any—'Starer.' I'm sure. Anyone named 'Dwight.'"

The postcard was an ordinary tourist's card, a glossy photograph of Death Valley in springtime: cactus flowers, sculpted and rippled sand dunes, a china-blue sky. No human figures in all that vastness. Deedee said, "Wow. I didn't know Death Valley was so beautiful. We should go there sometime...It must be for your birthday, Mom. See, this looks like 'Your Day, Lily'—then some words I can't read—'For this—these?—are the days of—regenance'—What's 'regenance'?"

Lily was staring at the red-inked message. She could not decipher a word. "—'vengeance,'" she said.

Deedee read haltingly, "'For these are the days of vengeance, that all things which are—willed—'"

"—'written.'"

"—'all things which are written may be'—what?—'suselled'?—is that a word?"

Lily said calmly, "—'fulfilled.' 'For these are the days of vengeance, that all things which are written may be fulfilled.'"

"Sounds like the Bible. Who's this 'Dwight,' Mom?"

The words, solemn and pitiless, had seemed to issue from Lily's throat without her volition. As if, after all, she was but a hollow reed.

Lily said, without looking, "I can't read the signature, honey. I don't know."

"Maybe it's a joke," Deedee said suspiciously. "The postmark isn't Nevada, see? It's Missouri. Mailed two days ago."

Lily took the card from Deedee and stood staring at it, at the dreamlike lunar terrain of Death Valley which she had never seen in person. For a long moment she didn't say a word; then, since Deedee was regarding her with frank curiosity, she said, "Yes. It's a joke, probably."

Why! Why would you do such a thing.

Why, after years of not writing, not calling. Never caring how I yearn for you just to know you're alive.

Why such a thing, at such a time.

Our birthday.

⁂

Quickly Lily hid away the postcard. As if it were something illicit, a secret; not taped to a wall of her workroom with dozens of other colorful cards but hidden meanly away in a drawer in a mess of pencil sketches, soiled rags. Where no one except Lily ever looked.

She would not have mentioned it to Wes even as a curiosity except that, at dinner, in the restaurant to which Wes had taken her and Deedee to celebrate Lily's birthday, Deedee brought it up. Saying suddenly, near the end of their meal, "Dad, did Mom show you the weird postcard she got today? Sort of a birthday card, with a Bible message. From Death Valley."

Wes had been enjoying the meal, and the evening; he was in a warm, expansive mood, ready to be entertained. "Postcard? Death Valley. No-ooo." He smiled at Lily, curious. "Who do you know in Death Valley, Lily?"

Lily said, "It—wasn't from Death Valley, actually. Just a tourist card. Postmarked Missouri."

"Well, who do you know in Missouri?"

"I was trying to think. A cousin, maybe. On my mother's side of the family. The signature might have been her name..." Lily's voice trailed off as if the subject, of so little importance, could not possibly be of interest to Wes.

That morning, there'd been no sign of cigarettes, or drinking, in Wes's office. Well, perhaps—a faint odor of smoke. Lily had not wished to go into the room and had in fact stood only at the doorway, peering inside. *Spying on your own husband! How dare you.* She was not a woman who snooped in another's private quarters, she was not a mother who entered even her daughter's bedroom when her daughter was gone. Wes had finally come upstairs at about 3 A.M. and he'd risen again at his usual hour of 7 A.M.; he laughed at Lily's concern, saying he wasn't a man who required more than a few hours sleep. He hadn't lit a cigarette in Lily's presence for weeks and, tonight, he was drinking only white wine, like Lily.

If only Deedee didn't persist! But she had an adolescent's sly maddening instinct for pressing seemingly small matters that vexed her mother considerably, though Lily would never have let on. Deedee said, "Y'know, Mom, when I first saw that card, it's weird somehow I thought it might be from Aunt Sharon. Today being your birthday, and all."

"Well, it isn't."

Lily stared at her water glass, a crystal goblet in which ice was melting. She wondered if Wes and Deedee were thinking how odd, Lily hadn't heard from her sister on their birthday. Lily had no idea where her sister was.

Deedee was saying, "You haven't heard from Aunt Sharon in a long time, I guess?"

Lily said, calmly, "It hasn't been that long. We spoke on the phone when—" trying to name a year, a date; a plausible recollection. "Sharon was involved with a dance troupe, in Miami, remember, and they were going on tour, I think to—Houston, Los Angeles. And after that—"

Deedee was saying disapprovingly how "weird" it was she'd never seen her own aunt; her mother's twin sister; how "weird" that Wes had never met his sister-in-law. "If Aunt Sharon's pictures weren't in that album, I'd wonder if she existed," Deedee said. "That's how weird it is."

Lily said, "Deedee, I wish you'd find another word instead of 'weird.' There must be plenty in the dictionary."

Deedee said, with the most innocent sly cruelty, "Those modeling photos are from a long time ago, Aunt Sharon was so beautiful and glamorous but she'd be kind of old now, I guess. She can't still be *dancing*."

Lily laughed. "Sharon is exactly my age, as you know."

"Well."

The three of them laughed. Deedee was, as often at mealtimes, showing off partly to amuse Wes; it was playful enough, but exasperating.

If I can get through this day, help me God, I will be fine. This is a dangerous day.

Wes was saying, "If I'd known, Lily, when I first met you, that you had a twin sister, I'd possibly have been intimidated. There's something strange about falling in love with a person who's actually *two*."

I am not two! I am one.

Deedee giggled mischievously. "'Strange'? *We-ird*."

Lily sighed, and tried to laugh; but it was painful to laugh; it sometimes happened that Wes and Deedee ganged up and teased her, and what more appropriate occasion than her birthday? She had to be a good sport. And Deedee was trying to be earnest, serious—"But, Dad, Mom and Aunt Sharon don't look like twins, judging by the photos. They aren't identical, they're only 'fraternal.' I mean 'sororal,' if that's a word."

It was a word, yes. A rarely used word. Lily had once looked it up in the dictionary, out of curiosity.

But she didn't say so, now. She said, an edge in her voice to show she was getting annoyed, "I think it's time for dessert. This is a school night for Deedee after all."

"Oh, Mom. It's your *birthday*."

"I've had plenty of birthdays. And I hope I'll have plenty more."

The evening had gone well. Better than Lily might have anticipated. She would have preferred to make dinner for them at home, of course; nothing made Lily happier than their domestic, cozy evenings; her most peaceful time of day. Especially if she'd been working intensely in her workroom, or at the college; if Wes didn't come home late from a work site, and wasn't distracted. Why do others make more of our birthdays than we do, ourselves? Lily wondered. Do they need to prove they love us, again and again?

She was smiling of course. She'd been smiling for hours. At the house, Wes and Deedee had given Lily their presents; a delicate heart-shaped locket on a thin gold chain, from Wes, who gave Lily jewelry every year oblivious of the fact that Lily rarely wore any jewelry apart from her wedding band and wristwatch; an immense clay pot of dusky-pink begonias for the window-bench of Lily's workroom, already crowded with plants, from Deedee. But Lily had been very pleased, and touched. She'd hugged and kissed both husband and daughter and stammered, "I—I love you!" and Wes and Deedee had been embarrassed and assured her they loved her, too.

You see how happy we are. My husband, my daughter.

It had been one of the surprises of her life, and one of the greatest blessings. How, when she and Wes had met, and had begun to see each other, he hadn't been jealous of her past; of what he would have been justified to perceive as her past. She was a young woman with an eighteen-month baby and no husband nor even the melancholy tale of a failed marriage; yet Wes had said simply *Tell me what you feel comfortable telling me, Lily. No more.* And so, hesitantly, feeling her way, for until that moment she hadn't rehearsed what she might say, how she would attempt to explain her peculiar circumstances, she said *He—Deirdre's father —isn't anyone I know—really.* Her heart had pounded with the audacity of her words, not a lie yet how far from the truth. *It was a—mistake* she said. And Wes startled her by laughing. Gently he said *Look, Deirdre isn't a mistake, is she?* and Lily said *No!* and Wes said *So you would not want him, the father, erased from your life, right?* and Lily said, contrite, *No.*

She'd known how she had loved Wes Merrick, then. A man so very different from her father; yet, like Ephraim Donner, a man of surpassing dignity, integrity.

A man with a beautiful soul.

During dessert, Lily was beginning to get drowsy. Wes and Deedee laughed, chattered. She had the idea they were oddly protective of her.

Across the crowded dining room was a frosted mirror on a wall and in this mirror the Merrick family was reflected in shimmering ghostly images. Lily had been watching half-consciously. As the wine went to her head—but she'd had only two glasses, hadn't she?—or three?—the reflections of the tall broad-shouldered man, the woman in a red dress and the teenaged girl became more seductive. Lily could not see their features clearly but they were obviously attractive, happy people. They belonged together, they were a family.

You see?

No, no!—Lily wasn't drunk.

Maybe just slightly giddy and extravagant blinking tears from her eyes kissing Deedee goodnight at the foot of the stairs and calling out so that Wes, hanging coats in the hall closet, could hear. "This was my most wonderful birthday ever! Thank you so much, both of you."

Deedee laughed and said, "Oh, Mom. You say exactly the same thing every year."

Lily protested, "I do? I don't! Wes?"

Wes was whistling, pretending not to hear the question.

"Well," Lily declared, "if I say it, I *mean it*."

Deedee called back over her shoulder, halfway up the stairs, "And you say exactly that every year, too, Mom."

The long day was nearly over: midnight.

Like making her way across the rock dam in the creek, stepping upon the shaky rocks one by one by one. Hoping she wouldn't fall into the chill swift-flowing water.

No telephone call had come. No message on the answering service when they returned from the restaurant. *Lily? Please call me, I'm in need of hearing your voice. Miss you.*

And when Lily had called that time, several years ago on their birthday, dialing the number Sharon had left for her, the phone had rung and rung. Area code San Diego, California.

Eventually, a few days later, a man had answered. When Lily asked to speak with Sharon, the man uttered an obscenity and slammed down the phone.

Lily was lying in bed, pleasantly tired. Arms and legs outstretched as if she were falling upward through the night sky. Drifting, floating. Wide undulating planes of sleep appeared to her like a puddled meadow. Wes hadn't come to bed again, apologized and kissed her and disappeared downstairs. And Lily lay in the big bed in the shadowy bedroom of the house she loved; the first house of her adult life; recalling with the vividness of a dream, how, after her father had died and the old farmhouse in Shaheen had been cleaned out (by Lily, mainly) from attic to cellar and the property sold, one rainy March day, ten-year-old Deedee snug in the crook of her arm, she'd settled into the sofa in the recreation room to look through the battered old photograph album Emmy Donner had kept.

Deedee was curious, of an age to be avidly interested in her mother's girlhood. And, of course, she'd wanted to know about her mother's twin sister who was "Aunt Sharon"—the glamorous and mysterious stranger. Aunt Sharon who'd promised to visit at Christmas, or for her and Lily's birthday in February, or for a week during the summer; yet somehow never came to Yewville. At the last minute postponing her visit.

But why? Deedee wanted to know.

Professional commitments!

That was what Sharon told Lily, and that was what Lily had to tell her family.

How fascinated Deedee was by the early baby pictures. Dimpled baby girls, *Rose of Sharon* and *Lily of the Valley.* Newly born, in their proud young mother's arms, like kittens whose eyes haven't yet opened. Emmy Donner liked to tell of how Rose of Sharon had been born first, an hour before her sister; at six pounds, thirteen ounces she'd outweighed the other baby girl by eleven ounces. Rose of Sharon had kicked harder from the start and cried louder and fretted more and nursed more hungrily at their mother's breast—*More, more, more!* For that was Rose of Sharon's way and it seemed natural that everyone should wish to please her.

There were the twin sisters in their look-alike polka-dot playsuits and in their Sunday dresses handsewn by their mother. Ashy-blond Rose of Sharon smiling happily at the camera as if understanding already at the age of three how photogenic she was; how beautiful in the glassy eye of the camera. And there was Lily of the Valley whose hair was several shades darker, shading into brown; a sweet startled-looking child whose smile was shy and partly hidden by her hand.

Thirty years ago. And more. Deedee was staring, blinking in wonder. She said, "Oh Mommy, I wish I had a sister, like you did!" Lily thought sadly, I wish you did, too.

Somehow it hadn't happened. Clearly, Wes hadn't much wanted it to happen. A part of his soul numbed by whatever he'd seen, endured or done in Vietnam forever hidden from Lily as the dark side of the moon is forever hidden, inaccessible.

As Lily turned the pages of the snapshot album with Deedee, she felt a bittersweet ache of memory; and a stir of apprehension. It had been years since she'd seen most of these snapshots. How many times as a girl she'd paged through it, how carefully she'd maintained it as a teenager, and, after Sharon left home to become "Sherrill"—the high-fashion model—Lily had faithfully affixed snapshots and photos into place, in chronological order. She, Lily, was the keeper of the Donner family album. The one who will remember.

A snapshot of the white-painted woodframe country church, the First Church of Christ of Shaheen, and Reverend Ephraim Donner and his wife Emmy on the concrete front steps their arms around each other's waist squinting in the sun. A snapshot, not a very focused one, of the church interior; twelve-year-old Lily self-consciously seated at the aged foot-pedal organ in a stiff-starched pink Sunday dress, black patent-leather shoes and white anklet socks, and her tall lanky father beside the organ holding a hymnal aloft. Poor sweet Daddy who'd been minister of that backcountry church for thirty-one years. Smiling into the camera as if into the eye of God. *Always know you are loved, children. Always in His heart.* Here, a picture of twelve-year-old Sharon in a pink dress identical to her sister's yet somehow prettier, and her black patent-leather shoes shinier, and her white anklet socks whiter. Rose of Sharon with wavy pale-blond hair to her shoulders, widened blue eyes clear as glass and a sweet rosebud mouth pursed in the very act of singing. Like an angel she stood at the front of the church, the youngest member of the choir. Joyously they sang *Jesus loves me, this I know. For the Bible tells me so.* While at the organ, pumping away at the wheezing foot-pedals, Lily lost her place hearing her sister's uplifted soprano voice penetrating the thicker, earthbound voices of the others. The congregation loved her, the elderly women moved to tears and the men staring open-mouthed. The other members of the choir deferred to the minister's daughter Rose of Sharon as an angel possessed of a God-given talent, and did not envy her.

As Lily deferred to her sister, too. Not out of envy but out of admiration.

Though knowing a Rose of Sharon very different from the shining blond angel-child the congregation beheld.

You're my slave you have to do what I say. And never never tell.

It was a miracle, a mystery—where the Donner twins' musical talent came from. Lily could pick out tunes at the organ without having had a lesson; after a few lessons from a neighbor, she could play the instrument—adequately enough to accompany the choir. (Not that she had any real talent, of course. Not for playing a keyboard instrument!) And Sharon had a naturally sweet, thrilling soprano voice. It was thin, breathless, inclined to waver and lacked resonance—but no one in the Shaheen area would notice.

Ten-year-old Deedee was intrigued by the numerous snapshots and newspaper clippings heralding Sharon's success, at the age of thirteen, in the STARR BRIGHT PRESENTS AREA YOUTH TALENT SEARCH 1972. Here, stuffed into the album, too many for all of them to be neatly pasted in, were dozens of pictures from that time: Sharon in a blue taffeta dress and high heels, thin and elegantly graceful as a long-legged bird, poised on a brightly lighted stage singing beside a piano at which a girl, her accompanist Lily, sat unobtrusively; Sharon being presented with a first-prize silver plaque and a gift certificate by the bronze-blond amply proportioned Miss Starr Bright, a middle-aged "media personality" of glamorous pretensions; Sharon wiping tears from her eyes, smiling at flashing cameras. What excitement! To have won first prize in the annual Starr Bright talent search! Miss Starr Bright had been hostess of a Buffalo television program for children popular in western New York in the 1960's and early 1970's and each year, with much publicity, she oversaw a "talent search." The competition was limited to children between the ages of eight and fourteen; Sharon, at thirteen, had entered just in time.

She'd won the silver plaque, and a gift certificate for $200 from one of the prestige Buffalo department stores, and of course she'd won local acclaim, publicity. Deedee didn't inquire what the cash prize was, any American child in the media era understands that winning is in itself the prize. And there was pretty *Sharon Donner, daughter of Reverend and Mrs. Ephraim Donner of Shaheen, New York, first-prize winner of the Starr Bright Youth Talent Search 1972* featured on the front page of the second section of the *Buffalo Evening News* of April 18, 1972. Deedee murmured reverently, "Wow."

Lily recalled how she'd been terrified, at the piano. She'd practiced the accompaniment to "I'm Always Chasing Rainbows" a hundred times yet at the crucial moment she came close to panicking, depressing keys timidly, missing notes, striking a flat instead of a sharp, but hurtling on, scarcely daring to breathe, as her amazing sister faced the audience beyond the blinding stage lights—more than one thousand people!—and sang, sang as if her heart were in the simple, sentimental words; as if, offering herself so, no panel of judges and the heavily made-up ex-"chanteuse" Miss Starr Bright could deny her victory. *I prayed to win, and I made myself win. We both won, Lily!*

Of course, that wasn't true. Deedee would hardly have thought so, staring at the numerous pictures of Sharon, reading through a batch of yellowing news clippings.

Deedee was equally fascinated by the snapshots that followed: lovely blond Sharon as a high school cheerleader, her hair in a sleek pageboy, a slim vibrant girl in a navy blue jumper and long-sleeved white blouse, the white terrycloth letters Y H S on her chest. By this time, the sisters were bussed into Yewville with other country children to attend school, a distance of eleven miles; seeming even longer on unpaved back-country roads; yet it was a place Sharon seemed precociously to know, and to thrive in, while Lily held back self-consciously, shy and overwhelmed at first. She was hurt when their new classmates inquired were they really twins? *twins?* but understanding the skepticism. They never wore matching clothes any longer, nor would Sharon allow Lily to wear her hair in a style resembling her own. If Sharon wanted shoulder-length hair, Lily had to keep her hair cut short; if Sharon decided she wanted her hair trimmed, Lily would have to let hers grow. *And don't hang around me for God's sake like some sad little puppy dog. And if you can't find anyone decent to eat lunch with sit alone and keep your dignity!* For Sharon hadn't time for Lily, at school. She'd quickly become one of the popular girls at Yewville High. Elected to the varsity cheerleaders when she was only a sophomore. Dating the school's most popular boys—including Mack Dwyer the senior football-basketball star whose well-to-do father owned Dwyer's Realty. Of course the Donners would not have approved of "dating" but Sharon—and Lily—conspired to keep them blissfully ignorant: Sharon simply stayed overnight at the Yewville homes of her girlfriends who were also popular, and also "dated." Somehow Sharon managed to win her parents' grudging permission to attend school dances, assured that these dances were rigorously chaperoned; there were several photos of such festive occasions, Sharon in gauzy prom dresses with spaghetti straps, Sharon posed smiling beside six-foot Mack Dwyer in a white dinner jacket, his arm around her bare shoulders. Their eyes blazing up in the camera's flash. Deedee asked, "Was he Aunt Sharon's boyfriend?" and Lily said, hesitantly, for she recalled that Sharon's relationship with Mack had gone mysteriously bad, and abruptly, "Not the only one, but the main one." Strange for Lily to encounter Mack Dwyer, now known as Michael Dwyer, in Yewville, and to realize that he, the former high school star, was now a man in his forties: still a "popular" personality, if shallow; his athlete's muscle lapsed into flesh, his still-handsome face stippled with tiny broken capillaries, the sign of a problem drinker; or one who'd been, as Lily had heard, a problem drinker until recently. "He's real good-looking, I guess," Deedee said, crinkling her nose, "but I don't like him."

Most of the remaining pages of the album were given over to Sharon's "professional" career as a model—interspersed, of course, with family snapshots of Lily and the elder Donners and other relatives and members of the First Church of Christ, at which Deedee scarcely glanced. Lily didn't blame the child: how ordinary, how *uninteresting* everyone else appeared, set beside glamorous "Sherrill." Sharon's modeling career began shortly after she won the Starr Bright competition: she was hired to appear in newspaper advertisements for the larger downtown Buffalo department stores, modeling "junior" clothes. Lily recalled the excitement of seeing her sister Sharon in these full-page ads in the *Buffalo Evening News*—the excitement of the telephone ringing, always ringing for Sharon. When she was seventeen, Sharon signed on with a Manhattan modeling agency; became "Sherrill"—sometimes with a last name, more often not; and, overcoming the Donners' objections, she quit high school, became a full-time model and moved to Manhattan. For the first year, things seemed to be going wonderfully well; Sharon claimed to be earning as much as $1000 a day, a figure almost unbelievable back in Shaheen. Then, suddenly, when Sharon was nineteen and on a shoot for *Vogue* in Mexico, she disappeared for four months; "drifted off" with a wealthy American man she'd met there; the agency hinted that drugs were involved; and "Sherrill" never returned to professional modeling again.

"Gee, Mom. Aunt Sharon is really pretty."

Deedee's words were hushed, in awe. As she contemplated the glossy glamor stills, now almost thirty years old. And the faded pages from *Vogue, Harper's Bazaar, Glamour, Mademoiselle.* Sometimes Sharon was hardly recognizable, elaborately made up, with dyed hair, or wearing a wig; a lovely slender girl's body encased in stunning, expensive, sometimes ludicrous clothes. Staring at this fairy creature, Deedee could have no idea, of course, of the heartbreak Sharon had caused in the Donner household; and of the havoc, eventually, in her confused life. Nor was Lily likely to tell Deedee.

The last photo of Sharon—"Sherrill"—had been taken sometime in 1978. A dreamy-eyed blonde with ivory skin, full sensuous mouth and size-four figure in crepey-black sexy clothes. *Look at me! Love me!*

"Is that all?" Deedee asked, disappointed.

"I'm afraid it is, honey."

There were no photos of "Sherrill" following the collapse of her modeling career. Her subsequent career as a singer-dancer, about which Lily knew very little, was not represented at all.

It had taken most of the morning to sort through the stuffed photo album and by the time Lily and Deedee had finished, Lily was feeling ill. *Why have you done such a thing, shown these pictures to Deedee? Risking so much, you must he mad.*

Long afterward, Lily was appalled at her own behavior. She couldn't comprehend it, for she might have simply hidden the album away as her mother had done, at the back of a closet, and never looked at it again.

When at last Wes came quietly to bed, after 2 A.M., Lily woke confused and asked him who'd telephoned, and Wes said no one, no one had telephoned, and Lily said, I thought I heard the phone ring, and Wes said no, sweetheart, you've been dreaming, and his weight in the bed beside her, his arm slung over her and his warm mouth in her hair were a part of the dream, the most precious part.

3
The Arrival

Here is how it happened, six weeks later on a brightly sunny cold afternoon in March.

Deedee was leaving the high school, walking with two girlfriends, when she happened to see, idling in the crescent-shaped asphalt drive in front of the building, a taxi: an unusual sight in Yewville, where there was a single taxi company, and not much demand for its services. And Deedee noticed, in the rear window of the taxi, just as the door was being pushed open, a face that was familiar to her—as familiar somehow as her own, and her mother's; yet a stranger's face, a face of strange, ravaged beauty, partly obscured by oversized sunglasses with very dark lenses. The woman removed the sunglasses as if to see Deedee more clearly. Her eyes were artfully made up, beautiful though ringed with shadows, fatigue. The woman's hair was pale, platinum blond, drawn back severely from her face into a chignon; her skin was ivory-pale, with a faint sallow sickly cast, as if she were only just recovering from an illness. Deedee might have estimated the woman was in her late twenties or early thirties, for any age beyond twenty is mysterious and "old" to a fifteen-year-old. Yet the woman was striking, stylish: her mouth was beige-pink, to mimic a "natural" look though it was anything but natural; she wore a cruel-looking silver ear clamp on her left ear, of the kind outlawed at Yewville High School, along with nose rings and more than three ear studs; and, as out of place in Yewville on an ordinary weekday afternoon as an evening gown would have been, a black satin quilted jacket with elegant boxy shoulders, black trousers with a strip of velvet at the crease, handsome black leather boots with a distinct heel.

"Geez," one of Deedee's friends whispered, "—who is *she*?"

"Not anybody's mother, from around *here*."

The woman had stepped out of the cab and was approaching Deedee and the other girls, but was looking only at Deedee; staring at Deedee with a strange, unnerving intensity. At last she said, "Deirdre—?" Her voice was hoarse, like a voice unused for a long time.

"Y-yes?"

"You know me, Deirdre—don't you?"

Deedee stared. Her face had begun to burn as if with fever.

Shyly she said, "Is it—Aunt Sharon?"

The woman in black gave a little cry, a half-sob, and came quickly to embrace Deedee, who stood unresisting, astonished, too taken by surprise to return the embrace. Dazed, she smelled the woman's strong perfume, sweet like overripe peaches, and a harsher chemical scent she could not know was the odor of bleached hair.

The woman stepped back from Deedee, smiling in triumph. "Yes! 'Aunt Sharon.'" Her eyes were delicately netted in blood. There were fine, near-invisible white lines in her forehead. Now Deedee could see that the woman was older than she'd seemed—obviously, Lily's age. And how like Lily she did look, in fact, except her features were more dramatic, exaggerated; as if Lily's pleasant plain-pretty face had been sharpened, given more definition, "beautified."

"Deirdre, get into the cab with me! We'll ride to your house."

And so, like an enchanted child in a fairy tale, Deedee got into the cab with her beautiful blond aunt Sharon, forgetting even to wave goodbye to her friends, and whoever else had come along to join them on the school steps, staring after the departing yellow-checkered taxi in amazement.

No warning!

Sudden as lightning striking.

On that day, a Tuesday like any other, Lily had been out of the house for much of the morning, attending a committee meeting at the college, doing errands, shopping; contentedly driving in the bright gusty air of March that smelled still of winter though with each passing day the sun was rising more confidently in the sky, cutting a broader swath. She discovered snowdrops, those exquisite, beautiful miniature flowers, newly opened amid the nacreous strips of snow bordering her front walk. At midday, the thermometer rose well above 32°F and the icy streets turned to slush; pedestrians were bareheaded, and some were without coats; reckless boys pedaled by on bicycles, eager to hurry the season. Spring! Spring in upstate New York!

This time, Deedee came bursting into Lily's workroom, smiling as she rarely smiled. Even before Lily saw the flowers in her daughter's hand, and absorbed the fact that they were Easter lilies, she knew that something irrevocable had happened.

"Mom? These are for you."

"For me?" Lily wiped her hands on her jeans and took the flowers from Deedee. Fresh-cut waxy-white lilies, long-stemmed, fragrant. But why?

Deedee was saying, excited, "Somebody's come to see you, Mom. To see us!"

Lily looked up to see Sharon in the doorway.

Sharon—"Sherrill." Her twin sister she hadn't seen in—how many years.

And how altered! Almost, in that first astonished instant, unrecognizable.

Sharon was smiling nervously, turning a pair of dark-rimmed sunglasses in her hand. "Lily, hello."

"Oh my God! Sharon."

Afterward Lily would think how ironic, she'd had no preparation after all. No premonition. At the time of their birthday she'd been thinking obsessively of Sharon, awaiting a call, or even a visit—but nothing. The nightmares had subsided, or she'd grown accustomed to them; absorbed them with such stoic determination they were forgotten by daylight. If, as it's popularly thought, twins have the psychic power to send each other messages, Sharon had sent her none.

The sisters stumbled together to embrace. If for a fraction of a second each had held back stricken, shy, not knowing if the other loved her, now they burned together with such urgency that Deedee, a witness, was deeply embarrassed. Her mom she could understand getting all teary and sentimental, that was what you'd expect from Lily, but Aunt Sharon who was so glamorous, sophisticated! In the taxi Aunt Sharon had told Deedee a little of her professional career in Miami and Los Angeles and Deedee had been impressed, a bit dazzled. But now both women were crying; crying messily, as people really do and not as they pretend on TV or in movies. The waxy-white lilies Lily was holding slipped from her fingers and fell onto the floor, so Deedee, grateful for an excuse to get away, deftly retrieved them and hurried to the kitchen for a vase: one of Mom's slender clay vases, perfect for long-stemmed lilies.

She was thrilled, enraptured. So this was her mother's "twin sister" Sharon! The most fantastic aunt, ever.

There were Sharon's several suitcases, an overnight bag and a heavy, bulky leather shoulder bag, carried by the taxi driver into the front hall. Quickly Sharon explained that she meant to stay in a hotel, or a motel; of course Lily protested, for Sharon must stay with them—"We have plenty of room, Sharon! I wouldn't hear of you staying anywhere else."

Sharon said, apologetically, "I know—I should have called before coming. But—I guess I was afraid."

"Afraid?"

"You wouldn't want me."

"Oh, Sharon!" Lily was hurt. "What a thing to say."

"I mean—your husband might not want me. You have your own life, your family—there wouldn't be room for me."

An air of childlike self-pity, so at odds with Sharon's glamor and poise! Lily seized her sister's hands—cold, thin hands—and squeezed them, protesting, "Of course there's room for you! How long can you stay?"

"Just a few days. Until Monday, I think."

"No longer? You've taken time off from work?"

"Yes, I mean no—I mean, I'm on leave. I'm a dance instructor at a school in Pasadena, but our spring session doesn't begin for a while." Sharon spoke carefully, wetting her lips in an odd compulsive manner.

"Dance instructor! Pasadena! That sounds very interesting, Sharon, why didn't you let me know?"

"But I did, I'm sure," Sharon said, staring at Lily. "I called you, I told you. Or I sent a card."

In the kitchen, Deedee was preparing a quick tea. She saw with relief that her mom and her aunt had stopped crying, at least for now, Sharon had carefully dabbed at her eyes, preserving most of her mascara. Strange that, if you took into account Sharon's two-inch heels, she and Lily were about the same height, approximately five feet eight; Sharon naturally appeared so much taller than Lily so much more poised, intimidating. Lily was the kind of woman you saw but didn't *see*—just sort of took for granted.

How elegantly thin Sharon was: though removing her quilted black satin jacket reluctantly, knowing Lily would be mildly shocked, disapproving of her thinness. "Oh, Sharon, are you—well? You haven't been ill, have you?" Lily asked, and Sharon said quickly, "No, no, I'm fine," sitting at the kitchen table, fumbling through her shoulder bag for something she couldn't seem to find, "—but if you had some aspirin, or painkiller—" So Deedee went to fetch some Tylenol, and Lily offered her sister tea, coffee, fruit juice, diet soda, and Sharon took coffee, black coffee, though saying, laughingly, she wouldn't mind something a little stronger: wine, maybe? So Lily said, "Of course! What am I thinking of, this *is* a special occasion." And took a bottle of red Italian wine from a cupboard, a very good wine, so far as Lily knew, and poured Sharon and herself two quite full glasses, and Deedee said with a playful pout, "Mom, what about me? I'm here, too." So Deedee was given a small amount of wine, and she and her mother and her aunt raised their glasses ceremoniously, and drank. And Lily said, smiling, though with an edge to her voice, "But why did you go to Deedee's school first, Sharon? Why didn't you just come here?"

It was an odd question, Deedee thought. Or maybe it was Lily's way of asking.

Sharon said, vaguely, "I—wasn't sure what the address was."

Deedee said, "Aunt Sharon recognized me right away! Didn't you, Aunt Sharon?"

So they talked for a while of that; of the meeting at the school; Deedee in such a thrilled, extravagant manner it was clear that the story would be told, and told, and told; for it had been, after all, very like something in a movie. Lily said she'd sent Sharon snapshots of Deedee over the years, and Sharon said yes of course, but not recently—"I'd have recognized Deirdre, anyway. Anywhere. I'm sure."

Deedee said warmly, "I'd have recognized *you*, Aunt Sharon. Mom has all your photos and things in an album, I've looked through it lots of times."

"Really! How sweet."

Lily was smiling her small fixed smile. The wineglass trembled in her fingers.

Lots of times? But why?

Sharon said, as if to placate Lily without seeming to do so (for to seem to placate Lily would be to indicate that Lily required placating), "—I just wasn't absolutely sure of the address. I didn't want to arrive at the wrong house. But I should have telephoned first, I'm so sorry." She was fumbling again in the shoulder bag, searching for cigarettes perhaps. The shoulder bag was made of a beautiful soft leather, russet-red; obviously very expensive, though much the worse for wear. Lily saw without meaning to stare that Sharon was wearing expensive-appearing jewelry, several rings including a large blue gem on her left hand, a sapphire?—and a platinum wristwatch that slid about on her thin wrist like a bracelet. Her throat was lined, more visibly than Lily's, and so she'd tied a black-and-gold silk scarf about it; a tiny label showed—Yves Saint Laurent. In the whorl of one ear there gleamed a cruel-looking silver clamp and around Sharon's neck there was a conspicuous gold chain, glittering like scales. Her platinum-blond hair had been skinned back so starkly from her face that the shape of her skull was evident; the hair was surprisingly thin, and did not have a healthy lustre. Lily felt a stab of apprehension for her sister, and for herself. *Was* Sharon ill? It would do no good to inquire directly; if you wanted to know any fact from Sharon, you would only learn it indirectly if at all. You would probably never learn it from Sharon herself.

Sipping wine, Sharon explained how she'd been traveling—traveling for weeks and had mislaid Lily's exact address; in fact, she'd blanked out on Lily's married name—"I mean, I know it of course; but I know so many names, they crowd one another out of my head." She and her dance troupe had been touring on the West Coast, most recently in Seattle, and had had quite a success; though, ironically, it looked as if the group was fated to break up "We have so many competing careers. Our agents are at one another's throats." Still, Sharon was smiling as she spoke; baring her perfect teeth in a smile of childlike hope, expectancy, yearning; the dazzling spotlit smile of "I'm Always Chasing Rainbows"; a smile calculated to melt the hardest of hearts, the most skeptical of judges. *Here I am! Don't send me away! I've come to you helpless.*

Lily had all she could do to keep from suddenly gripping her sister's hands, and hugging her again. Here was Sharon, returned to her! So unexpectedly.

Lily dreaded the moment when they would speak of their father. And of the Shaheen property. She hoped Deedee wouldn't be present, or Wes. She hoped she wouldn't break down into wracking sobs.

Lily poured Sharon a second glass of wine, for Sharon had finished her first quickly, swallowing down two of the painkiller pills; she was hoping, she said, to ward off a headache. Lily asked if Sharon would like to lie down, take a nap before dinner?—and Sharon said at once, no, she was fine; she'd flown into Buffalo the evening before, a long flight from Seattle, and had taken a

Greyhound bus to Yewville today, wasn't accustomed to bus travel any longer, the sort of Americans you meet, how *real* America is from the perspective of ground travel; but she was fine, fine. "'Starr Bright' sees America via Greyhound!" Sharon said, laughing, raising her wineglass to click against Lily's, and Lily laughed, too, but was puzzled—"'Starr Bright'?—why do you say that?" And Sharon, searching again in her shoulder bag, ignored the question, or hadn't heard; she was saying, chiding, "Lily, you should have warned me how changed everything is! The bus trip to Yewville was like a dream, one of those nightmares where things are familiar but changed, distorted. So much of the countryside is gone, the farmland! So many new houses, shopping centers—the highway is four lanes wide—the new bridge at Edgarsville Fairfield Park still looks the same. Yewville is a real city now, almost, isn't it?—like any other city in the U.S. The identical McDonald's, Wendy's, a Holiday Inn—gas stations, car dealers. The high school looks so different, I finally figured out it has a new facade, and an addition at the rear. And the old train depot—a restaurant! If the First Church of Christ is changed, too, or vanished, Lily, please don't tell me just yet, *I don't want to know.*" Sharon was smiling at Lily and Deedee, that dazzling forced smile; making a joke of her own agitation. "And, coming into town, everywhere I looked I saw names I knew, on billboards, signs—'Reigel Plumbing'—'Hendrickson's Fruit & Produce'—'Dwyer's Fence City.' All our old classmates, grown up."

Carefully Lily said, "It isn't Michael Dwyer—Mack—who owns Fence City, it's his brother Steve. His younger brother."

"'Michael'—?"

"That's what he seems to be called, now. Michael. He works for the mayor, heads one of the municipal departments. A few years ago he ran for state senator on the Republican ticket but lost—by a narrow margin." Lily paused, awkwardly. She'd never known why Sharon and Mack Dwyer had broken up and had never dared to inquire and now after more than two decades she would not have been able to surmise, seeing her sister's composed, slightly ironic expression. "It's Steve I know, from PTA. Michael Dwyer I don't know at all."

Sharon said evenly, "He'd be married, of course. With a family." When Lily vaguely nodded, Sharon said, laughing, "Everyone is married in Yewville! Of course."

"Well, some are divorced. Among our classmates. It seems to be going rapidly past us—life."

"Past some of us," Sharon said, sighing, "more rapidly than others."

Now she will speak of Father's death, Lily thought.

Instead, Sharon said brightly, "But *you're* happily married, Lily. And with a *daughter*."

Lily laughed, embarrassed; felt her cheeks burn, not altogether pleasantly; not knowing if Sharon was patronizing her? teasing? With such an elegant person, sincerity could seem artificial. Yet Sharon seemed sincere enough, inquiring after Wesley, whom she'd never met, listening as Deedee proudly explained her father's work, building houses and restoring older houses like the one in which they lived; Sharon said, smiling at Deedee, "*You* must be proud. D'you take after your father?"

Deedee glanced at Lily, and said, shyly, as if she'd only now just recalled, "Daddy's my stepdad. Actually."

"Oh. Yes. Of course."

There was a pause. Lily felt her temples throb. Her elation at Sharon's appearance was effervescent, like gassy bubbles that, burst, released a sickish aroma. *I am in danger* Lily thought.

But Sharon was smiling, and sipping her wine—"This is delicious, Lily. May I have a little more?" And talking of Yewville, and the neighborhood in which Lily lived; and of old classmates whom she hoped to telephone, perhaps even visit; if she had time. She was going to stay for only a few days, she was en route to New York to meet with her new agent. She'd begun to search again, more purposefully, in her shoulder bag; and Lily prepared herself to object, politely but firmly, if she brought out a pack of cigarettes.

Excuse me, Sharon, do you mind not smoking in the house? Sharon had begun smoking as a young teenager, a secret from their parents of course; a secret in which Lily had been a reluctant accomplice. In emulation of her precocious sister Lily had tried smoking, and had hated it. "Here! Lily, Deirdre—for you," Sharon said gaily, bringing out of the bag two gaily wrapped packages, gifts for Lily and Deedee.

Deedee, with girlish pleasure, opened hers: it was an exquisite necklace of emerald-green glass beads, turquoise stones and filmy speckled-golden feathers on silver links. "A Navajo keepsake," Sharon said. "Isn't it beautiful?"

"Oh *yes*."

Lily's gift was a heavy silver bracelet inset with turquoise stones. She slid it on: how inappropriate it looked on her wrist, glittering, regal. "I picked them up in Santa Fe," Sharon said, "on my way to"—laughing suddenly as if the very whimsicality of her words struck her—"wherever. *Here.*"

Deedee thanked her aunt Sharon profusely, and, except for shyness, would have hugged and kissed her. Lily thanked Sharon, and did kiss her sister's dry, heated cheek.

I should call Wes Lily thought. *To prepare him.*

Deedee stood at a wall mirror trying clumsily to fasten the necklace around her neck; the silver links, and then the feathers, caught in her thick springy hair. Sharon leapt up to help her with surprising energy. "Like this, Deirdre. Lovely!"

"Thanks, Aunt Sharon. Wow."

Deedee regarded herself with pleasure in the mirror, turning her head from side to side. The unusual necklace, silver, emerald-green, turquoise and fine, floating feathers, gave to her plain features a look of the exotic. Sharon stood close behind her, several inches taller than the girl, gazing intensely, almost greedily into the mirror. Her thin, beringed fingers rested on Deedee's shoulders. Lily expected Sharon to lower her chin to rest it playfully on Deedee's shoulder as she'd done years ago when they were girls together, with Lily.

We can't ever be lonely like other people.

We have each other.

Sharon said excitedly, "Lovely, isn't it? Lily, look: it brings out the greenish-blue in Deirdre's eyes."

Lily called Wes several times at his office, finally connected with him by way of the phone in his pickup truck as he was driving somewhere north of Yewville. The connection was poor, and Lily had to raise her voice, which was quavering with excitement, a strange wild elation. "Wes? My sister is here. My sister Sharon. She just arrived, she'll be staying a few days—" Wes said genially, as if from a long distance, "Well, honey, that's a surprise, but of course she's your sister—she's welcome." There was a pause, Lily could envision Wes creasing his forehead, rubbing fiercely at his nose. "As long as she wants to stay. Fine."

Lily felt immense relief. Lightly she said, "Wes, you don't need to say *that*," and Wes laughed, and said, "I was just hoping to impress you."

* * *

"Oh, Lily. It's lovely."

The lavender-and-cream guest room on the first floor, rear, had windows overlooking a side lawn of shrubs, evergreens and oaks; its own private door to the outside; a spacious closet and adjoining bathroom with gleaming fixtures and tile and a shower curtain smelling of newness. Lily realized, flushed with pleasure, helping Sharon hang some of her clothes in the closet, that she'd decorated this room with Sharon in mind. Unconsciously waiting for Sharon to come, to stay in this room.

Deedee had helped her pick out the floral cotton-and-silk bedspread in a vivid lilac print; matching pillows, curtains; the Laura Ashley wallpaper; the rich purple wall-to-wall carpeting that, though a bargain at a local rug store owned by a friend of Wes's, looked wonderfully luxuriant, expensive. Deedee had said it was a room for Princess Di.

You see, Sharon? For you.

Sharon said, her eyes widened, in a voice of utter sincerity, "Lily, how lucky you are! And how lucky I am, to be here."

Impulsively, Sharon gripped Lily's hands and squeezed them. A pang of happiness ran through Lily like an electric current. Lily recalled how, when they were girls, in high school especially when she'd feared she was losing her sister, Sharon would sometimes grip and squeeze her hands like this, in an ecstasy of emotion; confiding how someone, invariably an older boy, had spoken to her that day, or taken her for a ride in his car. How flattered Lily had been, singled out by Sharon's attention, which was like a dazzling blinding light.

Lily admitted, awkwardly, "I've been missing you so much, Sharon. I was hoping, in February—at the time of our birthday—"

Sharon was shaking wrinkles out of a glamorous silver lamé tunic, unless it was a minidress. Distracted, she said, "Oh, yes—our birthday. Actually, I was in Hawaii at the time, trying to get a little rest between engagements. I've told you about my friend James Fenke?—who owns a cable station in Pasadena?—he has a lovely house in Honolulu, on the water. A pink sandstone mansion. And such clean white *sand*."

Lily didn't believe she'd been told about James Fenke; but she murmured yes, to be agreeable.

"In Hawaii, you lose track of calendar time. Maybe there isn't even such a thing as time. So, if we had a birthday, I'm afraid I wasn't aware of it."

Lily laughed uneasily. "That's the wisest course, I'm sure."

Trying not to think *But why are you here, Sharon? Why now? After fifteen years, and more, of staying away. What motive?*

The last time Sharon had come home, to Shaheen, she'd been desperate. Suicidal. Eight months, three weeks pregnant.

As if reading Lily's mind Sharon said, in a neutral voice, "She—Deirdre—'Deedee,' you call her—is so"—her eyelids fluttered as if she were searching for the ideal, the perfect word, but could come up only with "—sweet."

"Oh yes, Deedee is. Except sometimes, on the surface, just slightly sarcastic."

"But intelligent, too. Like you. And so—grown up."

"Sometimes!"

Lily laughed. It was a mother's prerogative, to be affectionately critical of her child.

"She seems very—happy."

"Deedee is an American teenager, a sophomore in high school. She isn't happy twenty-four hours a day," Lily said reprovingly, sensibly. "But she's happy in her soul, I think. She's happy with Wes and me."

"God, yes. I can see that."

Sharon shuddered, as if the prospect of Deedee in another life had passed rapidly through her mind.

Lily was hanging up a pair of silky slacks, champagne-colored. There was a stain as of nail polish in the fabric but she hesitated to point it out to her sister. She said, instead, groping, almost shyly, "We all made the right decision."

"Yes."

"With each passing year, it seems more certain."

"Oh, yes."

"And it was—wasn't—so difficult after all. Deedee's birth certificate with my name on it—the doctor never doubted, you were me. I mean—I was you. He'd only seen us a few times, he wouldn't have guessed."

Sharon said slowly, as if the words gave her pain, "Because, yes—*we are twins*."

"And no one had seen either of us for weeks. At the campgrounds in the mountains. And people had thought I was living in Buffalo, going to school there—a place a girl could get 'in trouble' in." Lily paused, breathing quickly. She felt almost faint. "And Wes—has never asked questions. A girl can make a 'mistake,' plenty of guys make mistakes Wes says. I don't believe I have actually lied to him, I believe that in some way he *knows*; I mean, he knows the truth of my love for Deedee. And he's a man who lives in the present, rejoices in the present. He loves Deedee as much as he would if she were his own child."

"Well," said Sharon, sniffing, "*—that*, you don't know. No one, not even the man, would know."

"*I* love her so. Oh, Sharon!"

Lily's voice was pleading. She hadn't known she would speak in such a way, blinking panicked tears from her eyes.

Quickly Sharon said, "Don't worry, Lily! I haven't come back to—interfere. You must know that."

"It's just that I love her so—and she doesn't know."

"There's no reason for her to know. Her, or anyone. You kept your promise to *me*."

"Of course I did, Sharon."

Sharon said slowly, again as if the words gave her pain, "*You*—are *me*. You bore the baby, and the sin."

Lily laughed. "Sin?"

"In the eyes of the world, I mean. Not in ours."

"An 'unwed mother' isn't such an object of scorn any longer, or even pity. There are some—Wes included—who seem even to admire us."

"Still, there was sin. A loveless copulation, selfish drugged-out people. Deserving the worst." Sharon shuddered, as if revolted.

Lily persisted, trying to smile. "*I* don't believe in sin any longer, Sharon. I don't think I ever did, really. Even Daddy—he was no theologian, but he had a way of calculating Jesus' message so, after the crucifixion and the resurrection, it was all 'good news.' But I do believe in forgiveness."

"So do I!" Sharon said with a shrill little laugh. "I hope my own sins will be forgiven."

No maternal instinct in me she'd said fiercely, almost proudly. *No more than a bitch who devours her own pups*.

Though it didn't appear to be completely empty, Sharon was roughly zipping up the larger of her suitcases; shoving it beneath the bed before Lily could come help her with it. Her other suitcase, made of a chic dark blue weatherproof fabric, contained, like the Gucci overnight bag, mostly silken undergarments, stockings and toiletries. Something had spilled in it, cologne, hair spray, cosmetics. A sweetish-stale odor emanated from it which (Lily gathered) Sharon herself couldn't smell.

Now Sharon did search for a pack of cigarettes, in the shoulder bag. Her hand shook visibly as she placed a long filter-tip cigarette between her lips and lit it. Belatedly asking, "Do you mind, Lily? I'm kind of—anxious."

"No! Of course not."

Sharon sat heavily on the edge of the bed, and crossed her legs. Long swordlike dancer's legs. She tried to smile at Lily as if, for an alarmed moment, she'd forgotten who Lily was; why they were here together; like lovers thrown together, passionate yet exhausted. The skin beneath her eyes was discolored, crepey; very like Lily's, when she was tired. Yet the black mascara, even slightly smeared, gave her a glamorous, exotic look. The pupils of her eyes were dilated as if she were feverish, or drugged.

Lily did not want to think *Of course: she's taking something.*

Lily did not want to think *How many years has it been since my sister has not been taking something?*

Sharon spoke in a low hurried voice as if fearful they might be overheard. Her old air of secrecy, urgency. "It all seems so long ago now, doesn't it, like something in a dream! Out there in the country—another lifetime. Remember how we prayed? On the bare floorboards, the four of us? Praying. And what came of it was right, I knew in my heart." She paused, exhaling smoke. "I was so strung out on amphetamines, even the pain might've been happening to another person. It *might* have been you, Lily."

The sisters laughed together, thinly, wildly.

Lily said, "That's how it seemed to me, too. It seemed almost logical. Daddy promised that God would bless us, Jesus would watch over us. Almost, that night, I felt Him—His presence."

"I did, too. I did."

"Though I don't believe, really. I mean—"

"Oh, but we don't *know.* Don't say you don't 'believe,' Lily—when you don't *know.*"

Lily said, firmly, "The only thing that mattered was that the baby should be born, and live; and be loved."

"Yes."

"There's a sense in which a baby, human life, doesn't 'belong' to any individuals, anyway. Biological mothers, or fathers. It's life that begets life."

"God begets life."

"I didn't matter, or you. Or Daddy or Momma. Just the baby. God's will."

"'He hath led me, and brought me into darkness, but not into the night.'"

Lily was struck by the calm, clear, bell-like voice in which Sharon spoke these words, from—was it Lamentations? She, Lily, would not have remembered.

Lily said, "It might have been me, Sharon. Holding your hands, helping you give birth—those hours. So many times afterward I'd catch myself remembering *it had been me.*"

Sharon said, "You are her mother, not I; you, Lily, her rightful mother. That was God's will, He allowed us to know."

Lily felt compelled to say, for the sake of her own integrity, "I don't believe in the supernatural, in 'divine intervention' in human affairs. And yet—"

Sharon interrupted, "You do, Lily! You do believe! As Daddy and Momma taught us! When we were girls, you believed more than I did; you cried, remember how you cried, when Momma told us about the disciples betraying Jesus? And Jesus on the cross?—remember? That doesn't change. I thought it did, I thought I'd grown away from it, but God never changes. Even when we sin, Lily, even when we are cast low as swine, into the very belly of the beast—even then God *is.* His will be done. *You know that, Lily of the Valley.*"

The sisters stared at each other. Lily was so deeply moved, she could not trust herself to speak.

The gusty March afternoon had waned abruptly to dusk, Deedee was upstairs in her room, Wes hadn't yet come home. How strange this room in which they were together, a pretty feminine lavender-and-cream bedroom cozily lit—a bedside lamp casting a warm roseate glow onto the sisters' rapt faces. Sharon was smoking her cigarette in rapid puffs as if these mouthfuls of smoke were breath itself, pure oxygen. Lily was wiping at her eyes, smiling; about to burst into tears—she was so happy.

Yes. I know.

I am Alpha and Omega, the beginning and the end. The first and the last.

It had been more than fifteen years ago, in the late summer of 1981, that Sharon, "Sherrill," had come home to the Donners, despairing and suicidal and sick with pregnancy. She'd been abandoned, it seemed, by her lover in Mexico. She'd lost her employment as a high-paid fashion model. She'd refused to have an abortion for God had allowed her to know that abortion is murder. Yet, in Shaheen, hidden away in her parents' house, she'd raved of drowning the baby "like a kitten" if it was born; or stabbing the baby in her womb, the baby and herself. She'd wanted to die, she'd wanted the baby to die with her. Unless Lily would take the child as her own.

It could not be, yet so it was. So it came to pass.

For there was the holy power residing in Ephraim Donner: the power of Jesus Christ to heal sickness, to cast out devils. On their knees for ten hours praying, praying. Fasting, and praying. O *Lord have mercy. Jesus, help us. Though we walk through the valley of the shadow of death. Thy rod and Thy staff shall comfort us.* And so Jesus had seemed to speak to them, to suggest the wisest course. The sins of subterfuge and deceit in the eyes of mankind were of little consequence set beside the terrible sins of infanticide, suicide. For there had been no doubt among the Donners that Sharon was capable of acts of violence against herself and others. Had she not in her desperation slashed at the tender skin of her forearm with a razor, deep enough to sever an artery? Had she not raked her nails across her face, her breasts? Had she not swallowed pills that made her heart race and leap, cause sweat to ooze like oil from her pores? Had she not tried to starve herself to deny the baby growing in her womb? Had she not pinched her milk-heavy breasts? Raving *I am filth, undeserving of life. Take my baby from me and give her to God.*

It could not be, yet it was. So it had come to pass.

Sharon said, as if she'd been unconsciously reading Lily's thoughts, "Yes. You did that for me. You, Daddy and Momma—saving my life, which probably wasn't worth saving, and the baby's. And how did I repay you?"

Lily lowered her gaze as if to indicate she didn't know.

Sharon said sharply, "They didn't tell you?"

"I'm not sure."

"I stole their money, what little they had. Before I left without saying goodbye. Oh, Lily—it was only sixty-five dollars. Momma had maybe been saving it for years, in a bureau drawer. I would have stolen church funds except I couldn't get into the church office." Sharon had begun to cry almost without expression, her bluish-gray eyes glittering like glass. Yet she continued to smoke, sucking at her cigarette as if it were life to her.

Lily came near to choking, smoke stinging her eyes. "Oh, Sharon—you couldn't help yourself, you were sick. You weren't yourself, really!"

Sharon said, "That's so, Lily. It was as if *you* were somehow *me*; while I was—I don't know who. In Mexico, I was so Goddamned naive! In New York I could handle the glamor, the men—the attention; at least, I thought I could, though I'd gotten started with drugs there, mainly to fight exhaustion. And starvation! But I was being exploited all along, and it became obvious on the Mexico shoot. And then—that son of a bitch who 'fell in love with me'—talked me into quitting my job, traveling with him. He was 'an independent film producer'—'an associate of Bertolucci's'—'a friend of Dustin Hoffman's'—saying he was crazy about me, my face, my style; he wanted to marry me, finance films for me; I was going to be 'a new Grace Kelly'—he said."

Lily reached out to touch Sharon's hand, to clasp her icy fingers.

"Well. You couldn't have known."

Sharon said, with surprising fury, "It might have been so!—that's the irony. How do any movie actresses—Julia Roberts, Sharon Stone—Meryl Streep—get started, except by meeting someone who can help them? Someone with connections, with power? In fact he'd been involved in distributing a Bertolucci film in the U.S. He may even have known Dustin Hoffman. And I did look like 'a new Grace Kelly' if I was made up in that style. *I could be made to look like anyone!*" Sharon paused, smoking, brooding. Lily saw a vein throbbing in her left temple. "If only I'd had a better agent, someone who'd protected my rights, gave a damn about my future instead of simply raking in twenty percent off the top of my earnings. Oh, Lily, I know I was naive, I was selfish, and stupid, and getting pregnant—I must have been drunk at the time, or stoned out of my head. Yet—it might have been so, everything that bastard promised. *Everything might have happened as it was promised, like a fairy tale*."

Except, Lily thought, Deedee would not have been born.

Of course, Lily didn't say this. She was comforting her angry weeping sister as if she, and not Sharon, were the "elder." Lily of the Valley at whom no one ever glanced twice in the radiant presence of Rose of Sharon.

Sharon flinched in self-disgust, as if, another time, she'd been hearing, or sensing, Lily's thoughts. "Oh, Christ," she said, "listen to me. Always me, me, me! Blinded by vanity like that peroxide-blond 'Starr Bright' in her pancake makeup and false eyelashes and girdle! That old hag! And here I am, your sister 'Sherrill'—thirty-seven years old and ignorant as a country girl of thirteen."

"Sharon, you're too hard on yourself. You've always—"

"Does your husband know I'm here? Does he want me here?"

"Of course, Wes wants you. He's looking forward to meeting you at last."

"You called him, did you? Just now?"

"Yes."

Sharon was looking searchingly at Lily as if trying to determine what she really meant. She said, with a wan smile, "Well, I'll know within a few minutes. If he doesn't want me. And if so, I promise I'll leave, tomorrow. I would never come between you and your family, I promise."

Of course you won't, how could you?

Sharon had removed her tight-fitting leather boots, and was pacing about the room in her stocking feet, smoking, flicking ashes onto the deep-purple carpet. Unobtrusively, not wanting to seem fussy, Lily set one of her sculpted clay bowls on the bedside table, for her sister to use as an ashtray. Sharon had reverted to their previous subject and was lamenting, "Oh, Lily, how could I have stayed away, when Daddy died? And then the funeral—I was coming to the funeral, I *was* coming, but—my life became too complicated, somehow. I got sick, or—I had surgery. And it was too late."

Lily had once or twice inquired what the nature of Sharon's surgery had been, but Sharon's reply had been vague; she didn't think it prudent to inquire again. She said, consolingly, "I know, Sharon. It's all right."

"Did Daddy say anything about me—at the end?"

"Of course."

"Or had he forgotten me? Erased me from his memory?"

"You know better, Sharon. Daddy always loved you."

"But could he—forgive me? Stealing from him and Momma like that—"

"Sharon, you know what Daddy and Momma were like. They didn't need to 'forgive'—they loved you."

"But they loved you better—they must have. After what I did."

Sharon was watching Lily closely, anxiously. Lily felt her face burn with an emotion she could not have named.

Of course they loved me better, I was the daughter who loved them. I was the daughter who behaved like a daughter to them. I was the mother of their only grandchild. What could you expect, that they could love you more?

But Lily only repeated, quietly, what had been true enough:

"They always loved you, Sharon. It wasn't their way to compare us."

Sharon said, aggrieved, "Oh, I loved *them*! I just didn't have a chance to show it, as you did. I went out into the world, I didn't stay close to home, like you."

Sharon paused to light another cigarette, shaking out the match and tossing it onto the bedside table—not quite into the clay bowl. Unobtrusively, Lily put the match into the bowl, and handed it to Sharon to use. She said, "You've never asked about how Daddy died. You know it was cancer of the liver? But, at the end, it wasn't so bad actually. He was semiconscious much of the time, didn't seem to be in pain; kept drugged, I suppose. Wes had arranged for him to have a private room at Yewville General and we visited him every day, I was there through much of the day, for weeks, we talked, we even sang sometimes, you know how Daddy loved those old hymns. It was like Momma was in the room with us, we talked to her, too, sometimes. Daddy was a good man, Sharon; I know people would describe him as simple, a simple unquestioning Christian; but I always thought he was a good man in his heart, naturally; like Momma, too; their religion didn't make them 'good,' they made their religion 'good.' You know, Daddy was unusual as a preacher in that he didn't give much credence to 'evil.' Never preached much about the devil or hell. I think that people like him and Momma die more easily than others—I mean, people without bitterness or fear. They live more easily. So, when you didn't come to see him, Sharon, of course Daddy was disappointed, but he didn't stop loving you. He didn't judge you at all. He always thought of Deedee as your gift to—the world. He always had more faith in us, I think, than we could have in ourselves."

Lily was speaking quickly, pleadingly; never had she spoken at such length to her sister; but Sharon, pacing about, smoking her cigarette and giving off a hectic, perfumy heat, hadn't been listening closely. Strands of dry, ashy hair had escaped from her chignon; creases bracketed her mouth. She said, "God, I despise myself for not coming back in time! And now Daddy is gone forever. And

Momma. *I loved them so.*" Tears flashed in her eyes, glittering like the gold chain around her neck, and the cruel silver clamp in her ear. "It's just—my life is so complicated. Not like yours, Lily: I envy you! I had to take my chances when they came. You can't let personal life get in the way. It's like a—cruise ship casting off, and you're in danger of being left behind. A minute too late and you're on the dock staring after. Oh, Lily, you can't know how easy it is *not to exist.*" Sharon spoke excitedly, bitterly. Yet glancing at Lily to see how Lily was affected. She said, "Now God has run me to earth, Lily. I'm burnt out, exhausted. But God has His plans for me, He has determined not to allow me to rest but to make of 'Starr Bright' a scourge of sin, evil—emissaries of Satan. To repay Him for my wickedness when I was young."

Lily was perplexed, troubled. There was something in her sister's vehement words that struck her. "What do you mean, 'Starr Bright'? Why do you speak of her?"

Sharon frowned, and stared into a corner of the room as if into the distance.

"Did I say 'Starr Bright'? I didn't."

"'To make of myself a scourge of sin, emissaries of Satan'—? How? I don't understand."

Sharon changed the subject abruptly. She said, smiling sadly, "I used to be so *young,* Lily! Both of us—so *young*! Remember, you played the organ, and I sang at the front of the church and everyone stared at me, I was an 'angel' in their eyes. I could see myself in your eyes—all of you. Remember—" And Sharon began suddenly to sing, turning her eyes upward in a gesture of innocence too unstudied to be mocking or ironic, these familiar words:

"Rock of Ages, cleft for me!
Let me hide myself in Thee!
Let the water and the blood
That from Thy wounded side doth flow..."

Her voice trailed off, husky and cracked as if it had been unused for years. Lily was shocked at her sister's coarsened voice. *Why, she can't be a singer any longer. Her voice is gone.*

Sharon said, as if reading Lily's thoughts, "Lily, I'm run to earth. That's why I've come to you. God has run me to earth." Lily stood, and gripped Sharon by the shoulders. In her stocking feet, Sharon was Lily's height exactly. Yet how frail, how defeated she looked; how tired, ravaged; hiding her face in her hands. Lily said gently, "You can stay with me, Sharon. You can rest. You do seem tired—exhausted. You're welcome here, as long as you want."

"It isn't just that," Sharon said, shivering, "—but—also—someone is after me. Stalking me."

"Someone is after you—? My God, Sharon, who?

"He won't find me here with you, maybe. He thinks I'm a thousand miles away."

"But—who is it?"

Sharon shrugged weakly, as if it would do no good to name the man; as if his presence were ubiquitous, yet invisible. She lowered her voice. "A man. Death."

Lily said, frightened, "But—what do you mean? 'Death'?"

In a faint childlike voice Sharon said almost inaudibly, "Lily, you're all I have left in the world. Don't turn me away."

"Sharon! Of course not."

Lily embraced Sharon, hard. Her heart was pounding with certainty, elation. She held her weeping sister thinking *Yes, you're safe with me, I am strong enough, I will show you.*

4
"Starr Bright"

Not on the first evening of her visit but on the second, when she was feeling stronger, Sharon joined the Merricks for dinner.

When Lily returned home that day from a hurried afternoon of appointments, with groceries for the evening meal, there, to her surprise, was her sister in the kitchen. Smiling nervously at her, almost shyly.

As if she feared trespassing in Lily's territory, Sharon said, hesitantly, "Lily, remember that 'Mexican' chicken casserole Momma used to make? I saw you have some canned tomatoes in the cupboard, and rice, and chili powder—" Lily laughed, setting her bag of groceries on the counter. "And here's the chicken, and lots of other things. Let's get started."

It was as Lily had hoped but not as she'd expected.

My sister, visiting for a few days. Yes, we have so much to catch up on. Yes, we've always been very close.

Lily saw that, without makeup, Sharon's face was startlingly pale and sallow. But the deep shadows beneath her eyes were less conspicuous; she'd been able, she said gratefully, to sleep through much of the night—"Such wonderful quiet here!" Her eyes were quick-darting and still finely netted with blood; enormous in her thin face. She wore casual clothes: a black jersey blouse, a red silk scarf tied tightly about her hair, slacks of some oddly shimmering silvery-beige fabric. In flat-heeled sandals, working in the familiar space of Lily's kitchen, Sharon looked both sophisticated and almost ordinary.

All that morning and afternoon Lily had been thinking of what Sharon had told her the previous evening. *Someone is after me. Stalking me. A man. Death.* She felt a sensation of dread, perplexity.

Each time she'd tried to bring up the subject again, Sharon had managed to deflect it.

And now Deedee was with them, a cheery, enlivening presence.

Rare, Lily thought, bemused, for Deedee to be so enthusiastic about working in the kitchen, helping prepare a meal. Yet today, Deedee had volunteered to make dessert. She plied her aunt Sharon with questions—"I suppose you eat in restaurants all the time? When you're dancing?"—"Do people bother you, asking for autographs after a performance?"—"What do you think about when you dance, or is your mind filled just with the music?"

Deedee's aunt Sharon was circumspect in replying. As if, here in Yewville, her other life was distant to her, not very real.

In turn, Sharon drew Deedee out with questions about her life. Lily was surprised that Deedee answered so freely, and with such unexpected idealism. She told Sharon things she'd never told her parents: her hope of "traveling around the world someday, and keeping a photographic journal"—"making a contribution to society" —"writing poetry." It was touching to see how, in her glamorous aunt's presence, Deedee was so positive, vibrant, hopeful.

Proudly Deedee reported that her classmates had been asking about "the blond woman in the taxi who looked like a model or an actress"—but she hadn't identified Sharon except to say that Sharon was a friend of her mother's visiting for a few days. That was all.

Sharon leaned over to kiss Deedee's cheek, in gratitude. "Thank you, Deirdre. How thoughtful of you."

Sharon had made Lily, too, promise not to tell anyone she was back. In a day or two, Sharon said, she might telephone some old friends, relatives...or maybe not.

Of course Lily had agreed. She would have agreed to virtually anything Sharon requested, to please her, to allay her fears. Always there was something satisfying, even exciting, about a secret with someone both strong-willed and helpless-seeming like Sharon.

Even when you didn't quite know what the secret was, or might mean. What unknown obligations it might put you under.

*

The evening before, Sharon had been too exhausted, she'd said, even to meet Wes. She hadn't had any appetite for food but wanted only to soak in a hot bath, and go to bed early.

Well, maybe she'd have just a little to eat, if Lily didn't mind bringing her some fruit, cheese, bread. (Lily didn't of course.) And the rest of the wine they'd opened?

When Wes had come home, bringing a bouquet of long-stemmed white and red roses, he'd been surprised and disappointed to hear that his sister-in-law wasn't going to have dinner with them that night. "Is she sick?" he asked.

Lily bridled at the word "sick." It seemed somehow too blunt, vulgar; it could not suggest Sharon's fragile emotional and psychological state. "Not 'sick,' Wes," Lily said reprovingly. "Spiritually exhausted, I think."

Deedee explained that her aunt had traveled a long distance—from Seattle to Buffalo by plane, from Buffalo to Yewville by bus.

"Strange," Wes said, "she didn't call first. To let us know."

Wes was right, of course; yet Lily rather resented him passing judgment on her sister, about whom he knew nothing. That Sharon was desperate, fearing for her life—had no one to turn to, except Lily.

Run to earth. God has run me to earth.

Stalking me. A man. Death.

No, Lily wouldn't confide in Wes, about Sharon's secret. Until such time, if ever, that Sharon gave her permission. It would be their secret, among others of old.

Rose of Sharon, Lily of the Valley.

* * *

They were to have dinner in the dining room, by candlelight. A ceremonial occasion after all. Lily felt exhilarated as a young girl thinking *I miss a larger family, I have love enough for—more.*

When Lily introduced them, Wes and Sharon shook hands formally, rather shyly. Clearly, Wes was surprised at the woman he was meeting: judging by the glossy "Sherrill" photos he'd seen, and what he'd heard of Sharon over the years, he'd expected a glamorous, hard-edged person, and here was Sharon in her subdued, deferential, intensely feminine mode—her pale blond hair in a sleek chignon at the nape of her lovely neck, her clothes dark, sophisticated but conservative; a single gold chain glittering around her neck; small gold studs in her ears. Her face was pale, without makeup except for a light coral lipstick that gave her a youthful, vulnerable look, at least by candlelight.

His face flushed, Wes told Sharon how good it was to meet her, at last—"I've been hearing lots of things about you." And Sharon said, warmly, "And I've been hearing, from Lily and Deedee, lots of things, very nice things, about you, Wes."

A perfect answer. In Sharon's throaty, sexy voice. His name intimate as a caress: "Wes."

Sharon presented Wes with a gift, a small box wrapped in bright tinselly paper. Self-consciously Wes opened it to discover, of all things—cuff links. Lily hoped that neither Wes nor Deedee would make an awkward joke about the fact that Wes Merrick had never owned a shirt with French cuffs in his life, but Wes managed to thank Sharon sincerely enough. As if no other gift would have pleased him quite as much.

The cuff links were platinum gold with matching pearls on one side and the engraved initials *W M* on the other. Wes said, "'W M'—that's me, I guess," and Sharon said, "I hope you like them, Wes. I had them especially engraved for you."

An odd remark, Lily would recall afterward. But so many of Sharon's remarks were odd.

Lily was more troubled that the cuff links were so expensive a gift: did her sister really have that kind of money? Many of her things, Lily couldn't help but notice, were worn, frayed, even stained—though of high quality. And there was some ambiguity, about which Lily hadn't wished to question her, about exactly where Sharon was living.

Dinner went well, at least initially. The Mexican chicken was declared a great success. (Though Lily noticed that Sharon managed to eat only a portion of her serving.) Deedee took part in the adults' conversation in a manner that made Lily proud of her; and she looked transformed—her hair neatly brushed; fingernails cleaned and filed; wearing not her usual shapeless jeans, but a wool skirt and a white turtleneck sweater, and the striking Navajo necklace Sharon had given her. (Which Wes admired, too.) In emulation of Sharon's model posture, Deedee was even making an effort not to slouch as she usually did, sullenly self-conscious of her breasts; she smiled, not scowled, when Lily asked her how school had been that day. And Wes, though unaccustomed to guests at dinner, as to strangers in his household, was warm and engaged and welcoming to his mysterious sister-in-law.

Of course, Sharon was deftly flattering, subtle in her seductiveness. Lily had to admire her, though they were such very different people.

Fixing him with her somber eyes, Sharon said, "Tell me about your work, Wes. Your houses. It must be magical, building houses for people to *live in*."

Wes laughed, embarrassed. "It's magical when people pay me on time. *That* I appreciate."

Sharon said, leaning forward earnestly, "Yes, but you are doing something *real* in the world. Your work isn't just an idea—or shares in the stock market or—a performance. 'All flesh is grass, and the goodliness thereof.' But a house is real and human beings are affected by it and you are contributing to human happiness, Wes, and that's why I believe it's *magical*."

No one spoke like this in Yewville: nor in such a throaty, dramatic manner. Wes and Deedee gaped at Sharon, charmed. Lily smiled, thinking she hadn't heard Sharon speak like this since the evening of the Starr Bright Youth Talent Search 1972 when, before singing, Rose of Sharon Donner had introduced herself to the audience, utterly captivating them with her sweet Christian-girl idealism.

Wes was encouraged to talk about his work, his favorites among the area houses he'd been hired to restore; his ambitious plans for the future. Lily learned a few things she hadn't known and

Deedee, eager to be included in the conversation, said, with child-like enthusiasm, "Aunt Sharon, we can take a tour of Daddy's houses while you're here. There must be twenty really nice ones in town. And some new houses, too, on the River Road."

Wes said, dryly, "The money's in new houses, I'm afraid, not restorations. And in government contracts—which are out of my league."

Sharon sympathized. It must be so unpredictable, frustrating, to be in the construction business—"You never know how the economy might change." A Miami friend of hers, she said, had made millions of dollars building condominiums in the real estate boom in the 1980's—at least $100 million—and then, virtually overnight, the condos stopped selling, there was a glut on the market and even today many buildings are partially empty. "Last I heard, he had to declare bankruptcy."

There was a moment's startled silence. Deedee shifted in her chair and murmured, "Wow! One hundred million dollars." Wes laughed wryly, pouring more wine into Sharon's and his emptied glasses. "*That's* out of Merrick, Inc.'s league, for sure."

Lily said quickly, to deflect the subject from such daunting sums of money, "I don't really understand it but, in construction and real estate, doesn't everything depend upon the interest rate? When it's low, business is good; when it's high—"

Wes said, trying to be affable and not bitter-sounding, "You're screwed."

Deedee giggled reprovingly. "Dad-*dy*."

"No other word for it: screw-*ed*."

They talked about the economy and Lily was uneasy, hearing Wes so vehement, sardonic; she hadn't known the extent of his bitterness. He was telling Sharon that the Federal Reserve sets the interest rate—"As guided by the big American moneymen. The men who don't pay a penny in taxes. It isn't God on his throne who sets the rates."

Inevitably then they spoke of real estate in the Eden Valley, and in western New York generally. The region had been in a recession for some time; many factories had been shut down in Buffalo, Tonawanda, Port Oriskany. As for farmland—

Sharon said suddenly, to Lily, "And how is—the family farm?"

Lily had never heard the property described in such a way. Never in her memory had her parents' fifteen acres of rocky, partly wooded land adjacent to Reverend Donner's church been tilled except for Mrs. Donner's small vegetable garden. Awkwardly Lily said, "Well, you know, Sharon—it's gone. Sold. After Daddy died."

"Sold?"

Sharon stared at Lily. She did not appear to be acting, but utterly sincere. In the candlelight her eyes looked enormous, black with pupil as a cat's. Lily explained that she'd told Sharon, certainly; after their mother's illness, and then their father's, there were so many medical bills, and taxes on the property—"We would have loved to keep it but we had no choice, really."

"Lily, it isn't *ours?* It belongs to strangers? The Donner *family farm*?"

Lily said, faltering, "Sharon, I'm sure I told you," and Wes intervened, saying, "By the time your father died he was deeply in debt, Sharon. The land in Shaheen was sold for taxes and the old houses and outbuildings razed. *I* arranged for the sale, and I believe I got a good, fair price from a local farmer."

Sharon wiped tears from her eyes. Saying, to Lily, "But—it's *gone*? The house we grew up in? I dream of it so often, it's so real to me, I can't believe this—"

Lily apologized, guiltily, "Sharon, I'm so sorry. I thought I'd notified you, all along. It's what Daddy wanted, at the end. We—Wes and I—didn't feel we had any—"

"What about the church?" Sharon asked, suddenly sarcastic as a hurt child. "Has the 'First Church of Christ of Shaheen' been sold and razed, too?"

Lily explained that their father's church had relocated to the village of Shaheen at the time of his retirement. It was in new, larger quarters—much had changed.

Sharon protested, "I've always had this dream, Lily, of coming home. It's kept me going. 'In the valley of the shadow' it's kept me going. And now you say that our home is *gone*? And Daddy's church? And Daddy himself—*gone*?"

Sharon was staring at Lily with her bright, tear-glittering eyes, and Lily was staring at Sharon guiltily. Candlelight shimmered on the sisters' taut, pale faces; the air was charged as if with static electricity. Lily murmured another time, "I'm sorry, Sharon," and Sharon said in a wounded, wondering voice, "If only you'd told me, Lily, when the sale was. And when the funeral was, for Daddy. *I would have done anything to get here, to see him one last time.*"

Wes said, delicately, that certainly Lily had informed Sharon of their father's death; as of his long illness, and their mother's. And certainly Lily had informed her of the sale of the Shaheen property.

Sharon shook her head, as if not hearing. There was a tiny silver lighter in her hand, she lit a cigarette with shaking fingers. "How can Ephraim Donner be *dead*? He's so alive in my heart. I see his face, I hear his voice. The kind of man Jesus would have been—if Jesus had truly lived."

There was a bitterness here that alarmed Lily, frightened her. She thought *But you believe in Jesus, Sharon! Aren't you the one of us who believes?*

Sharon said, "I always thought *he* would outlive *me*. All of you in Shaheen would outlive *me*. And of course 'Deirdre'"—she turned suddenly, unexpectedly to Deedee, reaching out to seize the girl's wrist—"would outlive 'Starr Bright.' For God will use me as His wrath and His scourge, and then He will abandon me—I know. 'A sword shall pierce my soul.'"

The Merricks were amazed. Sharon released Deedee's wrist and lapsed into a brooding silence. She was smoking her ill-smelling cigarette as if it were her very breath.

Lily saw that Sharon was genuinely upset; it was obvious she was unwell, and not altogether responsible for what she said; another time she began to apologize, and Wes interrupted, annoyed now at both Lily and Sharon, "Excuse me, Sharon, but one crucial fact you should know: your father's estate, such as it was, was left to Lily."

Quickly Lily said, "Because, you see, Sharon, I was *here*—I'd been taking care of him. It hardly means that Daddy didn't love you just as much as he loved me."

Sharon was staring at Lily with her teary, glassy eyes. A look that seemed to indicate *Yes I want to believe you, yes please lie to me, how can you insult my intelligence by lying to me, you don't know me at all.* And still Wes was saying, more curtly than he probably wished to sound, he who avoided domestic confrontations however assertive he was with business associates, a man other men did not wish to cross, "As I said, Sharon, I happen to think I got a good price for the property. Maybe you'd like to examine the paperwork?"

Sharon said, grinding out her cigarette in one of Lily's fluted floral plates, "Thank you, no. I couldn't bear it."

Through this exchange, poor Deedee had become increasingly uncomfortable. Now she said, in desperate good spirits, so that Lily's heart went out to her, "Aunt Sharon, why don't we drive out to Shaheen, too? Along the River Road? Now that it's almost spring, the roads won't be so bad. I used to love going out into the country when I was a little girl."

Quietly Sharon said, with a glance at Lily sharply reproachful as a flick of a whip, "That's a kind, generous idea, Deirdre. But I doubt I'll be in Yewville long enough."

Lily silently protested *But you only just arrived yesterday, you can't be thinking of leaving already!*

Suddenly, then, interrupting their meal, there was a knocking at the back door.

"Who—is that? Don't let him in—"

It was probably just one of Wes's workmen, dropping by the house instead of calling as they often did, but Sharon reacted violently, almost dropping her wineglass, cowering in her chair like a frightened child. Lily explained the circumstances; no reason to be alarmed; they could hear Wes open the door, speak with someone named Eddy; but still Sharon was trembling, and then rueful, defensive. When Wes returned to the table, apologizing for the interruption, Sharon remarked if this were Los Angeles or Miami he wouldn't be so trusting about someone knocking at his door after dark, and Wes said, genially, "But this isn't Los Angeles or Miami, it's Yewville."

Lily felt a stab of pity for her sister. Neither Wes nor Deedee knew what she knew: that Sharon believed herself pursued—"stalked." She tried to imagine what it would be like, to be so panicked at the sound of someone knocking at the door; to be always so vigilant, nervously alert.

Someone is after me. A man. Death.

Lily contemplated Sharon, wondering if her story was true. Obviously, her emotion, her panic were genuine; the evening before, when Lily had held Sharon in her arms, comforting her, there was no doubt in her mind that something had happened to Sharon, to rouse her to such terror. But since she'd been a child Sharon had always exaggerated fears; embellished incidents to make her life more intriguing. Sometimes Lily thought it was unconscious, sometimes it seemed fully conscious. Sharon's clouded blue eyes demanding *Believe me! or I'll know you don't love me.*

Though there had been times, in high school for instance, when Lily had suspected that Sharon hadn't confided in her; hadn't told all there might have been to tell. Hiding away in a locked bathroom crying, and, in the night, prowling the house in secret... Something had happened between Sharon and her boyfriend Mack Dwyer, and out of hurt pride, or shame, Sharon had told no one about it. Not even her twin sister.

It was just nerves, Sharon said, the way she'd reacted to the knocking at the back door; truly, she was fine. She insisted upon helping Lily and Deedee clear the table for coffee and dessert, but she was unsteady on her feet and, in the kitchen, had to lean against a counter until a wave of dizziness passed. Lily wanted to say *Why didn't you eat more, and drink less?* Lily was annoyed, too, when Sharon declined the cherry cobbler Deedee had prepared for them, saying with a shudder she'd as soon eat broken glass as so many calories. Lily saw the look on Deedee's face: it would seem to her, and perhaps it had been intended to be, an allusion to her weight.

And wasn't there a not-so-subtle dig here, too, in Lily's side? *How can you, this girl's mother, allow her to be even a few pounds overweight? I would never allow it.*

Back in the dining room, Wes asked Sharon when she was scheduled to begin teaching in Pasadena. She looked at him so blankly he corrected himself—"Or is it Seattle? The dance school Lily mentioned."

Sharon said slowly, "I might not, after all. Might not go back. I'm on my way to—Manhattan. An old friend. We've both had heartbreak."

Deedee glanced at Lily, perplexed. Earlier that evening as the three of them had worked in the kitchen, quite enjoying themselves, Sharon had impulsively invited Deedee to fly out and stay with her when she got settled "on the West Coast."

Deedee said, uncertainly, "I guess you travel a lot, Aunt Sharon?" and Sharon said, "As long as I don't mind being manipulated by agents demanding fifteen percent of my income, I travel constantly." Wes asked, "When can we see you and your dance troupe perform, Sharon?" and again Sharon stared at him blankly, and Lily quickly intervened, "Sharon's dance troupe is disbanding, unfortunately." Sharon said, shrugging, "Disband*ed*, to be precise. Which is just as well. I'm ready to move on. The so-called glamor professions use women like Kleenex, then toss them aside. Exactly like Kleenex." She paused, reaching for another cigarette. "I knew Margaux Hemingway. We weren't close but we'd worked together on several shoots. She couldn't deal with it—the glamor, the excitement, and men—and what comes after. *I* survived because—I wasn't quite as successful." Her voice trailed off as she smiled mysteriously, recalling memories best unspoken.

Deedee, who'd read about Margaux Hemingway in *People* and had seen some morbid film clips on TV, asked Sharon what the former model and actress had been like, and Sharon said that Margaux had had her weaknesses like everyone else but lacked the strengths others had. Deedee asked, "*Was* it suicide, how she died?" and Sharon said bitterly, "It's always suicide, Deirdre," and Wes said, an edge of annoyance to his voice as before, as if he wanted to protect his daughter from such cynicism, "What do you mean by that, Sharon?" and Sharon said, "If they don't commit the act themselves, they drive you to it," and Wes said, "Who?" and Sharon said, almost spitting out the words, yet with satisfaction, grim pleasure, "Pigs and fornicators. Emissaries of Satan. 'He hath led me in dark places, as they that be dead of old.'"

The Merricks regarded Sharon with perplexity—was she joking? Or was she, uttering these strange, archaic words, deadly serious? Lily could not recognize the Bible verse, assumed it must be the Old Testament. There was a pale glisten to Sharon's skin and her beautiful dissatisfied mouth twisted downward in derision.

Lily thought to turn the conversation to another, more positive direction. "You'll love teaching, Sharon. Working with others is so rewarding! I was shy at first, but I've come to love my night class at the community college."

Deedee said, "Mom's students love her, too. They keep signing up for the course semester after semester, even the ones who can't 'pot' worth a dam."

Coolly Sharon said, "But my teaching will be different from yours, Lily. The Pasadena School of Dance is a professional school. We only accept talented students, only about fifty percent of our applicants; not just anyone, like a community college."

Lily might have been expected to feel insulted by this offhand remark, but instead she found herself laughing. How like Rose of Sharon, who'd pretended to be Lily's older sister in high school, insisting upon differentiating between them. Lily said agreeably, "No, my students aren't greatly talented as potters but they *try*. And I'm no genius, myself."

Deedee objected, "Mom, you're *good*. Mom made this vase here, Aunt Sharon, it's cool, isn't it?"

It was a slender, tubular ceramic vase of the color and sheen of mother-of-pearl, placed on the center of the dining-room table, containing the beautiful white and red roses.

Sharon touched the vase with her forefinger, almost in doubt. "It's very—professional."

"But to achieve this single vase," Lily said, "I had to make, and discard, probably two dozen. *That* isn't very professional."

Through the meal, Lily had been noticing how her husband and her daughter were gazing at her sister. With what intense, unwavering interest. Had either ever looked at her in quite that way? Even when Wes's love for her had been new, even when Deedee had been a baby? Lily was sure she wasn't jealous. Never could she be jealous of her twin sister. For what was Sharon but *a blond Lily, a far more beautiful and mysterious Lily?*

They talked of classes; of Deedee's high school, which had been, of course, Lily's and Sharon's high school, twenty years before; of teachers who'd retired, or died; of names, nicknames—"I wish I wasn't called 'Deedee,'" Deedee said suddenly, to her parents' surprise. "I hate that silly name."

Lily said, hurt, "But, Deedee—it's a sweet name—"

"It is not. Mom. It's a silly name."

Wes said, "Since when?"

"I don't know since when. Since always."

There was an awkward silence. Sharon said, carefully, "But the name 'Deirdre' is beautiful, I think. If I had a daughter—I'd like to have named her 'Deirdre.'"

Deedee frowned. "You think so, Aunt Sharon? 'Deirdre'? Isn't it kind of weird?"

"Certainly not. It's Irish, it's like poetry. 'Deir-dre.' Yes, it's beautiful."

This seemed to have settled the issue with Deedee, at least for the moment. Lily felt dazed, tricked; as if, under cover of caressing her, Sharon had pinched her, hard. *If I had a daughter, I'd like to have named her "Deirdre."*

In fact, Lily, her mother, and her father had named the baby Deirdre, after a distant relative of Lily's mother. Sharon who was "Sherrill" had had no interest in naming the baby, had never responded to news of the baby's name at all.

As if sensing the drift of Lily's thoughts, seeing the vexed expression on her face, Sharon said, reaching over to take Lily's hand and squeeze it, "Lily, I can't tell you how happy I am to be here. Thank you, all of you—for your hospitality. It's as if I was dead and now—I am alive."

Though she was looking very tired; there was a feverish edge to her voice. When Lily protested that she was exaggerating, she said, "No, it's true. I've been tormented, and put to the test; I've been made to pass through 'the valley of the shadow'; but I think I've come out on the other side now. Somehow you, Lily, here in Yewville, kept me alive. All these years. Even when I seemed to have lost you."

"Lost me? What do you mean?"

"Or maybe *you* lost *me.* Temporarily."

Wes said, "Sharon, you know you're welcome to stay with us as long as you like. If you need a quiet place to rest, to relax—"

Sharon laughed sharply, but her manner was flirtatious. "Is that a gentlemanly way of telling me I look tired, Wes? *Sick?*"

"Of course not. But—"

"But I am, of course—a little tired. I've been working hard. I've been run to earth."

"Well, we have plenty of room," Wes said, gesturing expansively. His cheeks were flushed from the wine, the good food, the intense conversation, so unlike the Merricks' usual dinners at home. "As Lily has told you, I'm sure."

Lily was still smarting, her heart pounding uncomfortably in her chest. *If I had a daughter. I'd like to have named her "Deirdre."* She wasn't quite sure what Wes and Sharon were talking about, and why Deedee was looking on with a wide, hopeful smile, the feathery-glinting Navajo necklace around her throat.

Lily had put on the Navajo bracelet, but it weighed so heavily on her wrist, and hadn't seemed quite appropriate for the occasion, so she'd removed it again. To wear another time, perhaps teaching her potting class. Her students, most of them adult women, would notice and admire it at once.

This? A present from my sister.

Oh, yes. I have a sister. I haven't mentioned her?

A twin. But not identical.

Dinner was over, it was nearly nine o'clock. Yet no one seemed eager to leave the table. As if the Merricks' strange, mysterious visitor, that fever-glow to her face and eyes, held them captives, willing captives. Sharon had been answering questions of Deedee's about her modeling career, about "Sherrill"; now suddenly she smiled, and said, "Oh, Lily—remember 'Starr Bright'? *She* started it all."

How odd, that Sharon had spoken that name several times since her arrival in Yewville. That transparently phony, showbiz name. Lily would not have wished to confess how she'd come to dislike the woman who called herself "Starr Bright," finally. That vain, self-promoting and bossy Buffalo TV personality who'd been fired from her job for driving while intoxicated, filed a lawsuit against the television station which she'd eventually lost, and ended her days, as Sharon probably didn't know, in a Buffalo detox center where she'd died of cirrhosis of the liver at the age of fifty-seven.

Her real name had been "Stella Breznick." She'd never married, had no children.

Lily said of course she remembered "Starr Bright" how could she forget the woman who after all had changed their lives? But Deedee insisted upon knowing more about Starr Bright; and Wes, though he'd grown up in Yewville, claimed to know nothing at all about her; so Sharon spoke animatedly, amusingly—"A busty blond Liz Taylor was what she tried to be, but she never got beyond *The Starr Bright Hour* on Saturday mornings, for children. Remember, Lily, how we'd write for tickets, weeks ahead of time? The tickets were free to children, but you had to reserve them. It was a long drive for us, thirty miles from Shaheen, and the studio audience had to be seated an hour before the show began. Daddy drove us a few times, and once or twice Momma, and what a treat it was! Except, having to get there so damned early, still you had to wait in line—"

With a startling vehemence Lily said, "Yes, and once inside the studio you'd wait, and wait—"

"—and the younger children would get restless, have to be taken to the bathroom—"

"—and everyone was so excited, but time seemed to stop—"

"—just waiting, and waiting—"

"—and finally Bessie the Cow would come out on stage, and we'd all scream—"

"—and the Ducklings and Goslings chorus, they were actual children, in costume—"

"—and Louie the Lion—"

"But still you'd be waiting, and waiting—"

"—because the show didn't actually begin until Starr Bright appeared, it was part-taped, and part-live—"

"—and always they'd say 'just a few more minutes, boys and girls'—"

"—'Starr Bright will be with you soon'—"

Sharon jumped to her feet, and pulled Lily from the table to join her, and the two women began singing, in mock child-voices, arms around each other's waist, the simple nursery-rhyme tune, the theme song of *The Starr Bright Hour,* which Lily would have sworn she hadn't known, had long forgotten.

> *"Starr Bright will be with you soon!*
> *Starr Bright will be with you soon!*
> *Starr Bright, Starr Bright!*
> *Starr Bright will be with you soon!"*

Lily was laughing giddily, seeing in Wes's and Deedee's faces a single expression of amazement, that she, Lily, wife and mother, was behaving in such a way. *Well, then, you don't know me, do you! No more than you know my sister Rose of Sharon do you know me, Lily of the Valley.* But abruptly then her laughter stopped, she felt weak, sickened; frightened; the way Wes and Deedee were staring, as if they scarcely recognized her, trying to smile, to see the joke. It came to Lily in a wave of panic that something terrible would happen, she was powerless to prevent it.

Once Lily went silent, Sharon too ceased her abrasive, jeering song. Her arm around Lily's waist that had been so tight slipped weakly away. She seemed suddenly faint, light-headed; leaning against the back of a chair; Wes leapt up to help her, but Lily was already gripping her sister's thin shoulders, gently yet firmly. "Sharon? What's wrong?" Lily asked anxiously. Sharon touched her fingers to her forehead, her eyelids fluttered. She whispered. "No—nothing. Just tired." But she was more than tired, clearly; the blood had drained from her face, leaving her haggard, aged. Strands of acrid-smelling hair had escaped from her chignon and her breath smelled of wine and cigarettes.

Wes suggested they drive Sharon to the Yewville General emergency room, but Sharon, trembling, pressed into Lily's arms pleading No! no! she was only tired, exhausted, she'd had too much to drink and wanted only to go to bed. Lily helped her walk cautiously from the dining room to the guest room at the rear of the house; Wes and Deedee followed uncertainly, not knowing what to do. "Don't let them look at me, stare at me." Sharon begged, clutching at Lily like a child, "—don't let them touch me, Lily! I'm so afraid." Lily assured her sister that no one would touch her except Lily herself, if that was what she wanted.

Long ago, when they were girls in Shaheen, sharing a single bedroom in which there were twin beds—how vividly it was returning to Lily, in fleeting patches of memory—she'd sometimes helped Sharon lie down on her bed and try to relax after one of her emotional outbursts (temper tantrums, "nerve-attacks" as their mother called them); their relationship at such times was that of nurse-patient; play of a kind, yet serious play. How startling that strong-willed Rose of Sharon, the master, should be so dependent upon Lily of the Valley, her slave; what pleasure to suddenly reverse their roles. Lily had not known whether even at such times Sharon remained in control; or whether somehow, as if by magic, she, Lily, had seized control.

More briskly than she meant, Lily told Wes and Deedee that everything was under control, and closed the door behind Sharon and herself. She helped Sharon lie down, removed her absurd high-heeled shoes, loosened her clothes. The gold chain lay glaring against Sharon's just slightly lined throat and though it could have weighed virtually nothing, Lily didn't like the look of it, and undid the clasp and removed it. Sharon was moaning how dizzy she was, how the room was spinning. Lily went into the adjoining bathroom to soak a washcloth in cold water, and brought it back to press against Sharon's feverish face. Sharon was trembling almost convulsively. Her teeth chattered. Feebly she clutched at Lily's hand. "Oh, Lily, forgive me, I'm so—afraid! 'Starr Bright' has done things and things have been done to her and—I will have to be punished." Lily asked, "Shall I call a doctor, Sharon? And make an appointment for the morning?" She meant to be practical, to hide her anxiety; she'd been good at playing nurse, quietly assuming her temporary control. Sharon pleaded, "No! No doctor! No one must know I'm here, Lily, you promised."

Lily said, stroking her sister's thin, frantic hands, "Yes, of course I promised! You're safe with me, Sharon."

In this way Lily Merrick's ceremonial dinner welcoming her lost sister Sharon back home was ended.

* * *

This talk of Starr Bright what was it but raving drunken nonsense.

After so many years. Lily refused to think of it, erasing her thoughts one by one like spraying a grimy window with cleanser and briskly wiping it clean.

And what did Wes know of Sharon. To speak of Sharon as he did.

Might Sharon have a drug problem? a drinking problem? mental problem? Shouldn't she see a doctor?

No, Wes knew nothing. A man could know nothing.

But she loved him. Wanted to be fair to him. Conceded yes her sister surely had problems, emotional problems after the way she'd been exploited. Psychological problems, yes possibly. And she'd drunk too much wine at dinner out of nervousness, excitement. Why had he kept filling her glass? You can hardly blame her for that.

Wes, in bed beside Lily. Saying softly Look I don't blame her, honey, I'm just concerned. For her, and for you.

Waiting for him to fall asleep. His prickling thoughts to shift from her.

Downstairs, was Sharon asleep? Or, like Lily, anxious, awake?

Run to earth.

God's wrath, and God's scourge.

In the guest-room bathroom Lily had seen: jars and tubes of cosmetics, lipsticks, a container of "ivory" face powder spilled as if with a shaky hand.

On Sharon's bedside table, face down, Lily had seen: a book with a cheap soft cover, fake gilt letters HOLY BIBLE.

STARR BRIGHT WILL BE WITH YOU SOON. STARR BRIGHT WILL BE WITH YOU SOON. STARR BRIGHT WILL BE WITH YOU SOON!

Beside the sleeping lightly snoring man who was her husband Lily lay part awake part dreaming in dread and anticipation.

III

YEWVILLE RESIDENT FOUND DEAD IN CAR
POLICE INVESTIGATE APPARENT SUICIDE

YEWVILLE, N.Y. (April 4) Stanley Reigel, 39, of 542 Brisbane Street, South Yewville, was found dead early Tuesday morning in his car parked in an empty lot of the Buffalo & Chautauqua Railroad yard.

Mr. Reigel, owner of Reigel Plumbing, was said by his wife Constance to have failed to come home after working late at his office Monday evening. He had informed her he would not be home for dinner because of "emergency bookkeeping matters" and when he failed to return home by 11 P.M. Mrs. Reigel made several calls to his office as well as to friends and acquaintances. At approximately midnight Mrs. Reigel and 16-year-old Benjamin, the couple's son, drove to Reigel Plumbing on Huron Road to find no one there.

At 6:45 A.M. Tuesday morning, Mr. Reigel's 1996 Ford Cutlass was discovered by Leo Mark, security guard for the Buffalo & Chautauqua Railroad, in a secluded area of the railroad yard. Mr. Reigel's body was in the backseat.

A preliminary examination determined that death appeared to have been caused by severe slashings of Mr. Reigel's wrists and forearms. An alleged "suicide document" is in the custody of Yewville police.

There are no indications of robbery.

Relatives of Mr. Reigel claim that he had no reason to take his own life. Eden County coroner Bill Early will be conducting an autopsy today. Anyone with information to aid in the police investigation is requested to call (716) 687-9592.

1
The Broken Bowl

Now the house at 183 Washington Street seemed, in Lily's eyes, to glow with a secret interior light. When she drove home and turned her car in the driveway she felt her pulse quicken.

She'd long been accustomed, during the day, to returning to an empty, rather lonely house. Wes was at work, Deedee at school. But now Sharon was visiting: Lily had only to enter the kitchen breathless and call out, "Sharon? I'm home."

Yes we've always been close. My twin sister Sharon and me.

Even with thousands of miles separating us. Even those years she was lost to me.

It was the second week of Sharon's visit. Time had passed with magical swiftness.

Lily had pleaded with Sharon not to continue on to New York just yet. Not in her shaky condition. Not with her migraine headaches, nausea and depressed appetite. It was obvious she needed rest and calm; she needed to gain at least fifteen pounds; to regain her old vigor and spirit. (Of the person who was "stalking" her—whatever danger he represented—Sharon declined to speak any further.) Apologetically she said, "Oh, Lily, I don't want to presume upon your hospitality—yours, and Wes's. Are you sure he doesn't mind if I stay a little longer?" and Lily said adamantly, squeezing her sister's hand, "Of course Wes doesn't mind! Hasn't he told you so, himself?"

Though Wes, being Wes, a naturally reticent if strong-willed man, was difficult to read. Having a stranger in his household clearly made him uneasy and self-conscious; equally clearly, he liked Sharon, whom he saw for only a small period of time each day, in the evening, and whom by accident he called "Sherrill" more than once—to his acute embarrassment. Sharon laughed nervously but assured him she didn't mind—"There are people who know me only as 'Sherrill' and not all of these people have been cruel to me. In fact, some have been kind."

Though he didn't tell her so himself—he left such issues to Lily, of course—Wes persisted in thinking that Sharon should see a doctor. Or a therapist of some sort. He'd had some experience with alcoholism—drug addiction—in Vietnam and elsewhere—and he knew the symptoms, he said.

Lily and Sharon quarreled—almost—about whether Lily should arrange for Sharon to be examined by a doctor. "You seem to be running a chronic fever," Lily scolded, "and I hear you coughing in the mornings. You might have a respiratory ailment that could be cured with antibiotics." Sharon said, with a little-girl air of pleading, "Lily, it's just these damned cigarettes. I'm trying to *quit*, I promise." Lily said, "But you scarcely eat. You say you're not hungry," and Sharon said, backing off, "No doctors! I can't bear being poked, prodded, pierced by any man, M.D. or otherwise—I'm terrified of needles." Lily said, "What about a woman doctor, then? I've heard of a new woman gynecologist who's said to be wonderful, very gentle. I would switch to her myself except I feel loyal to—" and Sharon said, sharply, "Damn it, Lily, *no*, It isn't like when we were girls, I'm not your slave now to be *commanded*."

Lily stared at Sharon. She was seated at her potter's wheel, in her workroom—Sharon in a chenille robe, barefoot, her damp hair wrapped in a towel, had come in to watch her work—but her hands and feet had ceased their motion. Her heart beat steadily, calmly.

"What? What did you say?"

Sharon said peevishly, "I'm not your slave, 'Lily of the Valley,' you're not my master, to tell me what's good for me—to command me at your whim."

But you commanded me. You were Rose of Sharon my master, I was Lily of the Valley your slave.

Sharon fumbled in the pocket of the robe, drawing out a pack of cigarettes. She was trembling but defiant; on the verge of an emotional outburst; it would be dangerous to push her, to upset her any further. So Lily bit her lip and suppressed her words and after a tense moment Sharon came to take her hand, her hand that was damp with clay, and, in an impulsive childlike gesture, in that way that endeared her to all the Merricks, she raised it to press against her own cheek—which was indeed hot, feverish. "Lily, don't be angry! Everyone can't be strong, like you."

One evening Wes returned home with a mysterious purchase, showered and came downstairs to dinner wearing a new shirt—a white cotton dress shirt with French cuffs. And the platinum-gold and pearl cuff links engraved "W M" Sharon had given him.

Lily laughed, and kissed him on the cheek. "Honey, what a surprise! You look so handsome."

Sharon was delighted, too. And Deedee, who said teasingly, "Wow. Daddy is becoming *style-conscious.*"

Wes, blushing, admired the cuff links, holding out his wrists so that they glinted in the cheery bright light of the kitchen. He complained of spending ten minutes getting the damned things through the slits in the cuffs—"But it's worth it, I suppose."

Lily was surprised, well Lily had always been surprised, by her sister's unpredictable behavior. Her unpredictable nature.

You would expect the convalescing "Sherrill" to be self-pitying and self-absorbed and oblivious of the tasks of running a household, such mundane chores as cleaning up after meals, running and emptying the dishwasher, keeping the downstairs rooms clear of accumulating debris like newspapers, spot vacuuming—but there was Sharon, sometimes wearing dark glasses, her hair hidden by a scarf, her face quite pale and resolute, throwing herself into housework; nerved-up, breathless, embarrassed if Lily or Wes should discover her, for instance, vacuuming the living-room rug, or, so strangely, as Lily discovered her one afternoon, on her hands and knees in the kitchen, scrubbing the floor with a hand sponge (when of course Lily had a sponge mop, clearly visible in the kitchen closet)—"I hope you won't mind, Lily, I just thought I'd help you out a little."

Lily was amazed. For Sharon had also scrubbed the sinks and the counters and the stove top and the oven with steel wool; she had sponged the interior of the refrigerator, loaded and unloaded the dishwasher; trimmed Lily's raggedy spider plants hanging above the windowsills. She wore Lily's loose floppy yellow rubber gloves but even so her carefully manicured nails had been cracked and broken. Her skin was sallow, even sickly, but glowing with satisfaction, pride. Lily thought *But my kitchen wasn't dirty!* She said, "Sharon, thank you. But should you be exhausting yourself? I thought you were going to relax today."

"Oh, no, I'm a dancer—I mean, I was. I need to *move.* I need to know I'm *alive.* And I don't want to be a burden on you and Wes, *please.*" This, from Sharon who as a girl had hated all household tasks, had performed them hastily and carelessly, with a look of being tortured; who, as an eighteen-year-old model, living in Manhattan in an apartment with maid service, had boasted to her sister back home in Shaheen that she never made her bed, never troubled to hang a towel evenly, or to pick up a plate after herself. *Heaven!* she'd laughingly described it.

Lily said, not knowing what she meant exactly, "But, Sharon—are you sure?"

Sharon laughed and said, "Sure about what? That I don't want to be a burden on the Merricks, or that I'm alive?"

A vague thought troubled Lily, a ridiculous thought never to be shared with another living being: that Sharon's eagerness to please was a mimicry, almost a parody of—well, Lily herself. Lily Merrick at the community college volunteering for committees which other, more seasoned and better-paid (male) faculty members avoided; Lily Merrick at PTA meetings, faithfully attending for a decade, resolutely smiling, good-natured, dependable; Lily Merrick who could be relied upon when others were too busy with their more important lives. Wes remarked of Sharon, after she'd volunteered to help him with his home office-work (Wes declined, of course: he didn't want anyone in his desk or files), "Your sister really isn't anything like I'd expected, you know? I'm wondering if you hadn't misrepresented her a bit, I don't mean consciously, but—unconsciously." Lily smarted, thinking *But you haven't met "Sherrill" yet! Wait till you meet her.* She said, "Well, but Sharon is older now, Wes. And she wants to make a good impression on you."

When Lily was home, in her workroom. Sharon frequently drifted in; wanting to watch Lily sculpting her pots; hoping she wasn't intruding. (Of course she was, to a degree; for Lily required solitude to do her best work.) Lily assured her sister she was welcome so long as she didn't smoke, though, invariably, after perhaps twenty minutes, out would come the pack of cigarettes from a pocket, and the little silver lighter with its mysterious engraved initials—not "S.D." but "P.B.," Lily had noticed. Lily would say, reluctantly, for she hated to be a scold, "Sharon, can you open a window, at least?" and Sharon would say, startled, as if, staring at Lily's swift-moving hands, she had no idea she'd lit a cigarette and sucked in and exhaled a luxuriant cloud of bluish-toxic smoke, "Oh—what? God, I'm sorry" hurrying to a window to open it, the damned cigarette gripped between her teeth.

No wonder you cough, no wonder you're sick, why are you poisoning yourself?

Like her admiration for Lily's married, maternal life generally, Sharon's admiration for Lily's work was enthusiastic, and seemed to be genuine. As she wandered about the workroom she frequently touched things—pots, vases, bowls. Some of these objects hadn't quite turned out as Lily had wished and a few were frankly misshapen, but Sharon had a kind word for all, as if she distrusted her judgment about such things or, more probably, felt that Lily, always the less secure of the two sisters, required indiscriminate encouragement. "Of course you're attractive, for God's sake,"

Sharon used to say, when they were in high school, "—we're *twins*, don't forget." It was meant to be a playful exaggeration of Sharon's own vanity, but clearly she was serious too. One day in Lily's workroom Sharon lifted Lily's most recent finished work, a heavy, glazed, earthen-hued bowl of about eight inches in diameter and five inches deep, a bowl Lily was hopeful about showing to a local gallery owner; Sharon turned it in her hands, a cigarette awkwardly burning between two fingers, as if it were a puzzle, and Lily at her potter's wheel, but no longer working, stared at her thinking *Don't drop it, please!* Sharon said, "Now, this is really beautiful, Lily. I hope you get a good price for it—one hundred dollars at least." Lily, who'd been hoping so, too, said, "Well. We'll see." Still Sharon turned it in her hands, peering at it, at eye level. Lily felt perspiration break out in tiny pinpoints all over her body. Sharon was saying that Lily's "talent for art" hadn't shown itself when they were girls, had it? and Lily pointed out that in their high school art class she'd done a number of charcoal drawings and watercolors and clay sculptures that their teacher had liked very much; she'd done illustrations for the school newspaper; she'd won a class day prize as "most promising artist"—but, still, Sharon shook her head, mystified. Lily knew that Sharon was recalling how their teacher had asked her to pose for the charcoal life-drawing sessions; how tranquil and aloof she'd seemed, and how beautiful she'd been, seated there on a stool at the front of the room, their teacher Mr. Hanson sketching her, himself. Twenty-five students, girls and boys of widely varying ability, staring at her, trying to capture her face, hair, shoulders in mere charcoal, on thick white paper. Sharon said, "I guess I don't remember. Are you *sure*?"

At last setting the bowl back down, carefully, onto a table. So Lily sighed with relief, thinking herself a bit ridiculous.

Lily offered to teach Sharon how to pot, but Sharon quickly demurred, saying you had to be "centered," didn't you, to be a potter?—"And I'm anything but." Lily said, "But maybe it would help you. It's calming, it's a meditation." Sharon laughed nervously, and prowled about the workroom, murmuring, "I read the Bible, and I pray. *That's* my 'meditation.'" It was a brightly glaring April day; not warm, but blindingly sunny; fearing migraine, Sharon wore smoke-tinted glasses even in the house, yet still flinched away from the windows. Her hair was skinned back behind her ears and in the unsparing light she looked both her age and exotic, with a model's gaunt hauteur. Lily stared thinking how strange, her sister's beauty was returning as if indeed she'd been convalescing in Yewville, absorbing nourishment and strength. Biding her time before moving on.

And where would she go, when she left Lily? Was there really anyone awaiting her in Manhattan?

In a corner of the comfortably cluttered room was a large cork bulletin board to which Lily had tacked all sorts of things—snapshots of Wes, Deedee, and friends; snapshots of pottery she'd given away or sold; a calendar; schedules relating to her teaching; postcards. One of the numerous postcards was of Death Valley; the colorful glossy photo of Death Valley in springtime, brilliant pink cactus flowers, eerily sculpted sand dunes, a sky so brightly blue it looked artificial. Lily saw that Sharon was staring at this postcard; she'd gone very still, the cigarette burning in her fingers. After a moment, aware that Lily was watching her, Sharon said, "So many postcards!—you have a lot of friends, Lily." Lily said, "I just haven't taken any cards down. They go back for years." Sharon said, "This one of Death Valley—it's very striking," and Lily said, frowning, "Which card is that?—I don't remember. It's years old, I think," and Sharon said, "I've been in Death Valley, in winter, that's the only time to drive in the desert. I'd been in Las Vegas with—a friend. A long time ago." Sharon's face was hidden from Lily, whose heart had begun to beat rapidly. Lily said, as if just recalling, "I couldn't read the handwriting on that card very well but I think it's from a cousin of ours—Louise Widener?—she moved to Ohio, I think, when we were in high school." Sharon marveled, "Are you still in contact with Louise?" and Lily said, "Well, apparently!" And laughed.

Sharon laughed, too. And began at once to cough—an ugly hacking sound. She backed away from the bulletin board and turned blindly and, still coughing, collided with the table upon which the glazed earthen-hued bowl had been placed; and before Lily could leap up to steady it, the bowl toppled to the floor—toppled, and shattered into pieces.

For these are the days of vengeance, that all things that are written may be fulfilled.

Lily hadn't needed to reread the Death Valley postcard, that drunken-scrawled red message. She knew it vividly, by heart.

"Oh, my God! Oh, Lily! I'm so *sorry*."

Of course, Sharon was appalled, crestfallen at the accident.

There was no doubt in either sister's mind—it had been an accident.

Sharon pleaded with Lily please forgive me! dropping to her knees to gather up the broken pieces even as, fighting back tears, her heart pounding in fury, Lily assured her it was nothing, not important, only a bowl—"Please! Never mind."

But asking Sharon to go away for a while, to leave her alone to sweep up the broken pieces by herself.

Guiltily Sharon pleaded, "Oh, but Lily—"

Lily could not trust herself to look at her sister. Sharon had removed her tinted glasses in a dramatic gesture to stare at Lily in dismay; she was visibly trembling, as if frightened.

Lily whispered, through gritted teeth, "Sharon, *please*."

* * *

Like Lily, Sharon was revulsed by stories of violent crime and tragedy and so she declined to watch TV news with the Merricks, nor did she apparently watch much TV at all. (There was a small set in her room but she'd mentioned to Lily she had yet to turn it on—"I don't want to contaminate my thoughts if I can help it.") For the first several days of her visit she'd avidly read the *Yewville Journal* in the kitchen, with Lily, particularly seeking out names of old friends and classmates; then, abruptly, in her impetuous way, losing interest.

Which was just as well, as Lily remarked to Wes. For the story of Stanley Reigel might have upset her.

It had been the Tuesday, April 4 issue of the *Journal* that carried the front-page news, complete with photograph and inch-high headline, of Reigel's death. Seeing the dead man's picture, reading of the "alleged suicide," Wes had been shocked; he'd known Stanley Reigel for years though they'd never been friends. And Lily was acquainted with Connie Reigel from PTA.

Naturally there was a good deal of flurried attention paid to the case by the local media, since such news—violent, mysterious death of any kind—was a rarity in Yewville.

Subsequent issues of the *Journal* and news reports on local television mainly repeated the original story, however; the basic facts remained unchanged. The county coroner ruled that Reigel's death was indeed suicide and that he'd been heavily drinking for hours before he died. Mrs. Reigel was unavailable for comment but relatives and friends of the dead man reiterated that he had no reason to take his own life; a friend, Michael Dwyer, an aide of the Yewville mayor, was quoted in the *Journal* saying that Reigel might have been having business troubles but there was nothing crucial that he knew of, and that he "just wasn't the type to commit suicide."

Wes had heard from mutual acquaintances that Stanley Reigel had in fact been having financial problems; drinking problems; and marital problems. He'd been separated from his wife intermittently for the past several years. Until recently, he'd been attending AA meetings but had begun drinking again. He'd been found dead in his car with a torn-out page from a Bible with verses marked in red ink folded inside his shirt—this was what police were calling a "suicide document."

A page torn from a Bible! How strange.

Lily and Wes took care to speak about Reigel's death in lowered voices, not wanting Deedee, in an adjoining room at the time, to overhear. Wes had had disagreements with Reigel over the quality of his work and his billing practices, and hadn't approved of Reigel's private life (Reigel was often seen in the company of women, in local taverns) but he was reluctant to speak ill of the dead. "Suicide is a terrible thing. For the survivors especially."

Hesitantly Lily said, "But everyone claims Stanley wasn't the type—"

Wes said bluntly, "Under the circumstances, everyone is the 'type.'"

It was that remote, eclipsed side of Wes Merrick speaking, that Lily feared. The Vietnam veteran, a battered survivor of alcohol, drugs, wartime horror—Lily dared not imagine.

Seeing the look in Lily's face, Wes immediately softened, taking her hand—poor sweet Lily, so easily upset!—and assuring her with a smile that of course *he* wasn't the type; not so long as he had her and Deedee. Lily kissed him, as if this was a truly placating remark, and pressed her cheek against his shoulder. She supposed that, in any number of Yewville households, in the privacy of their bedrooms, worried women were extracting from their husbands such assurances as she'd indirectly extracted from hers. For of all violence suicide is the most terrifying, as it is the most mysterious.

It occurred to Lily that Sharon probably knew nothing about the death and would not know unless someone told her, since she'd stopped reading the newspaper and never watched TV and, if she went for brief walks, wouldn't be speaking with anyone likely to inform her; Lily would caution Deedee not to bring up the subject. "In her state of nerves, anything can upset her," Lily said. "She'd gone out with Stanley Reigel, I believe. Just for a while, when we were all in high school."

* * *

There came Sharon somber and shyly repentant to the door of Lily's workroom. Asking forgiveness another time; berating herself for her clumsiness. "—I started to cough, got faint-headed—so dizzy I almost blacked out—lost my balance and next thing I knew—"

Lily interrupted the flow of rapid, anxious words with a touch to her sister's wrist. "Sharon, it's all right. It was an accident. I've broken plenty of bowls." Adding, not quite truthfully, "Bowls as nice as that one."

"But it was beautiful, it was special—wasn't it?"

Lily hesitated. "I can make another."

"Will you allow me to pay you for it, at least?"

"What? Of course not!"

"Suppose I'd bought it? And took it away with me? It was worth at least—five hundred dollars."

"Sharon, don't be silly."

"Then I'll know you aren't angry, Lily."

In a gesture Lily couldn't help but see as theatrical, but riveting, there stood Sharon in Lily's workroom drawing out bills from a wallet (sleek alligator hide, expensive, a large flat wallet of the kind a man might carry); as Lily stared in astonishment, Sharon drew out bill after bill—$50, $100 bills.

Lily was shocked. "What on earth are you doing, Sharon? What can you be *thinking*? Stop."

"But I want to repay you, Lily, however I can. Not just for the bowl I was so damned clumsy I broke but for—everything. My visit here. My being so welcome here."

"Sharon, you're our guest. I haven't seen you in years. I won't hear of it."

Stubbornly Sharon said, "But I do owe you money, Lily, don't I? You're just too generous to mention it. I borrowed money five or six years ago when I was down on my luck—in Houston, I think—I don't remember how much but I remember you came through for me." Sharon breathlessly pushed the bills at Lily, who was too surprised to know how to respond. "I have money, Lily—I'm not poor—men have paid what they owed me—some of them, at least. Just the groceries for my visit—won't you let me contribute something?"

"Sharon, you're our guest. This isn't right."

Lily had forgotten the money she'd lent Sharon; for it had been a secret from Wes, and being a secret from Wes had gradually faded out of Lily's consciousness.

"Can I give it to Deedee, then?"

"To—Deedee?"

"Or—isn't that a good idea?"

"I don't think that's a good idea."

Since their initial conversation about Deedee, Lily and Sharon hadn't spoken of Deedee in that way again; it was as if, altogether naturally, Sharon were truly the girl's aunt. This, too, Lily had nearly pushed out of consciousness as she'd been feeling, since Sharon's arrival, a sense of pride, elation, privilege in being a mother, and not a childless woman like her sister.

Sharon said, impatiently, "Then let me give something to you and Wes, for household expenses. Here."

Lily, embarrassed, refused to touch the money. But Sharon left it on Lily's cluttered workbench, a heap of crisp new bills—$2300.

2
The Secret Journey

Always unpredictable! Sharon had decided, she informed Lily, not to call her old friends and classmates, even their Shaheen relatives, just yet.

"All I really treasure of the past, Lily, is you."

She'd been looking through the old scrapbooks their mother had kept. Laughing, and crying; absorbed for hours; then bursting into Lily's workroom with a childish complaint—"The last part is so *messy*! Everything's out of *order*! So much is *missing*!"

As if Lily were curator of "Sherrill's" career.

As the days passed, however, Sharon grew restless; needed to get out-of-doors, to exercise her long lovely dancer's legs. Walking, even in the freezing mist, in the wind, in harsh sunlight, wearing her darkest-tinted glasses and a scarf tied tight around her head.

She'd discovered a frayed old coat of Lily's in the hall closet, a khaki-colored trench coat with a hood. It was a coat Lily would have sworn she'd tossed out years ago. Of course, Sharon could wear it all she wished. As well as Lily's boots.

"Where do you walk, Sharon? I'd love to join you."

Quickly Sharon said, "Oh, no. People would see you, Lily, and recognize you, and next thing you know they'd recognize *me*. And I'm not ready for that yet."

Though, now it was April and the days warmer, the wind likely to be from the south and not the chill Canadian north, Sharon was looking stronger, healthier. Of course she was still thin—far too thin, by Lily's standards—but some of the color had returned to her cheeks and her eyes were less blood-veined and there was an air almost of jauntiness about her, a smile playing at her lips.

Lily was disappointed, but supposed she saw Sharon's point.

"Well. Someday soon, I hope. Before..." Lily's voice trailed off, she might have been about to say *Before you leave us.* Or *Before it's too late.*

Sometimes by day, sometimes by night.

Slipping from the side door of the house, her private door.

Restless and excited and purposeful in her sister's khaki-colored coat worn with the hood. Even on overcast days wearing her dark-tinted glasses. Even, sometimes, at night.

Reasoning *If they are hunting "Starr Bright" they will not recognize me.*

Or, veins thrumming with one of her sparely administered speed capsules, of which she had perhaps thirty left hidden in the lining of her suitcase, *If I am "Starr Bright" I am invisible!*

In the frayed glamorless coat that was Lily Merrick's yet would not have been identified even as Lily Merrick's for it was one of how many hundreds, thousands of such coats in Yewville. In the black rubberized boots, she winced and laughed to see on her feet. So ugly! No style at all! Yet dear Lily her sister, almost-twin-sister, had chosen them of her own free will.

The first of her walks she'd undertaken shyly, when she'd only just arrived at her sister's. Not yet trusting her strength. Her brain dazzled by weeks of flight, body exhausted. When she'd been so jumpy the sound of a ringing telephone at the Merricks' or a knock at the door or simply Wes's footsteps (unconsciously heavy, urgent-sounding on the stairs to the second floor of the house) could throw her into a panic. But quickly she grew more confident, bolder. She slipped from the house and cut through the rear yard, through a gate in the wooden fence and into the alley behind; a narrow unpaved old-fashioned lane where trash cans were neatly kept and where some homeowners had garages, converted stables. This residential neighborhood had been semi-country not many decades ago. At East Avenue, she might cross to follow the alley to the end of the next long block; at Hawley Street she might cross to follow the alley to the end of that long block, where the houses and yards were smaller, though still neatly kept. Occasionally a cat would peer at her from atop a fence, or raise its tail to approach her, mewing questioningly in that way of an animal saying *Do I know you?* and Sharon would pause to pet it if allowed. Occasionally a dog would bark at her, friendly or otherwise, and she'd hurry on by. She might follow the alley to its end in a field below the Yewville Water Refinement Plant and above Route 209, a two-lane state highway of gas stations, fast-food restaurants and video stores and strip malls that had been rapidly thrown up in the 1980's. So far! The ordinary little alley that passed behind 183 Washington Street! Who would ever have guessed she, Sharon, presumed to be unwell, physically and emotionally a cripple, could have hiked so far, so quickly?

And so she might turn back, return home.

Or she might not.

A more circuitous route was also through the alley (for she would not have wished to be seen leaving the Merricks' house by the front, onto Washington Street) in the opposite direction, to Bank Street; across then to All Saints churchyard where, following graveled paths into the interior of the old cemetery, she might have been mistaken for a mourner—hooded head bowed in submission before weather-pocked crosses, wide-winged apocalyptic angels. (One afternoon discovering engraved on a black marble marker of 1859 *He hath led me, and brought me into darkness, but not into the night.)* At the rear of the cemetery was a secret way out through a partly collapsed stone wall, a quick glance behind her to see if anyone was watching *But no: God has rendered me invisible in His mercy* and she stepped through!

And followed then gropingly a rough-trodden path through underbrush and scrub trees that led gradually downhill, running parallel with East Avenue but hidden from view even in leafless late winter. Crossing then the raised meridian of the Buffalo & Chautauqua Railroad track. *And again no one to see! And no locomotive rushing at her.* Entering then breathless a jungle-like area of dumped debris, abandoned stained and torn mattresses and smashed lamps, ravaged furniture as in a vengeful holocaust of domestic bliss; a sight that left her panting with excitement as if such must be a sign sent to her, for her eyes only, from above. Crossing then an edge of the railroad yard where on the night of April 3 a pig would die bleeding to death behind boxcars derelict and lonely-seeming on rusted tracks. And so out to Depot Street, shabby row houses and vacant buildings, and beyond then a short block to State Road, Route 11, where there were no sidewalks, open areas of thawing mud bravely traversed in Lily's sturdy boots. Here too were gas stations, motels, X-rated videos and branch banks, a 7-Eleven store open twenty-four hours a day, the Circle Beer-Liquor-Wine and the Eight-Ball Lounge and Artie's Tavern. Also an upholsterer's shop, a dry cleaner's, Suzi's Chinese Take-Out, Rita's Beauty Salon. In the near but hazy distance, across four lanes of rushing traffic, was a new Ford dealership all gleaming vehicles and flapping flags, and, only just visible from the 7-Eleven, a high-rise Ramada Inn lifting from a landscape gouged out as if giant children had dug and maimed it with picks. Fifteen years ago all this had been open fields, farmland. Wild!

All flesh is grass, and all the goodliness thereof is as the flower of the field.

Where she'd seen, by the sheerest chance, unless of course it was a sign of God, a pickup truck bearing the broad white letters DWYER'S FENCE CITY hurtling by.

In disguise then as a plain, dumpy middle-aged woman with a sallow skin and no makeup, slumped shoulders in a shapeless trench coat, in mud-splattered and comically ugly rubberized boots, she purchased a carton of filter-tip cigarettes in the 7-Eleven; and a can of ice-cold Diet Pepsi, laced with caffeine, which she drank where she stood, thirsty as a dog. If the clerk was busy with other customers she paused to glance quickly through tabloid papers in search of news—"STAR" KILLER STRIKES AGAIN IN SAN DIEGO? —L.A. COP PSYCHIC UNEARTHS "STAR" VICTIMS BURIAL GROUND. She smiled to read of new outrageous and unsolved cases of murder and mutilation and bloody graffiti thousands of miles away. She smiled to think how "Starr Bright's" power would outlive even her who had brought it into being.

On April 4, April 5 and April 7 purchasing copies of the *Yewville Journal* since she no longer read it at home.

"*I* knew that guy. You'd see him around."

The 7-Eleven clerk, a stocky young man with slick quills of hair, a scruffy beard and a harsh asthmatic breath craned his neck to see what his customer was reading so intently between swallows of Diet Pepsi.

"Really?"

"Yeah. Reigel. Plumbing guy. He'd come in here for cigarettes —Camels. And next door." Next door was the beer-liquor-wine store. "He'd hang out at Artie's over there."

"He killed himself, they're saying. You believe that?"

Surprisingly, the clerk shrugged. Sharon regarded him slantwise through her dark-tinted glasses. "Sure. There's lots of people kill themselves, these days." He spoke sadly, as if recalling names, faces. "Somehow it's easier now."

"It's a sin, no matter what."

Sharon left the 7-Eleven as if she'd been obscurely insulted.

Across the way was Artie's—pink neon sign HAPPY HOUR HAPPY HOUR winking in the window. So inviting! She was dying for a drink. But a lone woman in such a place, packed at this time of day with men on their way home from work, truckers stopping for supper, even a plain, dumpy middle-aged woman with a sallow skin and no makeup, might attract undesired attention.

She wasn't prepared for any pig's company. Hadn't her protection with her. Not so soon after S.R.

Sharon entered the Circle Beer-Liquor-Wine to purchase a single half-bottle of wine. Chardonnay like the kind her brother-in-law had served at that first dinner they'd all had together—the Merricks making her feel so *welcome.* So *wanted.*

God, I love them all.

God, thank you for bringing me to safe harbor!

It was a thunderous late afternoon. Fluorescent lights illuminated ten-foot shelves, row upon row of gleaming bottles. All the customers except Sharon in her disguise were male; no one gave her more than a cursory glance; pigs' eyes sliding off her, a woman of no evident sex. *I am invisible, like God!*

Sharon located the wine she wanted. Her nerves were taut as piano wire, mouth watering for a drink. *Certainly I am not an alcoholic* she was explaining to her sister Lily, whose only fault was she pried into Sharon's life, forever *thinking thinking thinking* about Sharon and several times bringing up "Starr Bright"—why, exactly? *Alcoholism is genetic. No one in the Donner family was alcoholic. Momma and Daddy never drank for God's sake! So don't you look at me accusing me!* Lily's only fault was trying to tell Sharon what to do. Issuing commandments like when they'd been girls. When they were girls no longer.

Still, Sharon adored Lily. Lily, and Wes, and Deedee. What a happy family. What a good, decent, generous family. And what Wes and Deedee would never know, could never hurt them. Wild!

Sharon was about to bring the wine to the cashier's counter at the front of the store when she heard a familiar voice, and saw a tall, burly, graying-haired man in a light jacket pushing six-packs of beer along the counter—her brother-in-law Wes.

Wes Merrick, here!

Sharon held back, partly hidden by a display of discount wines. Thinking what a coincidence it was, she'd been thinking of the man and he'd appeared. She'd been thinking of him innocently and he'd appeared causing her heart to race as in the long-ago days when she'd see Mack Dwyer at school and feel an actual stab to the heart loving him so until he'd betrayed her.

Sharon could overhear Wes talking with the cashier whose name he knew, did she hear the name "Reigel"—"poor bastard"—"terrible thing"—couldn't be certain. In the weirdly convex mirror above the cashier's register was Wes Merrick's handsome ruddy face distorted yet to Sharon's eyes instantly recognizable.

Her brother-in-law Wes, in neutral territory.

Never glimpsed the man before outside the house on Washington Street—Lily's house.

Suppose they'd met by accident? The first day Sharon had come to Yewville. In fact she'd had a drink at a place next to the Greyhound station downtown before getting into a taxi. Suppose Wes had dropped in. An accidental meeting. It might have happened—why not?

Big-boned, clumsy-gentle. A fleshy mouth for eager damp kissing. A strong-willed man who would not be pushed beyond a point but until that point he's putty in your hands.

And how big a penis, blood-engorged to its full size, only Lily would know; and, being Lily, wouldn't ever tell.

It was unfair, Lily had always had all the luck. Not many boyfriends in high school but the few she'd had had respected her. Not crazy about her maybe, for how could any guy be crazy about Lily, but nice to her and decent as the guys tended to be to one another if they were friends; but rarely to girls; and never to Sharon. Who was the beautiful one of the Donner sisters, so unfair!

Not that Sharon had been seriously jealous of Lily. She'd had all the guys she wanted. Except they treated her like shit. Mack Dwyer who was the first she'd allowed to…touch her. That way. Mack she'd loved like crazy and would have died for and he'd gotten bored with her and treated her like shit saying *If you don't like it, leave me alone* but she was so weak, desperate in love and he'd passed her on to his buddies and even then…for a while… well, what could she do, she was just a kid. Stan Reigel had been one of them.

Well. *He'd* died. Twenty-two years afterward but that began to even things up, almost.

Yes, Lily had had all the luck without seeming to realize it. And still did.

"Mr. and Mrs. Wesley Merrick"—so most of the mail came, delivered to 183 Washington Street. Lily of the Valley, a married woman! A woman with a daughter! Who'd even come to resemble her, and Wes.

For unto every one that hath shall be given, and he shall have abundance: but from him that hath not shall be taken away even that which he hath.

Never had Sharon understood these harsh words of Jesus Christ, and she did not understand them now.

Wes had his wallet out, was handing the clerk bills. Sharon bit her lower lip smiling like a mischievous child thinking why not step out, declare herself *H'lo Wes! Can I ride back to the house with you, I've been getting some fresh air and exercise* and Wes would blink at her amazed *Jesus, Sharon—is that you?* And laughing she'd snatch off the dark glasses so he could get a good look liking it meeting her like this in neutral territory. And Lily who was "Mrs. Merrick" nowhere near. Wes would say *How about a drink, Sharon, at Artie's before we drive back* and Sharon would say, touching his wrist, *Hell, no, Wes, I have a better idea, let's get a bottle right here and we can park somewhere private and secluded—how'd you like that?*

Sure, he'd like that.

He was a man, any man's a pig in his innermost heart.

Instead, Sharon waited until Wes was safely gone from the store before coming forward.

Never, God help me! Never.

Never to Lily her own sister she adored. Lily of the Valley who was all that remained of the old, lost world of Shaheen.

That could not be part of God's plan for her—could it?

She was sickened thinking of it. Icy-cold in her bowels.

"Starr Bright" and—Wes?

Never had God suggested such. He had guided her across thousands of miles seeking sanctuary here. Where she might heal herself in Lily.

God, You would not be so cruel.

She would read the Bible that night until dawn seeking a sign, if any sign be offered.

3
Bleeding a Pig

There had been no plan, of that she would swear.

One day run to earth by her enemies and confronted with her crimes and made to plead guilty as "Starr Bright" butcherer of pigs and duly sentenced to death by the State of Nevada by lethal injection to which she would acquiesce as a lover the most passionate and voluptuous of her lovers she would so swear. No plan, no thought of vengeance bringing her east to home.

I don't want to kill. Not the most filthy of pigs deserving to die, I am Rose of Sharon, I am not one who kills.

That was so! God help her.

It was a safe harbor with her sister Lily she had wished. Only that. Lily whom she loved solely of the earth's inhabitants. Lily of the Valley who was her almost-twin and wiser than she in many respects. Lily she adored. Whose husband she would never *she would never!* seduce and bring to harm.

Wes who had opened his household to her though guessing (ah, she knew!) her sluttish past. Yet magnanimous, kindly. Like Christ extolling *Judge not, and ye shall not be judged; condemn not, and ye shall not be condemned.*

Though he look upon her with lust in his heart, knowing not it was lust for her he felt, she would never bring the man to harm.

Lily, I promise!

Certain too that there had been no wish of vengeance bringing her home to set "Starr Bright" upon those who had used her cruelly more than twenty years ago. Destroying her innocent girlhood with their grunting pig-lust.

Statutory rape, it had been. For Sharon had been only fifteen years old, her high school lovers had been seventeen and eighteen.

Mark Dwyer, Stan Reigel, Budd Petco—and others, their names faded as their faces. She would have supposed they might still be living in Yewville; but truly had not thought of them, not once, set upon her long pilgrimage home.

How "Starr Bright" eluded the police of several states alerted for a young glamorous beauty who did not exist.

How "Starr Bright" wiped away all fingerprints, all traces of her being in the wake of carnage. In Malibu shrewdly leaving behind twisted in the dead man's fingers three strands of hair taken from beauty salon debris in a Dumpster behind a strip mall. In Malibu as subsequently in Yewville leaving in the wake of carnage a single page torn from the Bible.

Yet not the Bible lying on her bedside table, which she believed Lily had seen. But the second of her Bibles, hidden in the lining of a suitcase. For the one Holy Book was her own, the other to be desecrated in the service of the Lord.

No. She'd had no thought of Dwyer, Reigel...the others. There had been no motive except wishing to be healed, bringing her home.

The ugly memory of the swimming pool at the park and the jeering boys *Hey Blondie Blue-Eyes! Don't be scared!* was fresher. Billy Ray Cobb had paid richly for that memory.

For where one pig could not be touched in vengeance, another might take his place; in butchery, one pig is identical with any other.

For truly she believed *God will not allow us to commit any act that is evil. That is not ordained by His wrath.*

In Yewville, she would consecrate herself to good.

In Yewville, she would emulate her sister Lily.

Truly she'd vowed. In her innermost heart. On her knees scrubbing the kitchen floor. Scouring the sinks, the grease-splattered interior of the oven. Speedy from a pill she'd swallowed one day when all the Merricks were gone and she was blissfully alone in the house kneeling panting in each corner of each downstairs room to swab it clean with wetted paper towels. And along the baseboards, crawling on hands and knees which was the only way to clean the room absolutely. In such a way erasing sin from the world. Never doubt, it can be accomplished!

Carefully rinsing each plate and each fork, spoon, knife in hot water before placing it in the dishwasher. Setting the kitchen cupboards in order—canned goods neatly aligned on the shelves, boxes in regimented rows. In the recreation room, dusting and polishing and taking up Deedee's tossed-down things to fold and set aside. Stacking magazines and papers as they accumulated. Cleaning with Windex the TV screen which she never watched.

So Lily laughed uneasily, saying Sharon, we don't live in a church!

Yet of course they did, not knowing.

Lily laughed saying *Sharon, you never used to be like this when we were girls.*

Sharon smiled in silence. Thinking *How many ways I didn't use to be when we were girls, Lily will never know.*

* * *

And then one day. Fourth day of her visit. Restless, and suddenly bored. Alone in the house. An actual house! Not a condo, and not rented. Lily had been begging her to see a doctor, *let me make an appointment please Sharon, get a blood test at least;* did Lily, did Wes, worry she was infected with AIDS? That was an insult if so. Never would God infect "Starr Bright."

Lily was out, Deedee was at school, Wes was at work.

There came "Sherrill" boldly to a mirror, trying on her wigs and examining herself critically. Only two wigs remained, curly strawberry blond and shoulder-length silky jet-black like Cleopatra. The others, utilized by "Starr Bright," had of course been carefully destroyed: burnt.

No evidence. No trace.

Restless in the strawberry-blond wig. And naked. Boldly prowling the house upstairs and down, in high-heeled shoes. (What if: a delivery man rings the doorbell, peers through a window, sees her, wild! Mistaking her for respectable Mrs. Merrick, wild!) She appeared floating as a ghost—a beautiful, naked ghost—in a mirror of the master bedroom upstairs; Wes would be lying, buck naked, giant erection flopping on his belly, on the bed. She used the adjoining bathroom which Lily had decorated in a fussy-pretty Laura Ashley style. "Sherrill's" naked buttocks on the powder-blue plastic toilet seat. Where Lily sat her bare ass. And Wes.

Used wads of faintly scented blue toilet paper to dry herself, fastidiously wetted from a faucet. Never, in "Sherrill's" romantic experience, do you know that within the next hour some ardent lover isn't going to want to kiss you *there.*

A vicious lover of hers, years ago hallucinating on peyote, Deedee's father possibly, now dead, once screamed at her *Wash yourself! Between the legs! I can smell you across the room!*

Wanting to die of shame, slash her breast, cunt, and wrists and *die.*

She'd tried. And no luck.

In Deedee's room she stood naked in high heels posed in a mirror. Ghost-body. One of the pigs had actually killed her and she was a ghost prowling a house in which she didn't belong. In which others were happy. Unknowing of their good luck, and happy. And that was unjust.

It *was* unjust, God must understand. Lily had all the luck.

Deedee's room was a dull-girl's room you could see. And Deedee for all her sweetness and admiration of Aunt Sharon was a dull girl. Wasn't beautiful, and would never be. Her features were only so-so. And that pudgy chin, nose. Baby-fat. At least fifteen pounds overweight. Why didn't Lily make the girl diet? Sharon had to laugh: Deedee more resembled Lily than she did her real mother, and more resembled Wes than she did the very man, that bastard, who'd fathered her. In a careless squirty-spasm in a Mexican hotel.

At least, Sharon thought she recalled Deedee's father. Though possibly she was mistaken.

In those days she'd been a careless girl. When you looked like her, you could be careless. Traveling with whoever was most crazy for her, could spend the most money.

Downstairs, Sharon prowled through Wes's office. Any secrets here? All men have secrets though possibly not at home. Not where someone might snoop. She drew her fingertips across the edge of Wes's desk, patted the seat of his well-worn swivel chair. He was a hefty, heavy man; with the look of an athlete beginning to go to fat; must weigh two hundred twenty pounds at least. Lily's husband! You'd have thought Lily Donner would have ended up with someone meeker, less manly. Sharon methodically looked through Wes's files and desk drawers where, she knew, Lily would never venture; discovering, in the lower left-hand drawer beneath a folder of tax forms a pack of Camels, two-thirds full. *And Lily was so proud her husband no longer smoked!* Sharon laughed. "Love you, big guy." She took one of the cigarettes to smoke in solitude, later, in her room. The cigarette was harsher than her own brand, lacking a filter-tip. The taste of Wes Merrick on her lips, tongue.

She'd found his name in the telephone directory—*Dwyer, Michael.*

On an impulse dialing the number but got only an answering machine. And a nasally woman's voice on the tape. Mrs. Dwyer? Furious, she laced her fingers over the phone receiver and grunted *You tell that fucker husband of yours to keep his filthy hands to himself fuck him and fuck you!* And slammed down the receiver. Panting.

"Oh my God, did I do *that*?"

Shaking, she'd been so excited. Hadn't known. A tight, keen sensation between the legs she hadn't felt in quite a while.

Wondering at the look on the woman's face. Serves her right, married to *him.*

Big Mack Dwyer. She'd wanted to die for. Almost did.

A sword shall pierce through thine soul.

Better luck with Reigel Plumbing. Just dialed the number, no secretary or answering machine, a man answered on the second ring. And "Starr Bright" begins cooing, as only she knows how. *Hello! is this Stan? Stan Reigel is it?* and he says *yes* and she says

Hey you'll never guess who this is back in town on a visit and he says *who?* and she says *C'mon hon: guess!* and there's a pause like the guy is blown out of his skull and in a lowered voice at last he says *Cindy?* and "Starr Bright" moans like she's hurt and mock-growls *Who the hell's Cindy? Better guess again!* And so it goes, back and forth for a while, "Starr Bright" is funny and easy going never in the slightest reproachful just out for a good time and sounding as if she's had a few drinks already this early in the afternoon finally cooing *Stan, honey, if you have a few minutes one night this week we could meet like old times and you'll remember me, fast.*

That easy. You'd never think so, but "Starr Bright" knows men.

So it had not been intended, had it? It had simply happened.

I accept my fate. I bow my head to Your will.

He'd picked her up at 10:30 P.M. of April 3, on Bank Street near Washington, where she waited sheltered in a darkened doorway of All Saints Church. There was a light drizzly rain, but freezing. And "Starr Bright" in miniskirt, high heels and silky textured black stockings.

And the sexy black lace gloves. A real turn-on, she knew from past experience.

Sliding into Reigel's 1996 Ford Cutlass. Perfumy, breathy. Long silky dancer's legs and tiny velveteen skirt, the curly strawberry-blond wig and makeup so professional it masked completely her washed-out skin. And glossy crimson lips pursed for kissing.

He'd whistled *Jez-us! Do I know* you?

Maybe not yet "Starr Bright" murmured giving the guy a peck-kiss *but you will, Stan-ley.*

His breath smelled already of whiskey. Good sign.

Stan Reigel she hadn't seen in twenty years. Thickset, balding, forty years old with a boy's pug face. (Would she have recognized him? Was this actually *him*? Good question.) He was asking nervously how's about a drink at the Eight-Ball or Artie's and she laughed, laying a black-lace-gloved hand on his wrist *Hell, no,*

Stan, I have a better idea, let's get a bottle and we can park somewhere private and secluded and get reacquainted—how'd you like that?

Stan liked that just fine.

Stan blinked dazed not believing his good luck.

Stan read *Playboy* probably. Back in high school, he'd groaned with the other guys over the luscious centerfold girl-bunnies.

And so in the Buffalo & Chautauqua Railroad yard where twenty-two years ago in the back of Mack Dwyer's camper guys had fucked Sharon Donner. Taking turns, drunk and giggling. She'd been drunk, too, and giggling feebly warding off their hands or trying to. Maybe she'd said no, maybe she hadn't.

When he began to fight her it was too late. She'd slashed as deep and unerring as "Starr Bright's" strength would take her.

Once they'd climbed laughing together into the backseat of the Ford Cutlass and eagerly he'd removed his coat, his shirtsleeves rolled up and trousers loosened. *Now d'you remember me, Stan?*

He'd been too surprised to scream. At first.

D'you remember me—now?

Now?

NOW?

She'd used a straight razor. She'd practiced the technique.

It was all "Starr Bright"—as when the lights came up blinding and she swiveled into her routine.

They would discover a tissue-papery page neatly torn from a Bible, the Book of St. John, 8. In red ink shaky block letters a self-hating drunk like S.R. might laboriously print SORRY FORGIVE ME. S. There was an urgent, loopy circle in red ink around verse 34: *Jesus answered them, Verily, verily, I say unto you. Whosoever committeth sin is the servant of sin.*

Tucked into the blood-soaked shirt against a dead man's heart.

"Alleged suicide"—she'd laugh over that, later.

Thinking how, in the Southwest and California, where "Starr Bright" had achieved renown, local cops wouldn't have come to such a conclusion.

*

At midnight telephoning Reigel's home number from a pay phone outside a gas station. Only two blocks from the darkened car where the pig was only just bleeding to death. But "Starr Bright" was flying high, "Starr Bright" was one to take risks. Wild! Dialing the pig's number and when a woman answered on the first ring she begged in a stricken little-girl voice *C'n I speak to Stan?—oh please!* and the woman asked *Who is this? What's wrong?* and the little-girl voice was wailing *Please please let me speak to Stan, I know he's there* and the woman demanded to know who this was and the little-girl voice interrupted *Mrs. Reigel he doesn't love you he loves me he's told me hundreds of times he can't stand you it's me he loves please tell him I'm sorry, I'm so sorry, I was wrong, I want to see him again, it's O.K. about what happened I forgive him*—and she's crying, sobbing as if her heart's broken, just a drunk hysterical young girl maybe fifteen years old young enough to be the pig-bastard's daughter.

4
The Happy Family

I am not what I appear to be in your eyes.

In all the world only one person knows my heart: my twin.

* * *

"That's quite nice, Janet—only just a little more on this side—yes, perfect."

"Becky, terrific! Didn't I tell you, last week?"

"Now don't be impatient, Anita: it's coming along nicely. It *is*."

Smiling, though she was rather tired this Thursday evening, Lily moved among her students in her pottery class at Yewville Community College. It happened that all her students this semester were women, eleven women ranging in age from twenty-six-year-old Becky, who was eight months pregnant, to seventy-nine-year-old Madeleine, who'd been a widow, as she'd briskly informed them on the first day of class, for a quarter-century; ranging in ability from Laurie, who'd taken art courses at the college for years, moving from instructor to instructor like clockwork, yet reluctant, as she grimly said, to "set out on her own," to poor Anita, who was no more than Lily's age but behaved like a woman of sixty, melancholy, long-faced, always breaking things, whose frequent unconscious sighs of *Oh! my goodness!* made them all laugh good-naturedly.

Lily loved teaching. She surprised herself by liking her students more or less equally, talented or otherwise. A class was like a family, really. If someone was lagging behind, you helped her (or him: sometimes, Lily had male students) catch up; if someone was in a bad mood, you teased her out of it. Lily had been teaching for only five years, and not each semester, but already she'd accumulated in the Yewville area dozens of former students who kept in contact with her; sent her snapshots of their new work, plus pictures of children and grandchildren. *A network of women. Sisters.* Wes was happy that Lily was happy with her teaching, as he often said; but he disapproved that she was willing to teach for such a relatively low salary compared to other, male teachers at the college. It was an old issue between them.

You undervalue yourself Lily. Consistently!

Well, at least I am *consistent.*

Lily didn't want to think about it. Already the spring term was half over, and she hadn't heard from the department head whether she would even be hired for the following fall semester, though contracts had gone out to other part-time teachers weeks ago.

Moving from student to student this evening, overseeing their diligent if frequently erratic work, the fashioning of generic pots, vases, bowls, "decorative objects for the home"—Lily felt strangely disoriented. As if she were in the wrong place, as in a dream. As if she should be elsewhere—but where? (At home?) She recalled her sister's tactless words: *But my teaching will be different from yours. The Pasadena School of Dance is a professional school.* Sharon had been rudely dismissive of Lily's work; but as so often with Sharon, accurate. Lily's students were not professionally committed to the art—or even the craft—of pottery, any more than Lily herself was. Most of them were middle-class housewives looking for something to do. Only one of them had the imagination of an artist—but she was fatally lacking the courage and self-confidence; a part of her wanted only to remain an amateur forever, basking in the praise of community college instructors. These were women, very nice women, who yearned to "express" themselves—to a degree. Like Lily herself. They were fond of Lily as an instructor and as a person and wrote admiring letters to her and about her, to the college administration. A network of women, former students of Lily Merrick. *They are your sisters, too. Can't you draw happiness from them?*

No, Lily thought sadly. I have only one sister.

Lily heard someone laugh. Startled, she woke from her reverie at the front of the room to discover the entire class smiling at her. "Must be contagious," Anita said wryly, "you're sighing, too, Lily!"

* * *

Lily was troubled about Sharon.

Obsessed with Sharon.

Wondering *Is she in danger, really? Who is after her?*

Has she brought my family into danger, too?

It was April 11. The length of the evenings and the intermittent warmth of sun-filled days seemed abrupt, disorienting. Some days —like this very day—were intoxicating with smells of moist earth, newly revived vegetation. In other years Lily couldn't wait for spring, this year she'd told Wes half seriously she wasn't quite ready for it.

Already, Sharon had been staying with the Merricks for two weeks and Lily had yet to suggest to Wes that Sharon was in some sort of danger, or believed she was. She couldn't violate her sister's confidence! And when she brought up the subject to Sharon, Sharon became flurried, agitated—"Oh, Lily! I can't deal with that now. I'm fighting a migraine, *please don't spoil this entire day for me.*"

So that, if Lily pursued the issue, she would be persecuting and harassing her sister, too.

The two-week period had been, for Lily, both dizzyingly fast and mysteriously slow; as if Sharon had been with them, in the downstairs guest room, for six months. The household was wholly altered by her presence. (And her absence: if Sharon was out on one of her lengthy walks, the question was when would she return? Rarely did she tell anyone she was slipping away from the house, still less where she was going, and for how long. Deedee reported having sighted Aunt Sharon in All Saints cemetery "as if she's praying or something"; Wes, driving on Hawley Street, was certain he'd seen her walking briskly along the back alley, in Lily's old trench coat and boots.) She'd changed remarkably since her arrival, when she'd been so exhausted and ill; now, her old vitality was returning, as if with spring, and her old restlessness, that air of stopped-up electric energy that had always made her attractive even to those others (girls, primarily) who'd disliked and feared her. *Can't resist me, don't even try!* she seemed to proclaim, baring her teeth in a beautiful gloating smile.

Now Sharon had more energy, ironically she hadn't nearly as much time for housecleaning of the fanatic, fastidious sort she'd done earlier. Carelessly, she tossed still-damp towels into the laundry chute, and required fresh towels daily; she changed the sheets on her bed several times a week, adding considerably to the volume of laundry Lily had to do. (Which most of the time Sharon was quite content to allow Lily to do, unassisted.) After dinner she drifted away as if oblivious of Lily and Deedee cleaning up in the kitchen, or, more frequently, she lingered over coffee with Wes, smoking a cigarette and querying him about his business, or the economy, or politics; to Lily's annoyance, Wes seemed suddenly to have all the time in the world for idle conversation, where once he'd rushed his meals, needing to return to work, if he'd come home to eat at all. But Sharon remained diligent about helping Lily prepare dinner, for it was a time when the sisters could be together, engaged in a practical, pleasant task. Also, as Sharon nervously joked one day, "You know, Lily, I like to see exactly what I'm *eating*. What it actually *is*. I've been poisoned by bad food too many times."

"Seriously? *Poisoned?*" Lily smiled quizzically.

But Sharon shrugged mysteriously. *For me to know* she'd tease when they were girls *and for you to find out.*

Though Sharon still declined to watch TV in the evening with whoever might be watching in the recreation room ("I just don't want to be upset by something I might see—a news bulletin maybe"), Lily had the idea that she turned on the set in her room occasionally. (Not that Lily was eavesdropping on her sister. But she heard faint voices in the room now and then when she passed by in the hall.) And Sharon was using the telephone, Lily knew. Who are you calling? Lily inquired, thinking Sharon would say the names of girlhood friends or relatives, but Sharon replied vaguely, airily, "Oh, no one special—just business, Lily. My professional life is damned *complicated.*"

Once she said rather sharply, "No, Lily. I am not calling any old boyfriends. I am not calling Mack Dwyer, *trust me*."

Another time, when Lily brought up the subject of their parents' graves in the Shaheen cemetery, asking if Sharon would like to visit them, Sharon said quickly, "I just can't be morbid-minded, Lily. Not at this time. I'm fighting for my life, fighting to *breathe*—can't you sympathize?"

Sharon began to leave the house more frequently on long restless walks, but she never invited Lily to accompany her. She was still fearful, she said, of being recognized.

"We'd look like sisters, side by side. In the open air."

Lily wanted to protest: Sharon so disguised herself in smoke-tinted glasses, her hair in a tight, thick twist entirely hidden by a scarf, her mouth a slash of crimson in a chalky face, how could anyone have identified her as Lily's sister?

She doesn't want me with her, Lily thought, hurt. *She's bored in my company already*.

It happened then that Sharon began to borrow Lily's car. Just for brief drives, she promised. Just to "get some air." Lily must have looked doubtful or reluctant at first, for Sharon said, with sisterly defensiveness, "Look, Lily, I have a valid driver's license from California, for God's sake." Lily murmured, "Yes, of course. I mean—I suppose." "Oh, you! Ridiculous!" Sharon snorted, and marched off to her room to locate the license, which was hidden away somewhere amid her things; Lily trailed after her guiltily assuring her there was no problem, no need to show her the license, of course she could borrow Lily's car.

Sharon said, huffily, "I'll bring it back in exactly the condition it's in, Lily. I *promise.*"

Watching Sharon drive her car, a no-frills economy Toyota, out of the drive and onto Washington Street and away, with a sudden spurt of speed, Lily thought how, as girls, Sharon had learned to drive long before she had. At first, Sharon had stealthily practiced on their father's old Nash, on a nearby country lane; in time, as a precocious twelve- and thirteen-year-old, she'd been instructed by older neighbor boys who were pleased to oblige her. (Lily watched, from the sidelines.) As soon as she turned sixteen, Sharon acquired her driver's license; at that age Lily was only just starting driver's education at the high school, one of the shyer, less confident students. Lily hadn't applied for her license until she was nineteen, by which time her sister was the high-fashion model "Sherrill" long departed from Shaheen and Yewville, living in Manhattan and boasting of driving a Mercedes coupe—"A gift from an admirer."

True to her promise, Sharon didn't cause injury to Lily's car. But she upset Lily, and Wes, by turning up unexpectedly at the high school to whisk Deedee off shopping at the North Yewville Mall, only just opened. There, Aunt Sharon and her adoring niece whom she pointedly called "Deirdre" visited only the most stylish stores, buying clothes, shoes, makeup for the girl. In all, Sharon must have spent $300, and paid in cash. Gap jacket and pants, Benetton sweaters. Polo jeans and bleached shirts, lace-up shoe-boots so clunky and ugly in Lily's eyes she had to know they were teenage high fashion. Deedee was euphoric of course, the happiest Lily had seen her daughter in years, but Lily was discomforted. "But Sharon, can you really afford all these things?" Lily asked, as if the mere outlay of cash were the issue. "What a question!" Sharon retorted, as if her very honor were at stake. "I'm not a housewife on a budget, Lily, dear I'm a career woman with my own income." Wes too was uneasy when Deedee, startlingly made-up in bright lipstick, eye shadow and eyeliner, modeled her "spring outfit" for him—snug pants, loose-fitting shirt and safari jacket; he told Deedee curtly that she looked "like something on MTV"—the channel of all channels Wes hated. In private, he warned Lily that he didn't want the shopping excursion repeated. "She's your sister. *You* make it clear."

One of the items of clothing Sharon bought for Deedee was a Gipsy Horse minidress of crushed purple velvet—size 8. Deedee's size was 12. "Deirdre and I decided she needs some incentive,

Sharon said. Lily asked, "'Incentive' for what?" and Sharon said, "To lose a few pounds, Lily. Obviously." Deedee, who was listening in, said, "Oh, God, more than a few!" sighing and pinching at her waistline, and her young, shapely breasts. "I'm *gross*."

Lily realized her daughter had already begun to cut back on food—no rich desserts, smaller second helpings at meals.

That evening Lily came to speak with Deedee in her room, gently scolding her for saying such things about herself. "Deedee, you're a lovely girl. Don't you know that?"

Deedee, sprawled across her bed, applying Revlon purple-plum fingernail polish to her nails, another gift of Sharon's, snorted and rolled her eyes. "Oh, Mom. You don't need to lie to make me feel good."

"Lie?" Lily was hurt.

Deedee said, sighing, as if it fell upon her shoulders to utter the most obvious, banal insight, one known to everyone except her dense mother, "Well, Mom, you never exactly tell the truth—do you? Not like Aunt Sharon. She just looked at me, and smiled, and said, 'Deirdre, you're fat.' I respect her for that."

I am not what I seem to be in your eyes.

When you learn, will you forgive me!

Lily's pottery class began more or less at 7 P.M. and was supposed to end at 10 P.M.; but her students lingered, of course. As usual, it was past 10:30 P.M. when Lily arrived home.

She was thinking about her sister Sharon, and she was thinking about her daughter Deedee.

I am not what I seem. Forgive me!

Someday, perhaps soon, she would have to tell Deedee that she was adopted; it was all the fashion now, such painful disclosures. But Lily's parents had believed that a child was far better off not knowing; and in Lily's case, when Sharon so adamantly insisted upon giving her baby to Lily, only under the condition that no one outside the family ever know the truth—what choice had Lily?

Fifteen years later, it seemed to her that her promise, made as much to her mother and father as to Sharon, still held; she could not see, morally, that a vow of such a kind would not be binding through life.

Lily wondered: would it be enough to tell Deedee that she was adopted, and not to tell who her mother was? (Lily hadn't any idea who Deedee's father was, and had been given to believe by remarks of Sharon's that Sharon didn't precisely know, either.) Deedee would want to see adoption papers; and there were none.

But to tell Deedee who her mother was, and to incur Sharon's wrath—that was impossible.

Mom, you never exactly tell the truth, do you?

It was a simple, uncanny insight. In her innocence Deedee had spoken more truly than she knew.

Yet how could Lily say *I am not your mother, I am your aunt.*

Your glamorous aunt Sharon—is your mother.

No, it wasn't possible! Even in her imagination Lily couldn't shape such painful words.

She would lose Deedee. She might lose Wes, as well.

Lily felt a wave of dizziness sweep over her, as if the very axis of her life were shifting. She had to grip the steering wheel of her car tight to maintain control.

But even before Sharon had arrived, with the explosive emotional force, in Lily's settled life, of a meteor, Lily had had a premonition of change. Some strange, frightening alteration as of the very molecules of her soul. Those dreams of last autumn and winter. Such disturbing, mysterious dreams. *You're my slave you have to do what I say. And never never tell.*

As if the cruel child Rose of Sharon had reentered Lily's life, commanding her to—what? What course of action, against her will?

And now Sharon was returned to Yewville, and Lily was the imposter.

Yet: was there a secret pleasure in all this?

A secret pleasure in the very fact of living a *secret*? As Deedee would say, with typical adolescent bluntness, a *lie*?

*

Turning into the driveway of her home, Lily felt, as always, her heart leap at the sight of the house; the downstairs windows, warmly lighted. There was a faint, chill fog, oddly stale-smelling, wafting across the lawn. How Lily loved her house, her home! It seemed to her a miracle that she, of all people, lived here.

Lily parked the Toyota in front of the garage, and hurried along the walk to the back door, and glanced into the lighted window of the recreation room to see a sight that stopped her in her tracks: there were Wes and Sharon on the sofa watching TV, each with a can of Wes's favorite beer in hand, and, on the floor between them, Deedee, hugging her knees to her chest. Reflections and shadows from the animated TV screen played across their rapt, smiling faces. Sharon was wearing a soft-looking pale yellow sweater Lily hadn't seen before, and her blond hair was newly shampooed and brushed, fluffed out about her face; she looked ten years younger than her age, startlingly beautiful. And there was Wes, ruddy-faced, grinning at the TV—Wes, who rarely had time to watch even news programs. And Deedee laughing. *A happy American family.*

Lily hurried inside, almost stumbling on the steps.

"I'm home!"

No one answered. No one heard. The TV must have been on too loud.

5
In Lily's Toyota

He hath led me in dark places, as they that be dead of old.

Driving slowly past the brick-Georgian house at 99 Parkway Lane. In the borrowed car driving slowly and thoughtfully and with no bitterness in her heart. For now "Starr Bright" was master, and would exact her vengeance methodically, without haste.

Not here, and not now. Another time. Soon.

Taking note that the house was of a style hardly distinguishable from its neighbors. Large, obviously expensive, a family home, six bedrooms at least. In "prestigious" Country Club Estates, where all the houses were new, large, made of brick: family homes. America is families, American homes are family homes. You observe them from the outside exclusively, at a distance. You would not be welcome inside.

In the directory she'd located him with no difficulty. A business phone and downtown Yewville address, and a home phone and address here at 99 Parkway Drive. *Dwyer, Michael D.* Lily had remarked she didn't think he was called "Mack" any longer but Lily would be mistaken. Mack's old friends, his high school buddies, certainly called him "Mack." An old girlfriend could only call him "Mack."

Remember me, Mack? No?

Sure you do.

Noting that the back lawn of the Dwyer home opened out onto the golf course of the Yewville Country Club, in mid-April puddled with sheets of glittering water amid the emerging green bright as artificial grass. Did Mack play golf now, like his father? The Dwyers' lawn, the lot, must have been two acres at least, larger than the Merricks' in an older residential neighborhood of the city but, being more recently developed, had fewer tall trees. There were open spaces between houses in Country Club Estates. You could not approach such houses from the street, or from the rear, without being exposed. But "Starr Bright" would never seek such entry.

And there appeared a great wonder in heaven; a woman clothed with the sun; and the moon under her feet, and upon her head a crown of twelve stars.

Not here, and not now. Another time. Soon.

It was a windy, chilly April day dazzling with sunshine. Shutting her eyes feeling the sun's warmth on her face she understood that it was the identical sun, the identical warmth, that had nourished her months ago in—had it been Nevada?—silently departing the room of the Paradise Motel splattered with a pig's blood yet "Starr Bright" herself spotless, untouched. *In His sign. In His terrible justice and mercy.* She had driven across the desert embraced by the emerging dawn, she had not been afraid, not even when a Nevada highway patrol car passed her, for His blessing was upon her, she could not be touched by mere humankind.

And so it had been, and so it would be. In all these months not once had she been in danger of being *seen, known, named.*

Driving now, in no haste, for never did "Starr Bright" act in haste, north to Route 209, which partly circled the city. She'd disliked Lily's little economy Toyota at first, it so lacked heft, dignity: but now she was getting the feel of it, the tight handling of the steering wheel, the low ceiling and cramped interior. Of course, "Starr Bright" was accustomed to luxury cars but this would do, in Yewville, for her purposes. And she was wearing, not Lily's old trench coat, but a newer coat of her sister's, a red plaid car coat with wooden buttons—a suburban-mother car coat! She loved it, such American anonymity. *I could be one of them—a mother. A housewife.* On her head was a tight-fitting beige knit cloche hat she'd bought at the mall the other day while Deirdre was trying on clothes and beneath the hat, hardly visible, silky jet-black hair, an attractive fringe of it across her forehead. And the smoky-black sunglasses of course. Without these, the sunlight would have pierced her eyes like ice picks.

Could have been a wife to him. And Deirdre our daughter.

Not fat "Deedee"!—but a lovely slim girl of whom "Starr Bright" could be proud.

But she would not remain in Yewville much longer. Following her date in a few days with Mack Dwyer she would depart.

Yet in no haste. Invisible.

She parked the Toyota at the rear of a strip mall on 209, behind Qwik-Photo. Approaching the rear entrance to the shop but instead quickly and deftly and without being seen searching through a large cardboard trash box out of which she selected a dozen prints apparently discarded for imperfections. And afterward parked elsewhere on 209 she sorted through the prints and tossed away all but one: a poorly focused snapshot of a girl of about twenty with a pretty, sullen mouth, lank dirt-colored hair, and eyes that stared as if about to burst from their sockets. *You don't know me Mrs. Dwyer but I know you. He loves me NOT YOU.*

Though undecided: if she should mail this snapshot and message to Mrs. Dwyer just before her date with Mack, or if she should mail it just after. Either way, the woman, the widow, would receive it the following day.

6
Lovesick

You're fat. But you needn't be. Exert your will! Be beautiful.

Lovesick Deedee drifted downstairs in the waning afternoon light to the rear of the house in the hope that her aunt Sharon's door might be open, or ajar; or her glamorous aunt might be in the kitchen preparing a cup of coffee and seeing Deedee would smile, hands on her hips. *Well, Deirdre! Hel-lo.*

Since the shopping trip, since Aunt Sharon had been the kindest to her that anyone in her lifetime had ever been, there was a special understanding between them. Deedee woke in the night startled and suffused with a sense of anticipation, keen almost as dread. *I love you, Aunt Sharon! Don't ever ever go away. Or—take me with you. Please.*

No luck this afternoon. The door of her aunt's room wasn't open, nor even ajar.

"Aunt Sharon?" Deedee knocked shyly on the door.

Her heart was beating quickly, her palms had broken out in perspiration. She had so much to tell her aunt: that morning she'd weighed herself naked on her scales, and her weight was just under one hundred twenty-eight pounds—a pound and a half down from the previous morning, and almost seven pounds down from her original, disgusting weight of one hundred thirty-five. But, after gym class, after having eaten nothing all day except a cup of watery plain yogurt and a half-apple at noon, she'd weighed herself again and her weight was one hundred twenty-six pounds and five ounces. *Fantastic.*

And she was feeling good. She was feeling great. Not lightheaded or dizzy but like her head was filled with helium-happy thoughts. *Fantastic!*

Aunt Sharon had predicted she could be wearing the purple crushed-velvet dress by May first if she truly wanted to; if her will was "concentrated" sufficiently. And so it would seem to be. *And so it would be.*

Upstairs Deedee's geometry homework awaited and a chapter to read in her history text and as usual there were damn old boring old household chores Mom was expecting her to do. But Deedee drew a deep breath and knocked again on her aunt's door, calling gently, "Aunt Sharon? It's me." Hearing then, or imagining she heard, a voice say *Come in!*

So she pushed open the door, which was unlocked. But the lavender-and-cream room, which smelled of perfume, cigarette smoke and something acrid and ashy, was empty. "Aunt Sharon? It's Deedee—I mean, Deirdre." She listened: running water? The shower in the adjoining bathroom? More than once, after showering, Aunt Sharon had allowed Deedee to perch on the edge of her bed and observe as she applied makeup to her face, or brushed and artfully styled her beautiful, shimmering pale-blond hair. (Aunt Sharon believed in being impeccably groomed for their evening meal.) Best of all, Deedee's aunt might offer to apply makeup to her face, too; or briskly brush and style her dense, springy hair, which was several shades darker than her aunt's. Once, Deedee had said, seeing her aunt and herself side by side in the bureau mirror. "We look alike, sort of, Aunt Sharon—don't we? A little?" The older woman had stared at her for a blank moment, meeting Deedee's hopeful eyes in the mirror, and Deedee was mortified thinking *Oh God! I've insulted her* but her aunt murmured something vague and pleasant that sounded like *That's sweet, Deirdre* and the painful moment passed.

Later, they'd shared one of Aunt Sharon's cigarettes. Deedee had choked a bit, coughed, her eyes spilling tears, and her aunt had laughed at her and tenderly touched the tip of a forefinger to her nose.

Exactly like me, Deirdre, at your age.

Sharing a forbidden cigarette, and sharing other confidences, was part of the special, secret understanding between Deedee and Aunt Sharon. And so when Mom asked, casually, in that way of hers that thinly masked hurt, *What do you and my sister find to talk about so much?* Deedee had shrugged and said, evasively, *Oh, Mom. Nothing.*

The guest bedroom, always so neatly maintained by Lily, and rarely disturbed, had become, by this time, wholly Aunt Sharon's room. Her fascinating things were spread out everywhere: clothing, lingerie, cosmetics, glittering bottles and jars and tubes. The closet was filled with more clothes, at which Deedee had been allowed to look, with her aunt overseeing to explain where she'd purchased what, for what occasion, and who had accompanied her, and what had happened; a sexy black silk Pierre Cardin pants suit, for instance, had been her outfit for an Academy Award ceremony in Hollywood she'd attended two years ago with Jack Nicholson and mutual friends. (Eagerly Deedee inquired what was Jack Nicholson like, and Aunt Sharon said, with a fastidious wrinkling of her nose, as if she both disapproved and was impressed by the man, *Exactly what you'd expect.* Deedee hadn't quite known what this meant but she'd giggled excitedly just the same.) There were wigs in the closet, too, "play-wigs" as Aunt Sharon called them. Rarely worn.

It was surprising that some of Aunt Sharon's jewelry, including the gold chain, lay atop the bureau, in plain view. Deedee went to examine the chain, which looked so beautiful around her aunt's neck, and which she so frequently wore. Then it was in Deedee's hands, lifted to her neck; Deedee noted its weight—of course, it was solid gold. Peering into the mirror, admiring the rich golden glow against her flushed skin, Deedee felt a thrill of—what? Never would she be beautiful like her aunt; but the possession of such a striking piece of jewelry would grant her a mysterious power.

"Deirdre! What are you doing?"

There stood Aunt Sharon behind her, staring. She must have slipped silently into the room; Deedee had not heard any sound, nor seen any movement through the mirror. Her aunt's normally smiling face was taut and waxy-pale and her eyes were narrowed almost to slits. And how harsh her usually welcoming voice.

Deedee began to stammer guiltily, "Oh, gosh! I'm sorry, Aunt Sharon, I—I was just looking at—this." In her fright she'd dropped the gold chain onto the bureau as if it were on fire.

Aunt Sharon was clearly angry, breathing quickly, but she maintained a cool poise. "It isn't good manners, miss, to enter another person's room uninvited. I'd have thought your mother would have taught you that."

Deedee saw that her aunt had just strode in from outdoors; she was carrying a tote bag, her hair was windblown and she'd just removed her dark-tinted glasses. Lily had taken the car for afternoon errands and Aunt Sharon might have supposed herself alone in the house.

Deedee was terribly embarrassed, her face flushed red as if she'd been slapped. "I'm so sorry, Aunt Sharon—I thought I heard you say come in. I knocked, and—I thought you might be in your bathroom. I—guess I don't know what came over me." And that was true enough.

Thank God, Aunt Sharon decided to forgive her. Deedee's repentance was so genuine.

"Well! You're here now. Good to see you, Deirdre."

Aunt Sharon dropped the tote bag onto the bed, went to shut the door to the hall, and, to Deedee's immense relief, managed a smile—almost, a smile of spontaneous welcome. Sitting on the edge of the bed, whose lavender-and-cream floral-print Laura Ashley comforter had the look of having been pulled up hastily over rumpled bedsheets, Deedee's aunt lit a cigarette; exhaled slowly, her eyes shut; recalled Deedee's presence and offered her a "drag"—which, under the circumstances, Deedee could hardly decline. Like an obedient child she took the cigarette from her aunt's just perceptibly trembling fingers (but how glamorous the nails: inch-long, maroon-polished and gleaming like lacquer), inhaled, choked, but managed, thank God, not to cough.

"And how've you been, sweetie? What's new?"

Deedee, grateful as a puppy for having been forgiven for her trespass, feeling the need to be praised and comforted, told her aunt, in some detail, of that day's weight loss—"I couldn't believe it. Aunt Sharon, what the scales said! It was so—*fantastic*."

Aunt Sharon murmured, "Hmmm!" as Deedee elaborated even further; she smoked her cigarette, glancing about the room. With a part of her mind Deedee understood that her aunt was distracted, still rather upset. *Please don't think I came in here deliberately! Please don't think I would spy on you! Steal from you! I love you.* Deedee complained that it was hard to diet when Mom was always vigilant at mealtimes—"It's like she wants me to stay *fat*. Her and Dad both. They say," Deedee continued, with an air of adolescent outrage, "—they like me *just the way I am.* Gross!"

But Aunt Sharon wasn't listening, perhaps; she startled Deedee by rising suddenly from the bed in a lithe, springlike motion at odds with her seemingly indolent manner; as if, like a cat, she'd sighted something moving outside the window—but, standing at the window, peering out, apparently she saw nothing. (The window, like others in the room, overlooked only an expanse of lawn, trees and shrubs and a glimpse of a neighboring house.) "Is something wrong?" Deedee asked, alarmed; but again, her aunt didn't seem to hear.

"Deirdre—has anyone unusual come to this house lately?"

"What? Who? I guess—gosh, no—I don't think so."

"Has anyone been making inquiries about me?"

"N-no, Aunt Sharon. Not that I know of."

"You're sure, Deirdre?"

Deedee nodded solemnly. She was sure.

In fact, it was so disappointing!—the girls who'd been curious about the glamorous blond woman in the taxi who'd called out "Deirdre" only twelve days ago seemed to have forgotten totally about her; and in fact forgotten within a day or two. Deedee had given brief, evasive replies to their questions, to discourage them from asking; yet she hadn't wanted the girls to *forget.*

Several of Deedee's closer friends had remarked upon her new clothes from the mall, and her experiments with makeup; to Deedee's delight, they'd noticed she was losing weight. They told her she was looking "great"—"terrific"—"really cool"—but Deedee hadn't been able to inform them proudly that it was the influence of her aunt—Aunt "Sherrill"—who'd been a top New York fashion model now with a West Coast modern dance troupe.

Her aunt who'd all but promised that she, Deedee, could come visit her in Pasadena this summer—*Stay as long as you like!*

"Your mother hasn't mentioned anyone making inquiries, either? —so far as you know?"

"I guess not."

"'Guess'—or *know*?"

"I think I—*know*."

Aunt Sharon, still visibly trembling as if, in fact, she'd seen something outside the window, decided to believe Deedee. In any case she shrugged, returned to the bed to sit heavily, smoking her cigarette and gazing at Deedee with eyes that were just slightly shadowed, and blood-veined; the lids, glimmering with silver-green eye shadow, were puffy as if she'd had a sleepless night or was running a fever. She wore elegantly fashioned white linen slacks, the cuffs of which were grimy; and a black sequined sweater with a stretched neckline, and canvas sneakers of the kind sold at Kmart, badly worn. Her glossy maroon lipstick was partly eaten away and her face was still tight-looking, pinched. Deedee was thinking *I will die if you stop liking me! If you stop trusting me!* She heard herself say how sad and lonely she felt at school sometimes, how bad she felt, that was why she ate more than she should, hiding away chips and candy in her room to eat while she did homework and sometimes in the middle of the night—"I just get so mad and so *hungry*."

Something in Deedee's whining, desperate tone roused her aunt to attention. The glassy eyes focused on her, suddenly sharp. "What's that? What's going on at school? Why are you unhappy at school?"

Deedee squirmed in embarrassment. It was an exaggeration to claim she was *unhappy*, exactly, only just not—*happy.* "Oh, I don't know, Aunt Sharon," Deedee said, gulping for breath, "—it's just the atmosphere, you know. I mean—the other kids—" *Don't pay enough attention to me.* "—sometimes they're cruel."

"Is a boy giving you trouble, Deirdre? Boys?"

Quickly Deedee shook her head, no. "Not exactly—"

Aunt Sharon said vehemently, "Deirdre, at your age boys are frankly pigs. You would not believe how filthy-minded a teenaged boy can be." She shook her head in disgust and wonderment. "Ordinary, 'normal' boys. The male sex in adolescence."

Deedee said uncertainly, "I—guess I don't know any guys that well. Aunt Sharon. The guys on the newspaper are sort of—quiet, nice—"

"They're different from us. Absolutely. With them, everything is sex, sex, sex. Sex, and hurting. To them, sex *is* hurting. All males are rapists only just looking for the opportunity."

Deedee swallowed hard. Her aunt's voice was so authoritative, so certain. The very word "rapist" was embarrassing: she'd never heard it uttered in such an intimate, face-to-face way by any adult.

"If a man—any man—any male of any age—could rape a woman, and kill her in that way, with his penis, hammering—hammering —hammering until she was dead—if he could do that, Deirdre, and get away with it, his identity unknown—he would. Are you aware of that?"

Deedee shook her head mutely, shocked.

"It's a fact of life, Deirdre. But a fact girls like you, good sweet middle-class girls, are protected from—that's to say, kept in willful ignorance. Until one day you find out—if you're unlucky—and after that, forever, you *know*."

Deedee could think of nothing to say except a muffled "Gosh."

Aunt Sharon continued, passionately, "That's why you must never trust them, Deirdre. Boys and men. You're young, and inexperienced, and your mother shields you—'protects' you. As she was protected, and as I was. We were led to believe that mankind is good—our father preached the gospel of Jesus Christ abiding in the heart of men and women—and we all know that Jesus is *good* —and so we weren't protected, and we came to harm. I mean—might have come to harm." Aunt Sharon paused, breathing quickly. She might have noticed the stunned, glazed expression in her niece's eyes for she relented, softening her tone. "Of course, not all men are wicked. Not all men are pigs. There are good men, too—like your grandfather Donner in fact, and like your—father, Wes Merrick—he's a good man, I'm sure. Though in Vietnam he was a soldier—a young man, male—" Her voice trailed off as if she'd thought better of what she was saying, and began again from another angle. "This diet of yours, Deirdre. Keep on with it! Already you look better, *I* can see the difference. And as you become more attractive to boys, remember: no trust. You control *them*—or stay away from them entirely."

Deedee, squirming, murmured a vague "O.K."

"You must carry yourself through life with dignity and courage, Deirdre! A woman walks on a high wire and men watch hoping for her to fall. Even good men—sometimes. They love helpless, hurt women! They call them 'good' women; they marry them. Independent women—women who walk alone—women like me—they call 'bad.'" Aunt Sharon laughed, as if she'd never heard anything so amusing. Her head fell back, the tendons in her throat were tautly exposed, her laughter was hoarse, a spasm rocking her body. Deedee grinned, and tried to laugh with her, yet somehow could not. She had the idea that her aunt was speaking with genial contempt of her mother.

Mysteriously Aunt Sharon said, "And if a brave woman defends herself—against male lust, cruelty—rape—they may charge her with being a criminal. They may try."

How strangely she was looking at Deedee. How almost—hungrily.

Still talking in this way, Aunt Sharon went into her bathroom; her manner was feverish, euphoric; it reminded Deedee of nothing so much as the way in which some of the girls at school laughed and shrieked together sometimes in the girls' locker room, or, more boldly, in the corridors between classes, when passing boys might overhear. Always, until now, Deedee had yearned to be a part of such strident hilarity.

Aunt Sharon opened and slammed the medicine-cabinet door, ran water into a glass, reappeared in the doorway, swaying, and swallowing down a pill, then another—"To ward off migraine." It occurred to Deedee only now that her aunt had been drinking; she must have gone out, for a drink, on foot. Deedee wished keenly that they might speak of other things but her aunt was squatting now beside the bed, rifling through her canvas suitcase. Deedee caught sight of, surprisingly, newspaper pages there, some of them tabloid size, with red banner headlines; it was one of these she selected, hesitantly at first, then handing it to Deedee with a flourish to read.

"Deirdre! Tell me what you think."

The paper was the *Inquirer,* the issue dated December of the previous year; the headline was SIX "STAR" MURDERS UNSOLVED, FEMALE SERIAL KILLER SOUGHT; the lurid, exclamatory feature, written in primer sentences, focused upon the butchery-murders of six men, whose pictures were shown, along with a graphic photo of a Las Vegas motel room splattered in blood and covered with cryptic star or pentagon symbols and the foot-high words DIE PIG FILTH DIE SATAN. Deedee's aunt was staring at her so avidly, it was hard for her to read; she kept losing her concentration; felt hairs stirring at the nape of her neck. Aunt Sharon was saying excitedly, "A Hollywood friend of mine—a close friend of Jack Nicholson's in fact—plans on doing a movie about this 'Star killer' if he can get financial backing. He'd like 'Sherrill' for the role. What d'you think, sweetie? Cool, eh?"

The other afternoon at the mall, Deedee had exclaimed "cool!" so frequently that her aunt had teased her about it. Now Deedee could only smile wanly. "I saw this on TV—I think. A while back. It's, well—" Deedee swallowed hard. The faces of the murdered men gazed out so *unknowing*; most of them *smiling*. One of them, "Herman LaPointe of Phoenix, Arizona," bore an unsettling resemblance to Wes Merrick, "—kind of sick, I guess. I mean—isn't it?"

There was a moment's pause. Then Aunt Sharon said, with an air of reproach, "It would be a fantastic role for my first film, Deirdre. It would be a true challenge and the results would receive a lot of nationwide attention—I'm sure."

Deedee laughed uneasily. "One of those movies Mom would never see." Then, she remembered: "Or you, either, Aunt Sharon. You hate that kind of 'exploitation'—you said."

"As an actress, I'd take any role that was a challenge," Aunt Sharon said coolly. "And so would you, Deirdre. If you were a professional."

"Like being a photographer, like in wartime—yes, I guess so."

But Deedee didn't sound very convincing. Her aunt took the *Inquirer* feature back from her, to return to the suitcase. Deedee saw that it had been folded, unfolded and again folded many times, with care.

The atmosphere between Deedee and her aunt had shifted. Deedee understood that something was wrong, she'd given the wrong, disappointing answer. Everything had gone wrong since she'd pushed open that door and come inside here uninvited!

Aunt Sharon sighed, and stretched; lit another cigarette, and clicked her little silver lighter shut decisively; cocked her head at Deedee, and said, with a droll smile, "Of course, I should expect nothing. These film deals have a way of dissolving into thin air—'Sherrill' knows." She spoke now with resignation where a minute before she'd been euphoric.

Deedee said, with forced enthusiasm, "You'd be great in movies, Aunt Sharon. Maybe—I could come watch, when it was being made?"

At the bureau, Aunt Sharon impulsively lifted the gold chain that Deedee had been so reckless in admiring, and held it out invitingly to the girl. She said, "I'm sorry I overreacted, Deirdre. My nerves! Your mother knows, my life is complicated in ways hers isn't; it's hard for me to adjust to Yewville, where basically nothing happens."

Deedee had a flash of a man's picture in the *Yewville Journal*—Stanley Reigel. His son Ben was a junior at the high school. But she wasn't going to contradict her aunt.

The older woman beckoned her, smiling; obediently Deedee went to her, and allowed herself to be positioned in front of the mirror, her aunt close behind her, raising the gold chain to her neck. How beautiful it was, glittering like a golden snake's scales! "You like this, Deirdre, do you?—you have excellent taste. So simple, classical—pure gold. A man gave this to me, in Las Vegas, ten years ago on my birthday. He was crazy to marry me—I loved him—almost loved him—but I had to break his heart." She laughed, sadly. "Here. Take it. It's yours now."

Quickly Deedee said, "Oh, no, Aunt Sharon—I can't."

"Why not?"

"Thanks, but I just *can't*."

Not knowing why, Deedee tasted panic; felt desperate to escape; the cold touch of the metal against her throat, her aunt pressing close against her from behind, her aunt's warm, somewhat stale breath that smelled of cigarettes and wine—no, she couldn't bear it.

"Mom says I shouldn't take any more presents from you, Aunt Sharon," Deedee said, for this was true enough. "She says and Dad, too—you're too generous with me."

"Too generous!" Aunt Sharon stared.

"After all those other nice things you bought me—" Deedee said awkwardly, easing away.

"But this is special, Deirdre," Aunt Sharon said, again lifting the gold chain. Her smooth forehead was knit in perplexity. "This has a sentimental value. If—"

There! Deedee heard her mother's car pull up the drive, and a moment later the car door slam. What relief she felt—it was hard to disguise it.

Deedee mumbled, "Mom's home," and headed for the door,

and her aunt grabbed her arm, gripping her almost painfully, and said, "Deirdre, you won't tell your parents about"—she hesitated, glancing toward the suitcase on the floor—"my movie plans, will you? That's our secret."

"I sure won't, Aunt Sharon!"

Seeming to know it would be the last of their secrets.

7
The Good Sister

It was not so easy to speak with Mr. Dwyer of the mayor's office as it had been to speak with Mr. Reigel of Reigel Plumbing but she had no doubt she would speak with the man soon, and so proceeded with her plan. En route to Rita's Beauty Salon to acquire strands of a stranger's hair she had a sudden attack of dizziness, had to pull Lily's Toyota to the side of the road. Oh God if a cop came by! asked to see her license!—a California license expired some time ago and maybe not exactly hers but one she'd borrowed from a friend or had been given. And she had no weapon to protect herself, none on her person. But recovered then after a few minutes for God had after all entered into a pact with her, a covenant. Completed the errand as planned, the hair in a plastic bag, so thirsty and her head pounding she stopped for a drink, just one, at the Ramada Inn at this hour of midafternoon when no man would approach her, and no man did. And on Bank Street at All Saints Church she marveled to see in the churchyard amid the grave markers "Starr Bright" resplendent in white her head lifted in pride and her blond hair afire and upon it a crown of twelve stars: how they blazed, blinded!

For my kingdom is not of this world.

Yet another day also in the Merricks' neighborhood ascending the long Hawley Street hill sighting a sturdy ugly-gray car approaching. Male driver in dark-tinted glasses and male companion glancing at her through the windshield of the Toyota impassive and unreadable. And she was alert but not panicked driving on impassive herself.

Plainclothes detectives. Unmarked police car.

Trying to recall if she'd seen this car before. Cruising Washington

Street, slowing in front of the Merricks' house. The unmarked cars were heavily reinforced, bulletproof. You could tell, if you knew what to look for. And the pig-look, unmistakable.

Yes but coming down from a drug high you're gonna be paranoid so factor that in always.

A guy had instructed her and she knew the wisdom of such advice. Yet: wondering if really she'd killed that one in Vegas, the one who'd been a cop, completely killed him draining the last drop of pig-blood from his veins. Deputy sheriff not of Nevada but some midwestern state. His name forgotten. *Had to break his heart!* For it was possible he'd lived.

Possible they'd all entered into a conspiracy. Police of how many states, counties. In which case the news released by Yewville police of Stanley Reigel's "suicide" was in fact a conspiracy to deceive.

Possibly they knew "Starr Bright" was here in Yewville, New York.

Known but not acknowledged.

So she drove, calmly, at twenty-five miles an hour which was the speed limit, past Washington Street. Would not return to the house for another hour minimum.

Though knowing of course they'd have the Toyota's license number in their computer. Obviously they knew to whom it belonged and the place of residence. And maybe—it made her crazy to think of this so really she shouldn't—like bringing a *lighted* match too close to her own hair—or singeing her eyelashes as once for some funky reason she'd done—just maybe they'd been questioning Lily. *Who is your sister? How long has she been residing with you?* But Lily of the Valley would never betray Rose of Sharon—never. *My slave. I command you. We can't ever be lonely like other people. I love you.* So she understood that Lily would never tell; not under torture, would Lily tell; but the man, the husband, his name temporarily blurred, the man who was Lily's husband—*he could not be trusted.*

Wes was his name: "Wes Merrick."

Casting his lustful gaze upon her, slow stunned smile of a guy feeling blood seeping into his cock, dreamy-eyed watching TV and their arms accidentally brushing together, the hairs stirring on Sharon's arm and she'd been ready for him, giving off every signal she was ready for him, sharing a final can of beer joking and kidding around and the girl, the sad plain fat girl, what was her name, Lily's daughter, poor Lily's responsibility—the girl grinning up at them like she's giving them permission to fuck right there on the sofa.

Why not? He was hot for it, and so was she.

Except: Lily'd come home.

Poor sweet stupid Lily of the Valley blundering in unwanted. Knowing what was what but, like Lily, pretending she did not.

Pretending not to know *If you died Lily your precious husband would want to marry me, just maybe I'd take the big guy up on it.*

But then inside the house suddenly she had one of her dizzy spells and began shaking and her teeth chattering like she was freezing and fuck it Lily was there, Lily was a witness and grabbed her to keep her from fainting crying *Oh Sharon!* so she felt her sister's concern for her, and her love. And Lily was the stronger insisting Sharon must see a doctor next morning, no more procrastinating. So in that moment of weakness she gave in.

For "Starr Bright" was brave as an upright flame fearing no earthly hurt. While "Sharon Donner" was a coward deserving the worst that might befall her.

Next morning of course she was fine. Changed her mind and called the doctor's office to cancel. And when Lily came to her room to get her she informed Lily she was fully recovered, she was fine and didn't need any doctor poking her with needles. So she wasn't going.

And Lily was almost speechless. Stammering, "Sharon, you p-promised! Damn you, you promised!" And Sharon laughed seeing her good-girl sister mad as hell, spots of color coming up in her cheeks. And Lily demanded, "Just what are you laughing at, Sharon?" and Sharon winked at her saying, "You."

Which really set Lily off.

Lily said, sputtering, "You promised! You promised, Sharon!"—as if they were girls of ten. "A blood test, at least, Sharon—obviously you're not well."

And Sharon said carelessly, stretching and yawning, so what if she was a little anemic, she was taking iron tablets. She didn't have leukemia for God's sake. She didn't have AIDS.

The look in Lily's face.

"Nerves. That's all."

Extending her slender beringed hands, beautifully manicured nails. Yes her hands trembled a little but so what? It was morning.

Lily said self-righteously, "Sharon, you don't *eat.* You push food around on your plate—you drink and you smoke your filthy cigarettes but you don't *eat.* You're too *thin.*" And Sharon retorted, "Yes? There's plenty of people—some of them right in this house—who think I look just fine at this weight. Ask them." And Lily said, the words spilling from her pent-up and painful, "And you're a bad influence on Deedee, she's starving herself, I'm afraid she'll become anorexic. Like *you.*" So they quarreled. First time in how many years. Sharon would've predicted she'd be cool, bemused, as "Starr Bright" looking calmly on, but there she was going hot in the face like her sister, heart pounding as if she'd snorted a line of coke. Cursing and pacing the room kicking at the bed, at a pillow on the floor, at her suitcase saying it was Lily who made her nervous, made her hands shake for Christ's sake always watching her! spying on her! just like when they were girls and Lily pretended to worry Sharon might get "in trouble" when she was simply jealous, pure and simple. Because she hadn't any boyfriends of her own. Saying, "I refuse to be dissected for your pity, 'Lily of the Valley.' You have no command over me now. I'm not your fucking slave. Nor am I a junkie—so fuck *that.*" And Lily stared at her dazed. As if not knowing what *junkie* meant. As if never hearing the word *fuck* hurtled at her like a glob of spit.

"And if you hadn't sold the family farm, I'd have a place to live," Sharon said furiously. "I'd have a chance to get well. I wouldn't be dependent upon your precious *charity.* You and your precious *Wes.*"

Lily protested, "Sharon, that isn't fair. It wasn't my decision to sell the farm, it had to be sold. I've tried to explain—"

"*You* want to believe I'm sick because it makes you so fucking *normal.* All our lives it's been *good* Lily and *bad* Sharon—right? You get off on that, right?"

Lily stepped back, as if Sharon's wild-waving hands frightened her. "Sharon, please. You can't believe that."

"If you want me to leave, Lily, just tell me. If you can't stand the sight of me!" Sharon's voice rose to a thin childlike soprano, blindly she would have rushed from the room but Lily caught her in her arms. The sisters struggled together, panting. "Stop, stop, just stop, Sharon just stop," Lily murmured, as she'd done when they were girls, and Sharon said, blinking back tears, "You don't really want me here, admit it, you don't have room for me in your life," and Lily murmured, "Sharon, stop, you know better," and Sharon said bitterly, "I don't know better! I don't belong here with you and your family I'm—trash," and Lily murmured as before to comfort her, to quiet her, and Sharon said, "I've fucked men for money, Lily. I've done terrible things. God has used me but God abhors me. God will cast me from Him. Lily, you don't know!" and Lily murmured, "Yes. I know you, I know your heart," and Sharon said, "You don't. You don't know me or my heart, you don't want to know," and Lily said, "Sharon, of course I know, you're my sister, I love you," and Sharon said, pushing at her, not hard enough to break Lily's embrace but pushing, nudging, as a fretting child might push against her mother's confining protecting arms, "How can you love me if you don't know me! You don't know my heart, Lily—you don't know 'Starr Bright,'" and Lily said, "I don't know 'Starr Bright' but I know you," and Sharon was crying, Sharon was crying in anguished furious sobs, and Lily said, maddening Lily as if no opposition in Sharon could dissuade her nor even discourage her from her path of righteousness, "Now let me drive you to Dr. Krauss, all right?" and Sharon lost control finally and screamed, "No, it is not all right!" and pushed Lily away, halfway across the room.

Thinking *Will I have to kill you, too, to be free of you?*

The sisters stared at each other. Their faces were damp with perspiration and their eyes dilated. In the kitchen Lily had turned on a radio, the local Yewville station was playing morning music, and now came a brisk cheery advertisement for a local car dealer, voices self-assured and optimistic and maddening too to "Starr Bright" who of all things despised hypocrisy. Saying, as if it were a curse, to Lily, " 'So then because thou art lukewarm, and neither hot nor cold, I will spew thee out of my mouth.' " Yet even now Lily stood her ground; did not retreat; fueled by the terrible strength of righteousness; the stubbornness of blind, ignorant love; saying gently, as if "Starr Bright" of all persons could be thus manipulated, "Sharon, I know you've been hurt. I know men have hurt you. I want to help you, you've come to me so that I can help you, only please let me!" And Sharon turned away cursing, and squatted beside the canvas suitcase, and removed from its lining a leather belt, a man's belt with a brass buckle, laughing, "Yes! I've been hurt! Hurt like hell, by men, yes!" rising to the rhythm of her harsh, panted words, draping the belt loosely about her hips, a belt twice the size of Sharon's slender waist; as Lily stared uncomprehending, poor Lily blinded by love as by an actual scrim before her eyes, and Sharon began to move her hips suggestively, lewdly, "Starr Bright" easing into her dance, grinning at her sister who continued to stare at her incredulously; her sister Lily who was the audience that "Starr Bright" had long sought, performing merely to men.

Lily said, "Who—was it? How did he hurt you?"

Sharon stroked the leather belt, looped her fingers sensuously about the oversized brass buckle slipping to her navel, laughed, mock-moaned and moved her hips and pelvis laughing at her sister's expression as she chanted to the beat, beat, beat of the dance—"Name's gone. *He's* gone. All of them gone. Ashes to ashes!"

8
Making a Date

She had faith, she'd never doubted. And at last connecting over the phone. In a soft sibilant voice of no reproach, still less accusation, saying, "Sure you remember me, Mack—'S.'" And the man who'd been Mack Dwyer repeated, quizzically, "'S'?" and she said, "—who was so crazy for you, she's never forgotten you," and Mack Dwyer said, "—What? *Who?*" and she said, "It *was* a long time ago…Mack," and Mack Dwyer said, uneasily, trying to laugh, "Nobody much calls me 'Mack' now," and she said, gently, still with no air of reproach or insinuation, "In my thoughts you're always 'Mack,' that's how I remember you," and Dwyer said, "Look, who is this, please?' and she said, "We were crazy for each other, couldn't keep our hands off each other. You were my first, Mack. Which is why I will never forget." And the man who'd been Mack Dwyer laughed again, uneasily, yet with an undercurrent of excitement, as if this were a game and he was late to catch on, saying, "Your voice does sound familiar…" and she said, "*Your* voice sounds familiar, Mack. Like yesterday," and Dwyer said, "But why wouldn't you give my secretary your name? Why is it a secret?" and she said, "Yes, I'd like to keep it a secret. If we get together. Maybe you would, too," and Dwyer said, his voice lowered, quickened, "But—who are you?" and she said, "Your little blond girl 'S'—from the country. The minister's daughter. Remember?" and there was a blank stunned moment, she believed she could hear an intake of breath and see the impact in the man's eyes, that astonished look of Mack's when, abruptly, more abruptly than he wished, he came, sometimes on her belly, or her thighs, or even her panties so she'd have to wash them out in secret not wanting her mother or Lily to know; and he murmured, "My God, is it—Sharon? Sharon—"

fumbling her last name, and she didn't help him out but said, "Might be it is," and Dwyer said, "But where are you?" and she said, "Right here in Yewville, Mack," and he said, "You went away? —you were a model in New York?—a famous model, people said. And now—?" and she said, for this was the truth. "Now I'm back in Yewville visiting, just a few days; seeing just a few, very special people; people I'd once—loved."

9
The Kiss

And in those days shall men seek death, and shall not find it; and shall desire to die, and death shall flee from them.

How could she sleep! Exhausted and her eyeballs seared in their sockets as if she'd been staring into the sun but how could she sleep! Nor even force herself to undress and lie down. Not in that bed, in those smothering bedclothes. Not in that room where the ceiling and walls pressed inward. Ridiculous floral curtains, floral-wallpapered walls—she wanted to scream with laughter. *As if you know me! As if any of you could know "Starr Bright."*

Every pig she'd bled to death, he'd been Mack Dwyer. Strange she had never comprehended that until now.

They'd made a date. The following evening. A weekday—a Thursday. Yes certainly he'd keep it secret. The date, and her name.

Except: how could she sleep between now and then?

Except: she couldn't risk one of her sleeping tablets, painkillers—couldn't risk drinking. For one drink is never enough.

Except: she was feeling sexy, hungry for—who?

Mack Dwyer. The first. *Which is why I will never forget.*

Impatiently she stripped. Let her clothes fall underfoot. The room was airless, smelling of her own heated body. Yet she was too shrewd to open a window even a crack—didn't trust what might be out there.

What right had Lily to embrace her. Making such a claim.

Love. I love you. My sister.

How she'd resented it. Lily was the stronger, always the stronger. No one had understood except Sharon. Not even Lily herself.

"Only 'Starr Bright' can match you, Lily."

That terrible strength of righteousness.

*

It was midnight, and then it was 1 A.M. and she could not sleep, and would not. Trying to calculate how many hours intervened between this moment of yearning and paralysis and 6 P.M. of the following day, when they would meet. In a motel room, off Route 209. Which Mack Dwyer would arrange. In secret.

There was bathwater running, pouring from the faucets. Almost-scalding water. Steam rising to calm her frantic thoughts. Except as she lay in the water naked, pale, forced to see how her breasts had shrunken and were almost flaccid, floating limply in the water, her mind leapt ahead to the motel room, and what would happen there.

Or had it happened already? Many times.

This will be the last. The last pig bled. God will release me—won't He?

She dared not inquire of God Himself. As she dared not gaze into the fiery sun for fear of going blind.

How quickly, she wondered, could she master him? She would not be using a straight razor this time, to be left with the dead man, as she'd done with Stanley Reigel and one or two others. She would use her own knife, for there was no possibility of "suicide"—this time. All that was required was leverage, and surprise; the man would be taken by surprise; naked, probably; and "Starr Bright" was practiced with naked men; once embarked upon a course of action, she would not be dissuaded; the first splash of bright arterial blood—

"Now you remember me?—yes?"

The nape of her neck against the cool porcelain rim of the tub. By degrees she was becoming calmer. Maybe she would have a drink—to help her sleep. But only one. To help her sleep. For she must not fail, and would not fail. For if she failed, "Starr Bright" would be apprehended; "Starr Bright" would be run to earth; "Starr Bright" would be exposed to staring, avid eyes; "Starr Bright" would bring shame and confusion upon Lily and her family. But she would not fail, for God would guide her hand. *For I have the keys of hell and of death.*

It was 1:35 A.M. She'd drifted into a dream, and was wakened suddenly. Hearing the door of her room being opened—so slowly! (Though knowing the door could not be opened, she'd locked it from inside.) And at once she was roused, vigilant. Sitting up in the now-tepid water, listening closely. It might be Lily—returned to seek her sister's forgiveness. It might be—Lily's husband?—whose name she'd forgotten in her distraction.

Yes, Wes. Maybe—Wes. She'd forgotten entirely about Wes!

* * *

By this time it was almost 2 A.M. But she dressed hurriedly, excitedly. Seeming to know he would be there, waiting.

In his office in the converted sunporch. Lily was always worrying her husband slept so poorly. Distracted by finances, Lily said. Didn't trust his bookkeeper, Lily said. People owe him money, Lily said. He tries to shield us.

Sharon bit her lower lip to keep from laughing, a good strong belly laugh. Knowing why Wes Merrick lingered in his office late at night; why he took his time going upstairs to bed with Lily.

"You know, too, Lily. Only you won't admit it."

It was an eye-catching, sexy outfit, but also easy to pull on over her head, a clinging red-jersey sheath she'd acquired in Palm Springs. The hem skimmed her knees, showing her long dancer's legs. No underwear. No stockings. Damp tendrils of hair clung to her forehead but she brushed, brushed, brushed her hair until much of it was dry, and fluffed out about her face. That schoolgirl look! Cheerleader look! "Guys love it." Hadn't time to apply makeup carefully for that would require forty minutes and he might give up waiting for her and go upstairs to bed, so quickly she rubbed foundation on her face, which was still, she believed, peering at herself in the steamy bathroom minor, a girl's unlined face if not seen in too revealing a light; and subtle spots of rouge on her cheeks; and glossy maroon lipstick making of her mouth a lovely open wound to be kissed, sucked, bitten, possessed.

She forced her bare feet into high-heeled shoes. Grunting with the effort. In a zippered compartment of the canvas suitcase was a blue-sequined purse and inside the purse "Starr Bright's" knife and these items she would take with her. For safekeeping or for protection—she could not have said, for she wasn't thinking clearly.

Long ago "Starr Bright"—the TV hostess, blond, busty, makeup like a thick crust over her tired-looking face—had told thirteen-year-old Sharon Donner and the others backstage *Once you get out there in the lights, kids—just trust your instinct. Don't think!*

It was the very best advice. It was the heart of show business.

She made her way through the darkened downstairs rooms and saw, unsurprised, that the light was on in Wes's office, and the door partly ajar. He'd been waiting for her!—but neither of them would acknowledge it, she supposed.

There was Wes oblivious of her, at his desk. Frowning at a computer screen, exhaling a cloud of bluish smoke. His thinning hair was disheveled as if he'd been running his hands through it and there were sharp creases in his cheeks like razor cuts. He wore those prissy reading glasses. His shirt was rumpled, opened at the throat, the sleeves carelessly rolled up to show thick, wiry hairs on his forearms. At his elbow, amid papers, was a tumbler of—what? Looked like whiskey or bourbon.

"Wes! Surprise."

The way he turned startled at her low, throaty voice, blinking foolishly, you'd have thought he hadn't been expecting her after all or possibly he'd given up hoping.

"Jesus. Sharon."

Stepping forward into the light she was enjoying the slow shock of the man's eyes taking her in, the clinging jersey dress, nipples poking against the fabric like buttons, and her long bare dancer's legs and the warm glow of her skin and the sexy high-heeled shoes that made her stumble just a little, laughing. "I didn't expect you'd be up, Wes," she said, reaching over to take his burning cigarette from an ashtray and lift it to her lips, which felt greedy, "—this hour of the night." He was staring at her, a faint smile stretching his mouth as if for a moment he couldn't think who she was, what good luck this was for him. But she felt a stab of disappointment—her brother-in-law was so *middle-aged.*

Waiting for you to come to me but you're too God-damned good for that so I'm coming to you.

He was saying, frowning, "Sharon, why are you dressed like that? You're not going out, are you?" Staring at her the way he'd stared at Deedee in her new clothes, perplexed and annoyed as by a riddle. And she said, "Hell, I couldn't sleep, my nerves!"—holding out a hand for him to see, trembling slightly, the cigarette in her fingers. "It's too damned quiet around here. Washington Street." She laughed, and Wes laughed, nervously. Not knowing why.

If he'd been waiting for her why was he wearing those ridiculous reading glasses. Bifocal lenses. That old-man look that was an insult to the glamor of "Starr Bright." Like some pig not taking time to wash, smelling of underarms and crotch. Cock tasting of piss. *Pigs.*

She was furious suddenly. But continued to smile the dazzling "Starr Bright" smile. Hugging her sequined purse against her breasts.

She told him yes she intended to go out, for a walk, a walk and a drink. She couldn't sleep she said it was so quiet her thoughts were like voices. And he said it was too late to go out, almost 2 A.M. and places would be closed. And she said she'd take a walk, then; would he like to join her? And he said, "You're not serious, huh?" And she said, flirting, but annoyed, "I'm not? Sure I am. Try me." And he said, "Lily told me you canceled the doctor's appointment, why?" And she said, angry suddenly, "Why? Whose business is it, *why*?"

Thought you weren't a fucking hypocrite, big guy.

Thought you weren't like all the rest.

They were talking, and they were almost arguing. So Wes went to shut the door. In case, far away upstairs, someone should be wakened, and hear voices.

He said, "I don't think you should be walking anywhere, Sharon, at this time of night." Looking at her, the spectacle of her, as if to say *And looking like you do.* And she laughed taking another drag on his cigarette. Saying, "What sexist crap. It's an insult. A man can walk at night anywhere he fucking wants, a woman's a prisoner? Fuck that." And again the man blinked at her dumbly as if he'd never heard such words before on a woman's lips.

She was hot in the face, incensed. She remembered the secret knife in her purse and dared him to put his hands on her. Telling "Starr Bright" what to do!

He was playing daddy saying how he and Lily were "both concerned" about her and that pissed her off, too, a husband-and-wife team shaking their heads over her. So she laughed, and shrugged, saying Christ she could take care of herself, she'd been taking care of herself since the age of eighteen when her God-fearing Christian family had washed their hands of her—"Cast me off as a polluted sinner. A *fashion model.*" But she didn't hold any grudge, you could see. She'd made her way alone. Modeling, and dancing; and dance instructor; and she'd be beginning her film career soon. So she didn't need anyone's help thank you nor anyone's charity.

It was like a TV speech. A close-up. She felt great, she felt in supreme control. "You know me, Wes—'Sherrill.' No last name. I've learned to take care of myself because there's never been anyone else."

Wes shook his head, laughed, leaning a haunch on the edge of his desk, a big-boned man going soft in the gut, but there was a certain bruised tenderness in his face, and the silvery-glinting stubble on his chin, and the graying wiry hairs on his forearms and at his throat—she felt a stab of desire, a scalding little needle at the pit of her belly. Every thought of Mack Dwyer had by this time evaporated.

Taking that hot soaking bath had been a great idea. She was softened up, moistened. This guy was sharp enough to get the signals, he'd had a lot of experience she was sure.

But surprising her saying, "Frankly, Sharon, I don't know the first thing about you. When I think I do, I learn I'm wrong." He paused, eyeing her belligerently. "Because most of what you've been telling us is bullshit, isn't it?"

Sharon stared at him not certain she'd heard correctly.

"What? Why—do you say that?"

"Isn't it?"

"I—I don't understand. What do you mean?"

It was like he'd slapped her in the face. Definitely she felt a sexual attraction for him, for his very belligerence; a sweet not-so-gentle throb in the groin. Laying a hand on his bristly forearm as if to both placate him and entice him. "Wes, I'm *hurt.* I'm—*insulted.* I just don't—"

"This teaching job of yours? At the 'Pasadena School of Dance'?"

"Yes, I—" She shook her head, confused. "No, wait. I've maybe decided not—"

"Well, there isn't any 'Pasadena School of Dance.' I checked."

Quickly she improvised, "Starr Bright" glib and inspired and daring him not to believe, "Oh, right! I guess it goes by another name—the school. And it isn't in Pasadena actually but in another town, for prestige purposes they align themselves with Pasadena—you know." She paused, breathing quickly. The fucker was letting her stammer and falter until her words gave out.

Wes said, "And this 'dance troupe' you've been traveling with—"

"I told you, we're disbanded. It's *over.*"

"And just why exactly did you come here, to visit Lily?"

"Do I need a reason? Lily is my sister—"

"Lily's been your sister for a long time. Why're you here *now*?"

Because I have nowhere else to go. Because I am run to earth.

She was furious! frightened! backed into a corner like a fucking rat! "Starr Bright" clutching the sequined purse and feeling the nudge, the impulse, how she might turn as if to leave and feign an attack of dizziness and when the man laid his hands on her slide the razor-sharp blade into his gut easy as you'd pierce a melon. A man, any man, daring to lay his hot beefy hands on "Starr Bright"!

But "Starr Bright" guided her in another direction. How much more strategic instead to go weak, or weak-seeming in the man's accusing eyes. Many times "Starr Bright" had humbled herself even bleeding in the mouth opening herself to a man's mercy. And this man she seemed to know having pillaged, raped, killed helpless women and girls in Vietnam in the guise of American soldiery and would surely do so still to this very day if granted immunity, and anonymity. So she was gripping his arm tighter and leaning on him for support and saying, her voice breaking, "Wes, if I didn't always tell you one hundred percent of the truth it's because I—I'm waiting to tell you. Just you. When we get to be better friends, when I can trust you."

Guardedly he asked, "Yes? And when's that?"

"I've been through some hard times—Lily knows. She's been so wonderful—generous—taking me in like this. And never a word of reproach."

"Right. I'd say, yes, she has."

She ignored his sarcasm. If you ignored a guy's sarcasm he sometimes dropped it.

Eyeing the amber liquid in that glass on his desk. Jesus, she needed a drink!

"When—can we get to be better friends? Oh, Wes, it's tonight I've got to live through somehow. I'm not looking beyond tonight."

Covering her face with the fingers of one hand. Her skin burning, feverish. It came over her like a wave of nausea, she wasn't wearing eyeliner or mascara, no dark glasses, her venous eyes and the soft crepey skin beneath them exposed, and he was standing close, she could feel his warm breath, this man peering into her very soul or seeming-so except "Starr Bright's" soul was one of those freaky distorting mirrors you looked into and saw your own mangled face.

He must've relented. There was the glass in his hand raised to her lips as you'd raise a glass to a small child's lips urging her to drink and she drank—bourbon. Sighing with relief.

"Oh God, Wes—thanks. I needed that."

She'd closed her fingers over his. Gazing up at him with hurt-swimming eyes.

He said, "It goes down smoothest after midnight, I've found."

"Yes."

She was liking this now. She was loving this. Loving *him.*

He opened a lower drawer of the desk and took out a bottle and splashed more liquid into the glass, filling it halfway and sipping himself and again offering it to her and again she drank and felt the wonderful warm liquid in her mouth, burning down her throat and coursing through her blood. *Love me! You're crazy for me, you know it.*

The sequined purse was awkward by this time in her grip, she laid it on the edge of his desk within reach, she was breathing quickly feeling the charge between them like the air before an electric storm and there she was saying, in the same soft, broken voice, the voice that was exciting this guy pouring blood into his cock like a faucet she'd turned on with her deft manicured fingers, how since she'd been a girl a minister's daughter but not the minister's favored daughter she'd always figured she was being punished ahead of time for whatever sins she might commit—"Like God's giving me a promise. Next time it's my turn."

Wes frowned. Like he was seriously trying to understand. "What's that mean? I don't get it."

"If you're hurt bad enough, Wes, God lets you know the reason for it will be clear someday soon. So it isn't, you know"—pausing, knitting her forehead as if the words were painful to shape—"just for nothing. No *purpose.*"

Again Wes surprised her, smiling. "Hell, Sharon. You believe that?"

"Of course I believe that. It's been my life."

"More bullshit."

"What? Now this is getting insulting, Wes—"

Don't you want me to confide in you? Open my heart to you?

He was saying, almost as if it embarrassed him, spelling out such elementary truths, "Look. The purpose of life is—more life. No purpose beyond that. No more plan to it than the species trying to keep going, reproducing all they can so some individuals survive. I wouldn't say 'God' has much of a hand in it."

"Why, Wes, that's a terrible heartless thing to say! And you the father of a child."

"Why? Why's it terrible and heartless?"

"It's—atheism."

"So? I'm an atheist."

"In the war? In Vietnam? Were you an atheist there?"

Wes's eyes clouded over. He'd been liking this and maybe it was a mistake to break the mood but she was pissed at him, the guy's cocksureness and it was scaring her, too—how casually he'd dismissed God like you'd dismiss some damn dumb embarrassing old nonsense you used to believe when you were a kid. "Sure," he said. "Vietnam. That's where I picked it up. That, and a heroin habit."

"Heroin!" She'd had a habit some years ago but maybe better not tell him, not yet. "So—what did you do in Vietnam? Lily tells me you've never told *her*."

Wes shrugged. "Let's drop it, Sharon. For now."

"You were liking it there, were you? Lots of guys did."

Wes drank bourbon. Wasn't going to say, was he. She laughed.

"You were just a young guy when you went in, weren't you? I bet you were hotheaded."

Again he said nothing. But just possibly he was liking this, too—some special memory he could play over in his mind. Like a scene in a movie he'd rerun lots of times.

"And the women, there? The girls? They all look so young, and the girls would've really been young. Twelve years old, ten…"

Stubbornly he stood mute, ungiving. As if by accident she nudged against him, the front of his trousers, Jesus he was hard, he was—*hard.* And laughed regaining her balance, clutching at his arm. Her long bare polished-looking legs in the sexy high-heeled shoes.

"Or, look"—she was giving him an out as if she'd just now thought of it—"maybe you don't actually remember? Maybe it's all kind of blank. Like some things you'd dreamt and what was real mixed in together and—you've given up trying to sort them."

He frowned, and shrugged. "Maybe."

"You never would've hurt anyone except you were made to. You were there and what happened could only happen there. And only that way, at that time. *I know.*"

He wasn't looking at her but at the glass in his hands, and again he drank, and she'd closed her fingers around his holding the glass and she, too, drank; and the warmth of the bourbon passed between them, delicious.

He said, not angrily, but bluntly, "In fact you don't know shit about me, Sharon. So let's drop the subject."

"Anyway it happened a long time ago. You weren't anybody's husband or father then, lots of things don't count then."

If you touch me, try to fuck me, I'll kill you.

Hey no, look: big guy, I'm hot for you. Try me!

He was asking her again why, why'd she come to Yewville, why at this time? Not when her father died, or her mother? What's the story? And she listened, nodding and trying to think, what had she been telling Lily, obviously Lily had confided in this man, Lily was her sister but had betrayed her. Saying she'd been missing Lily of course—for years. For all of her life away from Lily. But now, these past few months, now the dance troupe was broken up owing her money almost $10,000 she was resigned she'd never receive unless she hired a lawyer and brought a civil suit and the sons of bitches would declare bankruptcy and she'd be left having to pay the lawyer's bills—now also she had some personal problems, these past few months—she'd come home to Lily hoping to be taken in.

Wes was regarding her doubtfully. As if he wanted to believe but couldn't quite.

She said, tears starting in her eyes, "The truth is, Wes, I'm about run to earth. That first night you saw me—how panicked I was, when one of your workers knocked on the back door? I was scared of my life. I *am* scared of my life. There's a person after me who wants to—hurt me."

"Who?"

"A man. Someone I knew in Vegas and L.A. I can't talk about it."

"Have you reported him to the police?"

"No. I mean—yes. In L.A., he'd beaten me and I had to be taken to a hospital and the police were called, that's their policy. But I couldn't press charges. He'd threatened he would kill me if I did."

"Which hospital was this, Sharon?"

"Somewhere in L.A., I said! I don't remember the name, I was taken there by some friends, *bodily.* I—"

"Why's this person want to hurt you?"

"He thinks he's in love with me! He's jealous and possessive and has always had his way with women and I was the first to walk away from him, he says he'll make me pay for that, the insult. He'd threatened to throw acid in my face and he blackened both my eyes and—" She was wiping tears from her cheeks, startled at how feverish her face was. She hoped it wasn't flushed and unattractive, and this man standing so close.

"Does he know you're here?"

She saw where this was going and said quickly, "He has no idea where I am. He's looking for me, probably, in California. He doesn't know where my home was—*is.* As long as I'm here, I'm safe."

Wes was frowning. "But we should notify the police anyway. If he's threatened you."

"No! I can't."

"Why not?"

"I *can't.*"

Her eyes were hurt, helpless; a wave of dizziness rose in her and how natural it was for the man to catch her, steady her. And suddenly they were kissing.

Yes. Like this. At last.

A man's arms around her and she was clutching blindly at him, clinging to him; slipping her hand inside his shirt, greedily caressing his warm, muscled back. And he was moving his hands over her, moaning softly, his hands hard and deft and his weight pressed against her pressing her against the edge of the desk and she was thinking *He will force me now, he will rape me as he has raped children* and the thought was both terrifying and exciting; exciting and terrifying; "Starr Bright" stood a little apart seeing the man's hunger, and the woman's, how her arms were closed desperately around his neck, her parched lips aching pressed so hard against his, and her tongue seeking his; and the sequined purse pushed back into a pile of papers atop the desk, nudged by her thigh. *Pig! Like any pig! Adulterer and fornicator!*

But he'd ceased kissing her. He'd ceased, and stepped away.

Turned from her adjusting his clothing. She heard his labored breath and saw a flush in his throat, rising into his face; he would not look at her even as she tugged at his arm, frantically—"Wes, what's wrong? Be my friend!"

"Sharon, I—can't. Not this."

She pushed into his arms again, baring her teeth in a smile; she kissed him again, or tried to; but the man stood stiffly, his shoulders raised so she had to lift herself against him. "Wes, don't reject me!" she heard herself plead. "I love you."

Wes gripped her hands, gently detached her from him. It was impossible that this was happening—wasn't it? His face was terribly flushed, and his eyes were averted in embarrassment, shame.

He was murmuring, "This isn't a—good idea, Sharon. We'd better say goodnight now."

"But why?"

"You know why."

"Wes. I'm so lonely! So unhappy. The first time I laid eyes on *you*—"

"No. That's bullshit."

"—it's the truth, I swear! My feeling for you, Wes—"

"There's Lily. It isn't just you and me."

"But—Lily wouldn't know."

"*I* would know. And you."

"Wes, please—"

Don't make me beg, "Starr Bright" will not beg any man.

It could not be happening but it was: the man backed off from her, eluded her grasping hands, mumbling an apology she couldn't decipher for the blood roaring in her ears deafening her and dizzying her and she could not comprehend he'd walked out! Walked out of the room, and left her staring after him! This good man, this good, decent man her sister had married, a man "Starr Bright" had no power over, could not touch.

"Fucking *husband*!"

In disgust pouring the remainder of the bourbon into the glass, and raising it to her parched lips.

10
Revelations

It would have seemed at the outset the most ordinary of days—a Thursday in mid-April. Yet it would be the day of Lily's life she would never forget.

What a strange dream, or a jumble of dreams, she'd had the previous night. She'd been left exhausted! Waiting in line with her sister and other children to enter the TV studio theater in Buffalo where *The Starr Bright Hour* was broadcast. It didn't seem to matter if anyone had tickets—they had to wait, wait, wait. And at last they were allowed inside—forced to crawl on hands and knees through a tunnel of shiny tile that opened out into a cramped, low-ceilinged room of hurtful blinding lights and strange shadows harshly black as crevices in the very air. (Where were Mr. and Mrs. Donner? The sisters were alone, unaccompanied. There appeared to be no parents anywhere.) Overexcited, fretting children herded into rows of seats. A smell of wet wool, urine. Now began more waiting, waiting, waiting. Now began the confusion. The TV camera lights made their eyes ache. More children were being herded into seats that were already taken. Pieces of candy were tossed out into the audience and the children shrieked and scrambled for them. At last there came Bessie the Cow on stage—in a baggy spotted cow-costume with a silly cow-mask and lopsided horns. And Louie the Lion with an unconvincing mane and drooping tail. "They aren't even trying to fool us," Lily complained to Sharon, on the verge of tears. A seven-year-old knows such things! Yet the other children were in an ecstasy of excitement and anticipation. The chanting song began so loudly Lily's ears pounded with it *Starr Bright will be with you so-oon! Starr Bright will be with you so-oon!*

But "Starr Bright" never arrived. Lily woke with a headache, breathless and nauseated and exhausted as if she hadn't slept at all. But what relief to be out of that terrible, airless place! What joy, to be not seven years old but thirty-seven! She felt guilty, though, at leaving her sister behind.

And then there was the quarrel with Deedee at breakfast.

Mom please. Will you stop trying to monitor my life. Biting back tears Deedee had pushed past Lily and hurried from the house; on her way to school, having had only two cups of black coffee, not a morsel of food. In three weeks she'd lost twelve pounds and it was true the weight loss was attractive, the girl's round face now slimmer, prettier, and her eyes larger but bright with agitation, nerves. And her skin sickly pale. What could Lily who was her mother do except plead with her gently, reason with her, provide all the low-calorie foods she wanted, plan menus around her obsessive diet. (Lily had called friends who'd been in her predicament over the years, had been given good, if limited, advice.)

Lily said, "Deedee, you can diet, but you can do it reasonably, healthily. Try!" and Deedee said, sighing, too jumpy to sit at the table, "Mom, I hate that name 'Deedee.' Can't you call me 'Deirdre'!" and Lily said, smiling, "Well, then, 'Deirdre'—you can diet, of course, but can't you approach it more *calmly*?" and Deedee said, looking at her as if she'd uttered the most bizarre nonsense, "Mom, I haven't got *forever.* I'm already *fifteen.*"

As if fifteen were a tragic advanced age. As if time were running rapidly out.

Though she was desperate to escape, Deedee paused to take two cans of Diet Pepsi from the refrigerator to slip into her backpack.

Oddly, the name "Sharon" had not passed between them.

I can't blame my sister for what must be a weakness, a failing of my own.

* * *

"Excuse me, but will I be receiving a contract for next year?"

"Lily, what? A contract?"—as if he'd never heard of such a thing.

"A contract. A formal contract. For next year."

Entering the office of the art department chairman who was "Rob" to everyone on the staff Lily had felt sick with apprehension, nerves; out of nowhere, it seemed, she'd summoned up strength to make such a move, formulate such a request, at last; yet, once in Rob's office, invited to shift a stack of canvases (Rob was a painter with a controversial local reputation), she felt rather more anger, aggression. *You have no right to exploit me. To trade on my goodwill.* Rob's normally relaxed, somewhat condescending smile in Lily's presence had faded; he was rubbing at his nose, blinking at her as if wondering whether he'd heard correctly. Was this his most good-natured, self-effacing and dependable faculty member?—the wife of Wes Merrick? Lily had been teaching at Yewville Community College for years seemingly grateful to be hired at all, at any salary no matter how modest, and under any circumstances no matter how hasty, last-minute.

Lily Merrick's student evaluations were consistently the highest of any instructor in the small department, and Lily had frequently explained the fact away, as if embarrassed by it, "Well—my students are women, mainly. They get to be my friends." And the other instructors, most of them men, though liking Lily well enough and possibly even admiring her pottery, were quick to agree with her. *Women stick together. Can't trust women's judgment.*

Of course, Lily's occasional male students gave her very high ratings, too. But they liked her, it was presumed, because she was "so nice, kind."

There were two "stars" in the department: Rob, who was an action painter in the Pollock mode, thus expected to be absent-minded, or temperamental; and a two-hundred-twenty-pound bewhiskered scrap-metal sculptor from Buffalo who was notorious for canceling his once-weekly studio class, or showing up hung-over, morose and sullen. Both "stars" routinely received uneven, if not frankly low evaluations from their students; yet it seemed not to matter, their positions at Yewville Community College, and their salaries, were assured by generous contracts year following year. Lily had not wished to think of the injustice here, the unfairness; and so for years she hadn't thought of it; until, abruptly, it seemed only the other day after a conversation with Sharon about entirely different matters she'd begun to think about it; and to think about it seriously, practicably.

Saying now, "I was thinking, Rob, I'd like to apply to teach in Port Oriskany, if there isn't a position here. Lloyd Morgan"—Lloyd was chair of the department at the college there—"has told me he likes my work." This was true: Lloyd Morgan had been kind enough to send Lily a card, not long ago; but Lily hadn't been thinking of applying to teach at his college, a sixty-mile one-way trip, until this moment. *You see? I have other options. You mustn't take Lily Merrick for granted.* Rob was frowning, and tugging at his skimpy pewter-colored beard, which grew without a mustache on his upper lip and so looked oddly pasted-on, temporary. Clearly Lily's words were a total surprise to him; he'd perhaps expected her to have dropped into his office to invite him to dinner. But Rob was an affable individual, and he'd always liked Lily, her warmth, her reliable smile, her enthusiasm, certainly he understood her practical value to the department, and so finally, with a sigh, he nodded, and agreed, yes it might be a good thing for the college to offer her a formal contract, within the week—"Wouldn't want anyone to steal you from us, eh?"

Lily said, "I was thinking of a three-year contract, actually."

"*Three*-year—?"

"More or less what other adjunct instructors have."

"Yes, but—well, our budget—" Rob squirmed in his seat, tugged at his beard.

"And I think it's time for a raise, Rob, don't you? Approximately the same raise others have received."

"A—raise?"

And Lily smilingly improvised, naming a sum.

And so she left the Yewville Community College campus, driving her car out of the parking lot amid a festive glittering of chrome and windshields in the bright April sunshine. Smiling to herself, pleased, excited, a little frightened at her audacity.

About time, Lily of the Valley. What've I been telling you? All these years!

* * *

When Lily arrived home it was 4:20 P.M. and there to her surprise was Sharon awaiting her just inside the door, in the kitchen, smiling but impatient; obviously Sharon had been smoking, for the air smelled of it, but she'd gotten rid of the cigarette, and had made an attempt to air out the kitchen by opening windows, switching on the fan above the stove. Sharon was oddly dressed, in the rumpled old trench coat of Lily's she'd been wearing in wet, chilly weather; a black scarf tied tight around her head hiding every strand of hair, as if she were bald; ordinary stockings, flat-heeled shoes. Beneath the trench coat Sharon was wearing a dress but what it was, Lily couldn't see. The glamorous smoke-tinted sunglasses hid Sharon's eyes and her face had been artfully transformed into a model's flawless cosmetic mask. Before Lily could share with her sister the good news of her three-year contract and raise at the college, virtually before Lily could draw breath to speak, Sharon informed her excitedly that, at last, she'd gotten over her ridiculous shyness and called an old friend—"And Marnie's invited me over for dinner tonight, isn't that sweet of her?"

Lily said, "Marnie Spohn? I didn't—"

"May I borrow your car, Lily? Marnie lives just in—" naming a suburb of Yewville, "—it isn't far. Gosh, I'm so excited it's like a *date.* I haven't seen Marnie in—" Sharon's voice did not trail off so much as halt, as if she'd leave it to Lily to fill in the precise number of years.

Lily said, "Well, I suppose so, Sharon. But—"

Not knowing why she was faltering in her sister's exuberant, elated presence; why she felt almost childishly hurt; yes, it was hurt she felt—as in those painful days when her pretty sister would swing into the high school cafeteria with Marnie's crowd, an older crowd, cheerleaders predominantly, totally oblivious of Lily who often sat alone eating her lunch, or trying to.

(And on the school bus going home Sharon would take note of Lily's sullen silence, and ask her what was wrong, as if she didn't know; and Lily would complain dolefully, "When other people are around, you look through me like I'm not even there"; and Sharon exclaimed with sly, cruel wit, keeping her expression deadpan, "But I looked everywhere for you, Lily—I did. Are you sure you *were* there?")

Lily smiled now, recalling. If that was what it was, no more than adolescent hurt feelings surfacing after so many years, sheer sisterly jealousy, Lily would survive.

She said, though knowing Wes didn't approve of Sharon borrowing the Toyota, "Of course, Sharon. Take the car. And remember me to Marnie—if she remembers me."

"I will, Lily! I will!"

It was an odd, almost manic response. And Sharon hugged Lily with a strange urgency, as if she were embarking on a dangerous mission, and not simply to dinner a few miles away; as if she and Lily might never see each other again. Sharon's thin, beringed fingers were disconcertingly strong, as Lily had noted in the past. She wore a sweet, piercing perfume; though much of her head was hidden by the black scarf, her earlobes were exposed, and golden earrings dangled from them as in a cascade of coins; around her neck, just visibly glinting inside the trench coat, was the striking gold chain Lily gathered had a sentimental value to her sister. Sharon said, breathless, triumphant, "Don't wait up for me, any of you. I might be late."

Sharon hurried outside, gripping her tote bag. Lily wondered what she might be bringing Marnie. A gift? Lily had made no special effort to glance into the bag but had noted its contents appeared to be covered by a scarf or shawl.

Since the other day, when Sharon had behaved so defiantly,

with such actressy exaggeration, draping a man's brass-buckled belt around her hips and moving in a lewd, suggestive dance, a mockery of an erotic dance, Lily had felt uncomfortable in her sister's presence. Never could you predict when that other Sharon —"Sherrill"—or was it "Starr Bright"—might emerge, cruel and funny.

She'll be leaving me soon, she's become bored with me.

Lily watched as Sharon backed the Toyota around to drive out onto the street, in tight, anxious little jerks, foot on the brake, as if fearful of moving too quickly. Feeling again a small stab of almost pleasurable hurt, jealousy. She wouldn't have guessed that Marnie Spohn was anyone special to Sharon, no more than Sharon Donner was special to Marnie; and if Marnie had invited Sharon to dinner, why hadn't she invited Lily, too? She would know that Sharon was staying with Lily. And Lily hadn't seen, nor even heard of, Marnie Spohn in years.

Odd, Lily had the vague idea that Marnie Spohn had married and moved away from Yewville a long time ago.

She checked the telephone directory out of curiosity—no "M. Spohn." Of course, Marnie must be married. And Sharon had known Marnie's married name?

* * *

"Lily, last night I had a—talk with your sister."

"Yes? What about?"

Lily tried to smile. Seeing that Wes wasn't smiling. Her heart tripped absurdly. *He has fallen in love with her. He's finished with Lily now.*

"Different things."

Wes had startled Lily by returning home unnaturally early—only just 5:30 P.M. Not in recent memory had Wes Merrick come home so early even when, a few years previous, he'd been sick with flu. Now he stood awkwardly in the doorway of Lily's workroom, breathing harshly. His eyes snatched at Lily's, then shifted away; he was the kind of man who expects his wife to complete his thoughts for him; to articulate what he himself isn't quite able to comprehend.

Deedee had gone to a friend's house after school and Sharon was at Marnie's and Lily had been elated by the prospect of a free hour or more in which to explore a design for a large angular ceramic bowl, or sculpture; she wasn't yet sure which it would be; always in the past Lily's work had had a pragmatic function, it was a pot, or a vase, or a bowl, and could be justified as *serving a purpose*; but this design might be entirely different, and not at all "attractive"—she would wait and see. And now Wes stood in her doorway all but wringing his hands, clearly troubled and not knowing how to begin.

Lily said helpfully, "Sharon is out, visiting a friend from high school. I'm surprised—but relieved. Until today she hasn't contacted anyone in Yewville but us."

"Who? Who's she visiting?"

"A woman named Marnie Spohn. We went to school together."

Wes looked blank, the name meant nothing to him. "She's out, now? In your car?"

"Yes."

Lily steeled herself for the next of Wes's queries, for this was uncomfortably like an interrogation. But Wes said, instead, coming forward to touch Lily's arm, "Honey, it's hard to say this, but—I don't think your sister should stay with us any longer. I'd like you to ask her to leave as soon as possible."

"Oh Wes, why?"

This was not at all what Lily had expected. Yet she felt more stunned than relieved.

"She isn't a presence we want here. Especially with Deedee."

"You mean—the dieting? I've been talking to Deedee, I think she'll be more reasonable. This morning—"

"That, sure. But other things. The woman's general conduct—influence."

"Sharon has always been—flamboyant. A nonconformist. But she's good-hearted, so generous—"

"No, Lily. You're good-hearted, you're generous. Sharon is an opportunist and a liar."

"Wes! How can you say such things?"

"All day today, all last night—I've been thinking about her," Wes said slowly. He was caressing Lily's arm as if begging forgiveness. His skin was tired, coarse and sallow; his eyes were faintly bloodshot; his breath smelled just perceptibly of alcohol, and a flush as of guilt, or shame, suffused his face. "Last night Sharon came into my office around two. I was working on accounts. She was dressed to go out, she said she couldn't sleep, she wanted a drink, but I—discouraged her. From going out." Wes paused, looking anxiously at Lily. "She didn't tell you any of this?"

Lily said, "I didn't see much of Sharon today. She kept her door shut all morning and then I was out." Lily swallowed hard, frightened. "When she left for Marnie's about an hour ago she seemed very—excited. Hopeful."

"No matter what she seemed," Wes said impatiently, "you can be sure it isn't what she *is*. That woman has been lying to us all along. About the teaching position in Pasadena and the 'dance troupe' she claimed to be with and something so simple as where she's living now and why she's here."

"But—how do you know?"

"I know."

"The dance troupe—the school in Pasadena—"

"I *know*, I checked. And I asked her point-blank."

"I don't believe this. Sharon wouldn't lie to me."

"Well, she's been lying to me," Wes said angrily. "Maybe you and your sister share secrets I don't know about?"

Lily was alarmed at Wes's emotion; rarely in their marriage had he spoken to her in such a way, the way of a strong-willed, physically dominating man bullying a woman; agitated, confused, and taking it out on a woman. Lily said, "Of course, Sharon has confided in me over the years. I suppose you could say we have—secrets. We're sisters..."

"When it suits *her*."

"Wes, why are you so hard on Sharon? Why are you so angry? You've been saying you like Sharon, she wasn't what you'd expected."

"Because she's been lying to me, playing me for a fool. What is there between you that I don't know?"

Lily felt her face burn. She was angry, too.

"Wes Merrick, I will not be bullied."

"No one's bullying you, Lily. Just tell me is there something I should know, and I don't?"

Lily hesitated, hardly trusting her voice. She was so angry!

Pulling away from Wes, and when he gripped her arm pulling more decisively from him. And she'd been so happy! So pleased with herself, for once! Proud to anticipate Wes's response when she told him of her conversation with Rob. Thinking *I can respect myself now, I needn't cringe and apologize for my very existence.*

Wes said, exasperated, "Lily, God damn it!—I'm not accustomed to not knowing what's going on in my own house. I want your sister to leave."

Lily held back tears. "Wes, I've invited Sharon to stay for as long as—she needs to stay. You can see how she's been recovering, how much healthier she is. And she's been paying expenses. She would pay more, except I won't hear of it. She's our guest. She's my *sister*. She needs me, and I need her. I've been missing her for years. I've been—incomplete without her. Life hasn't seemed whole."

Wes said, "Lily, that's ridiculous. You sound like your sister now—exaggerating."

Was it true? Lily felt a suffocating wildness in her chest; in her throat and mouth; words not her own, yet clamoring to be uttered. *I hate you. I love her. No one is so close as Sharon and I. You don't know us. Leave us alone!*

More calmly Lily said, "I think, in fact, Sharon will be leaving soon," and Wes said, "Yes, but when?" and Lily said, recoiling from him, "Wes, your face, your eyes—you look so hateful. This isn't like you," and Wes said, flushing, "This isn't like *you*, and it's all her fault," and Lily laughed incredulously, saying. "We're adults—we don't blame other people for our problems," and Wes said, "Well, I do blame her. *I want her out of my house*," and Lily said, "It's my house, too," and Wes said, "And I want her out of

Deedee's life, completely," and Lily said, "But Deedee likes Sharon—so much. You haven't seen them together the way I have. I mean—the three of us, together. It's so important for Deedee to have an aunt." Lily was speaking rapidly, excitedly. She scarcely knew what she said. Her tongue was oddly numb as if losing sensation, becoming paralyzed. "It's wonderful for our daughter to have a *family*."

Wes was staring at Lily. "You and I are Deedee's family, Lily. We're all the family she needs."

"Wes, that's ridiculous. We're all related by blood—"

"Except me, yes?"

"What?"

"The three of you are related by 'blood'—Donner 'blood'—but not me?"

This was so: Wes was Deedee's adoptive father. But Lily had not meant it.

Yet she stood trembling, unable to protest.

Wes fumbled for a pack of cigarettes in his pocket and to Lily's dismay extracted one and lit it without apology. Lily could see the man's hands shaking.

After a moment Wes said, in a calmer voice, "Has your sister told you about this person who's stalking her?"

Lily said hesitantly, "Yes. But—"

"But you don't believe her?"

"Of course I believe her."

"*Do* you? I don't."

"I believe Sharon has had a difficult life. Her career might not be going so well as she says. It must be so competitive, so cruel! But she has her pride, she doesn't require our pity. She's still a beautiful woman and a gifted dancer and singer…" Lily's voice trailed off weakly.

Wes said, exhaling smoke in an abrupt, impatient gesture, "Last night Sharon told me that someone, a man, an ex-lover in California, has vowed to kill her. She fled him and she's hiding from him, is the story."

Lily said, defensively, "Sharon has always attracted men, not always the best kind of men. She's lived dangerously—sometimes. But—"

"But if she's in trouble, she should go to the police, Lily. We can't protect her."

"Of course we can protect her! How can you say such a heartless thing! Whoever this person is—he doesn't know she's here. She's safe *here.*" Lily paused, feeling the odd sensation in her tongue of cold, numbness. She could barely look at her husband; the acrid smell of his burning cigarette made her eyes sting. "Wes, did anything happen last night? Between you and Sharon?"

For Lily had to ask.

Wes sighed audibly. Pacing about Lily's workroom colliding with things, not noticing where he blundered; a large blind sweating animal in this unfamiliar, confining space. He said quietly, "I came close to—making a mistake with her, Lily. But I didn't, and I don't want to talk about it."

Lily heard. Through a roaring in her ears, Lily heard.

Of course she'd known, known something, had sensed something in Wes that morning when he'd risen earlier than usual and was out of the house while she was still upstairs; sensed something was wrong when Sharon kept her door shut through the morning replying in vague monosyllables to Lily's entreaties. *Sharon? Are you all right? Aren't you hungry? Sharon?*

How many entreaties, through a lifetime. Offering food, drink, solace, love to others. Risking rebuff, or simply silence.

"Lily? I'm sorry. I don't know what to say—I'm sorry."

Still Lily could not reply. She was faint, leaning against her workbench. The shattered pieces of the bowl she'd loved, the bowl Sharon had knocked to the floor, were still on the workbench, on a sheet of newspaper, as if Lily hoped to reassemble them; of course she could not, what a futile notion, she smiled sadly at such a futile notion, yet she hadn't been able to throw the pieces out just yet.

Lily said, "You've been so angry, Wes. I've never seen you like this."

"I'm not angry, Lily. I'm—scared."

"You! Scared..."

Wes said, "Since Sharon came into this house, things have been out of control. She's a disturbed woman. Very charming when she wants to be but it doesn't last. I think she's dangerous, and I want her out of here."

Lily tried to laugh. "Dangerous! Sharon..."

"She's crazy—in her soul. I've known people like that—not many—in Vietnam."

"Wes, what a thing to say, what an—accusation. Sharon is my sister—"

"Like I said, when it suits *her*. You hardly count in her life."

Lily drew breath to protest. *No!*

But it was true, probably. A simple fact. Anyone but Lily could see.

With deliberate fingers, Lily had been pushing pieces of the broken bowl into a heap in the center of the newspaper page; now she carefully lifted the corners of the page to secure the unwieldy, surprisingly heavy debris inside, and carried it to her wastebasket. She must have decided to clean up after all. Her next work, the ceramic bowl-sculpture, would be much more interesting than this had been. Perhaps a bit ungainly, even ugly. Beauty of a less harmonious kind.

Lily said, evenly, "You're attracted to Sharon, Wes. As a man would be. Any man. Of course." It was not a provocative statement but simply another statement of fact. But Wes responded hotly, "No. It was Sharon who sought me out, Lily. In one of her tight, sexy dresses and nothing beneath—*that* was obvious. Saying she couldn't sleep, she was lonely—" Wes paused, breathing harshly. It went against the grain of the man's temperament, to be informing on another; to be telling tales of another; alleviating his own compromised position by accusing another. Yet what choice had he? How otherwise could he explain? Lily saw with a rush of love for him, and sympathy, the helplessness in her husband's face: that her sister was making of Wes Merrick a person of the kind he himself despised. He said, in disgust, "Never mind. It's over. Nothing happened between us and nothing will. But I want the woman out of this house, Lily—or I'll have to leave, myself."

Lily cried as if stabbed to the heart. "No!"

It was then that the idea came to Wes. Lily saw it in his face, a look of fury and decisiveness, childish rancor yet adult rectitude.

I will cleanse my house of this pollutant. I will reclaim my family.

Striding to Sharon's room, pushing the door open (the guest-room door couldn't be locked except from the inside)—as Lily followed after, mortified, protesting, No! no! this is wrong, this is an invasion of Sharon's privacy!—but Wes in his wild mood paid her not the slightest heed. Impatient, muttering to himself, he threw open the closet door, pawed through Sharon's clothes on hangers and examined the floor, where pairs of shoes were arranged in rows; he inspected the bathroom, which badly needed cleaning; examined the glittering miscellany of items on the bureau top; yanked open drawers, rummaging inside—all the while Lily tried to restrain him, catching at his hands. No! how could he! Oh, Wes! On Sharon's bedside table was a Bible and this, too, Wes snatched up, leafed through, set down again; the floral-print comforter had been pulled up crookedly to the pillows on Sharon's bed, and this Wes pulled brutally aside, staring at rumpled bedclothes beneath as if he expected his sister-in-law to be hiding there; he checked beneath the pillows, and, as far as he could reach, between the mattress and the box springs; he bent to peer beneath the bed—hauling out Sharon's blue canvas suitcase, which was locked.

Lily was pulling at his hands, pleading. "Wes, no. Please let's leave now."

Wes struggled with the lock, might have broken it with his bare hands, recalled then a Swiss army knife in the hall cupboard and went to fetch it and forced the suitcase lock as Lily looked on helplessly, blinking back tears. "Look." Wes was lifting from the suitcase a remarkable assortment of things: several men's wallets, each empty; a man's platinum-gold digital wristwatch (flashing the exact time—5:49 P.M.), a man's gold signet ring, an Italian silk checked ascot scarf; and another Bible, smaller, cheaper, with tissue-thin pages; and, wrapped in a red rayon slip, what appeared to be a policeman's badge, gleaming as if it had been just recently polished.

Again Wes said, excitedly, "Look."

Lily stared at the gleaming object in her husband's fingers. "What—is it? Wes, I don't understand."

"'Sumner County, Nebraska, Deputy Sheriff.' My God."

Lily whispered, "But how could Sharon have gotten that?"

"How could she have gotten any of these things? She's some kind of thief."

"Oh, Wes! We don't have any right to violate her privacy—even if—"

"Yes, we have the right, *I* have the right."

Now Wes had discovered newspaper clippings, tabloid pages that had been carefully folded and placed inside the suitcase lining. He whistled thinly, holding these out for Lily to read; but Lily could not read the lurid banner headlines, her vision swam in a panic. Wes read aloud, haltingly, "'STAR' KILLER STRIKES 2ND TIME, VEGAS MOTEL, VICTIM 43, NEBRASKA SHERIFF'S DEPUTY'—my God. And here—the *Los Angeles Times* 'POLICE LINK SOUTHWEST MOTEL KILLINGS 'GORGEOUS' RED-HAIRED WOMAN SOUGHT.' Oh, Lily, Jesus…your sister must have killed these men. Killed them, stole from them." He read from another paper, "'A star, crudely drawn in blood, was left on walls in the victims' rooms.'…Look, here's the *Yewville Journal*—Stanley Reigel!—"

Lily began to faint, and Wes jumped up to steady her; he held her, and she clutched at him, terrified, unable to breathe; there was a violent pounding in her head as if an artery were about to burst; Lily was whispering, weeping, "We shouldn't have come in here. We shouldn't have looked. I knew, oh Wes I knew—we shouldn't have looked."

11
At the Starlite Motel, Yewville, New York

When, over the phone, he told her the name of the motel, she smiled happily—*A sign!*

You are sending "Starr Bright" a sign, thank you God.

That evening preparing for "MRS M DWYER" an envelope containing among other items the print of the angry-eyed girl. By this time half-convinced the girl was in fact Mack Dwyer's lover mistreated by him and vengeful as "Starr Bright" herself.

And the page carefully removed from the Book of John.

And hairs from the trash behind Rita's Beauty Salon.

These items to be left in the motel room, in the presence of the bleeding pig.

The letter she would mail afterward. Gloved hands always, no fingerprints to be traced.

And with this final sacrifice your destiny is fulfilled.

The man—"B. Decker" he would call himself—had made arrangements at the Starlite Motel on Route 209 North. Approximately four miles from Washington Street.

Pig-justice, he'd made the arrangements himself. She would be invisible. A shimmering upright flame, but invisible.

Arriving quietly at 6:05 P.M., parking at the rear. The room was 48 of the double-tiered mustard-yellow stucco building so of course she parked the Toyota elsewhere; partly hidden by an overflowing Dumpster, facing a canvas-covered swimming *pool.*

(Had she been here before? In summer? The swimming pool reminded her. There'd been a plastic mattress floating there,

American flag colors. A sharp stink of chlorine and a woman's shrill sexy giggling that might have been her own.)

Crossing the oil-specked pavement to the sidewalk running beside the motel, making her way limping slightly, favoring her left leg, to room 48 at the far end. If anyone observed he would see a woman of possible middle age in a shapeless trench coat, head covered with a dark scarf and face obscured by dark glasses and her shoulders slumped; despite the limp, she wore high-heeled shoes. And carried a tote bag.

If anyone observed.

And no one did.

The desk clerk on duty at the Starlite that evening would not have seen this individual at all. The desk clerk would have seen and spoken with and taken payment (cash: $55.75 with tax) from only "B. Decker" who'd telephoned the motel that morning to reserve a double room for one night.

For "Mr. & Mrs. B. Decker" of Utica, New York.

The desk clerk would claim to have heard no sounds—shouts, cries, screams. If there were such. For room 48 was at the farther end of the building, a very private room.

"B. Decker" had specifically requested a "very private, quiet room."

Not peace but a sword!—she'd wakened that morning with Jesus' voice ringing in her ears.

She had honed the knife carefully in the Macy's knife-sharpener in Lily's attractive kitchen. This was a ritual of love, even tenderness. Never any haste. Never hesitation.

At the rear of the Starlite there was a smell of garbage and diesel oil. Insecticide and disinfectant. "Starr Bright's" sensitive nostrils pinched. The pig's habitat, the pig's lair. For a confused moment she could not recall which of them would be awaiting her inside, with a bottle: the one named Cobb, the one named Fenke, the one named Marr, the one named Hughlings, the one named Salaman…

Not peace her pulsebeat urged *but a sword. Not peace not peace but a sword.*

For there had begun in Sharon's soul a counter-urging, a small pleading voice to which she dared not listen. Urging forgiveness, forgetfulness, What would Lily do in her place, what would Lily think? What would Deedee think? And the man, what was the man's name?—the man her sister had married not a pig but a good, decent man a faithful husband—what would he think of her, how would he judge her?

But no, she dared not listen. It was too late, "Starr Bright" had honed the knife, all was prepared as in an act before a live impatient audience amid dazzling blinding lights and sexy-throbbing drums.

Not peace! not peace but a sword. Amen.

Within an hour they were happily drunk, couldn't keep their hands off each other; or so it seemed. "Mack Dwyer"—the thick-waisted thick-bodied middle-aged man with graying hair combed in silly, hopeful strands across the flushed dome of his head, and "Sherrill"—as she'd asked him to call her—with glossy burnished red curls spilling to her shoulders, large mascara-rimmed eyes glowing with pale green eyeshade, beautiful glistening crimson-kissable mouth.

"Sherrill" poured drinks from Dwyer's bottle of Seagram's with the skill and poise of a cocktail hostess. Sipping very discreetly herself, urging the man on to more, more. And more. Cooing to him, soothing, murmuring, nodding enthusiastically. Listening with rapt attention. For Dwyer, like most men, had a lot to say. Oh yes, a lot to say. His fleshy mouth worked, his hands gestured. He had opinions, he had memories. He had hopes, plans. You listened, and you nodded, and you filled the guy's glass.

The pig does 99 percent of the work actually. You just sit back, wait.

"Starr Bright" would boast laughing to the cops.

It had been a mild shock, though—Mack Dwyer. So much older. Hardly the same guy. Looking like Mr. Dwyer—his father. He was still good-looking in a jowly way, women would be attracted to him, that air of confidence, swagger. But his face was starting to sag and his skin was of the hue and texture of cooked oatmeal. Now he'd removed his sport coat you could see the fistfuls of flesh at his waist spilling over his belt. Where once Mack Dwyer had been lean, muscle-hard, quick hands and feet, a panther.

Smiling she swooped to kiss him on the lips. Not a sensuous tongue-prodding kiss, not yet. More of a light teasing peck of a kiss.

"Wow! What's that for?"

" 'Cause it's so great to see you again, Mack. And looking so handsome like always."

Dwyer laughed grunting and reached over for her, as if to swing her onto his lap or onto the bed beside him; but quicksilver Sherrill eluded him, patting the back of his hand with her gloved fingers. It was a turn-on, tight red lace gloves with the red jersey sheath-dress hiked up to her thighs as she coiled herself in a chair; crossed her long lovely dancer's legs, gleaming in smoke-colored diamond-patterned stockings. *Take a good look, fella. Take an eyeful. 'Cause that's all you're gonna get of "Sherrill."* Thinking how strange that driving to the Starlite Motel, parking the Toyota and approaching room 48 she'd been feeling jumpy, anxious; wondering if maybe, this time, she should turn back. Lily's voice urging *Forgive him! Forget the past! Come home to us, Rose of Sharon!* But then at the door she'd pulled off the scarf and fluffed out her shiny red curls and removed the tacky trench coat to stuff into the tote bag and straightened her shoulders so her breasts emerged and wetted her lips and stepped into the light ready to see herself reflected in the pig's glistening-admiring eyes—Jesus, it felt so *right. "Starr Bright" in the right place at the right time and the rest of life is so boring.*

Noting how Mack Dwyer was breathing hard, staring at her in a slow-blinking way. Boyish, but dirty-minded. Sure. You could tell this guy was a small-town politician—even now, trying to figure out how he can fuck her, he's making gassy speeches.

And wearing a showy expensive wristwatch. Another digital with ebony face and flashing numerals exactly like—whose? The name was gone and the face except the "cabana" in Joshua Tree, the way the walls had shone afterward.

Sure she'd laugh telling the cops *I just liked to kill, it's a real rush. You should try it.*

Mack Dwyer was saying, phony-sincere, "Hell, I certainly did try to keep track of you, Sharon. I mean—'Sherrill.' People said you'd gone away, you were a famous model. Saw some pictures of you in a fashion magazine—fantastic! *I* went to Bucknell and flunked out first semester and my dad said he'd give me a second chance on the condition—" How earnestly the man talked as if Sherrill gave a damn, complaining of his marriage which wasn't "what I'd been looking forward to, frankly" and his kids who were "self-centered taking their father for granted" and his career as a Republican that was "on the upswing again after some rotten luck in the last election." Here was a man aggrieved, maudlin, in urgent need of female consolation. Here was a man deserving of a whole lot better than he had. Staring at Sherrill like she was a trick that might vanish. And tugging at his necktie, slick shiny red-striped tie selected for this special occasion. Saying, "It's terrific, Sharon, I mean 'Sherrill,' you called me like this. I was crazy for you, honey, back then, I really was; why we broke up *I* sure don't know," and she laughed and said, "You don't, huh, Mack?" and he said emphatically, shaking his head so his jowls quivered, "I *don't*. But I have this feeling you blame me, right? It was something I did or said, right? Shit, I know I was an s.o.b. my last couple years of high school, you girls shouldn't have spoiled me so I lost perspective—you know?" and she laughed saying, "So I guess it was our fault, huh?" and he reached for her again playfully and clumsily and not yet dangerous and she was able to elude him leaving him panting. "Jesus, Sherrill! You're so beautiful. Your eyes, your skin—hair—that dress—you do forgive me, don't you?" and she said, in a sexy-throaty-teasing voice, "Now why would I need to 'forgive' you, Mack? You got a guilty conscience?" and he said, with boyish contrition, "It *was* my fault, wasn't it? What'd I do? Was it—oh, Christ I remember: this girl from Stillwater was going out with Budd Petco and she and I sort of traded dates—at Wolf's Head Lake?—and you hid in the girls' changing room crying I guess and wouldn't come out, Budd said—" and she said, smiling sharply, "No, Mack. Sure wasn't me," and he said, "It wasn't?" and she said coolly, "Some other girl of yours, hon," and he said, sipping at his drink, "Could've sworn. Pretty girl with red hair, freckles all over..." and she said, bemused, "You remember 'Sharon Donner' with red hair and freckles?" and he said cagily, "Hmmm, sweetheart, the age I'm getting to, I don't know what the hell I *do* remember," and she said, smiling, lazily stroking the shining calf of one of her legs as if unaware of how provocative a gesture it was, the perspiring man only a few inches away staring at her, "You remember your senior prom. I was your date," and Dwyer smiled again in his sheepish-boyish-lewd way murmuring, "Mmmm, yeah, I guess I do—sure," and she said, "You and your football team buddies got me drunk and—you know," and he said, shifting his shoulders excitedly, "'Got you drunk'—I don't remember that, Sharon. Hell, I got pretty smashed myself," and she said, teasing, playful, poking him in the thigh, "What you guys did to me in your father's van, remember that van?—wasn't so nice," and he said, frowning, staring into his glass for a moment before drinking, "Look, I don't remember that, I was smashed out of my skull," and she said, shaking a forefinger at him, close by his flushed face, "Piggy-piggy! *Was* Mack naughty? 'Big Mack' and his team buddies?" and he said, defensively, "I don't remember anybody doing anything they didn't want to do," and she said slyly, "It was statutory rape, Big Mack," and he repeated, doggedly, "*I* don't remember anybody doing anything they didn't want to do," and she said, "'Statutory rape'—rape by the statute," and he said, "There sure as hell wasn't any *rape*, that's a laugh," and she said, "Because I was only fifteen," and he said, making a snorting noise like laughter, "Hell, *I* was only seventeen, or—" and she said, "Eighteen, actually," and he said, "Well—whatever. We were kids," and she said, lightly, in a kind of singsong, "And I didn't say yes, Big Mack, not yes to five guys," and he said, "Yes, but you did say yes—you didn't say no," and she said, "Maybe you didn't hear," and he said, "In fact I was smashed out of my skull, that's the fact, I don't remember any of this," and she said, laughing, "Oh, well—boys will be boys, eh?' and he said, with a heavy sigh, tugging at his necktie, "I guess. Now I got kids of my own, sons, who don't listen to me," and she was laughing at his look of physical discomfort, an aroused, sweating male, an upright thick-bodied pig in clothes too tight; and playfully she raised her leg, and drew the instep of her high-heeled shoe against his thigh and side, poking, tickling, and he gaped at her in startled delight, and she leapt to her feet now displaying her slender body, stretching her arms, in a pretense of kittenish yawning, showing the tip of her pink tongue between crimson lips.

As if the musical tempo had been quickened, now the action would begin.

"O.K., Big Mack, strip."

"Huh?"

"Strip."

Running her tight-gloved fingers through the man's disheveled hair and, when he lunged for her, leaping back agile as a dancer or a gymnast. "Hey! Whew!" He'd exploded in laughter, spilling whiskey on his trousers.

She, too, was panting. And perspiring. But loved the feeling, like a cocaine high. Commanding, "'Starr Bright' says *strip,* fella."

Laughing, eager, Dwyer stumbled to his feet. She danced away, keeping him at arm's length. She was snapping her fingers and moving her eel-like body in tight, erotic contortions, laughing at his dazed expression, commanding, "Strip! It's time—strip for 'Starr Bright'!" and Dwyer said, blinking, "Who's 'Starr Bright'?" and she was pivoting away, keeping the room's sole chair between them, singing, "—'gonna be with you soon! Gonna be with you so-oon!'" and he tried to fall in with her mood, swaying-drunk, saying, "If I strip—you, too, sweetheart? You're gonna strip, too?" and she said, "Right! Just turn your back, honey," and he said, with babyish inflection, "Don't wanna turn my back, wanna watch," and she darted at him to run a quick-caressing hand down the front of his thick body to his bulging groin and he shuddered as if struck by a current of electricity, his eyes lost focus, and she laughed saying, "'Starr Bright' will teach you tricks she learned in New York—L.A.—Acapulco—Paris—Tangier—*Hong Kong*!—but Big Mack's got to turn his back first," and she was dancing, shaking shoulders, hips, pelvis, "—then there's gonna be a nice sur*prise*."

So Mack Dwyer trustingly turned his back on her, muttering and laughing to himself; panting as if he'd run up a flight of stairs; fumbling to remove his white cotton dress shirt that was sweated through under the arms and across the back, tossing his tie into the air, undoing his belt, his trousers. Nor slackening the beat though regarding him now with a look of loathing, she reached for the blue-sequined purse and removed the knife; her protection; pearl-handled stainless steel carving knife remarkably light in the hand with a five-inch blade honed to razor-sharpness that afternoon; the knife that fitted her right hand perfectly; the knife that steadied her hand so it ceased to tremble; the knife that thrilled her like a baptism, it felt so *right.*

Every time, so *right.*

Dwyer clumsily stripped to his shorts, cotton boxer shorts, she noted with disdain the flaccid fat at his waist, the pocked thighs, pallid legs. The boy Mack was gone, a stranger had taken his place yet must be punished. She hid the knife behind her back as he turned to face her expectantly.

His heated face sagged in disappointment.

"Eh, Sharon honey? What's wrong?"

She was smiling at him, shining. An upright flame, a woman clothed in the sun and upon her proud head a crown of twelve blazing stars. And in her sexy high-heeled shoes, her supple legs as far apart as the tight sheath dress would allow, a dancer's or an athlete's pose, poised in readiness.

The wild music pounding between them faster and faster had ceased now, abruptly. Whatever mood, rudely shattered.

Dwyer's bloodshot eyes lowered, to his own body. He said, mumbling in chagrin. "Guess I—I'm changed some, eh? Not like eighteen."

Still she said nothing, smiling; poised in readiness. At a short distance a car door slammed, a car was driven noisily away. The man was abashed and apologetic but beginning to be annoyed, a sullen droop to his mouth. "Sharon, you're not changing your mind, are you? Because if you are this is a helluva time to—"

Now bringing the glittering knife around so he could see it, moving deft and unhesitating and bent slightly at the knees, feinting the blade toward him as he stared, astonished, backing off, eyes widened as in a caricature of incredulity and alarm. He was gasping for breath, "—wait, no, what—is this?—what the hell —oh my God, wait, Sharon—" as astounded as if the very earth had opened up before him about to suck him down to oblivion. He backed clumsily away, aside, shaking his head murmuring no, no, no and she discerned in his dazed eyes how he would make a desperate swipe at her, hoping to send the knife flying from her fingers, imagining her fingers weak, imagining her a weak woman easily intimidated by a man's superior strength; and so seeming to invite him, taunting him; and he *did* move, but so clumsily, stiffly, his athlete's reflexes long since blunted, she had no difficulty leaping to one side like a cat, and swinging the blade in a swift powerful arc even as the man's arm was moving in an arc of its own so the blade caught him in the palm of his hand slicing the skin in a deep four-inch laceration from which bright blood at once erupted, and as he whimpered in pain clutching the wrist of that arm she drew the blade swiftly along his forearm, this time in a deep six-inch laceration, beautiful to her eye—"There, pig! Now you know 'Starr Bright.'"

She paused to switch on the TV. Network evening news in too-vivid color.

Dwyer stumbled backward in panic, against the edge of the double bed, nearly falling; blood flowed in two streams down his uplifted arm, dripping to the carpet. She did not give him time to recover from the shock of the assault nor even to breathe but advanced upon him, smiling, "No, I haven't changed my mind, Mack, 'Starr Bright' never changes her mind," and he was begging, pleading, "Wait, no—Sharon, please you don't mean—can't mean—help me I'm bleeding, my arm—I swear to God I'm so sorry—" and a thought came to her, it was perhaps not a thought of her own but one sent to her from God for *in these days shall men seek death, and shall not find it; and death shall flee from them* so she circled the trembling man urging "On your knees! Pray to God to save you!" and Dwyer sank to his knees on the bloodied carpet staring at her, trembling with terror staring like a transfixed animal, and she was speaking calmly to be heard over the animated TV voices, "Yes, pray! Pig-rapist, pray! 'Our Father who art—' *Pray!* 'Starr Bright' didn't do this for Stan Reigel but she will do it for you, Big Mack, remember Stan-the-Man your team buddy?" and Dwyer failed to comprehend so she repeated her words and this time a sick comprehension dawned in his eyes, his body stricken with grief for its own mortality, so she commanded him again, pointing the bloodied tip of the knife at his throat, "Pray, pig! If God has mercy, 'Starr Bright' has mercy, if God has no mercy, how can 'Starr Bright' have mercy? 'Our Father who art—'"

At once the terrified man began, "'Our F-Father who art—in H-Heaven'—"

So Mack Dwyer, forty years old, naked except for sweat-dampened boxer shorts, knelt on the soiled carpet of room 48 of the Starlite Motel, Route 209, Yewville, New York, in the early evening of a Thursday in April, praying for his life. As "Starr Bright" looked on, an empty vessel to be filled with God's will.

12
Rose of Sharon, Lily of the Valley

There is evil that takes hold of people, that isn't born in them; the way a thistle seed takes hold in soil. There is evil that is allowed into the heart, invited in.

In a suspension of dread Lily awaited Sharon's return. In the pretty lavender-and-cream bedroom that had been Sharon's. She sat on the edge of the bed, she stood, paced about, gazed worriedly out the window into darkness; sat again, weak, sick with anticipation of what was to come. Spread out on the floral-print comforter were a dozen or more newspaper clippings and pages, a *Newsweek* feature with the lurid title "First 'Big League' Female Serial Killer Strikes in Southwest, California," at which she couldn't bring herself to look; and the wallets, the wristwatches, the leather belt with the brass buckle, the Nebraska sheriff's deputy badge. Wes had opened both windows to dilute the stale odor of strong perfumes, cigarette smoke. Lily wondered whether the odor would ever entirely fade from the room.

She'd been crying, and there was a choked, constricting sensation in her chest. In her fist she held a damp, shredded tissue. In another part of the house Wes was pacing, smoking. From time to time she heard his footsteps approach—he returned to stand in the doorway, looking at her. He'd wanted to call the police immediately but Lily had pleaded with him, "Wes, no. Please. Let me speak with Sharon first. Just the two of us."

Wes had said, almost angrily, "Lily, your sister is insane! She's a homicidal maniac."

Lily had pressed her fingertips against her eyelids. Her head swam. Wanting to protest *I can't believe that. There must be some explanation. It can't be as it seems!* But she said nothing.

At least, Deedee wasn't home for this. She was staying overnight with a girlfriend—fortunately.

Lily began to cry again, Wes knelt beside her and held her and in a gentler voice said, "The woman might be dangerous. Lily. She is dangerous," and Lily said, "Not to us, Wes," and Wes said, "To anyone! She's insane." But Wes relented, and agreed to let Lily speak with her sister alone, for a short while. Assuming Sharon returned at all.

He would remain, he said, downstairs, in his office with the lights out. Never far from a telephone.

How she loved him, Wes Merrick, her husband! Foreseeing that, when this nightmare ended, when Sharon was gone from them, and their happiness restored, she would never tell him who Deedee's mother was, she would never confess she had no idea who Deedee's father was. For such "truth," though factual, was not the truth of the heart. Such "truth" was not worth a moment's pain suffered by another.

To live with a secret, secrets—and to live happily.

What is this but the human condition?

So Lily told herself, tears like acid scalding her cheeks.

It was at 8:40 P.M. that Lily saw a car's headlights turn into the drive.

Sharon returning home from—wherever she'd been.

Lily steeled herself. Rising to stand beside the bed, clasping her hands together in an unconscious attitude of prayer, then dropping them at her sides. She knew that, in his darkened office, Wes stood rigid as well, waiting.

Sharon must have seen the lighted windows of her room, must have seen Lily inside, hesitated for a moment before opening the door and stepping into the room. And in that instant seeing Lily's expression, and the items spread out onto the bed; her eyes locking with Lily's in the full force of recognition.

"So, Lily. You know."

"I—don't, Sharon. I don't understand."

"Yes. You do."

Lily would recall afterward the flatness of her sister's voice. The look almost of relief in her blood-veined eyes.

Sharon came into the room, breathless, stumbling in her high-heeled shoes as if she were drunk, or dazed by a drug; the tote bag slipped from her fingers and fell to the floor, and Lily could see inside what appeared to be, among other things, a curly red glamor wig and a blue-sequined purse. Sharon was wearing Lily's old trench coat, unbuttoned; beneath, slacks and a sweater; the flawless cosmetic mask looked like crust on her strained face, her crimson lipstick was eaten partly away and her mascara was smeared. Her hair, visibly thin in the direct overhead light, was damp, as if she'd only recently showered. She moved slowly as if her joints ached.

Lily said, faltering, "But—what? What should I know, Sharon?"

Sharon said, shrugging. "It's true. What the papers say. I'm the one. I killed those men."

"Sharon, no! My God…"

"Who broke the lock on my suitcase? Wes? Good. I'm glad. I'm tired of running, I'm run to earth." Sharon glanced around, squinting, as if seeking Wes out; but Wes was not visible; she laughed, and raised her voice, "Wes! Good! Call the police! *I'm so tired.*"

Lily would have gone to Sharon to take hold of her hands but Sharon brought her hands up close to her body in an odd shrinking gesture, shutting them into fists; as one might do not wanting to be touched; not wanting another to be contaminated by one's touch; as if her hands were soiled. It was an unmistakable gesture and though Lily could see that her sister's hands were clean, perhaps scrubbed clean, the thought came to her *She has killed someone, tonight. She has just killed.*

Lily was crying, "Sharon, my God, why?" and Sharon said, as if confused, "*You* didn't know, Lily? Didn't guess?" and Lily said,

"How could I guess—such a horror! It can't be true, can it?" and Sharon said, flatly, "Eleven men. Pigs, not men. God guided my hand, Lily. And another," drawing from the trench-coat pocket a man's digital wristwatch to toss onto the bed amid the others. Lily stared at first uncomprehending. "Sharon, who?"

"Guess, Lily of the Valley."

"Mack Dwyer—?"

"A pig who used to be 'Mack Dwyer.'"

Sharon tried to smile, wanly. Lily was appalled, even at such a time disbelieving. "No! Sharon, I can't—"

"Where's Wes? Has he called the police?"

"No!"

"No?"

Sharon was peering toward the doorway, the darkened hall. She seemed confused. Her bloodshot eyes were shiny yet unfocused. Her damp pale blond hair had been expertly fastened at the back of her head in an elegant French twist from which a few tendrils had escaped. In the high-heeled shoes she stood swaying, shivering.

Now Lily took her sister's hands, gently pried open the fists; held her hands tightly in both her own; Sharon's hands were icy-cold, tremulous. There was only a faint fragrance of perfume about Sharon, a smell rather of soap, shampoo. *She has showered off his blood. She has washed herself clean.* Lily pleaded, "Sharon, tell me there's some—mistake?"

"No. No mistake."

"But—why?"

Sharon said, with sudden passion, "Why? You know why, *Lily!* They were pigs who didn't deserve to live! 'Starr Bright'—her revenge."

"'Starr Bright'—?"

"God guided my hand, Lily. Now God is done with me. This"—indicating the things on the bed—"you—and Wes—it's a sign, God is done. It's over."

"But, Sharon—"

Moving still in that slow, arthritic way, blinking rapidly as if to get her vision into sharper focus, Sharon went to the tote bag and took from it the blue-sequined purse and opened it and held out for Lily's horrified examination a knife, a kitchen carving knife with a gleaming blade, and Lily recoiled, and Sharon laughed saying, "No, no, it's washed clean, the pig's blood is gone." This, too, she dropped onto the bed with the other items.

Going then like a sleepwalker to the telephone on the bedside table, to Lily's amazement fumblingly dialing a number and saying in a husky, hoarse voice, "H-hello? Police—?" and Lily cried. "Sharon, no!" and snatched the receiver from her, and put it back.

"Why did you do that, Lily?"

"Sharon, not yet! Not yet! It's too soon."

"No, it's time, Lily. God has abandoned me and I'm so tired, it's time."

Lily pleaded, "No, no, no," pulling Sharon into her arms, sinking onto the edge of the bed, and Sharon swayed, stumbled, sank to her knees beside her, limp and unresisting and beginning at last to sob, as she'd done when they were girls, in the identical posture years ago in the farmhouse in Shaheen in their shared bedroom on the second floor beneath the wind-ravaged eaves, begging forgiveness of Lily of the Valley, for she was Rose of Sharon who'd wronged her, or had wronged someone, or had been wronged by someone, insulted, injured, cut to the heart, trembling with rage, indignation, sheer unnameable passion. Lily was stroking her sister's head, her sister's thin shoulders, Lily whispering, "Thank you for coming to me, Sharon, for coming back to me," and Sharon said, "Help me, Lily? Don't stop loving me?" and Lily said, "I'll never stop loving you, Sharon," and Sharon began to pray, "'Though I walk through the valley of the shadow of death…'" and Lily joined her, "'…I will fear no evil: for thou art with me: thy rod and thy staff they comfort me…'" and that was how Wes discovered them, a few minutes later.

13
"Deirdre"

It wasn't at Ali's house they had supper but at the mall where Ali's mother let them off. They ate at Pepe's Pizzeria or rather Ali ate and Deirdre drank two large diet Cokes saying that's all she wanted, she wasn't hungry. And at Pepe's there were three guys eyeing them, older guys from another high school who followed them into the movies sitting in the row behind them and cracking jokes, laughing and when the movie ended they asked the girls if they'd like something to eat, the girls said O.K. but they couldn't leave the mall because Ali's mother was picking them up at nine, and Ali and Deirdre went to the women's room whispering and giggling together, and Deirdre was feeling just a little light-headed, nothing serious but that weird thing with her eyes like she was seeing double and needed to blink hard to clear her vision, but Ali gave her another diet pill and that helped, actually she felt terrific, both of them felt terrific giggling about the guys whose last names they didn't know but they'd seen them around the mall, sure. The girls lit up a single cigarette for a quick smoke to share and Deirdre's gaze kept drifting to the mirror, not knowing if she liked what she saw there, or whether it scared her, her hair in the new way, the face that was hers yet not exactly, the slimmer cheeks, large startled-looking eyes outlined in black like eyes in a drawing. She was excited, maybe nervous a little, her fingers trembling as she approached the mirror gravely to smear Plum Moon maroon lipstick on her mouth, her wound of a mouth, raw and hungry.

THE
END

“The Murderess”

Many years ago in Sharon Springs, Vermont, Anne-Marie Thayer crouched at an upstairs window (might it have been in the attic?—the air was so dense, so oppressive) watching that woman, *the murderess*, swimming in the Thayers' pool. Her fists trembled; her face felt scorched; she was engorged with hatred. "Why don't you go away and leave us," she whispered at the ducked head, neatly white in its rubber cap, and the slow measured graceful arms that drew the body fish-like across the length of the pool, "why don't *you* die…drown in the bottom of the pool…go away and leave us."

Anne-Marie had been fifteen at the time. Possibly sixteen: though in later years she would have wished herself younger. The violence of her hatred for her father's cousin, for the infamous Constance Price, was that of a child: a fixed, ferocious, rather astonishingly innocent wish that the woman would simply disappear. She had come out of nowhere, nearly; she could then disappear just as easily. It was not necessary for her to die, Anne-Marie thought, in fact her death, here at the Thayers' summer place, would only add to the furious dismay and embarrassment and revulsion Anne-Marie had been feeling all summer. It would give her friends and their parents and the local people who lived in Sharon Springs all year round more to gossip about: Have you heard what has happened at the Thayers', have you heard the latest….

But there was little likelihood of the woman dying, Anne-Marie thought, her mouth small and pinched and pitiless, as she spied upon Constance Price from the window. Little likelihood of her drowning. She swam with a certain matronly caution, a contemptible prudence, not so foolishly timorous as Anne-Marie's mother but hardly as confident as Anne-Marie herself: she was not, so people said, as strong as she appeared.

Anne-Marie shut her eyes suddenly. The heat of the attic room pressed against her temples; she felt dizzy, helpless. The small brave figure in the pool disappeared. There was no pool, there was no swimmer. No quiet rhythmic splashing. All the world slid away like sand through outspread fingers and Anne-Marie was left with only the greed, the almost lustful greed, of her secret wish. Oh my God why don't you *die*.

She swam in her old combed cotton tank suit, defiant in the rain.

The murderess had been in the pool when the sun shone that morning, and afterward she'd lounged with Anne-Marie's mother on the flagstone terrace, and then Robin Wilks had strolled over from next door, idle and chattery and inquisitive, and the morning stretched into lunch, and Anne-Marie hid upstairs, whispering to herself, pretending to be going through old trunks and crates and boxes. Her mother called for her. What was she doing, why didn't she join them. Was she still rummaging through that hopeless junk…? What on earth did she expect to find? Treasure? Mrs. Thayer's voice was querulous, jittery, and gay all at once. Anne-Marie had tried to mimic her many times but she was inimitable. The best strategy was to simply say nothing, to indicate acquiescence in silence; to be docile; daughterly.

But that morning she had shouted down the long crooked crazy stretch of stairs: "I'm not looking for anything! I'm cleaning up this disgusting mess!"

Shortly afterward rain-clouds appeared in the northern sky, a not-infrequent sight. They were blown down from Quebec, across the scattered mountain range, swollen and hearty and smug. One minute there was sunshine, Mrs. Thayer lamented, and the next minute thunderclouds and rain. Anne-Marie thought that the pinnacle of Bloodroot Mountain, off to the northwest, looked most dramatic when thunderclouds loomed up behind it. She did not mind overcast weather, not even the rain, she said; *she* was not a tourist in this part of the world.

So she swam in the rain. Despite her mother's protests, and Constance Price's odd look.

Twelve laps. Fifteen. Seventeen, eighteen, nineteen....

She was a tall girl, with well-developed arms and shoulders and legs; her breasts were small, her stomach hard and flat; her hips were lean and almost boyish. Colorless brown hair, fair eyebrows, skin that burned too easily in the summer and chapped too easily in cold weather. Brown eyes. A small vulnerable mouth. In dread of seeing by accident the woman she was fated to become—plain, she supposed, with her father's too-ruddy skin and her mother's blinking hopeful eyes—Anne-Marie avoided studying herself in mirrors for long periods of time. It was a blessing that the cabinet mirror in the old third-floor bathroom, which she insisted upon using this summer just as she had insisted upon using a high, narrow, out-of-the-way room at the top of the house, was so mottled and vague. It seemed to cast a veil over her features, blurring them, softening them, so that she need not directly confront herself. Sometimes she whispered to that cringing image endearments calculated to comfort and yet to mock: You poor thing. *You.* Broken-out forehead again, eh? Hair stringy but what do *you* expect.... You're not Constance Price, are you.

From the screened-in porch her mother called out: "Anne-Marie, I'm afraid of lightning, what if lightning strikes the water...? You come in here, now. Anne-Marie?"

The raindrops were hard and cold and rather shocking on her face. And there was a wind; a sudden change of temperature. One minute it was a pleasant August day, and then it was chilly as mid-October....Anne-Marie closed her eyes and propelled herself through the water without joy. Twenty laps. Twenty-one. She had been an excellent swimmer only two summers ago and it frightened her that now she seemed to be losing interest. In school, she had always been eager to swim; now she halfway sympathized with the girls who sat out the period, offering excuses of varying plausibility.

"Anne-Marie—? Don't you hear? I just saw a flash of lightning—"

Exhausted suddenly she turned to shout something at her mother. And lunged for the side of the pool. Her breath was ragged and almost painful, her heart was pounding, she was really cold, shivering with cold; there was nothing pleasurable about the water at all. But facing her mother she could not resist a resigned, spiteful grimace, quick as an arpeggio.

"Go to hell," she murmured.

But not loud enough, of course, for Mrs. Thayer to hear.

And was the woman really a murderess?

Yes. In fact she was.

It was a matter of public knowledge, it was on the record forever: Constance Price had committed the act of murder.

"Of course there were mitigating factors," people said. "There were circumstances. For instance...."

"What is she like? Does she drink?"

"Does she play golf?"

"Did she really inherit his money?—*his?*"

A woman of forty-three with faded gold hair, hollow eyes, hollow cheeks. A long narrow face that struck Anne-Marie as repulsive: not because it was ugly but because it had obviously been beautiful at one time and was now ravaged. There were shadow-marks beneath the eyes as substantial as if someone had smeared them on, there were lines on the cheeks that looked like rivulets made by tears. A repulsive woman, Anne-Marie thought, shivering. In perpetual mourning. Deathly.

"Why do you half-close your eyes like that?" Anne-Marie's father asked one evening. "It it something new? A new fad?"

Blushing, Anne-Marie opened her eyes wide.

"You're behaving very oddly," he said, squaring his shoulders. That afternoon he had driven up to Sharon Springs from New York City and the creases on either side of his mouth showed a certain belligerent strain Anne-Marie and her mother recognized at once. Now he sat at dinner, eating quickly. He was by nature a happy, gregarious man—so he described himself to people outside his family—but something was always pulling him down, some great poisonous toad was always squatting on his chest. It was a tradition in the family that Mr. Thayer was revived in the country, at the summer place; it was said of him that he "came alive" in Sharon Springs. His people had owned this house for a very long time: a Captain William Thayer had built it, or part of it, in 1760. (There was a brass plaque on the outside of the house—Mrs. Thayer made certain that the boy who did their lawn kept the evergreens from obscuring it.) When Mr. Thayer was not in good spirits in the country he cast about to discover why. If his wife Ginny was not to blame with her harmless cocktail prattle, or the enormous house itself with all its problems—("We own a white elephant in Sharon Springs," Anne-Marie told people, smirking, yet a little vain, "it was built in the eighteenth century and has two furnaces and is falling apart and it really *is* white—peeling white with Greek Revival columns and a hundred windows: it looks like the setting for a murder")—why then his daughter, who so resembled him, must be to blame.

She was lazy, and then again she was exasperatingly energetic. She knocked things off tables. She walked too heavily, especially when barefoot. She was dreamy, not-there, maddening; and then again she was too intense, jumpy. He could not tolerate her coming to the dinner table, even in the country, in those grotesque short shorts, and with her hair falling in her face. He had asked his wife Ginny to speak to her in private about that, and about her posture. Hadn't she any sense of her own body, hadn't she any pride? Since his cousin Constance had come to visit a month ago Anne-Marie had been behaving more strangely, and more maddeningly, than ever. She refused to speak directly to Constance and did not even look at her. In the woman's presence she simply went blind—or half-shut her eyes so that the lids trembled. Her voice, which was normally rather strident, became whispery and mock-reverent. *Not-there* was the girl's strategy.

"I asked you if there was something wrong," Mr. Thayer said, staring down the table at her.

That evening, a rainy disappointing evening, there were no guests. Only Constance Price, sitting as usual across from Anne-Marie at the oval walnut table, her head slightly bowed as if with the weight of her braided and coiled hair. Mrs. Thayer in a sleeveless dress splotched with great gay sunflowers sat at Anne-Marie's left, in fretful silence. Someone else had been invited—who had they been?—a couple new to the village, who lived the rest of the year in Boston—they'd begged off for some reason, a child's illness, an unreliable babysitter. Rain drummed against the high old-fashioned windows and further distorted the antique glass.

"If you have difficulty with your vision," Mr. Thayer said, not unkindly, "we can make an appointment for you with an ophthalmologist. You can ride back to the city with me, even, if it seems very serious."

"I don't think—"

"We could arrange for next week, maybe. A week from Monday."

Anne-Marie opened her mouth to protest, then sat mute. Her eyes filled with tears of hatred. And shame: for Constance Price was a witness.

"All right," she said in her new, faint voice. "Thank you."

"What? I didn't hear that."

"Yes. Thank you. *That will be fine*."

"Why don't any of your friends come over this summer?" Mrs. Thayer asked.

Anne-Marie, leafing through an old copy of the *Saturday Evening Post* from a pile of magazines stacked beside the fireplace, shrugged her shoulders and did not bother to reply.

"You didn't quarrel with Dolores again, did you? And that nice girl from last year—the one who played tennis so well—Edith Dacey—"

"Edith isn't up this year. She's in Europe."

"Alone? By herself?"

"How would I know?"

"But Dolores? I saw her and her mother over in Woodstock a few days ago, I waved but couldn't stop—I was driving and they were walking and—"

"I see Dolores," Anne-Marie said patiently. "I see her as much as I care to. She's just down the hill—there's no problem."

"Last year there were two or three girls, you had such a good time with the pool—"

"People have their own pools."

She swatted at a large black spider, scurrying groggily across the floor. It left a considerable smear on the slate.

"How ugly," Mrs. Thayer said, staring in disgust at *her*.

But not an hour afterward she asked, again, crinkling her eyes as she did when she meant to be charming, or when she'd had too much to drink, why none of Anne-Marie's friends came over that summer.

"You know," Anne-Marie said.

"What?"

"You know why."

"Why?—Because you don't invite them."

Anne-Marie said nothing.

"And why don't you invite them?"

Anne-Marie stared at her bare dirty toes. The big toes were giants, the little toes stubby. The nail of her right toe was thickened and somewhat discolored: the boots she'd insisted upon wearing all winter were too tight but she had not wanted to give them up. Even now the toes sometimes hurt. It had bled beneath the nail, in near-invisible bluish streaks.

"You know why," she said hoarsely.

"Poor Connie. Just because of *her?*"

In a bright green dress with a halter top, her hair newly blond and curly as a poodle's, Mrs. Thayer drew back like a woman in a play; like an amused sophisticated woman in a light summer play. Her eyes crinkled all the more. Her lips stretched into a doubting, and somewhat mocking, smile.

"You hadn't better let your father know about this," she said.

"He knows. Obviously."

"He's her only relative—he's all she has. And after that operation last year—"

"He is not Constance's only relative," Anne-Marie said, shutting her eyes. "That's bullshit."

"Anne-Marie."

"He isn't all she has! And anyway what difference does it make! She was living in Washington, wasn't she, she had a job there, she was—"

"It was Oregon. Portland, Oregon."

"She was living alone there, wasn't she? Why for Christ's sake did she have to come back east—"

"She isn't well, you know that, don't talk so loud!...There's nothing wrong with Constance visiting us," Mrs. Thayer said. "Your father wants her here. I want her here. She's a remarkable woman, she gets along very well with our friends...."

Anne-Marie made an amused, sobbing noise.

"Everyone has commented on how charming she is, how soft-spoken, and attractive, and...."

"Do they ask about the murder? The shotgun?"

"Anne-Marie, it wasn't murder. You know that."

"What her husband looked like afterward?—what it felt like to pull the trigger? And all the police—"

"It wasn't murder. You don't understand these things. The poor woman was acquitted, we're all simply trying to forget, it was a tragedy of course but—"

"*It was a tragedy of course*," Anne-Marie said, raising her eyebrows like her mother. "But for who? For him?—or her?"

"It was self-defense. There were mitigating circumstances. Her husband was a beast, a— Why are you laughing? There isn't anything funny about this."

"Her husband was a beast. He drank, he gambled, he beat her up, he ran around with queers, he threatened her with a hunting knife, he did all sorts of fanciful things, he got his head blown off, he left her a million dollars: I agree, it isn't funny. It just sounds funny."

"Most of the money went to the lawyers, as you know. And it wasn't a million. It was nowhere near a million."

Anne-Marie staggered past her mother, pressing the palms of both hands against her temples. She would burst into tears in another moment, she would scream unforgivable things at her mother. As it was she said, "You—you only want her here for how bizarre it is—so people can say *Aren't the Thayers generous, aren't they liberal*—so they can say *Isn't Ginny Thayer daring—imaginative—*"

"Anne-Marie, that's ridiculous—"

"I hate you! I hate us all! I wish, I wish," she said, blundering into the doorframe, sobbing hoarsely, "I wish we were all *dead*."

In dark green sunglasses, in a denim skirt that fell just below the knee, Constance Price walked the mile and a half to the village of Sharon Springs; or across the Revolutionary War Memorial Park to the old Episcopal Church and its hilly, crammed churchyard; or along the Green River; or along the narrow, crazily slanted lanes of Sharon Springs where most of the houses were historical landmarks—some covered in brown shingleboard, some white like the Thayers', one or two immensely and absurdly regal, year-round mansions made of stone and timber. She swam in the morning, walked in the afternoon, visited the little library in town, did not shy away from speaking to friends of the Thayers who spoke to her on the street. She was, Anne-Marie could see, conscious of herself and her special destiny at all times. As if she knew herself being watched, spied-upon. *The murderess did this today. The murderess did that. She was reported to have walked as far as the village limits of Chittendon today, obviously the woman is restless, bored, lonely, uneasy....*

Once, back in June, strolling along an unpaved road with Dolores Foss, Anne-Marie saw her father's cousin ahead and could not avoid speaking to her; and introducing her to Dolores.

Dolores did not hesitate to shake hands with Constance and say, "I'm very happy to meet you, Mrs. Price."

And Constance smiled her cool startled smile and said, "I'm very happy to meet you, Dolores."

A minute's awkwardness: Anne-Marie's stammering: and then somehow, somehow (Anne-Marie was never able to comprehend how, afterward; not even years afterward) Dolores and Constance were talking quite effortlessly about Middlebury College, and the language program there, and the possibility of Dolores's taking a course in Chinese next summer though she wouldn't have graduated from high school yet; and it was revealed that Constance Price, many years ago, had taken courses in Oriental culture; she had in fact majored in art history at Barnard and had always planned to continue her studies with a concentration in....

When Anne-Marie and Dolores walked on, fifteen or twenty minutes later, and Constance Price was out of earshot, Dolores said in a warm, wondering voice: "But she's so *nice*."

Anne-Marie laughed coarsely. She was still trembling from the outrage and shame of the encounter. "But why shouldn't she be nice, Dolores. What are you getting at?"

Thereafter she avoided Dolores.

And the other girls as well, the two or three she knew. They were shallow anyway, the spoiled daughters of wealthy idle parents who had nothing better to do than gossip....What was the notorious Constance Price really like, they wondered. Was she at all "repentant"? Had her life been completely ruined? Had she spent any time in jail?—not even overnight? No? Yes? But surely she has had psychiatric treatment? And the Thayers: did they really feel safe with her in the house, did they really feel comfortable? Could they sleep well at night?—These were questions Anne-Marie felt flying about her head when she bicycled through the village.

Dolores called only once, a week after the encounter with Constance Price. "Hey," she said. "Anne-Marie."

Anne-Marie mumbled a reply.

"What's wrong? Is something wrong?"

"What?"

"Is something wrong?"

Anne-Marie, blushing angrily, could think of no reply.

Dolores chatted for a few minutes until her voice faltered. And then the girls backed away from each other by making vague, tentative plans to meet, and Anne-Marie hung up, and that was it.

*

"You've kept my friends from me this summer," Anne-Marie whispered to Constance Price, who sat pretending to listen to a conversation between Robin Wilks and Anne-Marie's mother and a handsome graying couple new to the area who were somehow associated with a Festival of the Arts at Dartmouth. "You've poisoned everything."

Constance smiled at Anne-Marie whenever they met. The smile was calm, measured, courteous and without meaning. As the weeks passed Anne-Marie came to see it as mocking. *If you want to ask about it why don't you. If you're curious like everyone else. You hate me and want me gone: why don't you speak up? Coward.*

But she said only, once, as Anne-Marie climbed out of the pool in haste as she prepared to enter: "Is something wrong?"

In Southampton, six years before, Constance Price had shot her husband Travis Price with one of his hunting guns. There were no witnesses: the shooting had taken place in the Prices' bedroom very early one morning, one Sunday morning in June.

Robin Wilks, a bachelor in his fifties who spent July and August in Sharon Springs each year, and travelled about the world as a cultural journalist for *Time-Life* the rest of the year, queried Ginny Thayer so gravely and so politely on the subject that one would not have known he already knew everything about the case. So Anne-Marie judged, sitting with them, sucking iced tea through a straw and trying not to laugh.

"It was a terrible, terrible thing," Mrs. Thayer sighed, "poor Lowell was very upset as you can imagine though the two of them were never close.... I mean they hardly knew one another, they're cousins twice removed. It was such a tragedy."

"I remember it very vaguely from the newspapers," Robin Wilks said. "The usual sensational headlines...."

They spoke softly as though Constance might overhear. But in fact Constance had driven over to Hanover that morning, to use the university library.

"Didn't she stand mute at the arraignment and make no attempt to defend herself..." Robin Wilks said.

"And there were so many ugly, hideous stories!" Mrs. Thayer said, shuddering. "That dreadful husband of hers. We never met him, of course—never knew him. It was all quite a surprise to us. To Lowell and me. But he was evidently in the habit of bringing home with him all kinds of.... And he abused her, evidently, and threatened her...." Mrs. Thayer glanced over at Anne-Marie who was staring blankly at her. "Well, it was a horrible thing and all we want is to forget it. The poor woman is still young, she's hardly my age..."

They were silent for a while. Anne-Marie finished her drink noisily and Robin Wilks lit a cigarette, tapping it thoughtfully on the back of his hand. "And after the acquittal she went to England, didn't she, and then came back to the States and got a job, at a girls' school, wasn't it, in Connecticut? And a parents' committee got her fired. I remember reading about that a few years ago just by accident.... Or do I have the sequence jumbled?"

"It's just a tragic thing that we're trying to forget," Mrs. Thayer said firmly. But her skin glowed; her small hopeful eyes had brightened. "Of course we never talk about it with Constance. She's the most reserved, dignified person.... I've never even heard her raise her voice. Not once."

"It was certainly generous of you and Lowell to invite her here," Robin said.

"Oh no! Not at all. I mean—was it? But why," Mrs. Thayer said, confused, smiling, "why do you think so? She hasn't anyone else—She's all alone—she *isn't well*, you know—"

"Everyone thinks it was very generous," Robin said expansively.

"Everyone? But—Well—She isn't any trouble at all, not really," Mrs. Thayer said, blushing with gratification. "In fact she's almost too quiet, too detached—secretive in a way—Do you know what I mean? Have you sensed that about her, Robin?"

"I think I have," he said slowly, nodding, avoiding Anne-Marie's beacon-like glare. "Yes. Indeed I think I have."

*

Why did you do it, Anne-Marie asked.

Because I wanted to, Constance said curtly.

Yes but why. Why, Anne-Marie whispered, frightened of the woman's calm expressionless gaze.

Because I wanted to, Constance said. Which is why we do everything we do.

* * *

The murderess was quite striking in a long skirt, aqua with faint golden-green streaks, and a white silken blouse. Her hair was austere and regal as usual but did not seem to weigh so heavily upon her head. There was color to her face, especially her cheeks; and her thin nervous smiling lips were a dark pink. So, Anne-Marie thought shrewdly, a transformation. Witch-like. And would it do the trick?

She was not a beautiful woman and would never be beautiful again. But it was no puzzle, that a business associate of Mr. Thayer's, up for the weekend, should be talking with her animatedly, and at such great length.

What were they talking about, those two?—off in a corner so long?

Anne-Marie drifted by, checking ashtrays; checking for crumpled-up cocktail napkins and toothpicks that might be lying about on the floor. Such a din of voices! Exclamations, laughter, ritual noises of pleasure and well-being and hope. But what were *those two* talking about?

She wondered—did he know, had he been informed of the woman's past, what she had done? Had her father explained the "circumstances"?

Anne-Marie was last at the buffet table, last of all, behind even the most dilatory stragglers. It was her strategy to stay clear of the others in order to more accurately observe.

"Anne-Marie? There's a seat here," Constance Price said, raising her eyes to Anne-Marie who passed by wraith-like. "Your mother has brought some extra chairs out...."

Anne-Marie did not hear. She carried her plate of food to the far corner of the terrace where her father and several others were seated. She would have left the lighted area and walked to the very edge of the property, as far away from the gaiety as possible, except that her absence would be noticed.

* * *

By accident—or was it by accident—Anne-Marie ran and dived from the side of the pool one morning when she could bear it no longer (the last week of August was bitterly disappointing: a chilly rain and no more than a few hours of sun and her parents' guests hogged the pool and what was Anne-Marie to do, prowl about the old house as she'd done most of the summer, poking in trunks and boxes and closets, sniffing out mildew and rot, allowing herself a minute's weeping over charming clumsy little drawings she'd done as a child of three or four, stuffed now in a box in what had been the "art room" on the closed-off third floor—what was she to do, play another dispirited game of backgammon with her mother or solitaire with herself)—and entered the pool at such an angle that her legs, her knees, struck Constance Price's back, and the woman cried out in pain and surprise, and lost the rhythm of her breast-stroke, and swallowed water, and began to sink—

It happened so quickly, and Anne-Marie's legs were numbed with the pain of that astonishing impact, and she too gasped and swallowed water and threshed about in panic—

When she reviewed that moment, as she was to do many times: countless times: she was always to say that it had been an accident. She'd run across the grass, she'd been certain no one else was in the pool, she'd simply dived in without looking and in the next instant there was so much confusion and pain and alarm and—

Did you almost drown, people asked.

No. I don't think so. Not me.

Did *she* almost drown?

Reviewing that moment, contemplating that moment, Anne-Marie would often begin to tremble uncontrollably. And if Constance Price was not nearby she would say, quite frankly: She did drown. She did. She was dead—almost. Her heart had stopped. I know it. I know it.

But you saved her.

I saved her, Anne-Marie would say, shutting her eyes. I pulled her into the shallow end and up onto the cement and I did all the things I'd been taught to do like a mechanical doll I did them, I did them, I straddled her and pressed my hands against her ribs as I'd been taught in swimming class and I wasn't even crying, I wasn't even begging her to come back, I did what I was taught to do and after ten or twelve or fifteen times she began to choke, and cough, and vomit spilled out of her mouth and she was alive again—

"Anne-Marie likes to exaggerate," Constance sometimes said. "Of course I wasn't dead. I don't think, really, that I was even unconscious. I had an idea of what was going on...."

"You were unconscious," Anne-Marie would say, stricken and amazed, and staring even now with wonder at Constance's face. "You weren't breathing any longer."

"It was like a dream, I can half-remember it. Apart from my back it didn't even hurt very much."

"It hurt, it hurt," Anne-Marie would say, gripping her fists between her knees and rocking lightly, as if she were trying to bear the pain of it, trying not to give in to it herself. "Oh my God it hurt. But you came back: you didn't die. As soon as I saw you were vomiting I knew you wouldn't die and I hadn't killed you."

"Of course you hadn't killed me," Constance would laugh. "What a thing to say—! If I had died, if I *had* drowned, it wouldn't have been your fault—it was just an accident, a foolish accident. I think we were both equally to blame."

"Do you? *Do* you?" Anne-Marie would ask with her doubtful, radiant smile, brushing her forefinger beneath her nose and sniffing like a child. "Oh I don't. *I* don't. But then I know better."

* * *

After the accident Constance spent a few days in bed, and on the wicker chaise longue in the old sun room, convalescing. She was groggy from the pain-killing pills she'd had to take; she spoke slowly and carefully, like a woman trying to wake from a dream, too confused to be frightened. Anne-Marie never left her. When she was able to go outdoors Anne-Marie supported her, walking with her arm about her waist.

They avoided the pool, avoided that side of the house. In an overgrown, dragonfly- and butterfly-busy old garden they sat, sunning themselves, talking. One day Anne-Marie stammered out the single line of poetry she thought the most moving she'd ever come across, the most gripping—*I see a whale in the South-sea drinking my soul away*—and then could not speak, the moment was so tense. Constance Price did not laugh at her agitation, she did not even murmur agreement; instead she reached over to squeeze Anne-Marie's clenched hand.

By Labor Day Constance was well enough to drive to Hanover, where she and Anne-Marie went to an arts exhibit. They walked slowly about the campus of Dartmouth and had a late lunch in a beer garden, sitting at a table made of an enormous old wooden cable spool; acquaintances of the Thayers saw them, and unfortunately came over to join them, but they were able to slip away before long without appearing rude. They strolled back to the arts exhibit and Constance bought Anne-Marie a hand-wrought silver bracelet. "Oh but why?" Anne-Marie laughed, blushing. "It's so beautiful but— But why get it for *me*—"

"Well, you saved my life after all," Constance said.

Anne-Marie glanced at her but could not determine if she was mocking, or sincere. But the bracelet was quite lovely: she could not refuse it.

* * *

When Anne-Marie graduated from high school she spent the summer travelling with Constance Price in Italy, France, Spain, and England; her postcards to Mr. and Mrs. Thayer were breezy and euphoric, but disturbingly enigmatic—for though Anne-Marie was to begin classes at Sarah Lawrence that fall she made no allusion to college, or to returning at all. Nor did she write letters, or telephone home as her parents had wished.

"It was that woman," the Thayers were to say, afterward. For years afterward. "That murderess…"

Anne-Marie enrolled in classes at the Art School of the University of London, and majored in art history, and in time did graduate work in her field of specialization—Symbolist art, with a special concentration on the work of Lucien Lévy-Dhurmer. She lived with Constance Price for a while, then travelled about on her own, then moved back to London to rent a flat a few blocks from Constance's flat in Kensington; in all that time she never asked about Constance and the murder, Constance and the famous sensational shameful murder. Nor did Constance speak of it.

Why did you do it, she wondered.

Because I wanted to.

Yes—but why?

As the years passed she no longer wondered about it, in fact no longer thought about it. Apart from the Thayers everyone forgot both Anne-Marie and Constance.

—Though once in Heathrow Airport Robin Wilks came upon them, the two of them, waiting for the arrival of a plane from Amsterdam, had it been?—waiting for a friend. It had been many years but he recognized Constance at once, and Anne-Marie in a minute or two.

Constance Price was by that time in her late fifties, somewhat heavier, but still a very attractive woman. Her pale, thinning hair was fixed in a knot at the back of her head; she wore a dark, wine-colored suit; she gave Robin Wilks her hand and was courteous with him though it was evident she did not remember him at all. Anne-Marie was a tall, slender young woman of about thirty, soft-spoken, shyly bold—she asked with a droll downturning of her mouth if he still spent summers at Sharon Springs, and if her poor mother was still flirting with him—more attractive than she had been as a girl. They talked briefly of the States, of New York City, of Vermont, of various national and international events; of Robin's planned retirement in another year; of Anne-Marie's classes (she taught at a small college south of London); of Constance's plans for travel; and very gingerly, and adroitly, of the Thayers' disappointment in Anne-Marie. Evidently the girl still went home fairly often, at least once a year, but she had no wish to live in the States and there was usually a quarrel, so it was difficult—a difficult situation.

But Robin, afterward, reflecting on the two of them—on how they had looked before he approached them, talking together earnestly, animatedly, as if they had just met or were new acquaintances or were a mother and daughter who were exceptionally close, did not suppose that it was a difficult situation at all. They were lying, he thought. Guilty and lying.

SOUL/MATE

For Han and Bill Heyen,
"soul mates"

PART
ONE

I

Dorothea Deverell knew herself at a disadvantage.

On this drizzly misty evening of November 14, driving in her secondhand Mercedes to the dinner party that would forever alter the course of her life, Dorothea—thirty-nine years old, widowed for fourteen years, and for all of those years childless—felt the sharpness of disadvantage like an early, ominous, shivering presage of the flu: and did not like the feeling. She did not like it because it was too familiar.

She was already twenty minutes late for the Weidmanns' dinner party (which she did not much want to attend, in any case, since her lover and her lover's wife were also to be guests), and she had been so delayed in leaving the Institute (where she was assistant to the Director, a charmingly incompetent gentleman who not only publicly claimed he could do nothing without Miss Deverell's help but saw to it that the extravagant claim was daily, even hourly, substantiated) she had not had time to hurry home, bathe, calm her thoughts, and change into something more formal, and more feminine, than the navy cashmere suit she had worn that day to work —a Chanel ten years out of date, elegantly shabby, with raised slightly knobby shoulders and long sweeping skirt to mid-calf that gave her the look, as her lover, Charles, once remarked, of a sweetly befuddled prioress in a nineteenth-century French novel. Dorothea dreaded being late for any occasion. however innocently, out of a fear that those awaiting her might guess she really did not want to come at all; sociable gatherings, though the very life's blood of the unmarried and the staple, so to speak, of her administrative work at the Institute—she was in charge of scheduling lectures, chamber music concerts, art exhibits, trustees' meetings, charity functions, luncheons, receptions, and many another gregarious event at the community-minded Morris T. Brannon Institute—often filled her with a mysterious malaise.

That morning Charles had telephoned her in her office to ask if she was going to the Weidmanns' tonight, and Dorothea had said in a weakly ebullient voice, "Of course—I wouldn't miss one of Ginny's lovely parties for the world, would you?" "God, yes," Charles said. He spoke with more than usual vehemence; he was no more naturally sociable than Dorothea, though, like Dorothea, he usually managed to acquit himself well at such events; even, upon occasion, to shine. He was a tall lean greyhound sort of man, in his late forties, with sandy-silvery hair, a fair face splashed with pale freckles, a frowning smile, somber pebble-colored eyes beneath rather prominent brows—trained in the law but reserved, even shy. Ah, yes, enormously shy! He and Dorothea Deverell had been romantically involved with each other, to the ambiguous degree that they *were* romantically involved with each other, for more years than Dorothea cared to recall. "And is Agnes coming too?" Dorothea heard herself ask, rubbing harshly at an eye; and Charles said, "She plans to be, yes," with a just perceptible sigh, an exhalation of breath Dorothea would not have noted had she not had so many years' practice. "Well," she said. "Well," Charles said. The line went silent, though not yet dead; like two shy, bumbling adolescents they did not want to say goodbye. Finally Dorothea said, in a resolutely neutral voice, "I'd heard from Ginny that Agnes was sick," and Charles said quickly, "She *was*, last week, with a migraine headache, and nerves, and—the usual. But she's better now. And she intends to come to dinner tonight; she wouldn't miss one of Ginny Weidmann's parties, she says, for the world." "How nice," Dorothea said dryly. Her lips twitched in a fierce little smile, but of course Charles Carpenter, miles away on the far side of town, could not see.

Ginny and Martin Weidmann, whom Dorothea had known from the days of her marriage—her young, doomed husband had been in fact a classmate of Martin's at Williams College—lived in the most fashionable section of town, in a splendid old "Italianate

Victorian" house with a square central tower, tall narrow fretwork-framed windows, steep shingled roof. The very street was antique and otherworldly: cobbled, in chronic need of repair, banked in so severely at the curb that Dorothea invariably scraped the lower edges of the Mercedes' fenders whenever she parked in front of the house—as she was now doing. "Why am I here?" she cried aloud. She foresaw that it would be one of those evenings when nothing would happen that had not happened countless times before.

Judging by the cars parked on the street and in the Weidmanns' circular driveway, all the other guests were here. She recognized the Carpenters' white Cadillac, on the opposite side of the street, poised as if for a quick getaway. Impractical eye-catching white had been Agnes' choice though she rarely drove the car; Charles did all the driving.

Dorothea rang the doorbell breathlessly and smiled her bright beautiful smile as Ginny embraced her and scoldingly greeted her—"You're almost half an hour late, Dorothea! It isn't like you! We were all worried!" Inside, the hum and buzz of conversation filled the downstairs, like a familiar piece of music; there was a delicious odor of roasting lamb; smells of wine, flowers, fruit. The Weidmanns' black maid, Tula, came to take her coat away, and for a blurred instant Dorothea had a consoling glimpse of herself in Ginny's antique Venetian mirror—she did not look nearly so haggard as she felt. Her burnished-mahogany hair fell smoothly about her face as if it had been conscientiously brushed, her large intelligent brown eyes shone with expectation. "How lovely you look, Dorothea, all the same!" Ginny said ambiguously. "That suit is so becoming!"—with a fleeting frown that cut Dorothea's heart. (For it meant, didn't it, that the suit had become by now too familiar? that it wasn't at all the sort of thing Dorothea should have worn this evening?) Ginny was perfumy, chatty, Junoesque, her hostess gown as splotched with color as chintz wallpaper. She was a dear friend of Dorothea's who did not in truth know Dorothea very well; one of those older, dauntingly generous married women who see it as their task to find the perfect mates for their unmarried female friends. Over the years Ginny had introduced Dorothea to so many eligible bachelors, Dorothea swung between a sense of guilt for having failed her and a sense of outrage for being so frequently hauled up on the auction block, against her will and, indeed, often without her knowing what was going on—until it was too late. She had begun to feel like one of those suddenly stubborn mares who at a certain weary age refuse to "stand" for a stallion and have to be impregnated, if at all, by artificial means.

Thus Ginny Weidmann—who meant, of course, only well—was now hurriedly briefing Dorothea on the subject of tonight's candidate, another in her seemingly inexhaustible store of very nice men, gentlemanly men, business associates of Martin's. "Why do you look so surprised, Dorothea? Surely you haven't forgotten? I *told* you I was inviting Jerome Gallagher tonight, didn't I?" Ginny asked.

"Yes, I'm sure you did," Dorothea said quickly.

Wineglass in hand, husky voice lowered, Ginny provided Dorothea with a hurried compendium of facts regarding Mr. Gallagher to which Dorothea made a spirited pretense of listening. Surely this too was familiar? She understood that, remaining unmarried for so long, she was a sort of enigma to her friends and that after a certain period of time there is something disquieting, even disagreeable, about an enigma. She was trained as an art historian at Yale; traveled and studied abroad in her early twenties; came home and met, fell in love with, and married a young French architect, newly an American citizen, named Michel Deverell, who died in an automobile accident on a Boston expressway, aged twenty-eight, when Dorothea was herself only twenty-five years old and recovering from a miscarriage suffered in the seventh month of a difficult pregnancy. And how quickly the subsequent years had passed, how swiftly and seemingly without event her life was passing from her! There was Charles Carpenter, whom she had known since her marriage, and whom, for the past eight or nine years, she had loved, but their affair, their friendship, was a strictly private matter, suspected perhaps by some—by Agnes Carpenter? by sharp-eyed Ginny Weidmann herself?—but not known: decidedly not known. It was Dorothea's custom, when asked discomfortingly personal questions, to say simply, "I was married once, a long time ago; my husband died when I was twenty-five. I've worked for the Brannon Institute since 1982." She did not willingly elaborate; though shy, she was also stubborn, the sort of person, usually female, who so subtly shifts the subject away from herself, and onto others, the finesse of the maneuver goes unremarked. Vaguely it was thought that Dorothea Deverell had been pregnant when her young husband had died and had lost her baby as a consequence, was thus a doubly tragic figure, and this misconception Dorothea could scarcely correct, for it belonged to the genteel mythologizing of her life to which she had no access: like the belief that she was, for all her well-bred delicacy of manner, actually a woman of enormous unexercised passion (like the proverbial virginal prioress) and that she was an heiress of considerable means who did not therefore require serious advancements in position or salary at the Institute—this, the most invidious notion of all, based on the evidence of haphazard items inherited years ago from an elderly great-aunt, including the 1979 Mercedes-Benz 500 SEL, which was always stalling on the expressway, a well-worn natural stone marten coat several sizes too large for her, and various pieces of costume jewelry, furniture, and household goods. If the mythologizing did not represent her, neither did it betray her, and Dorothea took care not to contradict its general outline. She knew that she was locally admired, even, to a warming degree, well liked: she was lovely, she was reliable, she was beautifully mannered, she was *good*. Yet even to her face people evinced airs of pity, for, having such advantages, why then did Dorothea Deverell appear so disadvantaged? At the last dinner party at the Weidmanns' she'd attended, not so many months ago, at which, thank God, Charles Carpenter and his wife had not been guests, a well-intentioned older gentleman had inquired of her at the dinner table, in full hearing of the others, why a pretty girl like herself wasn't married, his very words being, unblushing, in fact quite forceful and accusing: "Why isn't a pretty girl like you *married*?" And Dorothea had smiled and had replied, sweetly enough, though inwardly trembling and feeling a rude hot blush rise up into her face, "I was, once—when I *was* a girl."

And the entire table went silent, eyes averted. For a space of several awkward seconds.

Now Ginny was saying, "Oh, and another thing. What *is* this campaign of Roger Krauss's against you? I hear such—"

They were midway in the Weidmanns' polished and sparkling foyer, about to join the festive group in the living room, when, to Dorothea's dismay, Ginny did a characteristic thing—even to laying an exclamatory hand on Dorothea's arm and squeezing. Having just thought of this new subject, Ginny, who was all spontaneity, emotion, and thoughtlessness, not unlike an overgrown bullying child, could not keep it to herself for a more felicitous moment but had to thrust it immediately at Dorothea, as if, indeed, thrusting it into her appalled face: "I hear such disturbing things, Dorothea, *really!* We must talk!"

"But now? Must we talk of that terrible man now?" Dorothea cried with a despairing little laugh.

The older woman, regarding her with some concern, relented and merely shook her head, making her diamond earrings flash and her splendidly glowing red-rinsed hair catch the light. Dorothea's heart panicked in her breast. She had now to compose her face, her very self, as best as she could, entering the living room in which her unacknowledged lover awaited her—her lover, and the others. Ah, how she did not want to appear in their eyes as she so sadly, emphatically, felt: one of those persons of whom the world says with surprise and pity, But how unfair! how unfair, her life!

Dorothea Deverell had fallen in love with Charles Carpenter by degrees; even, it might be said, against her will. She was a woman of principle and she did not believe in provoking others to violate principle—and Charles was of course a married man. However unhappily and pointlessly, a married man. At every step she had warned herself, *You'll regret this!* like a brash child venturing out onto thin ice, ever outward onto thin thin ice, wind wailing in her ears and heart pumping: *You'll regret this! You'll regret this!* How very unlike the precipitous headlong plunge into passion, emotion, and eventually grief she had experienced with the young French architect. (Dorothea had known her husband so briefly, if tenderly, it seemed natural for her to think of him in formal terms. And, dead at twenty-eight, he would remain forever young.) Charles Carpenter was a partner in a prestigious Boston law firm for which Michel Deverell's architectural firm had done some work; thus the two couples came to know one another socially, if not intimately ; but it was during Dorothea's first flush of local renown, when she was establishing herself as a new bright cultural presence in Lathrup Farms (a suburban village, resplendent on Boston's North Shore) that she became reacquainted with the Carpenters: with Charles in particular.

One Sunday afternoon he had appeared seemingly out of nowhere close beside her to touch her shoulder and murmur, "Dorothea? Might we talk? alone?—for a minute—back along here?" as with a surprisingly forcible grip of her elbow he led her along a rather slippery marble walkway out of sight and earshot of a crowd of others; and Dorothea, frightened, excited, guilty, had known at once what the man intended and how she would respond. The occasion was a large cocktail reception for some charity purpose held in one of the area's stately old homes, a neo-Georgian mansion overlooking the Bay, one of those from which Mrs. Carpenter had mysteriously absented herself, requiring of her husband that he convey her apologies and offer, never quite convincingly, an explanation of some kind—usually having to do with health. It would be false to say that Dorothea had not been aware of Charles Carpenter for some time, and aware of his interest in her; that she did not bloom in his company, enlivened by his wit and the vigor of his conversation; that she had not in fact often sought him out at such gatherings, as a way of establishing that the gathering, for her, had some human validity. And now Charles was saying in a hurried undertone, staring at Dorothea's face, "I don't want to embarrass you, Dorothea, and I certainly don't want to alarm you, but I seem to have fallen in love with you, and I thought that you should know."

Dorothea said softly, wonderingly, "Yes."

So it began, their romance, their mildly adulterous friendship, with Charles talking and Dorothea listening: an attractive couple in young middle age whose rapt interest in each other would have been (perhaps was?) self-evident to any incidental observer. So long a widow in her own and the world's imagination, Dorothea had felt herself comfortably a virgin again; her womb, emptied of any substance, was again a virgin's womb, chaste, tight, and inviolate. Hearing Charles Carpenter's faltering, agitated, but finally quite moving declaration of love and his desire to see her privately, as soon as possible, if only she would allow it, Dorothea remained strangely calm: as (so memory cruelly tossed up to her) she'd been, at first, when news came of Michel's death, and she had stood in their little rented Beacon Street apartment listening, nodding, head bowed, nothing to say, only a few practical questions to ask. If her eyes had flooded with tears they were not so much tears of emotion as simply a nervous response, as if she had been slapped hard across the face. *You'll regret this!* she told herself coolly, but there she was agreeing just the same to see Charles Carpenter, a married man, the very next evening. And to tell him, as he loomed dangerously near to her, squeezing her hand in his, that she was very fond of him too: she'd long thought of him, she said, as a special friend, to whom she might have turned in time of trouble.

Yet, after the early delirium of intimacy, the fierce whispered declarations, vows, promises, proposals, their feelings for each other quickly acquired a kind of equilibrium, or stasis. Charles telephoned—or did not telephone; they met surreptitiously once, or twice, or three times a week—or did not meet at all. So weeks yielded to months, and months to years. Eight years? Nine? There were periods when Dorothea seemed in retreat, as if gripped by conscience; there were periods when Charles seemed in retreat, as if nettled or hurt by Dorothea's display of conscience or stricken by his own. As passion waxed in one it was likely to wane in the other, following a melancholy law of human paradox, so that if Charles suggested telling Agnes everything and asking for a divorce, Dorothea was likely to resist, uneasily reminding him that his wife was not a well woman and would be humiliated by such an event; if Dorothea in an outburst of temper suggested that she'd had enough of subterfuge, she would be seen with Charles publicly or not at all, Charles might point out, reasonably enough, that it was she, with her sensitive position at the Institute, who would suffer the more—"Of course I want us to marry, I want it with all my heart, but is this the right time? Have you thought it through seriously? Have you considered the consequences?" Not for nothing was Charles Carpenter trained in the law.

And so—the years. Dorothea had her work (she was generally believed to be next in line for the directorship at the Institute, when the current director, Mr. Howard Morland, retired: Mr. Morland was sixty-six, no longer much engaged in his position, and very fond of Dorothea Deverell); and Dorothea had her friends, her numerous friends, one of whom was Charles Carpenter. She had the vague hazy warmly comforting conviction that, yes, she and Charles would one day be married, and there would be, in town, a new Mr. and Mrs. Charles Carpenter; perhaps they would live in a new house, in her fantasy one of the fine old restored eighteenth-century houses in the Weidmanns' neighborhood. When the time was "right." (Or had Charles said "ripe"?—his voice often dropped to a murmur in Dorothea's presence.)

Charles's wife, Agnes, remained oblivious of her husband's love for Dorothea Deverell. Or, if suspecting, had made up her mind not to care. She had become with the years one of those women, not uncommon in tightly knit social circles, who exudes an air of disappointment and irony like a pungent perfume assailing the nostrils of others. She dressed expensively but carelessly; her skin was sallow and unhealthy, and her eyes puffy-lidded; her round stolid face was a defiant pug's face, with the liverish cast of a being of action who has for mysterious reasons refused to act, so that her energy, her very life, had backed up in her, choking her. It was not known in Lathrup Farms whether she drank because of chronic ill health or whether her chronic ill health was the result of her drinking; whether she was "difficult" because she drank or drank because she was "difficult," trusting to alcohol to free instincts that social decorum would otherwise have suppressed.

In the many years of their acquaintance, Dorothea's only intimate encounter with Agnes Carpenter had been an embarrassing one. She had come upon the woman in a powder room one evening at one or another party, the wife of her lover, whom she envied, and feared, and hated, and often pitied, and there was Agnes Carpenter in a gold lamé pants suit leaning and swaying over a sink, so drunk her eyes were squeezed shut and her skin had gone a dead doughy ghastly white, and when Dorothea offered to help Agnes pushed her hands away blindly, crying, "Don't touch! Don't touch!" but then, a moment later, she begged, "Oh, God, help me please—" turning and staggering as Dorothea caught her in her arms and, in one of the toilet stalls, held the poor woman's shoulders while she retched into a toilet bowl, vomiting in long shuddering heaves. The bout of sickness had lasted perhaps ten minutes, during which time other women, venturing into the powder room, discreetly backed out again, leaving Dorothea Deverell to the task: which of course she acquitted ably, like a nurse's aide, hardly seeming to mind (though of course she minded terribly) that her black silk dress with the countless shimmering pleats was splashed with Agnes Carpenter's foul-smelling vomit while Agnes Carpenter's gold lamé came through unscathed. And after that unfortunate incident Agnes Carpenter's public manner with Dorothea Deverell was distinctly formal, if not chill.

Telling Ginny Weidmann about it (for she'd been, for all her scruples, unable to keep it to herself), Dorothea had said with a nervous laugh, "Now the woman is my enemy for life!" and Ginny had agreed, though not laughingly. Ginny said, "Agnes Carpenter is the kind of person you wouldn't choose for an enemy, any more than you'd choose her for a friend."

At the Weidmanns' elegantly set dining room table, amid the flutter of candle flames and the sparkle of silverware and the rich fragrance of rack of lamb and vegetables, Agnes Carpenter sat in a pose of polite attention, not swiftly but methodically draining her wineglass and allowing it, as if absentmindedly, to be refilled by Martin Weidmann. Talk ranged up and down the table—politics, a local art exhibit, mutual friends, a best-selling novel, the latest real estate development scandal—while Agnes Carpenter fussed unconvincingly with the food on her plate, cutting it up, Dorothea noted, into small pieces, and mucking the pieces about and leaving most of them. If Charles saw he naturally gave no sign; but perhaps, caught up in the conversation, glancing frequently at Dorothea, he did not see, exactly—for what after all could he do? She is a strong-willed woman, Charles had remarked to Dorothea once, rather vaguely, and Dorothea had not disagreed. Though thinking, What of me? Have I no will at all?

But she was determined to enjoy herself. As always, at the Weidmanns' table, the atmosphere was lively, exclamatory, irreverent, a bit loose at the edges, punctuated by Ginny's interruptions—"You did *what*? You said *what*?"—and by Martin's braying laughter. The food was superb, the wines delicious (and expensive); in twin etched-glass bowls at the center were pale yellow rosebuds that gave off a muted fragrance. In addition to the Weidmanns, the Carpenters, and Dorothea, there were three other guests: a striking Cleopatra-looking young woman in her late twenties named Hartley Evans, a new friend of Ginny's who worked for a Boston television station; a youngish jowly man named David Schmidt, who worked, as he rather too frequently mentioned, for a prominent brokerage firm in the city; and Jerome Gallagher, Dorothea's dinner companion for the evening, a tax lawyer whose habitual expression was sharply quizzical, as if he were hard of hearing, and whose bald head shone fiercely in the candlelight, like polished stone. We have all been brought together for a purpose, Dorothea thought, but what is the purpose? Is life, even in a world of couples, too lonely otherwise? Tonight she felt more than ordinarily on display since she and Charles were seated almost directly across from each other and obliged either to talk or, pointedly, not to talk to each other; and there was the distraction of Jerome Gallagher, Ginny's eligible bachelor of the evening, introduced to Dorothea with the aside, "You two have so much in common, I *envy* you!" So blunt a prognosis had the temporary effect of making them both tongue-tied, frowning Mr. Gallagher in particular, but, after some awkward false starts, Dorothea at last asked the inevitable question, "What sort of work do you do?" And Jerome Gallagher proceeded to tell her. She knew she could relax for the duration since as a female listener she was hardly required to respond except in monosyllables of agreement, enthusiasm, or wonder. Except for Charles Carpenter, men never asked Dorothea about her work.

Mr. Gallagher talked and Dorothea half listened, observing Charles and thinking how odd, how ironic; in the man's actual presence she often felt estranged from him, as in her reveries (indulged in daily, or rather nightly) she did not, even as she acknowledged his attractiveness: that angular fine-boned face, the light splash of freckles like raindrops, the alert intelligent eyes. And he dressed inconspicuously well, not stylishly but decently, wearing, Dorothea saw to her pleasure, a beautiful silk necktie she'd given him (and which Charles had had to mention to Agnes as an impulsive purchase of his own) and a fine bluish-gray pinstripe suit that fitted his tall lean frame elegantly. A man one might kill for, Dorothea thought, if one were that sort. That morning Charles had said he would rather have stayed home, except for seeing her, but he seemed to be enjoying the dinner party as much as anyone at the table, having struck up a spirited debate with Schmidt, a very vocal and opinionated young man (conservative, Republican, scornful of "federal restraints"), and the exotically made-up Hartley Evans (inky black hair smooth and synthetic as a wig, enormous blue-lidded eyes wide in perpetual surprise), in which Ginny Weidmann participated and to which Agnes Carpenter made a perfunctory pretense of listening, using the excuse of a change of plates to light a cigarette: parchment-colored cigarettes, Egyptian, which gave off a sharp acrid stench and within seconds drifted to Dorothea's sensitive nostrils and eyes. If Agnes had eaten little she had drunk much; her fleshy face seemed about to shift its contours; she laughed for no specific reason and raised a chunky hand to her brow—her enormous dinner ring, a square-cut jade bordered with diamonds, catching the light aggressively. Her damp derisive gaze shifted to Dorothea's face without taking hold, as if Dorothea's place were empty.

Why will you not give him up? Dorothea silently pleaded. When you don't love him? When you are standing in the way of others' happiness?

Then, to Dorothea's horror, conversation at the table shifted suddenly, like a landslide, and within seconds the subject was the "power struggle" at the Brannon Institute, in particular the unconscionable tactics employed by a new member of the board of trustees named Roger Krauss, in promoting a protégé of his while systematically denigrating Dorothea Deverell—from the position of being, as Krauss insisted, not at all anti*woman* but anti*feminist.* Krauss, who had been named to the board the previous spring, had taken public exception to several of the programs Dorothea had scheduled, most notoriously (for he had published an attack in the Lathrup Farms weekly paper) a traveling exhibit of women's sculpture; he was condescending or outright rude to Dorothea when they were thrown together, talked behind her back to other members of the board and to the director, Mr. Morland. That Krauss had his own candidate for the directorship, a nephew-in-law currently working at the Whitney Museum, was part of his campaign against Dorothea, but he was clever enough to present it only as a part; his real objection to her taking over the directorship, he said, was ideological. He would not trust her, he'd several times declared, not to "subvert" the Institute for her own political ends.... Dorothea laid down her fork in dismay, felt her face go painfully hot and her heart beat sullenly against her ribs. This was the very topic she dreaded their taking up, and the worst of it was they were obviously not so much taking it up as reverting back to it, as if, before Dorothea's belated arrival, they had been discussing it, and her, at length.

Her eyes snatched at Charles's, seeking solace. He was staring down at his plate as if sharing her discomfort. It pained Dorothea the more, wounded her in her pride, that her lover had learned of her predicament before she had explained it to him, before she had transformed it into a dryly amusing little anecdote, to mitigate her shame. Ginny was saying angrily, "It just seems to me so outrageously unfair that Dorothea, who has done a damned good job at the Institute, should be obliged to defend herself after all these years—and to defend herself against such spiteful attacks!"

Martin agreed, and so of course did Charles, who was still staring down at his plate, his lips pursed; the new people—David Schmidt, Hartley Evans, Jerome Gallagher—looked thoughtful if rather neutral; but Agnes Carpenter, exhaling smoke through both nostrils in a lavish gesture, said, "But Roger *is* excessive. It isn't his nature to do things by halves."

Ginny said, "A scorpion has its nature too!"

Unperturbed, Agnes Carpenter said, "Scorpions aren't required to be lovable. Only to be scorpions."

At this rather unthinking remark there was a startled silence; then Martin Weidmann came gallantly to Dorothea's rescue, and Charles said something impatient, and Ginny, excited, held forth at some length, the words *unfair, unjust, outrageous, misogynist* flying about Dorothea's head like crazed wasps. She tried not to listen; tried to smile, as if not minding in the slightest; wondered how it would be received if she simply rose from the table and left the room and stayed away until the subject was changed. The problem of Roger Krauss and his heartbreaking campaign against her was one Dorothea dealt with by not thinking about it at all:

simply blanking the horror out, as a dirtied wall is whitewashed, crudely and expediently.

Social life! Dorothea glanced at her watch and saw that it was only five minutes to ten. It seemed much later. There was a salad course yet to come, probably cheese and fruit, and of course dessert, coffee and liqueurs, and the rest, another hour at least to be endured before she could slip away home to fall exhausted into bed to dream of one day marrying Charles Carpenter and living a normal blessed life in a lovely old Lathrup Farms house, with a walled garden perhaps, and in cold windy weather Charles would build a fire in the fireplace, applewood for fragrance, and they would sit close together on the sofa clasping hands staring mesmerized at the dancing flames thinking *How lucky we are! How happy we are! How did such good fortune befall us?* Dorothea's eyes flooded with moisture as if flames were indeed singeing her eyeballs. Beside her Jerome was saying stiffly, "This fellow Krauss sounds like bad news. You might think about bringing a lawsuit against your employer, you know, if they do ease you out, if there really were promises made about advancement. Women are doing it all the time, these days."

Dorothea excused herself and hid away in the Weidmanns' gold-wallpapered little guest bathroom as long as she dared, and when she returned to the table, thank God, the subject of Krauss had been dropped and a fresh subject taken up. The salad course was just being served, and Martin Weidmann was opening another bottle of wine, and Agnes Carpenter was lighting up another parchment-colored cigarette and exhaling smoke through her nostrils. Dorothea thought of Toulouse-Lautrec, who dined frequently at the Eiffel Tower, and who said. "One place I do not have to see the Eiffel Tower is inside the thing."

And then the doorbell rang. And everyone went silent. And Ginny cried, "Who can that be?" as if, her table being full, no one else could possibly turn up at her door.

They listened as Tula went to answer.

*

"What a surprise! What an enormous, *lovely* surprise!"

The unexpected visitor was a great-nephew of Ginny Weidmann's named Colin Asch: a tall too-thin boy with shadowed eyes, a delicate-boned asymmetrical face, lank pale hair that fell nearly to his shoulders. Dorothea, quite taken by his appearance, would have put his age at twenty-three or -four. He wore a soiled sheepskin windbreaker with a broken zipper, khaki trousers, a black cashmere sweater badly stretched at the neck, and no shirt beneath; his skin was sallow as if with fatigue, and his chin and cheeks were lightly stubbled; pulled reluctantly into the dining room to meet his aunt's friends, he blinked, and frowned, and squirmed, like a nocturnal animal rudely confronted with light. With a maternal solicitude in which delight and accusation contended, Ginny several times exclaimed, "But we were expecting you *last* week, Colin! Weren't we, Martin? Where on earth *were* you last week? Of course it's all so vague, the way you young people live your lives!"

Except that Ginny's arm was linked through his, the boy looked as if, in a paroxysm of embarrassment, he would have liked to run out of the room. Dorothea felt sorry for him, hauled like a prize of some sort into his aunt's dining room, exhibited to her friends. (Ginny's own grown children, about whom Dorothea heard a good deal, were well adjusted, happy, moderately successful, and not in much need of their mother's fervent attention.) The boy stammered an apology and said he hadn't meant to interrupt a party, but by now Martin too was on his feet and insisting Colin should join them at the table; it was unthinkable that Colin not join them, plenty of room and plenty of food and surely Colin had not eaten: "You look," Martin said jovially, "as if you haven't eaten in weeks!"

"But maybe Colin would like to freshen up a bit first," Ginny said, belatedly noticing her nephew's disheveled appearance and the look of pained pinched fright about his eyes. "Would you, dear? And then have a little something to eat? Why don't you take him upstairs, Martin? He can change, if he'd like to, into something of yours."

With a desperate shoulder-squirming maneuver the boy wriggled free of Ginny's grasp, repeating that he hadn't meant to interrupt a party; he never went where he wasn't invited; he'd see them again some other time.

"But you *are* invited," Ginny persisted.

And Martin, laying a heavy paternal arm across the boy's narrow shoulders, said warmly, "You can't run away when you've only now arrived!"

Colin Asch stammered and resisted a bit longer, but the Weidmanns, united, were clearly too much for him, too practiced at this sort of benevolent bullying. Though Dorothea exchanged a swift amused look with Charles—how like Ginny and Martin this scene was!—she felt relieved at the outcome: that this lonely appearing melancholy young man should be cared for, at least temporarily, and made to join their company. There was something striking about him, his eyes, his face, his very stance, to which she could not have given a name, yet which seemed to her both exciting and familiar. In any case his presence in the Weidmanns' overheated dining room would give the evening a distinct note of validity.

In a flurry of excitement Ginny and Tula laid another place at the table, close beside Ginny at the head, and in a dramatic undertone Ginny said, "The poor boy! Poor Colin! He had had such a tragic life!" All her guests leaned forward expectantly; Ginny glanced toward the foyer and the stairs, as if to reassure herself that Colin and Martin were safely out of earshot.

"The first thing, which some of you may have read about, or I've told you about, years ago—it must have been fifteen years ago—Colin's parents' death and the way they died; it was too ghastly! Too terrible! My niece and her husband and Colin, who was twelve at the time, were in their car, my niece's husband was driving, and it was raining, and they were going over a bridge in the Adirondacks, just south of Lake Placid, one of those metallic-mesh bridges, or whatever you might call them—you know the kind, so particularly slippery—and this bridge was narrow and not in good repair and there was another car coming from the opposite direction and somehow my niece's husband lost control of his car—I really do think the other driver must have been speeding, or driving dangerously, but that was never established—and struck the railing, and the railing broke, and they plunged into the river. The boy managed to get out and swim to the surface, but his father and mother were trapped inside the car, in only about eight feet of water, so the boy tried to save them, diving back down trying to get the doors of the car open, trying to pull his mother free, and then his father; he'd dived back into the water a dozen times by the time police arrived, isn't it just hellish to imagine? My poor niece, who was so sweet! Her poor husband! But the poor boy most of all, to endure such a nightmare! Because he'd tried to save his parents and he'd failed, and"—here Ginny's voice dropped tremulously, and she glanced again back toward the stairs, one beringed hand pressed against her breasts—"and they said he'd been raving and delirious when the police came; he'd fought the police, insisting his parents were still alive and he could save them; the poor child, imagine, only twelve at the time and always so sensitive—he had musical talent, a lovely soprano voice, he had a talent for drawing and painting; my niece herself was an artist, she'd taught for a while at Holyoke—and it was said that Colin had gone mad in those minutes, that his mind simply shattered."

The very candles on the table seemed to shiver; Dorothea felt a pang of creaturely sympathy and horror, recalling in that instant the black engulfing wave not of madness but of the acquiescence to madness, to whim, accident, chance, fate, that had swept over her and threatened to drown her when Michel Deverell died.... I know now that God, as principle or presence, is sheerly madness, Dorothea had thought calmly.

In the silence that followed Ginny's account, Agnes Carpenter said, in the vague surprised tone of one who, expecting to be bored, is not after all bored, "Yes, I remember that. That freak accident. The boy trying to rescue his parents from the submerged car. It was in all the papers. There were photographs. I remember." As if delivering a coup de grace Ginny said quietly, "But that isn't all. There is more."

A few minutes later Martin returned to the table, having left Colin Asch upstairs to shower and change, and hearing Ginny's recitation of yet more tragedy, or wretched bad luck—following his parents' death Colin had been sent to a boarding school for boys in New Hampshire, at which the headmaster was discovered to have "preyed" upon certain of his young charges, evidently including Colin—he said in a reproving voice, "Ginny, I really don't think Colin would feel comfortable if he knew you were talking about him. He was quite anxious to leave, and I assured him it would be a quiet evening."

"But he can't hear us, he won't know," Ginny said.

"The important thing is he's so much better now," Martin said, "compared to the last time we saw him. We wouldn't want to upset him."

As if Martin had merely confirmed her point, Ginny said passionately, "That's the courageous part of it. The noble part. How the boy has been in and out of hospitals half his life, not exactly mental hospitals, please don't misunderstand me, but clinics of one kind or another, being treated for depression and anorexia and God knows what all else. After the scandal at the boarding school —the headmaster committed suicide, in fact—Colin had a breakdown and couldn't eat, couldn't sleep, refused to talk or respond to anyone, even had to be fed intravenously for a while, against his will. Then he recovered, to a degree, and was sent off to live with relatives in Baltimore, but that didn't work out for some reason, so he went back to another boarding school. Over the years most of the family has chipped in to help, and there was some insurance, of course, from his parents' deaths, and even a lawsuit some of the boys' parents brought against the school in New Hampshire—what is the name of that place, Martin?"

"Monmouth Academy," Martin said reluctantly, "but I really don't think you—"

"—which the school settled out of court, and all of this helped the financial problem somewhat, but only somewhat. Fortunately Colin is so bright and quick and serious about his studies, at least initially, he has managed to win several scholarships since graduating from high school—if in fact he ever did graduate from high school; I'm not sure on that point." Ginny paused breathlessly, glancing again toward the upstairs. There was no sound, no evidence of movement; Dorothea had a sudden surrealist vision of the fated boy, having overheard his aunt's somehow too animated voice, deciding on the spur of the moment to take revenge against her by slashing his throat in her bathroom. "But he has done well in recent years. I mean, fairly well. His life is a bit mysterious actually. He had a scholarship to the Rhode Island School of Design, and then he disappeared and turned up in New Mexico living with a colony of artists, and then he was backpacking through Europe and no one knew his whereabouts for months, and then—do you remember, Martin?—we ran into him, almost literally ran into him, in San Francisco, when we were out there for a convention of yours. He seemed to be alone, and he said he had a job as a salesman of some kind, door to door. He didn't seem eager to spend much time with us."

There was a pause. Hartley Evans asked, "Where does he live now?"

Ginny said, "That's it—no one exactly knows! He was in Europe this past summer, Amsterdam and Heidelberg mainly; then he backpacked through Germany and Italy and wound up somehow in northern Africa; and then a few weeks ago he telephoned us saying he was going to be driving through Boston, but the evening we expected him he didn't show up. Knowing Colin, we didn't worry too much, but Martin did check with the police, and there was nothing, and he never called of course to explain, and now tonight: here he is. He's such a sweet boy—you can see it in his eyes. And the tragedy of his young life—you can see *that* in his eyes. I wish there were more he would allow Martin and me to do, to help. But he has his pride too. He's twenty-seven years old, a grown man. He has his pride."

Martin said jovially, "Now, dear, I think that's enough."

Dorothea had listened intently to Ginny's account, wondering why she was so strangely moved. She recalled the philosopher's cryptic observation: Terrible experiences give one cause to speculate whether the one who experiences them may not be something terrible. She could not remember the name of the philosopher but knew he must be German.

When Colin returned to the dining room and was again rapidly introduced to the Weidmanns' guests, he had so radically altered his appearance—having showered, shaved, combed his damp pale hair back from his forehead, put on a fresh white shirt and a navy-knit tie of Martin's—Dorothea did not think she would have recognized him. Though exceedingly self-conscious, a bit embarrassed, even sullen, about the mouth, he managed to take his place at the head of the table, beside his beaming aunt, and he managed to smile—even, shyly, to laugh—as he began to eat. (He was clearly hungry, yet picked about in his food like a fastidious child.) Dorothea saw that his eyes moved quickly and ceaselessly from one guest to another, one face to another; she imagined that for a beat or two he lingered at her own, frankly stared, and then moved on. He knows we have been talking about him, Dorothea thought uneasily. *He had gone mad, in those minutes. His mind had simply shattered.*

But he was hardly mad now: edgy and self-conscious but subdued; in his uncle's clothes, several sizes too big for him, he looked mysteriously chastised. He was a handsome young man, very nearly a beautiful young man, Dorothea thought, with his long Roman nose, waxy pale at the tip, and his well-shaped mouth, like something sculpted in stone. Indeed, there was something lapidary about him, particularly in profile; of whom or of what was Dorothea reminded, by his profile? Had he lived to be born, my own son might be sitting in that place, Dorothea thought. It was a wholly senseless thought which she discounted and forgot at once.

With unsteady fingers she reached for her wineglass and saw to her surprise that it was empty.

The subject of Germany was raised (presumably because Colin Asch had recently been there?), and the men at the table, and Hartley Evans, were discussing it: the political phenomenon of the "two Germanys," the division of East and West ("like warring twins," Charles thoughtfully said), the primitive or mystical belief in a special destiny for that nation—or for any other nation, in fact. Martin asked Colin's opinion, and there was an awkward pause during which it appeared that Colin might not have been listening; then he glanced up, shifted his shoulders like a recalcitrant schoolboy, and gave, in a rapid murmured voice, a most remarkable little précis—succinct, pointed, intelligent. So far as he knew, he said, from talking with people his age, particularly in Heidelberg where he'd studied for a while, the younger generation did not think in such outdated mythic terms at all: for them, East Germany and West Germany were two quite separate nations, and the fact that they would never be united did not trouble them, or deeply engage them, in the least. "They are more concerned with ecological matters," he said. "They are concerned with American and Soviet missiles." He paused. His mouth worked oddly. "The future. Not the past."

"Oh, but I find that so hard to believe, knowing what we do of the Teutonic character," Hartley Evans said, pursing her glossy scarlet lips and frowning pedantically. Wine and rich food and the excitement of an attractive young man at the table—more obviously attractive, in any case, than David Schmidt, the broker's assistant, to whom Ginny had pointedly introduced her—had enlivened the young woman, loosened her, brought even more color into her cheeks. She was one of those women who perceive of social intercourse in such circumstances as a near variant of the sexual, requiring some of the same feints, jousts, and rejoinders. But Colin Asch did no more than glance at her, and mumbled something inaudible, and stared down at his plate, fumbling his fork; and the subject was snatched up, like a football, by David Schmidt, who had spent six weeks in Munich recently and who knew a good deal about "the Federal Republic—and the other" and was not shy about informing his listeners of what he knew.

For everyone excepting Colin Asch the salad course was now over, and a delicious salad it had been, with several kinds of greens, including arugula—a favorite of Charles Carpenter's which Dorothea never failed to serve him when he ate dinner at her home, as he sometimes, though infrequently and always surreptitiously, did—and indeed the subsequent course was cheese and fruit, pungent imported cheeses and luscious Concord grapes; though by now Dorothea's appetite was quite quenched. She noticed that Colin Asch was eating oddly, even furtively, rather like a sick cat Dorothea had once owned—the poor creature, afflicted with what turned out to be pneumonitis, had been starving but had been unable to eat, repeatedly lowering her head to her food and then looking up helplessly at Dorothea. The sight had filled Dorothea with a terrible anxiety, for what could be done? So too did Colin Asch bring his fork to his mouth, then lower it; raise it again and take a small quick bite, chewing with an expression of scarcely concealed distaste.

Sharp-eyed Ginny Weidmann, just returning to the table from the kitchen, cried, "Colin, is something wrong? You aren't eating."

Colin shook his head and mumbled no, nothing was wrong.

"The meat? The *lamb?*" Ginny asked, as if something crucial were at stake. "Can't you *eat* it?"

Again Colin replied in a mumble, lowering his head. A panicky expression crossed his face.

"But you seem to have eaten some of the vegetables, haven't you?" Ginny persisted. "Oh, dear, are you a *vegetarian?* Colin? Is *that* it?"

Colin shifted his narrow shoulders in a paroxysm of embarrassment or annoyance, meaning possibly yes, possibly no; meaning, Leave me alone. But Ginny Weidmann would not let him off so easily. He was hungry, she said; he must eat. He was alarmingly *thin*. So Tula was charged with taking away his meat-and gravy-contaminated plate (though with a stiff sort of dignity Colin had not acquiesced to this) and bringing another, heaped with steaming vegetables in almost comical profusion. A harsh ruddy blush by now mottled the young man's face, prominent as a birthmark. To draw attention away from him, so that he could, if he wished, eat,

Dorothea threw out a remark on some cheerful neutral subject, which was taken up hopefully by Charles Carpenter, but unfortunately Agnes Carpenter was not to be deterred and asked of Colin Asch, in a voice both belligerent and coquettish, whether he belonged to a religious cult that forbade the eating of meat or whether not eating meat was—well, a quirk of his own?

This, Colin simply did not answer, not rudely, but as if he had not heard; and Agnes Carpenter asked her question again, louder, and added. "But do you eat eggs? Or cheese? Do you wear *leather?* I bet you're wearing leather *shoes!* A leather *belt!* What I find so annoying about vegetarians is their self-righteousness; I mean, we don't harangue them, why should they harangue *us?*" She appealed to the table, as if inviting complicity. "It's like those people who do volunteer work with the homeless, feeding the homeless, that sort of thing, and make the rest of us feel guilty simply for existing."

"Well," Martin Weidmann said with an embarrassed laugh, as if summing up the subject, "these things are controversial, of course. Like abortion, or air pollution. But who would like more wine? Jerry? Dorothea? Your glass is empty."

Agnes Carpenter persisted, looking at Colin Asch. "But do you belong to a cult? One of those exotic Indian religions, with the gurus who own Rolls-Royces? I hope not!"

Colin Asch, impassive, his face stony, said, with a patience that struck Dorothea as heroic, that, no, he did not belong to any cult, but he did belong to the Animal Rights League; and he was a vegetarian, but he didn't make a habit of haranguing others to believe, or to behave, as he did. He added, mumbling, "As you would, if you knew."

"'Knew'?" Agnes Carpenter asked sharply. "What does that mean, 'knew'?"

"That we are all sentient creatures. That, in our consciousness, we are one."

"Including animals?"

"Yes. Including animals."

"And what does the—whatever it is, that you belong to—"

"The Animal Rights League."

"—and what is *that?* Do you campaign against laboratory experiments; do you break into zoos, that sort of thing?"

"Agnes, why don't you let Colin eat his dinner?" Charles Carpenter said, suddenly exasperated.

"But I am simply *asking*. I'm sure he would like to *tell* us."

"Our organization is based upon the premise that human beings are not superior to animals," Colin said, beginning to speak agitatedly, "but that human beings *are* animals. It is not a pejorative term, 'animal,' but a simple description of biological reality. Animals have personalities, animals have emotions and beliefs, and some animals have languages—"

"Does a sponge have 'personality'?" Agnes interrupted.

And David Schmidt, meaning to be amusing, said, in an undertone, "A spider? A slug? What about bacteria?" Hartley Evans giggled. Jerome Gallagher laughed.

No one meant to be cruel, but the effect upon Colin Asch was to silence him, in mid-sentence. He laid down his fork—dropped it, really—and made a gesture of pushing his plate away from him. His mouth was working as if words churned inside, unable to break free. Though Martin Weidmann was saying loudly, affably, in the voice of a well-practiced host, that no one need defend himself and no one need take offense, Colin pushed his chair back from the table, and stood, and said in a quavering voice, "*Homo sapiens* is not the only species on earth. *Homo sapiens* has the power to destroy many of the other species and to destroy itself, but it is not the only species on earth, nor is it above and beyond and superior to creation, as you would know if you looked within yourself, if you made an attempt to transcend your vile human selfishness—"

"Colin, dear," Ginny cried, "do sit down! Please!" With a strange tight smile Colin said, "The suffering of animals is no less because it lacks a language. Like the suffering of infants."

There was a pause. Agnes Carpenter, startled, relenting, murmured something conciliatory; Martin repeated that no one should take offense; Ginny, roused to maternal solicitude, pleaded with Colin Asch to sit down and to finish his meal. There was salad to come, she said pleadingly, and dessert; surely he wanted dessert? Pecan pie with whipped cream? "We understand about the animals, Colin, really we do," she said. "Animals do have personalities, dogs and cats certainly do, and horses; they're quite strong-willed really, we all know that. Won't you sit down, dear? We promise you can eat your meal in peace."

"Do you!" Colin Asch said angrily.

The atmosphere was highly charged; everyone was looking at everyone else in alarm. What had happened? And why? In the silence Dorothea spoke, in a peculiar slow voice, as if the words were being coaxed from her against her will, "But animals too eat one another. We, I mean—since we are animals. It is something of which we should be ashamed, but even shame is not enough to defeat hunger."

Colin Asch looked at her steadily, stared at her. His lips had gone white, like a wound from which blood has drained. After a long moment he said, simply, "Yes. You are right." Yet he continued to stare at Dorothea for another beat or two, while the others shifted uneasily in their seats.

In the end Colin Asch allowed his aunt to coerce him into resuming his meal; true to her word, she saw to it that he completed it in peace. He said nothing further. He did not so much as glance at Dorothea. Then he excused himself, and went away upstairs, and was gone. And by midnight Dorothea Deverell was safely home, by a quarter past midnight she was soaking in her bath (for going immediately to bed, tonight, would have been unthinkable), giddy with exhaustion yet queerly exhilarated, stirred. Why had she said the strange words she'd said to Ginny's great-nephew? And why had he looked at her so intently, his eyes narrowed and damp, the skin about them appearing bruised? Saying good night in the Weidmanns' foyer, Charles Carpenter had pressed Dorothea's hand hard; and he too had looked at her intently, with a flattering sort of interest, his warm gaze one of tenderness and affection, yet mute. Why could he not speak except in pleasantries? Banalities? She supposed he would telephone in the morning as he frequently did, and she supposed she knew of what their conversation would consist. *I love you, you know. Yes—and I love you.* He would want to know more about hateful Roger Krauss and the "campaign" against Dorothea, and Dorothea, wincing, would assure him it was nothing, really; nothing at all, really; had not Mr. Morland virtually assured Dorothea his position when he stepped down?

(But perhaps I will bring a lawsuit against the Institute after all, Dorothea thought, amused. As my lawyer friend Mr. Gallagher has suggested. For why not? What's to be lost? My precious "femininity"?)

Soaking in her bath, belatedly a little drunk, Dorothea breathed in the warm fragrant steam that smelled like narcissi; she imagined she could hear the telephone ringing in the next room but of course that could not be. Charles would never call her this late; that wasn't in his character.

When was the last time they'd made love, like real lovers? Weeks ago. Back in September. In Dorothea's chaste white wicker bed, enclosed by Dorothea's chaste Laura Ashley floral wallpaper. *I love you, you know. Ah, yes!—and I love you.* They had not spoken of marrying for some time, not even to advise each other solemnly against it. They had not spoken of Agnes Carpenter for some time except in the most general of terms.

Dorothea lay luxuriously in her bath in the warm fragrant water, noting idly that her breasts, her creamy-pale unused breasts, floated gently, like balloons, and that the dark wiry hair between her legs, scratchy to the touch, was obscured by the water's rippling soap-bubbled surface. She stretched her rather long legs, pressed her toes against the hard rim of the bathtub. *I love you. His mind had simply shattered.* The gentleman to whom Ginny Weidmann had introduced her tonight had asked if he might telephone her sometime the following week; might she be free for dinner sometime soon, perhaps a concert in the city? She'd been vague and polite, not quite looking him in the eye. Thank you, yes. Perhaps. Sometime.

She was nodding off to sleep, in the bath. The day had been so incalculably long.

A boy's face appeared suddenly: blunt, bold…the eyes searing, knowing. Not a human boy but an angel: a fierce bellicose archangel, out of Michelangelo perhaps, blowing his doomsday trumpet, cheeks puffed and forehead cruelly creased. Colin, his name. He'd stared at her, in front of the others. But what was his last name? She was too drowsy to remember.

2

Colin Asch had been forced to kill before but never so dispassionately. So without premeditation.

A clean sort of XXX, he was to note in his Blue Ledger in carefully printed block letters, *uncontaminated by desire.*

It had happened in innocence. It had been the consequence of actions not within his control. He'd left Sea Breeze Village (several acres of condominiums) early in the morning of November 10, driving out of Fort Lauderdale in the red '87 Mustang with the sliding sun roof the woman had given him, which she surely wouldn't call the police to get returned, and just south of Daytona Beach on I-95, maintaining his usual steady unobtrusive speed of sixty-five miles an hour, he happened to see, one lane over to the right, one car length ahead, a car he thought at first to be identical with his, lipstick-red, two-door coupe, good condition except for streaks of corrosion on the fenders, but it turned out to be a Toyota of about that year, and what drew his attention to it like a magnet was it had a sliding sun roof too *and the roof was partway open and there was a hand stuck through it wriggling the fingers to taunt him.*

Or was it a signal?

(In the open air! Drivers on all sides! The Florida State Highway police patrolling in unmarked cars!)

Colin's immediate and instinctive response was to brake, slow his speed, let the Toyota move ahead. Because the disembodied hand (it was the driver's hand: he had only one hand on the steering wheel) was so distracting, vertical in the air like that. Because the eye is drawn irresistibly to such a thing, against the mind's will. Because looking at it while he was driving, staring at it, was dangerous; what if he had an accident? Colin Asch was by temperament and choice the sort of person who neither shrinks from trouble nor seeks it *but if this was a taunt or a signal what then?*

Slowing his speed didn't help: the Toyota slowed too. Kept the distance fixed between them. Aloud he murmured, half sobbing, "Why don't they leave me alone!" He had cash on his person, nearly $1,000 in various denominations, thus a form of anonymity, thus clean and pure, but there were credit cards too. Certain goods in the trunk of the car.

You need to concentrate at such times. Need to be alert at every pore.

The Toyota in the right-hand lane was a mirror twin of his car, and in it a driver (male, alone) was arrogantly sticking his hand up through the sun roof, making a fist, flexing the fingers. What did it mean? Was it directed at Colin Asch, or simply at the driver of the red '87 Mustang? It might have been a fag sign too, Colin thought. He speeded up to pass, but the sight of the disembodied hand through the roof was *so distracting so insulting so dangerous* he lost his nerve and fell back. He was in a sudden panic, fearing the loss of control of his car.

But he played it cool. Inside, he wasn't emotional really; he could enter the Blue Room, breathe in its chill numbing air; he was going to be untouched. Had not he impressed Dr. X (the most recent of Colin Asch's many psychiatrists, psychotherapists, spiritual counselors, et al.) with his "integral" personality? his maturity? his healthy optimism tempered by a healthy sense of realism? That look in the eyes (so important to make eye contact with the fuckers) that meant intelligence, patience, humor? Pointless to risk so much. And the credit cards, one of them for Neiman-Marcus of Palm Beach, in a name clearly not his. And the goods in the trunk which *were* his by rights, but still it was risky.

North of Daytona Beach, about thirty miles from Jacksonville, the driver of the Toyota exited at a rest stop. Colin Asch followed. For some miles he had not been taunted by the disembodied hand, but the point had been established. To prepare himself he'd whistled flawlessly from start to finish, not missing a note or a beat, the languorous first movement of that Beethoven piano sonata known as the "Moonlight." An insipid sentimental title, not Beethoven's. But it had stuck.

There he was, suddenly, the driver of the Toyota: medium height, medium build, black bushy hair, glasses, teacherly, short-trimmed beard, denim jacket, jeans…not so much as glancing over at Colin as Colin nosed the Mustang into the space beside his. Cool. He'd locked his car and gone off in the direction of the men's lavatory.

On the rear bumper of the Toyota was a sticker: ANIMALS ARE ONLY HUMAN TOO. What was that supposed to mean? Was it some kind of joke? Colin Asch detested bumper-sticker jokes; they interfered with your thoughts. The Toyota had District of Columbia license plates and a Georgetown University parking decal. In the back seat were scattered books, pamphlets, articles of clothing. Though Colin Asch stretched and yawned, a lazy relaxed look should anyone be watching, in fact he was scrutinizing the rest area: just about deserted except for a station wagon with Iowa license plates, a camper with Ontario license plates, and a diesel with its motor running on the far side of the rest rooms. The place smelled of damp and loneliness.

Stealthily, Colin's fingers tried the door on the passenger's side of the Toyota. But it was locked. And the sun roof too was shut.

In the men's lavatory with its powerful stench of disinfectant, Colin Asch struck up a conversation with the driver of the Toyota, remarking on the bumper sticker—What's that mean, *animals are only human too?*—and the young man said he was an activist with an organization called the Animal Rights League; the bumper sticker was just a sort of joke. Easygoing enough but he didn't seem inclined to linger so Colin asked another question or two, learning that the organization was comprised of a coalition of animal lovers, conservationists, philosophers (academic), and lawyers; their project was to "define" and "protect" animal rights, to expose inhumane practices regarding animals in our society, and to publicize abuses *all the while behaving as if on the road there'd been no signal between them*, so Colin too played it ingenuously, nodding and smiling his boyish sweet attentive smile, beautifully lashed russet eyes fixed to the other's ordinary mud-brown eyes behind the lenses of his glasses, two youngish males measuring each other maybe, but it was a public place; anyone could walk in at any time.

The guy was a fag but not acknowledging it? Seeing that Colin Asch was not the man he'd thought he was?

Or was it something else entirely?

The animal rights man, a professor at Georgetown, philosophy, might have thought it strange that Colin Asch was so absorbed in their talk that he followed him out of the lavatory without using it, but he gave no sign, captivated perhaps by Colin's bright flattering sincerity and the evidence he gave as if off the cuff that he too was a sharpie, remarking how he'd always thought it disgusting the way animals were exploited by man, raised to be slaughtered and eaten, tortured in laboratories in the name of science, but the tricky thing was as Jeremy Bentham argued (wasn't it Bentham? one of those hard-nosed Utilitarians?) that there are no rights outside the law, you can't have "rights" without "law" since there is no natural law, no moral law, only transcribed man-made laws in certain carefully delimited political contexts—which took Colin's listener so by surprise he really opened up, talking warmly and excitedly as if he'd found some long-lost friend or brother. That was the effect Colin Asch generally had on people when he tried.

The man's name was Lionel Block; they even shook hands. Colin showed great interest in reading Animal Rights League literature, thanked Block kindly for giving him a pamphlet ("The Metaphysics of Animal Awareness" by Lionel Block), stood beside the Toyota turning pages, seeing photographs of hideously burned, scarred, mutilated animals...including wild creatures that had gnawed off their own paws to free themselves from traps. Block was talking but Colin Asch wasn't listening. Tears of hurt and rage slowly filled his eyes. He said quietly, "You will go to any extreme, won't you?—people like you."

There was a startled silence. Colin grinned at Lionel Block, who was frowning at him as if he hadn't heard.

Overhead, high, an airliner was passing. On the interstate, traffic passed in a steady droning stream. The diesel was starting up on the other side of the rest rooms, heaving into noisy motion like a prehistoric beast. The station wagon was gone, the camper too. Colin said, "That signal you were making back on the road—what did it mean?"

"Signal? What signal?"

"With your hand. You know. Through the sun roof of your car."

Block adjusted his glasses on his nose, peering at Colin as if he didn't understand. His hair, bushy and kinky, was receding from his forehead; he wasn't Colin Asch's age after all but some years older. When he asked again, "What signal?" Colin made the gesture himself, with his right hand, flexing the fingers lewdly. Block stared. He said, "I wasn't making any signal. I was trying to keep myself awake."

"Awake?"

"The cold air, the wind—it's just a way of keeping from dozing off," Block said uneasily. "When I drive alone I get hypnotized from watching the pavement, so sometimes I open the sun roof a little. Just some crazy thing I do."

Colin regarded him levelly, smiling as if they shared a secret understanding. "So that was it!" he said. "All those miles I thought you were making a signal."

They stared at each other. The rest stop was a desolate place, back far enough from the highway so that no one driving past could see, or would care to make the effort of seeing. At any instant, however, someone could exit, drive right up to within a few yards of Colin and Lionel Block, and this Colin liked, sort of. It kept him on his toes. He had the wire loop prepared in the right-hand pocket of his sheepskin jacket, and his finger crept in, to caress it. He winked, and grinned, and said, "You certainly fooled me! Made a fool of *me!* Misreading you the way I did."

Block licked his lips, trying to smile as if mirroring Colin Asch's smile but with little success. His eyes gave him away; they were the eyes of a badly frightened man. He said, "Well, I guess you did. Misread me. I'm sorry." He rubbed at his nose with blunt stubby fingers, and a gold signet ring gleamed on his left hand. "Now if you'll excuse me—I have to leave."

"That sort of thing is distracting, you know," Colin said. "At high speeds. Making signals to other drivers and confusing them."

"But I wasn't making signals! Jesus Christ, I never dreamt anyone was watching. Or, if watching"—Block swallowed clumsily in mid-sentence—"paying any attention."

"It was a false signal, then," Colin said brightly. "A false alarm."

"I—I guess so."

"You just said it was, didn't you?"

Colin stood quietly, unmoving, his head slightly lowered as if he were preparing himself for a struggle. He had tied his longish hair back in a careless ponytail at the nape of his neck, but several strands had worked free and were blowing across his face. He brushed them irritably away from his lips; he couldn't bear hair on his mouth, his own or anyone else's. Then he returned his right hand to his pocket, fingering the wire loop. He carried an eight-inch switchblade in an inside pocket, and there was, in the trunk of the car, the woman's snub-nosed little .38-caliber Smith & Wesson revolver, but it would be the wire loop, the wire noose, this morning. He said softly, "No one likes to be manipulated."

Block stammered, "No one was manipulating anyone! I'm sorry if you misunderstood!" He would have pushed his way to his car, pushed Colin Asch aside, but courage failed him. Thus far they had not so much as touched. "Look," he said, pleading, "this is crazy, isn't it? Are you joking? Are *you* crazy? You must know I didn't mean…if it was some sort of hand signal, some sort of secret signal, Christ, I swear I didn't know, I've never heard of such a thing. Don't you believe me? Anything I did I did in absolute innocence! And I certainly wasn't aware of keeping pace with you, you and your car."

Colin said, winking, "OK, but tell me. Why did you select me? I mean, why me? How did you know?"

"Look, I'm going to have to get some help, help from the police, if you don't let me by." A rim of white showed above the dark dilated pupils of his eyes. His breathing was harsh. *At this point*, Colin would afterward note in the Ledger, *he seemed to comprehend his error and the fact that there would be no turning back.*

Still they discussed the matter further. Like reasonable men. Colin was saying that Block wasn't going anywhere until he explained, and Block persisted in saying there was nothing to explain, and Colin said, what the signal meant, and how he knew Colin was in the car behind him, *how he'd known when Colin himself could not have known.* He was gripping the wire noose, calculating the motions he'd make, observing himself from a distance or, as if it had already happened, on film. Block might have been a match for him if he'd tried, but like most men of his type (Colin Asch knew the type) he wasn't going to try, scared shitless just by some stranger looking at him the wrong way and saying things he wasn't prepared to hear. Thus Block was backing off, looking confusedly around for help while at the same time hardly daring to take his eyes off Colin's face. But there was no help. No one would come. Out of a mottled bluish sky fat raindrops fell as if idly, erratically, striking the asphalt pavement, the men's red-matched cars. Block was saying in a broken voice, "Let me alone—I'll get the police," and Colin said, following him, though not yet hurried, "Hey, man, I only want to know why of everybody out there on the road you selected *me*, why *me?*" and Block said, "But I didn't," and Colin said, "Why, for this? For now? For what you're forcing me to do?" and Block lost control at last and shouted, "But what am I forcing you to do?"

Four days later, late in the evening of November 14, Colin Asch arrived at the Weidmanns' home in Lathrup Farms, Massachusetts. He was driving the red '87 Mustang. He was spaced out and tired—hadn't eaten in a long time. Hadn't washed (except for his hands), hadn't shaved (hadn't had the opportunity). He'd planned on stopping in Baltimore (where, guilty and reluctant, and maybe a little scared, they'd have to take him in) but for some reason kept on driving. North to New York, north to Massachusetts. Boston. Reasoning it was wisest under the circumstances. No one would ever catch up with him, but distance helps.

He'd promised his Aunt Ginny he would visit them anyway; she loved him and would take care of him, and even if she asked too many bossy questions he could handle that, no problem about that. The husband he could handle too. No problem. He didn't lack for cash—he had now about $1,075 in his wallet—but that wouldn't last forever and he was tired, suddenly so tired. The good feeling had propelled him for days, but now it had left him as it always did like water draining out of a sink and there he was in Lathrup Farms, at his aunt's house, knowing she'd take him in. "She is one of the few people who believes in me," he said aloud, as if to another party. And it was true. The other sons of bitches were always waiting for him to make a misstep, waiting to find fault, commit him to medical treatment. But his Aunt Ginny loved and trusted him; she'd taken him in for a while after the scandal broke at school, Mr. Kreuzer found dead and all that. Just to think of her was to forget, sort of, his actual age, and to half think (as in a dream) that he was some other age, years younger. But it was all subjective, after all.

In the Blue Ledger where he kept account of his life he'd noted only *B.L. 781011Alf.* regarding what had happened in Florida, reversing initials and numerals in case anyone ever read what he'd written. He knew there were professional code breakers who worked for police and the FBI, but that didn't worry Colin Asch in the slightest. To break your code they first have to find your code. They have to find you.

There were guests at the Weidmanns', seated at the dining room table, but everything was stopped for Colin as soon as he stepped inside the door. His aunt greeted him as if she'd been waiting for him all these days, hugged him hard, fussed over him. Powerful waves of shyness and pleasure alternated in him, raising heat into his face.

Ginny Weidmann was a large soft perfumy woman, not bad-looking for her age—about fifty, Colin guessed—with a bright made-up face and intense eyes. The kind of female who, if you closed your fingers around her upper arm, you'd leave prints in the flesh. But sharp-eyed and no fool: she was biting her lip, trying to gauge the extent of his hunger, his tiredness, all he'd been through these past few days. Even noticed the marks on his hands, the shallow reddened scratches, saying half accusingly, as if Colin were much younger than his age, "Oh, Colin—what on earth have you done to yourself? And where have you been?"

She sent him away upstairs to shower and change; his Uncle Martin was a good generous-hearted guy taking him in hand—here's the bathroom, he told Colin, and here's a closet of shirts and things; anything you need give me a holler, you promise?—and Colin, a little breathless, promised. His eyes were filling with tears at this welcome. When he was alone in the shower, lifting his face to the hot stinging spray, he said, "They know they can trust me—they're not like the others." If he'd barged in on his uncle down in Baltimore, the old fart might have sent him away again; Colin wouldn't have put it past him. I'll go away, I didn't mean to interrupt, he'd have said, polite as he was with the Weidmanns, and the old bastard might have taken him at his word. Which was why he hadn't gone to Baltimore after all. Or one of the reasons.

It was six or seven years since Colin had been in the Weidmanns' house, but he remembered it clearly. In certain respects he was gifted with a photographic memory: he gathered, from things people told him and from things he read, that his mind wasn't like other people's minds but capable of summoning back memories vivid as dreams, frequently so real they left him shaken and aroused. So the Weidmanns' big Victorian house entered, came flooding back as if he'd left it only last week. The carved archways and molding, the tall narrow many-paned windows with their elaborate curtains and draw drapes; everywhere you looked, antique furniture and Oriental carpets and polished hardwood floors. Cut-crystal chandeliers, stained-glass window in the foyer.

The smell of freshly polished silverware. Of freshly cut flowers. Of money.

There'd been talk of the Weidmanns taking Colin Asch in after the accident in which his parents drowned (which he thought of as simply the Accident—when he thought of it at all), and again after the trouble at the Monmouth Academy and Colin's breakdown and hospitalization. But their children, a boy and a girl Colin's age, he'd blanked out their names, had opposed it. They'd been jealous of him, pretended to be afraid of him. The little fuckers.

"But I'm here now."

He was grateful for the hot splashing water, the fragrant soap. It was the least they could do for him—his own blood kin, after all. He shampooed his hair roughly and rinsed it, surprised at its length. He didn't want to be mistaken for some hippie queer. Out of the shower, dripping, he dried himself in an enormous towel the size of a beach towel and combed through his snarled hair with a stainless steel comb that must have belonged to his Uncle Martin—this was Martin's bathroom—then shaved with a razor he found in the medicine cabinet—his uncle's too, he assumed—hands shaking slightly so he had to go slow, didn't want to nick himself. In the mirror his expression was guarded, self-critical. He'd always been aware of his remarkable good looks—a Nordic angel, Mr. Kreuzer used to call him, mocking and loving—but he knew that good looks can be lost rapidly, in a few months, a few days, a single hour if it's the right hour. His eyes looked shadowed even in the bright overhead light, and the whites were lightly threaded with blood as if he hadn't slept in days. (About that—sleeping—he wasn't too clear. He guessed he'd slept in the car in hidden places off the highway, curled up in the back seat with the .38 revolver under him.) They would feed him here in this house, and they would see to it that he slept, rested, regained his equilibrium. They were good people, the Weidmanns: Ginny especially. If only she wouldn't try to overdo it.

Colin's hands ached where the wire had cut in deepest. He had not noticed at the time or afterward, driving gripping the steering wheel tight. He had not wanted to use gloves with the wire noose because it was tricky enough handling it with his bare hands. He thought of surgeons, their manual skill, precision: required to wear the thinnest of gloves when they operate, because they need to feel what they're doing and the instruments are so delicate. And if the membrane of the glove is pricked, and if blood from the patient seeps through, there is the danger of AIDS. Except for AIDS he'd go to medical school and train to be a surgeon. You're born with the touch, it's said, or you are not. You are or you're not. Like musical talent, which Colin Asch had had too, as a child.

"It's so fucking *unfair*."

He couldn't have said what was unfair but he felt it keenly, and he knew too that they were talking about him downstairs, hearing of his "tragic" life, et cetera, shaking their heads and murmuring the usual banalities. If the Weidmanns went too far with that shit they'd regret it.

It burned his ass too that his Uncle Martin (so-called uncle: the two of them weren't related by blood, and even if they had been he'd be Colin's mother's uncle, not Colin's) just naturally assumed he hadn't any decent or even clean clothes of his own. Wear anything you like, anything that comes close to fitting, the smug old fart had said, showing him shirts, a rack of neckties, letting his beefy hand fall on Colin's shoulder as if he had the right. Maybe he was queer too, like the bastard back at the rest stop. His uncle's age, you might as well try anything.

So Colin, his heart beating sullenly, selected a plain white cotton shirt, a plain navy-knit tie; the neck and shoulders of the shirt were too big for him but he liked it, sort of, when clothes didn't exactly fit, gave him a boyish even a waiflike look, a real advantage. He'd always been young, and he'd always looked younger than his age. There was a real advantage in that; he thought of it as a kind of lever.

He sat on the edge of the Weidmanns' bed, pulling on black silk socks. Wild! A few days ago he was on the beach in Lauderdale, greasy hair blowing in his mouth, and now he was here! The master bedroom was a spacious high-ceilinged room with green silk wallpaper, thick white wall-to-wall carpeting, most of the furniture oversized—big four-poster antique bed, big bureau, big full-length mirror. If he had time he'd investigate but he hadn't time, they were awaiting him downstairs; he *was* hungry. In his uncle's cuff link box he found a pair of gold and onyx cuff links which he slipped into his pocket; in his aunt's jewelry box he found a pair of gold and diamond earrings which he also slipped into his pocket, reasoning that, with all the Weidmanns had—and of course Ginny's really expensive jewelry was locked safely away—they wouldn't miss these small items. In a dressing room alcove he found his aunt's handbag, or one of her handbags, a red leather Gucci, quickly extracted the wallet and from that a few bills, two tens, a twenty, a five, reasoning they wouldn't be missed, so many bills remained. And the bitch had credit cards, of course. They all did.

"It's the least you owe me. Fuckers."

When, downstairs, he entered the dining room it was like stepping out onto a stage: he could feel the electrically charged air, his mere approach giving off sparks. Ginny with her big mouth and probably Martin too had set him up perfectly so now there were these assholes, solemn-faced, gaping at *him*: Colin Asch. He just took over; he had them all. But he played it cool, knowing everybody likes sweet shy boys, tongue-tied boys, *orphan* etched into their faces. And no reason he could have named except he'd actually looked through some of the material in the back seat of the Toyota, felt a sudden kinship of sorts with the victimized animals, legs in traps, wired up for experiments in laboratories, chickens with their beaks chopped off, monkeys with skulls sawed open—*Christ, what a world of suffering! Why does God allow it to happen!* —so when he picked up his fork it seemed to him that he'd be the kind of person who couldn't eat meat, who was too pure to eat meat, and the rest of them would have to acknowledge it. Thus within seconds the taste and even the smell of the lamb roast was nauseating.

This caused a flurry of excitement too, his aunt fussing over him and sending the little black girl away for a clean plate; Colin liked it but squirmed with embarrassment. Sons of bitches looking at him imagining themselves so superior, taking pity on Colin Asch.

One by one he took them in. Tried to memorize names—his short-term memory was fantastic when there was some purpose for it.

The youngest woman at the table was "Hartley," about thirty years old, little-girl good-looking, black glossy hair, bangs to her eyebrows, fleshy red mouth he imaged sucking him off, and that expertly; and within days. "Charles Carpenter," a mild-mannered but probably shrewd-minded coldhearted son of a bitch, mid- or late-forties, lawyer, and well-to-do. His wife, "Agnes," a drunk with a soft ruined face, heavy-lidded eyes, too much jewelry hanging on her with a mineral glitter as if out of spite (the woman's jade dinner ring was the size of a robin's egg), but Colin connected with something in her, something sour and peevish waiting its turn. And there was a guy his age or a year or two older, "Schmidt," by the look of him a young lawyer or a young stockbroker, nattily dressed, smug, hopeful, trying to impress the table (trying to impress "Hartley") with some crap about West Germany. And there was another man whose name Colin hadn't caught—he'd have to ask before the evening broke up—pinch-faced, bald except for patches of grizzled gray around his ears, nervous, sad, heavy-hearted, Colin could see, or sense; in his early fifties maybe, or older. And quietest of them all a woman named "Dorothea Deverell" who was a friend of Colin's aunt, creamy-pale skin, large intelligent eyes, watchful too, very still, hard to estimate her age but Colin supposed she must be in her mid-thirties…who did she remind him of? She wore her dark hair brushed back from her face and fastened neatly at the nape of her neck by a tortoiseshell clip. She looked down the table at him intently, he had the idea respectfully. It occurred to him that she was a good person, she had a good kind decent generous soul; like a spark the idea ignited in his heart, pulsing warmly through his blood. Later that night he would note in the Blue Ledger, *I think so. Of course I can't be sure.*

Though probably little or nothing would have come of this insight—Colin Asch was visited with so many insights, sometimes within a single hour—had not, a little later, this woman spoken so strangely, and so...purposefully. To him. In front of the entire table.

Exactly how it happened he wouldn't be able to recall, afterward, trying to record the episode in the Blue Ledger. Carpenter's wife, Agnes, had been questioning him about vegetarianism, asking did he belong to a cult, coming fairly close to insulting him—it was really surprising how hostile the bitch was *for no reason at all simply for the hell of it*, which Colin Asch could understand but which didn't mean he liked it or liked being mocked in front of a little audience including the hot-looking girl with the eyes and the pouty luscious mouth and Miss Deverell, who looked pained at the attack—but he maintained his composure, observing himself carefully as if indeed he were on stage as years ago he'd studied a videotape of Colin Asch on an actual stage—he'd played the role of Mark Antony in Shakespeare's tragedy at the Monmouth Academy and everyone marveled over his acting skills, most of all Mr. Kreuzer who had directed the play—so there was no temptation to lose control, start stammering, saying things he'd afterward regret. In fact the nastier Mrs. Carpenter became the nicer Colin Asch could be; there was a palpable rhythm to it, like two people on a teeter-totter, or fucking; which was maybe why Mrs. Carpenter persisted, when everyone else was on Colin Asch's side and casting her disapproving looks. Colin got to his feet so agitated he didn't know what he would say; the words just came out of him: "The suffering of animals is no less because it lacks a language. Like the suffering of infants."

That got them. That got them! Agnes Carpenter had to back down, knowing she'd pressed him too far. And the others said things, tried to gloss over the awkward moment, fat blowsy Ginny Weidmann trying to slide her arm through his as if she had the right. "We understand about the animals, Colin, really we do," she said anxiously. "Won't you sit down, dear? We promise you can eat your meal in peace."

Colin wrenched away from her. "Do you!" he said.

Thinking: You can all go fuck yourselves.

It was at that moment, in the startled silence, that the woman Dorothea Deverell spoke. A stranger to Colin Asch yet clearly sensing his inner distress. Saying *in a weird quiet premeditated voice* words of a higher consolation: "But animals eat one another too. We, I mean—since we are animals. It is something of which we should be ashamed, but even shame is not enough to defeat hunger."

Colin stared at her through a watery red haze. How strangely she'd spoken, how unexpectedly! To him! Piercing his heart!

There had never been anything like it before in his life.

Thus the ugly moment passed, and Colin Asch was able, with dignity, to resume his place at the table, and his meal: for which he was indeed ravenously hungry. And afterward, upstairs in the room these kindest of people had provided for him, he had recorded the incident in the Blue Ledger as best, considering his exhaustion and agitation, as he could. *Animals eat one another too. We, I mean...Even shame is not enough.*

A beautiful woman. "Dorothea Deverell." A stranger to Colin Asch *yet mysteriously knowing him;* knowing how he craved understanding, sympathy, consolation. *The gist of it is, hunger sanctifies!* he recorded.

An utterly simple truth which it was required a stranger tell him, lest false guilt contaminate his soul.

So Colin Asch, though by nature the roving kind—or is it roaming? —restless to the very marrow of his bones and drawn, it sometimes seemed, by the sun's westward movement across the sky, to movement of his own, allowed himself to be cajoled by the Weidmanns into staying on in Lathrup Farms for a while. Through Thanksgiving, at least. Until he knew more clearly what his plans for the future were. (He wanted, he said, to look for a job. Maybe later return to school. There were so many good schools in the Boston area. Many job prospects too, he guessed. At RISDE—the Rhode Island School of Design—Colin Asch had been an outstanding student; certain of his instructors had praised and encouraged his talent, as an artist and as a graphic designer. There was a future awaiting him, they'd said.)

So he said yes. So he said Thank you from the bottom of my heart.

And meant it! God, yes.

"Everybody else treats me like"—he paused, reflecting—"dirt."

"Oh, now, Colin dear, that can't be true," Aunt Ginny said reprovingly. "Can it?"

He was twenty-seven years old, in December to be twenty-eight years old. Alone. Unmarried. No true family. In Europe it was several times said of him he was "so uniquely American," but in America what could be said of him? He carried innocence about him like a radiant heat, shining in his beautiful eyes, coursing through his veins. His handshake, his touch, communicated warmth, strength, modesty, a special destiny. Knowing nothing of his tragic background, women adored him for the hurt in his face, and his manliness. Some men too adored him, and some men feared him. *And with good cause!* as he noted, amused.

Of the several XXX incidents recorded in the Blue Ledger, only one was female. And that, in one of the western states, in so blurred a passage of Colin Asch's life (someone had turned on Colin Asch to the powerful visions of mescaline) it scarcely counted. Might in fact have been a dream. Contemplating the cryptic abbreviations in the Ledger regarding that incident Colin Asch was as puzzled, or nearly, as a stranger to the Ledger might have been. He'd forgotten the girl's name, the girl's face, even the means of death! Which was not consistent with his character.

Before Fort Lauderdale and the sixth-floor condo in Sea Breeze Village, Colin Asch had been living in Miami, and before Miami he'd been living in Houston, and before Houston he'd been traveling in Morocco (where one evening in Tangier he knocked on the door of the American expatriate writer Paul Bowles—and was admitted), and before Morocco he'd been traveling in Greece, Germany, Holland.... Before that was the United States: a brownstone in Brooklyn Heights where he'd lived with some of the members of an experimental troupe of actors. And before that a string of shitty manual jobs, servile jobs, in the New York area. And before that...things were vague. Patches of his adult life were shifting out of focus like his childhood, which was so distant from him as to have happened to another person. Barely remembered on the far side of a river.

These things he yearned to tell the Weidmanns' friend Dorothea Deverell. How he was cursed with too many talents. Music, art, writing, acting, science, "the art of human relations"...all beckoned. Yet in none thus far had he managed to succeed while others, less talented, had forged careers. "So damned fucking *unfair.*"

The truth was that much that had happened to Colin Asch in the course of his life, beginning with the Accident surely, but perhaps beginning at birth, had happened merely in his vicinity. Apart from his will and without his guidance.

Thus "praise" and "blame" are equally unmerited.

Thus "he" (agent) and "it" (action) are falsely separated.

Thus even the most general time demarcations—"past," "present," "future"—are invalid.

For in the Blue Room (which at certain times Colin Asch was privileged to enter) all things become one. The fierce blue light erases all shadow. There is no gravity, no weight. Not even "up" and "down"!

Purification is the goal. The means scarcely matter.

Absolution.

Sanction.

As Colin Asch would explain to Dorothea Deverell. When he saw her again.

*

Each day Colin Asch scanned the newspapers hoping to find an account of the episode recorded in the Blue Ledger as *B.L. 781011Alf*. But there was nothing. Days passed, and a week —and there was nothing!

"Fuckers."

It angered him that his victim Block, who had in the end put up a desperate struggle to live, like a maddened animal, and had given Colin Asch quite a workout should not merit even an inch of newsprint here in the North. Nor was there anything in *Newsweek*, to which the Weidmanns subscribed. You would think the Florida state police and the highway patrol would talk to reporters about having come upon a "perfect crime"—for, if it was not perfect, where was the perpetrator?

"Yeah," Colin said, snorting in derision. "*Where is he?*"

He considered writing messages to the police down there. Maybe the Jacksonville police too—maybe they were involved. Just to bum their asses a little. Give them a hint who they were dealing with. And maybe to Georgetown University where Block had taught—ANIMALS ARE ONLY HUMAN TOO might make a good cryptic message.

But why do the bastards any favors?

Also, Colin was getting absorbed in matters up here. Looking for a job. Making contacts. Making the right connections.

It did not worry him in the slightest that police might in some way trace him…as if they could trace his footprints in the sand leading them right to *him!* Not once since the age of fifteen, when he had first killed or been forced to kill, had Colin Asch been linked to any of his murders; so far as he knew (admittedly, he could not absolutely know), his name had never been on any list of police suspects. The police, like everyone else, or nearly everyone (for there was the one tenth of one percent who stood apart from the herd) were just too stupid.

Colin Asch had in fact always relied upon the world's stupidity as a factor in his own talent. Amid a herd of slow-witted bovine beasts he was a leopard capable of running at speeds up to seventy-five miles an hour—a flash of burnished flaming light. In Florida he had not been rushed; he had been methodical as always, knowing that, as soon as he returned to his car and drove away, he could enter the Blue Room and float weightless there for miles, hours, in an utter bliss of childlike innocence; thus he followed his self-prescribed stratagem of the Baffle…meaning that he deliberately, and with boyish pleasure, fucked up the scene. He dragged the body into a scrubby littered area behind the rest rooms (scolding it for its heaviness and its inclination to snag on tree roots, bushes, and the like, as if even in death Block was being uncooperative) and there pinned a page torn out of a magazine from Block's car onto Block's sweater, reasoning that, when police discovered the body, they would think that the photograph on the page (of AIDS patients in a Washington clinic) had some relevance to the victim's death. Next he found several lipstick-stained cigarettes where someone had dumped them in the gravel, and these he tossed into the Toyota, on the floor by the passenger's seat and in the rear. A condom from his own wallet he tore out of its foil wrapper and tossed both condom and wrapper into the back seat. Then, with Block's car keys, he scratched nonsensical letters and zodiac signs on the hood of the Toyota; then locked the car doors; and, still not hurrying (though a car with Georgia license plates, heavily weighted with children, had just driven into the rest area to park some distance away), he wiped the surface of the Toyota everywhere his fingerprints might conceivably be found. Then he got into the red '87 Mustang and drove away—and did indeed enter the Blue Room almost immediately, sucked breathless into it, like a soul into heaven.

3

Poor man, Dorothea Deverell thought, staring. But surely he can't be totally blind? Out by himself like this?

The gentleman in question, a timid rather stooped figure in dark glasses, wearing a tweed cap, a loosely belted trench coat, and unbuckled galoshes, was making his way across the foyer of the Brannon Institute, tapping the marble floor with a white-tipped cane and following at a slant in the wake of others entering the recital hall; it was nearly 4 P.M. of a dark wintry Sunday at the end of November, and people had come to hear, in larger numbers than Dorothea Deverell had dared hope, the British soprano Natalya Lowe sing Schumann, Brahms, and Poulenc. Always anxious before such events (as indeed before any event that might be said to be her responsibility or, in retrospect, her fault), Dorothea found herself more anxious than usual this afternoon: a pitiable figure, no doubt, to those who knew her, in her elegantly cut black silk dress with the high neckline and the countless shimmering pleats. There were pearls screwed into her ears, and pearls around her slender neck, and she was very pale and smiled steadily. She had worried that no one would show up for the recital, though the event was advertised as free. She had worried that Miss Lowe, known to be temperamental, would not herself show up. Or that her accompanist would raise further objections to the conditions of the recital hall and the piano he was obliged to play. (This high-handed individual had decided, late Friday afternoon, to reject the Institute's Steinway concert grand, insisting that another be rented for the performance.) And Roger Krauss, who hated Dorothea Deverell, had come, with another trustee and his wife; and Charles Carpenter, who loved Dorothea Deverell, had not yet come—and perhaps would not. Standing by the entrance, smiling and waving and calling out greetings to friends, she felt her heart congealing to ice; she could not have been more uneasy if she herself were going to sing. And it was all so absurd. And so excessive. And futile.

Which of the philosophers was it who observed that the natural bent of things is toward chaos, and that order itself is unnatural? For there is only one way for things to go ideally, and any number of ways for things to go wrong.

Seeing that the man in the dark glasses was headed waveringly in her direction, Dorothea quickly came forward to assist him. "Sir? May I?"

Though startled, he acquiesced immediately to her hand on his arm, smiling inside his gingery-gray beard and murmuring, "Ah! Thank you! You're very kind." Had he been standing at his true height he would have been a head taller than Dorothea Deverell, but he walked in a hunched, crablike manner; it would have been difficult to determine his age. Not young, certainly. But how old? As Dorothea led him slowly down the wide center aisle of the hall and to a choice seat in the third row he apologized for being a nuisance; he wasn't, he said, totally blind, but had a fair amount of vision in his left eye, at least if the light was good; most of the time he had no difficulty getting around.

"You aren't a nuisance," Dorothea protested. "We're very happy to have you here." In her excitable mood she spoke almost gaily; she had no idea what she said. (For perhaps Charles Carpenter had arrived by now? was watching her help a blind man settle into his seat?)

Though Dorothea would have liked to flee, the man in the dark glasses unexpectedly thrust out his hand at her and said, "My name is Lionel Ashton—may I ask yours?"

"Dorothea Deverell," Dorothea said.

Mr. Ashton did not release her hand quite so quickly as she might have wished; his grip was strong. He had heard of her, he said; didn't she have something to do with the Brannon Institute, wasn't she well known in Lathrup Farms? He squinted frowningly up at her through the smoky black lenses of his glasses; you could see nothing of his eyes inside. In the foyer he had seemed timid and hesitant, but he exuded a curious sort of authority now, bent upon deterring Dorothea though he sensed her eagerness to hurry off. His voice was husky as if unnaturally lowered and much of his face was concealed, by the glasses, and the tweed cap (in style though not in quality resembling a British workingman's cap) pulled low over his forehead, and the bristling little beard that reminded Dorothea of a Scotch terrier's fur. How odd that I have never seen him here before, Dorothea thought. When she finally excused herself to back away, he called after her, "Thank you again, Miss Deverell! I'm not a man who forgets kindness!"

It was just past 4 P.M. and the recital hall was agreeably filled. Dorothea dismissed the girls who were handing out programs in the foyer and remained to hand them out herself to last-minute stragglers. But there were few. She stood smiling vaguely toward the front doors, waiting. As she so often waited. Perhaps I am of that breed of women uniquely qualified for waiting, she thought. Behind her the doors of the recital hall were shut; after a pause the first vigorous notes of Schumann's "Widmung" were sounded; a powerful soprano voice, so much larger than life, seized control of all imaginations. That is the way to do it, Dorothea thought, staring toward the entrance. Though she had signed on Natalya Lowe for this engagement back in March and had been quite pleased at the prospect of bringing the soprano to Lathrup Farms, in Dorothea Deverell's own Sunday afternoon recital series, now, she scarcely heard—

The outer doors opened another, final time, and two Lathrup Farms matrons, sumptuously clad in fur coats and hats, hurried inside, bearing with them a bone-chilling gust of air.

Dorothea Deverell took her place inside, at the rear of the little hall, sitting alone, hands clasped on her knees. She was thinking that since Roger Krauss had begun his systematic campaign against her she had become conscious of doing many things wrong.

It was like proofreading for the dozenth time a passage of her own careful prose to discover, to her chagrin, that she'd made a typographical error of the most blatant kind.... The other day, doing galleys for next season's calendar, she had come upon "arists" where "artists" was meant. And she had read this so many times.... The error was trivial yet it filled her with dread: for if the eye trickily fills in where there is a significant absence, what does that portend for our reading of the world? and our sense of ourselves in the world?

Where previously, at the Institute, Dorothea had carried on in a bliss of well-being, assuming that, underpaid as she was and uncomplainingly overworked, she had the general support of the community behind her, now she supposed that was not the case at all and never had been. She was well liked, of course—how many times had people said, conspicuously in her hearing, *Isn't Dorothea Deverell marvelous!*—but she was liked as other civic-minded women in the community were liked, and her talents, such as they were, set beside those of a man—any man?—were likely to be discounted. In this affluent suburban village many women, the wives of prominent citizens, exerted themselves in volunteer work; yet their exertions were likely to be erratic, unreliable, and even, in certain comical instances, seasonal. With these, Dorothea Deverell was surely lumped: which was, she supposed, no one's fault but her own. For in what ways *am* I different?

She was keenly aware too of the many missteps and blunders of her daily life. Returning from the grocery store with fruit already bruised, overpriced items she must have selected without seeing. Mislaying things, losing things. Forgetting things. Spilling things. Allowing herself to be cheated in stores because she was absent-minded, inattentive...for her life pushed forward in its subterranean way with little vigilance and self-protection. She believed, at times, that she was under the spell of an interior voice she did not quite recognize: chiding, nagging, questioning, narrating. The voice passed judgment on Dorothea Deverell, and this judgment had the power to silence her. Ah, what would it be, Dorothea thought, to have the confidence to so powerfully (yet tenderly) declare oneself to the world as the soprano Natalya Lowe declared herself? (Miss Lowe was now singing Poulenc's beautiful little cycle "Tel Jour, Telle Nuit.") Does the power of one's voice come first, or is confidence required for power? Dorothea wondered.

Over the telephone Charles Carpenter, to whose elusive figure Dorothea Deverell's hopes for "emotional happiness" were affixed, had murmured apologetically that he would not know until the last minute if he could come to the recital. "If I'm not there I suppose I won't be coming," he had said. Dorothea laughed. "Your logic is amazing." "But I do want to come. You know I do." Adding, after a wistful pause, "Just to see you, Dorothea." Carelessly, Dorothea Deverell said, "Ah, Charles, you can see me any time!"

When the recital ended and Miss Lowe and her accompanist were warmly applauded, Dorothea woke from her trance and applauded happily with the rest. Despite her distracting thoughts she had noticed that the middle-aged singer, still flamboyantly beautiful, or at any rate "striking," had developed a slight hoarseness at lower levels; and her upper register of passion and substance seemed rather willed—if not frankly simulated. In the middle range Natalya Lowe was most effective; thus in the middle range she poured out her soul, or gave a convincing impression of doing so. In any case we are an audience of amateurs and not difficult to please, Dorothea thought. She clapped and clapped until her hands stung.

Overall, she was so pleased with the event she had herself arranged that she did not even dread the wine and cheese reception to follow, at which Dorothea Deverell would function as hostess for two-hundred-odd people. The color had returned to her cheeks, the light to her eyes. The dry cleaner's had done a superb job with her black silk dress. She had forgotten her enemy Roger Krauss entirely. She had forgotten the importunate blind man whose grip had been so insistent. She had forgotten—almost —that Charles Carpenter had again disappointed her.

⁂

Next day at noon, crossing the small park attached to the Institute (the Morris T. Brannon Institute was housed in the English Tudor mansion that had been the home of the wealthy industrialist-philanthropist Josiah Brannon, and the property included several acres of land), Dorothea happened by chance to notice a solitary figure on one of the park benches…bareheaded, very blond…in a patch of wintry sunshine, *The Selected Poems of Shelley* in his hands. It was the very paperback edition Dorothea had owned since college, thus the cover was familiar; and familiar, too, the young man who sat so intently reading. He was long-limbed, lean, boyish, with a bright blue scarf around his neck and a soiled sheepskin jacket: ah, Ginny Weidmann's nephew Colin. Dorothea hesitated, wondering if she should say hello; but he was so absorbed in his book and had not seen her. Dorothea Deverell was the kind of person, inexplicably shy at selected times, who, seeing even old friends and acquaintances on the street, was inclined to turn quickly away if she herself had not been detected.

Afterward, however, she thought of the young man with pleasure: so romantically alone, in a chilly deserted park, in the middle of the day, reading the poems of Shelley! I envy him, I suppose, she thought.

That night she felt urged to telephone Ginny Weidmann, to thank her, belatedly, for the dinner party; and to apologize for not having telephoned sooner. As a single woman in a world dominated by couples Dorothea Deverell could not dispel the notion that any social invitation made to her was proffered out of kindness, if not charity; she had to keep in check a propensity for excessive, guilty gratitude. But Ginny Weidmann was primarily interested in critiquing Agnes Carpenter's behavior that evening —like other Lathrup Farms women, she did rather resent the fact that Agnes Carpenter was Charles Carpenter's wife, now that the woman had grown so charmless, and so unapologetic as well. "I simply can't forgive her for attacking my nephew after I'd confided in her, in her and in all of you, about his—his sensitivity,"

Ginny said. "The poor boy has had breakdowns, he's been hospitalized, and he has made such a—I really don't think it's excessive to say he has made a valiant effort, a heroic effort, to live in the world. The vegetarianism is only a phase, I'm sure, and it isn't after all *criminal*."

There was a pause. Dorothea too felt a thrill of maternal, or perhaps sisterly, solicitude for the beleaguered young man. "How is he?" she asked. "I assume he's staying with you and Martin for a while?"

Unhearing, with passion, Ginny said, "*How* do you think Charles endures that woman? He is such a superior human being himself—but I do think he carries loyalty rather too far, don't you? There is something so annoyingly old-fashioned about Charles Carpenter, don't you think?" Dorothea murmured mere sound: neither assent nor dissent. The subject of Charles Carpenter, as conversation, filled her with a profound unease. Ginny plunged on. "Martin believes that Charles is a 'desperately stoical' man and that it is his religion that keeps him from divorcing her. These old Episcopalian families, these stubborn old *Bostonians!*"

Dorothea thought, Charles Carpenter is no more religious than I am. She said, "Well, you can see that Agnes was a very attractive woman at one time. She still would be, in fact, if—"

"Oh, Dorothea! Just *stop!*" Ginny said. "You carry that sort of thing too far!"

What sort of thing? Dorothea Deverell wondered.

Ginny Weidmann went on to speak in a hostess's effusive terms of Jerome Gallagher, who had been "quite taken" with Dorothea—"As I'd predicted, Dorothea; why were you so worried?"—and of her glamorous young friend Hartley Evans: "Isn't Hartley beautiful? Just so—sharp and quick and *contemporary.* She telephoned last week to ask if Colin might be willing to be interviewed on one of the television station's talk shows, about his animal rights work and vegetarianism. Martin and I were delighted—Colin needs to be involved more with the world, the work-a-day 'real' world—and to our surprise he agreed. 'If you give me moral support, Aunt

Ginny,' he said. He's such a shy boy at heart, but as you might have noticed he can be amazingly articulate, even eloquent, at times. And he's *smart.* He hopes to get a job in the public sector of some kind, so meeting people at Hartley's station will be a step in the right direction, we think—actually, he happened to mention just sort of casually that he had been an assistant to a German public television producer in Heidelberg, a sort of American consultant, I gather. Isn't he remarkable, really? And so sweet." Dorothea said, as if she had been bullied into it "Yes."

"He's going to be staying with Martin and me for a while—there are so many excellent universities and art schools and God knows what all else in this area, and he intends to go back to school in a year or so. The awkward thing is, he hasn't much money but he doesn't want to be a burden on us. Becoming an orphan at the age of twelve was probably more traumatic in certain ways than having been an orphan at birth would have been, since the boy has his pride after all."

"Yes," Dorothea said, not certain that this was true but for some reason keen upon pursuing the subject. "But does he have many friends? Girlfriends?"

Ginny said, "No—and yes. Because he's so itinerant he doesn't have friends in the usual sense, I mean they're all scattered, but as soon as he settles down he starts attracting them. Hartley, for instance—she's such a sophisticated young woman, but she seems quite taken by Colin." She paused. "I do wish he'd find the right girl and marry her. I'm conventional enough to think that might be the only solution to his problem."

"His problem?"

"The trouble is, Colin is so damned trusting. He's an idealist. He has always wanted people to be perfect, and when that doesn't work out he becomes disillusioned, sometimes bitterly. I'm not clear on the details, but evidently when he was living with one of his father's brothers in Baltimore and going to college—the state university, not Hopkins; he'd applied at but been rejected by Hopkins, which hurt him a great deal; after all, he *is* so bright!—

he was involved with a man or men later arrested for drug dealing, and check forging, and somehow poor Colin got roped in with the others and actually arrested. It was a mistake of course and the charges were later dropped but it was upsetting. And there were other things," Ginny said vaguely, thoughtfully, "other unfortunate incidents that grew out of his naivety. In some respects, you see, Colin Asch is still a child. An unspoiled, *natural* child. What is that European term, it applies to children abandoned in the wilds, and brought up by animals—"

"'*L'enfant sauvage*'—"

"For instance, day before yesterday Colin insisted upon taking Martin and me out to dinner, to celebrate, he said, just the fact we were all alive—it was so touching. He has surprised me with flowers several times—the other day I walked into the bedroom and there was a bouquet, lovely red roses, waiting for me; I simply broke down and cried; my own children, you know, would never, *never* have—well, you know. They completely take Martin and me for granted. But Colin, it seems, takes nothing for granted. He is so eager, so hungry somehow—so curious. He has been asking, for instance, Dorothea, about you."

"About me?"

"Asking how long we've known you. What sort of work you do, what sort of life you lead. I told him just a bit—I hope you don't mind."

"Oh, no," Dorothea said. "Not at all." Though thinking, My marriage. My "tragic" marriage. She could envision the gusto with which Ginny Weidmann told of Michel Deverell's death; recounted the old, now so very maudlin tale of Dorothea Deverell's miscarriage, which she was sure to place after the death. Yet it did not fail to please her, even as it discomfited her, that Colin Asch, that intriguing young man, should inquire after Dorothea Deverell at all. The situation was a mirror of sorts in which Dorothea might view herself from a new and unexpected—and possibly advantageous—angle, but she did not want to pursue it. Her vanity was to deny all impulses of vanity in herself.

Before they hung up Dorothea said she hoped to have the Weidmanns over for dinner soon, before Christmas certainly: "And your nephew too. If it wouldn't bore him to join us."

"Oh, I'm sure Colin would be delighted," Ginny said, though her voice had gone slightly vague. "Actually he's gone a good deal—says he is acquainting himself with this 'new untouched part of the world'—he usually comes home after Martin and I are asleep. During the day he is job-hunting, and at night I suppose he's making friends, meeting other young people. We've given him a key of course and he's perfectly considerate—never makes the slightest noise—moves through the house like a ghost."

"Excuse me? Miss Deverell?"

Dorothea Deverell looked up from her desk to see, poised in her doorway, having somehow slipped past her secretary, Colin Asch himself—the young man's expression tense, his jaws set, as if he had been steeling himself for some time for this moment. Afterward Dorothea would recall how unmistakably, how seemingly naturally, their eyes had locked; how immediate her own reaction had been, of surprise, recognition, embarrassment. She felt a rude hot blush rise into her face.

It crossed her mind, perhaps unreasonably, that Ginny Weidmann was responsible; she'd sent her nephew over to say hello to Dorothea Deverell.

But Colin had plans, it seemed, of his own. Tall, lanky, very nervous, with the bright blue scarf wound about his throat, looking both shy and in a way belligerent, he had come to ask Dorothea if she remembered him? and would she like to join him for lunch?

"I just happened to be in the neighborhood, Miss Deverell," he said quickly, as if an explanation were required. "In fact I was just looking at the watercolor exhibit here, it's very good, I think; whoever chose the show has excellent taste—watercolor is the most difficult medium of all, you know. In art. The painting has to be done almost in a single gesture; there isn't any room for error or hesitation. But—but I guess you know all this." In Dorothea's little office the young man's voice had taken on a raw adolescent soaring tone; he stopped speaking abruptly.

Dorothea told Colin Asch that she was terribly sorry—"I'm afraid I haven't planned on eating out today." She was so taken by surprise that she too stammered a bit. Her reply, curter than she'd intended, threw Colin Asch into a blushing confusion; he apologized several times; he should have known, he said, that a person in Dorothea's position would be busy. Dorothea said perhaps they could have lunch another time—for she saw the hurt in his face and did not want to send him away so rudely. She asked after the Weidmanns; she asked how Colin was getting along in his job search and drew him out further on the subject of the watercolor exhibit at the Institute (the paintings were early, minor work by John Marin which Dorothea thought interesting, if not profound—others had their doubts), which allowed him to speak with more purpose, in fact quite impressively. His favorite watercolors, he declared, were those of Winslow Homer.

"And of his it's the Maine ones I prefer, and the ones painted in the Caribbean. The Adirondack paintings look like superior magazine illustrations, don't you think?"

Dorothea, startled, said that she thought so, yes. Yes, she'd always thought so.

So they began to talk more easily. Almost casually. And Dorothea invited Colin Asch to have a seat (there was a cushioned ladder-back chair, not often used, perpendicular to her desk), feeling a belated regret that she had so precipitously declined his invitation. Clearly Ginny Weidmann's nephew was one of those persons, rather like Dorothea Deverell herself, who not only dreads being rejected but dreads the yet more subtle social circumstance of forcing another to do the rejecting.

(But why was her heart beating so erratically, and why the unpleasant heat in her face? Was it that Colin Asch's awkward manner—so at odds with his striking face and the slapdash youthfulness of his clothes—reminded Dorothea of the boys of her remote youth who had acutely embarrassed both herself and themselves by asking for "dates" in high school?)

When, ten or fifteen minutes later, it might have seemed time for Colin Asch to leave—when he had in fact risen slowly, with a look of abstraction, to his feet, looming tall above Dorothea's desk—he again surprised her by saying, with a wistful boyish smile, "Are you sure, Miss Deverell, you won't join me for lunch? Somewhere close? It wouldn't really take long."

Dorothea laughed hesitantly and heard herself say, "Well—I guess we could." For there was no reason after all why not. Adding, as Colin Asch helped her with her coat, "But please do call me Dorothea."

"Dorothea!" the young man said happily, as if testing the very syllables.

Outside, in the chill thin winter sunshine, there was some hesitation about whether they should simply walk to "a tearoom sort of place" two blocks away, where Dorothea often had lunch with friends, or whether they should, as Colin Asch suggested, go to a restaurant he'd passed a short distance away, L'Auberge, since, after all, he had his car, and it was no trouble to drive. Dorothea protested that L'Auberge was too expensive but somehow it came about that she acquiesced, and a minute later they were driving along the boulevard in a handsomely gleaming silvery-green automobile for which, nonetheless, Colin Asch felt obliged to apologize: it was a second- or third-hand Olds Cutlass Calais which he had recently bought on a trade-in and, now that he was its owner, did not altogether like. To make conversation Dorothea volunteered information about her inherited Mercedes, which so frequently stalled at crucial moments, like expressway ramps, and Colin Asch nodded vigorously and said, "Yes. Aunt Ginny was telling me. All sorts of good things come your way—you're the kind of human being they happen to."

Dorothea said laughingly, "Ah, hardly!" But Colin Asch was unhearing.

At L'Auberge there was valet parking, but Colin Asch did not care to entrust his car to the black-liveried "valet," insisting upon dropping Dorothea off at the canopied entrance and parking his car himself; and, inside, in the rather romantically murky twilight, it developed that, though Colin Asch had made a reservation, and the table indeed was in readiness, he was not dressed "in appropriate attire"—that is, he was not wearing a coat. That he wore jeans, that he was tieless, seemed not to matter—but he was not wearing a coat. In the exigency of the moment Dorothea did not have time to think it odd about the table reservation, for now there was a spirited exchange—good-humored for the most part, yet quite serious too, like a game of tennis between well-matched players—between Colin Asch and the maitre d', the former insisting that his clothes would be wholly appropriate in the most chic, exclusive clubs in Manhattan, hence why not here in suburban Lathrup Farms, the latter insisting that the dress code was not of his invention but it was his responsibility to enforce. Catching sight of Dorothea's look of sympathetic worry, Colin Asch decided abruptly to give in and wear the dullish gray shoulder-padded "sports coat" provided by the management, though it was far too large for him and, as he laughingly said, not his style. Thus the early part of their conversation at lunch was taken up with the absurdity of conformist behavior, which in lightning-quick leaps Colin Asch related to the Inquisition, and the Holocaust, and the subjugation of women through the centuries, and the stoning of Socrates—or did Socrates die some other way? Colin asked, seeing perhaps the merest flicker of an expression on Dorothea Deverell's face. She said, "He was given hemlock to drink." And added, for the situation seemed to require such grand, summary, thoughtful statements, "He died nobly."

"He *did*," Colin Asch said emphatically. "He absolutely *did*."

And then they were talking—or at any rate, and very animatedly, Colin Asch was talking—of Percy Shelley: of *his* death; of the ignorance of the world that had so vilified him, the English establishment in particular, how they'd virtually driven him to his death by drowning, a death Colin Asch thought as clearly a suicide as

Chatterton's. "In my opinion," he said emphatically, "both suicides were mistakes: poets of such genius had not the right to cut off their lives so prematurely and give counsel to their enemies."

Dorothea, who had been talked into sharing a carafe of rather delicious red wine with Colin Asch, agreed, and said, "Who was the poet—I think he's a contemporary—who said that suicide is pointless; 'it happens anyway'?"

At this Colin Asch laughed with enormous appreciation, as if Dorothea had said something very witty.

Which perhaps she had?

Though Dorothea Deverell had been taken to dine at L'Auberge any number of times since moving to Lathrup Farms she did feel, in its pointedly "gracious" atmosphere, distinctly out of place; not in her manner, or in her appearance (for in fact Dorothea was perfectly if accidentally dressed for the occasion in a dove-gray silken wool dress with a belt that emphasized her slender waist, and good patent leather pumps, and a necklace of amber stones Charles Carpenter had given her for her thirty-seventh birthday), but in her temperament: for places that seem to require of one an obeisance to their pretensions ran against the grain of her spirit; and, more practicably, she worried that Colin Asch—so touchingly anxious that wine, food, the table, Dorothea's seat at the table, be perfect—would spend far too much money on this supposedly casual and impromptu occasion, even if, as she would insist, she paid half the bill. (She began to worry too that he would not allow it.) Yet it did stir her vanity that, so unexpectedly, on an ordinary weekday, she *was* here, and not at the clattering female-thronged tearoom where the management and the waitresses smiled at her familiarly and knew beforehand the dishes she would order; or, worse, at her cluttered desk at the Institute, distractedly spooning yogurt into her mouth or gnawing at an apple, or a croissant, while frowning over material that Mr. Morland, in what Dorothea thought of as the man's wholly factitious premature senility, had dumped into her lap. Here at least, in this elegant setting, amid the flash of cutlery and gilt-edged china and the murmurous intonations of the wine steward—and had not Dorothea, entering, glimpsed several acquaintances dining here today too? including, even, a ripple-haired gentleman who at first glance resembled Mr. Roger Krauss, the trustee who bore her such spirited ill will?—Dorothea Deverell might be mistaken as a person of consequence. For why otherwise would so striking a young man, in a modish black silk shirt and very casual jeans, a young man not related to her or in any way obliged to her, be addressing her with such interest and exuberance? Why would he listen so attentively to her every word, as if he meant to memorize it?

Colin Asch was saying, "I was afraid you wouldn't remember me, Dorothea."

Dorothea said, as if in gentle reproof, "Of course I remembered you."

"But you must meet so many people, in your position—so many important people."

"Not so very many. And not so consistently important."

"Ah, but I find that hard to believe!"

Colin leaned eagerly forward, his elbows on the table, regarding Dorothea with intense, rather quizzical, warmly brown eyes. His face with its fine-cut features seemed illuminated from within; he smiled repeatedly. He had brushed his long pale hair deftly back from his forehead so that it fell, in languid waves, behind his ears and curled over his collar. He had shaved carefully and anointed himself with a faintly scented lotion. His fingernails were short, as if bitten, but scrupulously clean; on the third finger of his right hand he wore a gold signet ring; a high-tech digital watch with an iridescent black face gleamed on his left wrist. In the oversized sports coat with its bulky shoulders and wide lapels he looked like a boy whimsically disguised in his father's clothing.

As the meal progressed without incident—the smiling young Italian-looking waiter had shrewdly deferred to Colin Asch's authority from the start—Colin visibly relaxed, as did Dorothea. There was, even, no fuss about the menu, or the food; since the vegetarian dishes did not seem particularly appealing, Colin Asch ordered soft-shelled crabs, saying that, since coming to stay with the Weidmanns, he had had to modify his vegetarian diet to a degree. "I didn't want Aunt Ginny to be preparing special meals for me," he said.

They talked for a brief while about vegetarianism, and animal rights, and the philosophical problem of what constitutes consciousness, personality, and selfhood: if the ability to use language is necessary to a definition of "selfhood," what then of brain-damaged human beings who have no language? Are they any more "animals" than normal human beings? Are animals who respond to or (in the case of certain celebrated chimpanzees) actually learn to use language more "human" than these afflicted people? But then—for Colin Asch's transitions were abrupt—they were talking about the Marin watercolor exhibit again, and about "great art" and its effect upon the soul, and what art schools in the area would Dorothea recommend? Colin intended to apply sometime soon. He asked about her background, her training, and wondered if he too might apply to Yale, then discarded the notion; Yale was probably one of these snobbish intellectual places, like Johns Hopkins, Harvard, Princeton, that looked down their noses at you if you didn't have the right degree. "It must be wonderful, Dorothea," he said, smiling quizzically, "the kind of job you have. At the Brannon Institute. Aunt Ginny was telling me a little about it." He paused. "And about you."

Dorothea's face, which showed her emotions far too nakedly, must have stiffened in apprehension, or in pain, for Colin Asch quickly amended, with a delicate sort of tact, "I mean—how active you are in the community. How much everyone likes you, how many friends you have."

The words hovered oddly in the air as if challenging Dorothea to refute them. But they were true enough, she supposed. Hardly the whole truth but true enough.

With a queer ducking smile she said, "And not a word about my 'tragic' life?"

Colin Asch laughed, baring his teeth in a sweet spontaneous

gesture, like a muscular reflex. "Ah, my aunt is very good at 'tragic' lives!"

To Dorothea's relief he did not pursue the subject but went on to talk, with his characteristic effervescence, of other things, and Dorothea was spared the obligatory recital of personal facts that had so sadly but inevitably calcified, with time, into mere facts—the romance of the "whirlwind" courtship, the brief marriage, the subsequent widowhood. In telling new acquaintances about her background—for, invariably, they asked, as Dorothea Deverell asked after theirs—Dorothea found herself in the ironic position of stimulating sympathy, even, in her more sensitive listeners, emotion, in which she could no longer truly share. Thus in their early rather giddy rather disorganized meetings Charles Carpenter would allude as if guiltily to the shock she'd had to bear so many years before, and how brave she'd been, and so on and so forth, embracing her, kissing her, in a passion that seemed as much reverential as sexual, so that Dorothea had to resist the impulse to say, in healthy exasperation, "But Michel has been dead for a long time! *You* are the man I adore!"

Near the end of the meal it seemed to Dorothea that Colin Asch began to speak more rapidly; his talk was bright, brilliant, funny, electric. It was late—nearly two o'clock—but he insisted that Dorothea share a small light fruit soufflé with him and have coffee, or tea—herbal tea?—which the smiling young waiter went to fetch. When Dorothea dared broach the subject of halving the bill—"You can't really afford this, aren't you looking for a job?"—Colin Asch stared at her for a startled, hurt instant, as if she had said something incomprehensible. "But of course not, Dorothea," he said softly. "Of course *not*."

As they were leaving the restaurant Dorothea encountered, to her extreme embarrassment, Roger Krauss, in the boisterous company of several men, doubtless businessmen like himself, and Mr. Krauss, a thickset bulldog-looking man in his late fifties, with dark thick hair rippled across the crest of his head and sharp shrewd maliciously merry eyes, not only advanced upon Dorothea with an exuberant mock-friendly greeting—"Miss Deverell! I *thought* that was you inside!"—but stood in such a position in front of the coat check counter, unbudging, that Dorothea had no choice but to introduce him to Colin Asch, with the low murmured words, "Colin is Ginny Weidmann's nephew, he's visiting them for a while," though there was no reason surely—surely!—for any explanation. Colin Asch, flush-faced from the excitement of the meal, just zipping up his soiled sheepskin jacket, flashed Krauss an eerily beautiful smile, like a muscular reflex, and shook his hand too, vigorously. In the company of his grinning friends (to whom, Dorothea knew, he'd been speaking of her) Krauss backed off, pulling a sporty black lamb's-wool astrakhan hat down low on his brow and saying, "How nice of *you*, Dorothea, to entertain the boy!"

The riposte was pointless but cruel; cruel because pointless; and Dorothea was so silent on the drive back to the Institute that at last Colin Asch said, in an almost frightened voice, "That man—is he an evil man?"

Dorothea laughed and said, "Oh, hardly evil! Just not so very nice."

"He seemed to know you," Colin said hesitantly.

And Dorothea said, "He's someone connected with the Institute—one of the trustees," but because the day was so brightly sunny, the mere fact of driving in Colin Asch's handsome Cutlass Calais so innocently pleasurable, she decided to say nothing more of Roger Krauss; or even, so long as it could be postponed, to think of him. There would be ample time for Krauss later, at home. In her bath. In her bed. In the blurry hallucinatory hours of the night when Dorothea Deverell was so frequently wakened from sleep as by an urgent voice in the very room with her: and lay awake, most nights, for a long time, stiff and resistant and helpless.

Colin Asch persisted, glancing at Dorothea, "He seems to have upset you, though. What was the name? Roger Krauss?"

Dorothea said, almost gaily, "He didn't upset me at all. I'm not that easily upset."

At the Institute she thanked Colin Asch for the elegant lunch—overpriced as she'd feared, but delicious. "Now I hope you and the Weidmanns will come to my house for dinner sometime soon, before Christmas at least," she said, shaking the young man's hand; and he, frowning, purse-lipped, retaining her hand just a fraction of a second too long, said, "Christmas is a long way off, Dorothea."

Dorothea Deverell lived, alone, seemingly by perverse choice, at the curve of a cul-de-sac called Marten Lane; there were no more than six or seven houses on the lane, each old, made of brick or stone, possessed of a crumbly storybook sort of quaintness though not—yet—certifiably "historic." Dorothea's house, bought with a small legacy when she was thirty-one, was made of an alveolate gray stone; the date 1878 had been chipped into one of the front steps. There were, facing the street, two square-cut windows on each of the floors, framed by black shutters in need of fresh paint; the roof was black-shingled, with a look of pushing downward, like a low brow. Inside, the first-floor rooms were large enough, without being spacious; the upstairs rooms, three bedrooms and an old-fashioned bath, were rather cramped. The single staircase at the center of the house was narrow and steep as farmhouse stairs—"Of course this was a country place when it was built," Dorothea felt obliged to inform visitors new to the house. "It was probably a farm; this area was outside the village limits." There came then the inevitable exclamations—how lovely, how perfect for you, how lucky you were to find it—and these facts Dorothea knew to be true. An irony of her circumstance was that, at the time she had been distractedly house hunting, she had resolved she would find a place, for herself, for life; she would never remarry, would never again expose herself to the risk (now needless: for wasn't she self-supporting?) of unspeakable loss. And it was Agnes Carpenter, at that time more generally sociable and even, it had seemed, tolerably fond of Dorothea, who had told her about the house, urged her to telephone the elderly owner (a widow) before the house was officially listed with a realtor.

Though renovated at some expense by previous owners—new kitchen, new electrical fixtures, new plate glass windows to the rear—Dorothea's house exuded, still, a broody damp air, as if sullen secrets were retained in its walls that no amount of light or cheery interior decorating could dispel. And the ceilings, while not literally low, had the look of so being; Dorothea's guests, entering her dining room, nearly always glanced up at the ceiling, and the taller men had an instinct to duck. Entering Dorothea's bedroom, Charles Carpenter too glanced upward, a faint nervous smile on his lips. He was a tall man, about six foot two, and low doorways made him uneasy.

In the house, Dorothea's favorite room was not her bedroom, despite its romantic memories and hopes, but her living room downstairs, which centered upon a large fieldstone fireplace, and which she had furnished with a mélange of things, some from the days of her marriage, some inherited, some newly purchased: a marble-topped coffee table with Italian Provincial legs, a pair of Queen Anne chairs cushioned in dusty rose, an impractically cream-colored sofa in spirit like a chaise lounge, outfitted with numerous pillows, upon which, in the evening, she liked to lie. There was a faded Chinese rug laid upon the hardwood floor that was too small for the room, but no matter. There were hanging plants, plants on windowsills, potted plants listing in corners. There were four antique clocks of which three were in working order but struck the hour at unexpected times; Dorothea liked their waywardness, suggesting as it did that time did not matter but might be a function of individual eccentricity. The coffee table was heaped with magazines and books, for Dorothea Deverell had become one of those persons who begins one book, lays it down and begins another, lays that down and begins yet another, and so until several are in orbit simultaneously; none powerful enough to dispel the others, yet none so negligible as to be shelved or tossed away. Since girlhood Dorothea felt obscurely that to open a book—a serious book, at least—was to enter voluntarily into a contractual relationship of sorts with its author: one was obliged to stay with it until the end, or, at the least, out of civility, one was obliged to make that effort. She read too with an almost fervid concentration, a groping sort of intensity, as if in pursuit of elusive life-altering truths or ghostly images of herself tossed up in distant mirrors in unknown rooms. And the old romance of reading returned to her, that evening, curled up on the sofa in her rather shabby cashmere bathrobe, her paperback of Shelley's *Selected Poems* in her lap.

She read, pausing now and then to recall that day's so very unexpected excursion and to wonder at Ginny's young nephew, who had orchestrated it—in fact (recalling the reservation, made without Dorothea's knowledge) engineered it. In his presence Dorothea had felt alternately charmed and overwhelmed; now she was left, as with the aftertaste of too much wine drunk at too early an hour, slightly disoriented. The flamelike intensity of his being was admirable but exhausting: she would not want to see Colin Asch again soon, or too frequently—the remainder of her afternoon at the Institute was headachy and fatigued, as if the hour and a half spent at L'Auberge's darkened interior had sucked her vitality from her even as it nourished her. (For the food had indeed been delicious, quashing the need for Dorothea to prepare any evening meal for herself at all.) At one point, driving her back to the Institute, Colin Asch had said apologetically that he hoped he hadn't talked too much and hadn't interrupted her too frequently —it was an old habit of his, he said, but only when he was in the presence of certain people. Most of the time, he said, he spent by himself, in silence, and that silence spilled over—he had used those actual words, "spilled over"—into time spent in company with other people; but when he was in the presence of certain people something seemed to happen. "I guess I'm just lonely. For the right kind of friend." This, Dorothea had not wanted to pursue. She'd murmured something about his aunt's having told her that he had a good many friends—hadn't that young woman Hartley

Evans telephoned him?—but this Colin Asch himself did not care to pursue, as if unworthy of their attention or as if in fact he hadn't given it much thought.

Like many quiet, intelligent, congenitally introverted people, Dorothea Deverell prided herself on her powers of analysis, of self and others. They were not assertive powers in any public sense, but they gave her solace at such times, for it seemed to her that the puzzle Colin Asch represented—Ginny Weidmann had referred to him as a "mystery" but surely that was exaggeration?—could be logically worked out if Dorothea applied herself to it. For one thing, the young man's attraction for her, very likely temporary, was that of a son for a mother. (It would not surprise Dorothea in the slightest if she resembled the long-dead Mrs. Asch. She would ask Ginny to show her snapshots.) But the primary fact about Colin Asch was not really that he was an orphan—there are many orphans, after all—but that he was a remarkable person: possessed of a lightning-quick mind, a true if mercurial intelligence, a lively tireless curiosity, and, rare in a young person, a respect for the feelings of others that had seemed, at times, almost morbidly heightened. He had watched Dorothea's face closely; he had stared almost greedily—like an infant staring up at the adult faces above it, equipped by nature with the neurological mechanisms that would provide in time a decoding of their bizarre utterances, but only in time.

How exhausting, though, such sympathy! Dorothea thought. Her impetuous young escort had several times, and always successfully, made a stab at guessing her thoughts.

Like Dorothea Deverell herself, though in a more extreme fashion, Colin Asch had yet to "connect" with life. You could see it in his frank innocent open gaze before he opened his mouth to say a word. He had no career, and his prospects were as unformed as those of a bright eighth-grader. Too much attracted him—indeed, enthralled him. A young man of his gifts who spent his time driving aimlessly about the country, dropping in on relatives on the spur of the moment, or backpacking through Europe or northern Africa—clearly, no one had taken him in hand; no one had forced him to apply himself to the effort of growing up. It was admirable perhaps that he was looking for a job—Ginny Weidmann seemed to think so—but for what sort of job was he suited? His chatter about himself that day, both evasive and artless, had indicated he had never completed any course of study, had never earned any degree. Art school seemed the most pathetic sort of chimera.

Dorothea perceived in Colin Asch, as in herself, a fatal lack of strength, drive, ambition. Not an excess but a deficiency of ego was the problem. He was a young man who could assert himself with parking-lot attendants and waiters but had clearly failed at asserting himself in the matter of life. A tempestuous uncharted energy, like that of Shelley's West Wind, seemed to blow him about from place to place, and Dorothea had winced slightly at his ready employment of the word "evil"—even while doubting that he meant it in any literal sense. It was a child's word, and it had sprung childishly from his lips. But he had not meant it, Dorothea concluded—he was too like herself.

When Charles Carpenter telephoned that evening (by the ease of his voice Dorothea knew he was not at home but at his office in Boston, perhaps, or in some neutral place) and asked Dorothea about her day, she did not tell him about Colin Asch, reasoning that the little excursion would never be repeated, but she did tell him how cozily content she was, how almost blissfully happy, curled up on her sofa, reading a yellowed paperback book dating from her Bryn Mawr days; and what was his opinion of such verse—

Drive my dead thoughts over the universe
Like withered leaves to quicken a new birth!
And, by the incantation of this verse,

Scatter, as from an unextinguished hearth
Ashes and sparks, my words among mankind!

Be through my lips to unawakened earth
The trumpet of a prophecy! O Wind,
If Winter comes, can Spring be far behind?

"Beautiful, isn't it?" Dorothea asked, a little breathless. "We take Shelley for granted."

"Yes. Beautiful," Charles Carpenter said.

4

"Beautiful."

Colin Asch's breath streamed whitely from him, warm blood-heated vapor that immediately turned cold. Almost directly overhead a full moon shone: bone-white, powerful as a beacon of light, making his eyes ache pleasurably. Moonstruck: what did it mean? Was it real, was it a scientific fact or some old archaic superstition? *I was moonstruck*, Colin Asch would afterward record in the Blue Ledger, but he would not record his nervous excitement, his hopeful smile as he lifted the heavy binoculars another time. *Not to blame: MOONSTRUCK.*

Inside the warm-lit house some fifty or sixty feet from where Colin Asch stood in the shelter of a snowy Douglas fir, she lay curled on a sofa in the innocence of believing herself unobserved. Colin understood by her position, bare feet tucked beneath the hem of the beautiful green robe, pillow behind her at about the height of her shoulder blades, that this was a familiar pose, a favored place: *no one had ever seen Dorothea Deverell quite like that, nor had she ever seen herself thus.*

The telephone had just rung, and Dorothea Deverell had set aside her book, and now she lay back with the telephone receiver crooked against her left shoulder, the fingers of her right hand twining…nervously? happily?…in the phone's tight-curled cord. Colin wondered to whom she was speaking, but it was true wonder, not jealousy, for it made him happy that she was happy, if those were the valid signs of happiness he observed in her face.

This was not the first time that Colin Asch had positioned himself shrewdly in such a way as to observe unobserved Dorothea Deverell, but it was the first time he had trespassed on her property, the first time he had watched her in the sanctuary of her home *where, that night, she was doubly safe*, protected by the walls of the house and by her friend outside. Thus he felt no guilt, or nearly none. He guessed that, if Dorothea Deverell suspected his presence, she would throw open the door of the house to call to him. *Colin, is that you? Colin? Why are you outside in the cold, why don't you come in here…?*

He could imagine her voice, that lovely lifting bell-like voice.

But of course she was still on the telephone, still curled up so comfortably on the sofa, her mahogany-dark hair glossy in the lamplight, her pale skin with a look of alabaster radiance, for even if one day Dorothea Deverell should suspect that Colin Asch was observing her at such private times or more public times, he understood that she was the kind of woman, a natural-born lady, who would never want Colin to know that she knew…for the specialness between them was just this: that each "knew" while appearing not to "know." For this knowledge if too crudely revealed would ruin everything, the very sacredness of the understanding…like acting in a play while simultaneously "acting" and aware of both the audience and yourself, thus the danger of forgetting entire passages of dialogue, bringing the play itself to a premature end.

But she knew. Didn't she know? She knew—in a way. As Colin Asch had known immediately. Weeks ago. The first exchange of glances, the startled recognition. *Soul-mate* was Shelley's word, *soul-mate* the word of the poets. *Mate of one's soul*, and it is through the eyes the souls initially declare themselves, while words, groping, barely adequate, can only follow.

And that day—their time together. When she'd listened so kindly, with such sympathy. Her smile, her warm intelligent eyes, her small hand warm and dry in his, yes thank you, thank you it has been a lovely surprise, though he understood she'd shrunk a little from him too; he would have to be careful in the future not to overwhelm her.

Talking too much, asshole. Cool it.

Guess I'm just lonely. For a friend.

Afterward for a long time he was scared and excited, eyes kept filling up with moisture, spilling over, running down his face, and his pulse was fast, faster than he liked, as if he'd swallowed something unknowingly or been injected in a vein without his knowledge or signed consent. Driving the Olds along streets he didn't know, on the expressway going west for a while, laughing, talking to himself, for a while singing fragments of church songs ("Come, O Holy Redeemer" was the one he seemed to know best) from his days in the boy choir before his voice changed, those days (years) remote to Colin Asch now and indifferent as a scene in a photograph or glimpsed on the far side of a river, and you can look at it, even hear it, without the contamination of emotion or desire; it is all other people, and they have nothing to do with you. Toward night when the streetlights switched on—*how he loved that instant! like the first instant of creation!*—the mania began to stabilize; he was able to meet H.E. as they'd planned in Luigi's near the television studio and she had good news for him about the job he'd interviewed for, though she was pouty and sullen at first because out of innocent forgetfulness and not calculation he was almost half an hour late, but he was so sweet he was so apologetic so loving she forgave him of course and they went back to her place and Colin Asch was laid and that stabilized him a little more, *You're so beautiful Christ I'm crazy about you can't get enough of you love love love you baby,* so sincere and almost pleading as if he were frightened of her of the power she'd have over him when all the while his brain was working fast and smooth as a machine and he explained that he couldn't stay the night since his aunt and uncle were expecting him and he was already late. Thus he got away just past 10 P.M., kissing her at the elevator his arm so tight crooked around her head she winced in startled pain and their mouths bruised together, tongues sucking like the real thing *oh sweetheart I'll call you tomorrow try to see you tomorrow if I can wait that long* in the elevator descending wiping lipstick and spittle from his mouth but he liked her really, *did* like her—she'd kept her word about helping him and the job would be his *Colin Asch's first step in the television business* though he'd have to hold out for a slightly higher salary, he'd earned more than that as a taxi dispatcher and a lot more than that working on an offshore oil rig in the Gulf of Mexico a couple of years ago. "Are you serious about that salary?" he'd ask, smiling his sweet quizzical smile; then he'd say with a soft little laugh, "Well—I guess you are." He got in the Olds and drove up to Lathrup Farms, parked at the mouth of Marten Lane in the shadows where no one was likely to notice the car, then crossed silently slantwise through lots neighboring 33 Marten Lane where Dorothea Deverell lived—tall beautiful fragrant trees lightly encrusted with snow, and the rears of the houses exposed like sawing through a skull: wild!—but he took no unnecessary risks, this wasn't the time, eyes dilated in the dark and senses alert as a wild animal's in the presence of its enemies, until he was at the rear of Dorothea Deverell's stone house where he'd never been before (though he had twice during the day when he knew Dorothea Deverell wouldn't have been home strolled past the front with no intention other than simply recording with his eyes), standing crouched in the shelter of an evergreen, raising the binoculars shakily to his eyes. And there suddenly she *was*. There—she *was*.

Lying on the creamy-colored sofa, scattered pillows around her, vivid green robe, the peep of bare toes, expression somber, intense, wholly surrendered to the book she was reading—which he saw with a thrill of pleasure was Shelley's *Selected Poems*: his very book! She knew nothing of him of course. Sensed no alien presence. He would stay only a few minutes, then leave as quietly as he'd come, for the last thing on earth Colin Asch wanted was to frighten or upset or in any way embarrass Dorothea Deverell: "I'd rather blow out my brains."

In the stark unflattering sunshine of midday Dorothea Deverell had looked to Colin Asch's sharp eye slightly less beautiful than he recalled from the evening when he'd first seen her, and on the afternoon of the music recital through his magical smoked lenses, but now by lamplight the woman's youthful beauty was restored.

Alabaster-smooth skin, eyes so dark as to appear black...the curve of the brow, and the narrow curve of the nose...the perfect slightly pursed (wetted?) lips. As she read Shelley's poetry she was sounding the words to herself like music. She read the poetry as if by that means she were reading Colin Asch.

No human face but the sculpted face of Saint Teresa. The Italian sculptor Bernini. Was it Bernini? The perfect face—*was* it Saint Teresa?—lifted in dreamy ecstasy, sleepy eyelids hooded, and there stood before her a smiling angel with a golden spear just drawn back from plunging the weapon into her heart—or was it Leonardo? In that instant Colin Asch was excited *but made no move to touch himself not wanting to desecrate the moment.*

Moonstruck.

He lowered the binoculars to give his numbed forearms a rest, then raised them again. Old-fashioned heavy binoculars but high-powered: he'd found them poking around in the Weidmanns' basement gathering dust on a shelf with broken-stringed old tennis racquets, the kind with wooden frames. If he had asked his aunt or uncle for the use of the binoculars they would have said yes of course but he was too shrewd to ask: never ask any more favors than you require. Just take. *And keep your mouth shut.* (Colin intended to replace the binoculars as discreetly as he had replaced the diamond earrings and the onyx cuff links when he decided to stay with the Weidmanns as their guest...though he hadn't troubled to replace the money in Aunt Ginny's purse, knowing, rich bitch, she'd never miss such small change, and she hadn't, and even if she had would she dare accuse him to his face...*him?*)

Inside the house, the telephone conversation had acquired a new urgency. Dorothea Deverell no longer twined her fingers in the cord but was gesturing with that hand, sitting up, speaking intently...frowning, and smiling, and smiling frowningly, even nodding, baring her teeth in a grimace of emotion. What was she saying? Was it a quarrel? Suddenly, the perversity of the situation struck Colin Asch: for Dorothea Deverell, showing emotion, waving her hand in the air, behaved, as people do in such instances, as if the party at the other end of the line could see her while knowing of course that he (or she) could *not*—yet, simultaneously, unknowingly, *she was in fact being observed through binoculars.* And for the first time Colin Asch felt a wave of guilt, shame. For he was taking advantage of the woman he admired most in the world, and he could not rationalize that this would have given her pleasure—ah, hardly!

Yet he did not lower the binoculars. It was late—nearing midnight. The white-glaring moon had shifted its position overhead. As if sensing his presence, Dorothea Deverell glanced upward, staring at the window, frowning severely—but Colin knew she could not see him; he was too far away, and hidden; and, in any case, the windowpane of a lighted room, at night, reflects only the interior of the room. Dorothea Deverell ran her fingers through her hair in a sudden impatient gesture that seemed to Colin out of character. Was she about to cry? Was she laughing? A spasm of unreadable emotion passed over her face. *What was she saying? To whom was she saying it? And at so late an hour? A lover? Did Dorothea Deverell have a lover?*

Colin Asch took a step backward as if someone had shoved him.

"I wouldn't like that."

This was not the first time in Colin Asch's life that he had been drawn powerless to resist into the orbit (as he thought of it, and wrote of it in the Blue Ledger) of Woman; for there had been, many years before Dorothea Deverell, the summer when Colin Asch was thirteen years old living with relatives and he'd gone with them to their Wyoming ranch where there was a woman named Mindy—or was it Mandy?—the young blond wife of a neighboring rancher with whom Colin's relatives were friends, and this woman taught Colin to ride a horse, and this woman saw in Colin's face what no others wished to see. Too bad you aren't my kid! she'd joke, roughing his hair, giving him a poke in the arm as boys do with one another, but she had her own children, horse-riding loud-mouthed children who hated Colin Asch, and that summer he'd followed her with his wide staring sleepless eyes and was discovered several times outside her house in the early morning before sunrise where he hadn't any reason to be or any right so there were cruel jokey things said and she stopped coming around and Colin knew they all talked behind his back; thus before they left at the end of August he took his revenge and though no one could prove it had been Colin Asch who had set the fire they seemed all of them to know; thus he came to hate Mindy (or was it Mandy?—he hated even the name) and the family he'd lived with, whose name he had never recorded in the Blue Ledger. And at the Monmouth Academy there was Mrs. Kendrich, the chaplain's wife who had befriended Colin Asch from the start, giving him books to read and offering critiques of his poetry and praying with him, and when the rumors began of the headmaster's secret circle it was Mrs. Kendrich who went to Mr. Kreuzer; thus there was bitterness between them and division at the school…and the night that Colin Asch discovered the body in the bloody bedclothes and ran outside barefoot in the snow it was Mrs. Kendrich who found him… who saved his life. And at the inquest she had protected him.

And there were one or two others recorded in the Blue Ledger—no more. In the course of fifteen years, no more. And none of the women had been so wonderful as Dorothea Deverell: none so beautiful, and none so well-bred and ladylike, so refined, so intelligent too—*for Dorothea Deverell was a match in intellect for any man.* (Only by chance, by way of a remark of Colin's aunt, had he learned that Dorothea was the author of three small art books: monographs, with color plates, on the American artists Isabel Bishop, Charles Demuth, and Arthur Dove! Of course she was too modest to have mentioned them herself when Colin had asked about her work.)

And she is an heiress. One day (perhaps) to inherit yet more.
And she is independent of any man.
And she is pure. And good. And yet unjudging.
Of the one tenth of one percent of the world's population that

stands apart from the rest she is clearly one of us—yet speaks softly and sympathetically.

Her influence is palpable as the moon's on the tide but it is an influence for peace, for calm, for love, for surrender. Not the fierce pounding surf but the gentle lapping on the beach like the approach of sleep. Like the joy of the Blue Room itself—no sound, no shadows! No gravity!

So Colin Asch recorded in the Ledger, sitting on his bed, 4 A.M. and as awake as at midday and writing, writing…his pen moving rapidly across the page as if entranced with no regard for lines, margins, red-inked columns. (The Ledger, appropriated from a closet of office supplies at the Monmouth Academy, was an accountant's book, of an awkward size, its covers of stiff cardboard and much battered and stained over the years. Especially toward the front pages were missing, crudely torn out. Other pages were covered in handwritings of various types, in various shades of ink, predominantly blue but also green, red, purple, and crimson; there were erasures that had resulted in serious tears, mended with transparent tape; there were sections crossed out so elaborately that *no one not even Colin Asch himself could have deciphered them.* For the past six years or so the code Colin used had been consistent but before that he'd used other far more tricky codes; thus if he looked back to earlier entries he was often stymied by their meaning though he never doubted that, had he the time and patience to puzzle over them, he could crack his own ingenuity!) Like a man running with a pyramid of eggs in his hands, heartstoppingly beautiful exotic eggs he saw them, the aqua of robins' eggs but larger, painted eggs perhaps as at Easter, like a man entrusted with beauty of exquisite fragility he was desperate to record certain wonders, *to set down permanently certain visions and revelations entrusted to him,* which had their focus entirely upon Dorothea Deverell and granted no significance at all to the fact or facts that so pleased others—that of the numerous job interviews Colin Asch had had in the past two weeks several offers had been made to him *and excellent offers too for prospective employers were bowled over by the young man's appearance manner intelligence sensitivity wide-ranging background and experience in many walks of life above all by his ability to speak and to "relate,"* and he had decided after all to accept the position at WWBC-TV though the beginning salary was modest and might forestall for a while Colin Asch's moving to an apartment of his own. How exciting, dear, how lovely, Aunt Ginny'd said, clasping his hands warmly; you could see the affection shining in the old girl's eyes, Aunt Ginny was one of the few people on this shitty planet who gave a shit for Colin Asch and he knew he could rely on her, if there was some stiffness beginning with Martin Weidmann—and Colin Asch's powers of detection were raised to the nth power in such matters, *just try to put something over on this boy you cocksuckers*—he knew she would protect him, take his side, for it would come to that eventually, in such circumstances living in such close quarters like a family though the Weidmanns had had sense enough to give Colin his own key and to allow him complete privacy, still it always came to that in the end—a woman bravely defending Colin Asch against some detractor or enemy.

"Fuckers."

And then, a moment later, since the hoarse word hung strangely in the air: "But things are changed now."

It was true: Colin Asch had a job in television, he'd performed so charismatically on the talk show—Dave Slattery's *On Your Toes*—calls to the studio Hartley said were five to one in his favor which was "fantastic" and "unprecedented" because Slattery's viewing audience was usually conservative if not reactionary and Slattery did his best to trip people up on camera but Colin Asch maintained his good-natured calm smiling dignity remembering always to look directly into the camera with the red light burning *to make eye contact with the invisible television audience;* thus he won even Slattery's grudging respect it seemed—and viewers you would not predict to be tolerant of weird ideas like vegetarianism and the "rights" of animals, not least Colin Asch's long shining Christly pale hair, were wild for him as Hartley Evans said. And she said, each time she introduced Colin Asch to one of her co-workers, "He's a natural for the medium."

And indeed Hartley Evans's co-workers liked Colin Asch very much too. Shook his hand warmly and sincerely. Congratulated him. A few days later in the studio the manager interviewed him just casually over coffee in Styrofoam cups; yes there was an opening, a sort of assistant's assistant, you could say it was a sort of internship, not much salary to begin with but "there's definitely a future," and Colin told him of his experience in Germany and also a job he'd had with a small television station in Galveston, Texas, sure he could get references if that was necessary, if that wouldn't hold things up—"I'm eager, you know, to get *started*." The manager shrugged off the need for references in this instance, the job was practically on-the-job training after all, a handshake and it was settled, and Hartley Evans slid her arms around his neck afterward, nuzzling and biting his lower lip, fiddling her fingers in his hair as if she had the right, but Colin Asch was suffused with pleasure and allowed it, allowed her anything she wished, childishly passive even malleable in her hands until of course it was time for him to assert his dominance, enter her between her legs, "make love" as it was called—his mind floating and skittering free of his laboring body there between the slightly fattish white thighs opening and closing in an increasingly frenzied rhythm until with a scream (Colin Asch could not have said it was from her throat, or from his) it was over, and an hour later it seemed, though in fact it must have been the next morning just before noon, he dropped by the old renovated Tudor mansion that was the Brannon Institute just to inform Dorothea Deverell quietly but proudly that he had a job—"I'll probably be on camera in about six months"—with WWBC-TV in downtown Boston, his face lighting up happily *at her face lighting up happily* at his good news. He was mildly disappointed when she confessed she hadn't seen the talk show, rarely watched television she said, but clearly she was impressed by the position, by what it meant for Colin Asch's future in the media; he heard himself saying excitedly that "the electronic media is the soul of America, the communal soul," and with this Dorothea Deverell puzzlingly concurred, and though he'd meant to mention her books to her—that he intended to buy them, to read them, to discuss them with her—he'd had time only to skim through his aunt's copies thus far—it was wild! so many interviews for jobs, so many telephone calls, in the past five or six days!—all that slipped from his mind in the exigency of the moment but he came to his senses quickly when Dorothea Deverell invited him to sit for a few minutes, realizing that he'd better be discreet and get the hell out: he knew she was busy (the telephone had rung on her desk, she'd put the call on hold) *and he was busy too*, expected down at the studio early that afternoon. Just thought I'd drop by to say hello, he said, and Dorothea Deverell smiled and said, Any time, Colin, and all accomplished smoothly *absolutely naturally with not a single misstep.* At the door hesitating, glancing back—"I suppose I share your disdain for television, Dorothea, but it *is* a job: a beginning."

And she said at once, "Oh, yes, of course."

> *The world is a lonely place, lonely as the grave. We live in silence primarily—and in solitude—and this fact the "media" would deny. From this flows the power of the "media" for both evil and good.*

These observations Colin Asch recorded thoughtfully in the Blue Ledger, after his first week as assistant manager's assistant at the station. One day soon he would reveal his findings to the television audience—if the fuckers who ran WWBC gave him a chance.

"—I mean it just seems so damned unjust that a woman of Dorothea's qualifications and, let's face it, her *quality* should be treated like that," Ginny Weidmann was saying into the telephone, as Colin casually passed the door. "Especially since Howard Morland has always been so fond of her and these past few years—*is* it his health? is it his heart?—he has certainly taken advantage of her goodwill, and, you know, her capacity for—*I* don't know—her capacity for not wanting to see the truth of the situation. I'm not saying of course—who am I to say?—that Roger Krauss's nephew or whoever he is isn't qualified, for all any of us knows even more qualified—no, but I *didn't* say that, Sandra! For God's sake don't misquote me!—but I *am* saying that Dorothea has a right to the directorship, a moral right, quite apart from her qualifications, and the board of trustees should be forcibly reminded of that if necessary." She paused; she listened; Colin Asch, hovering just beyond the doorway, paused too, his heart going hard but slow in his chest. Ginny said with a harsh exhalation of breath that might have been a sigh, "No, nothing is definite, it's all just rumor. Martin says we should let things develop as they will—for one thing, Howard hasn't officially announced his retirement—and Dorothea's programs this season have been so successful, I'm sure even Roger Krauss can't fault them—I really can't see, you know, how the board could vote against offering her the directorship, how, you know, they could actually *do* it. I mean, Evelyn Mercer is a trustee and she is such a sweet, basically a sweet decent fair-minded woman—of course she *is* the only woman; that's one of the problems. Roger Krauss has made it into such an issue of sex—of gender—talking so irresponsibly as if Dorothea has her present position only because she *is* a woman and that the board did her a favor by hiring her!"

Colin, in his car, driving in early evening traffic along the boulevard, on his way to inspect an apartment in Lathrup Farms Mews—a brand-new apartment-condominium complex actually located in the suburb of Danvers, immediately adjacent to Lathrup Farms: Colin was "looking at" apartments now—whistled from start to finish, flawlessly, that classic song of Schumann's, "Widmung."

December 19: Colin Asch is twenty-eight years old.

Lying awake sweating and calculating…if there were some tactful way of allowing Dorothea Deverell to know of the birthday he was sure she'd want to have him, and the Weidmanns of course, to her house for dinner, for hadn't she promised weeks ago and she surely did not seem to be the kind of person, the kind of woman, who fails to honor her promises, he has happened—ah, really just by chance! *really* by chance!—to see her now and then in the village, in Lyman's (the quality grocer where Ginny Weidmann shops too, and Colin cheerfully goes on errands when he's in the mood) and in the dry cleaner's and in the library where it's clear everyone knows her name, everyone likes her—*faces lighting up as she approaches, as if she were bringing a warmth of pure radiant light*—and in the drugstore making purchases, her back to him poised and straight in the attractive black cloth coat with the filmy fur collar, then crossing Main Street to the parking lot to her car, the classy Burgundy-red Mercedes Colin Asch has come to know so well, he observes quietly from a post near a building just to see: if the car's motor starts, or if, you can't always tell, the car's wheels might spin in the ice; there is a treacherous layer of hard rippled ice beneath the powdery snow, and Dorothea Deverell might need help....

Colin Asch broached the subject casually to his Aunt Ginny, not that Dorothea Deverell might want to have a birthday party for him of course but that he, Colin, wanted to celebrate by taking the Weidmanns out to dinner—the restaurant of their choice, and perhaps Dorothea Deverell would like to join them?—but as Colin should have known, Ginny insisted she would have the dinner herself, at home; she hadn't known the nineteenth was Colin's birthday—and it was coming up so quickly! why hadn't he given her warning?—and he really was spending too much money on restaurants, wasn't he—her fond worried eyes searching his—but Colin wasn't listening to every syllable; he nodded, winced, said a little impatiently, "OK, but do you think your friend Dorothea would like to join us?" and Ginny hesitated a moment before saying of course, she'd call Dorothea, that *was* a good idea, but she'd thought—again searching his eyes quizzically—"Probably you would like me to invite Hartley? Aren't you and Hartley...?" and her voice trailed off discreetly and in a moment of hauteur Colin said, "Hartley and I are—" as if really he couldn't imagine what Ginny was thinking of, what the precise literal even clinical term was; thus it fell to the fat-faced busybody cunt to supply it, not "fucking" (as perhaps she was thinking; the old girl knew which end was up) but "—seeing each other? Quite often? That's the impression I have—am I mistaken?"

Colin was back on his heels now. Cool it. Easy. Saying, smiling, "I guess that's right, Aunt Ginny. I'm so grateful to you for introducing us." He paused, and they smiled happily at each other, like conspirators. "Hartley is such a special person."

"She is, she is!" Ginny said, as if the issue had been in some doubt. "So you'd like me to call her, then? For Saturday evening?"

"And your friend Miss Deverell too?"

"And Dorothea too—of course."

Afterward Ginny said almost accusingly, "Colin, I'm really so glad you told me your birthday was imminent. It would have been a pity for none of us to know. Are there other things about you, dear, you should tell us?"—smiling, as if teasing—"other secrets?"

Colin laughed. "Not a one, Aunt!"

But to Colin's regret Dorothea Deverell could not come to his birthday party: terribly sorry, she told Ginny, she had another engagement that night.

Mailed him a birthday card, however: tasteful, attractive, but just a commercial card. From a gift shop. No present, no other acknowledgment. If he was disappointed—and, yes, he was—he hid his disappointment so thoroughly that everyone (the Weidmanns, H.E. looking prettier than usual in something soft, lacy, pastel; Colin Asch often had that effect upon even the strongest-minded "career woman") had a great time, a memorable time, Colin Asch telling amusing fantastical stories about travel in Europe, travel in North Africa, the vicissitudes of life "on the bum" on the open road, and truly he liked making people laugh, especially people who were fond of him, people who were on his side; you could see the excited emotion shining in H.E.'s big sensational mascaraed eyes: now this was a girl (not a girl, precisely: thirty-one years old) who adored him, adored his cock, anything he wanted to do to her he'd be welcome to do, in time, if (as of course he would: Colin Asch was no jerk-off asshole male chauvinist) he took it slow enough, gradual enough, didn't lose his cool with her little-girl simpering and not wanting him to see her in the shower, the droopy big-veined breasts, the lardish thighs, potbelly, and her skin a little coarse without the thick pancake makeup, Jesus how he resented her going crazy the way she did as if for the show of it coming to orgasm like he was killing her or something breaking his rhythm and concentration which really pissed him off it tempted him to the cruel cruel thought of jerking his cock right out of her at the crucial moment as he'd done with one or two cunts in the past taking Colin Asch for granted, or why not—just a casual quicksilver thought: *not serious!*—actually kill the cunt closing his two big thumbs around her throat—the carotid artery, is it?—see how she likes it then, moaning and gasping and screaming bloody murder in his ear then sobbing afterward saying his name like an incantation *like she had the right* simply because he'd told her he thought he was in love with her he'd never met a girl like her and so on and so forth, it pissed him off too that she was that eager to believe, wrung his heart with pity and *he hated pity: all it did was weaken.*

"Thank you all very much... this is maybe"—eyes filling with tears like genuine pain—"the happiest birthday of my life."

So that's it, asshole.
Colin Asch's twenty-eighth fucking birthday.

And Christmas too came and went and Colin Asch saw nothing of Dorothea Deverell but was relieved to hear she'd gone somewhere to visit relatives—"distant relatives I think," a woman friend of the Weidmanns told them, "poor thing, distant relatives is all she *has*"—so he felt better immediately and in the Blue Ledger charted his plans for the New Year. Impatiently he thumbed through the earlier pages seeking, what was it, that Roman saying Mr. Kreuzer had printed on the blackboard, how the class had shivered when he translated it, and the strange knowing set of his eyes drifting as invariably they did onto C.A., the tall stiff pretty boy in the first row, what the fuck was it, and where?—then suddenly he'd found it, was staring at it. Handprinted block letters in smudged India ink: *Mors tua, vita mea*.

He smiled; he saw what he must do. And she would never know—never know a thing!

"Your death, my life."

PART TWO

5

"Yes? Who is it?—What?"

Dorothea Deverell, heart beating rapidly, fists instinctively raised as if to protect her face, was wakened from a deep, near-narcoleptic sleep by a sound as of something, or someone, in the room with her. A murmured word, a sharp inhalation of breath, a shifting (not precisely a creaking) of her bedroom floorboards… and suddenly she was awake and badly frightened.

She lay shrewd and unmoving. She heard nothing. She told herself calmly, There is no one in this room with you and there is no one in this house with you…as you know. As always at such moments of crisis Dorothea Deverell's interior voice was brisk, pragmatic, and scolding, though her vision, struck so rudely from sleep, was blurred as if she were peering through an element dense as water. What had she heard, if she'd heard anything? It was early, still dark, too early for mourning doves in the eaves to disturb her with their melancholy cooing, or for the notorious sanitation truck, or the newspaper delivery.…A jetliner passing overhead, perhaps. Yes. Making windowpanes vibrate, casting a malevolent fibrillation to the very air. That seemed the most likely explanation.

Dorothea's fear retreated but did not vanish, like shadows dimmed by light. She drew the covers up to her head, tried a childish maneuver of hiding her eyes, pressing her face against the pillow.…She tried to take comfort, as ordinarily she would have done, that she was in her own bed: returned home after ten days' absence, amid her own cherished things, beneath her own ceiling, set soon to embark upon one of Dorothea Deverell's flawlessly executed professional days. But these thoughts aroused an unexpected pang of dismay, like muck unwisely stirred. Today was

January 4, the first Monday of the new year, and though she had fled the holidays in Lathrup Farms to force herself to a decision about her future, she had failed to come to any decision: the new year, stretching off interminably, would be a more strained variation of the old.

She'd gone away, in dread of the "holidays"—that debilitating season in America when stable men and women begin to quaver, and the unmarried, like Dorothea Deverell, are made most keenly to feel the pathos of their situation—to a small inn in Framington, Vermont, telling no one except Charles Carpenter about where she was going; she'd gone away alone to contemplate her life: as she thought of it, wryly, when in the mood for wryness, the ruins of her life. For she knew very well—how could she not know?—that her days at the Brannon Institute, where she had been so happy, were numbered and rapidly diminishing, and she could not much longer deceive herself about Charles Carpenter—that happiness of any sane sort lay in that direction. They had quarreled bitterly over the telephone; they had said bitter things. Dorothea Deverell, gentlest of women, had heard herself say to the person whom of all the world she loved the most, "To put it crudely, Charles, you seem to be waiting for Agnes to get seriously sick and die—you won't take the first step either to divorce her or to break with me."

Before Dorothea left for Vermont, Charles Carpenter had insisted on seeing her, to plead with her another time—not to lose patience with him, or faith in him, not to cease to love him: for what would his life be, without her? "What exactly is your life *with* me?" Dorothea had inquired, not archly but quietly, with the air of one asking a quite serious question; and Charles Carpenter, burying his face in her neck, had murmured, "Just—my life." He had tried to talk her out of going to Vermont by herself, especially at such a time. It would make her all the more lonely. It would make her morbid. (Charles knew that, during the first summer of their marriage, Dorothea and her husband had driven together through New England, had stayed in romantic country inns.) But most of all, he would miss her enormously: "It's so much more painful at this time of year to feel yourself alone," Charles said, rubbing his eyes with both hands, "when you can't actually find any time to *be* alone, to breathe. When you're jammed up against other people and obliged, like them, to be having a good time."

Dorothea ignored Charles's gentle attempt at wit; such attempts, on both their parts, were also usually gestures at reconciliation. She said, unfairly, "You could come with me." He said, staring, "Ah, but Dorothea—that's what I can't do." And so it went, for they had had this conversation or its variants many times before; if one spoke impetuously, like Dorothea, the other had hardly any serious need to reply in defense—for in this case Dorothea knew that Charles Carpenter was not a man who took his responsibilities lightly: he had an emotionally unstable wife who did not so much threaten as indicate, by her reckless behavior, the continuous possibility of suicide, and he had (the burden, Dorothea thought, of "had"!) aging parents in Boston, supremely nice people, for whom he represented the sole means of emotional support. As a partner at Bell, Carpenter, Smith & Lowe he had also, at this time of year, the duty to put in an appearance at any number of festive holiday affairs, ranging from black-tie dinners to the company's annual Christmas party for its employees. Running away to a romantic inn in the Green Mountains had the appeal only of the impossible.

Dorothea said, "What I really intend is to spend some uninterrupted time being depressed. I realized, the other day, with the telephone ringing a half dozen times in an hour, it's been a while since I've had the solitude for it. When you're working you really can't settle into being depressed in any systematic way."

Charles laughed as if startled. Though he knew Dorothea Deverell more intimately than any other living person knew her, he professed frequently to be startled by her most candid remarks, as if they were out of character. He said, "You're joking of course?"

"Oh, of course." Dorothea laughed.

They kissed, shyly at first, then with increasing urgency. Dorothea felt her lover's suddenly aroused desire with a pang of unease and excitement. For Charles Carpenter *was* another woman's husband: Dorothea Deverell was trespassing; surely this constituted transgression? surely both were behaving criminally? Charles murmured, "Should we go upstairs? Dorothea—darling? Could we?—at least for a while?" but Dorothea said unexpectedly, "No, please—it would only make leaving harder." "But which of us is leaving?" Charles said, hurt. And then, seeing Dorothea's face, "I seem to have ruined your life after all. And I meant, you know, only good." Dorothea said impatiently, "Don't talk like that—you speak as if I were a victim, that my life were over! We both knew you were married, from the start. We both knew." "But I'm preventing you from—from meeting other men," Charles said humbly. And Dorothea, stepping away from him, laughing, a catch of despair in her throat, said, "I meet other men all the time! I wouldn't lack for escorts, really! It's just that, compared to you, they exert no special fascination." The image of Ginny Weidmann's young nephew flashed to Dorothea's mind—the fine cheekbones, the intense intelligent eyes—but was as swiftly banished. She paused. She said, "Jerome Gallagher called the other evening." "Who?" "Jerome Gallagher, you remember—the man Ginny introduced me to, back in November. At that dinner at their house." Charles frowned as if suddenly vexed. "Yes. That dinner," he said flatly. "The evening Ginny Weidmann's strange nephew appeared," Dorothea said, as if it were necessary to elaborate. She knew Charles did not want to be reminded of the evening since, by the end of it, his wife had drunk so much that she swayed visibly on her feet and had to be helped by Charles simply to rise from her place; yet she heard herself saying, in a bright, neutral tone, "What did you think of him, Charles? We never really talked about him: Colin Asch." Charles passed a hand over his eyes; his skin was unevenly flushed, almost ruddy. He was standing in Dorothea Deverell's charmingly furnished living room, on her exquisite old Chinese rug, as if, for the fraction of an instant, he himself were about to sway on his feet—to pass so rapidly from the exigency of sexual desire to the ellipsis of discourse might not be, Dorothea was afterward, repentant, to think, altogether healthy. But his voice was clear enough, if not indeed brusque: "I didn't think anything of him at all."

Charles Carpenter had extracted from Dorothea Deverell a vague sort of promise that she would telephone him from Vermont sometime during the holidays; but this, after all, she did not do: to her vast defiant relief she did not do. (How many times in recent years Dorothea Deverell had been reduced to the shameful act of telephoning her lover and hanging up quietly when his wife answered, she would not have wanted to calculate, nor would she in her pride want to acknowledge, even to herself, how frequently, with no excuse whatsoever, she had driven past the Carpenters' handsome old colonnaded house on West Fairway Drive.) So for the duration of her retreat they had been chastely out of contact, which seemed to Dorothea both bracing and very sad, for she missed him terribly, missed even the special pang of not seeing him that we feel only when living in close proximity with the one whom we are forbidden to see—for distance, in matters of romance, is a powerful analgesic.

She was therefore relieved to discover, amid the pile of cards, letters, and packages of various sizes that had accumulated in her absence, a handwritten letter from Charles Carpenter, which she ripped open at once and quickly scanned: but it told her, in its carefully chosen, rather Augustan diction, nothing she did not already know. Her heartbeat, painful at first, had subsided by the end of the letter to its normal rhythm. Did I expect him to break it off? Dorothea wondered. Charles is not after all the one to break things off. One of the packages was auspiciously large, gift-wrapped, from Saks, with no other return address and no signature on the MERRY CHRISTMAS card from the store; Dorothea opened it slowly and lifted enthralled out of the tissue paper a white lace formal blouse—or was it a little jacket?—exquisitely beautiful, and in her size—size 6—and there was a matching skirt, floor-length, silken wool, dazzlingly white. It was so lovely a gift, so unexpected—Dorothea had bought nothing for Charles, had insisted they not exchange presents this year—she began to cry in hoarse gasping sobs.

"It's too good for me; I don't deserve it!"

Upstairs in bed she had been so besieged by unwanted thoughts she'd given up trying to get back to sleep; and rose, and showered, and dressed, and began the long day, setting herself in motion like a clockwork doll though it was not yet 7 A.M. In the inn at Framington, in her single rather chilly room with its impeccable antique-imitation furniture and windows overlooking the village green, Dorothea had managed to sleep heavily; yet she had not on the whole felt refreshed, but groggy, headachy, edgy, apprehensive—as if her flight from home had been perilous, exposing her to hairline fractures of the psyche she might not otherwise have noticed. Sleeping was always a problem for Dorothea; if she slept well she tended to feel guilty for having done so, as if it were a symptom of encroaching sloth and deterioration; if she slept poorly, she spent the better part of the day yearning to return to sleep. In Vermont she had not wanted to think that there might simply be something wrong…some growing unease in her soul, as of premonitory alarm. Waking several times in the night as she'd wakened this morning, as if something, or someone, were in the room with her. Or watching her. Or merely thinking of her.

And when, twice a day, except on the very coldest days, she left the hotel to trudge along the snowy country roads, she had to fight the panicky sensation that she was being followed. Followed! Dorothea Deverell in an old-fashioned fur coat, fur hat pulled down low on her forehead, knee-high boots…so bundled up as to appear ageless, sexless. She knew it was absurd; she knew it was groundless, such fear, such bone-deep *apprehension.* In a stained old volume of Montaigne's *Essays* found on a shelf in her room she discovered a poisonous gem set in the midst of Montaigne's affable prose, a quotation from Pythagoras, translated as *Good is finite and certain, evil is infinite and uncertain.* The insight made a sudden, sickening impression on her—"Of course!"

Yet she managed to enjoy herself nonetheless. She was tough, hardy, resilient: yes, and stubborn to the core. She'd brought along an entire suitcase of work—Institute matters, and correspondence, and notecards, slides, and drafts of a book-length essay on Charles Burchfield for which she had signed a contract with a New York publisher of fine art books—and she managed, on those long uninterrupted winter days in her room, to accomplish a good deal. Her meals were provided, her room briskly cleaned and aired and restored to her. There was no television set in the room. There was no telephone. The Brannon Institute was closed for the holidays so there was no pressing need for her to think of it. Or of Mr. Morland, who for all his sweetness seemed to be avoiding her lately. Or of Mr. Krauss, who, that day in the French restaurant, had so pointedly not avoided her. ("How nice of *you*, Dorothea, to entertain the boy!") After a late dinner in the inn's low-beamed dining room Dorothea propped herself up cozily on her bed and read one or another of the numerous books she'd brought along with her, the majority of them newly purchased novels in smart bright eye-catching jackets. She favored long, weighty novels, novels densely textured (if not snarled and knotted) as life, in which she might lose herself for hours at a stretch. And she had, too, her old companionable edition of Shelley's poems.

And now it was January 4, a blowsy overcast Monday morning, and Dorothea Deverell was back in Lathrup Farms, set in motion, in perpetual motion she sometimes thought it, but determined to acquit herself fully. She might resign her position at the Institute before it was required of her—before Mr. Morland called her in for that embarrassed regretful conversation. She might send out letters looking for new employment, she might put her house on the market, might move away; anything was possible since there was no one to prevent it. She switched on the lights she customarily switched on when preparing to leave the house for the entire day, these truncated winter days, and turned up the volume on the radio (as Michel had insisted: loud voices in a house discourage would-be intruders). She went into the freezing garage and climbed into her car, breath steaming, gloved hands cold on the steering wheel, wondering why, in this familiar setting, she felt so apprehensive, so anxious...as if the very silence surrounding her were taut with expectation. And opaque, and dense. Impermeable even to her screams.

Something is going to happen, she thought. Or has already happened.

Dorothea Deverell, much praised for the quality and efficiency of her work and her unfaltering good grace in its execution, had never wished to confront her admirers with the rejoinder: But what is the alternative? My efforts are in the service of a single grand effort, the combating of loneliness.

It had been so since early childhood, interrupted for the space of some swift-passing months during her brief marriage (and briefer pregnancy); then resumed again, with pitiless exactitude, after her husband's death. Work was the blessed anodyne, the *there* to which, in times of stress or despair regarding the worth of her own being, she might retreat. It was the inevitable completion of the task, and the resumption of the life to which it was presumably marginal, that constituted the problem.

Yet at times of supreme concentration, Dorothea Deverell was energized, even quite happy—and it was this mood, intensified by the solitude of the early hour at the Brannon Institute and the agreeable surroundings of her office (a surprisingly capacious room with lustrous cherrywood paneling and old-fashioned mullioned windows reaching nearly to the fifteen-foot ceiling), that Dorothea's assistant, Jacqueline, interrupted at 8:55 A.M. when, still in her coat, breathless from the stairs, her fox-slanted eyes moist from the January cold, she burst in upon Dorothea Deverell to say, "Dorothea! You've been away! Have you heard? Did you read? About Roger Krauss—?" Jacqueline was a solidly built flamboyant attractive woman in her mid-forties, mysteriously married yet hinting of an acute disappointment in marriage, given to irreverent asides meant to placate, or support, or entertain Dorothea

Deverell, to whom she was wonderfully loyal and with whom she must have felt her fortunes at the Institute bound. They had worked together for six years, and though Dorothea did not wholly trust Jacqueline in matters requiring tact and diplomacy, especially over the telephone, she could hardly imagine the Institute without the woman's ebullient presence.

Now Dorothea Deverell and Jacqueline stared at each other, and Dorothea felt her heart clutch, for she saw in Jacqueline's excited glistening eyes—ah, what did she see? Jacqueline, still breathless, was saying, "It was in the papers day before last, how he died—Mr. Krauss; one of our trustees, you know," she said unnecessarily, as if, at this date, Dorothea Deverell might not know who Roger Krauss was, "—the victim of some sort of sex thing, not just robbery, and there's all sorts of rumors, but anyway, the thing is," Jacqueline said, now briskly unbuttoning her coat, "the man is *dead*."

Dorothea had hardly taken all this in. "What? What has happened?" she asked faintly.

"The night of New Year's Day. In a parking garage, in the city. Mr. Krauss was killed."

"Mr. Krauss?"

"Yes. Him. They don't know who did it yet." Jacqueline was trying very hard not to exude an air of cruel satisfaction. "But they didn't mention us, they didn't mention the Brannon Institute—in the papers, I mean—mainly his business reputation, who his father was in Boston, and things like that, and it was on the television news too, of course, like it's all some sort of big scandal that might open up." Jacqueline paused, regarding Dorothea Deverell intently. "So that's the man who tried to pass judgment on *us*, Dorothea, on *you*, writing such nasty things in the paper about our exhibit last spring, and now—look what has happened to *him*!"

"Roger Krauss is dead? He has *died*?"

"Not just died," Jacqueline said impatiently, drawing a newspaper out of her handbag with a flourish, "but been *killed*. 'Garroted,' the police called it."

"Garroted!"

The word hung in the air of Dorothea Deverell's office like an exotic obscenity.

Alone in her office, door shut, telephone off its hook, Dorothea with trembling fingers spread open the creased pages of the *Boston Globe* that Jacqueline had provided her, to read, with shock, dismay, and an incredulity that deepened, rather than diminished, with the passing minutes, of the violent death of Roger Krauss, fifty-six years old, "area businessman and philanthropist": he had been strangled with a wire bound tightly around his neck and also wantonly stabbed in the eyes and groin; robbed of his wallet, wristwatch, cuff links, tie clip, ring, even his belt, hat, and necktie; found in his car, a two-month-old Lincoln Continental, at 4:40 A.M. of January 2, behind the wheel, in a pose very like that of a living man, by the attendant on duty at the high-rise parking garage on Providence Street near Tremont. Krauss's car was on the third level of the garage and no one had heard any struggle. His parking ticket had been stamped for 8:15 P.M.; the attendant then on duty had no memory of him, since business had been brisk at that time, but the late-night attendant remembered his returning on foot sometime around 3 A.M. and taking the elevator, though there had been no exchange of words between them. He also remembered having seen a young, or youngish, black man wearing dark glasses, a goatee, stylish fawn-colored suede clothes, and carrying what appeared to be a clarinet case, around that time too, but he had not caught a very clear glimpse of the man. Police detectives said that Krauss's murder did not seem to have been simply a mugging death, on the evidence of the extreme violence done to the victim (Krauss's eyes had been "severely gouged" with his own car keys, and the murderer had razor-slashed his groin through his trousers) and other details, which at the present time, in the interests of their investigation, they did not care to divulge.

In the earlier part of the evening Krauss had had drinks with friends at the Ritz-Carlton and had spoken of going on to have dinner with other friends, unnamed. Divorced for the past eleven years, he had maintained a small apartment on Beacon Street but spent most of his time in his Lathrup Farms residence. Dorothea read that he had been active in civic, church, and charity organizations. He had graduated from Harvard Business School. He had served in the U.S. Air Force as a first lieutenant. He was survived by two sons, Roger Jr. and Harold.

"How horrible!" Dorothea whispered.

The accompanying photograph was of a younger Roger Krauss, hair darker, features sharper, expression more affable than Dorothea recalled. She studied it and could not see in that face the face of the man who had mocked her so openly a few weeks ago; she decided she would expel that unfortunate memory from consciousness since it did not do the poor dead man any credit, nor did it do Dorothea Deverell credit, to insist upon remembering. It is enough that he is dead, Dorothea thought, not knowing, perhaps, what she meant. She felt only pain for Roger Krauss now, a rush of sympathy, and pity for the ignominy of his death—its slightly shady aura, against which he could not protect himself.

So Dorothea Deverell read the article, and reread it, and sat at her desk for a long while, as if entranced or struck dumb. Then she folded the paper carefully up, put her telephone back on its hook, and resumed her day.

But it was not so easy!—there were telephone calls from friends; there were messages for Dorothea to return calls (one of them from "C.C." at his business number—a rare request); there was above all the sparked-up presence of Jacqueline, who, though Dorothea pleaded with her to let the subject drop, could not forbear hurrying out at noon to buy the late-morning edition of the *Globe*. "They caught him! The killer! It looks like!" Jacqueline reported, again breathless, and laying, uninvited, the newspaper across Dorothea's desk. Two other secretaries joined them to read of the newest development in the Krauss case: police had arrested a suspect who answered to the general description of the killer, a black man, unshaven, thirty-two years old, with a record of several convictions for muggings and armed robbery, picked up on a street two miles from the parking garage on Providence at 1 A.M. of January 4. The man had been in an "intoxicated state" and had "offered resistance" to police officers. He was wearing a new suede jacket similar to the one worn by the killer and could give no satisfactory explanation of how he'd come into the possession of Roger Krauss's wallet and credit cards. No photographs accompanied this article. "Well, that was quick!" Jacqueline said, mildly disappointed.

Dorothea Deverell leaned forward suddenly and pressed the palms of her hands against her eyes, as if she felt faint, an uncharacteristic gesture in the presence of others. Asked if anything was wrong she said, almost inaudibly, "Of course something is wrong—a man is *dead.*" Her reply was prim, not quite what she'd intended; Jacqueline and the secretaries retreated, as if chastised. She heard them whispering in the corridor outside her office and went to close her door. She telephoned Charles Carpenter but was told of course that he wasn't in—it was twelve-thirty and he wasn't expected back in the office until after two and who is calling please? Dorothea said quickly, "Thank you, it isn't important, I'll try another time."

Next, she would have liked to see Howard Morland, not to discuss the death of Roger Krauss of course (that would have been unthinkable) but to exchange New Year's greetings perhaps, and to take from the elder man some measure of patrician calm or consolation; but as Mr. Morland's secretary explained, he would not be returning for two weeks—he was vacationing in the Caribbean. "Of course," Dorothea said. "I'd forgotten."

For the remainder of the afternoon she worked with sporadic flashes of efficiency and zeal, trying not to be distracted by thoughts of the dead man, or of the ugly circumstances of his death, but haunted by such words as *garroted, eyes gouged, razor-slashed, mutilation.* She tried too not to hear, as if echoing lewdly in a closed corridor, *How nice of you, Dorothea, to entertain him!* I do not want to think ill of the dead, Dorothea Deverell instructed herself, but what is to be done if the dead thought so ill of me? But at 4:00 P.M., when most of the Institute staff was still working, Dorothea gave up the effort, which had brought on a headache and an inexplicable sense of malaise, and shut up her office and drove out of the parking lot as if released from a prison.

Yet she did not want to go home. She was fearful, for some reason, of going home.

The lovely white outfit Charles Carpenter had given her—did it not resemble a bridal gown?

Was it a bridal gown?

"And we promised we wouldn't exchange presents this year," Dorothea said aloud, in a tone of faint protest. But of course she was quite excited too. She would not have wanted to say *quite* how excited.

Charles must have repented, then, for allowing her to go off by herself to Vermont.

Yet his letter—so staid and circumspect, so typically *lawyerly*—had made no reference to the gift at all.

"He bought it at the last minute," Dorothea said aloud. "He bought it on impulse."

Driving in her car she began almost immediately to feel better, much better: as if the phenomenon of even moderate speeds, the achievement of even a modest number of miles between herself and the Brannon Institute, were mysteriously tonic. And she'd driven so many miles the previous afternoon, from Vermont! Soon she found herself beyond Prides Crossing, beyond Beverly Farms, headed, it almost seemed, for Maine.... She parked her car at the end of one of the cliff roads, on a high bluff overlooking the Atlantic, and sat there dazed and exhilarated, as if she had come an enormous distance simply for this: this brilliant waterscape of purples, blues, and greens, choppy and white-crested with foam, like a Winslow Homer painting. Despite the cold she got out of the car, standing for a while looking—staring—at the ice-bound shore, and the riotous waves, and the glowering winter sky, her hair whipping crazily in the wind and her eyes filling with tears. This was not like her, was it! This was not like Dorothea Deverell, was it! She felt an uncanny sort of life, *livingness*, thrumming through her...she felt flooded with strength, purpose, hope, resolve. Her enemy was dead and she was alive. It was so simple a thing it might have been overlooked.

She stood there for a while, hugging herself, shivering, her face damp with tears that began, in a light film, to freeze on her cheeks. She stood there until the air turned dark, gradually at first and then abruptly, as with the rushing of thousands upon thousands of dark-feathered wings. But there were no birds, were there? She glanced up, startled. Only the massive snow-laden clouds. Only the oncoming night.

"Wasn't it shocking! Yet, at the same time, you know, not really surprising," Ginny Weidmann was saying. Her manner was somber, even grave, but resolute; she glanced up to take in Dorothea Deverell with the others. "It seems the man led a double life."

"Why? What do you mean?" one of the women asked.

"Sit down, Dorothea, and let Martin get you a drink; you look lovely," Ginny said. She lowered her voice. "The police found pornographic material in his car, you know. It wasn't in the newspapers. Videocassettes, magazines." She lowered her voice even further. "*Male* pornography. *Homosexual*."

"Really?"

"Roger *Krauss?*"

"They found a ticket stub in his pocket, too, from some X-rated theater," Ginny said. "Martin doesn't like me to speculate," she went on hurriedly, while Martin was out of the room, "but the police themselves have speculated that he might have picked up the man, the young black man, you know, in the theater, and was bringing him back home with him. Which would explain—certain things."

"Oh, but it's so hard to believe of—"

"—so hard to believe of *him*—"

"Roger Krauss, of all people—"

"Oh but, these days, you can't *tell*—"

"—can't predict—"

"Yet with Roger you could, actually," Ginny Weidmann said reprovingly. "Remember his campaign against Dorothea? Against 'feminists'? Clearly, there was an emotional bias against women."

The gathering of some six or seven people looked to Dorothea for confirmation; but she murmured only a few ambiguous words and must have shown her discomfort, for they let her off lightly and returned to their spirited analysis of the "mystery" of Roger Krauss without her—clearly the subject was in full throttle and must be allowed to run its course. Several times Ginny Weidmann interrupted to say passionately, as if in Dorothea Deverell's stead, "None of it surprised *me.* There was a logic to it all along, to *me*."

"But has the black man confessed yet? I heard on the news this morning—"

"He claims he is innocent, of course—what can you expect?"

"The evidence does certainly seem—"

"—*very* damaging!"

There was a collective pause. The doorbell rang; another friend or neighbor had arrived. Again it was murmured, in an air of amazement, "But who would ever have thought it—of *Roger Krauss?*"

It was Sunday evening. Ginny Weidmann had telephoned Dorothea Deverell the day before, inviting her to drop by for a drink, just a handful of friends were coming over, not a party but an impromptu gathering; we haven't seen you since before Christmas, Dorothea, where on earth have you been keeping yourself? So, with mild reluctance, Dorothea came to the Weidmanns', both dreading and anticipating further talk of Roger Krauss, about whom she had heard so much this past week from various sources and with whose name her own seemed, at least temporarily, so unhappily bound. The "homosexual" details Ginny Weidmann had just now supplied were new, however, to Dorothea, and affected her more powerfully than she would have wished to acknowledge. As talk swirled about her head she sat unmoving on the sofa, her drink untouched in her hand, thinking, So that was it. It was nothing personal, then.

Dorothea had come to her friends' home for consolation of this sort, perhaps; or out of simple loneliness; or fear; or guilt. (Though why should she feel guilty?) Since the Carpenters' white Cadillac was not parked outside, Dorothea knew that Charles would not be here; yet she had unconsciously prepared herself, stiffening slightly, for the man's possible presence—his eyes, narrowed, moving quickly and warmly onto her, as, invariably, they did, in these sociable circumstances. But there was no one. That is—there were several men, including (Dorothea saw belatedly) Jerome Gallagher; but there was no Charles Carpenter.

Dorothea had seen her lover, however, the night before last, briefly, and had several times this week spoken with him on the phone. He had been very kind and understanding about what he called, with an air of mild repugnance, the "Krauss affair"; had not pursued the subject with Dorothea, as if sensing (ah, Charles knew her so well!) how she would have begun to feel guilty about it. (Though why should *she* feel guilty?) And there was the tantalizing, one might say unnerving, puzzle of the Christmas presents; the one Charles Carpenter had indeed sent her (a kidskin jewelry box trimmed in sterling and tortoise) and the one Charles Carpenter had *not* sent her (the white lace jacket and matching skirt). The little jewelry box had been gift-wrapped and mailed from a prominent Boston jeweler's with a card enclosed, *Love always, C.*, and this Dorothea had discovered on Monday evening when she opened the remainder of her mail. Two presents, then? She had been, in her absence, the recipient of not one but two Christmas presents? "If you gave me the jewelry box, then who gave me the—other?" Dorothea had asked, for a moment almost frightened; and Charles Carpenter said with a careless, hurt laugh, "If *you* don't know, Dorothea, how the hell should *I*?"

But Dorothea had not wanted to guess.

Just as she was preparing to leave the Weidmanns', for the others were going on to dinner at a local restaurant and she did not care to join them, there appeared, belatedly, with boyish smiling apologies, Ginny's nephew Colin Asch, in the company of the glamorous Cleopatra-looking girl, whose name, for the moment, Dorothea could not remember; and she understood, suddenly, by way of her absurdly pounding heart, that it had been an error for her to have come here. For here, so abruptly, was the boy—the young man—Colin Asch: with his uncannily lapidary features, like a brash Renaissance archangel come to life, the shock of his white-gold hair, his beautiful crafty eyes...looking at Dorothea Deverell with a curious intimate intensity, as if they were old, very old friends, or blood relatives, or a kind that scarcely need greet one another in public. But there were handshakes all around, there were introductions, for not all of Ginny's guests had met her nephew—"really my grandnephew"—nor had they met Hartley Evans, who was, it quickly developed, the new anchorwoman for the weekday evening news on WWBC-TV, thus locally known, and the object of immediate and spirited attention. Dorothea Deverell, on her feet, meaning to leave, had nonetheless to linger, to smile and listen and disguise the queer emotion she felt at the sight of seeing—ah, so companionably! so *easily!*—Colin Asch with Hartley Evans, or Hartley Evans with Colin Asch (the young woman was standing close beside him, had entered the room with her arm conspicuously linked through his, as if to proclaim they were lovers)—these tall, attractive, radiantly happy young people who, by contrast merely, made everyone else in the Weidmanns' living room appear dimmed and middle-aged. Dorothea Deverell felt a stab of—was it envy? jealousy? simple dismay? or a vicarious sort of pleasure, harsh and unexamined, in the young lovers' very physical presence?

Both were buoyant, nerved up, like performers who find it difficult to leave the stage; or perhaps they'd been recently quarreling—or making love. Dorothea, smiling, looked from one to the other. Hartley wore more jewelry than, even, she'd worn on the evening of the Weidmanns' dinner party, and her glossy black hair framed her face perfectly, sleek as a helmet; her eyes and eyebrows were elaborately traced, her eyelids shadowed in pale silvery blue; her fleshy lips a perfect luscious crimson. And her skin, her young skin—in the lamplight, at least, it was virtually poreless: perfect. Yet the surprise of the evening was Colin Asch, who had had his long hair cut and styled, perhaps with an eye toward television performance, and who wore not his slapdash late-adolescent's outfit but a camel-hair blazer with gold-glinting buttons, a creamy-beige turtleneck sweater, impeccably creased navy-blue trousers. On his right hand was the gold signet ring, on his left wrist a handsome platinum-faced watch Dorothea had not seen before. Studying him as, for the moment, he stared smiling at Hartley Evans (who was entertaining them all with an anecdote about having met recently, and interviewed, former Secretary of State Henry A. Kissinger), Dorothea began to feel uneasily that something was wrong: or was not, in any case, altogether right; for how could *this* young man—healthy, energetic, eyes shining with scarcely suppressed excitement, fingers twitching as if in rhythm with an interior music—have stepped from that *other* young man, Ginny Weidmann's "tragic" nephew, who had seemingly washed ashore at the Weidmanns' home back in November, barely two months ago? That evening, Colin Asch had been a lost soul: dazed, bedraggled, sallow-skinned, quixotically idealistic. (Is he still involved so passionately in animal rights? Dorothea wondered. She'd heard no word of it from Ginny in some time.) Now he looked supremely like a young professional man, confident in his own abilities but respectful—even, seemingly, reverent—of his elders. The two cannot be the same person, Dorothea Deverell thought, amazed.

At this moment Colin Asch glanced at her as if, indeed, he'd heard her speak; and their eyes held; and, feeling a wave of faintness suddenly, Dorothea Deverell explained that she was leaving—was already late for her next engagement. Colin Asch said, simply, "I'll walk you to your car, then, Miss Deverell—I mean Dorothea," taking her elbow gently and escorting her from the room, turning away with such unstudied abruptness from his girlfriend and her charming banter that one had the sense, a rather chilling sense, that he hadn't been listening to her at all, or to anyone. He was vivacious, keyed up, as if pleasantly intoxicated, and indeed Dorothea smelled alcohol on his breath; he was chatting of cheery inconsequential matters, complaining funnily about WWBC-TV and the "media mentality" with which he had to contend, but they were anxious to keep him, promising him he'd be broadcasting soon, but maybe he'd quit anyway, go to work for a competitor—"*That'd* shake them up, the buffoons"—glancing at Dorothea with a sudden liquid look. "But you don't watch television, do you, Miss Deverell? Dorothea? And why should you, with your superior sensitivity, your mind on *other things?*" Dorothea laughed, as if with fond familiarity the young man were teasing her, parodying her high-flown cultural pretensions, but of course he was not; he spoke with absolute sincerity.

In the Weidmanns' foyer Colin Asch helped Dorothea on with her coat, the heavy gleaming beautiful old stone marten fur, and she prepared nervously to explain it to him, the fact of it, an inheritance from an aunt—for she herself did not believe in the cruel custom of raising and slaughtering animals for their skins—but he was humming happily, as if taking no notice; then he broke off to remark that he hadn't seen her in a very long time he missed her sort of he'd liked that lunch that day he'd been disappointed Dorothea hadn't been able to come to his birthday party of course it was planned at the last minute and why Aunt Ginny hadn't called Dorothea sooner he didn't know, that's about the only thing in Aunt Ginny's character that could stand some improvement—"Her habit, you know, of tossing things together at the last minute, telephoning people, as I guess she did yesterday, to invite you all over." He was standing behind Dorothea, tall and suddenly very still, his hands on her shoulders. "But it was very thoughtful of you, Dorothea. That card. That birthday card," he said quietly. "I've kept it, I'm treasuring it. I won't forget it."

Dorothea laughed again, uneasily, and their eyes met in the mirror beside the door, and she thought, He is the person who sent me the present—of course; but at the same instant two facts were unmistakably clear: she had not the courage at this moment to mention the present to him and to ask for an explanation, and Colin Asch, sensing that she knew, was too tactful, or too crafty, to bring it up himself. Our secret remains our secret, he might have been thinking, smiling dreamily into the mirror.

Colin Asch walked Dorothea Deverell out to her car, which was parked in the Weidmanns' circular driveway, fresh-shoveled snow on all sides; his step was ebullient, and he was whistling the opening bars of a familiar melody—hauntingly familiar—was it a song of Schumann's? He hadn't troubled to put on his topcoat but he'd placed jauntily atop his head a black lamb's wool astrakhan hat—"Do you like my new hat, Dorothea?" he asked with a boyish hopeful smile. "I just bought it, at a post-Christmas sale, in the village—one of those fancy men's shops where Aunt Ginny buys things for Martin."

An excess of information seemed, here, to be proffered; yet Colin Asch's manner was wholly ingenuous, and Dorothea said, as if praising a child, "Yes, I do like it, it's very—handsome."

"You know, Dorothea," Colin said, opening the door of her Mercedes, mimicking a bow from the waist, "I sort of thought you might like it."

Dorothea Deverell gathered her skirt around her—it was a multipleated hunter-green jersey-wool skirt, a rich beautiful fabric hardly at all eroded by time—and slipped into the car. She was breathing rather quickly, like a girl; and Colin Asch, not unlike an impetuous suitor, leaned on her car door and peered down smilingly at her. His breath steamed and faded, steamed and faded. His lips seemed to twitch involuntarily, lifting upward in a white wolfish grin. As if they'd been quietly talking about this subject, he said, "Yes, it's strange how, sometimes, a despicably evil person who doesn't deserve life has it taken from him. As if there were after all justice in the world, as certain of our great visionaries and poets have believed." He paused, and added, *"As if."*

Dorothea shivered and fumbled in her purse for her car keys. Were they talking now of Roger Krauss? She nodded vaguely; she murmured a vague assent. Thinking to change the subject, to make a kind of closure, she said, almost gaily, "You and your young woman are a very striking couple—you seem so happy together."

"Do you like that type? Really? Ah, I see you're being polite, Dorothea." Colin Asch was leaning over Dorothea's car door, pensive, quizzical, arms dangling. The astrakhan hat gave him an exotic, foreign look and had slid forward on his head, as if it were a size or two too large for him. In a lowered voice he said, "She imagines that she is in love with me—wants to have my child, and all that! She'd suck my life from me if she could. The marrow out of my bones."

This sudden unsolicited confidence left Dorothea Deverell nonplused. What to say? Why was Colin Asch looking at her so oddly, as if inviting complicity? She had begun to feel rather nervous, wishing that this strange young man would step back from her car and allow her to drive away. He was gazing down at her at such an angle, he had all the advantage; Dorothea could only crane her neck and squint uncomfortably up at him.

"I don't take the flesh that seriously, to tell the truth," Colin Asch said with a negligent shrug of his shoulders. "Only the spirit. The soul."

Pointedly, Dorothea lifted her car keys out of her purse; her smile had grown strained.

"But you, Miss Deverell—Dorothea—is there someone you're in love with?" Colin Asch asked suddenly, impulsively, as in a headlong plunge of unconsidered words. "That no one knows about—except him?"

Dorothea flinched, as if the impetuous young man had reached out to strike her.

He added quickly, "Look: you can tell me. You can trust me. *I can keep a secret.*"

Though she was inwardly trembling, with fear, with indignation, with simple shock, Dorothea managed to say quietly, "I don't divulge secrets promiscuously, my own or anyone else's. Now may I close my car door? I must leave."

Like a hurt, obstinate child Colin Asch persisted. "I *can* keep a secret, Dorothea. No force on earth can pry a secret out of *me*."

Dorothea Deverell made no reply, switching on the car engine. She was terrified suddenly that Colin Asch would touch her—would reach down gropingly, like a blind man, and stroke her hair.

Instead he sighed, and settled the hat more firmly on his head, and said apologetically, moving to shut Dorothea's door, "The primary thing is, you *are* happy—these days—with the coming of the New Year and all that? You *are* happy, Dorothea?"

"Yes," Dorothea Deverell said, almost angrily. "Very."

For so, after all, she was.

6

It made him happy if she was happy if those were the valid signs of happiness observed in her face.

But she seemed not to trust him yet, fully—he had not proven himself to her all the way.

After he was promoted at the station maybe, or quit and got a better job somewhere else. Maybe. After he moved into the new apartment. Champagne celebration! Black tie! A limousine to bring her! And she'd wear the beautiful clothes he bought her, dazzling white, pure, perfect on her. "La Belle Dame sans Merci." (Which Mr. Kreuzer read to the class slowly mesmerizingly so you could feel the beat, the diminished stress in the final line of each stanza, and his eyes had drifted out to young C.A. slouched in his seat by the window staring down at his hands impassive, transfixed, *I saw their starved lips in the gloam, / With horrid warning gaped wide, / And I awoke, and found me here, / On the cold hill's side,* and after the last words faded there was a silence so tense so haunted he wanted to scream to scream to scream to destroy it utterly but he'd only stared, impassive, at his hands.)

But should Colin Asch do the preparation of the food himself, or should he buy it? The greatest chefs in the world were men; it required a special touch. Not just any asshole could prepare gourmet food or even make the wine selection. Or should he order it from a caterer? His aunt would know. There were places like that all over in the well-to-do suburbs: food caterers. Thriving businesses. "The fuckers have so much money out here they have to eat it, shit it." One thing was certain, they wouldn't cheat him.

And what about furniture for the apartment? Didn't you have to order it weeks ahead of time? Months? It was going to be tricky getting more $$$ from his several sources when he hadn't made a move to repay any of it. The $$$ from K.R.'s wallet (for so in the Blue Ledger he was officially recorded) was a nice surprise but hadn't gone far, and the credit cards were worthless in such a circumstance; you'd have to be high on crack or coke or some other kind of shit to try it, like the black guy they picked up, poor sad dumb motherfucker asshole what'd he *think*—it was manna from heaven? and the fancy suede gusset-sleeved jacket too? There was H., and there was S. (whom he'd just met, out here in Lathrup Farms in the village bookstore), and there was X, Y, Z; he'd never lack for ways of picking up small change, but G. was getting worried, drawing out cash for him (last time $1,500: for the camel-hair jacket, shirts, merino wool sweater, decent haircut—it hadn't gone far) on her credit card, fearful of writing another check though she had her own personal account: "Now don't breathe a word of this to Martin, please!" she'd warned, as if C.A. of all people required warning. In childlike gratitude he'd smiled, lifting the old girl's hand with its glittering diamond ring; he'd pressed his forehead against the back of her hand in childlike fucking gratitude, Don't know what I would do without you, dear aunt, you saved my life when I came here and you took me in, not like the others: there is no one like you in all the world. Oh, dear Aunt G.

Now if M. died, one of these days? Mugged in the street, shot in his car, *not* in the vicinity of Lathrup Farms however—you wouldn't want anyone to think it had anything to do with his home. Even breaking and entering, and he's shot defending himself, because G. too might be involved and you wouldn't want that; no, that was out, or at least that was somewhere ahead in the future. Too many things to think at once.

Also, it's always riskier where there is a blood relation, where they can figure out motives. XXX uncontaminated by desire is the highest achievement. But emotions intrude. Like with K.R., he'd hated the fucker so, by the time he got to him. And other things too. Other things intrude.

*

"I saw that."

"Saw what?"

"You and her. The one you've got a crush on."

"What—?"

"You know!"

"No, I don't know. You tell me."

"That woman with the pale moony face—the stuck-up one. Your aunt's friend."

"What about her?"

"What's her name?"

"Never mind her name, what about her?"

"I said I saw you. You and her."

"Saw what, cunt?"

"You and her! *You and her!* You never look at me like that!"

Colin Asch stood tall as if on stilts, cracking his knuckles that were suddenly very bony, and sort of magnified: first the left, then the right. Eyelids slid over dry achy eyes. They were high—but rapidly descending. All that $$$ and the bitch was bringing them down. As she'd done, stupid cunt, too many times. Wild wet hurt eyes that looked almost crossed, and the mascara blurring. And the nostrils wet with liquidy snot. And the wet red mouth dribbling.

"Sweetheart, I look at you like that all the time."

"Fuck that! Fuck you! I want you out of here!"

Colin Asch began suddenly to whistle. It seemed the necessary response. Head thrown back and lips pursed as for a sucky sucky kiss of the highest order. Whistling "The Bolero"; otherwise there was the danger of something happening. *They tempt you with loss of control. It is that above all to be RESISTED.*

He'd lied to her about where he was the night before and why he'd missed work—the third or was it the fourth time he'd failed to show up, and who got blamed but her? Was there another woman, was it *that woman?* "She looks old enough almost to be your mother," And what about the apartment he was looking for, why wasn't she being kept abreast of what was going on? Or was he planning to move and not inform her?

Her voice went on and on, beyond "The Bolero." He stripped to his underwear, he was so fucking warm. Beads of sweat on his forehead, trickling down his sides. She was saying, laughing angrily, "Sometimes there's a part missing in you, Colin; sometimes you scare me, you're so—" though he'd explained it all smoothly and satisfactorily, he thought, and now in her wildness the cunt was mucking it up again, which he could not allow to upset him. His thumbs deftly pressing against the big bluish throbbing arteries in her neck…or maybe he'd take hold of her shoulders and slam her against the wall, the floor, the doorframe, anything hard enough to crack her skull. At a certain point of spiritual intensity *all becomes unbearable—or bearable. It is that point that must be reached.*

He'd stripped to his undershorts, sweating and panting. The whistling was fading out the way a radio station fades, then suddenly it's gone. In the doorway of her cheap glitzy bathroom he switched on the fluorescent tubing and said, "What are you doing in there, sweetheart? What're you doing in the tub like that?"

He came closer, peering. His nostrils were widened with the smell of it.

Behind him she was saying, "Colin? What? What are you—?"

He played at the half horror he actually did feel. Peering at the spectacle through his fingers.

"Sweetheart? Hartley? *What did you do to yourself?*"

She came up behind him, scared, padding barefoot, heavy on her heels but not daring to touch him. Saying, "Colin? What's wrong?"—trying to look over his shoulder at what was in there, in the tub. *Sometimes there's a part missing in you Colin you're so—* Then she did touch him, her fingers brushing his wrist, but he didn't feel it.

"One side of your head is broken," he said. "There's blood in the water. Hartley? Sweetheart? What happened? *What did you do to yourself?*"

High and wobbly on stilts he freaked her out, seeing it there in the tub, seeing her, the vision so powerful she saw it herself, or almost. Begging him to stop. Begging him for Christ's sake please stop. He advanced to the bathtub talking to what was almost there, the dead female lying naked in the scummy water, big breasts floating, nipples like bruised eyes. There was coagulated blood from the gash from the rim where the skull had cracked; the fingernails and toenails had turned blue. In amazement and pity Colin Asch crouched over the corpse, speaking to it while Hartley Evans tugged at his arm, laughing shrilly, begging him please for Christ's sake to stop—"You're driving me crazy. *You're crazy*."

They were in an elevator together and the cable'd snapped. Was that it? Next time she spoke of D.D. he would kill her—it was that simple. He guessed she knew. Or maybe, cow cunt, she didn't know. In bed afterward burying his face in her neck saying Love, love, love, having trouble staying hard enough to enter her then when he did she winced as if in pain and he lost it, started to slip out, he thought of hurting her finally and unmistakably so she'd let him go but then he thought of D.D. and of how *she* would be saddened by this, if she knew…shocked, saddened, disgusted. After all she expected so much more of Colin Asch. *Please Dorothea I want to be good. I am trying to be good.* Deciding then not to fuck H. or to frighten her but begging her instead for forgiveness, like a child sobbing; she knew he was an orphan didn't she, she'd wrap him in her arms in forgiveness wouldn't she, of course she would. *Please help me Dorothea to be good.* And as if by a miracle the meanness drained from him.

And in the morning neither C. nor H. would remember a thing. Or almost.

K.R.8821Am was the notation. So terse, elliptical. A code not even the FBI could crack.

But inadequate to convey all he'd felt. After so many hours, days, of stalking. *And then the world became so suddenly perfect. PERFECT.*

Someday he would share his secrets with her; he would lay the Blue Ledger itself in her lap and invite her to read. In a calm lucid voice like a broadcaster's skilled voice he would say, "You see, it's like Euclid discovering the truths of geometry. The pure inviolate absolute truths of geometry. Not *inventing—discovering.*"

And the euphoria that followed, though it was finite, was so very real. The blueness of the Blue Room: he'd take her there too. Someday.

She looks old enough almost to be your mother: the words flung out haphazardly, cruelly—inaccurately. For D.D. hardly looked old enough to be Colin Asch's mother, nor did she in the slightest resemble Colin Asch's mother so far as he could recall her. Mrs. Asch, dead, drowned, so many years ago. A soft-bodied vague woman with artistic pretensions, a coarse braided rope of blond hair like a peasant girl's, nervous squinty eyes and nothing of Colin Asch's fine-boned features in her face: nothing. He had the snapshots to prove it! She'd smoked cigarettes compulsively; she stank of cigarette smoke. She'd smoked cigarettes *while bearing Colin Asch in her womb.* If she loved him he did not remember. If she loved him, "it wasn't anything personal; she'd have loved anyone in the same circumstances." Mr. Kreuzer had made the boys snigger, shocked, quoting them some ancient king or soldier who'd disparaged his brother—*Why should I honor him just because the two of us came out of the same hole?*

And then there was Mr. Asch, whom Colin Asch remembered even less clearly. Dead, drowned. A Manhattan textbook publisher of whom no one had ever heard until the news went out over the syndicate wires about the submerged car, the twelve-year-old boy who'd dived and dived and dived from the riverbank to save his doomed parents.... Colin Asch remembered none of it afterward, or very little, knowing mainly what police and others chose to tell him, and he hadn't asked questions because he'd never been that kind of child. *Think of your mother and father in a better, finer world, with God,* Mrs. Kendrich said, touching his cheek. *Drive your cart over the bones of the dead,* Mr. Kreuzer said, touching his cheek. There was a burial site, a joint grave marker, in Katonah, New York, but it wasn't Colin Asch's responsibility and he had neither seen it nor thought of it in years.

"And the body's cells change completely every seven years."

The $638 cash out of K.R.'s wallet was his reward, also the platinum wristwatch fancy tie clip crocodile belt cuff links silk rep tie shoes fancy fur astrakhan hat the fucker'd been wearing—*to the victor go the spoils.* The hat especially: you couldn't say that Colin Asch was timid, wearing the hat for all to see should they *see.* But no one save D.D.—of course—had the power to *see* Colin Asch in his truest self.

He'd stood close behind her easing the fur coat onto her, helping her with the sleeves. Lovely silky blackly iridescent fur—was it maybe mink? Nearly a head taller than the woman, he'd observed her greedily in the mirror, her dark beautiful worried eyes, the faintest of white lines bracketing her mouth, gaze veiled by thought; he was saying how thoughtful of her it had been, sending him a birthday card—"I've kept it. I'm treasuring it. I won't forget it." His voice close to quavering.

For of all the world, who had treated him decently, like a human being—like a human *soul*—and not some piece of mere shit you could slight, and insult, and forget, and cast disapproving looks at (like his asshole "Uncle" Martin'd begun to do), or tell to get out, go away and crawl into a hole maybe and die? *Of all the world no one save D.D. cared for him, or knew him.*

She knew of course that Colin Asch was the person who'd sent her the Christmas gift: the lace jacket, the floor-length skirt. The instant their eyes had met *despite the presence of the jabbering others* that fact was established. Thus there was no need for the woman to press Colin Asch's hand and whisper "Thank you" to him, though when they did shake hands—this being the style of affluent America, vigorous sincere-seeming handshakes all around, men and women both—the communication came to him by way of the warmth and surprising strength of her hand. *Our secret remains our secret—ours alone.*

And when he'd popped the hat on his head, feeling buoyant, nerved up, just the slightest bit crazy with the risk of it, and the joke of it too, D.D. had taken it in knowingly, those dark worried eyes lifting to his (for of course she would fear for his safety, having no knowledge of his past accomplishments or of the ingeniousness of the Baffle, no practical knowledge of the stupidity of the police) and had said she'd liked it: "It's very handsome!"

At her car they'd spoken quite directly. Now she knew, if she had not previously known; now he knew that she knew—*there was forever that bond between them* as if when he'd lowered the wire noose so swiftly and cleanly over the fucker's head, when instantaneously he'd jerked it tight, tight, tight, her fingers had guided his own, had fitted themselves to his, warm, soft, surprisingly strong. Thus with Colin Asch's sworn enemies: he'd known what he wanted to do and he had done it! and it was *done!* She would not have wished to witness the actual event, for pity was a fault in her perhaps, as in Colin Asch, or was it rather a magnanimity of spirit—like the great poets and visionaries who seek to embrace the All—so the actuality, the fact of it, would have frightened her, dismayed her, that Death after all is but a feeble word, a mere syllable, to set beside Dying—its physicality. its awful ignoble convulsive struggle—and the sudden stench of shit in the fucker's pants, the transformation of R.K. into K.R., into mere meat. The man had been strong, but Colin Asch with his rock-hard shoulder and arm muscles, the powerful tight muscles of his thighs too which, by way of leverage, he brought to bear upon the victim; ah, Colin Asch that radiant angel boy was stronger!—always stronger! "Did you doubt me, Dorothea? Because I seemed to be taking so long? You should never doubt me, Dorothea."

She had allowed him to know, in parting, that she would never divulge his secret—of course. For it was her own secret as well. And that, yes, he'd made her happy—*"very."*

Which, after all, had been the point of it.

ANYTHING DONE HENCEFORTH IS BLESSED
BECAUSE IT EMANATES FROM THE SOUL

Thus Colin Asch wrote in the Blue Ledger that night.

*

The Blue Ledger, precious as Colin Asch's very life, for in a sense it *was* his life, was sometimes carried in his duffel bag, sometimes locked in the trunk of the Olds, less frequently hidden between the bedsprings and the mattress of his bed in the spacious silken-wallpapered guest room the Weidmanns had given him, rent-free, since his arrival in November. But it was there, in that room, that the Blue Ledger showed signs of having been disturbed—taken from its secret place, probably looked into, if not minutely scrutinized, then replaced, *but clumsily replaced!* so that Colin Asch with his sharp eye and instinct for danger knew what had happened at once. His nostrils contracted as with a sudden virulent odor.

"I will have to kill her after all—if she was the one."

The thought upset him, and saddened him—his aunt was one of the few human beings on the planet he'd thought he could *trust.*

But when he went to her, speaking quietly, smiling, his shut fists hidden behind his thighs, the woman professed such innocence, and ignorance, Colin understood she hadn't seen the Ledger after all; she knew nothing about it. Shrewdly Colin had not mentioned the notebook, only the fact that someone had been in his room going through his things rearranging his things without his knowledge or permission *and he didn't like it.* "I thought, you know, Aunt Ginny," he said, beginning to get a little breathless, "that no one would dare violate my privacy in this house. That I could trust people in this house of all the fucking places in the world." Ginny Weidmann's eyes widened and grew moist. She said, "I suppose—it might have been Tula."

Colin said, still quietly, "I asked you not to let her in my room didn't I."

"Yes, dear, and I explained to her, but—"

"I said I'd do my own fucking cleaning, didn't I."

"Colin, dear, please—please don't be angry," Ginny Weidmann said. "I'm sure it was an innocent mistake. I'm sure that Tula just forgot. Or she may have misunderstood my—"

"You told her to clean in there, didn't you? 'Cause you were worried I wasn't cleaning up my own crap, weren't you?"

"No, dear, I'm sure that I—I don't remember *precisely*—"

" 'Cause you didn't trust me. To keep things clean. And I told you the first day, I told you, I can't bear it that a black woman has to clean up after me, I can't bear it; I *told* you, I *explained*, and you said you understood." The injustice of it ran like a flame over his brain, his soul. Still, he managed to control his voice. "Just because we have white skins and they have black skins, and we've exploited them through the centuries, and the conditions are still slave conditions, *only the proportions have been altered*."

"But Colin," Ginny Weidmann said, removing her half-moon reading glasses and setting them nervously aside, "Tula has worked for us for years! I'm sure she is very fond of us!"

" 'Tula,' as you call her—though she doesn't call you 'Ginny,' does she—hasn't worked for *me* for years."

"But she—"

"She hasn't worked for me for years!"

He backed out of the room and she followed him, apologizing, weakly protesting, her nephew who was rapidly losing control of himself *for as sudden sometimes as sexual desire it sprang up in him: the need to do hurt! to restore balance! justice!* Literally wringing her hands, and her pop eyes swimming with tears. "Colin? Do you really think it's—wrong?"

In another part of the house the black maid was vacuuming. The sound ran through Colin Asch, pulsing with the rage of his own blood.

"For us to hire them? Whites? *Blacks?*"

Colin Asch backed away from the woman, his hands in front of him now in a gesture of angry submission. He wasn't going to hurt her; *she was one of those he wasn't going to hurt* no matter how she tempted him. Blowsy cow with her face all gummed up, fifty-five years old and the "red rinse" glimmering in her hair, not to mention the diamonds—*ah yes the diamonds*—on her left hand winking and jeering at him. He'd helped himself to small change out of her purse now and then, and he'd walked off with tiny crap items no one'd ever miss around the house, a three-inch carved jade elephant on the mantel, a little silver bowl or cup some businessman had given Martin Weidmann in 1977, plus some tacky gold cuff links in the bottom of Martin's jewelry drawer in the bedroom with a look of never being used, but the big things he'd drawn magic circles around *not to cross into and violate* since Colin Asch knew from past experience that once he got started it was very difficult to stop. "The final thing is, you've got to mash in their brains." But the bitch had a nerve—you had to hand it to her—waving her jewels in his face when she knew Colin Asch had nothing, and no prospects: hadn't been able to enroll in a fancy Ivy League college like her shithead children; thus he was fated to occupy an inferior position for life—or was he?

He'd run upstairs to the room to get his duffel bag (in which the Blue Ledger was carefully secreted; hand over hand he tossed things in, panting, as Ginny Weidmann, frightened, tried to placate him. But Colin Asch was not a man to be placated. *His integrity would not allow it. His very soul was sickened.* So upset he'd begun to stammer, telling the ignorant white woman who was his aunt that she and her kind should be ashamed of their exploitation of the black underclass—"Paying an entire class of human beings to shovel up your shit for you. And boasting it's 'employment'! And boasting it's 'wages'!"

Here was Ginny Weidmann crying at last, Ginny Weidmann who'd never in her blind complacent life been so attacked, so *exposed*, it was like he'd slapped the bitch in the face the way she cringed, staring at him, like Moses and the burning bush you'd think, like Jacob and the angel, so Colin Asch felt sorry for her—almost—as she pleaded, "Colin? Colin? I'm sure that Tula likes us, forgives *us*. And she needs the money I pay her, and I tip her too, Colin, I try to be generous."

Colin felt a stab of pity for his aunt, sympathy almost; he was yanking the new merino sweater down over his head, heather-colored it was, beautiful hand-knit wool, $198 marked down to a bargain $125 for the post-Christmas sale in the Village Haberdashery where he'd bought it; he was brushing his hair irritably out of his eyes, trying to explain to his aunt patiently as you'd explain to a child or a retarded adult that it was the capitalist class structure that was the tragedy, that she and Martin were as much victims of it as Tula—"If her people were trained for decent-paying jobs, if they were college-educated like most middle-class whites, they wouldn't have to work as slaves for you, or starve."

Ginny Weidmann stood watching Colin Asch, a crumpled tissue pressed against her mouth. Her eyes, swimming in hurt, followed him as if without comprehension. She cried, "Colin, dear—what are you doing? Are you packing your things? *Are you leaving?*"

Politely but emphatically he shifted her out of his path and went to the closet. Fuck it: he'd have to make several trips, what with the new clothes and the books, and that pissed him, definitely—it'd have been the shrewdest maneuver to pack up the car on the sly, then simply walk out, shutting the door behind him. Or could he talk Aunt Ginny into giving him a hand?

"You're—leaving? Like this? Just walking out? Like this? Without even saying goodbye to Martin?"

Colin Asch cast the woman a look meaning yes. Meaning *how can you ask?* Meaning *you are the one who has forced this, not I.*

Of course he had a place to go, he had places—Christ! more than he could count!—but he hadn't yet signed the lease for the apartment, he'd been about to sign then got worried then made an appointment to see the other apartments, Sylvan Towers was one, Fairleigh Place the other, couldn't decide between the two since the rent was about the same and both buildings advertised "no fee"; then Susannah—Mrs. Hunt; he'd met her in the Bookworm—the sable coat attracted him first then the strong snubbed profile then the quick-darting eyes with a look of something knowing, ribald, in them—and she'd been attracted (that was obvious) to him: mop-headed and a bit sullen like a college kid home on vacation and had been quarreling with his parents wandering now in the only bookstore in town with an expression of faint incredulity *You call* this *a bookstore!—this?*—and he'd been on one crutch, his right foot bandaged, a skiing accident at Vail, or was it Switzerland—"People like you better if you're crippled or maimed somehow"—then Susannah Hunt insisted he look at an apartment in her building, Normandy Court, which he liked a lot; it sort of bowled him over with the view of the edge of a park and a balcony where, mornings, he could have breakfast, and the walls were such a pure spotless white and the hardwood floors so gleaming—two bedrooms, two baths, unfurnished—a long living room with glass along one wall where he'd have the celebration party for Dorothea Deverell when she got her promotion—you could fit fifty people in there without much trouble—and the kitchen, though small, was all modern fixtures and really cool: "This place could turn me domestic," he'd said, rocking back on his heels, and Mrs. Hunt, laughing through her cigarette smoke, squeezed his wrist and said, "I have the identical kitchen, Colin, and it hasn't done a thing for *me*."

So he went there. Not to the apartment but to Normandy Court, where Susannah took him in. The Weidmanns he told her had this weird marriage where the wife drank all day and the husband had his own life practically; it sort of reminded Colin of this man who'd been killed in the city—what was his name, Robert Krauss? Roger?—a successful businessman and all that but unraveling at the edges, hanging out with weird people, rough trade maybe; yeah he'd made a pass at Colin, sort of, but tentative enough to pretend that wasn't it at all; he felt sorry for them they were well-intentioned people basically very nice very kind very generous but pathetic like so many people out here—"I guess you don't fit the pattern at all, Susannah, *you* must be lonely here aren't you?"—and that was the right thing to say since Mr. Hunt was gone (gone where? married a younger woman?) and the kids were grown up and gone and there was bad blood all around, Colin Asch could smell it.

*

He would tell her *there is no door but the way in is everywhere. Like God whose center is nowhere and everywhere at once.*

Long ago, on the far side of the river...coming in breathless out of the freezing wind into the hotel lobby grand as the interior of a cathedral, and his mittened hand had slipped free of his mother's gloved hand, and he was drawn forward staring at the enormous Christmas tree which was like no other Christmas tree he had ever seen because it was not *green* but *white*, and covered in eye-sized blue lights that winked on and off to a quick nervous beat, and glittering blue glass ornaments the size of a man's fist...and the air pulsed a chilly blue, finely vibrating with the voices of strangers and their heavy footsteps. He had stared in astonishment at what wasn't a real Christmas tree or even the idea of a real tree but the representation of a wholly artificial tree that nullified the idea of a real tree because it was perfect...it was white, it was manmade, it would never die. The entire domed alcove of the lobby in which it stood was blue, a thin cold artificial blue, and there were mirrored walls lightly frosted with artificial snow in which a child with pale blond hair and a small pale face stood transfixed, as if paralyzed by the sinister wonder in which he was enclosed: there was a child in the mirror and a child in a mirror in that mirror reflected from the opposite and adjoining walls, and in these other walls there was a child in a mirror contemplating a multiplication of children in mirrors seen from the side, from the rear, seen full-face, seen in their entirety and in fractured segments, a child repeated endlessly yet always the same child, identical and unmistakable, the eyes snatching here and there, and back again and there, finally staring aghast into Colin Asch's stricken face. How could it be? And yet it *was!* The front of his head as it was ordinarily seen in a mirror yet every other angle of vision simultaneously as God would see so that the child was both inside himself and outside, and there was no child! And the air thrummed blue and was beautiful!

Like dying, he would tell her, *but not needing to go away to see what it would be like, after you were gone.*

*

In the Blue Room he could float for hours. For hours stretched like days, like an unbroken stream of fat clouds stretched across the sky. *And no one could touch him: he was bodiless, weightless, shadowless. Floating.*

He'd known what he had wanted to do, and he had done it. Thus it was *done*.

And it could never be undone.

Not by any power on earth.

Not by any power in the universe.

Not by the power of God—if there was a God.

XXX performed deftly and with precision, after days of admitted frustration, anger that interfered with his sleep and even his digestion since he'd been unable to get close to the target or, if he'd been able to get close, the circumstances (other people close by, witnesses) weren't congenial for what he wanted to do. He knew that Miss Deverell might be waiting…wondering. Why was it taking Colin Asch so long to intercede in her behalf? After that lascivious look the fucker had dared give them, slitting his eyes and oily mouth in insult, as if, for that alone, he wouldn't be punished!—as if for that instant's assault, which pierced Miss Deverell sharp as a blade *as Colin Asch with his senses keenly alert understood,* he wouldn't be punished by all means available! "Though he was dead, the fucker, when I did the other, I guess"—meaning the gouging of the eyes, which was an impulsive thing, sort of wild, whimsical, and cutting him up as he'd done with the razor, which he'd more or less planned depending upon the circumstances. For split-second timing of course was crucial. You had to know what you wanted to do, and you had to know how to do it. Fast.

And then you had to know how to make yourself vanish. *Fast.*

But for days prior to the execution of the plan he'd been balked and made a fool of, sort of. Like he had a hard on that couldn't be discharged and he was getting meaner and nastier almost in a frenzy in that state. Like it was R.K.'s fault that C.A. couldn't get close to him, to use either the wire or the razor, not one not two but three actual times he'd thought *This is it* calmly and methodically, but the situation had shifted at the very last moment like a picture suddenly blurring out of focus...which had surprised him so much he hadn't had time to be scared until afterward, thinking of it. For if Colin Asch's luck had not held, if he hadn't a special destiny but was just an ordinary man, he'd be under arrest now, maybe, or he'd have been forced to kill another person, or more than one other person...not skillfully but desperately, in a panic.

"But of course Colin Asch's luck held."

It had been a sign of genius to darken his face as he'd done with theatrical makeup, and wear the woolly little goatee, which he'd worn once before with success, and of course the dark glasses that were practically wraparounds so his eyes were totally hidden...and a black wool cap fitted like a swim cap on his head, to hide his hair...and the fawn-colored suede outfit meaning he was a certain class of black, had money, taste, personal style. And the clarinet case. *Genius shows itself in detail; in detail is the mark of the artist.*

So Colin Asch allowed himself to be glimpsed by the parking attendant who would be the only witness. The only surviving witness.

R.K. had taken the elevator up into the parking structure so C.A. took the stairs, not altogether certain which level R.K. was on but there was no problem locating him—in his dark topcoat and asshole astrakhan hat, weaving a little as he approached his car, drew his keys out of his pocket to unlock the door. The lateness of the hour and the semideserted garage made everything still. *A certain holy quality to it. Shadowless.* C.A. swallowed hard, feeling that little kick or trip to his heart that meant he was approaching the edge of what he'd been born for, *what was necessary to exact, to restore balance.* The secret was control. The secret was easing into the Death axis where you become the agent of Death in full control of Death, not its accidental victim or witness. So there appeared on level 3B of the parking structure this light-skinned youngish but old-fashioned kind of affable Negro, middle class you'd guess, professional class, strolling openly and in no hurry toward a Datsun hatchback parked a few spaces from R.K.'s

Lincoln, a coincidence the two men were going to their cars at the same time but nothing more than a coincidence surely, and when R.K.'s eyes lifted narrowing a bit in his direction the black man nodded respectfully and glanced away as you'd naturally do in such circumstances; then he glanced back as if in recognition, smiled tentatively, said in a lilting friendly absolutely unintimidating voice, "Mr. Krauss, is it?" and Krauss it was, thick-bodied, thick-necked, eyelids mildly inflamed with a long night of holiday drinking, lips pursed, baffled but not wanting to make a social blunder, so the black man said quickly, in his rich low melodic voice, "Wouldn't expect you to remember me, Mr. Krauss, but we met a few weeks ago, I think, out in Lathrup Farms, at a concert, a recital, at the arts center—wasn't it Howard Morland who introduced us?"

So, the setup: and R.K. naturally fell for it, it *was* innocent-seeming certainly, even in such deserted surroundings smelling of concrete and cold and dirt, and there's a well-dressed artsy-type black man extending his hand for a brotherly handshake and R.K. has no choice but to shift to a magnanimous liberal-hearted white in fact nodding in a semblance of recognition, friendly too and extending his gloved hand in that automatic response you can trigger in strangers if the right cues have been signaled as, here, with clockwork precision, they have been signaled. And easing in snaky-quick and close the affable black begins a smile not to be completed as a smile, exactly.

"Fucker! Did you think you could escape *me!*"

The assault by the agent of Death is so swift, so unexpected, the fur hat knocked from the head, the wire noose forced down and tightened in the same fluid motion, there is no time for anything more than a faint gurgling protest, a muffled dreamlike shriek of astonishment as the eyes bulge outward, the skin darkens with blood swelling within seconds like the skin of an overripe tomato about to burst, then the victim is on his knees flailing, convulsing, tearing with his nails at the unbelievable pressure around his neck choking the life out of him in beats in perfectly calibrated beats—

clockwork that can run in one direction only and can never be controverted not even by the power of God.

Thus the victorious hunter stands over his fallen prey whose death he has earned, whose death is *his.* Legs apart, knees bent, muscles strained to their fullest, expression thoughtful, patient—for the death convulsions are the *streaming-out of life* in the one that yields to the *streaming-in of life* in the other.

Did you think you could escape *me?*

Mr. Kreuzer had revealed to C.A. and a very small number of other privileged boys the secret of the X-factor, which democracy and Christianity and "archaic ethical remnants" sought to deny, but which manifested itself in the very genes and chromosomes of the biological organism—that approximately one tenth of one percent of the species *Homo sapiens* was destined to rule the rest, by way of superiority of intellect, personality, spiritual and physical strength, and that intangible element in the human psyche known as will. "Will is the conduit of fate," Mr. Kreuzer said. C.A. had not at first—for he was very young, a mere boy, a mere *angel boy* in whom his *devil twin* still slumbered!—comprehended. *Will is the conduit of fate.*

Thus when one is beset by emotion, by raw unmediated impulses flying like maddened wasps about one's head, it is *will* that must prevail, as *will* prevailed in Colin Asch, after the XXX on January 2, successfully completed, and the life that had luridly coursed up into him by way of his tingling hands and arms was almost too potent to be contained, he wanted to shriek, he wanted to laugh, to shout!—wanted to proclaim to the world what he had done and the justice of it! At the same time he wanted to get out of there as quickly as he could and had to resist the panicky instinct to run (for what if someone should step out of the elevator, push open the door to the stairs? What if the parking attendant below should have heard the sounds of struggle and was coming up to investigate?), but he had *plans*, he had a *method*, he had a *discipline* that could not be violated. So he willed himself to perform those acts that in his imagination he had already performed, calmly, even coolly, despite his pounding heart and the sweat running in tiny tickly streams down his sides, despite his shaking hands: the appropriation of certain items of clothing and jewelry, and of course the wallet (thick with bills and credit cards), *to the victor go the spoils*, and he had time too for punishing in certain requisite ways, the eyes that had given her insult, the groin, the fat cock, no matter the heaviness of the body in death, mere insensate *deadness*. For the revenge was hers, and must be exacted in full.

"I am the mere agent."

Then he placed the ticket stub he'd shrewdly acquired earlier that evening (at a porno movie house showing the double New Year's Day feature *Boys of the Night* and *Secrets of the Nazi Storm Troopers*) deep in the dead man's trouser pocket; then he heaved the body up and into the Lincoln, positioning it behind the wheel, head back against the headrest as if, indeed, merely resting, and stiffening arms crossed in the bloody lap. Then he removed from its Saran Wrap wrapper a wadded rag soaked in paint thinner, which he tossed into the back seat of the car; then he placed, in the car's trunk, beneath a rubber mat, three fag porn magazines purchased several weeks before, when he had first fashioned his plan—one of them dated January 1988, the others older, stained and rumpled, secondhand.

The genius of the Baffle is simplicity: *give the fuckers one main thing to think and they will think it.*

These actions Colin Asch performed deftly and pleasurably in less time in fact than it would afterward require him, in his aunt's home, sitting Indian-fashion on his bed, to record them, codified, in the Blue Ledger.

And then he took the stairs swiftly down to the ground level of the parking structure, encountering no one, being seen by no one, and on the ground level he waited patiently, perhaps ten minutes, until the attendant was occupied with a customer, and then he walked unhesitatingly out onto Providence Street—a free man. At this late hour (the dead man's watch, slipped on Colin Asch's wrist, read 3:20) the street was deserted except for a scattering of parked cars and a solitary police car easing through the intersection. By now Colin Asch felt so cleansed of all emotion, so pure, so child-like, so righteous, so spiritually replenished—*XXX performed to balance injustice, "eye for an eye, tooth for a tooth"*—that the sight of the patrol car made no special impression. And, in any case, it was headed in the opposite direction.

7

On a snowy Monday in early February, Mr. Howard Morland, tanned and rested from a protracted vacation in Barbados, dropped by Dorothea Deverell's office at the Institute to invite her, as if impulsively, to have lunch with him at his club that day. "The two of us have," he said, with the faintest of embarrassed smiles, "a little catching up to do."

Dorothea Deverell said without thinking, "Oh, but I'm afraid I can't, Howard—not today. I really have too much work to do. I wasn't intending to go out for lunch at all." Seeing Mr. Morland's look of gentlemanly disappointment—or was it, yet more subtly, a look of commingled pity and impatience—Dorothea felt her face begin to burn, as if she had been caught out in a social error. Yet she persisted. "I mean," she said, in a faltering voice, "there really is so much that should be done."

Mr. Morland merely laughed and backed off, with a dapper little salute. "Of course, Dorothea," he said, "I understand. But perhaps you could see me in my office? Sometime this morning? I promise not to encroach upon your time."

"I can," Dorothea said, swallowing hard. For of course this was the summons she had been awaiting. "I mean, I will."

When, an hour later, Dorothea entered the director's office, ushered inside by his smiling secretary, she found Mr. Morland seated not at his desk but in a black leather recliner with a raised footrest; he unwound himself from it and made a sort of belated gesture of getting to his feet, even as Dorothea told him not to bother. They were old associates after all: never intimate, but perhaps familial. "How lovely you look today, Dorothea!" Mr. Morland said, as he almost always did, shaking Dorothea's hand, as he almost always did, with a boyish vigor that never seemed less than genuine. Standing hardly taller than Dorothea Deverell at five feet five inches, Howard Morland was the sort of smallish compactly wiry man who, adept at such ferocious games as squash, racquetball, and handball, enjoys making larger men, and some women, wince at the strength of his handshake. But Dorothea had long ago learned to brace herself against it.

The first several minutes of any conversation with Mr. Morland in his capacity as director of the Brannon Institute were invariably given over to obfuscatory chatter, involving an exchange of social information: health, recent activities, news of mutual friends. Dorothea complimented Mr. Morland on his tan and asked an apposite question or two about the Morlands' house in Barbados. Where usually this preliminary ritual of talk chafed at Dorothea's nerves, for Mr. Morland with his feckless aristocrat's poise seemed to consider everything with equal seriousness, this morning she was grateful for it. Though she smiled readily and laughed at Mr. Morland's jokes—for Dorothea Deverell too had poise—the blood had drained out of her fingers and toes with startling abruptness, and she suspected that she looked rather pale. She was uneasy about the conversation to follow and could not imagine what course it would take.

She knew, however, that Roger Krauss's name would never be mentioned. It had never crossed Mr. Morland's lips in the past, when Krauss was so pointedly alive, and it would never cross his lips now that Krauss was dead.

Howard Morland's office, originally a drawing room in the Brannon mansion, was half again as large as Dorothea's, with the same elegantly high ceilings, tall narrow windows, and fine woodwork. In addition, Mr. Morland's office had antique furnishings from the estate, including, on the walls, costly works of art—an exquisite sun-drenched Bonnard, a small murky Corot oil. There were long Spanish lace curtains framed by heavy velvet drapes, there was an Irish crystal chandelier, there was a stately travertine marble fireplace of the hue and seeming texture of curdled cream. A model of the old ideal of connoisseurship, Mr. Morland's office was less an "office"—with vulgar connotations of practicability, routine, work—than a self-regarding display of wealth and taste. Entering it, seated in it, Dorothea Deverell had never once thought, in her six years as Howard Morland's assistant, that she might some day inherit it; her hopes for advancement had always been abstract. For certainly she did not deserve such splendor.

Just as Howard Morland was known for his habits of obfuscation, so too was he known, by his professional colleagues at least, for sudden, sometimes dizzying transitions of subject. One moment he was chatting amiably, and at length, about the "marvelous wild monkeys—so shy" of the Windward Islands; the next he was telling Dorothea Deverell, in the same tone, his smile undiminished, that he had, at the previous Friday's meeting of the board of trustees of the Institute, made the date of his retirement official: June 1. "And I requested of them, and they concurred—I should say, Dorothea, unanimously and enthusiastically concurred—that you be named the next director." His smile deepened; his beautifully capped teeth shone whitely. Because of his tanned face his hair too shone white, a benign snowy innocent sort of white, still quite thick. "Dorothea? Did you hear? We want you to be the next director of the Institute."

Dorothea Deverell, listening intently, had not, somehow, heard.

But she managed to smile and to nod, murmured a few confused words of assent, felt her eyes fill quickly with tears, as if swelling. She had to resist the impulse to say to Howard Morland, whom, suddenly, she saw as a beneficent father, her friend and protector all along, "But the directorship is too good for me—I don't deserve it."

She said instead, "I'm very honored."

Mr. Morland went on expansively to tell Dorothea of the circumstances of the board meeting, in which, of course, he had played the major role: what was said, and by whom; how very highly Dorothea's unique talents were regarded; their fear that (for there had been recent rumors) Dorothea might seek employment elsewhere. He told Dorothea the board hoped, if she accepted the terms of the directorship, that she might want to take over the responsibilities of "acting director" in a few weeks, to make the transition less difficult.

"With an immediate adjustment in salary, of course," Mr. Morland quickly added, misinterpreting Dorothea's lowered gaze.

So they spoke of practical matters, and problems that had accumulated in Mr. Morland's absence; and the remainder of the historic conversation, for Dorothea, passed in a drunken sort of blur —for she feared she might burst into tears, and Mr. Morland would be obliged to comfort her. Yet she was not untouched by a sense of irony, knowing that, had not Roger Krauss been removed from the board of trustees by death, and had not the circumstances of his death been so inescapably lurid, it was quite doubtful—ah, quite!— that the director of the Brannon Institute would be having this particular happy conversation with his assistant; he might indeed be having a very different sort of conversation altogether. (Yet he is not aware of this at all, Dorothea thought. The fact of Roger Krauss has been removed from his memory entirely.)

She thought it amusing too, more innocently so, that Mr. Morland should solemnly propose an interim assignment as acting director as if, for the past several years, that had not been, *de facto*, Dorothea Deverell's very position at the Brannon Institute.

Yet when she rose to leave and Mr. Morland again shook her hand, or, rather, clasped it almost tenderly, Dorothea felt tears of gratitude rush into her eyes, tears of relief, of sheer girlish joy. Now my future is clear, she thought. A part of my future at least.

"I had always intended this, you know, Dorothea," Mr. Morland said warmly. "You to succeed me, I mean. I hope, dear, you never had any cause to doubt—?"

In a tone of equal warmth, her eyes shining with emotion, Dorothea Deverell exclaimed, "Never!"

When she returned to her office on the second floor, there stood Jacqueline happily awaiting her, and several other staff members —for of course the secretarial staff had known, since the board's meeting on Friday, of Dorothea Deverell's promotion. "*This*," Jacqueline said half accusingly, handing Dorothea a single long-stemmed rose, ruby-red, in a slender glass vase. "Why did you think *this* was on my desk? Did you think I just bought it, for myself, for no reason? To liven up Monday mornings?"

Dorothea accepted it from her, blushing with pleasure. She hadn't noticed the rose on Jacqueline's desk at all.

Later, she telephoned Charles Carpenter at his office, to tell him her remarkable news, which, to Charles Carpenter, did not seem so very remarkable, "It's about time," he said. Grimly, with a husbandly sort of loyalty, adding, "Those bastards." But Dorothea refused to allow him to take that tone and spoke of how exceedingly gracious Howard Morland had been, and sincere; and not a word of course of her old enemy Roger Krauss. "I should hope not," Charles Carpenter said. "I should think, rather, they all owe you an apology—starting with Howard. He has been slipping by on charm for the past sixty-odd years."

In recent weeks, since Dorothea's retreat to Vermont, she and Charles Carpenter seemed to have drifted closer together; they were in one of their cycles of intense, almost sibling intimacy, speaking with each other daily, sometimes twice daily, on the telephone, though they usually did not see each other more than once a week. Charles confided in her that he spoke to her more frequently than he spoke to his wife, and always about more significant things. For which, I suppose, Dorothea thought, I should be grateful: *there is that at least.*

Charles did congratulate her on the promotion, however; he was happy, he said, that she was happy. "Now my future is clear, in Lathrup Farms," Dorothea said jubilantly. Then added, lest her lover be hurt or alarmed, "A part of my future at least."

(Though Roger Krauss had been dead hardly more than a month, the subject of his death, and its shocking circumstances, was no longer much discussed in Lathrup Farms; other matters, less scandalous but gratifyingly local, had come to the fore. Out of a dread of seeming to delight in another's ill fortune, Dorothea Deverell did not follow news of the police investigation in the papers, if, indeed, there was news; nor did she participate in conversations that drifted onto that topic. In time she might even convince herself that Mr. Krauss had merely been baiting her, taking a devil's advocate sort of stand vis-à-vis "feminism," as often, in social situations, meaning no real harm, otherwise good-hearted men will do. To think of him as her enemy was surely to exaggerate? "I must guard against that sort of thing."

It was Dorothea's vague understanding that the mystery of the murder was more or less solved; that the police had their man; that there would eventually be a trial. And this too, this public posthumous death ritual, she would make every effort to ignore in the interest of maintaining that purity of conscience, or soul, that seemed to her as much a part of Dorothea Deverell's identity as her dark brown eyes, her dark brown hair, her creamy-pale skin, her delicate frame.)

On the day that Dorothea Deverell's promotion to Director of the Brannon Institute was made public—by "public" meaning simply its release to the Lathrup Farms weekly, where it was featured in a prominent article—she arrived home from the Institute at about 6:30 P.M. and had scarcely taken off her coat and begun sorting through the morning's mail when the doorbell rang. As if, she thought, someone had been waiting for her. Or had followed her home.

It was Colin Asch, whom she had not seen for weeks, with a bouquet of flowers. "I hope you don't mind, Miss Deverell! I just wanted to drop by, you know, to congratulate you!"

Dorothea was startled to see him, so tall, so blond, so palpably *there*—yet rather happy too, for she'd been thinking of him, and in a way missing him. She invited him inside, and offered him tea or some sherry—"Thank you, you're very kind, why don't I have whatever you're having: tea?"—and put the flowers in a vase. A half dozen gorgeous flame-colored gladioli. Each stem was about three feet tall, each blossom the size of a man's fist. Dorothea laughed aloud at the prodigality of her young friend's gift. She felt suddenly quite giddy, festive. "Sherry," she said. "And what the English choose to call 'digestive biscuits.'"

They sat in the living room, Colin Asch rather shyly, at first, on the sofa, whose excess of little pillows seemed initially to confound him; Dorothea in a facing Queen Anne chair. How larger than life her visitor appeared, and how enlivened, keyed up, physically *busy*—leaning forward to examine books and magazines on Dorothea's coffee table, craning his neck to see the framed Oriental woodcut on the wall behind the sofa, smiling, smiling, like a child on a rare excursion, or a lover newly admitted to the very bower of bliss. He wore a sports coat in bright Harris tweed, and striped tweed trousers, not quite matching the latest in men's fashions presumably; his white-gold hair was cropped short at the sides and back but rose in thick tufts at the crown of his head. A scrim of pale beard glimmered on his jaws and cheeks, and this too Dorothea seemed to know was fashionable—though why it should be, she hadn't the slightest idea. And was that an earring in the young man's right earlobe? Not an earring precisely but a sort of clamp, gold or brass and rather cruel-looking?

In a high rapid self-conscious voice Colin Asch was explaining to Dorothea, as if some sort of explanation were expected, that he had actually heard of her good news from his Aunt Ginny days ago—"But she cautioned me not to be premature. To wait, you know, for the official release." His expression shifted as if in mimesis of his days of anticipation and impatience. "It's such wonderful news, Miss Deverell—I mean, Dorothea! And so deserved!"

Dorothea thanked him and tried, after a discreet pause, to deflect the subject from herself, asking after Colin Asch's job at the television station and where he was now living—she'd heard, she said, that he had found an apartment somewhere in Lathrup Farms? It struck her at the time, though less forcibly than it would afterward, as odd, just slightly odd, that a young man whom she scarcely knew should be so impressed by—indeed, so emotionally caught up in—her modest professional success. And the way he looked at her, his beautiful eyes widened in respectful admiration: it was all rather odd. But flattering.

When Colin Asch told Dorothea that he no longer worked at WWBC-TV but had a "much more challenging" job in public relations with a firm here in Lathrup Farms, she recalled vaguely that Ginny Weidmann had told her something of this and of Colin's rather abruptly leaving the Weidmanns' house. She recalled too that there had been some unpleasantness—hurt feelings on Ginny's part—and something more, but for some reason it had all faded from her memory; perhaps she hadn't wanted to believe anything less than good of Ginny's extraordinary young relative. He was saying, with an embarrassed shrug of his shoulders, "They didn't want me to leave the television station, and it was all rather awkward at the end. In fact, a competitor of theirs found out I was leaving and made me an offer *over the telephone*—which left me a little breathless. But I had had it up to here, Dorothea," he said, drawing a forefinger swiftly across his throat, "with the media and their pitiless emphasis on *popularity.* The only question such people ask themselves is, 'Will it sell?' Or, 'Will advertisers like it?' The content of a typical television program is always subordinate to so many other factors, so many other *trivial* factors—I mean, it's an insult to the human species! At least," he said, lowering his voice, "it was an insult to *me.* They practically begged me to do a pilot show, a sort of high-level interview program like on public radio, you know, where the interviewer really knows his material, reads a lot of books and things, to prepare, and I was tempted, sort of, but not, you know, really seriously—what the media takes from you ultimately is your soul, Dorothea: nothing less. So I quit. Walked away. And had the good luck to walk into another—well, a much better job."

Dorothea Deverell, rather dazzled by the rapidity of her young friend's recitation and the intensity with which he regarded her, could only murmur, banally, "Good for you!"—though the thought occurred to her that public relations, as she understood the field, could not really be much of an improvement over television.

Colin Asch finished his glass of sherry, and licked boyishly at his lips, and laughed, and said, "I know what you're thinking, Dorothea—"

"Yes?"

"—that a job in public relations is the same kind of thing as a job in television, that the goals are sort of basically the same—an emphasis upon surfaces, images, and all that. But no, actually," he said, frowning, "it isn't like that, actually. I mean, it can be, and probably is, in most circumstances, but this position that I have, assistant to the art director at L.L. Loomis and Company—d'you know them? ever heard of them? they're a state-of-the-art kind of company, first-class, upbeat, sort of wired, but wired in a *good* way—the director's a guy about my age, only a few years older, really great to work with. In fact I was thinking, Dorothea, on the way over here—I mean, I have another reason, a primary reason, for being here—but I was thinking, sort of, I could help you out, I mean at the Institute, with publicity for your programs and exhibits, that kind of thing—I mean," he said, breathless, "if you wanted me to."

Dorothea smiled, as if ruefully, and said, "Yes, publicity hasn't been one of our strong points. I never seem to—"

"It isn't just *informing* people of what you're doing, it's *forcing* them to take notice," Colin Asch said passionately. "Some of the programs you sponsor, they're so good, they're so deserving of a much wider audience—they're as significant as anything going on in Boston, in my opinion, or in Cambridge—but the masses have to be alerted. Not that you'd want too many people of course; the auditorium wouldn't hold them. But the art exhibits, that's different, they'd space themselves out sort of naturally I'm sure." Seeing Dorothea's smile he asked, "Is something wrong?"

"I was just thinking, Colin, that it has never yet been a problem for us, at the Institute: an excess of people—of 'masses.'"

"Well, I know," Colin Asch concurred, with a sheepish smile, "it's been a small operation, mainly local, serving the community and all that. But now that you're in charge it's a new era, sort of—has got to be. Maybe you could give me your schedule for this spring—before I leave—so I could get started, just sort of unobtrusively? I mean just on my own." As if to discipline himself for speaking so excitedly he came to a full stop; Dorothea saw his jaws clamp. Then he said, "I mean *just* on my own, Dorothea. Don't worry about a fee. *Pro bono*."

Dorothea said, uncertainly, "That would be very kind of you."

"Oh, no! I'm not kind! I'm just—a cultural emissary!"

Colin Asch had settled almost comfortably into the sofa, with the pillows neatly positioned beside him. He now crossed one long lanky tweed-clad leg over the other and chose a biscuit from the plate Dorothea offered him. She saw that he was wearing enormous running shoes, in shades of lavender. And was it possible, in 20 degree weather?—no socks.

He said, as if to prod her into speaking a bit, "But it *is* a new era, Dorothea. With a woman in charge, and all."

Dorothea Deverell did indeed have plans for change, and newness; but she supposed she had better go slowly and not worry, or annoy, or offend the rather conservative board of trustees and the faithful little corps of volunteers, mainly female, who supported the Institute. But she confided in Colin Asch that, yes, she was intending to broaden the scope of the lecture series in particular: the former director had not wanted her to bring in a "controversial" speaker, a woman defense attorney who worked with battered women and children in Boston, and this excellent woman she would certainly engage for next year; and she would invite poets now and then; and in two or three years, when a former professor of hers at Yale retired, a distinguished art historian in the Renaissance, she might arrange a sort of *Festschrift* in his honor, inviting a number of art historians in his field, including former students, to give public lectures…and it would be tied in, of course, with an art exhibit.

"Those are wonderful ideas," Colin Asch said, staring at her. "Those are—I mean, those are *brilliant* ideas."

So encouraged, Dorothea Deverell was led to confide in her young friend even more, some of it sheerly speculative, and all of it unformed, inchoate: she foresaw an education series, she foresaw extensive renovations in the building, she foresaw new additions—a wing better suited for art exhibits, a new auditorium. She said, breathless, "I was telling a close friend about some of these things the other day, Colin, and he said, as if he were startled, 'I hadn't realized you had such ideas, Dorothea,' and I said to him, 'I've never had power before, and power brings ideas.' He looked at me strangely, then, and said, 'I suppose it *is* a matter of power ultimately, the realization of ideas.' I couldn't help replying—though I didn't at all want to offend him!—'Not *ultimately*, but *immediately*.' And then," she said, laughing almost girlishly, "and then he really did look at me strangely."

But Colin Asch was not to be drawn in with Dorothea Deverell's laughter. He said soberly, brushing a crumb or two fastidiously from his lips, "Yes, the average man is very jealous of a woman's 'power.' Who did you say was your friend?"

"Charles Carpenter," Dorothea said. (But why had she told Colin? She hadn't meant to.) Her cheeks pulsed with warmth; she added, apologetically, "You wouldn't remember him, but he—"

"Of course I remember him," Colin Asch said. He cast his eerily dazzling smile up at Dorothea as if she were teasing him. "A lawyer. A friend of the Weidmanns'. His wife attacked me on the issue of my vegetarianism. She was drunk—she was a drunk. Yet, do you know, Dorothea, Mrs. Carpenter tried to make it up to me afterward? Sent a check for two hundred dollars to me for the Animal Rights League, by way of my aunt."

Dorothea Deverell stared blankly. "She did? Agnes Carpenter?"

"Wasn't that kind of her?" Colin Asch said. "Even if she was expiating a guilty conscience."

"Yes," Dorothea said slowly. "It was kind of her." She added, not knowing what she meant, "Many of the most generous things in life, I suppose, are done to expiate guilty consciences. Which doesn't make them any—"

"Any less generous."

There was an uneasy pause. Dorothea offered her visitor a second glass of sherry, which he accepted with thanks—"It's delicious!" She had the distinct impression that he was turning over in his mind a question of some blunt direct sort regarding Charles Carpenter, and she wanted neither to hear it nor answer it.

She said, "Ginny was telling me you've found a new apartment?"

Colin Asch nodded and caressed the metal clamp in his ear. "It's called Normandy Court, do you know it? No? I'm on the eleventh floor, overlooking a little park. A friend—a new friend—is sort of helping me finance it, until I get settled in at L.L. Loomis. That's her Porsche I'm driving too—though maybe you didn't see me drive up in it?—a 1986 model I have an option to buy if I like it. Sweet little car, and *fantastic* apartment. Which is why I'm here, Miss Deverell, I mean Dorothea—I hope you'll come to see me there, and let me make dinner for you? I was thinking some sort of celebration dinner, you know, in honor of your promotion? I'd invite Aunt Ginny and Uncle Martin too, they're such wonderful people, and anyone else you'd like and my friend Mrs. Hunt, Susannah Hunt, I guess you know her?—sort of?—she says she knows you. Just a small intimate dinner. *Please say yes.*"

"Why, yes—of course," Dorothea said slowly. "If—that is—"

"It would mean so much to me! It would be such an honor!"

"If you don't think it would be too much—"

"How does March fifth sound to you? A Saturday? Eight P.M.?"

"As far as I know that date is—"

"The actual reason I have to postpone the dinner so long," Colin Asch said with a pinched, pained look, "is I can't depend upon the furniture people to get the furniture to me before then. This beautiful glass and chrome dining room set—first they promised it in three weeks, now they've extended it to five, the bastards! And this beautiful Halogen lamp I bought on sale, right off the floor, marked down from $460 to $399, a real bargain, when they delivered it the base was scratched—so I refused to pay the C.O.D. charges and sent it back. *But I still want it.* Some items are in the apartment, like a nice off-white sofa, actually sort of resembling the one I'm sitting on, but others aren't, so Susannah has lent me some stuff of hers in the interim. But by March fifth everything should be perfect. By March fifth everything *will* be perfect."

Dorothea said weakly, "But I can't allow you to go to any trouble, Colin. Or spend much money—"

"How can it be trouble, Dorothea," Colin Asch asked, regarding her with hurt eyes, "if I am doing it for *you?*"

Dorothea was holding her sherry glass in both hands, to prevent its trembling. She thought, what does he want from me?—and why? With a pang of chagrin she remembered the Christmas present, the unexpected and, indeed, unwanted gift; and meant to mention it to Colin Asch before he left the house. And Susannah Hunt: how did this ingenuous young man become involved with *her?* Dorothea Deverell could claim no firsthand knowledge of the woman but had heard startling tales, over the years, revolving around her legendary rapacity for men (including young men) and her squabbles, legal and otherwise, with her former husband, a prominent local physician. Once, at a cocktail party, Dorothea had spent an anguished half hour observing, out of the corner of her eye, her beloved Charles Carpenter in a spirited, laughter-punctuated conversation with the glamorous divorcée; to her mortification she had happened to glance across the room to see Agnes Carpenter similarly observing the couple...staring at them with a Gorgon's unwavering eye. How sisterly she'd felt toward poor Agnes in that instant! How united in their mutual helplessness!

She had never said a word about the episode to Charles Carpenter, nor had he said a word to her.

Now she said to Colin Asch, in a neutral voice, "Are you no longer seeing that young woman from the television station? What was her name?—with the lovely black hair—"

Colin Asch said vaguely, "*That* didn't work out."

Dorothea said, "Didn't it? I'm sorry."

"Oh, don't be sorry! Really—don't be," Colin Asch said. He grinned, and uncrossed his long legs, and ran a hand roughly through his hair. "Hartley was too intense. She wanted too much from me. We just weren't, you know, each other's destiny. Also, Dorothea," he said, lowering his voice, "she had a cocaine habit. An expensive one."

"Cocaine!"

There was an awkward pause, and Colin set down his sherry glass and rose to his feet. He consulted the platinum watch on his wrist and said, reluctantly, "Well, I suppose I should be leaving." Then, in virtually the same breath, he said, "Your house is so beautiful, Dorothea! Do you think I could see the rest of it?"

Dorothea heard herself say, "Of course."

Her mind leapt ahead to the upstairs: in what condition was it? Must she show her impetuous young friend everything—even her bedroom? Her closets?

Seeing her expression Colin said, "Unless it's too much trouble? I mean—you must be exhausted from your long day."

"Oh, no, it isn't too much trouble." Dorothea laughed.

And then the telephone rang.

She excused herself and took the call in the dining room, absentmindedly watching her visitor through a mirror—in fact, through two mirrors—without his awareness. The caller was a woman friend named Merle, an intelligent, rather lonely married woman with whom Dorothea Deverell sometimes went to the ballet, and though Dorothea tried to cut the conversation short it seemed that Merle wanted to talk: wanted rather urgently to talk. "May I call you back? I have a visitor," Dorothea said. She saw, in the living room, Colin Asch in his boxy Harris tweed moving with astonishing swiftness from place to place, like a big feral cat on its hind legs…scanning the books in her bookcase, checking the things on her fireplace mantel, lifting and setting down a little ivory box on a table…trying, with a practiced twist of his wrist, the lock of her terrace door…tiptoeing to the foot of the staircase and peering up, frowning, into the shadows. (But why? Dorothea thought, fascinated. I am not up there: I am down here.) The inside of her mouth seemed to be coated with a thin scummy fear, and it was with relief that she saw the tall blond figure pass out of the mirrors' range. She murmured to Merle in as kindly a voice as possible, "I'll have to call you back later. I can't talk now."

When she returned to the living room, however, Colin Asch was awaiting her with a quizzical, radiant smile. He held an art book of color plates by the American artist Alice Neel—"*This* is an original talent!" he said. He queried Dorothea Deverell about Neel, and Dorothea told him some of what she knew and offered to lend him the book—which he accepted with gratitude. He was so eager to learn, so much the ingenuous student, her suspicions of him seemed unwarranted.

Indeed, in the face of the young man's dazzling personality it was difficult to form any negative judgment of him at all.

Dorothea was telling Colin Asch about the background of her trio of dwarf Portuguese orange trees in their green ceramic pots, arranged along the southerly wall of the dining room—the tour of the house seemed, mercifully, for the moment at least, forgotten, or held in abeyance—when the telephone rang another time. A spasm of anger ran over the young man's face, but he clenched his jaws and said, "You're a very popular woman, Dorothea!—or I've come at the wrong time."

"I'll tell him to call back," Dorothea said apologetically.

But it was Charles Carpenter, with whom she did want to speak, as he wanted, it seemed quite urgently, to speak with Dorothea. Might he drop by, Charles asked, on his way home? He was still in Boston, and he'd had a very difficult day.

"Is something wrong?" Dorothea asked, alarmed.

"What is it?"

"I'll tell you when I see you, Dorothea," Charles Carpenter said.

Dorothea said softly, "Is it—?"

"About you, and me? Yes it is, dear," Charles said. "And Agnes."

Dorothea Deverell, standing in the darkened dining room, the telephone receiver pressed against her ear, could make no reply. She knows, she was thinking calmly. Now it will be all over between Charles and me.

Charles said, "Is someone there, Dorothea?—with you?"

Dorothea, staring sightlessly at the floor, pointedly not looking into the mirrors, murmured vaguely, "No, not really."

Her lover did not register this ambiguity, or subtlety; he said, "Then I'll be seeing you soon, Dorothea. In about an hour."

Dorothea said, dumbly, "Tonight? Ah, yes. Of course."

They said goodbye; and like a sleepwalker Dorothea returned to her visitor, who was standing, as if at attention, in exactly the same spot he'd been standing when the telephone rang. This time, Dorothea suspected that he had been listening to her conversation. She could not recall if she had spoken her lover's name and was too exhausted suddenly to care.

Colin Asch was examining with reverence a Chagall lithograph of sleeping lovers framed and hung prominently on Dorothea's wall, a gift from Michel Deverell's grandfather, on the occasion of their wedding; a mysterious and beautiful work of art at which, in truth, Dorothea Deverell rarely glanced, it had become so familiar to her with the years and was, over all, so melancholy in its associations. The artist had signed *Marc Chagall* in pencil, in the lower right-hand corner, and it was to this signature that Colin Asch pointed, exclaiming, with touching naiveté, "He really did sign it himself, didn't he! This must be a real collector's item!"

Dorothea said, "It's only a lithograph—one of many copies."

She told Colin that the telephone call had been an important one, and that someone was coming over that evening to see her; she was sorry to be unable to take him on a tour of her house, but another time, perhaps…?

"Yes," said Colin. "I understand."

Dorothea felt like a guilty wife or courtesan in a Molière farce, ushering out one male to clear the way for another: though why she should feel guilty, and why such circumstances, edged with hysteria, might be imagined as crude farce, she could not have said. God knows there was nothing amusing about it.

At the door Colin Asch said, "You won't forget March fifth, Dorothea, will you? Eight P.M.? I'll be sending out invitations as soon as I can, but please mark the date."

"I will," Dorothea promised. "I will mark the date."

She could make out, at the curb, in the dim light of a streetlamp, Colin Asch's borrowed sports car. Small, sleek, classy. Dorothea feared he would impulsively invite her to go for a ride in it, and that, against her will, she would hear herself accept.

On the front step Colin Asch shook her hand vigorously, clasping it just a beat or two too long. Dorothea said carefully, "What exactly do you want of me, Colin?"

It was the first time in her life she had ever spoken so, to any human being.

Colin Asch blinked at her as if she had slapped him. He said, hurt, "I don't 'want' anything of you, Dorothea. It just makes me happy to think—I mean, to *know*—"

"Yes?"

"—that you are here. That you exist." He spoke slowly and painfully, not meeting Dorothea's eye. "That, you know, our lives are…parallel."

Dorothea waited, but he said nothing further. Tears of relief sprang into her eyes. She said, squeezing his hand, "That's very kind of you, Colin. You're a remarkable person. I feel the same way about you—you've put it very gracefully."

"Then that's everything," Colin Asch said gravely, backing away.

She watched him hurry to his car, knowing that, before he climbed inside, he would turn and wave to her, just once. As he did.

She was thinking shrewdly, Parallel lines never meet.

*

Awaiting Charles Carpenter, Dorothea Deverell changed from her gray jersey dress to a plaid woolen skirt and an oversized Shetland sweater and put on low-heeled shoes. She carried the vase of tall flame-colored gladioli out of the living room, where they were far too exclamatory, and walked from room to room before setting them down in a twilit corner of the dining room. Then she made herself a cup of strong tea and stood in the kitchen drinking it. She was too agitated to sit down; seated, she would hear her heartbeat too clearly. She was thinking that her life of nearly the past decade was coming to an end and that, for all its frustration, intermittent humiliation, and heartbreak, it had been a comfortable sort of life. She had been happy, really—less a married man's mistress than a married man's second, and far more companionable, wife. Her mother's words rose to her memory. "You go on for years and years doing the same things, not even thinking how happy you are, then suddenly one day everything is ended"—this sad, stoic observation on the occasion, when Dorothea was a senior in high school, of her father's first operation for cancer. Now Dorothea thought, Yes. But I will have to bear it.

And then, to her astonishment, within the hour Charles Carpenter brought her entirely unexpected news: "I've spoken to her, Dorothea. I've told her!"

He hadn't yet removed his overcoat, which smelled of cold, and was slowly removing his hat, a gray fedora Dorothea Deverell thought very handsome.

He said, "Did you hear me, Dorothea? *I've told her.*"

"Told her—?"

"I mean, I've begun to tell her. At last!"

Dorothea stared at Charles Carpenter, whom she had rarely seen so excited; so agitated. She backed off, rather frightened—then stepped forward into the man's hard, clumsy embrace—they grasped each other like guilty children and staggered together in Dorothea's little foyer.

Charles was saying triumphantly, "Last night—and this afternoon, over the telephone! I've made a beginning, at last! Now there is no turning back!"

As if yoked together they moved blunderingly into Dorothea's kitchen, where, uninvited, Charles Carpenter located a bottle of Irish whiskey in one of the cupboards and poured himself and Dorothea drinks. In the living room they sat on the sofa amid the scattered pillows, clasping hands as Charles Carpenter talked and Dorothea Deverell listened wide-eyed and disbelieving.

"Out of nowhere suddenly—we *weren't* arguing; our silences are far, far worse than speech—I simply said to her, 'We don't love each other, Agnes, why do we remain together?' and she cast me a look of absolute loathing as if I'd violated a sort of secret between us, and when I tried to continue she got up and left the room, as she has left at other times, simply walking away—*as if I didn't exist.* But I followed her, and insisted we talk, and we did, or I did. I mentioned the possibility of a separation, and she screamed at me, 'I'll never consent. I'll kill us both first!' Later, she accused me of wanting to kill *her;* I knew she wasn't well, she said; and what would my parents—'your precious parents'—say; and my business partners—'those fellow hypocrites.' She slammed out of the room, and I didn't follow her for a while; then I went upstairs where she was waiting but she'd locked the door, and—and so it went. For hours! Literally for hours!" He stared at Dorothea, smiling strangely; he was grasping her hand in his so hard she winced in pain. Several times he said, wonderingly, "But I've made a beginning, at last. I've made a beginning—at last."

Dorothea said faintly, "I'm so glad, Charles."

"My parents *will* be very upset, and I dread telling them, but it can't be helped. They've tyrannized me—us—with their good, sweet, uncomplaining, exemplary natures for too long. Being good, you know, is a kind of blackmail, it holds the rest of us in thrall. Agnes has always known this—known she could rely upon my 'good' nature, my fidelity, my absurd sense of conscience. Ah, yes, she has known! She has *capitalized!* Now she can enjoy a sort of martyr's pleasure, a mean bitter pleasure, casting me as the villain, a 'typical middle-aged asshole'—those were her words—and reaping sympathy and pity, or so she thinks. As if any of our friends are hers, any longer! As if anyone but her husband has been able to tolerate her, for years!"

So Charles Carpenter talked; and Dorothea Deverell, in a trance of amazement, listened. Could she believe what she was hearing? But what *was* she hearing? In the midst of a passionate tirade on the subject of Agnes' excessive drinking, Dorothea interrupted to ask if the word "divorce" had been uttered, and if Agnes had said anything about consulting a lawyer—and Charles Carpenter stared at her, as if unhearing.

He said, passing a hand over his eyes, "She will retain a lawyer who's an enemy of mine—I know it."

Dorothea said, "*Our* relationship should be kept a secret for the time being, shouldn't it?"

"Dorothea, I don't see how it can," Charles said. He had removed his suit coat; now he tugged irritably at his tie. A fine film of perspiration glistened on his face. "I thought, you know, that that was the point of—all this: my speaking to her, bringing things out into the open. Perhaps, in terms of timing, with your appointment and all at the Institute, it isn't ideal, but as I said I hadn't planned it—just suddenly out of nowhere, out of our damned glacial *silence,* I began talking and haven't been able to stop. You know I love you, and I want to marry you; surely you don't expect me to *deny* you? To Agnes or to anyone?"

Dorothea had to resist the childlike impulse to shut her eyes tight. She said, "But have you told her, Charles? About—?"

"One of the things she screamed at me was, 'There's another woman, isn't there?'—and I didn't answer; I managed somehow to deflect the question, but a while later she returned to it, and said, 'Is it Dorothea Deverell?' and I'm afraid, Dorothea, under the pressure of the moment I said 'No.' I went on to say, 'The deadness in our marriage has nothing to do with any third party, as you certainly know,' and that distracted her enough to—Dorothea? Are you all right?"

Dorothea was clutching at Charles Carpenter's hand with both her hands. "Did she—did she really say that? 'Is it Dorothea Deverell?'"

"Yes. She did. She isn't an unobservant woman, after all."

"But you told her 'No.'"

"I told her 'No' as a means of telling her something else—eliding speech, in a sense—not very courageously, I'm ashamed to say, but in the desperation of the moment expediently; I didn't want Agnes, in her rage, to involve *you*. To pick up the telephone and call *you*. That would have been unthinkable, dear."

Dorothea was still clutching Charles's hand in her hands, and now she leaned forward suddenly, as if faint, and pressed her forehead against it. She was thinking, What will happen now? What will happen—now? She murmured, "So you've told her, Charles, at last!" Dazedly she kissed his hand, her face damp with tears—she had not known she was crying. She whispered, "I love you," and Charles Carpenter kissed her warm forehead, whispering, "I love *you*," passionately, repeatedly, as if he were making a formal vow.

"Now maybe we can give up all this—subterfuge. This damned demeaning subterfuge. I am at fault, for postponing a break with my wife for so long; in retrospect I'm appalled at my cowardice. My 'goodness.' My very sense of myself as citizen of a community! You've been so patient, Dorothea, a saint, really—having such faith in *me*. But now, soon, we can live together, openly—we can be married, and live together, in a house of our own—like normal people." He laughed excitedly, as if the single glass of whiskey had gone to his head; he slung an arm around Dorothea almost roughly, hugging her close. "Imagine, Dorothea darling: married. *Like normal people.*"

"Yes," Dorothea Deverell said. "Yes," she wept, though in truth she could not imagine it. Not after so many years of hope.

So, that night, after Charles Carpenter left her—they had gone at last up to Dorothea's bedroom to make love, as ardently as if for the first time—Dorothea Deverell lay wakeful, rigid, her eyes starkly open and her brain a storm of thoughts. Like maddened wasps the question assailed her; *What will happen now? What will happen—now?* Though she tried to think of Charles Carpenter, and her love for him, and the possibility—or was it, now, a probability?—of their being married someday soon and living in a house of their own—indeed, Dorothea had just the house in mind, or its type: Georgian revival, elegant, stately, though not large, in the older "good" section of Lathrup Farms—she nonetheless kept envisioning Agnes Carpenter, her rival, her sister rival, lying at the very same moment sleepless in *her* bed, in *her* bedroom, on the other side of town—she envisioned the woman's stunned, creased, aging face and those terrified glaring eyes—*Is it another woman? Is it Dorothea Deverell?*

I had so much rather be an object of her selfishness, Dorothea thought miserably, than have her be the object of mine.

So Dorothea passed a hellish night, the first, she presumed, of many to come; and *this* the consequence of her happiness—hers and Charles Carpenter's. By morning she had made up her mind, and telephoned Charles at his office, and told the astonished man in a rush of words that he should wait—they should wait, *must* wait—and not do anything further to upset Agnes.

"To upset Agnes?" Charles Carpenter asked, as if he had not heard correctly.

Dorothea said, "Please don't be angry, dear, but I—I can't bear to hurt her. I can't bear it that you and I, in our selfishness, should hurt her. In time, perhaps—in a few months, gradually—it could all be explained to her, but not so suddenly—so cruelly. It's like murder! such an assault! And there are two of us, Charles, and only one of her: think of how she must feel!"

Charles protested, "*I* don't want to hurt Agnes either, but it has to be done. In fact it has been postponed far too long, as I thought you'd agreed. If you and I are to—"

"All those years I envied Agnes and felt such bitterness toward her, or thought I did, and now I find I—simply don't want to hurt her. Can't bear to hurt her. You loved her once, didn't you? And she loved you surely—didn't she? She hasn't been well for years; she will only begin drinking more heavily—"

"Dorothea, for God's sake, you sound hysterical. Where are you, at home? Haven't you gone to work? I'll come over—"

"No, don't come over! Not now!"

"You sound so upset—"

"I *am* upset; we must rethink this!"

"But I thought, last night, we'd come to a kind of conclusion—"

"Did you say anything more to *her*, last night? When you went home?"

"No. Not to Agnes. But to you, Dorothea, I mean—I talked to *you*—I thought we'd come to a kind of conclusion, Dorothea, didn't we?" There was a pause; Charles Carpenter was breathing heavily, like a man who has been taxed to the limit. This side of him, this sense of an impatience, even anger, barely restrained, was new to Dorothea Deverell, and intimidating. "And now," he said bitterly, "now you're withdrawing from me. Now you mean to deny *me*."

"I certainly don't! I love you. But there *is* Agnes, she *does* exist, other people do exist in the world, and we can't simply trample over them. Only think," Dorothea said in a hoarse frightened voice, "of how, at this moment, she must feel!"

"I'm thinking rather more urgently of how I feel," Charles Carpenter said.

"But I—" Dorothea began.

But in that instant the line went dead: for the first time in Dorothea Deverell's life someone had hung up on her.

A few days after Colin Asch's visit with Dorothea Deverell a packet came for her, special delivery, containing a sample of the invitation card Colin meant to send out to the guests for Dorothea's dinner party.

Colin Andrew Asch
requests the pleasure of your company
to celebrate the appointment of
Dorothea Deverell
as Director of the Morris Brannon Institute
on Saturday, March fifth, nineteen eighty-eight
at 1104 Normandy Court, Lathrup Farms, Massachusetts
R.s.v.p. *Eight o'clock*
Telephone: 617-555-5825 *Black tie*

The paper was stiff ivory; the print elegantly, one might say a bit pretentiously, engraved. Holding it in her hand, Dorothea laughed aloud in embarrassment. "This is impossible." Why did that good-hearted young man forever teeter on the brink of absurdity, making too much of too little, pouring his emotions into vessels too frail to contain them? In his letter he requested from Dorothea a list of people to whom he should send invitations; informed her that, on the evening of the party, a chauffeured limousine would pick her up and bring her back home; and that, if she had liked it, and if she was "so disposed," she might wear to the party a "recent Christmas gift, from an anonymous admirer."

"Impossible!"

When, however, Dorothea telephoned Colin Asch to protest, as diplomatically as possible, the unneeded formality of the invitation and its "self-congratulatory" tone, he countered with the argument that the appointment *was* an honor and she *was* to be publicly congratulated. "You are not congratulating yourself, after all; it's your friends who are doing so." Dorothea had not the heart to tell him that, indeed, a banquet of sorts in her honor was being organized by the Friends of the Brannon Institute, for early September after Howard Morland officially retired, and that other dinners and gatherings of an informal nature were planned, and would be planned—Lathrup Farms being Lathrup Farms, after all. In an outburst of defensiveness, as if Dorothea had challenged him on some very deep issue, Colin told her that everyone to whom he'd spoken about it thought it was a great, a fantastic idea, and his Aunt Ginny was frankly jealous. "She tried to preempt my party, in fact—'Why don't we do it at my house, Colin, we have more room over here'—but I told her absolutely *not.* It's *my* idea and my apartment. It's *my* celebration dinner for *you.*"

Dorothea gently objected that she found the very idea of a celebration embarrassing; Colin Asch said at once, with the energy of a high school debater, speaking rather loudly into the phone, "But embarrassing for who? *Whom?* You can't think exclusively of yourself at such a time, Dorothea, you have to think of your friends too, don't you? Like, they want to honor you, they'd be cheated if you backed out—right? It's like certain great people who die, you know, and say in their wills they don't want any funeral or fuss; in a weird way it's sort of *selfish*, I always thought, to deprive people of—you know, certain ceremonies. What would human existence be like, Dorothea, without ceremonies? I don't mean crap like Christmas, Easter, that worn-out dead kind of stuff; I mean, you know, something living, springing from the *heart*—"

So in the end, fairly bludgeoned by her young friend's passion, which after all outweighed her own aversion to the project, Dorothea Deverell gave in and withdrew her objections. Even to the slightly silly formality of the card. Even to the admonition "black tie." She neglected to mention the limousine, and the Christmas gift, the lovely white lace and wool outfit—though she intended, at the time of the party, to consent to neither. Her primary anxiety about the dinner was not in fact such details but the guest list: whether she dared invite Charles Carpenter without inviting Agnes, and without Agnes' knowing about the party; how, given the protocol of such things and the endogamous nature of social life in Lathrup Farms, the finesse might be managed. Though Charles Carpenter was still furious with her and might refuse to come in any case…he loathed black tie occasions. And matters at the Carpenters' home were, as he grimly and accusingly said, at an impasse.

In the end Dorothea decided simply to invite Charles, by himself, with an invitation sent to his office. Perhaps, by March 5, he would have forgiven her.

8

What do you want of me, Colin? she'd asked, raising her lovely troubled eyes to his, and without thinking he told her what was in his heart surging and pulsing in his blood strong enough to choke him *I don't want anything of you Dorothea only that you exist, that our lives are parallel* and so saying he saw the happiness lighting up in her eyes like sudden candle flame. Backed away trembling in dread of being drawn by those eyes into saying more, revealing more, before she was prepared to hear.

"I was only the agent—yours."

Subsequently he would record in the Blue Ledger:

> *Parallel lines never meet!*
> *Except in the eye!*
> *—like at the horizon!*
> *Thus in the eye of the mind parallel lines* NEVER FAIL *to meet!*

He'd subsequently record too in abbreviated codified fashion how he had driven off from 33 Marten Lane, then parked the Porsche (which was handling beautifully—a dream car at last) on a side street then doubled back as he'd done in the past always with conspicuous success having calculated the most direct route that answered to the demands of safety and common sense through Dorothea Deverell's neighbors' back yards, in only one instance a dog yapping like crazy in what looked like a glassed-in rear porch—but maybe nobody was home?—but anyway C.A. never hesitated never panicked knowing this was a special night for him *nothing can touch you at certain illuminated times when all that is "out there" emanates in fact from the soul*...just jogging along like he's a weird local guy actually *jogging*...except not on the street but across the back yards of his Lathrup Farms neighbors...in six-inch crusty-icy snow in new Nike running shoes and no socks. So you get a little snow in your shoes, what the fuck: "The main thing is, it's healthy."

At the rear of 33 Marten Lane, Colin Asch stood panting, staring into the warm-lit interior of the very living room in which *Jesus! wild!* he'd been sitting in a few minutes before *what a weird shift of perspective!* except now Colin Asch was gone, also Dorothea Deverell was gone, that very sofa with the little pillows perpendicular to the fireplace, and the rose-colored chair in which she'd been sitting smiling at him her sherry glass held in both hands her mood gay, bright—*How beautiful* she'd said, taking the gladioli from him *thank you so much Colin, you shouldn't have*—and the gladioli were there in the tall cutglass vase proudly on the mantel *but Christ! how weird it all looked from outside the window like he almost could (like when he was acting, on stage) watch himself perform from outside himself.* He'd forgotten the fucking binoculars. Thus had to approach the house closer than the other times. Crouching just outside the terrace window, the big plate glass window that was the entire wall on that side.

D.D. had gone upstairs maybe but he waited, C.A. had all the patience in the world, warmed now by the sherry she'd given him, the cookies, the taste of the sugar still in his mouth, crystals on his tongue, all the patience in the world *there's a certain holy quality to this: shadowless* and they'd shaken hands goodbye, her eyes shining with affection for him and approval of him *Just to know that you exist* and she'd said *I feel the same way about you—you've put it very gracefully.* Thus he waited, and after a while D.D. reappeared, looking young as a schoolgirl in a plaid pleated skirt and yellow sweater but unsmiling now, worried, distracted, the man who was her secret lover was on his way but it was not a visit that promised pleasure, or solace—"Could be he's giving her a hard time." Colin Asch felt a stab of hurt and resentment when Dorothea removed the vase of flowers, his flowers, from the mantel, carrying them out of the room *as if by a directive of the invisible lover.*

(Whom he guessed to be the man whose name she'd uttered, "Charles Carpenter," the friend of the Weidmanns'—middle-aged cautious-looking sort of Englishy fucker, lawyer, well-to-do—of course Colin Asch remembered him, never forgot a name; and the wife, Agnes. Had the audio equivalent of a photographic memory: perfect recall. He had tricked D.D. into saying the name aloud: "Charles Carpenter." And shrewdly he knew by her liquidy gaze and the softness of her voice, *That's him! that's the man!*—for it's a fact that when you're in love with someone you say the name as much as possible, for instance at the present time Susannah Hunt was in that stage where she said his name constantly—"Colin, *Col*-liin"—sort of mock-crooning, caressing, teasing, parodying (lest her young lover beat her to it: S.H. was the kind of woman who'd had some bad experiences with younger lovers, Colin could sense) some of the things they were doing, or maybe just the fact that they were doing them at all plus saying the usual words like *I love you I'm crazy about you* like *you're so beautiful* like *Oh God that was wonderful* like nobody had ever said such words before but you had to believe they were true, and wanted to.)

And there suddenly the man was, in Dorothea Deverell's living room where, a short while previously, Colin Asch had been: Charles Carpenter himself. Looking taller than Colin remembered. And so earnest. So *excited.* A drink in one hand, and his other hand grasping D.D.'s, dragging her along. As if he had the right.

Thus Colin Asch was forced to crouch shivering in the snow amid the sharp-needled evergreens while inside the lovers had their surreptitious meeting—*an assignation* it would be termed—sometimes kissing, embracing...then drawing back again to talk... and D.D. was crying it seemed...and Carpenter tried to comfort her when it was obvious *he* was the one causing *her* grief—hadn't she been radiant with happiness a short while before, in Colin Asch's company?

So he watched. Couldn't hear what they were saying. Not even their voices, which were seemingly raised now and then. You had to figure it: the fucker was a married man cheating on his wife, thus disloyal, dishonest; D.D. was foolish to trust him; *didn't* trust him, probably; if she was happy with him with being in love with him why was she so agitated now? Why was her face shining with tears? *And she'd hidden Colin Asch's gorgeous flame-colored gladioli for this man.*

How long this went on, the two of them talking, embracing, kissing, Colin Asch could not have said, an hour perhaps, or more; he'd slipped into a trance like dreaming with his eyes open not minding that his feet were fucking cold and there wasn't any moon to soften things, staring at the man and woman inside the house only a few yards away but *distant*...this weird sensation rising in him like almost coming in his pants like observing a target ignorant of being observed thus *your power is infinitely magnified while theirs is diminished* to the point finally of extinction. Then abruptly the two of them got up from the sofa and left the living room, passed out of Colin Asch's vision, so he climbed up onto the terrace to look inside—couldn't see them—in a reflex gesture tried the door: but naturally it was locked. (The kind of lock he could jimmy open, though, in maybe thirty seconds.) Was Carpenter leaving finally? *Or were they going upstairs to D.D.'s bedroom?* Colin backed off from the house, sliding and stamping in the glazed-over snow to disguise his footprints, but he couldn't hear voices at the front door or the sound of a car door being slammed and so forth, which meant the two of them had gone upstairs leaving him behind in the freezing cold like a mongrel dog, not that a dog would be treated with such insult—it was the time of evening when human beings sat down together to share a meal, to partake of a ceremony, not be kicked out into the fucking arctic cold, and he'd had the distinct impression she was meaning to invite him to dinner, of course she was meaning to invite him to dinner, after the tour of her house, then the fucking phone rang, then it was *him*—Carpenter—the fucker. In a sudden rage that came over him like a spasm of hiccuping he thought of hiding in Carpenter's car in the back seat and when finally the bastard got in and drove off he'd allow him to get a certain distance then at a light or something he'd just reach up and around and get him in a choke hold the kind that the police are trained to use *pressing on the carotid artery to cut off circulation to the brain, one two three four five! presto!*—then just calmly get out of the car and walk away—"Sure, I could do that. Easy." But he had an even more convincing flash like a dream of him ascending the stairs in the house moving like a sleepwalker like Shelley who said *I go my way like a sleepwalker until I am stopped and I never am stopped* up the stairs into her bedroom where it would be darkened but he'd see them clearly the two of them asleep, naked after love, love-making *though in truth it was unimaginable that Dorothea Deverell would do such a thing really* nonetheless he saw them asleep and he saw himself standing over them and he had a knife in his hand, or a razor…and as Charles Carpenter slept Colin Asch gracefully sliced his throat—it was part of his pride to do things with grace like they were effortless though all of his life, his ingenuity, his physical conditioning went into the smallest gesture!—and somehow Carpenter just bled to death without waking…nor did *she* wake… for he could not imagine it, could not imagine any of the scene, except that *she* continued to sleep oblivious of what Colin Asch was doing, of what must be done *for her own very sake: her happiness.*

But this vision rose and fell away in a quick flash like the flash of a car's headlights, blinding one instant then gone the next, though leaving Colin Asch dazed and weak in the knees…like, once, naked except for a thin undershirt, he'd stood on a carpet kneading his toes in excitement and terror and Mr. Kreuzer'd reached out to touch him, the hot little pulsing knob of him, and in that instant he'd come, standing, whimpering, scared, a stream of semen shooting out thinly from him and arcing, and falling…and Mr. Kreuzer said, "*That* was precipitous, Colin."

Weeks later on the afternoon of March 5, Colin Asch in his newly purchased tuxedo was setting the dining room table for dinner, his pulse already fast though he'd taken two Quaaludes that morning, whistling a jagged dissonant version of "Traumerei"—which he'd once played, straight, on the piano, aged eleven—talking to himself to cheer himself up—*tonight's the night! after so much anticipation! Colin Asch's social debut in Lathrup Farms!*—and he stood for a long moment with the place card in his trembling fingers that read in elegant old-fashioned script *Charles Carpenter*—Colin had done the place cards himself, every one of them: black India ink, a snub-tipped drawing pen—thinking he had to make up his mind soon what to do about Carpenter. Or if he should do anything at all.

March 5: Colin Asch woke before dawn thinking at first he was in Susannah Hunt's oversized perfumy bed but, no, she'd laughingly kicked him out early the previous night, a telephone call had come from her fiancé (as she called him), this old guy sixty-two or -three who owned condominiums in the Caribbean, an ex-physician, ex-partner of her husband's, but Colin Asch didn't pay much attention to the details, nor did Susannah Hunt, most of the time, but "Honey, I have to look out for my future, don't I?" So Colin woke in his own bed, his mind immediately flooded with panic thoughts of that evening's party, the first dinner party of his life, the many guests who were coming, and Dorothea Deverell herself.... He was a novice at such things, a mere baby the women were calling him, thus Susannah Hunt and Ginny Weidmann were helping out and he'd contacted this fabulous caterer everyone recommended, yes the guy *costs* but it's *worth it.*

Naked and shivering with anticipation, Colin Asch walked through the rooms of his apartment laughing like a child—"I own this! Jesus! I own *this!*" Staring blinking at the mirrored walls in which his handsome form glided and the high-class furniture he'd bought, the way everything went together, the modulation of the colors, the *shapes* and *figures:* "Fantastic." At the Rhode Island School of Design and that art school in New Mexico he'd checked into for a semester Colin Asch had been told he had a natural genius for interior design, a magical eye, and the name of that particular game is BUCKS they told him, none of this artistic-integrity shit, but you just sort of naturally take for granted a talent that comes so easily so he'd never tried to work his way into the field. But here was this stupendous apartment, the living room and the dining room especially, looking like something in *Art & Architecture* and maybe the Lathrup Farms weekly might do a photographic feature on it, "contemporary bachelor living" maybe: the white walls with the brass mirrors and the wall that was almost entirely glass and the long oatmeal-colored sofa with its dozen designer pillows and the tub-shaped suede chairs in umber and mustard yellow, the twin Halogen lamps (tall graceful black poles, shallow white globes) and the thick-piled creamy-white wall-to-wall carpeting, the dazzlingly beautiful glass-and-chrome dining table and the sideboard and Colin Asch glided about naked partly aroused in ecstasy, also in a kind of disbelief—"Hey: I own *this*." He would worry about making the installment payments when the time came.

You're some kind of a neurotic perfectionist, Susannah Hunt told him fondly and chiding, and he'd answered proudly, You can't get anywhere in this shitty world otherwise, and she'd laughed and said, For some of us, trying to be perfect only slows us *down*.

Dorothea Deverell too had that insight into his character; the last time he'd telephoned her—anxious to know if she had the date for the dinner party right, the time for the limo, and so forth, *he couldn't bear it if something went wrong! if he was publicly humiliated at the outset of his social career in this affluent Boston suburb!*—she'd said, Aren't you making too much of this, Colin? of *me?* and he'd laughed nervously and said, gazing at his reflection in one of the brass mirrors like some young British actor on a BBC television program, all elegant cool, the last word in absolute fucking charm, "Ah, but I've just begun, Dorothea! *Watch me!*"

But what about the dining room chairs? They were three-legged, which he hadn't exactly noticed when he bought them. Sitting on them could be tricky because they wobbled slightly, but if you sat carefully and didn't shift your ass around they were OK. Colin Asch stood biting his thumbnail wondering if he should warn his guests tonight about the chairs, just casually, or say nothing.

He saw too suddenly that there were black scuff marks on one of the walls from the fucking furniture delivery men and it looked as if—from this angle, the sun glaring the way it was—the windows were rain-splotched, and he'd washed them himself the other day, a long hard job, thus it sickened him if he'd have to wash them a second time, not that he minded the literal expenditure of energy (he had plenty of energy) but the idea of it, the repetition of an action already performed, *asshole repetition of something you've done once and were pleased with,* demoralized him—it was a sign of the inferior man, the slave mentality, and not that of the master.

A flood of panic hit him then that even the Quaaludes could not forestall. That he'd made a mistake and could not alter the course of time to undo it. Like the car skidding and crashing through the rusted bridge railing and into the water, and not even God himself could reverse time if the fucker'd wanted to.

The day before he'd been in a weird wired state too at L.L. Loomis, bossed around by his so-called supervisor, Jay—the bastard's actual name was Jason—who behaved in a systematic patronizing manner toward Colin Asch, handing him crap assignments any asshole could do like double-checking galleys and pasting labels on packages, running errands to the printer like a mere messenger boy, it'd been weeks now since he started work and he was yet to be allowed to experiment with design and layouts—Jay's fear of Colin Asch's potential talent was transparent; also, the fucker was jealous of Colin's connection with Susannah Hunt, who was an old, good friend of Mr. Harris who owned the business.

Jealous too of the sexy black Porsche Colin Asch drove, and the stylish clothes Colin Asch wore, and the luxury apartment he knew about (from Colin's chatting with the office girls) but would sure as hell never see. Thus referring to him not quite behind his back as "glamour boy," "angel puss," and "blond beast."

Just give them a chance to see how imaginative you are, honey, how shrewd and sharp, Susannah Hunt told him, and this Colin certainly intended to do but had been thwarted thus far by the selfishness of Jay—though sensing himself a popular addition to the office staff. But day following day his supervisor was still with him, ignored his smile, his good-natured placating remarks, sure the bastard was jealous, paunchy fag-looking guy in his early thirties, probably he knew about Colin Asch's big dinner party to which he wasn't invited so he was pushing Colin all that day, then finally when he told Colin to run some crap back to the printers to have it reset Colin said quietly, "Fuck you: I'm not a gofer," and Jay said excitedly, as if he'd been waiting for this, "That's exactly what you are, glamour boy, so move your ass."

In an instant the revelation burst in Colin Asch that the force inside "Jay" was giving permission to the force inside "Colin Asch" to confront it and destroy it if he could, but Colin sat quietly, unmoving, his mind working quickly, he didn't want to disappoint Susannah Hunt was the primary thing, when she had such faith in him and had helped him so much, lending him money as she had and possibly there would be more to come (though "lending" was sort of ambiguous since maybe she'd never get around to actually asking for it back) and he had to be reasonable: he knew this was a trial period for him at the public relations firm and he had only to work hard and succeed and later when he was promoted to the top or had maybe moved on to a billion-dollar company in Boston or Manhattan he'd tell them all to go fuck themselves.... Christ, he could understand how ex-employees so frequently returned to offices and factories and this poor bastard the other day in Kansas City spraying innocent people with bullets in a post office he'd been fired from, Colin could understand that mentality for sure but he'd never fall into so crude a mold for the simple reason he was too smart. *Once you lost control it's all over.* So he lifted his eyes to those of his frowning supervisor and managed a childlike hurt smile and said, repentant, "Well, I guess you're right, Jay. Thanks for reminding me!"

*

Thoughts of Jay were getting scrambled into thoughts of Dorothea Deverell and the upcoming party so he spent a while with the Blue Ledger soaking in a hot bath trying to work things out *control is the essence of survival* taking another Quaalude *anything done henceforth is blessed because it emanates from the soul* but still he was feeling weird so he got dressed and drove by the caterers' to see how things were going, drove to a florist's to buy razzle-dazzle flowers—a dozen ruby-red roses, big bunch of purple dwarf iris, big bunch of mixed gladioli, Colin Asch's favorite flower—then came back home and made a few calls, one of them to the limousine rental and another to Susannah Hunt, who didn't seem to be in the apartment or in any case wasn't answering her phone, and one of them to Aunt Ginny, who said, "Colin dear *please* don't worry—the caterer will take care of everything, or almost everything, but would you like me to come a little early, to help out?" It was only 5 P.M. but he decided to get dressed anyway, putting on the tuxedo he'd bought the week before at the Village Haberdashery, 20 percent off the ticketed price, the ivory-white silk pleated shirt and the embroidered red silk vest and the black bow tie, and staring at himself in a full-length mirror Colin Asch felt chilled, he looked so good, an old melancholy washed over him like dirty water—*Why has this young man blessed with such looks such brains such talent been treated like shit all of his life?*

To which there was no answer.

Barefoot in his formal attire Colin Asch spent an hour and a half fussing over the table settings, arranging and rearranging the floral displays, positioning the place cards—twelve guests at his table and the guest of honor was obviously to be seated at one end of the table and the host at the other but where to put Charles Carpenter, for instance? and where to put his VIPs as he thought of them, the Director of the Brannon Institute himself Mr. Morland (who had initially declined Colin's invitation but then, on the basis of Colin going personally to speak with him, consenting) and his wife, and Tracey Donovan, the young woman from the *Lathrup Farms Monitor* who covered area "social and cultural" events. Also there were the Weidmanns, and there was Dorothea Deverell's assistant, Jacqueline, and an unknown factor named Paul Wylie who was another Institute worker, Colin hoped not a guy his own age or type, and a second unknown factor but probably harmless, a woman friend of Dorothea Deverell's named Merle Altman. Five men and seven women which presented a problem he couldn't solve to his satisfaction and where should he put Susannah Hunt, on his right hand as she'd naturally expect or midway down the table next to Carpenter maybe? She knew Carpenter, she'd said, and liked him. A lot.

Colin checked the champagne another time, counted the wine bottles—Martin Weidmann had advised him on the wine and he hoped to hell he could trust his judgment—and there was the brandy, and the crème de menthe, two or three other fancy liqueurs he picked up just in case, and on the shelf carefully wrapped in a Kleenex the pulverized pill he meant to sift into Dorothea Deverell's drink or possibly her coffee at the end of the evening: he'd forgotten the specific name of the pill but it'd been one of the giant white ones, one of a very few remaining from his stay with the woman in Fort Lauderdale. "Better put it in my pocket," he said aloud, and did.

As promised, the caterers arrived precisely at 7 P.M. so Colin began to feel a little more relaxed; then the Weidmanns arrived at 7:30 and he felt better still, in fact moved almost to tears by the very sight of them—Aunt Ginny a good-looking woman in an aqua cocktail dress with a sequined bosom, Uncle Martin in black tie like some handsome old graying business executive in an advertisement—*the only living relatives who cared a fuck about Colin Asch.* Aunt Ginny kissed him and moved on into the kitchen to take charge, and Martin seemed impressed with the apartment and the furnishings and asked after Colin's new job and told him he looked great in his tux and Colin blushed with happiness and stretched his arms to ask, like a boy asking his father, if maybe the sleeves weren't a little short?—did his cuffs stick out too much?

"They look fine," Martin said, pouring himself a drink. "Those are interesting cuff links," he added, and for a dizzy moment Colin thought the cuff links were actually Martin's, then remembered of course they weren't.

"Oh, these? They were a gift," he said, holding out his wrists for Martin to examine them, gold with ruby and onyx insets. "Sort of a private joke; this woman I used to know called me 'Colin' like with a 'K'—you know, like a German pronunciation: *Kol*in—so she had these cuff links made up engraved with a 'K'."

"Interesting," Martin said. "And how's my old friend Susannah Hunt?"

Then it was 8 P.M. and Colin Asch's guests began to arrive; so many slow dragging hours and now everything seemed to be happening at once, everyone was arriving at once, there were guests like Paul Wylie and Mrs. Morland whom Colin had never set eyes on before, and there was Susannah Hunt in a glamorous black satin dress fairly bursting in the bosom, diamonds glittering on her fingers and at her wrists: Mrs. Hunt who discreetly pecked him on the cheek and breathed in his ear, "Hel-*lo* Colin!" And there suddenly in the crowded little vestibule stood Dorothea Deverell in her fur coat, bareheaded, smiling at Colin Asch and extending her hand—and Colin couldn't help himself, he stared at the woman for just a fraction of a second too long: she was so beautiful, she was so perfect, *she had come to him.*

Her appearance so dazzled him, he hadn't time to be disappointed that Dorothea had not come alone as he'd fantasized her, in the elegant Cadillac Brougham limousine, but had had the driver pick up two other guests, her assistant Jacqueline and her friend Mrs. Altman. As if Colin would derive any pleasure from hiring a car at $110 an hour for *them.*

But Colin Asch, greeting his guests, showed none of this; he was shaking hands, being introduced, stooping to hear names. Dorothea Deverell seemed quite impressed, perhaps even startled, by the splendor of Colin's apartment—"But how beautiful, Colin! How *unique*."

"Is it?" Colin asked eagerly. "Do you think so?" When he helped Dorothea remove her coat he saw to his immense satisfaction that she was wearing after all the costume he'd given her—the exquisite lace jacket and the long white wool skirt. Again he stared at her, not knowing what to say. His eyes misted over. Finally he whispered, "Thank you, Dorothea," but the Weidmanns were swooping upon her, she and Ginny embraced warmly as sisters, and the doorbell was ringing again, and someone opened it to another stranger, a snub-nosed smiling woman—and Colin walked off like a sleepwalker with Dorothea Deverell's fur coat to lay it tenderly across the bed in his bedroom exhilarated by the knowledge that, if all else failed, *she had come to him: to Colin Asch.*

Through the lively cocktail hour Colin shrewdly rationed his drinking; he had a naturally speedy naturally wired sensibility which alcohol sometimes exacerbated, so he played it cool, acting the perfect host, introducing guests to one another where required—not that he knew these people but he'd quickly learned their names!—overseeing conversations then easing away tall and handsome and seemingly poised: What a remarkable young man, what an extraordinary young man, he's Ginny Weidmann's nephew, who *is* he, an actor? an artist? a young business entrepreneur? He found himself oddly shy in Dorothea Deverell's specific company but was otherwise in control, or nearly—he had only to clamp his jaws shut when there was the danger of talking too fast and too much. The tuxedo was a little warm but impeccably tailored, his new dress shoes gleamed darkly, at the age of twenty-eight he was clearly approaching the prime of his young manhood *and perhaps this evening and the night to follow would constitute the pinnacle of his life.*

"Didn't I tell you, dear? Everything is going beautifully," Aunt Ginny said.

And Colin, wiping his forehead with a handkerchief, said, "Thanks to you, Aunt, it *is*." In truth he was getting a little resentful of the woman's supervision of the caterer's assistants as they were serving the hors d'oeuvres, for whose party was this anyway? "I owe you everything!" Colin said.

He was grateful though for Susannah Hunt's glamorous presence, and for the chaste distance she maintained between them—would anyone know, could anyone *guess*, what their relationship was? And it quite flattered him that perky little Tracey Donovan, the media representative for this social event, seemed so sincerely impressed with Colin Asch's guests and with his apartment and with *him*—asking him numerous questions about his public relations career, his past television experience, his travels in Europe and North Africa—"We'll have to get together soon for a full-scale interview!" Mr. Wylie, with whom Dorothea Deverell was earnestly discussing a painter of whom Colin Asch had never heard (Burchfield? Charles Burchfield?) turned out to be, to Colin's relief, no rival of his but a stocky sweet-faced man of youngish middle age with tortoise-shell glasses; and Charles Carpenter, for whom he had a certain nervous edgy excitable feeling, was quite gracious to him, gentlemanly and charming, including Colin in a conversation (about politics? Soviet–U.S. relations?) he was having with Howard Morland and Martin Weidmann as naturally as if they were all friends—neighbors, peers, equals. Talking with them, offering his opinion, Colin was flooded with a sudden happiness: *the happiness of a man among men.* Why had he been cheated of this all his life?

It absorbed his rapt attention, that Charles Carpenter was Dorothea Deverell's lover and no one knew save Colin Asch. He was their protector, in a way. You could think of it that way.

He yearned to draw Charles Carpenter off into a corner of the room and say confidentially, man to man, "I know, Charles. But your secret is safe with me."

Carpenter had a tall, slim, slightly round-shouldered figure, probably rather slack-muscled at his age; his hair appeared grayer than Colin recalled. His long lean horsy face was handsome but creased as if with worry or tiredness…still, Colin could see why Dorothea Deverell or another woman might admire him. So *reasonable.* So *solid.* So *patrician.* So like the father you'd maybe choose if you were a baby again. And had a choice.

Which wasn't the way the fucking world was constructed.

Then they were summoned to dinner, and there were exclamations at the splendor of Colin Asch's table—the scented candles, the roses, the gleaming English bone china and sterling silverware—and after all his guests were seated and the champagne poured, Colin resplendent in his tuxedo and red silk vest rose to toast Dorothea Deverell in a high, quavering voice—"our guest of honor: one of the most accomplished women of her generation"—and Dorothea laughed, exclaiming, "My God, Colin—really!" as if they were old casual friends, but Colin insisted and spoke excitedly of the several books she had written, and her years of dedication to the Institute, until he fell abruptly silent and stood staring down the length of the table at her—he had more to say but could not utter the words. In any case the mood at the table was festive and unserious, Colin Asch's awkwardness scarcely mattered, went perhaps unnoticed, so he ended, blushing, "—anyway, let's drink a toast to Dorothea Deverell, and wish her health and happiness forever!"—and the moment passed.

Colin sat down. His head was ringing as if it were inside a clapping bell.

He wanted suddenly savagely to murder everyone. All of them.

No—he was in a giddy exhilarated mood. Never in his life had he attempted anything like this: an ambitious dinner party. He was telling the women close beside him that he thought there was nothing happier on earth *than to bring people together in festive settings.* Susannah Hunt, pleasantly drunk, lifted her glass and cried, "I'll drink to that!"

Now there followed the elaborate procession of courses, the realization of Colin Asch's fevered consultation with the caterer and his several changes of mind: oysters forestière followed by chateaubriand of beef with espagnole sauce and wild rice and intricately cut vegetables followed by a salad of red lettuce and Belgian endive followed by French cheeses followed by strawberry chiffon pie followed by coffee, tea, liqueurs in tiny sparkling glasses, Swiss bitter-chocolate dinner mints…and though Colin Asch who'd paid for all this tried gamely to eat he had not much appetite. He'd gotten hooked on the champagne and red wine, alternating glasses until the champagne ran out, doing a good deal of talking and laughing less fearful now of getting loud *he had every right to enjoy himself freely at his own fucking party* entertaining the entire table with anecdotes of travel in Germany, Greece, Morocco…and then there was a general conversation about a racial incident that had taken place in Roxbury a few days previously in which Colin Asch as a former "television person" could participate, his opinion in fact solicited by none other than white-haired aristocratic Howard Morland, who was clearly quite taken with his young host…and talk shifted to AIDS, and to politics, and to an event that was scheduled soon to occur at the Brannon Institute, and to area restaurants, particularly several new and highly recommended restaurants of which Colin Asch had not heard, thus could inquire (of the gourmet Paul Wylie) after them…and the meal was passing swiftly or was it passing with dreamlike slowness…and Colin Asch saw that Dorothea Deverell was happy…*was* happy…engaged in conversation with friends at her end of the table and hardly more than glancing now and then (ah, how discreetly! how *skillfully!*) at her lover Charles Carpenter, who in turn did not frequently glance at her; they must be old well-practiced lovers, accustomed to such situations.

But Colin Asch had the power to end all that.

There was spirited conversation about the stock market, and Third World poverty, and the ever-imminent "global crisis," and when the way cleared for Colin to volunteer his opinion he launched into a lengthy earnest explanation of the X-factor in human genetics—did they know that one tenth of one percent of the human race is instinctively bred to lead the remainder? that there are by nature "master" beings and "slave" beings? that social institutions that fail to acknowledge this are doomed? A sharp slightly shrill edge to Colin Asch's voice signaled to certain of his guests that this subject meant a great deal to him and perhaps at the moment he was not to be contradicted, but others registered nothing out of the ordinary so there followed a lively discussion, confused and disjointed and a bit combative, until Colin heard himself talking too loudly and clamped his jaws prudently shut, making an effort simply to smile, to nod, to let the ignorant assholes talk, he was magnanimous enough to accommodate dissenting points of view. The bosomy perfumy women at his end of the table were united in any case in trying to make him eat—"Colin the food is *delicious*, you simply must *eat it*"—and Colin fumbled with his fork and chewed a bit and swallowed, washing whatever it was down with a big mouthful of red wine then shaking his head like a dog to clear it, staring down the length of the table past the tall glittering candles and the ruby-red roses in their crystal vase at Dorothea Deverell so beautiful in her white lace jacket, her eyes shining like a young girl's. He raised his voice to thank them all, suddenly, "For coming here! Tonight! For being my friends!" His mouth worked as if puzzled: "I want to be your friend! To be one of you! I *am* one of you, for Christ's sake!" He was breathing quickly, almost panting. Their many eyes both intimidated and excited him. He added, gripping the edge of the table as if he feared falling from his chair: *"I want to be good!"*

This released a chorus of protesting voices, primarily female, Ginny Weidmann's and Susannah Hunt's the most earsplittingly soprano: "But you *are* good, Colin! You *are* good! You are an *angel! Silly boy, Colin!*"

So that quieted him for a while, stirred his emotions so he was in danger of crying, his head lowered and his eyeballs sliding as if greased in their sockets: weird! Then suddenly it was nearing the end of the meal—*so suddenly coming to an end!*—and Colin Asch lurched to his feet, inspired another time, smile wide and bright as a jack-o-lantern's, and again he lifted his wineglass high above his head and proposed a final toast: "To somebody not with us tonight who made all this possible"—and there was a flurry of amused quizzical speculation about who this mystery person might be—but Colin Asch winking and grinning refused to say, repeating, "To someone not with us tonight who made this all possible *by being not with us tonight*"—and at this Dorothea Deverell flinched visibly and cast Colin a look of such shocked disapproval, such transparent warning, he bit his lip and went silent, swaying at his place smiling stupidly the glass still lifted above his head…the gaiety at the table awkwardly fading…until Mrs. Hunt in throaty dry Tallulah Bankhead style said, "No doubt an absent parental figure—the very best kind." And this naturally provoked a fresh round of mirth, at least in those ignorant of Colin Asch's "tragic" background.

Then Colin was sitting again, his heart pounding wildly.

Thinking: She saved me.

Thinking: Saved us both.

With the excuse of wanting to help serve the coffee and tea in person Colin Asch was able, unwitnessed, to stir into the cup of herbal tea intended for Dorothea Deverell the finely ground drug he had prepared, as easily and innocently as if he were stirring sugar into it, and this he served to her without arousing the slightest suspicion, and returned to his seat at the far end of the table nursing a final glass of red wine and watching her sip at her cup—until finally it was emptied. Horse-sized barbiturates, his female friend in Fort Lauderdale had called them, prescription pills strong enough to knock out a horse, and to this, yes, Colin Asch could attest. Though he scorned reliance upon drugs, mainly.

And then it was midnight and the party was over—a fantastically successful party but now at last over—and Colin Asch stood in his miniature foyer saying good night, shaking hands, thanking his guests for having come, and there stood wrapped in her fur coat prepared for the cold lovely Dorothea Deverell with heavy eyelids and an unfocused sort of smile…teetering on her white satin high heels to lean forward to kiss Colin Asch on the cheek as if they were the oldest and dearest of friends *as if they had known each other all their lives.*

"Thank you, Colin. It was wonderful."

"Dorothea. Thank *you*."

*

While the caterer's assistants labored to clean up in the kitchen, Colin Asch retired to his bedroom to change from his formal attire to jeans and a black turtleneck sweater and Nike jogging shoes. So wired by this time he could barely contain himself, he did push-ups on the carpet—fifty-five, fifty-six, fifty-seven, then gave up counting—till finally the hired help went home and things were quiet as the tomb, yet still shrewdly he forced himself to wait another forty-five minutes before leaving in the low-slung black Porsche for 33 Marten Lane.

9

The telephone was ringing persistently, jarringly, in a distant room. Or was someone speaking to her from a distant room. She could not make out words, only murmurous modulations of sound; she could not see, though her eyes were open. Nor could she move for her limbs were paralyzed…heavy and leaden as if waterlogged.

It was frightful, horrible: yet, becalmed in her bed, paralyzed, she was not capable of feeling such emotions. Her own interior voice, muted, solicitous, was both warning and gentle admonition: *This is your punishment. This is your reward.*

"How can it be? My God!"

When, early in the afternoon of Sunday, March 6, Dorothea Deverell finally woke from her heavy stuporous dreamless sleep—the sleep of a dead woman—it was to the appalling knowledge that she had slept for nearly fifteen hours.

Her bedside clock showed 2:40. She thought at first that the electricity must have gone off and that somehow (she was too dazed to have reasoned how) day and night were reversed.

When she tried to get out of bed she was too weak; her legs would not hold her. A tiny pin might have been dislodged in her upper vertebrae, for her head rolled helplessly on her shoulders. "What has happened to me? Was I drunk last night?" Her eyeballs were as seared as if she had been staring for hours into a naked light, and the interior of her mouth was parched, scummy, vile; her nostrils were so pathologically dry she felt them as twin passageways leading up into her brain. Not in recent memory had she felt herself so thoroughly debilitated, so ingloriously *wrecked.* "But did I make a fool of myself?" She wondered if she would dare telephone Charles Carpenter to inquire. Though surely it would be more prudent to say nothing, in the hope that nothing would be said to her.

A vertiginous five minutes was required simply to get Dorothea Deverell from her bed and into her bathroom; wherein, in the mirror above the sink, a wan, etiolated face awaited her. Another half hour was required to get her but partially dressed and downstairs...descending the staircase like an invalid who can no longer trust in the efficacy of her own limbs or the substantiality of the physical world to support her. How her head ached, how her eyes burned! How thoroughly wretched she felt! She saw that the folklore of the classic hangover was needed to mitigate its sickening horror. To suggest that the drinker has brought his misery upon himself, thus is, after all, in control of his fate.

Yet she could not recall having drunk more than two glasses of champagne at Colin Asch's party, and perhaps a single glass of red wine. Or had she drunk more, half consciously? Had she blacked out on her feet? She could remember virtually nothing of the ride home in the limousine, or of undressing for bed....She knew herself a woman unaccustomed to alcohol; yet, more to the point, unaccustomed to such fevered celebration, such an insistent focusing of others' attentions upon her: Dorothea Deverell. It left her giddy and childlike and wholly uncritical, as if, unprepared, a reckless hiker in the mountains, she had gone too high too quickly.

She could not tolerate so much as the thought of breakfast, but stood at the sink drinking ice water and trying not to notice how her hands shook. If this is your debut into a new life, Dorothea, her interior voice admonished, perhaps you are unfit.

Toward evening, by accident, she discovered that her rear terrace door was unlocked. This was a rude little shock—though she must have left it unlocked herself since, so far as she could judge, nothing in the house seemed to have been taken, or even disturbed; there were no footprints visible on the carpet. In the excitement of the past several weeks she'd become careless, though; increasingly, break-ins and acts of vandalism were being reported in the North Shore area. You must get a burglar alarm installed,

Charles Carpenter repeatedly urged her, and repeatedly Dorothea promised, yes, she would.

She checked the upstairs, and nothing there appeared to have been disturbed either.

Belatedly, still feeling rather dizzy and unreal, Dorothea made her bed and picked up, in the room, her white silk slip which the night before she had tossed on a chair, her brassiere and underpants lying on the floor, the exquisite white outfit Colin Asch had given her for Christmas unceremoniously draped across her bureau.... She checked it anxiously for stains but found none: white is so beautiful and so impractical. It was a costume Dorothea Deverell would never have chosen for herself, even granted the willingness to pay an inflated price for clothing, yet she liked it very much, now; prized it, in fact; for she'd looked really quite remarkably beautiful in it the night before, as if the bloom of her young womanhood had been restored. To see Charles Carpenter's eyes drifting to her, dwelling upon her, in love...in what must be called, for all Dorothea Deverell's mincing behavior of the past several weeks, a husbandly sort of tenderness...how could she fail to be grateful for *that*? And Colin Asch had been naïvely happy to see her in it, ignorant of the fact that the reasons for her having worn it were sheerly expeditious: she had so forestalled planning what she would wear to the dinner party, she'd gone through her closet only the afternoon before, in mounting anxiety, to discover that really she had nothing suitable: no evening dress except a burgundy velvet sadly worn at the elbows and seat and a long black rayon skirt that was rather battered-looking at the hem and, in any case, rayon.

But fortunately she had white satin shoes to go with the jacket and skirt, and a white beaded bag. Which went perfectly.

PART THREE

10

The call came for Dorothea Deverell late in the afternoon of April 11, a windy, sun-splotched day. She would remember it forever as the second of the telephone calls to abruptly reorder the course of her life.

Dorothea was in her office at the Institute—her old office still, since Mr. Morland, though rarely at the Institute these days, had yet to vacate his—engaged in a somewhat groping conversation with a Lathrup Farms matron who, newly widowed, was considering giving a sizable donation to the Institute in her late husband's name with the proviso that she "maintain some say" as to its specific use. To this, Dorothea felt she could hardly object; yet, recalling past episodes in the previous director's experience, when such provisos brought with them unanticipated problems, she was reluctant to simply agree. Perhaps Mrs. Harmon would like to join the Building Committee? the Programs Committee? Perhaps she would like to be an honorary member of the Friends of the Morris T. Brannon Advisory Council?

To these suggestions the impeccably dressed Mrs. Harmon made no reply, as if unhearing, but, smiling tightly at Dorothea, said in a small, stubborn voice, "The thing is, Miss Deverell, that I want Edgar's name to be preserved. I want to be certain that it not be *forgotten*."

"Of course," Dorothea said, nodding in sympathy, "I understand." She was about to say more when there was a sudden knock at the door, curt and sharp, and in the same moment Jacqueline entered, with a look so unlike her usual—so stricken, so apologetic—that Dorothea's blood simply ran cold.

"Miss Deverell?" Jacqueline said, "I'm so sorry to interrupt you and Mrs. Harmon, but there seems to be an emergency call for you."

"Ah, really! Is there! Then I'll take it in the other office."

Dorothea spoke almost calmly. Her family was so attenuated by this stage in her maturity, the pool of her blood relatives so shrunken, there could be no emergency in her life excepting one pertaining to Charles Carpenter.

He is dead, she thought, lifting the receiver.

For, after all, hadn't she lived through this horror already? In the distant past, as in a distant lifetime?

Thus it required several seconds for Dorothea Deverell to realize that it was Charles Carpenter who was on the line and that it was he to whom the horror had in fact happened.

He said, "Dorothea? Agnes is dead."

Dorothea gripped the telephone receiver hard and sat on the edge of a table. Uncomprehending, she said, "Agnes is—"

"Agnes is dead."

"—dead?"

"Just now. I mean—I've found her just now. In the house." He spoke in queer uncharacteristic gusts and waves. Dorothea could hear noises, men's voices, in the background. "I'm here—at the house. The police are here. The ambulance too—but it's too late, she's dead. Dorothea? I found her just now—a while ago, I mean. There hadn't been any answer all day when I called her so I came over and let myself in and went upstairs thinking she was, she might be—you know how she has been—thinking she might be sick, or unconscious, in her bed. Thinking she might have fallen and injured herself. I called her name and there wasn't any answer so I went upstairs and the bathroom door was shut and locked, and I forced my way in, and there she was—I mean, *is;* I think she still *is*, unless they've moved her—in the bathtub. In the bathroom. Upstairs. She—seems to have had an accident."

Dorothea's eyes immediately flooded with tears. "My poor darling," she said. "Oh, my poor, poor darling Charles! How terrible! For Agnes! For Agnes, and for you! Shall I come over there, darling? What can I do?"

"It seems somehow she *drowned*," Charles said wonderingly.

"In only a foot or so—how many inches could it be?—of water. I found her lying there in the water—the water was stone cold—her face was submerged—I checked for a pulse but couldn't find one. It was horrible! Her lips were purplish-blue. I knew she was dead."

Charles Carpenter paused. In the background someone, a man, was shouting directions. Dorothea wiped at her eyes and said, "Charles? Are you all right? You've had a terrible shock, shall I come over? Or would I be in the way? I had better come over."

He said half accusingly, "She'd been drinking. She reeked of it. There were bottles in the bedroom, bourbon and gin. That must have been it—that, and the other."

"Yes? What other?"

"You know—I've told you. The drugs. The sleeping pills. And there were diet pills too, for a while. I don't in fact think that Agnes ever gave up any prescription willingly; I think she simply changed doctors. My God, I *told* her, I *warned* her! And she refused to listen! These past few weeks, Dorothea"—Charles had moved to a residential hotel in Boston in mid-February—"have simply been hell. She has been—had been—simply impossible. The drinking, the raving, the abuse, the threats, the terrible, unforgivable things she said—ah, but I've told you enough of it already, dear Dorothea. I can't heap such filth upon your head, I can't—I don't dare—" He was speaking more and more rapidly until finally he stopped; and Dorothea, her heart pierced, could hear him sobbing. How she longed to hold him in her arms, to comfort him. For surely she had the right? Surely she, of all living beings, had the right?

Dorothea offered again to come to him but Charles rather curtly told her no, he didn't think that was a good idea right now; he would speak with her later, try to see her later that evening if possible—if the police were finished with him by then. "I'm sure they have questions to ask of *me*," he said, with a sudden grim gust of humor. "The husband is always the first suspect."

"But Charles—"

He hung up abruptly—in other circumstances, it would have

been rudely—and Dorothea Deverell was left gripping a telephone receiver tight against her ear, listening to a dead line. She thought, Yes? What if—*if Agnes Carpenter's death were not accidental, but deliberate?* Since the Carpenters' separation Agnes had repeatedly threatened to kill herself, had several times threatened to kill both herself and Charles. Dorothea burst into fresh, despairing, bitter tears.

"That terrible woman—*it would be just like her.*"

After a tactful several minutes Jacqueline poked her head into the office and, seeing the state Dorothea Deverell was in, went to comfort her. What had happened? Why was she so upset? Dorothea said in a rapt, slow voice, "It's horrible: Charles Carpenter's wife is *dead*, she has *died*, it must have been only a few hours ago." Jacqueline expressed surprise and sympathy, to a degree: she didn't after all know Mrs. Carpenter, though she was acquainted with Mr. Carpenter. Dorothea murmured, "Horrible, horrible," pleating the fabric of her skirt, tears streaming unimpeded down her cheeks.

"But how did it happen?" Jacqueline asked.

"An accident," Dorothea said. "I don't suppose they quite know, yet. He said—Charles said, Charles Carpenter—he'd come home and found her in—oh, Jacqueline, it's so terrible! So sordid, somehow!" Dorothea began to weep harder, helplessly, for Charles's sake; and for poor wretched Agnes': and for herself too, perhaps—the guilt of it, the shame of it, the misfortune. For at this point, in the late afternoon of April 11, when, as the pathologist's report would later disclose, Agnes Carpenter had been dead approximately nineteen hours, it had not yet begun to occur to Dorothea Deverell that the death of her lover's wife, whether by accident or otherwise, might be a factor in her good fortune.

If Jacqueline was mystified by Dorothea Deverell's passionate grief, and the look of frank shocked guilty fear that showed in her face, she had the discretion not to show it; she was a kindly woman, for all her occasional caustic wit, and she seemed to look upon Dorothea Deverell—her superior at the Institute—as a personal charge, an innocent very much in need of a protector. As Dorothea wept and murmured repeatedly, "Horrible, *horrible*," Jacqueline sent Mrs. Harmon away and must have told the others simply to go home (it was the end of the working day for the staff) without disturbing Dorothea. Afterward, Dorothea would recall how readily her assistant had absorbed, not so much the fact of Agnes Carpenter's death as of Dorothea Deverell's emotional connection with Charles Carpenter.

Has Jacqueline known all along? Dorothea wondered.

Has everyone known, all along?

The fact of death is public: what is personal yields to the impersonal; even one's body shifts out of one's unique possession, no longer tenanted. So there was a funeral for Agnes Carpenter, which everyone in her circle, or in Charles Carpenter's rather wider circle, attended. There had been, prior to the funeral, an autopsy; there would be, in ten days' time, an inquest. The county coroner would file his report. The local newspapers would print whatever seemed "newsworthy"—not a good deal, for neither Agnes nor Charles Carpenter was a public figure—but it rankled Charles that the information should be so freely printed, that the Carpenters had been "formally separated, divorce pending" at the time of Agnes' death. Most distressing, the Carpenters' home on West Fairway Drive—in particular the Carpenters' bedroom, and Agnes bathroom—was thrown open temporarily but aggressively to a team of strangers: investigating detectives, police photographer, fingerprint man, pathologist. Though there appeared to be no evidence of foul play in the death—no fingerprints found other than those of the dead woman and her husband, no forced door or window, no sign of theft—the investigation would turn upon whether Agnes Carpenter had died accidentally or by her own hand.

Charles Carpenter was surely not a suspect in his wife's death, as he had jokingly remarked to Dorothea, but he was questioned repeatedly, to the point of despair and exhaustion. To his distress (and to Dorothea Deverell's) two crumpled sheets of stationery were discovered in a wastebasket in Charles's former study, with the words "Charles" and "Dear Charles" written on them, in Agnes' very shaky but recognizable handwriting: raising the possibility of a suicide note, thus suicide.

"Agnes would not have done it," Charles Carpenter said, many times. "She was simply not the *type*. She was not the *type*."

But hadn't she threatened suicide, by his own account? Might not her death have had a good deal to do with the pending divorce, the separation?

With lawyerly doggedness Charles Carpenter repeated, "My wife would not have done it. She was not the type to take her own life. I knew the woman for more than twenty years—*and I would swear under oath*."

But hadn't there been planned, the investigating officer persisted, for next Monday, a meeting between the Carpenters and their lawyers, to discuss the terms of the divorce? Did Charles believe it could be nothing more than a coincidence that his wife should die only a few days before this meeting?

Charles Carpenter said angrily, *"I would swear under oath."*

Days passed, and Dorothea Deverell was to hear many times her lover's account of how, concerned about his wife, he'd gone to the house and discovered her body; in his bereavement (and Charles Carpenter was truly bereaved) he seemed under a spell, or a compulsion, to tell and retell the story, to dredge up new details, as if desperate to get it right. And, relaying his story to others in abbreviated form, Dorothea too came under the spell of the need to get it right.

As if we are testifying in a court of law, Dorothea thought. Like criminals on trial, to be judged by the sincerity of our words.

According to the pathologist's report, Agnes Carpenter had died in her bath at approximately 9 P.M. of April 10. Charles had last spoken with her late in the evening of April 9, and they had had a vicious quarrel. "Her final words to me were, 'You deceitful son of a bitch!'" Charles said. "And then she slammed down the receiver and practically broke my eardrum." Agnes had been drunk, irrational, vindictive—the previous week she'd telephoned Charles's parents to tell them what a "lying hypocrite" their precious son was, which greatly upset them; now she was threatening to make a visit to Charles's law partners to tell them what he was really like. "I didn't want to provoke her even by pleading with her," Charles told Dorothea. "I dreaded her guessing you—somehow knowing it was *you*."

"But it seems so unfair," Dorothea said guiltily, stroking her lover's hair. "That you should bear the brunt of all that alone."

"Agnes was my wife," Charles said. "In a sense none of this had anything to do with you. I mean—I love you and want to marry you of course, but Agnes and I had fallen out of love with each other a long time before. Our marriage had been dead for years before you and I met." He spoke briskly; he was nodding, telling himself this story too as if its veracity were unquestioned; which perhaps it was. "I've come to see, Dorothea, that you have nothing to do with it—any of it. The ugliness, the scandal. You are really quite innocent, darling, of it all."

As if he knows how hopeful I am, Dorothea Deverell thought humbly, of being told so.

Yet she could not resist speculating: "I wonder if, you know, there was anything we might have—I might have—done…to prevent it."

"Nothing," Charles Carpenter said emphatically, "Absolutely nothing."

And then he might retell the story another time, in a slow, wondering voice: evoking for Dorothea a vision, very nearly cinematic in its fluidity, of how, having telephoned Agnes without success on the morning of April 11 and intermittently throughout the day, he'd driven to the house…knowing something was wrong as soon as he saw not one but several newspapers lying on the sidewalk. And that day's mail was still in the mailbox. And he'd unlocked the rear door and gone inside, entering through the kitchen, dismayed at the overflowing trash can and the plates messily stacked on the counters and in the sink and even on the floor. And the numerous empty gin, bourbon, and wine bottles in plain view. (For the past three weeks Agnes had refused to allow their cleaning woman to come to the house: she didn't want her "poking her nose in my business.")

Charles called Agnes' name but there was no response—nothing.

"The radio was on in the living room, turned up high, which struck him as strange. During the daytime, when she was alone, Agnes frequently turned on the television, even when she was too restless to watch; but the radio, rarely.

"Agnes?" Charles called. "Where are you? It's Charles."

He dreaded what he might find upstairs, in their bedroom. He halfway feared she might be hiding and would rush out to attack him.

He was appalled by the condition of the bedroom: the bed unmade, bedclothes disheveled, blinds drawn, everywhere items of soiled clothing underfoot. And here too were empty bottles. And the close stale air reeking of alcohol.

"Agnes?" he called. "Where are you?"

Several times she'd fled from him in a rage and locked herself in her bathroom, so it did not surprise Charles that, when he tried her bathroom door, it was locked. "Agnes? *Agnes?*" he said. He was not yet alarmed but he seemed to have a sense, he didn't know but he *knew*, that this was no ordinary episode in their lives. He called to her, pleaded with her to open the door, and when there was no response he threw his weight against it and forced it open and found Agnes inside, naked in the bathtub, slumped over, her head partly submerged in the water.... He knew in an instant that she was dead: the bathroom smelled of deadness. Yet he could not believe it, really, he shouted her name, felt for a pulse, tried to lift her from the tub as if to revive her. She was not breathing and her lips had turned a ghastly purplish-blue, her skin horribly white and puckered from the water. Her eyes had rolled partway back into their sockets as he had never seen human eyes before. He knew she was dead but could not believe it: he knew the woman's stubbornness, her perversity—and this seemed to him, in his shock, in that suspension of feeling that shock initially provides, a part of her subterfuge, her ill will and hostility. "Agnes! Agnes! *Agnes!*" he shouted.

Then in a panic he ran to telephone the police. And an ambulance.

Like a terrified child he begged them to come help him. "My wife—she isn't breathing! Please help me! Help us! The name is Carpenter, we live at Fifty-eight West Fairway Drive—"

Awaiting their arrival he ran back and forth between the bathroom and an upstairs window from which he could see the street, as if under a compulsion to check every few seconds to see that Agnes was really in the state in which he had described her… now that he had made the calls, now that the outside world would know of what had been until now a sheerly private matter; he had a childish expectation that perhaps he'd made a mistake and Agnes was not in fact dead but playing some sort of cruel trick on him.

He thought, But these things don't happen to people like us.

And afterward, when the house was open to strangers, and teams of men entered it freely, including a police photographer, a youngish bearded man in tinted sunglasses who took numerous photographs of the naked woman in the scummy gray water who had been Charles Carpenter's wife, he thought, as a corrective: If these things can happen then we weren't the people we imagined we were. All along, we had been other people.

"I suppose I actually felt, on a purely unexamined level," Charles Carpenter told Dorothea Deverell, "that, living in that particular house, on West Fairway Drive, in Lathrup Farms—being, you know, the sort of person I believe I am—I would be spared such monstrosities. And could spare others from them."

Dorothea Deverell said naïvely, gazing up into Charles Carpenter's face, in love, "But Charles—you *are* that person!"

⁂

Dorothea Deverell was not of course the only friend who comforted Charles Carpenter during this period of grief and upset—the Weidmanns, among others, rallied to him—but she was the friend upon whom, most clearly, he depended. And with the passing of days, weeks, eventually months, it would become yet clearer that their connection, their emotional rapport, went deeper than simply friendship. For Charles Carpenter was often at Dorothea Deverell's home for dinner (though he did not stay the night), and friends who invited one to their homes began quite naturally to include the other. If a general communal curiosity was aroused by such practices—if, behind Dorothea's and Charles's backs, gossip of various degrees of intensity made the rounds—they were not to know of it directly; though Dorothea, forever sensitive to emanations in the air, supposed that people must be talking—"They would hardly be normal, otherwise."

For gossip after all is the very soul of a community: evidence that it is not a mere mechanical gathering of individuals but a living organism with its own life's blood.

And one day Ginny Weidmann impulsively telephoned Dorothea Deverell, to ask her friend point-blank, "Are you—? And Charles—? Is it—Dorothea, *is* it true?"

Dorothea had long ago prepared a dignified little speech with which she might explain herself to such friends as Ginny Weidmann; she would say, "I don't know precisely what you are asking, Ginny, but I can tell you—yes, Charles Carpenter and I are very good friends; yes, I suppose we are in love; but Agnes Carpenter knew nothing of it and it had nothing to do with the disintegration of the Carpenters' marriage—that marriage had been, as everyone knows, dead for years." Now, however, confronted at last with the actual question, Dorothea Deverell merely said in a quiet, hopeful voice, "Yes."

And then there came the inquest, in late April, at which, to Charles Carpenter's (and Dorothea Deverell's) immense relief, the verdict of accidental death was given.

According to the county coroner, the specific cause of Agnes Carpenter's death was drowning; there had been water in her lungs. But the alcoholic content of the deceased's blood was so high, and she had taken so many tablets of Valium, that she'd clearly been unconscious, even comatose, at the time of her death.

And she had a medical history of alcohol and drug abuse.

"So they chose not to make an issue of the 'suicide' notes after all," Charles Carpenter said. "I suppose they didn't think it was worth the effort—trying to build a case against me on such slender evidence."

"A case against you?" Dorothea Deverell asked, puzzled. "But wouldn't it have been a case against poor Agnes, arguing that she had meant to take her own life?"

"But Agnes is dead," Charles Carpenter said carefully. "And I, as the surviving husband, stand to collect her estate—and her life insurance, which would have been null and void in the case of self-inflicted death." He paused, as if mildly ashamed, not quite looking at Dorothea. "I thought you understood, dear. The usual terms of life insurance…?"

And now the realization swept over Dorothea: for of course she knew, or must have known. Charles Carpenter was the beneficiary of his wife's estate as Dorothea had been the beneficiary of Michel's estate years ago. At the time, she had been too distraught with grief to think about money or to care about her financial situation; at this time, she simply did not want to know.

Charles said, placatingly, "We can give most of it to charity, in Agnes' name."

Dorothea Deverell knew that for some time, even before the Carpenters' formal separation, Agnes had been willfully negligent about money, as a way of asserting herself against Charles; her excuse was always that it was *her* money—she had inherited approximately $2 million at her mother's death. Her personal checking account was often overdrawn and her record of it unreliable; though she seemed to have little to show for it, she ran up large, frequently unexplained bills on her credit card. "She is trying to drive me mad," Charles complained, "and she is succeeding." He was the one in charge of all financial matters, as he was in charge of household matters—the overseeing of workmen, repairmen, the weekly lawn crew during the summer months. One of Agnes' chronic habits was to lose receipts and even, it seemed, to lose or misplace cash. Like many women who are affluent yet have no work, thus no salaries, of their own, she harbored a curious ambivalence about money in the abstract: clearly she relished its use, as an expression of personal power, while at the same time she disdained it. Her cynicism was not without its lyric side; Dorothea recalled her once saying, at a social gathering, "Money *doesn't* buy happiness—but it makes it irrelevant." Charles Carpenter had visibly winced.

After Agnes' death, Charles and his accountant tried gamely to make sense of the woman's financial records. There were many errors, many missing items, and, dating from the last six weeks of her life, at least one mystery: On March 7, Agnes had made out a check to an individual (or a business) called, simply, "Alvarado," for $7,000; on April 10, the day of her death, she had made out a check to the same party for $8,500. Charles had no idea who or what "Alvarado" was: a store? an independent money manager or investor? Nor did anyone in the Carpenters' circle of friends know. "She could not after all have spent fifteen thousand five hundred dollars on alcohol and Valium," Charles grimly observed.

But he was satisfied that the mysterious expenditure had nothing to do with his wife's actual death. For what connection could there possibly have been?

These matters, and numerous others, Charles Carpenter routinely shared with Dorothea Deverell; as she shared with him, perhaps to a lesser extent, matters pertaining to the Morris T. Brannon Institute. Charles's mourning for his difficult wife was taking the form of a protracted quarrel with her, which, being wholly one-sided, *his*-sided, could not fail to yield frustration and anger; this,

Dorothea was more than willing to indulge, out of guilty complicity. She might try to comfort her lover in his grief, but she would never have wished to quarrel with it. She foresaw how, as if inevitably, she and Charles Carpenter would become a couple in Lathrup Farms society, even before they were married and living in the same house; as Ginny Weidmann said, they were a "perfect match."

Dorothea smiled suddenly, unexpectedly.

For she *was* happy.

Since Colin Asch's extravagant dinner party in her honor, Dorothea Deverell had been very kindly disposed to her friend Ginny's young nephew. She invited him to the cocktail reception for a new art exhibit at the Institute and there introduced him to a number of the trustees and members of the Friends—older, well-to-do men and women, for the most part, of the kind socially receptive to the emanations of "youth." She gave him inscribed copies of her handsome books on Isabel Bishop, Arthur Dove, and Charles Demuth; in lieu of the dinner party she owed them—for this wasn't after all a period in Dorothea's life when she felt up to the demands of a dinner party—she invited the Weidmanns and Colin to be her guests at a performance of the visiting New York City Ballet in Boston and took them to dinner beforehand at a restaurant near the theater. More importantly, she suggested to Mr. Morland, who immediately agreed, that Colin Asch be added to the Institute's payroll as a "consultant for publicity"—as it was, Colin had been helping in a casual, unsystematic way, placing notices for upcoming Institute events in Boston publications and getting local radio and television stations to add such notices to their cultural calendars. "Our office has been mailing out press releases, as they're called, for years, with a minimum of success," Dorothea told Colin, mystified. "How is it these people have listened to *you?*" Colin merely laughed, embarrassed, and said, "I suppose it does require a certain knack. A minor talent for coercion."

He was touchingly grateful to Dorothea for adding him to the

Institute staff and thanked her repeatedly. "The consulting fee is very modest. I'm afraid," Dorothea said, pleased that Colin Asch was pleased, "but maybe, one day, we might have enough in the budget for a full-time director of publicity—"

"Oh, I doubt that I could work here full time," Colin said quickly. "It's just, you know, the honor of it. The association. The Morris T. Brannon Institute." He paused. He smiled his spontaneous sunny smile at Dorothea, which never failed to move her. "But—who knows? I can't make predictions, in terms of my career. Modeling is a notoriously unpredictable profession."

"Modeling?" Dorothea asked, amazed. It was the first she had heard of it.

It seemed that Colin Asch had quit L.L. Loomis in mid-March; he'd been approached by one of the firm's clients, Elite Models—"'Elite Models at Affordable Prices' is how they advertise themselves"—to sign on with them as a photographer's model, primarily for men's fashions. Of course he had not ever envisioned himself as a model since he was rather critical of his appearance, and skeptical too over the very idea of peddling one's looks on the market.... Though he had not been particularly happy at L.L. Loomis, where his talent and energy were being suppressed, he'd hesitated to leave since a job in public relations might have led to something in artistic design, even in architectural design, someday; but here suddenly was this exclusive modeling agency begging *him* to give *them* a chance. So he suffered through a week of terrible indecision; once he had an offer to leave, and an excellent offer at that, everyone at Loomis naturally wanted him to stay—even the supervisor who had been so cold and so transparently jealous of him. "But finally I decided to quit and try my chances at modeling," he said. "After all, I'm twenty-eight years old and not getting any younger."

Dorothea Deverell listened to Colin Asch's words as she might have listened to the speech of an exotic foreigner or the song of an exotic bird. Surely he was, as canny Howard Morland had said of him, a "golden boy—hardly a member of *our* modest species." She did not envy him the adventure of his new profession—the very thought of "peddling" one's looks in public dismayed her—but she did envy him the brash vitality of youth. And she had no doubt that, if he did not give up too quickly, he might very well succeed.

Almost apologetically she said, "How meager it must seem, then, to be asked to serve as a consultant for us. The Institute isn't very glamorous, I'm afraid." Colin Asch fixed her an almost defiant look. "As if, Dorothea, *I* should be concerned with 'glamour'!"

A week later, however, near the end of April, he dropped by Dorothea's home uninvited to show her his portfolio of photographs. "I just thought, you know, you might be curious," Colin Asch said. Most of the photographs, he explained, as Dorothea turned the pages slowly, were the property of the agency; the half dozen at the end were the first prints of a "shoot" he'd done the previous week for the fashionable men's store Tatler & Co. Watching Dorothea's face, he exuded an innocent, boyish vanity. "It's weird seeing yourself as an object," he said. "But I guess it sort of puts things into perspective."

Does it? Dorothea wondered.

She had made them a pot of herbal tea; she'd laid the bulky portfolio down on the dining room table and was examining the glossy photographs in sequence, thoughtfully, as if they were—as, indeed, perhaps they were—works of art. It was clear that Colin Asch wanted her to contemplate these images of himself as a model, but it was not clear to Dorothea how she was expected to respond. "How striking!" she murmured. "How unusual!" She found herself staring at a photograph of a very blond very arrogant-looking young stranger posed leaning against a Jaguar sports car parked amid the dunes, the point of the photograph being, evidently, the Italian designer's suit the young man modeled, with exaggerated shoulders and a slim waist and wide lapels. "I don't think I would recognize you," Dorothea said, laughing uneasily. "It *is* you? Colin?"

"Oh, you'd recognize me, Dorothea," he said, seriously. "You and I would know each other anywhere."

There was the formidable young blond man posing in jodhpurs and a polo shirt that fitted his slender yet muscular torso tightly; there was the young blond man in a fashionable ribbed sweater and blue jeans and running shoes; there, lounging on sunlit stone steps redolent of the Mediterranean (though photographed, surely, in the Boston area), his hair glaringly blond, his eyebrows nearly white, eyes obscured by tinted Polo glasses. In one photograph, over which Dorothea chose not to linger, he was nearly naked—wearing only snugly fitting jockey shorts. In all the photographs Colin Asch seemed far more sinewy, muscular, *masculine*, than Dorothea would have thought him had she simply envisioned him, summoned an image of him in her mind's eye. For was he not, still, the waiflike boy who had turned up at the Weidmanns' house back in November and who had stared so appealingly at Dorothea Deverell? And if he was no longer that boy, what had become of that boy?

She looked up at Colin Asch, who, standing with a teacup in one hand, his other hand crooked at his waist, elbow akimbo, was looking expectantly at her, and saw that, yes, the young man who stood before her was indeed the monographic young man of the fashion photographs; he had supplanted entirely the skinny boy with the limp ponytail, the sallow grayish skin. The carnivore had supplanted the vegetarian.

Unless, she thought, there had never been any vegetarian, from the start. Only the carnivore.

But these were fleeting, unfocused thoughts, themselves supplanted, in the next instant, by others—for Colin Asch with childlike eagerness seemed actually to be waiting for a judgment of some sort from Dorothea Deverell. "Do you," he asked, with a gesture toward the portfolio, "do you think I have a future there, Dorothea? Or do you think it's all some sort of—I don't know—chimera? It *is* an exciting life, but it's tough, too—like, you know, 'dog eat dog'; you're in such immediate and continuous competition with other models, I sort of wonder whether my nerves can stand it."

Dorothea Deverell said, closing the portfolio carefully, "But it seems you're more than merely promising, Colin, it looks to me as if you have arrived," and a moment later wondered at the odd jocular confidence of her remark. Did she mean it? Did she even know what she was talking about? Her professional world was in no way contiguous with that of modeling.

But it was the reply Colin Asch most avidly wished to hear; his face lit up like a child's. He said, humbly, "Thank you, Dorothea. For your faith in me. There's no one whose opinion means more to me than yours, and your—faith in me. I'll always remember it."

So Dorothea could hardly retract her statement, or even qualify it. She said, "Are there other 'shoots' planned soon?"

"The head of the agency told me that too, in effect, what you said, Dorothea," Colin said thoughtfully. "And the photographers I've been working with. 'Naturally photogenic,' they're saying—that's a sort of buzzword in the profession. Of course, I can hardly take credit for it," he said, with modest dip of his head, "it's just an accident of genetics. When I was a schoolboy at Monmouth Academy there was this teacher of mine, he was also the headmaster of the school; he'd say he had faith in me too, could see in my face I had some sort of special destiny and he wanted to guide it, he said, but..." Colin Asch's voice trailed off dreamily. For several seconds he stood, teacup in hand, staring not at Dorothea Deverell but through her, at a space that excluded her; she felt suddenly, though not for the first time, the fact of his extraordinary loneliness. "But something happened to him, and things changed. It's such a sad thing in life, isn't it, Dorothea," Colin Asch said, frowning severely. "That things *change?*"

Dorothea, in whose imagination visions of poor Agnes Carpenter had been dominant for days, since the news of her death two weeks before, said merely, "Yes."

"They told me I should get 'investors' in my career, 'shareholders' to help with expenses," Colin Asch said suddenly, in a derisory voice. "A top model, you know—the head of the agency thinks I'll be tops in maybe five, six months—can make a million dollars a year, two million, but there are expenses to begin with, and I have my apartment and my furniture and my car—payments, I mean, rent and insurance and that sort of thing," he said, speaking quickly, laughing. "I'm just so damned ignorant of that side of life, so helpless, like, you know, an *idiot savant* or something—Mr. Kreuzer, my teacher, he used to say, 'All you need, Colin, is someone to take you in hand, someone who loves you'—but, Jesus, Dorothea, I told them I just couldn't do anything like that!" he said vehemently. "I mean, after all, peddling myself to my friends? I told them no, I refused to do that sort of thing, I'd rather quit right now than—than do that sort of thing."

Slowly, almost awkwardly, Colin Asch took up the outsized portfolio and prepared to leave, his movements rather studied; so that Dorothea, ever conscious of her role as—and her limitations as—a hostess, had the distinct impression that her young friend was waiting for—hoping for—an invitation to stay awhile longer. It was Saturday evening; surely so handsome and dashing a young man would not be spending Saturday evening alone? Dorothea felt a pang of guilt, but her evening was taken: given over to Charles Carpenter, for whom she would prepare a meal here at home, in truth the happiest most idyllic sort of evening she could envision, though their conversation would almost surely be centered upon poor Agnes and the ramifications of her death…and Colin Asch, for all the appeal of his boyish loneliness and his young man's swaggering glamour, simply had no place in it.

At the door Colin Asch said, as if eerily, and not for the first time, he were capable of reading Dorothea Deverell's mind, "*That* was so sudden, wasn't it?—Mrs. Carpenter's death the other day."

Dorothea said, startled, "Yes—yes, it was."

"Did you know her, Dorothea?"

"Not really. No—not well."

"You're closer to Mr. Carpenter, I guess."

"Yes," Dorothea said uneasily. "Charles and I are quite close. He has been"—and this was vague, fumbling—"involved in activities at the Institute for years. A very cultural man, a—a man who likes to involve himself in cultural things. Though with his job it's—"

"Susannah Hunt was telling me Mrs. Carpenter had been an alcoholic for years," Colin Asch said gravely. "Sort of emotionally unstable? And the Carpenters' marriage wasn't, I guess, too happy. They didn't have any children?"

"No," Dorothea said. She would have liked to end the conversation but had no idea how, since Colin Asch was standing with his back to her front door, and the door had not yet been opened. "They didn't have any children."

"*That's* a blessing, then," Colin said. "Though I guess, at their age, the children would be all grown up, mostly. Even out of college."

"I suppose so."

"Susannah was telling me Mrs. Carpenter might have taken an overdose of pills? Like, I mean, on purpose? She'd left some letter or something behind that the police confiscated?"

"No," Dorothea said firmly, "there was no letter."

"There was no letter?"

"Not that I know of."

Colin Asch soberly pondered this: not disbelieving, merely thoughtful. The brass clamp in his ear—he was wearing it again, after an interim of weeks: fortunately he'd left it off for his own dinner party—flashed rakishly; his punkishly styled hair lifted in tufts from his forehead. He smiled suddenly and said, almost in a whisper, "Mrs. Hunt is the kind of woman, she makes things up, and it isn't even lying, really, it's just—fabrication. In fact, you know, *she* drinks a lot too. I think that's why she's going around saying all these things, these sort of unverified things, about the Carpenters—she's afraid she might end up like Agnes Carpenter." He paused, nodded, not seeming to see the look of apprehension in Dorothea Deverell's face, and said, in a derisive dismissal, "Next thing you know, she'll be telling lies about *me*."

It was a balmy misty day with a palpable taste of spring in the air, so Dorothea accompanied her young friend to the curb, to his car—the black Porsche, low-slung, polished, expensive-looking. (But was that a dent in the rear right fender? And was that a hairline crack in the front windshield?) She wondered if the Porsche belonged, still, to Susannah Hunt, or whether Colin Asch had bought it from her. The peculiar outburst about his finances, about "investors" and "shareholders" in his career—which, discreetly, Dorothea Deverell had seemed not to hear: even should she be inclined to do so, Charles Carpenter would be severely disapproving if *she* invested in Colin Asch's modeling career—indicated a concern with money of an extreme kind. (Which did not in fact surprise Dorothea, who had wondered from the start how Colin Asch could afford so luxurious an apartment, with such luxurious furnishings, and such tastes. Surely Susannah Hunt was not supporting him entirely?) Guilt tugged at her like a mild ache; she could of course help Colin out if he was terribly in need of cash but she worried that lending him money would humiliate him and giving him money would insult him. At their luncheon at L'Auberge he had looked as if she'd slapped him when she had merely suggested paying her half of the check.

"It was sort of like Krauss's death—I mean, unexpected," Colin Asch said, tossing the portfolio casually into the car and swinging in behind the wheel. "But sort of expected, too, in the context of the life. If you knew the life." He took down a pair of Polo driving glasses from the sunscreen and fitted them on his face. Immediately he became the very blond very arrogant young man, a Greek god-like young man, in the fashion photographs. And he was wearing white: a white linen sports coat with a mint-green collarless jersey shirt. Dorothea Deverell, not knowing what he said exactly, was smiling uncertainly down at him. "If you know how to read it," he said with an enigmatic smile.

"Read it?"

"Like, you know, Dorothea, things in code."

And then, in keeping with his glamorous persona, he drove off.

Afterward, preparing dinner and awaiting Charles's arrival, Dorothea Deverell reviewed her conversation with Colin Asch and felt increasingly uneasy. What had he been talking about? She seemed to have nodded there, at the end, and given him her hand in farewell. Had Colin Asch, for all his pride, really wanted Dorothea to "invest" in his career? Or had he been sincere in his dismissal of the very idea? He had spoken almost angrily, after all, of the prospect of peddling himself to his friends.

No, Dorothea thought, finally, he can't have meant it.

She would not in any case mention the possibility—or even its impossibility—to Charles Carpenter.

For Charles did not approve of Ginny Weidmann's nephew; it seemed he had not approved of him from the start. Dorothea had several times tried to argue in Colin Asch's behalf but Charles had remained unmoved. "But Colin is so appealing, so likable," Dorothea said, "so eager, like a child, to be loved," and Charles replied, "That's in fact why I don't much like him—why I resist."

That evening, at dinner, Dorothea described Colin Asch's brief visit: his portfolio of photographs, the prospect of his new career. But Charles did hardly more than murmur in response, like a jealous husband. In exasperation Dorothea said, "*Why* don't you like Colin? He likes you; he has told me. He very much admires you."

"Does he?"

"He has told me so himself."

But Charles Carpenter was not to be drawn into discussing a subject against his will. He would rather, Dorothea supposed, settle into the sort of melancholy, tender, brooding exchanges they'd had for days on end, circling around the subject of Agnes and the degree to which they might consider themselves involved in her death.

Impatiently, Dorothea said, "You don't really have any reason to dislike Colin, do you?"

After a brief pause Charles Carpenter said dryly, "Only my sense, darling, that the young man is a psychopath."

Dorothea stared, as shocked as if her lover had reached out suddenly and struck her. "A…*what?*"

"You heard me perfectly plainly, Dorothea. A psychopath."

*

Dorothea Deverell had heard perfectly plainly but did not choose to consider her lover's words. They were cruel and vindictive; they did not reflect very nobly upon him.

Yet they abraded her nerves; and she had cause, a few days later, to remember them, meeting Susannah Hunt in a village store and having a painful conversation with the woman. Out of nowhere a voice rang out: "Dorothea Deverell! It *is* you!" She looked up startled to see Mrs. Hunt, floridly made up, elegantly dressed, headed in her direction, as if they were old, intimate friends—or enemies with a score to settle. In a louder voice than was required, Mrs. Hunt said, "I *thought* that was you, Dorothea, but you're looking—well, you aren't looking quite yourself somehow."

To this semi-accusation Dorothea Deverell could think of no adequate reply, so stood mute, smiling, expectant, a ream of typing paper in her arms. She had hurried into the Village Stationer's to make a single purchase and truly had not time to linger and chat, as the formidable Mrs. Hunt seemed inclined. "I don't believe I've seen you, you know, since the night of Colin's party. *Your* party," Mrs. Hunt said, as if Dorothea needed to be reminded. "Have you been well? And Charles Carpenter—has *he* been well? Such a terrible, terrible shock. I'm still shaken by it."

Susannah Hunt was a powerfully attractive woman, tall and full-bodied, with an air of desperate chic. She had outlined her wide mouth in a chalky cranberry shade and colored her eyelids pale blue, but both her mouth and her eyes appeared puffy. Something stylishly severe had been done to her hair, which was dyed a flat, lusterless black, razor-cut close to her head. As she spoke Dorothea was vaguely aware of a gentleman friend waiting for her at the front of the store, an older, white-haired man, deeply tanned, in a navy blue blazer with a nautical look to it; but this friend Susannah Hunt herself seemed to have forgotten. She was standing close to Dorothea and smiling rather strangely at her, asking after Colin Asch, whom, it developed, she had not seen in a while—twelve days. Uncomfortably, Dorothea said, "As far as I know, Colin is well. He seems to have embarked upon a new—"

"He's a *model.* Isn't that extraordinary? But so somehow *right*, don't you think? Since he's so very attractive and there's so little a man can do with being attractive—a heterosexual man, I mean—except *be.* A model, or an actor, that's about it," Susannah said in a bright dazzling rush of words. She smiled at Dorothea but her eyes were cold. "Did you say you'd seen him? He's always talking of course about *you*—how you gave him a start, so to speak, here in Lathrup Farms. When he'd just about been desperate—penniless. Working practically as a beach boy—in Florida, was it? Key West?"

"I—I don't know about that," Dorothea said.

"A very attractive young man, in any case," Susannah Hunt said.

"I suppose he is, yes."

"And sweet."

"Yes."

"But with such a violent temper! At times."

Seeing Dorothea's disbelieving look, Susannah Hunt drew a hand lightly across her brow, as if to indicate an injury to her eye. She gave off a rich, disturbing scent: expensive perfume, red wine. Was the woman merely drunk? Drunk and histrionic? Dorothea wished to think so. "At times, indeed," Susannah said, sighing.

Dorothea would have moved on, but the woman blocked her way. She asked her now whether she had heard from Ginny Weidmann recently, whether Ginny saw much of her nephew these days. "I don't like to call her, you know," Susannah said. "She has become so sort of mother-henish over him. So proprietary."

Dorothea thought. She had not spoken with Ginny Weidmann in more than a week but was reluctant to convey this information to Susannah Hunt, whose intimate, rather belligerent manner she did not at all like. "I'm afraid I don't know," she said. "Now if you'll excuse me—"

"He stays away overnight sometimes. Colin does. He never used to, you know—he was wild about that apartment. 'The center of the universe,' he called it. 'My sanctuary.' Now the little bastard simply disappears without explanation…a day and a night, two days, two nights...leaving me practically *frantic.* But you don't know where he is, Dorothea, you say, or whom he might be with?"

"No," Dorothea said coolly.

"Yet you and he are so *close*."

This too had the resonance of an accusation, to which Dorothea Deverell felt no inclination to reply. The heady discomforting scent of perfume and wine was now unmistakable, emanating from the other woman; Dorothea had the idea that Susannah Hunt, now regally drawn to her full height, swaying as if indignant in her high-heeled alligator pumps, was debating whether to challenge Dorothea head on or grant her a mocking sort of victory.

Then, as if suddenly remembering her gentleman friend at the front of the store, she gave way and relented, allowing Dorothea to pass by to the cashier. She said, "Next time you do see him, Dorothea, tell him *hello* from me. From Susannah. And that's all. And that's *all*."

"Yes," Dorothea promised. "I will."

So, with a shudder of repugnance, she escaped. Thank God, she thought, Colin had eluded that terrible woman.

11

Where did the money go? Where, when Colin Asch had sure as hell earned it, sweated for it, did it *go?* The phrase "cash flow," which he didn't entirely understand, stuck in his brain: yeah, it *flows*, all right, sure does *flow*! "In one fucking direction." In the Blue Ledger when he could force himself to sit still he made his calculations, in pencil, in pencil with a good eraser, but what he needed was one of those little Japanese pocket calculators. To take the burden of mathematics off his brain.... He'd try, God knows he'd try; then the injustice of it rose like vomit to the back of his mouth and he threw the Ledger down and walked fast through the rooms of the apartment, almost trotting, slapping at his bare thighs (hadn't he gotten dressed yet? but what time was it?), trying to figure out why Colin Asch always needed money, money and more money, always more fucking money, when there was after all money coming in: *flowing* in. Or had been until the other day when he realized he'd better stop for the time being.

Running needless risks, jeopardizing his future. And now Dorothea Deverell had trusted him with an executive position at the Institute; he didn't want to disappoint her.

Still, it was a task for Colin Asch in this weird electric kind of state that'd settled onto him to sit quietly to figure his next moves out in the Ledger, let alone meditate as his soul urged—"The kingdom of God is within! Within!"—let alone endure with grace the shooting sessions, the protracted scenes of passivity, even helplessness, the photographers giving him instructions, herding him here and there like a clumsy calf, or actually positioning, touching him—arms, legs, head. The other day he'd caught the fuckers exchanging glances behind his back but gave no sign, just continued smiling—compliant—"professional" in every regard. When all he wanted to do was tear their throats out with his teeth.

In a year, he'd been promised, he'd be one of the top Boston-area models. Thus he *was* trying—subordinating himself to his intellectual inferiors.

"Colin Asch is learning. A lot."

Also with Susannah: screaming at him, threatening to go to the police or to her lawyer, actually daring him to hit her like it was Colin Asch's manhood and dignity she challenged, though the cunt liked it, being hit, fairly hard but not too hard, never any blood—"They tend not to like actual blood." But he'd backed off from her, laughing, saying, Wow. Wow. *Wow*. Saying, Lady, you don't *know*. The first time she'd started hinting about wanting her money back, her "investment," he'd had the quick sort of floating idea why not strangle this woman and dump her body out in the dunes, but it wasn't a serious thought; after all there was Dorothea Deverell in his life now—just thinking of her calmed him, to a degree. So he'd kidded Susannah out of her rage or whatever it was—"All she ever needs is a good hard fucking"—and afterward in the steamy bathroom he wrote in the mirror in tall block letters HEY I WANT TO BE GOOD!!!!

The money, though. Did Freud say money is shit? For it *is* shit. Surely. Money-grubbing capitalist-imperialist society where human beings are forced to peddle themselves in the market...if not their actual flesh (like your million-dollar fashion models) then their talents, their brains, their souls. If Susannah followed through with her threat to stop paying her share of his rent at the Normandy Court he'd have that added expense, plus the payments on the furniture et cetera and incidental expenses and of course the $$$ he wished to hide away as a nest egg...for the Emergency. (For Colin Asch sensed that the time rapidly approached when he would feel the need to terminate this phase of his life, as, in the past, he'd terminated other phases; he'd maybe have to go into hiding at an hour's notice, with Dorothea Deverell as his friend and companion perhaps or maybe just alone: thus $$$ sequestered safely away *hidden right here in the apartment* was of the utmost priority.)

"The money, though."

In the secret Ledger's account there was D.T./2300/"M" (meaning that Tracey Donovan, the perky little plump-assed reporter for the local weekly, had handed over to Colin Asch a check for $2,300 payable to "T. Manatee"—her notion of his professional modeling name); and there was W.G./3500/"A" (meaning that a Lathrup Farms widow named Gladys Whiting, to whom in fact Dorothea Deverell had recently introduced him, had invested $3,500 in his career as "A. Avalon"), and there was C.A./7000/"Al" and C.A./8500/"Al" (meaning that Agnes Carpenter before her death had invested a total of $15,500 in Colin Asch's projected career as a handsome if temperamental blond model named "Alvarado")—*yet still it wasn't enough.*

Was he adding wrong? Subtracting wrong? Monthly expenses multiplied by twelve plus incidentals plus 15 percent set aside for the Emergency....It seemed that, the more cash flowed *in*, the more cash flowed *out*, and there was nothing he could do to prevent it. "Sometimes I feel, Dorothea, as if the top of my head is about to explode. *I don't think I'm going to make it.*"

Bare-assed on his tacky little balcony leaning against the railing, his eyes filling slowly with tears. A soft spring breeze stirring his hair...but which spring was it? *When I'm thirty I will cut my throat. I don't want to live past thirty.* Not knowing what the fuck to do next...sensing he hadn't better try to see Dorothea Deverell for another few days, though he could try to calm his thoughts thinking of her. And it came back to him in a flood of warmth how one day Mr. Kreuzer had placed his hand over his when he was writing or doing algebra, guiding Colin Asch's thin hand with his, his cold faltering hand enclosed in the other's big-knuckled hand that carried such heat, guiding Colin's pencil that way, helping him, and all the trouble to come wasn't so much as a premonition then; he'd felt his eyes fill with tears...what kindness, what relief. Just to know somebody gives a fuck about you.

But that sort of tender solicitude is rare.

"If you know how to read it."

Watching her face: and she'd blinked at him, mildly puzzled it seemed, her brown gaze imperturbable, opaque. Silent but squeezing his fingers as if in warning *don't say it*, as if to warn *yes—but don't say it*. And he'd sped off from the curb exhilarated as a smartass teen-aged kid—couldn't help showing off in the Porsche.

Though Dorothea Deverell had disappointed him too. Not inviting him to stay a while longer...not inviting him to stay for dinner when he had a strong hunch that Charles Carpenter would be coming over and the three of them would have gotten along so well, Colin just knew it. Actually, that was his plan. Sort of. Like Dorothea Deverell and Charles Carpenter would take in Colin Asch like married couples sometimes do, especially older married couples with no children or with grown-up children like the Weidmanns. Now that Carpenter's wife was safely out of the way, the two of them owed Colin Asch a favor, after all. If only they knew.

(Did they know? Did *she* know? Sometimes Colin believed she must...like about Krauss; he was certain she knew about Krauss... but the other he wasn't so sure about, actually.)

"It's the stillness in her."

That night, after the celebration party where they'd all been so happy, Colin Asch had come to her house in secret like a sleepwalker drawn to his fate. Not knowing what he would do but knowing, trusting; his instinct would guide him, for what did not, in this blessed state, emanate from the soul? In her presence *Colin Asch was elevated he was refined he was purified* like the petals of a flower opening innocently in the sun. High on champagne and red wine and one or two other factors, the smiles and warm handshakes of his good friends—*I want to love and be loved! Is that too fucking much to ask?* And Dorothea Deverell had kissed him on the cheek, thanking him for his kindness. And flying high but fully in control he had followed her afterward to her house in the night and with a miniature screwdriver he forced the lock of the rear terrace door; then he was standing inside in the dark that was so familiar to him as if he'd been living here all his life just as she was living here, *as much at ease.* This fact he would later note in the Blue Ledger. With a pencilized flashlight he illuminated his path to the stairs and upward…a narrower staircase than he recalled, and strangely steep, like a staircase in a dream… and maybe he *was* dreaming, for there was no fear in it: Colin Asch ascending to Dorothea Deverell unhesitating and lithe as a panther *knowing no harm could come to him or to her as all emanated from the soul.*

In her bedroom in the shadows he felt his breath quicken, for there, suddenly, she was…asleep and breathing heavily, hoarsely, as if straining for oxygen…*there*, only a few feet away, unknowing! "Dorothea. I won't hurt you." He drew nearer, stood above her, staring in amazement in rapture nothing raw or crude, nothing sexual—though, yes, there was *that* (feeling the blood rush into his penis like a faucet turned suddenly on), but so much more than merely *that.*

Wouldn't touch himself. It wasn't like *that* at all.

The thin beam of light darted and snaked about the room. Seeing that the room too was familiar, the low ceiling slanted at the front windows, the shape of the windows, the doorframes, teasingly familiar as if without being conscious of their union he'd seen them for years through her eyes. Thus *he could not be touched! could not be stopped!* Standing above Dorothea Deverell as she slept staring at her sleep-struck face as (when? where? he thought, yes, it had been recent) in one of the hospitals where he'd made his way by stealthy night to a young woman's room thus to contemplate her in her sleep and that too a heavy drugged sleep, a sedated sleep, the kind mimicking death but it isn't the real thing of course. The skin like alabaster; the dark disheveled hair on the pillow; the eyes (so beautiful! so *knowing!*) shut in sleep; the lips moist and open; the breath coming deep, rhythmic, labored…to which he tried to fit his. "Dorothea. It is I, Colin Asch; *it is I.*" Why was he trembling, when he wasn't frightened or even unduly excited? Why did his heart pound so heavily, as if he felt he were trespassing, doing something wrong? Through the fragrant dark dense as water Colin Asch could plunge to her, dive to her, take her up in his arms rescue her from all harm. It was his mission, his fate. He'd never have hesitated. *My life for hers!* he thought gaily.

But she slept, unknowing. And there was no danger. The room with the low slanted ceiling and the floral wallpaper and the gauzy white curtains like a dream solidified around the dreamer. *We could die together. Tonight.* Excited, he pulled the black turtleneck sweater off over his head and let it drop. His hands were clumsy in the tight kidskin gloves, but that couldn't be helped. On a bureau were her clothes and on a nearby chair, tossed down; she'd barely managed to get undressed for bed he supposed: there, the white lace jacket, the long white skirt partly on the floor, a white silk half slip and a white brassiere; and touching the fabric Colin Asch couldn't help himself, he removed one of the gloves and held it gripped between his teeth and pressed the silky underclothes against his bare chest managed to force the slip (so fragrant! charged with electricity sparking in his hair, his eyelashes) down over his head, his mouth dry with anticipation, dread of what might happen, *or had it already happened and the woman was dead...?*

(But only if Colin Asch was trapped, boxed into a corner. Only if there was no way to accommodate his dignity, pride, manhood. Never would he force her however—"I promise"—or even beg as Mr. Kreuzer had in the end, fumblingly pressing the very razor into the boy's fingers, daring him, or actually wishing him to use it—"What more perfect death than death-in-union? Two-in-one? Forever?")

Afterward he would not remember precisely but it was like a dream in teasing fragments, the emotional tone of it and not details or images or uttered words. Colin Asch crouched over the sleeping woman slowly tremblingly drawing the covers off her, ascending, like a beam of light...no shadows! no gravity!...and she continued to sleep unknowing, trusting in him—a woman in a nightgown bunched at her knees, a woman with a petite skeleton, flat-bellied, her breasts flattened too as she slept lying on her back but slightly twisted as if she had fallen from a great height—and Colin Asch bent closer, staring, the silk slip in tight folds over his chest, fragrance easing upward, his eyes filling with tears like pain. In an ecstasy, nearly blinded, he knelt at the bedside and pressed his burning forehead against the woman's bare foot…the pale bare foot, cool as stone, and as smooth.

I want to be good!

I want to destroy the world.

Days or maybe weeks later the mood shifted suddenly like the spring woods, turned shitty; Colin Asch was susceptible at this time of the year, the axis of a new fresh head-splitting season when you're supposed to be happy like the rest of the assholes, lifting your face to the sun, sniffing the earth, the moisture, the warmth, melting snow and dripping eaves and rivulets of water running fast in the gutters; and he made the effort. Christ the fuckers had no idea what an effort it was, how he loathed them manipulating his very body daring to touch his very skin which pained him, it was a true complaint—hyperesthesia, they'd called it, like the outside layer of his skin had been peeled away thus medicines were required but he hadn't had those medicines in a long, long time—"I don't like any doctors fucking with *me* like I was just some mere body or something," he'd actually told the judge who'd heard his case, but that was a long, long time ago, in another spring. Anyway he made the effort. Allowed himself to be made up—"You're a little *pale*, Colin, also there's some shadows under your eyes: see?"—and made the fucking effort trying to joke with the photographer, to turn their relationship into *something warm something real something other than the merely commercial* for he'd been thinking he would like, really, to be a photographer—but a true photographer—taking portraits of distinguished people traveling around the world for (maybe) *Time* magazine, or *Life*, or the *Boston Globe*; it was unnatural for a man of Colin Asch's energy and temperament and imagination, above all, dignity, to be so passive, so putty-in-the-hands like the other models (those narcissistic assholes, pretty-boys crazy in love with their own reflections), when he was an artist himself: and that primarily. Thus he gritted his teeth, and smiled, and tried hard, showing how serious he truly was, how eager to cooperate, during one of the breaks asking the photographer about his background, what kinds of work he did, what kinds of contracts were necessary, and was photography school actually a good or necessary thing or could you sort of pick it up on your own—"Provided you had good advice, I mean." Of course Colin Asch had been enrolled at the Rhode Island School of Design. He'd been told he had almost too much talent for one individual—"It sort of all condenses, y'know, if you have too many things to think about, too many currents pulling at you—like a paragnosiac fugue."

Bob the photographer peered at Colin Asch over his heavy white coffee mug steaming coffee and said, "Like a *what?*"

"Paragnosiac fugue."

"What the hell's that?"

Blinking and smiling his dazzling white smile, drawing his fingers swiftly through his newly shampooed hair—"Oh, I forget."

Then seeing how Bob looked at him not knowing if he should smile or not as (maybe) Bob'd looked at Colin Asch a few too many times for his own good (the fucker: telling tales on him like all the rest he didn't doubt), Colin Asch quickly added, "Just like a nervous spell, sort of."

"Oh," said Bob, still looking at him, still holding the coffee mug steaming in front of his mouth. "Is that it."

He wanted to plead with her; he was surrounded by mental and spiritual inferiors—except of course for her and Charles Carpenter (if Charles Carpenter would only *see!*)—thinking sometimes he was swimming to save his life, desperately flailing his arms to keep from sinking, drowning: "The worst kind of death, Dorothea. You don't know."

It was moist warming air that upset him. It was the acceleration of the earth. The approach of the summer solstice *before he was prepared.* This year held a threat of being worse than the year before, scaring him with its excitement and violence like pelting rain against the windows and the roof of the car, like thunderclaps the smell of lightning—his sense of smell was so heightened at these times, like a dog's actually. I'd have liked to be a dog, just, y'know, trotting around sniffing, seeing the world through my nose, Colin Asch had told one of his doctors when the fugue had just about lifted and he was himself again or nearly; the fault lay with the impure PCP he'd dropped which left one of his temporal lobes short-circuited (or so he surmised: the doctors gave him and his fellow victims double-talk in which you couldn't believe or confidently disbelieve)—all this he would explain to Dorothea Deverell one day soon. That it scared him, things speeding up as they sometimes did. "And I haven't touched any PCP for years."

Which was true. Absolutely incontestably true.

Of course Colin Asch could not confide in Dorothea Deverell *everything.* That he was tortured not knowing, not being able to decide, what exactly to do about the Carpenters: to eradicate the husband, or the wife. There were powerful arguments on both sides. There were voices yammering on both sides.

For one thing, he hated Charles Carpenter, didn't he, for supplanting Colin Asch in Dorothea Deverell's affections; if Charles Carpenter died it would fall to Colin Asch to comfort her, and no one else. *Our mutual tragic lives. Life?*

But he couldn't be blind to the fact that if Charles Carpenter died, or was killed suddenly, Dorothea Deverell would be terribly upset: brokenhearted. "Christ, it might *kill* her." And he didn't want *that.* No—scrutinizing his soul—he didn't want *that.* "What I want is happiness for her, and happiness for me. But Dorothea must come first, otherwise there is no *me.*"

Knowing this he was flooded with relief like simple happiness, or happiness like simple relief. He did after all want only to be good *in homage to the goodness in her.*

Thus he inwardly debated. Thus the thoughts rose and fell and drifted and faded and reemerged in his head as he stood on his balcony in the soft spring rain...or drove the Porsche along unfamiliar highways...or posed near-naked, his head tilted at an insufferable angle, modeling sea-green swimwear coyly bulging at the crotch, eyes opened wide despite the glaring brain-frazzling lights. For hours, or was it weeks, Colin Asch analyzed the possibilities open to him, and to her. Yes, he wanted only what would yield happiness to her—"So Mrs. Carpenter must die." It was that simple. Inescapable.

XXX performed out of humane indifference, disinterest. For he had nothing personal against the woman, in fact he felt clean and neutral toward her, he'd forgiven her for challenging him that night at the Weidmanns'—in truth, she'd played into his hands like the two of them were performers and the others mere spectators—and he had been pleased he could convince her that the young blond New Wave model "Alvarado" had so promising a future why not invest $10,000 in his career? and she'd thought about it awhile then said she would limit herself to $7,000: "But don't tell my husband! Don't anybody"—she'd begun giggling, the alcohol flush warm in her cheeks—"tell that coldhearted *prig*."

Of course not, Mrs. Carpenter.

Thus in his unhurried reverie Colin Asch came to the conclusion clear as Euclidean logic that Agnes Carpenter, and not Charles Carpenter, must die. So clearing the way for Dorothea Deverell and Charles Carpenter to wed. So ushering in, in time, a new ménage in which more and more frequently young Colin Asch would be included: weekends, special holidays, birthdays. It would be the most natural thing in the world; older childless couples often take up younger unattached men. A kind of spiritual adoption.

"You will never be lonely again."

"Why, Colin. That is, Alvarado. How nice. Finally."

Seven-thirty P.M. of April 10, Colin Asch has rung the doorbell of the residence of Charles and Agnes Carpenter, 58 West Fairway Drive, Lathrup Farms, Massachusetts, eight-inch stainless-steel switchblade knife in his right-hand coat pocket, small tidy fragrant bouquet of flowers (daffodils, carnations, yellow tulips) in his right hand, and after a wait of five minutes or so he's being invited inside by the lady of the house: his second visit to this house, and his last. "Come in, come in," Agnes Carpenter says airily, "Just in time for a drink"—swaying a little on her feet leading the way into the semidarkened not-entirely-clean living room where the smell of cigarettes and alcohol is strong. Colin Asch thanks her and goes out into the kitchen himself to fetch a vase and water for the flowers, since it's the least he can do under the circumstances. From the other room Agnes Carpenter calls to him half accusing half teasing and he doesn't quite know what she is saying but he answers, "Right! Good! Great! *Yeah!*" Bottles on the kitchen counter, on the floor, dirtied plates stacked in the sink; his nostrils pinch in fastidious disdain. For who would think, contemplating the outside of the Carpenters' fine old colonial, it would be in this condition inside?

In the living room Agnes Carpenter has prepared Colin Asch a drink, a dandy big Scotch to match her own, handed him with shaky beringed fingers, and Colin Asch sets the bouquet atop the fireplace mantel ("*That's* nice, thank you," Agnes Carpenter barely murmurs) and accepts the drink, smiling his sweet cheery boyish dazzling smile but not drawing off his tight black kidskin gloves; he's too shrewd to be leaving fingerprints anywhere around here. He sees that the poor bitch had hurried to make herself up when she heard the doorbell—quick-powdered face, sad-glamorous crimson lipstick, some attempt at fluffing out the permed dry-as-straw colorless hair; and she'd buttoned (crookedly) up to her wrinkled throat the emerald-green brocaded Japanese housecoat or kimono she's wearing: not knowing who might be ringing her doorbell this time of evening but hoping for a pleasant surprise. Peering worriedly at her lanky visitor through the squares of stained glass framing the door until, yes, yes, finally, she recognized him—her young friend Colin Asch, her secret investment "Alvarado." Recognized him and opened the door wide.

"It *has* been a long time…hasn't it? At least a month?"

Giving Colin Asch a pug-dog look of reproach, moist eyes narrowed, and he likes it since there's invariably an edge of flirtatiousness to such reproach, allows him to shake his head, baffled, and smile sheepishly. "Gee, Mrs. Carpenter—I mean Agnes—I meant to call but I've been so busy these past six weeks, I guess your investment is really going to pay off 'cause Alvarado's phone practically never stops ringing—"

And Agnes Carpenter exercises her power by interrupting, careless-seeming, "Not at all! Not at all! I've been busy too! I quite understand!" She lowers her voice mock-dramatically: "All I was, actually, was a tiny bit concerned, Colin, that you *were* still around. That you hadn't disappeared."

Tall blond natural-aristocrat Colin Asch fixed the woman with his wide-open quizzical eyes. "Disappeared? But *where?*"

Agnes Carpenter laughs sharply as if he has said something intentionally comic.

They sit; and Agnes talks. In surges and gusts like someone who has not had the opportunity to talk in a long time. She is semi-drunk; not quite slurring-drunk; some color in her sallow cheeks and a look of sudden light in her bloodshot eyes. *With a tinge of regret C.A. touches the weapon through his coat pocket. Why is it the fate thrust upon some of us, to bring not peace but a sword?* Self-consciously Colin Asch settles himself in a velvet loveseat facing Agnes; close by a brass and mother-of-pearl mahogany cabinet that looks Mediterranean and antique. He listens politely to his hostess's yammering, crosses his long sinewy legs, shifts his shoulders inside his striped boxy double-breasted coat, nervously straightens his tie (a beauty, a creamy silk Dior with a pattern of tiny black horse-figures—Valentine's Day gift from Susannah Hunt): all to suggest that he's charmingly ill at ease in this plush bourgeois setting—he's an innocent, even naive young man, of the sort the modeling profession might well take advantage of: and predatory women. Agnes Carpenter pauses in mid-sentence, to squint at him. "Your gloves—why are you wearing gloves?" she asks. Colin

Asch says, embarrassed, "Oh, these? I'm so anxious these days, I'm back in an old bad habit of biting my nails till they bleed—the thumbnails especially—so the doctor said, he said the very best method, the most practical, is just to wear gloves. Until the anxiety lifts."

"Until the anxiety lifts," Agnes Carpenter echoes, suddenly touched. "But you know, Colin dear boy, that might not happen for a long time. With some of us—a long, long time."

Surreptitiously Colin Asch glances at his platinum-band wristwatch. Seven-forty already: he hopes to be out of here and in rapid motion by nine-thirty.

Unless he can wrap it up earlier? The woman *is* getting drunk.

And there is another drink, for Agnes, while Colin Asch (like a young athlete in training) nurses his, and more talk, the conversation swerving and lurching along a track very like the one it took on Colin Asch's previous visit in March. "I suppose you have heard? I suppose everyone is talking about it, laughing behind my back? Charles wants a separation; he says he wants a *divorce.* And only out of spite! Only to hurt me! Because"—and here Agnes begins laughing, laughing and coughing, wheezing, her jowls quivering, in mirth and indignation—"he knows I know *him*, inside and *out*. There's no mystery to Charles Carpenter to *me!* To his wife! I don't doubt he has a woman friend with whom he imagines himself madly in love—some cold greedy ambitious young woman twenty years younger than he who flatters him sexually—if it's possible to flatter my husband sexually without bursting into laughter. These pseudo-'liberated' young women today, they're all stalking other women's husbands since there aren't enough heterosexual men to go around. But the hilarious part of it, Colin, or the tragedy, take your pick, is that no man is a mystery to his wife—no wife is a mystery to her husband." Agnes Carpenter pauses, laughs derisively, succumbs to a fit of coughing, wipes her mouth on her sleeve, *the lovely emerald-green fabric despoiled by a gesture of slovenly drunkenness that fills Colin Asch with revulsion and pity. And anger.*

"Someone should put you out of your misery, Agnes."

"What? Don't mumble, please!"

"Someone should take you out, out on the town, like," Colin Asch says, wildly improvising, as if he too is on the brink of being frankly drunk and in a party mood, as, perhaps, having swallowed down a bennie or two before coming over, he is. "A good-looking woman like you, cooped up in here. It's a great house but, well, it's just—an interior."

Agnes Carpenter laughs shrilly, as if her young male visitor has said something not only intentionally comic but profound. "Christ. Are you *correct.* It's, whatever it is, just an *interior.*"

So the minutes pass. Colin Asch tries to calibrate the degree of the woman's drunkenness vis-à-vis the actions he requires her to perform.

Since as "Alvarado" he is hoping for another generous check, another gesture of faith in him as a top-rank model, he naturally turns the conversation in that direction, and Agnes Carpenter willingly follows, for isn't there something titillating? salacious? about the very notion of a male fashion model? Thus, minutes of banter, some of it gay and flirty and some of it—"D'you think, dear Colin, or, I mean, 'Alvarado,' d'you think, being in such close contact with some of those people, there's any danger? for instance, of getting AIDS?"—rather nasty, and at last Agnes Carpenter heaves herself up from her chair to lead Colin Asch into another room—Charles's "den" as she bitterly calls it—and to make out a check for "Alvarado" (who has, so very shrewdly and prudently, his own savings account in an area bank from which all monies will be withdrawn first thing in the morning of April 11) for the sum of $8,500. The grim satisfied smile on the woman's pug face suggests that she is doing this primarily to take revenge upon the absent, so conspicuously absent husband: there is a happy violence in the very swash of her signature. The bedrock of personality shows through the scrim of girlish intoxication: flushed and panting slightly, Agnes Carpenter hands the check to Colin Asch as if handing the young man her virtue, or her very life, and says very nearly the same words she'd said the first time: "But don't tell my husband, he would so strongly disapprove. That coldhearted"—and she searches for a word—"bastard."

"Of course not, Mrs. Carpenter," Colin Asch says courteously, examining the check to see that the date, the sum, the spelling are correct and the signature reasonably legible. "'Alvarado' never tells."

"I've asked you to call me Agnes, for heaven's sake!"

"Agnes, then," Colin Asch says, suddenly high with sheer simple happiness *that sometimes though not always precedes the entrance to the Blue Room,* "for heaven's sake!"

Now that the financial transaction is completed, Colin Asch is all business. When Agnes Carpenter turns as if to leave her husband's den, asking if Colin would like his drink freshened, he says quietly, "No—we have a little more business here." The check is safe in an inside pocket and the eight-inch stainless-steel switchblade knife is in his hand, opened. "Pick up the pen again and write a note to your husband," Colin Asch says, having located, in one of the messy desk drawers, a rose-tinted and -scented stationery pad with *From the desk of Agnes Carpenter* engraved at the top. There is a pause of several seconds, several long seconds, during which Agnes Carpenter stares uncomprehending at Colin Asch and at the knife he holds, its gleaming point not precisely aimed in her direction but its significance unmistakable. At last she says, hoarse, blank, "*What?*"

"I'm not going to hurt you, Agnes, you have my word on that, but like—as I said, there's more business here. Write a note to your husband. Here. On this pad here. With this pen here. 'Dear Charles.' Come *on.*"

But Agnes Carpenter continues to stare. Too shocked, too puzzled, too—oddly, even now—trusting, to be frightened. "But Colin, what are you—? What on earth is—? That knife—what *is* this? Colin? What—"

"I'll explain it all later if there's time," Colin Asch says briskly, handing her the pen, nudging her to write. "But for right now I'm requesting your cooperation: 'Dear Charles.' Write, right here. Right *now*."

"But Colin—that knife? Is that a real knife? Are you—is this—are you going to rob me? After I did so much for—"

"And now a little more, Agnes," Colin Asch says. Ah, what a model of calm, equanimity. Afterward he will record in the Blue Ledger, *XXX performed clean & ingenious & UNCONTAMINATED BY DESIRE.* He explains to the astonished woman that he isn't going to hurt her—naturally not—he doesn't want to hurt her 'cause he likes her, admires her, but he's pressed for time and will she cooperate? It isn't a robbery, no such thing, Colin Asch is above the crudeness of armed robbery, housebreaking, pillage, desecration, that sort of thing, but she had better obey his instructions since he has a complete scenario in mind—"And I'm pressed for time."

Several times Agnes Carpenter, now beginning to be frightened and, so suddenly, quite sober, asks, "Are you going to hurt me? Please—are you going to hurt me? Oh, Colin, why do you want to hurt me?" and several times, with growing impatience, Colin Asch says, baring his perfect teeth in a smile, "I don't *want* to hurt you, Agnes, that isn't my intention," and, finally, the blood beating hotly in his eyes, a sort of choking band tightening invisibly around his chest, he says, *"Take up the fucking pen, Agnes. Do as I say."*

So Agnes Carpenter takes up the pen and, as Colin Asch stands over her, begins to write, in a badly shaking, terrified or drunken hand, *Dear Charles*—but Colin Asch nudges her hand, and the pen makes a wavering skidding mark. "Start again. Do it over. This time just 'Charles.'" And as Agnes Carpenter writes *Charles*, Colin Asch again nudges her hand and spoils the second note, and Agnes Carpenter has begun to cry in helplessness and terror and, just maybe, hurt feminine pride, for she'd thought this young man had liked her, had been in an oblique way attracted to her as women of any age and any condition of physical decline or mental disorientation are led to think despite the strong counterminings of rationality.

"Thank you, Agnes," Colin Asch says quietly, taking up both notes and crumpling them and dropping them—how very mysteriously! how seemingly purposelessly!—into the wastebasket beneath the desk. "And now," he says, waving the knife as if negligently, as if it were but an extension of his hand, "now we go upstairs."

"Are you going to hurt me? Oh, Colin, please—"

"No one is going to hurt you, on that you have my word," Colin Asch says, as if speaking prepared lines, calm poised controlled at the very brink of an outburst of euphoria but knowing how to keep himself from being sucked over the brink like forestalling the moment of orgasm for as long as possible. "But we're going upstairs now, Agnes. We're taking along something to drink and we're going to continue our visit upstairs."

So Colin Asch leads his tottering hostess into the other room and loads his arms with bottles, Scotch, gin, bourbon, whatever, and he helps her forcibly up the stairs as she shifts from terror to defiance to pleading to weeping to threatening—"If you don't let me go, If *you* don't go, and go *now*, I-I-I will call the police"—and back to pleading again, which is the note upon which, mainly, her life will end: "But *why*, Colin?—how *can* you, Colin?—when I gave you more than fifteen thousand dollars; I've been so *nice* to you, Colin—"

Upstairs, briskly efficient as a film director. Colin Asch instructs Agnes Carpenter to go into her bathroom and draw water for a bath—yes and dribble in some bath salts, like that—and take off her clothes—*as if quite naturally she is going to take a bath.* When she balks he lifts the knife to her throat: "Do it, Agnes." So she does it. Obeying clumsily yet eagerly, like a frightened child, for after all Colin Asch gives the impression (no matter what his actions suggest) that he will not harm her if she follows his instructions step by step, for why should he harm her (he's behaving so rationally!) if she follows his instructions step by step? "Do it. And you have my word, I won't hurt you."

Agnes Carpenter, naked, is a piteous sight. Her stout fleshy self quivers with animal fear. And, in these awkward circumstances,

Colin Asch isn't able (as in truth he would like for *there is nothing personal about this sacrificial action, nothing contaminated with mere desire*) to glance away. Large flaccid drooping breasts…large flaccid drooping belly…creased lardy hips, thighs, buttocks…a rough patch of graying-brown pubic hair…knees oddly bruised, discolored…but the calves of the legs rather slender, and the ankles…and the small white feet, the very toes quivering with terror. *Don't hurt me.* And Colin Asch assures her, *Of course not.*

The luxurious bathroom with its lemon-yellow tiled walls and its several mirrors and its gleaming ceramic sink and oversized tub is filling up quickly with steam. There's a festive air to this, the heady scent of the Scotch (which Colin Asch urges Agnes Carpenter to drink: it will make things much easier for her), and the bath salts (it's one of the scents Susannah Hunt favors and were he a nostalgic person which of course he is not *he hasn't time* Colin Asch would recall how in the early days of their friendship he and Susannah splashed about in Susannah's oversized fake-marble tub together playful and conscienceless as children and *not once did Colin Asch fantasize killing or even humiliating the cunt*), and swaying dangerously, with Colin Asch's assistance, Agnes Carpenter manages to lower herself into the warm lapping water, and then she's settled weeping and shaking her head from side to side as if in disbelief, why why *why* has this young man turned against her, *why* is he doing this to her when she meant only well she meant to be good to be kind to be generous to open her heart to him, and now he's handing her her glass of Scotch and urging her to drink, and he has located a container chock full of Valium capsules in her medicine cabinet, and these capsules one by one he is urging her to take, to swallow down—like this, Agnes, come on—he gives the impression of an individual both plunging headlong into the future and restraining himself, under extreme duress, like a precision machine vibrating finely with energy.

For the next forty-five minutes, never hurrying the action, Colin Asch forces Agnes Carpenter to swallow down approximately fifteen tablets of Valium, and at times she resists, and at times she acquiesces, her feebly hysterical weeping now intermittent. Near the end of the siege she tries to shake herself awake, tries to open her eyes, unfocused crescents of bloodshot white, and her swollen lips move—"Let me go, don't hurt me; *why?*"—so faint Colin Asch can barely hear but he says, laying one of his gloved hands lightly atop her head, "I won't hurt you, Agnes—you won't feel a thing." Then her head rolls slack on her shoulders, her pale breasts appear to float like dead things, her mouth falls open… she is out, unconscious: breathing heavily, hoarsely.

Colin Asch, sitting on the toilet seat, sweating amid the fragrant steam, waits a few minutes longer. It is eight-thirty-five. Maybe Agnes Carpenter will cease breathing, with no violence done to her? Maybe, by herself, she will sink helplessly into the bathwater and drown?

Colin Asch doesn't want to contemplate the doomed woman too intimately. *Pity is the most destructive and the most useless of all human instincts* he'd written in the Blue Ledger years ago, after an incident long since forgotten. *Pity weakens. Pity unmans.* Hadn't Colin Asch once lost all control and run outside half naked, barefoot in the snow?

"You won't feel a thing."

The mania is almost upon him like a giant bird gripping its talons in his shoulders but how calm! how cool! how controlled! he remains. Carefully emptying bottles of liquor into the sink and running the water hard to carry the smell away then taking the bottles into Agnes Carpenter's bedroom (where in fact there is a half-empty bottle of Dewar's on the bedside table) and letting them fall where they will. The bedroom is large and luxuriously furnished like the rest of the house but in extreme disorder, bureau drawers hanging open, clothes underfoot, bed unmade, a lampshade crooked, over all a sour sickish odor. "Disgusting." It is an irony not lost upon him that, before he leaves, he will have to straighten things up a bit, for, though he intends to take one or two or three small items of a kind that won't be missed, he doesn't want the police to suspect that there was a stranger in the house, an intruder...the first thing the fuckers will look for is evidence of theft.

In the bathroom Colin Asch carefully wraps towels around both his hands and stoops over Agnes Carpenter, or over Agnes Carpenter's body—the woman is so insensible now, so comatose, it hardly seems that any spirit inhabits that flesh. But as he forces her head down into the water she begins to resist—not fighting exactly, or struggling, but tensing—and suddenly her hands rise out of the water as if to grip his, so Colin Asch releases her and steps quickly away.

"Not true violence but a death by natural causes. Or nearly."

So he waits. Patiently. A trifle impatiently. Beginning to pace about. In and out of the bathroom...in and out of the bedroom... down the stairs...where, in the living room, it occurs to him suddenly to switch on the radio. The fucking house is too *quiet.* What if Agnes Carpenter wakes up and begins screaming hysterically into that *quiet?*

Through a front window Colin Asch nervously observes the street, the sidewalk. Deserted. Peaceful. (He parked the Porsche blocks away, of course.)

It is eight-fifty. He finds himself lifting the telephone receiver, involuntarily dialing Dorothea Deverell's number. He stands listening to the ringing, the ringing, the ringing...his heartbeat pleasantly fast. As if he is in two places at one time. As if he has forgotten some danger close by. "Hello? Yes? Who is it?" Dorothea Deverell says, a little breathless. Colin Asch listens to her voice but does not speak. *I am your agent. I am Death's force.* "Hello? Is anyone there?" Dorothea Deverell asks. Even now she is composed, rather excessively formal; as if guessing that, whoever it is who has called her, he means no harm. *My love for you is beyond any love previously known to man.*

Dorothea Deverell hangs up the phone and Colin Asch thinks, Yes, good, it would be wrong to bring her into this action unprepared. XXX performed in utter solitude and dispassion.

"I will tell you sometime. There is nothing I will not tell you, sometime."

He returns the receiver to the cradle and hurries back upstairs, imagining he has heard Agnes Carpenter struggling in the bathtub but to his relief (he doesn't want violence!) she is lying slack-jawed, boneless, unconscious...and when, this time, his hands wrapped in towels, he squats over her to force her head beneath the water she no longer resists. "Yes. Like this. It will be over in a few minutes." The life seems to have gone out of her already, leaving her rubbery and docile, like a balloon; he presides over her drowning, her death, with no extraordinary difficulty, XXX performed with an almost surgical precision, holding her there for a long, long time...a long dreamy heart-pounding time. Feeling the joy of release bubbling in his veins. In his very spinal column. Sweet and explosive as sexual orgasm but cleansing. And innocent. Blameless. Shadowless.

"Didn't I promise you, Agnes? You wouldn't feel a thing."

Recorded in the Blue Ledger as *C.A. 888104am.*

> *A sensation of extreme lightness as if a weight was being removed from my chest. And I could breathe again LIKE SURFACING FROM WATER.*
>
> AND NOW FOREVER AND EVER I AM FREE! FREE TO BE GOOD! *FREE TO BEGIN MY ENTIRE LIFE OVER AGAIN PURIFIED AND BLESSED!!!*

"But Dorothea, it didn't last long this time. In the Blue Room, that good feeling—something went wrong!

"Dorothea? Something has gone wrong!"

Afterward, and in the days following, he scarcely took much interest in reading about Agnes Carpenter's death in the newspapers, for it wasn't (after all) a murder case...the police, the assholes, considered it an accident. They had found no evidence of foul play and no evidence of theft. And Charles Carpenter seemed to have believed that no one was with his wife at the time of her death and that "nothing was missing" from the house. (When of course, following his custom, Colin Asch had appropriated a memento or two. And he'd taken $130 from a surprisingly large wad of bills—$288—he'd found in Agnes Carpenter's purse.)

But the pleasure of it all seemed diminished, he didn't know why.

And there were worries about money: expenses, monthly payments.

Even with Agnes Carpenter's check for $8,500 Colin Asch didn't have enough money.

"It's all so demeaning, Dorothea."

The capitalist-imperialist society was at fault. Forcing its citizens to sell themselves on the open market, *prostitute themselves like mere meat.* Colin Asch was coming to despise all that had to do with modeling, with the exploitation of his physical being, the contamination of the spirit within.

And, by the end of April, by the first days of May, Colin Asch was in a stage in which he could barely tolerate Susannah Hunt's presence *yet dared not offend her irrevocably.*

Her voice, her air of perpetual hurt and reproach, her melting eyes, her painted nails drawn slowly and seemingly provocatively up his arm: "Colin? Honey? Don't you love me anymore? God damn you, what *is* it?"

Colin Asch shut his eyes, and kneaded her flesh, and buried himself in her, and fucked her, as best he could. He did not want to hurt her, still less did he want to kill her. Knowing well that, in such cases, the lover is always the first suspect.

"So demeaning, Dorothea!"

And the new season. Spring.

"Too much light."

12

Late in the warmly sunlit afternoon of May 8, a Sunday, Dorothea Deverell was working at the rear of her house, in her garden—if "garden" was not an overly ambitious term for so modest and circumscribed a space, in which, this spring as most springs, she intended to plant only the hardiest, most reliable of annuals—when she heard, in alarmingly rapid succession, the doorbell to the front door ringing and a hard and prolonged knocking. Her immediate sensation was fear, even dread—but there could be no more bad news, could there? so soon? Charles Carpenter was coming over, but not until six; nor would Charles Carpenter, even under extreme duress, have made such a racket at her door. Dorothea envisioned a neighbor come to inform her that her own house was on fire, or an official serving a subpoena.

She was hurrying to the front door when the knocking abruptly stopped. And when she opened the door she saw no one there.

Yet she had scarcely time to consider if it was a prank or something more urgent, for already, at her rear—calling to her through the house from where he stood on the terrace—her importunate visitor announced himself: Colin Asch. "Dorothea? I'm here, I came back here, I thought you might be back here," the young man said apologetically, and rather excitedly. "I'm sorry to disturb you. I hope I didn't scare you!"

Dorothea, who was in fact quite shaken and annoyed but supposed she would readily recover, said, "No, Colin, of course not," not seeing at first as they approached each other to shake hands in greeting that Colin Asch looked distinctly odd: his smile stiff and excessive, his forehead creased, his eyes moist and blinking and narrowed as if the sunlight blinded him. "Of course not, Colin," she said, as if a conventional femininity (in which the perhaps bolder accents of femaleness did not obtrude) obliged her to tell lies, to put others at their ease.

"I thought maybe you'd be out back, just not answering your door 'cause it's Sunday or something," Colin said, shaking Dorothea's hand—in fact, squeezing it, hard—and fixing her a look in which subtle reproach and forgiveness contended. "Or maybe somebody else was here. But there's nobody here? Or is somebody coming over? Later, I mean? You can tell me: just be direct. *I'll leave if I'm not welcome*."

Dorothea saw to her mild surprise that her young friend was carrying a duffel bag of remarkable shabbiness slung over his shoulder, and that his clothes, though no doubt "fashionable" in the new aggressive style she made no effort to comprehend, were strangely rumpled, even creased, as if he had been sleeping in them. A metallic blond stubble glinted on his jaws, which had, as he continued to smile, a predatory thickness to them Dorothea had not previously registered; a bluish vein, wormlike, angry, defined itself prominently in the center of his forehead. His eyes *were* alarmingly moist—was he about to cry? Or had he in fact been crying? Dorothea, sensing an emergency, her instinct for maternal solicitude immediately aroused, assured Colin Asch that no one was expected for some time and that in any case he was welcome, of course. "Please sit down," Dorothea said, "and tell me what's wrong."

"How do you know—why do you *think*—something is wrong?" Colin Asch challenged her.

"You seem so—"

"You *know* something is wrong," Colin Asch said reprovingly, letting his duffel bag fall at his feet, "so why ask?" But he sat on Dorothea's sofa heavily, as if suddenly exhausted, his shoulders hunched and his head lowered, turning his head in jerky little tics from side to side as if he were trying to ease its stiffness. Dorothea could hear him panting and seemed to sense, from a distance of several feet, the powerful emanations of heat that rose from him. Even as she ventured to take a seat in a chair facing him Colin Asch got abruptly to his feet, as if too restless to remain in one place. "You left this open," he muttered; he strode to the terrace door, and shoved it shut, and locked it. Then, for a brief moment, he stood at the plate glass window staring out. What did he see? Did he see anything? Beyond the young man's tall, rangy, somehow electrified figure the solace and simplicity of Dorothea Deverell's garden—the evergreens and newly leafed deciduous trees, the whitish slanted sunshine itself—seemed now remote, inaccessible. Something terrible has happened, Dorothea Deverell thought. And I am involved.

Yet with reasonable calmness she asked, "Colin, what *is* it? Please tell me."

"Oh, I think you know," he said quietly.

"What, Colin? I didn't quite hear."

"I think you know, Dorothea."

"Know? Know what?"

He rattled the handle of the terrace door, saying, "This is the kind of lock that burglars can force easily. It isn't a *safe* or a *smart* kind of lock."

He returned to Dorothea's sofa and sat, again heavily, sighing, belling out his cheeks, in a juvenile expression of extreme fatigue. But his skin was flushed with excitation; there were slight tremors in both his eyelids. With increasing uneasiness Dorothea waited for him to explain himself but instead he made a desultory show of examining books on her coffee table—a gigantic *Matisse* with hundreds of color plates a well-worn paperback of Montaigne's *Essays*. (Dorothea had brought the Montaigne back with her from Vermont but had never quite finished reading it.) Colin frowned over the *Essays*; said, with no transition, "Except for today, I mean—this morning—not *that*; *that* was only a mistake." He paused, watching Dorothea. "The other two, I mean."

Dorothea said, swallowing, "I'm afraid I don't understand, Colin."

"Don't you!" he laughed. Then: "Who did you say was coming here today? You said somebody's coming? Is it Carpenter? *Him?* When is he coming?"

"At—at five."

"*Is* it Carpenter?"

Dorothea winced inwardly at the name, so unceremoniously uttered. "Charles Carpenter, yes."

"He's coming at *five?*"

For a long strained moment Colin Asch stared at Dorothea as if he were trying to determine whether she lied or spoke the truth. Dorothea was beginning to be seriously alarmed. He has hurt someone, she thought. Or someone has hurt him.

"*He's* a friend of mine too but he doesn't know it," Colin Asch said slowly. "He thinks—I can sense that he thinks—he doesn't like me."

"Of course Charles—"

"He doesn't *know* me. He's *prejudiced.*"

"Oh, but I don't think—"

"But you're my friend, Dorothea, aren't you? and I can trust you?"

"Of course, Colin, you must know by—"

"You can trust *me.*"

"Yes?"

Seeing Colin Asch's look of bravado and hurt Dorothea Deverell felt a sudden urge to go to him, to lay a hand on his overheated forehead and brush his damp hair from his eyes. How unlike his usual composed self he appeared, how raw-edged, how without defenses! Yet she was not so forthright a person; she remained seated, fixed in place, staring, in dread and fascination.

"No, I have to modify that, I'd have to say that you are my only friend, Dorothea," Colin Asch said, shaking his head gravely. "Not Charles Carpenter. Not now, and maybe never. And I don't trust him—how the fuck could I trust him—he's a lawyer, isn't he? And a lawyer is an officer of the court, isn't he? Isn't that his allegiance?"

"Colin, dear, please—you're frightening me," Dorothea Deverell said. She would have risen from her chair but she seemed to know that the sudden movement would upset him; and she had after all nowhere specific to go. "Can't you tell me what has—"

"Dorothea, I'm just not *happy!*" he said petulantly. "For years, in school, I was the good boy, the 'little angel,' the superachiever, and now, headed for thirty, I'm getting frankly *tired*—I mean spiritually and morally and not just physically *tired*—fucking *tired*. This constant pressure to excel, to claw my way to the top. Competing with people who might be friends, forced into savage competition like you are in a mercenary society like ours—it's invariably the shitty end of the stick for someone who's sensitive. I know you probably don't feel it, Dorothea, you're different—you've always been different; you hold yourself above such things —but *I* feel it—Christ, do *I* feel it!"

Dorothea said, inspired, "Did you quit your job, Colin?"

"Yes," Colin Asch said vehemently. "I quit my job."

"But—so soon?"

"Quit Elite Models—'Elite Models'!—Friday morning in the midst of a big-deal shoot! Told them all to go fuck and just—quit. Walked away."

"But, Colin, I thought you—"

"No, I never liked it, Dorothea: I loathed it. Peddling my flesh like I was some kind of—meat or a prostitute, or something. I saw the look in your eyes when you examined the photographs, Dorothea, I *saw*; it was for that revelation I came." He paused, breathing hard; he was rummaging through the duffel bag at his feet, Dorothea could not imagine what connection there might be between the young man's fierce contemptuous words and his pawing about in the duffel bag, but she sat watching, fascinated. He has hurt someone, she thought calmly. It is for that reason he has come to me.

"Y'know this Roman emperor Caligula, Dorothea?" Colin said conversationally. "My teacher Mr. Kreuzer—Mr. Kreuzer was headmaster of the school but he taught English too—he told us how Caligula said he regretted 'the world didn't have a single neck so he could strangle it'—*wild!* That stayed with me all these years: 'a single neck so he could strangle it.' I know you won't agree—you're so *good*, so *nice*—but that's the way a lot of people feel a lot of the time. Winding up invariably with the shitty end of the stick year after year."

And then he spread out on the carpet the several items he

wanted Dorothea Deverell to see and was gazing expectantly up at her, his pale eyelashes trembling and his eyes brimming with moisture. In that instant Colin Asch reminded Dorothea Deverell of her mother's father, elderly, partly paralyzed, aphasiac after a severe stroke, gazing up at her from his hospital bed with his single sighted eye and waiting with intense excitement for her response.

A pair of man's gold cuff links, a smart new-looking man's leather wallet, a square-cut jade dinner ring edged with small diamonds—how could Dorothea respond? What could these items possibly mean? "My treasure, Dorothea," Colin Asch said, lightly mocking "for *you*."

The beautiful dinner ring, so large as to resemble costume jewelry, did look teasingly familiar to Dorothea; the other things meant nothing at all. She smiled uncertainly at Colin Asch as if this were a mere game: a riddle, perhaps. "But Colin, what are they? Whose are they?"

Still lightly mocking, Colin Asch said, "You know, Dorothea."

"But Colin, I—"

"Don't you?"

Dorothea Deverell, on the verge of exasperation, spread her fingers wide, helpless. "Colin, I'm afraid I don't. *I don't know*."

Is there an authentic premonitory instinct, Dorothea Deverell would afterward wonder, or do we simply fill in the spaces of our ignorance retrospectively, claiming a superior wisdom where there was only—ignorance?

It was true, she had thought intermittently of young Colin Asch often that winter, and well into spring; she had brooded in her customarily inconclusive way upon certain actions of his, and certain enigmatic remarks ("Oh, you'd recognize me, Dorothea—you and I would know each other anywhere"), and had been haunted by, if not indeed frankly baffled by, certain postures and assumptions, granted even the profundity of her involvement with Charles Carpenter and with his grief and distress over his wife's death.

(Weeks after the accidental drowning it was the rude shock of its initial pronouncement that lingered, still, in Dorothea Deverell's imagination, possessed of the nearly cryptesthetic power to arouse in her, at weak, unguarded moments, a paralyzing sense of guilt and shame.) Yet she would have to confess that she had not thought of Colin Asch in any exact, any *real*, relation to herself; she would have said that she did not think of the unique young man in any exact relation with anyone at all—not excluding Ginny Weidmann, his very blood kin. For surely there was something innocently transitory about him? For all the blond, muscular, sinewy *physicalness* of his person, something fleeting and insubstantial? To which the words "fickle" or "shallow" or "unreliable" or "uncontrolled" did not in all fairness apply?

How very strange Dorothea Deverell thought it, that having expressed such childlike delight in his "position" at the Institute, Colin Asch had twice failed to show up for meetings in April; what news she had of him, from Ginny Weidmann, was scattered and vague. She had the impression of a life being rapidly lived, too rapidly, perhaps; but it was not *her* life, and she had no right, certainly she had not the requisite knowledge, to pass judgment. For, involved with Charles Carpenter as she was, and more in love with him than ever before, she simply did not have time to think about Colin Asch, still less to worry about him. Since that peculiar episode when, unbidden, the young man had dropped by Dorothea's house to show her those amazing photographs of himself as a model, she had heard very little of him, or from him: and had not sought him out. Maybe later, in another year, when she and Charles Carpenter were in some way settled, "established"... maybe at that time, if Charles were willing, she might befriend young Colin more attentively: invite him for dinner, include him in gatherings, help to advance and promote him. Until then, her own life and her own work claimed all her energies. And what was Colin Asch but a being *sui generis*, of no age precisely, speaking with no discernible American accent, possessed seemingly of no background, no personal history? "He is a will-o'-the-wisp," Dorothea Deverell decided, as if she were affixing a label to a work of art and having done with it.

She did not consider that in fact she had no clear idea of what a "will-o'-the-wisp" actually was; it was the lightness, the musicality of the term, that charmed her.

Now Colin Asch sat on her sofa, smiling, watching Dorothea Deverell with moist glittering eyes, informing her in a matter-of-fact voice that he had killed both Roger Krauss and Agnes Carpenter—and he'd done it for her. As her agent. In her name.

"Not that they didn't deserve it, Dorothea," Colin Asch added, with a derisive twist of his lips. "They did! Him especially! It was a *pleasure*, with him! The son of a bitch!"

And Dorothea, bathed in cold as if a glacial wind had penetrated the walls of her snug little stone house, simply stared at him, her mind blank with growing horror. "What—what did you say?" she several times asked in a whisper. She could not believe Colin Asch's words yet knew, as if a lock were clicking into place, that they must be true. She knew—yet could not believe. This so very kind so very generous so very warm and affectionate and sympathetic young man—a killer?

What had Charles Carpenter called him? A psychopath.

Yet Dorothea said faintly, blunderingly, "I don't believe it, it isn't possible."

And Colin Asch said, as if reprovingly, "Look Dorothea, there's nothing to discuss. I mean like, what's there to *debate*? They weren't the first people I've killed and I doubt they'll be the last. You know what Shelley said of himself: 'I go my way like a sleepwalker....I go until I am stopped and I never *am* stopped.' Sure! It's like that! If you cover your tracks, if you're reasonably careful and brainy—who's to catch you? The police don't know that much, they work with probabilities and not possibilities...*probabilities* not *possibilities*. You supply them with some clues that fit together—with a baffle, some little story they can tell themselves—they fall for it every time; you know why?" He smiled so broadly at Dorothea, his lower face seemed nearly split in two. " 'Cause they're human! They want to believe that things add up, make sense, come neatly together. There's never any motive for any single thing Colin Asch does that anyone could calculate, which is why nobody will ever catch Colin Asch—nobody."

"But why—"

"These things I brought you, they're mementos, the ring especially—take it, try it on! Like I said, there's nothing for us to *debate;* it isn't a matter of *talk.*" Colin Asch kicked the ring in Dorothea's direction—it rolled along the carpet toward her chair. His action was the most wayward, abrupt, and unexpected that Dorothea Deverell had ever encountered in him; she couldn't help flinching. He said, as if confidentially, "The weird thing is, Dorothea—I mean this really makes you believe in destiny, karma—the thing is I picked out that ring in five minutes, at Aunt Ginny's that night, y'know, when she made me join you people and sit at the table; there I was in your presence, Dorothea, without knowing you, and there I was looking at a woman's big fancy glamorous dinner ring, without knowing *her*, but sort of guessing I'd get that ring one day, one day I'd slip it into my pocket—Colin Asch restoring a little balance to the world. Go on, Dorothea: try it on."

Dorothea was staring at the ring at her feet—a square-cut jade stone edged with small diamonds, in a white gold setting. It was exquisitely beautiful. She could not bear its lying like that on the floor; she picked it up, turned it in her trembling fingers. Yes, it was Agnes Carpenter's; she remembered it now. "But how, Colin, did you get it?"

"Took it."

"Yes, but how?"

"Out of her bureau. In the bedroom. A fancy little jewelry box with a lock that wasn't locked—the ring was the only thing I wanted." He sighed and squirmed about on the sofa, as if with irrepressible energy. "Though Christ!—I could use the money."

Dorothea swallowed. "I mean, Colin," she said carefully, "how did you get it? How did you get the opportunity? I don't understand:

this is Agnes Carpenter's ring, and Agnes Carpenter is dead; she died by—"

"She didn't die: I killed her."

"You—killed her?"

"I *told* you, Dorothea," Colin Asch said, making a snorting noise, bemused, dismayed, and slapping both hands against the sofa. "I *told* you I killed her, and I killed the other one—who else was there to do it? Your boyfriend Carpenter? Like hell!"

"But I can't—"

"No need to look at me like that, Dorothea, it wasn't any special effort. I mean, it was easy—it's always been *easy.* What's so fucking hard is"—and here his voice dipped, and his face took on an expression of simple regret—"this sort of life here, that you have—this sort of daily life, *living* it, making sense of it as you go along or maybe not making any special sense of it but just—going along. *That's* hard. The other is *easy.*"

"You are telling me, Colin, that you actually—killed?"

"Sure! Why not? People get killed all the time, don't they—somebody's got to do it!" He laughed, as if he'd said something extravagant and witty. "Once I get the idea figured out it isn't difficult to execute it. Like, you know, making up your own movie or play in your head. Everything that exists in civilization, Dorothea," he said, tapping his forehead, "comes from in here—the human brain. Once you get the idea, the rest comes naturally. But the idea, first—that's the trick. That's genius."

Dorothea laid the jade ring carefully on the coffee table. The gold cuff links and the leather wallet remained where Colin Asch had deposited them. She was blinking rapidly, for her eyes were filling with tears of shock and disbelief. *Was* she in shock? Her hands and her feet had gone icy cold, the interior of her mouth extraordinarily dry; she feared that, if she got to her feet, she might faint; yet she had to get to her feet. She had to get away from Colin Asch—had to go for help.

But it was Colin who rose, fairly leaping to his feet. "I'm dying of thirst!" He went out into Dorothea's kitchen; she heard him open and shut the refrigerator door. Somehow, on tottering legs, she followed him, a terrible roaring in her ears, her vision nearly gone. "This is delicious—just what I need!" Colin said happily, drinking orange juice directly from the quart bottle. He stood, head back, legs spread, emptying the bottle.

Dorothea felt rather than saw the floor rise swiftly toward her; there was a sharp cracking blow against the side of her head. She'd lost consciousness for what could not have been more than a split second—then woke, lying on the dining room carpet, her head ringed with pain, while Colin Asch crouched over her. Repeatedly, he uttered her name, begged her to be all right. "Don't die, Dorothea! Don't *die!*" He ran into the kitchen to dampen a towel to press against her face. When she was sitting up and had more or less recovered, he said, repentantly, "It's my fault. I upset you, I guess. You're a sensitive woman—I should have known."

He helped her into the kitchen, where she sat, sat and stared at him: stunned, perplexed, rather blank. What had he been telling her? That he'd killed two people, or more? That he was a killer. He—her friend? Her friend Colin Asch? She thought, I must telephone the police. I must get help. It had not yet occurred to her that she was in the presence of a dangerous man.

Nor did he seem to her mad. He was pacing about the kitchen talking excitedly but lucidly, berating himself for his "insensitivity" and then, in the next breath, declaring that "it couldn't be helped" —Dorothea had to *know* because she had to *help him.* (But what was he expecting, Dorothea wondered. What did he want of her?) If his manner was extravagant, histrionic, hadn't it always been so? The brass clamp flashed in his ear as his eyes flashed, and his quick nervous smile; the heat that almost palpably radiated from him might have been mere high spirits, energy, the hyperkinesia of youth. Dorothea said, "You didn't really, Colin, did you? What you said—"

"Didn't really *what?*"

"—Agnes Carpenter, and Roger Krauss—"

"Yeah? What?"

"Didn't—*kill?*"

The very word stuck in Dorothea Deverell's throat.

Colin Asch regarded her with bemused eyes. She saw that his face was angular and lean, the bones of the cheeks, brows, and forehead far more prominent than she remembered. He had lost weight—too much weight. His face gleamed with perspiration like anger, and his striped sports shirt was soaked through beneath his arms. "What did you want me to say, Dorothea? No? Is that what you want to hear—no?"

"Just—tell me the truth."

"OK: the truth is yes."

"But—why?"

"I told you, Dorothea: for you."

"For me?"

"For *you*. But also, like, 'cause I wanted to—Colin Asch never does anything that isn't *ordained*."

"But I don't understand," Dorothea said gropingly. "You have come here today to tell me—"

"I've come here today to tell you that I'm not *happy* the way I deserve, that things are *fucked up*, that I need your help, Dorothea—your *advice* and *consolation!*" he said in a high plaintive voice. "I need some sign from you that things are all right. That, you know, things are—in place again."

"In place?"

"Like you said once about appetite, people doing what they have to do, like carnivores and their victims—I forget the exact words; I have them written down—it was a way of explaining, it made sense. And you looked at me too like you knew me, you recognized me. And I recognized you."

He fell silent, contemplating Dorothea Deverell; Dorothea could only shut her eyes. She tried to comprehend: If Colin Asch were a murderer and if he were confessing two of his crimes to her, did that mean that a murderer was confessing to her—to Dorothea Deverell? And, if so, did that mean she must bear witness against him?

But I am his only friend, she thought.

She said, with more resolve than she felt, "But, Colin, you must know that I will have to inform the police. If what you say is true—"

"The police? You think so? Yeah?"

"—there seems to have been a terrible, tragic misunderstanding, and I—"

"Nobody's informing the police of anything, Dorothea," Colin Asch said matter-of-factly. "It's got nothing to do with them; they're completely at a distance. It's got nothing to do with Krauss and Mrs. Carpenter either, much—it's just between you and me. Which you knew all along."

"But—"

Colin shouted her down: *"Which you knew all along!"*

Dorothea flinched as he went to the telephone and knocked the receiver off the hook. In an instant he was enraged, out of control. "You're not telling the police and you're not telling anyone! I'd have to kill us both right now, right here, and I'm not fucking ready!"

After several seconds the telephone began to emit a series of harmless warning beeps; then went silent.

How silent, indeed, Sunday afternoons were, in the leafy cul-de-sac at the end of Marten Lane!

Dorothea thought, So that is his plan.

She thought, So Charles and I will never marry after all.

She'd begun to cry without quite knowing it. Colin Asch said sullenly, "We'd better go." When he went into the living room, to retrieve his duffel bag perhaps, Dorothea decided to make a run for it—thinking, in her desperation, she might go next door, scream at her neighbors to call the police—but of course Colin Asch easily caught her: she'd barely gotten out the side door, would have had to grope her way through the darkened garage to another, outer door. Hurt, fierce, incredulous, Colin Asch cried, "I knew it! *Now I can't trust you either!"*

His grip on Dorothea was surprisingly strong, practical, not in the least hesitant. Dorothea, struggling, weeping, felt his warm moist breath like a dog's against her face and smelled the harsh acrid odor of his perspiration. For the first time the fact of the young man's physical self, his sexuality, struck her.

"We'd better go," he said. "Before Carpenter comes. 'Cause I *am* ready for him."

Seemingly out of nowhere Colin Asch had drawn a pistol. It had a long smooth barrel and a handsome carved wooden handle, like a work of art.

So, at 4:50 P.M. of Sunday, May 8, began what would be Dorothea Deverell's nearly one hundred hours of terror: though "terror" as such, with its intense, visceral, adrenaline-charged distress, could hardly be sustained for so prolonged a period of time. Afterward, contemplating the wild, doomed flight on which Colin Asch took her, Dorothea would recall feeling alternately resigned and fatalistic as if, in a sense, she were already dead and merely enacting a prescribed role; and alternately hopeful, even optimistic—as, perhaps, condemned prisoners feel, anticipating the reprieve they know cannot come.

Before they left Dorothea Deverell's house, Colin Asch forced her to go upstairs to her bedroom so that she could change her clothes; it was his idea that they would be less readily identified if they looked like two men. That was the first baffle, he said. (Dorothea believed the word was "baffle" but did not inquire.) So, trembling, biting her lip to keep from crying, Dorothea Deverell, her captor close by, changed from the attractive clothes she had so deliberately put on earlier that day—a beige pleated skirt in light wool, a hand-decorated wool-and-cotton sweater—into navy blue rayon slacks, and an old gardening shirt, and an old sweater. Colin Asch insisted that she pin up her hair and wear a hat, and to this too Dorothea acquiesced, though the only suitable hat was a very old mothball-reeking green angora cap she'd worn one winter to keep her ears warm and forgot she still owned. Take whatever you need, Colin Asch instructed, having gallantly located one of Dorothea's suitcases and holding it open for her—underclothes, socks, another shirt and another sweater, toiletries—then he led her into her study where he insisted she bring along some books and "things you're working on—you might not be back for a long time." In the kitchen he loaded several grocery bags with food from Dorothea's cupboards and refrigerator, whistling as he did so, exclaiming to himself, not unlike a boy about to embark upon an outdoor adventure. How innocent he seems, Dorothea thought, in wonderment. The long-barreled pistol was stuck, with rakish insouciance, in his belt.

"OK! Great! Let's go!" he said.

Not the black Porsche but another automobile entirely awaited them in Dorothea Deverell's driveway (later to be identified as Susannah Hunt's 1988 Audi, though outfitted with license plates from the Porsche: Mrs. Hunt would be found dead, strangled, in her bed in her Normandy Court condominium), its rear seat and trunk partly filled with Colin Asch's things, but there was space for Dorothea's too. Handing her the keys Colin told her she should be the first to drive. "It will be more practical for me to drive after dark." He spoke with a husbandly solicitude.

And, later, when he took over the wheel for a long siege of driving—by that time they were well into New Hampshire, on northwest-bound Route 89—he extracted from Dorothea the promise that she would not try to escape from the car by doing anything crazy or reckless like opening her door while they were in motion, nor would she make signals at people in other cars; if she involved others, Colin warned her, he'd be forced to shoot them dead: "You'd be signing their death warrants, Dorothea."

So she obeyed. Rather like a zombie, or a robot.

Thinking repeatedly, this can't be happening…such things do not happen to people like us.

It seemed like a very long time before they stopped for what remained of the night. Somewhere, Dorothea had the groggy idea, in upstate New York, in a desolate wooded area off the expressway. Colin Asch, unable to stay awake any longer, positioned himself to sleep with his arm around Dorothea's shoulders and his head resting hard against hers, so that he would be immediately wakened if she tried to slip free. That way, there was no escaping him, even in sleep. Even in the fitful, twitchy, hallucinatory bouts of sleep to which each succumbed.

"Won't you please reconsider?" Dorothea Deverell was not quite begging but speaking quietly, practicably "I'm sure that allowances might be made if you haven't been well, if you've been"—she hesitated to say the word "hospitalized"; now driving the Audi, her eyes aching with the light as if she'd been ill, she scarcely dared glance over at Colin Asch, her captor—"not *well.* I mean, if you have a history of—of episodes."

Colin Asch, arms folded, lying back in the passenger's seat with his head against the window in a sullen sort of pose, merely grunted.

"I would tell them how considerate you've been of me," Dorothea said carefully, wetting her lips, "how you haven't"—and again she hesitated, not wanting to say the word "hurt"—"haven't threatened me"—though this was not quite true: he'd threatened her after all. In a desperate little plea she concluded, "But you're so intelligent, Colin! You must know the police will pick us up soon!"

"A lot of things can happen, Dorothea, before that happens."

They stopped for gas. They stopped at a truckers' restaurant where Colin, pistol inside his shirt, bought hot food, coffee. They stopped on a lookout point—a "scenic site"—in the Adirondack Mountains not many miles from the Canadian border. Dorothea's mind worked swiftly and with seeming proficiency but to no purpose. She would signal someone (at a gas station, at a restaurant, beside the road, in another car) to get help; she would escape from her captor (perhaps wrestling with him for the gun); she would call attention to them, or to the car, in some way: the same few thoughts repeating endlessly, to no purpose. She thought of Charles Carpenter, who had by now come to her house and found it empty—her car still in the garage but some of her clothes and possessions missing, food missing from the kitchen. Would he know? But how would he know? And when he called the police how would they know? Several times she broke down, sobbing, near-hysterical, and Colin Asch said, rubbing his own eyes roughly with a fist, "Just don't give *in*, for Christ's sake."

As if, Dorothea thought, amazed, their predicaments were identical; they were united in their desperation to escape.

It had been Colin Asch's bold intention to cross the Canadian border into Quebec, but each time they approached the customs and immigration checkpoints—at Trout River and Hogansburg, in New York, and at Derby Line, Vermont—he changed his mind; wisely, no doubt, for by this time there must be a police alert out for them, or for their car. (Dorothea did not know that Susannah Hunt was dead but Colin had told her that the car was registered in Mrs. Hunt's name.) On this protracted giddy headachy second day of flight they drove in wayward looping circles, so far as Dorothea could judge, mainly along narrow mountain roads, where dusk came prematurely and brought a feathery barrage of snowflakes. "This is madness, Colin," Dorothea said. "We simply can't keep this up."

Colin Asch yawned brutally and said, "You want to stop, then? You're ready?"

At least, she thought, Charles has been spared.

But Colin Asch's mood was rather more nervous, petulant, and distracted than murderous; he drove along ever-narrowing roads, turning up forks, reconsidering, backing out again, as if guided by instinct; bringing them at last to a deserted lakeside area of cottages and lodges, Glace Lake the name. Was this near the place where his parents died? Dorothea wondered.

At the far end of a rutted lane was a lodge of weatherized logs in mock-Swiss chalet style; a shingle above its front door announced LAND'S END. As Dorothea Deverell, reeling with exhaustion, stepped out into the freezing air, it struck her as the most bitter sort of irony that she might very well die here.

Colin Asch adroitly forced a door at the rear of the house and let himself in and came to the front door, where, not having moved an inch, Dorothea awaited him. She'd begun to cough helplessly.

She was on the verge of illness: a raw burning ache had established itself in her throat, and she felt the early symptoms of bronchitis. Almost shyly, apologetically, Colin said, "OK, Dorothea, come inside! I'll unload the car. Maybe you can find a hurricane lamp or something."

"Yes," Dorothea said tonelessly.

She came stumblingly inside the unfamiliar house where the long-confined air, smelling of dirt and damp, was as cold as outside. A cruel parody of a homecoming, she thought. A parody of a honeymoon.

Fearing a caretaker at Glace Lake, Colin hid the car somewhere to the rear of the house and shrouded the windows; smoke from the chimney was unavoidable—he had to start a fire in the fireplace. (The gas stove in the kitchen was disconnected; the electricity was turned off.) Clumsily, her fingers stiff, Dorothea prepared a makeshift sort of meal for them, using the fireplace. It was sobering, how ferociously hungry each of them was—no matter the metallic taste of the soup, heated in a stained saucepan, or the bread's staleness. They devoured hunks of cheese, slices of turkey breast, raw carrots. Like animals, Dorothea thought, feeding.

Then she slept close beside the fireplace, or tried to, in a kind of delirium; her teeth chattering with cold, misery, simple dread of what was to come; waking to spasms of coughing and pain in her throat and chest. Her captor was too excited to sleep—he'd boasted that he needed no more than three or four hours of sleep for every twenty-four—he spent much of the night (Dorothea gathered) prowling about the house with a flashlight; then, near dawn, she woke with a start to a pressure on her leg—and there was Colin Asch, curled up innocent as a child, or a large dog, heavily asleep on the floor close by her with his face pressed against the calf of her right leg. His pale beard glinted like silver, his mouth was slack, his breath moist and gurgling.... Dorothea hugged herself in the frowsy-smelling blanket Colin Asch had located for her in one of the closets and stared at her captor, her friend, her former friend; whom after all she had never known. Colin Asch was mad, but what *was* "mad"? That the young man had evidently killed two quite innocent people, and for a purpose he could not explain; that he felt not the slightest twinge of remorse, or, indeed, full consciousness of his actions; that he fervently believed Dorothea Deverell's life and fate were inextricably bound up with his own: these were mere facts that lay upon the surface of his being like the fact that he had blond hair, brown eyes, a strong-boned angular face. Such facts described but did not define him.

In the morning a chill glowering sunshine penetrated the coverings Colin had affixed over the windows; with the return of day, or daylight, a sense of ever deeper malaise overtook Dorothea Deverell. As, noisy, ebullient, whistling to himself in a display of cheery high spirits, Colin prepared breakfast, Dorothea made little effort to help; she was sick and would be getting sicker: her limbs stiff, tears dried in her eyes. She could not imagine what she looked like, what desperation flickered feebly in her face; nor did she care. She wondered why, during the night, she had not taken advantage of the darkness and fled.... Surely Colin Asch would not shoot her in the back? Surely that was not to be her fate at his hands?

That day, intermittently, when she dared, Dorothea tried to engage Colin Asch in conversation, frankly pleaded with him. What did he hope to accomplish, hiding out here in the mountains? How long could they endure it? What did he intend to do next—or if they were discovered? Colin Asch told her airily that he was sorry things had turned out exactly as they had. "But, Dorothea, after all, none of this is my *fault*." In a tone of mild reproach he told her that he would have continued on his way, back in November, pursuing another phase of his life, if it hadn't been for her—"Like there was a promise you made to me, Dorothea. That first night."

"Promise? I don't understand."

"Yes, Dorothea. You do."

Colin removed the coverings from the windows, and opened the rear door of the house, but did not leave the house at all; nor did he allow Dorothea to do so. He was jumpy, apprehensive, breaking off in the middle of a sentence to cock his head and listen: was it a loon on the lake? an airplane passing high overhead? a chain saw in the distance? a scrambling, as of squirrels, in the eaves? He fingered the pistol, checked the bullets in the revolving cylinder, laid the barrel alongside his nose as if in a parody of contemplation, strode about with the gun loosely stuck in his belt. Dorothea eyed it, thinking: Am I required to try to take it from him and use it against him? Is that expected of me? There was no vision of Dorothea Deverell, no extravagant cinematic daydream, in which, for even a fleeting moment, she could imagine such an act: she no more wanted to shoot Colin Asch than she wanted to be shot by him.

Colin squatted on his heels in front of a ramshackle bookshelf, pulling out and leafing idly through old copies of *National Geographic*, *Audubon*, *Arizona Highways*. There were United States and world atlases; an incomplete set of *Collier's Encyclopedia.* He told Dorothea in a dreamy voice that he'd always been fascinated by maps and travel. Maybe he was Marco Polo, reincarnated! "If I had my life to relive that's all I would do, I think—get in motion, and stay in motion—let momentum carry me. And you could do the same, Dorothea! Evil begins with stopping: with entropy."

From time to time during that long hallucinatory day and the next, Dorothea was uneasily aware of Colin Asch regarding her in silence; she perceived, with a despondent heart, that he was contemplating her death. Hers, and perhaps his own: murder and suicide. Was that not romantic? Was that not the logical end to their story? As if merely conversationally, Colin Asch said, "My book here—I'm going to be writing in it soon. I have to think what I mean to say 'cause there isn't a lot of time, you know? You could write in it too, if you wanted. I mean at the end. The last pages."

"Is it a journal?" Dorothea asked.

"It's my life. In words."

The notebook was oversized and substantial, with badly worn blue-gray covers: a kind of account book, or ledger. Colin was not precisely offering it to Dorothea (who did not in any case want to touch it), but he leafed through it in such a way that she could see some of the pages: tight, condensed passages of script, lines that were presumably poetry, sections meticulously crossed out in bands of black ink. Stroking the pale stubble on his jaws he said dreamily, "What I want to do is bring it up to date. Up to the present hour. From a perspective, you know, of great distance. Like God looking down." Dorothea murmured a vague soft assent but drew no nearer. "You couldn't read it, actually, most of the pages," Colin said apologetically. "It's in code."

"Ah, yes, I see—code," Dorothea said.

"To keep the fuckers from sticking their noses in my business," Colin said, smiling bitterly. "After my death."

The interior of the lodge was furnished in a spare yet slapdash manner, the large main room in particular: there were dusty old woven "Navajo" rugs laid upon the floor, and mismatched stained furniture, and lamps with torn shades, but, here and there, substantial and attractive items like the Shaker-style rocking chair in which Dorothea sat and the long narrow churchly-looking table at which Colin Asch sat for hours, writing in his notebook, alternately rapidly, as if he were inspired, and then very slowly. For long dreamy periods he simply gazed out the window (he was seated in such a position as to have a clear view of the lane, and the lake) or in Dorothea's direction. We are a grotesque parody of domesticity, Dorothea thought, but of what sort of domesticity *is* the parody?

She seemed to know that, if she survived, she would remember this interlude for the remainder of her life: not the episodes of confusing action and violence (for she understood that violence was unavoidable) but this protracted and seemingly idyllic scene in which, only a few yards away, her young blond captor Colin Asch sat brooding over his notebook like an unusually intense schoolboy immersed in his lesson. Outside the day was slowly warming; the air smelled wetly of spring and of plenitude. In the Scotch pines that ringed the house, jays called to one another in urgent, throaty, liquid notes, a spring song that, to Dorothea's ear, had always the sound of bubbles musically ascending.

Colin Asch read to Dorothea Deverell a stanza of a poem of Shelley's he had transcribed, he said, eleven years before, "Never guessing how I'd be reading it to *you, today!*" It was not a stanza Dorothea immediately recognized, nor could she in all honesty have attributed it to Shelley, for she had neither read nor thought of Shelley's poetry in months.

> "'*The everlasting universe of things*
> *Flows through the mind, and rolls its rapid waves,*
> *Now dark—now glittering—now reflecting gloom—*
> *Now lending splendor, where from secret springs*
> *The source of human thought its tribute brings—*'"

Colin Asch's voice trailed off as if this were not in fact the end of the stanza but a weariness had passed over him suddenly, touching Dorothea Deverell as well. And outside, in the pines, the jays continued to sing.

In all there would be four days of captivity; it would end, and end abruptly, in the late afternoon of May 11. But almost immediately Dorothea Deverell began to lose her sense of time and of spatial distance, as one whose proprioceptive instinct is dislodged loses all sense of the body's unique and indefinable territoriality. Or as the web of memory itself is altered by the mildest of brain lesions.

It seemed to her in her weakened emotional state that Charles Carpenter's love should have had a greater power to protect her. But it was distant, and its force hourly ebbing. She thought, I am alone.

Except for my captor.

She was sick: wrapped in her frowsy blanket though it was midday and May. From childhood she'd had respiratory illnesses of varying degrees of severity, and certain symptoms frightened her, for they might signal a headlong plunge into fevers, wracking chills, convulsive coughing spells. Her lungs were congesting, and her chest felt as if an invisible band were slowly tightening around it. Her eyes watered with tears of hurt and indignation.

But she was watching (and could not help but admire) Colin Asch on the floor in front of the fireplace doing push-ups—how rapidly!—how like a slightly frenzied machine!—as the little blue vein defined itself ever more palpably in his forehead and his face grew visibly hotter, ruddier. He counted ninety before stopping. And then he did sit-ups; fingers linked at the nape of his neck, elbows expertly swung around to touch his knees in an alternating pattern. And then—as if his mad energy could in no other way be contained—he jumped up and, panting, glistening with sweat, chinned himself on the doorframe. Though he was so thin that his ribs showed through his damp T-shirt, the muscles of his shoulders, arms, and back appeared hard and prominent. "...twenty-eight, twenty-nine, *thirty!*"

Performing for Dorothea Deverell but never so much as casting a single glance in her direction.

In plain view, atop the table, lay the long-barreled revolver.

Dorothea, eyeing it, thought, I must make the effort. She calculated there were six feet separating her and the gun; and that, when Colin was distracted, she need only throw off the blanket, lunge forward, snatch it up in both hands....She would turn it against her captor and stammer out an entreaty, or a threat: *I will pull the trigger if you don't obey me!* But hallucinatory images assailed her of Colin Asch simply wrenching the gun from her grasp or, worse yet, the gun firing by accident, a bullet tearing through Colin Asch's chest or face.

"You could have taken the gun any time you wanted, Dorothea," Colin Asch said, as, at dusk, they ate one of their crudely improvised meals. "But you didn't. You could have shot me down dead and you'd never have been charged for a thing, and that means you don't want to go back any more than I do."

Dorothea said quietly, "That isn't true."

Colin said, "Yeah, it's true."

Dorothea said, "Colin, you must know—it isn't true."

"It *is*."

So with the stubborn purposelessness of true intimacy, they quarreled; until finally Dorothea turned away, choking with indignation, hurt, dismay. She seemed to recall how, in childhood too, the salt taste of tears was the very taste of humiliation.

"If you're wondering, the way I did it was I got her drunker than she was, and fed her some Valium from her medicine cabinet, and held her head under the water till she stopped breathing. She didn't feel a thing!—just like I promised her. Not like that son of a bitch Krauss," Colin Asch said with a spitting gesture. "I wanted him to feel it all the way, and he did."

It must have been very late. Dorothea's watch had stopped running. Colin Asch was feeding, page by single page, the book he called his "blue ledger" into the fire. Dorothea did not want to ask why.

"It's a weird thing," he said almost conversationally, ignoring the look of revulsion on Dorothea's face, "how good you feel doing something you know is right. Like, after all, there're so few times in your life you really know you're standing in exactly the right place at the right time. Like you're not even yourself any longer but an agent of history. Of Death."

Dorothea shuddered, and said, "I should think it would be better to be an agent of life."

"When I kill someone I am the agent of Death," Colin Asch said slowly. He was detaching pages from the front of the notebook, ripping them carefully from the binding: he'd rekindled the fire, and it burned with a disconcerting Currier & Ives cheeriness. The lighted warmth, cast upward on Colin Asch's angular, pale face, gave his cheeks a look of boyish ruddy health. "When it's done it's done forever. *And no one can controvert it.* Think of that! Try to realize that, Dorothea! When you put something in the world, or love something in the world, or, say, you yourself are in the world, it's all fucking vulnerable—it can end at any minute. But the agent of Death—that's different." His voice rose tremulously. He grinned into the firelight. "Yeah. *That's* different."

"You're talking simply about destroying things, taking life away—"

"You don't know what I'm talking about, Dorothea," Colin Asch said, " 'cause you've never done what I have done. And if you had, you'd know."

"But—"

"If you had, you'd know."

Dorothea began sobbing, and the sobbing turned into a spasm of coughing that left her throat raw. Earlier that day Colin had expressed concern for her and murmured something vague about taking her to a doctor or to an emergency room. "Or maybe I could go by myself to some drugstore and get you penicillin." In a nervous reflexive gesture he'd checked the pistol another time for bullets, swinging the cartridge holder out. Dorothea had wondered how he'd known her bronchial condition required penicillin but she said nothing about it, and in any case Colin seemed to have forgotten within the hour.

Now he said, as if talking to himself, "You don't want to go back any more than I do. I know. It's a matter of honor and integrity—think of Christopher Columbus carried back to Spain in chains! The fuckers! What they want is to make people like us grovel, beg for mercy. But why the fuck should we? It's a question of freedom. It's power—doing things the way you want them done, becoming the agent of your own life. And death."

Dorothea made an effort to control herself. "But I don't want to die," she said.

"When I was twelve, and my parents died, there was this weird force drawing us off the bridge and through the railing—into the water—I could *feel* it, almost," Colin said, beginning to speak in an agitated voice, "but I thought—you know how you do at that age—I thought I could fight it, *controvert it!* There I was, diving into the water, swimming down, trying to get the car doors open, trying to pull them out—my mother, my father, first the one then the other then first one again then the other—like there was some kind of crazy thing in me too so that after a while I wasn't even thinking, didn't have any volition, or will; it wasn't Colin Asch but just my body, my muscles. But the fact was I failed. The lesson I was meant to learn was—I failed. Life goes in one direction only, like a river flowing or like gravity—you can't controvert it."

Deeply moved, having dreaded another sort of narration entirely, Dorothea said, "But you were very brave, Colin! And so young...."

Colin shook his head violently. "There was nothing brave about it; I don't know what 'brave' is. It was just this asshole kid trying to do something he wasn't meant to do so a lesson could be taught about it. Life goes in one direction only."

"Ah, Colin, surely not!"

He tore off another page and dropped it into the fire. Dorothea had a glimpse of a surface of neat block letters in a variety of shades of ink; there were tiny drawings too, or doodlings, in the margin; she would have liked, in that instant, to snatch the page out of the fire and save it. But it burst into flame and vanished.

"Did that happen anywhere near here?" Dorothea asked. "Your parents' accident?"

"No. Nowhere near here," Colin Asch said. "Hundreds of miles to the south."

Dorothea Deverell did not believe she was asleep but there, unaccountably, was her mother...her young mother with loose flying hair and dark smooth golden skin...striding through a meadow of tall grass, shading her eyes and calling *Dorothea! Dorothea!* A scattering of tiny yellow butterflies surrounded her. The game was that Dorothea's mother could not detect the giggling little girl crouched hiding in the grass so Dorothea leaped up to surprise her, feeling a wave of joy so intense it turned to pain in her throat... and then she was coughing violently, and awake, returned confusedly to herself, sitting in a patch of wan sunlight in an opened doorway strange to her in a place strange to her and someone was approaching, speaking to her in a peremptory, suspicious voice: "Hey, what the hell are you doing here, lady?"

A burly old man in soiled overalls and a railway worker's cap, with a flushed bewhiskered face and small narrowed eyes: the caretaker for Glace Lake?

And some thirty feet away, behind him, beside a pickup truck parked in the lane, stood a teen-aged boy with what appeared to be a rifle slung loosely in the crook of his arm.

Dorothea waved at the old man to come no nearer, trying to warn him, her voice raw, cracked. "Get away! Don't speak to me! There's danger!"

But the old man took no heed; excitable and emboldened, having sized up Dorothea Deverell as no one he need fear, he said loudly, belligerently, "Just what the bejesus are you doing here, lady? This is private property—don't you know?"

At this point two events happened with near simultaneity: the boy by the pickup truck shouted out something to the old man Dorothea could not quite hear (except for the word "Grandpa," which she would retain for a long time), and, easing up noiselessly behind her, as if, these many hours in "Land's End," he had primed himself for this very moment, Colin Asch gracefully leaned over Dorothea's head in the doorway, and aimed the pistol at the old man's chest, and fired. Dorothea screamed as the old man spun partway around and fell; Colin leaped to the walk crying "Fucker! That'll teach you! I'll kill you all!" He sighted the boy in the lane but the boy turned to run; Colin pursued him and fired a single shot but almost immediately returned, cursing, infuriated, as Dorothea knelt beside the dying old man whose chest was already soaked in blood and whose face had gone, with terrifying swiftness, a sickly ashen gray. "A doctor—call a doctor! Oh, Colin—an ambulance!" Dorothea said.

Colin Asch stood over his victim and almost idly aimed the pistol again, at the old man's forehead.

"Here's your doctor, you old fart. *Didn't I warn you all!*"

And then it was the end, or nearly.

Dorothea found herself cringing in a corner of the kitchen, then in the tiny lavatory adjacent to the kitchen, sobbing hysterically, as

Colin Asch, enraged, incredulous, stomped from room to room, from window to window, shoving furniture into place to establish what reports of the siege would subsequently call a "barricade," cursing, talking loudly to himself and to Dorothea, whom he berated for having been discovered and for having forced him to shoot the old man without adequate preparation. First, Colin had had the idea that they must flee, in the car, but he'd immediately changed his mind, reasoning that "they" would be waiting for him since the road led in only one fucking direction thus they'd have him trapped like a sitting duck; they'd set up a roadblock or wait in ambush; the only strategy was to stay where they were and see how long they could hold out—"Fucking Christ I've already wasted three bullets!"

Banging on the lavatory door with such violence that the feeble lock sprang open he shouted at Dorothea, "It's all happening too fucking fast! I'm not ready! *You're* not ready!"

And indeed from this hour everything happened with dream-like rapidity and logic, as if the unnatural stasis of many hours were breaking, pent up and malevolent, about their heads. There came to Dorothea's ears, within minutes it seemed, the sound of a police or ambulance siren, and a second siren, and a man's voice, garishly amplified through a bullhorn, shouting instructions to "you!—inside that house!"; the sound of other voices; and Colin Asch's at first unrecognizable shouting (so raw, so despairing and *young*) from one of the barricaded windows—he was armed, he said, and he had a hostage. And there was the deafening sound of gunfire, and breaking cascading glass. The image of Charles Carpenter's face passed swiftly through Dorothea's vision, but it was a face of studied calm, remoteness. He knows nothing of me, she thought. It was all a dream.

For the duration of the siege—three and a half hours in all, though most of that time was spent in shouted instructions, commands, repartee of a kind—Dorothea Deverell remained where she had crawled to hide, shivering with a hot rank animal fear and gradually passing beyond panic and into a stage very like catatonic bliss: as if, in this nearly sculptural mimicry of death, she might magically be spared death.

Yet even then, amid the chaos of men's voices, random and seemingly theatrical displays of gunfire, and the outraged heavy footsteps of her abductor as he charged past her hiding place to commandeer one or another window (it would have been held grievously against him by the county sheriff and his deputies, had he survived, that Colin Asch had given them so pointlessly difficult a time in "rescuing" the fallen old man whom they could not have known with certainty was dead)—even then, in the very cynosure of madness, Dorothea Deverell would have found it exceedingly difficult to believe that Colin Asch who so admired her and was her friend truly wished her harm.

"He would *not*—would he?"

But at last Colin Asch came for her, and presented her briefly at a window, to prove, since proof had been demanded, that his "hostage" still lived; then he walked briskly away into a room at the rear of the lodge, presumably the safest, most barricaded of the rooms, a bedroom with a fieldstone fireplace in which, so very unexpectedly, a fire was burning—for Colin was occupied in tearing pages from his mysterious blue notebook and feeding them to the fire, and in this he wanted Dorothea's help. Repeatedly he said, with jaw-gripping fury, that he wasn't ready! wasn't ready!

Finally he threw what remained of the notebook into the flames and watched it ride their crest for a long moment, and that was that.

He had then, in his right hand, a long smartly gleaming knife at which Dorothea stared without recognition; staring too at Colin Asch's face—why had she never noticed it before, that thin sickle-shaped scar over his left eye? His mouth moved but she could not make out the urgent words. There was too much that was urgent, that was loud and jarring and unceremonious, for her to absorb. Colin Asch was telling her what must be done since there was no escape and no going back. "All that's finished now."

He pressed the knife into her fingers and closed his strong fingers over hers, saying, "Like this," and Dorothea was uncomprehending but not at first resistant for was this young man not her protector?—but when the edge of the blade touched her throat Dorothea screamed and pushed away.

So Colin had to forcibly reposition her—by now the two of them were squatting beside the fireplace and Dorothea's back was close against the wall—and press the knife into her fingers another time, saying, in a pleading, accusatory voice: "But it's time! Don't make me do it to you alone!"

"No—let me go!" Dorothea cried.

And Colin said, as if reasonably, bringing the blade up against her throat, harder this time, "We love each other, Dorothea—we haven't had to say so."

And Dorothea said, "I don't love you well enough to die with you!"—struggling against the young man with a reserve of strength she could not have known she possessed. She succeeded in prying the knife from Colin's fingers, using her nails to lacerate the backs of his hands and his face. "Let me go! Let me go! Let me go!" she screamed. In the startling sweaty intimacy of their near embrace she sensed in him an absolute surprise—consternation—as if he could not believe that Dorothea Deverell would resist this death ceremony, or would resist with such hysteria.

The knife clattered to the floor—but Dorothea's strength, having flared up, now died away; a moment's struggle had consumed it. Colin snatched up the knife and held it as if threateningly against his own throat, saying, hurt, reproachful, "Dorothea? Don't you want to? Don't you love me? You'll let me do it alone?"

"Don't."

"You'll let me do it alone?"

Regarding Dorothea Deverell intently yet calmly, as if he were staring into a mirror at his own reflection, Colin Asch brought the end of the blade against his throat, against an artery he'd groped to find with seemingly practiced fingers. In the instant in which he brought the blade powerfully downward and slantwise against his throat his eyes became entirely black, all pupil, as if with an unspeakable pleasure. Dorothea screamed for him not to do it, shutting her eyes, steeling herself against the warm splash of arterial blood that would explode upon her and mark her for life. For of course it was too late.

13

"Dorothea?—where are you?"

Too much light.

EPILOGUE

They were not yet married but were shortly to be so, on the last Saturday in September—the very eve, coincidentally, of Dorothea Deverell's fortieth birthday; which would subsequently prove to be the happiest birthday of her adult life. But for months, on the weekends, they had been house-hunting, looking for the perfect house: the house that would somehow erase, or at any rate counter, their memories of the past. In secret they hoped for a house that might combine the most prized qualities of the houses they were leaving while suggesting, publicly, neither house—for Dorothea Deverell and Charles Carpenter, as lovers, were duly guilt-ridden and supposed they would forever remain so, in a luxury of self-recrimination no amount of penance could absolve.

Many have sacrificed, Dorothea thought, who dare not give themselves in love. *That* prim virtue, at least, she would be spared.

The house they had almost definitely decided to buy, in an older residential area of Lathrup Farms near the Brannon Institute, was, finally, not perfect, but they were keen to buy it just the same—a small white brick-and-stucco with Greek Revival features, tall slender fluted columns, an elegant portico, tall windows; an interior that, in its current unfurnished state at least, with high ceilings, white walls, and gleaming hardwood floors, suggested the austerity of a Dutch interior out of Vermeer—a tabula rasa of a kind that cast an immediate, potent charm over them both. Walking through the house on her initial visit, Dorothea Deverell had squeezed Charles Carpenter's arm in a fearful sort of delight. Yes! Here! This is it! We are home! She would retain the house's quality of austerity, a wonderfully light-flooded sharp-angled purity; but there would be hanging plants, and richly colored carpets, and interesting but not obtrusive contemporary furniture. She had not the slightest intention of relocating her charmingly mismatched things in a new setting: she would sell some of them and give the rest away to Goodwill. Like Charles Carpenter she wanted most desperately to make a fresh start on neutral territory. After all, neither was lacking in funds.

The sale of Dorothea's house had brought her unexpected revenue: as if by magic the property had quadrupled in value during the nine years Dorothea had owned it. And Charles Carpenter's Fairway Drive house had sold for much more. And there was his late wife's estate as well—estimated, even after inheritance taxes, at more than $2 million. For Agnes Carpenter, though having filed for divorce from Charles, had not yet cut him out of her will; her husband remained her chief beneficiary.

When first told this astonishing news Dorothea Deverell had felt a pang of chagrin, a sense of sisterly hurt, for Agnes' sake. "It does seem so unfair for her, somehow," she told Charles Carpenter. "So much the sort of thing that, in her ironic cast of mind, she might have anticipated."

"But only in essence," Charles said. "If she'd truly anticipated it she would have cut me out at once."

"Still," Dorothea said, "it seems unfair."

"But why, Dorothea? If *I* had died when Agnes had died, if that madman had killed me instead, *she* would have inherited everything," Charles said reasonably. "It hadn't crossed my mind to cut her out of my will, so long as she was my wife."

Thinking of these things—even as she'd resolved not to think, still less to brood over them—Dorothea Deverell drove to the beautiful white house on L'Arve Place one afternoon in early September: twenty-two days, to be specific, before the wedding. She had picked up a key from the real estate agency; she wanted to make another final visit to the house (she'd already made several "final" visits) before she and Charles signed the purchase papers. The house loomed in their imaginations with the monumentality of an Egyptian pyramid, nearly!—they joked that buying it together seemed a more daunting step somehow than getting married.

It was past 5:30 P.M. when Dorothea arrived and let herself into the house by way of the front door; Charles was to meet her there as close to that time as he could manage. But she liked it that she'd arrived before him; she walked through the beautifully empty rooms breathing in with gratitude the ineffable odor of vacancy.... There were no mirrors remaining on any of the walls and no casual reflecting surfaces. What pleasure, Dorothea thought, to be so totally *alone:* not even one's own face to intrude.

Though, these days, Dorothea Deverell was looking extremely attractive; her skin plumped out slightly with health, and less pale than it had been; her eyes clear, if frequently bemused; her hair richly dark and glossy, its several strands of gray, silvery-gray, and white hairs quite distinctive. Since the terrible events of the previous spring she had become less fretful over trivialities, less impatient, demanding, and critical of herself. It was a quality of middle age, she supposed, but not of middle age exclusively. The persistent narrating voice of thirty-odd years, forever detached, clinical, judgmental, and subtly disappointed in Dorothea Deverell's performance, whatever that performance was, had been, during her convalescence, replaced by other, more benign and forgiving and even encouraging voices. These were to be quite explicitly traced to their sources: the excellent doctor who had attended her in the hospital (Dorothea had been there for three weeks), her warm and unfailingly supportive circle of friends; her associates at the Institute; Charles Carpenter above all. As a hospital patient Dorothea Deverell had learned the virtues of passivity and obedience in small things; she had pleased others simply by regaining her health. She had pleased herself too by recovering sufficiently to return to work on the first Monday in June and to take up quarters in Mr. Morland's old office.

There had been a good deal of disagreeable, even sensational, attention focused upon Dorothea Deverell, of course, but Charles Carpenter had shielded her from most of it. No media interviews, no strangers knocking at her door. He had not shown her the newspaper accounts of the abduction and its aftermath, nor had

Dorothea asked to see them. It would have given her no pleasure to see Colin Asch's photographs in the newspaper; the less so, since, by way of an incidental remark of Jacqueline's, she gathered that some of the modeling shots had been used.

But the police had been very nice, very courteous, patient and undemanding in their questions. There were the three Boston-area killings credited to Colin Asch, and the killing at Glace Lake, and it seemed there were others in other states, or their likelihood, but the evidence was inconclusive. Dorothea told the police, and retold them, all she knew of Colin Asch or could honestly recall. By way of her experience as a "witness" she came to understand why, in criminal cases, reports of eyewitnesses are notoriously unreliable: what the witness believes to be clear remembering is in fact fabricating, filling in the gaps, misremembering, and what is "remembered" becomes subsequently this misremembering, ever more emphatically reiterated. The precise events of the abduction—for "abduction" was the public, the inevitable word—had begun to fade in Dorothea's memory almost immediately afterward, as our dreams so quickly and teasingly fade even as we labor to recall them; her physical collapse had surely exacerbated the emotional trauma (the bronchial condition had become lobar pneumonia by the time she was taken to a hospital in Massena, New York, following the siege at Glace Lake), thus her memory was further confused by delirium, feverish bad dreams. Extreme illness frequently mimics psychosis, in which the cacophonous images of the unconscious fly loose: Dorothea Deverell was so sick as to have conflated, to her shame and distress, the deaths of the mass murderer Colin Asch and her young husband Michel Deverell ...as if Colin Asch's death, which she had witnessed, were in some way Michel Deverell's death, which she had not.

For these reasons her account to the police was tentative, hesitant, qualified. Most of her statements were preceded by *I think* or *I seem to remember.* There was revealed to be an intermittent amnesia concerning the one hundred hours—"one hundred hours" being the neutral euphemism Dorothea Deverell herself preferred—which

Dorothea could not penetrate. Had her abductor struck her, pummeled her, tried to strangle her? No, said Dorothea Deverell; yet the medical reports listed bruises on her body, reddened marks on her throat. Had her abductor threatened her life? No, said Dorothea Deverell, not exactly. Yet hadn't he tried to kill her, at the end? Hadn't he held a knife blade against her throat, at the end? Yes, said Dorothea Deverell but…but it was somehow not *that.*

Asked to explain herself, Dorothea could not, quite. Her words were faltering and inadequate.

She was capable, however, of recalling vividly the details of the "cold-blooded" shooting of the caretaker at Glace Lake: the exact circumstances of Colin Asch's first shot, and his second. Only Colin Asch's words, if he had spoken at all, eluded her.

Over all, she could not remember much of what Colin Asch had said to her during the one hundred hours. The doorbell had rung at the front of her house, she had hurried to answer it, and then…. The sound of the young man's voice was beginning to fade; even more strangely, his face. "It's as if Colin stands on the far side of an abyss," Dorothea told Charles Carpenter, "speaking to me, trying to explain himself, in a normal voice—but a normal voice, under the circumstances, isn't sufficient. *I can't hear.*"

"Then don't, for Christ's sake," Charles Carpenter said. "Let it go, Dorothea."

"But—"

"Let *him* go. The contemptible son of a bitch."

When he was forced to speak of Colin Asch, Charles Carpenter's usually composed face was contorted by a grimace of sheer loathing; the mere name upset him. For it was the general if unproven hypothesis that Colin Asch had had an exploitive sexual relationship with Agnes (thus the two checks to "Alvarado"—identified by bank tellers as Colin Asch), as he'd had with Susannah Hunt and almost certainly with Roger Krauss. Of this, Charles Carpenter simply could not bear to think.

Her medical examinations had shown of course that there had been no sexual assault upon Dorothea Deverell, no sexual activity of any kind. But had Colin Asch threatened her with rape? with any sort of sexual violence? "No," Dorothea Deverell said, "he did not." For this she knew with absolute confidence.

Now Dorothea found herself standing on the stairway, her hand resting on the banister, in the house on L'Arve Place, thinking of these things: the very things she had vowed she would not think about, particularly in this new setting. "Let it go!" she said aloud, and hurried up the stairs.

The master bedroom had tall windows facing south and west; the westerly windows were flooded with sunshine of a mellow, autumnal cast; Dorothea felt its warmth on her face like the gentlest of caresses. In this room there were faint rectangular marks on the walls from mirrors and other hangings, the ceiling was blistered in several spots, thus they would have it all redone; the walls repapered in something light and restful to the eye…*not* a print of any kind…an ivory-beige perhaps. Dorothea liked that color and hoped that the Carpenters' master bedroom, which she had never seen, had not had walls in that shade.

And plain curtains, satin and damask. And a new carpet laid upon the floor.

At a front window she watched as Charles Carpenter's car was parked at the curb; she watched as the man's tall, elegant figure emerged. Like a young girl awaiting her first lover she watched him approach the house, then ran breathless to the staircase outside the bedroom door to wait for him to appear below: she'd left the front door unlocked.

"Dorothea? It's Charles." His voice lifted uncertainly. "Where are you?"

Dorothea Deverell leaned over the banister; there was something wonderfully playful, prankish, about seeing the top of Charles Carpenter's head while he had no awareness of her presence. She laughed happily and called down, "I'm here, Charles—come up!"

THE
END

"An Unsolved Crime"

But would the prongs be sharp enough?—we wondered.

Ammonia or rat poison or lye—wouldn't he smell it?

We giggled until we were weak. We upset the Chinese checker board and the marbles rolled onto the bedspread and onto the floor, rolling in every direction, under the bed—where there were always dust-balls, though Momma cleaned once a week—and into the corners of the room. I stepped on one, once, and lost my balance and almost fell down.

You laughed at me. Hid your face in your hands and laughed, laughed, in silence.

Lenny, aren't you stupid! Big dumb stupid Lenny!

Your shoulders shook with that silent, painful laughter. When you took your hands away from your face you weren't a girl any longer—ugly-pale, tired, washed-out, even the freckles on your forehead were faded, strange, like those coin-sized spots on Grandpa's hands.

What are you staring at? you cried.

I couldn't speak. My eyes stung, I had been laughing so hard. Now I couldn't speak. You had been so pretty as a little girl, everyone had fussed over you, your red-orange curls and your big brown eyes and your freckles and your snub nose and…

Stop that! Stop that staring at me and thinking about me! you screamed.

Still, I am thinking about you.

The years, the years: wide and tumultuous and mock-blank as the Alder River. They exist, we exist, we are doomed to think about one another as if we were still there, living together in that house. All of us, living together. In that house. We are doomed to think about one another as if we were still alive. We are doomed to think.

Remember the rustling of the cornstalks, the wind in the corn, late August and the parched ghostly sounds, remember lying awake, in the heat, awake, listening?—thinking? The moon is the same moon. I saw it the other evening. That moon! It's so bright, so obvious, there's something terrifying about it, the defiance, the refusal to be subtle; and it never changes. Nothing changes. They may have razed the old house—carted the aged bricks away, or left them to lie in a heap—they may have levelled everything, let the cornfield go wild, and the pastures—they may have built a six-lane highway through the property by now—I never inquired—but nothing changes, everything remains. Fixed. Stuck. There. Then.

You should not have laughed at me. Why did you laugh?

Distance, people claim, conquers all. It's a new slogan—put distance between yourself and your troubles and be a new person. I am not being ironic. I never joke. The jet-plane confers absolution upon any sinner: simply put distance between yourself and your sin. I want to believe this. I am old, but not old enough to have become legend; I am not yet mythological. Still human. Still here, fixed. In this new age I fly from continent to continent, I sleep dreamlessly, hurtled above the clouds. They are filmy and disappointing, these clouds; how different they looked to us, from below! At the edge of the plains the clouds hung thick and brooding and sly, jockeying for position with one another, changing from minute to minute. You could not trust the sky, especially in the spring. Those winds, those lightning-storms! Dust-spirals dancing across the yard!...A tornado struck the Richters' farm, a mile away, demolished the silo, threw fenceposts and farm equipment all around, but killed nobody, not even a chicken, and he—our father, I mean—was troubled by it. *Just a baby tornado, he said, that means that it might come back again real soon, might strike us next time.*

Now the skies are different. Perhaps they are as evil, but their evil is monotonous; one soon falls asleep. Returning from Rome our plane circled Kennedy Airport for two and a half hours and did I feel apprehension, was I sick with dread? Not at all: I dozed. Dreamless except for the rustling of the cornstalks, the August wind that lifted the curtains on your window—organdy, weren't they?—pale yellow? And the smell of the sick-room. Medicine, fever, despair. Exultation.

Distances are illusions today. You watch a film, a kind of cartoon animated by living actors and actresses; you leaf through a glossy, up-to-date magazine, reading articles about technology and world famine and drug addiction and Washington and new "life-styles" which you have read before, in other magazines, all with glossy important covers; you fall asleep to avoid conversation with whoever sits beside you—so often, lately, it has been a woman my own age, a widow, always a widow, eager to talk, lonely, alone—you fall asleep in one time-zone and awake in another. Life is so easy now, when nothing matters.

Time, too, is an illusion. Must be. People are always saying so, aren't they? Each of the glossy magazines contains an article about a mystical-minded physicist, usually a Nobel Prize-winner, who makes sly, teasing proclamations about the nature of time. It doesn't exist. It's a fourth dimension. We are trapped in three dimensions and cannot escape and cannot—unless we are physicists with a poetic inclination—even comprehend the nature of our entrapment. It hasn't been so many years, then, since we were brother and sister.

Wait....

The curtains were pale yellow, yes, but dotted with white—dotted Swiss curtains. Momma made them on the sewing machine. You helped. You were ten years old. I was thirteen. It was the winter he came to live with us, you were ten years old and I was thirteen and Momma was—we didn't know it at the time, we didn't know such things—only thirty-four. A girl, really. A silly weepy frightened country girl. It wasn't her fault, then. We hated her and blamed her and even plotted against *her*...for a while, a few weeks; but we never meant it. Did we? I'm sure we didn't. We didn't really hate her, either. They told her to get married again, what would happen to the farm if she didn't get married again, soon, what would happen to Elsa and Lenny without a father...? Oh they told her, they nagged her! I heard them! Sell the farm, they said, and move to town. Sell the farm. Or get married.

She got married.

He sold the farm.

She must have loved us, she made those curtains for your window, and skirts and blouses and jumpers for school, and even shirts for me, though I didn't like them and refused to wear them: they didn't look right around the collar. There was already a Montgomery Ward store in town, a big three-story building in the center of town, why not buy clothes there, weren't they cheap enough, good enough? She must have loved us to fuss so. Now you'll have a father again, she said. Oh she loved us, she loved us! She was so stupid.

The citation claims that I have written over two hundred stories. I have "contributed" a great deal to contemporary literature. I am not famous, as television performers are famous, but the universities compete with one another for me—they wish to confer honorary degrees upon me, they wish to bribe me with citations like the one I have before me, which I have lost interest in reading—what are these words *about*?—whom are they honoring?—and in my practical old age I accept at least one invitation out of ten. I have nothing else to do, the lease on the "maisonette" in Coral Gables is up and I didn't renew it and so I must take to the skies, crossing and recrossing the continent, crossing and recrossing the Atlantic Ocean; and plans are forming, obscurely, as if without my knowledge, that have to do with a cultural ambassadorship to such distant cities as Tokyo: my sense of humor is such that I will not resist.

Two hundred stories, a dozen plays, one ambitious but ill-fated novel—an "interesting failure"—ignored for decades, barely tolerated, and suddenly in my mid-sixties—a few years ago—proclaimed as a "modern master," heralded and lifted high and graced with prizes, isn't time kind to those who merely endure, aren't young people kind to those whom their parents' generation has scorned? —and distance, too, is kind. My Midwestern accent sounds slackly elegant, an antiquated music, when I am far from home. (I am always far from home.) Time, distance, skies, clouds, cornfields, the dry crackling breezes of August, two hundred stories, academic gowns of light wool, black wool, and ludicrous caps that make my poor head sweat, speeches that ramble on for hours, it seems—for hours, while we suffer!—and some of the speeches are my own, some of those silly self-important voices are my own, mine. I say anything, I say everything. I am applauded. Not yet senile, I sometimes exploit the possibilities of senility: the slow, slow, ponderous, solemn, absolutely sincere expression of the obvious. They applaud. It is their wish. Now that I am going blind and I wear these extraordinary goggle-like contraptions—my eyes swim in the lenses like demented fish—no wonder people stare at me with such pitying attention—no wonder they invite me everywhere—it is their collective wish to applaud so that auditoriums tremble with their good nature, their zest, their respect for one who has "accomplished so much." I could stand at their podiums and explain that the two hundred stories were attempts to tell a certain story that never got told, that I am too old, now, and lazy, and arrogant (though you would not think so, staring at my tranquil, much-wrinkled face), and have lost my faith.... But why should I trouble my audiences, why should I mar the good-natured enthusiasm of these ordinary afternoons? It is not subtlety that is invited to receive honorary degrees.

Mr. Breslow, one of my hosts is saying, in a clear well-modulated voice, would you like to meet...? Would you like to wash up before the luncheon, or take a nap...? Would you like...? Would...?

You are alive, even now. Facts surround you. You are a wife, or were; a mother; a grandmother. These facts are not exactly lies but they obscure the truth and for that reason you and I never meet, never even speak over the telephone; what a shame, people whisper, imagining there is ill-feeling between us. The fools! They know nothing. They have nothing to do with you and me. *What a shame....*

Facts surround me also. I curl up behind them, safe, mocking, unassailable. One drink at five o'clock, another with dinner (usually around 7:30) and perhaps a nightcap, that's all, that's absolutely all, and then I sleep, dreamless, inside my wall of facts, my accomplishments and citations; there, I am unassailable.

Mr. Breslow, they murmur. Mr. Breslow. Reverent silence. A droning high-pitched elderly voice, not mine—can it be mine, that Midwestern jabbering?—then the applause. I am at ease with words, I can make them do anything, like a stage magician I draw them out of my sleeve and wave them about in shabby-elegant circles, I smile the benign mocking smile of the unassailable, I am not listening to my words or to the applause, I am thinking of the cornfield and the pastures and the barns and the eroded bank above the river, where he fell and died, Oh!—what a death!—the bright blood splattered on the dry rocks, August and the riverbed so shallow, moss on the rocks dried to a queer papery white you could peel off in one strip if you were careful; I am thinking of those things and of the high narrow red-brick house and the steep black-shingled roof and your room and your curtains and the sky framed in the wall like a cheap bright print of the kind sold at Montgomery Wards and how we plotted, snickered, giggled, setting up the board for our game of Chinese checkers, or shuffling the soiled, sticky cards for another game of gin rummy, or euchre, or double solitaire. We took turns shuffling. Sometimes the cards stuck together, sometimes you dropped them, exclaiming, angry, overexcited, and I told you to be quiet, and shuffled them myself. The fact is that you were sick in bed for eight months. You had pleurisy, then you had—what?—the doctor called it "flu"—you were too weak to get up, Momma worried that you would die, would waste away and die, poor Momma, and Momma's husband worried, too, his eyes snatched at me downstairs and once, in the cow barn, oh yes, once, he knew, he knew, and stared at me to see—did I know?—but I played dumb sunny innocent Lenny, I gave the bastard no hint at all. Breslow, Breslow, Breslow was our name, Elsa and Lenny's name, and his was something else. Do you know, I've forgotten it?

It's recorded somewhere. On the death certificate, which the county coroner signed. On the grave marker.

Perhaps it is because of him we quarreled, you and I? Or because of the inheritance? Because of the furniture or the chinaware or—or what? Our grandmother's rag-rug cushions, her hand-sewn quilts, all that junk stored in the attic? The debts?...But there must be a reason, they whisper, there *must* be a reason. Elsa never speaks of Len, Len never comes to visit Elsa, never sends her his books, not even a Christmas or a birthday card. A childhood squabble, that must be it. Resentment. Jealousy.

Let them whisper, let them invent stories. One by one they are dying off anyway. One by one we are dying off. Who will remember *him*...? His own people are scattered. They don't exist. If I could write the story of his life I would erase all of them, I would return to zero, never give him a chance to destroy us. *We* had no quarrel with each other. We were brother and sister, we were Breslows, we sent our trembling ghost-selves through the darkened house, seeking him, groping our way to him. (He had no name, it was always *him, he, his.*)

Death-by-poison: weren't horsetail and jimsonweed poison, and the berries of the yew tree? And of course there were other poisons around the farm, poisons of all kinds. Arsenic (for rats, gophers, woodchucks, porcupines). Lye. Toilet cleanser. Ammonia. Turpentine? And gasoline. Someone had poisoned our collie a few years earlier: he came to the back door, clawing at the screen, whining and shuddering, dying, and I couldn't help him, there was nothing I could do, nothing. I wept and wept. So did you. Who would do such a thing, poison a friendly dog like that!...Such a terrible death, that noisy strenuous eye-rolling agony!

(That's the way *he* should die, I told you; you shook your head from side to side, eyes shut tight. No no no no. A crime. A terrible sin. And we would be discovered, wouldn't we? He could smell the poison. Taste it.)

We argued, we dreamt. Long agitated dreams. The heat of summer, the airlessness of August. There was the possibility of ground glass, which I had read about in a detective novel, one of those cheap paperback books that began to fascinate me, when I was only eleven or twelve, leafing through them in the second-hand store in town while Momma looked at appliances. Glass ground fine as sugar! And, like sugar, sprinkled onto his food!

Elsa, you could have done it easily. When you were well again, and helping Momma with the meals again. Downstairs in the kitchen, Elsa's ghost-self, Momma's back turned for a minute and—and it would be done—and he would be doomed. So easily! He wouldn't have known, might have thought the gritty taste was just salt. He ate so fast anyway, didn't know what he was eating, stuffed himself, jaws grinding and his entire face moving, moving in rhythm with his jaws, his eating. Ate so fast, tasted nothing. Pig. Animal. In his guts there would have been such agony, such agony....

Elsa?

There would have been vomiting, there would have been blood coughed up. Ground glass: they would know. The sheriff would be called, we would be questioned, we would be discovered. Unless Momma was blamed? But we didn't want Momma to be blamed, poor silly Momma.

Elsa, why are you whipping your head from side to side, why are your eyes shut tight?

One of us giggled and couldn't stop.

One of us began to cry.

Outside the house, then; in the hay barn or in the fields. A crowbar, a mallet, a sledgehammer, pounding pounding pounding against his head. Do you think I'd be afraid? Do you think anything could stop me once I got going?...An unsolved murder. No one would know. It could have been done by a thief, maybe. There were thieves in the area, in Yewville, even in Marsena. Someone had broken into the hardware store and took some equipment and was never caught. Someone had broken into Dan McPhee's house last summer when everyone was away at the beach. And was never caught....I could kill him with the pitchfork, I said. Could walk right up behind him in the hay barn and let him have it. Between the shoulder blades. Through the heart. (But would the prongs be sharp enough? What if he didn't die? What if he turned around and saw me and although I struck what if it wasn't enough to kill him and I lost my strength and dropped the pitchfork and....)

One of us began to giggle, hands pressed against his mouth.

Then we'd hear him on the stairs. Wasn't that *him*? Those footsteps?

Sometimes he walked right past your door, walking heavily so that the floor shook. Went to the big bedroom and fell onto the bed, clothes and all, dirty shoes and all; exhausted from the day's work. Sometimes he stopped outside the door to listen. And we were quiet, we were frightened and quiet. But sometimes he opened the door without knocking and stuck his head inside and his eyes were queer, narrow, as if he expected to see something blinding....(What did he expect to see? Did he know I would be there, pretending to shuffle the playing cards, or shaking the dice in the little black cup?)

He opened the door without knocking and leaned inside and looked at you. And looked at me.

Said nothing.

The first time it happened, you were mute for almost a week.

What's wrong with Elsa, I asked, what's wrong with the baby?—the little cry-baby!

(I was jealous of you then.)

Red-orange hair, curly hair, just too pretty-pretty, everybody's favorite and of course I was jealous. We weren't friends then. You were ten years old, I was thirteen. You hated me, didn't you? Or maybe you didn't. I had other friends, a boy who lived in Marsena, a boy in my grade at school, and the Richters' grandson who stayed with them sometimes. I rode my bike out on the highway, all the way to Marsena, all the way to Childwold and back. You couldn't ride such a distance and you were afraid of the big dogs that chased us. I didn't like you. I didn't think about you at all....The first time it happened, you didn't tell me because we weren't friends, you didn't tell Momma either, he warned you what would happen if you told.

Then he let you alone for a long time.

Then it happened again, again, he must have been drunk, it was after one of the trips to town, he'd gone alone and stayed all day and Momma was in the cellar when he came back, and you were washing your hair in the bathroom, and he came in without knocking, and shut the door and locked it, and where was I, where was I…? Upstairs, doing my homework? Must have been.

Momma was back in a few minutes, she had three quart jars of canned tomatoes, she put them in the refrigerator, she didn't even know he was home. There was no sound from the bathroom: he put his hand over your mouth. And you didn't cry out anyway. You didn't cry out, didn't struggle?

Didn't move?

You were crying then for hours, for days. Weeks. Years of it: I can hear you even now. Your skin turned sallow, there was something sickly and babyish about your smile. Cringing, grinning….I wanted to slap you. I couldn't stand it, watching you. So skinny, your collarbones showing, the calves of your legs like sticks: and you kept dropping the cards when you shuffled them. Oh hell! Look what I've done! Damn it, damn it! Whimpering, a five-year-old's voice, and you were twelve at the time.

Plans, vaporous calculations. Strident dreams. Scenarios: I would do this, you would do that, the two of us would….We argued quietly, crazily. No one could hear. We argued about the pitchfork, I tested the prongs and they seemed sharp enough, we argued about who should find him, what we would tell the sheriff's men. We argued about the poisons. Which one to use? Then there was the shotgun, his shotgun, .16 gauge, kept in the storage closet downstairs, not loaded, could I load it, could I actually walk with it to where he was, seek him out, could I…could I pull the trigger? Impossible. But he might have an accident with the gun somehow. Someday. It happened all the time, it was written up in the papers all the time, certainly it could happen to *him*.

But who would find him? When would it happen? Where would Momma be? How could it seem like an accident?

Shoveling the driveway with him, one winter morning. Breath steaming about my face. He was a few yards away, his back to me. The snow-shovel? But it was too light, it would never kill. You were in the house, you weren't thinking of us, there were no plans for this, our digging through the snow that had drifted across the lane, the two of us alone together, his back to me, panting, grunting, alone, unknowing. It was ten below zero. The wind moaned through the screen of pines and the sky was a fierce bright crazy blue. Haha! You knew nothing about this, this supreme moment. But I lived through it, Leonard lived through it, a wool cap pulled down tight onto his forehead, overshoes buckled to mid-calf, his movements uncoordinated in that clumsy wool-lined jacket, heart pounding so violently there seemed to be something wrong with his eyesight. The day darkened, then went light again. Too light. There were splotches of sunshine, there were sudden shadowy cracks. I stared at his back. I stared at his head. (He wore a wool cap also, navy blue.) Now, now, now.... But no.

Panting, trembling. So cold! The wind made my eyes water. I couldn't see. I was going blind, going crazy. You knew nothing about it, you were safe in the house, not even thinking about Lenny. Not even thinking about *him*.

Nothing happened that day.

How could anything have happened? The snow-shovel was made of aluminum, it was too light. I worked with him, obedient. Eyes watering. It was cold, cold. But I worked with him, shoveled the lane out to the road, a quarter-mile, and some of the drifts were five feet high. Then we had breakfast together: scrambled eggs and Canadian bacon and toast and warmed-up mashed potatoes from the night before. His face was ruddy, his cheeks burned. Called me Len, Lenny. Sonny. Hard work. Men. Father and son. Didn't eat so fast that morning, seemed to be tired from the exercise. Not in good condition now: going to fat. Must have been in his late forties or early fifties. Never thought about such things at the time, adults' ages.... The radio, weather report for the area, more snow expected, temperatures going down even farther the next night, what did I think of that?—and no school either. A little vacation, eh?

I tried to answer, tried to smile. But my face was stiff from the cold.

He fell silent and finished eating.

What was there to say?

Six months later he was dead.

Fingerprints, footprints. I am running all over, grinning to myself. Across the pasture, behind the barn, through the bindweed and the burdocks and the jimsonweed. A ghost-self but nonetheless aching. Love, what is it, what was it? Where? We dreamt his death together until it blossomed in him, in his brain. What is death, what is playing at death? You weren't pretty any longer. Your wrists were so thin, I could have snapped them between my fingers. I wanted to scream at you, wanted to slap you. How could you let him! Why hadn't you fought! Standing there frozen, paralyzed, helpless, it was like me standing there with you, that filthy bastard grunting and moaning over us....

Who knew? Nobody knew.

But there were witnesses.

I was a witness, listening. Absorbing. Decades later I hear the voices again, yours and mine, I hear *his* voice, I can see him squeezing you against him, running his hands over your breasts, your tiny breasts, pressing so hard against your ribs that they ached afterward, grasping you by the back of the neck, holding you against him, close, close, rubbing against you slow and hard at first and then faster, frantically, his grip hard, impersonal, no one you knew, no one who was aware of you, not even your stepfather and not even a man but just anyone—anything—a force jamming itself against you harder and harder.

Afterward, pleurisy. Fever. "Flu." Weight loss of twenty pounds. Afterward, your head on the pillow as if you were too weak to raise it. Ghastly-pale, ugly, listless. Where is your spirit, Momma asked, what has happened? Such parched, dry lips. And that queer smile of yours, without humor: the thin lips drawing slowly back from the small, perfect teeth.

Afterward, his warning: don't tell anyone, don't ever tell anyone, something terrible will happen if you tell anyone.... On the stairs, his eyes snatching at me, I was going downstairs and he was coming up, how easily I could have...could have thrown myself upon him...the two of us falling back down the stairs, his head thumping against the edge of a step, his outcry of pain, surprise, his knowing cry, now it was going to happen, now; but no, nothing.

Never.

Yet how easily, how easily....

The other night he spoke to me in a dream. He visits me often, a presence, in work-clothes of a vague, indistinct type, his face not completely formed, his gray eyes blurred. He said: I do these things so that there will be nothing remaining, for you. I do these things so that you will be perfect.

I ran at him, in the dream. Yes. I really did. My dream-self is young and vital and rather stupid. He leaps into action, all arms and legs. He is invincible. He giggles, wipes his nose on his sleeve, springs into action. Tumbles down stairs, rolls over and over, his strong fingers closing about his victim's throat, his voice rising higher and higher, like a siren, too ignorant to give up when his victim evaporates. Who are these people, inhabiting us? Who are we, to contain them?

I wrote tentative stories about you and him, and me. Over the years I must have written hundreds of pages. But I tore them up, I threw them away, sat with my fingers pressed against my eyes, helpless, motionless, bewildered. In one of the stories he didn't really touch you: it was all innuendo, sly and cruel and yet chaste. In another, he tickled you, kissed you, wrestled with you; all in play. And, at first, you giggled, you responded in delight. (You were a lonely child, weren't you? Like me.) Then, as the seconds passed, you became frightened. *It* happened, then, and he let you fall free.

In another of the stories, hardly more than a sketch, he made love to you in your bed, in your sickbed, with the wind blowing the dotted Swiss curtains into the room.... In another of the stories you screamed, you fought, it was necessary for him to smother you. (I couldn't continue the story: I slipped into his head, I began to plot with him, to calculate how your body would have to be carried out of the house and thrown into the river, weighted down, so it would never, never be discovered.) Dreams, wisps, vapor, the peculiar patterns of the spirit, certain intolerable rhythms....

At the State University, a freshman, tall and gawky and bespectacled and earnest and perhaps pitied by my roommates, before they discovered how intelligent I was: a freshman, composing stories and poems for extra credit in English 1, hour after hour remembering, describing, inventing. "An Unsolved Crime." My slight stammer was mastered by sheer willpower. My nervousness was tamed by a methodical, compulsive reliance upon a schedule. Hour after hour, discipline, order, sanity, cunning. The death of the stepfather: a heart attack. Calling to the stock, angry, stooping to pick up a stone to toss at one of the cows, then the darting pain, the horrible gripping pain, the blackout, the collapse, the fall. Down the steep hillside, down, down into the dried riverbed. Coronary thrombosis, they said. The county coroner. Filled out the death certificate and signed it.... Sentences composed, sentences crossed out and rephrased. The way that bright blood looked, on the parched boulders! The way his body looked, suddenly small, harmless. Death isn't death but dead, merely. Dead.

Death isn't death but dead, merely. What do you mean by that, Leonard? My freshman English instructor was an aging young man, partly bald, earnest as I but not so exaggerated.

I can't... can't... I can't explain....

Death isn't death but dead, merely. Which means...?

My stepfather fell and died and was dead, we found him dead, he died one morning, early one morning, just died, died, went out to bring the stock in and something happened and he lost his footing and slipped—fell—hit his head on the rocks below—

I fell with him, plunged after him. My head rang. Someone was sitting at a desk listening to me, politely, my theme in one hand and a cigarette burning in another, someone was listening, wasn't sneering, but I plunged after the dying man, lost my footing and fell after him. I had pushed him so hard, you see. Ran at him. Both hands, palms of hands, fingers spread, struck at him hard, hard, no time to think, no time for him to turn and discover me. His death stank in my nostrils.... You ran up behind me, close behind me. Is he dead? Is he dead? Dead?

Sentences composed slowly and laboriously, hour upon hour, year after year. I was an undergraduate. Years passed and I was gone from the Midwest; lived in England; seemed to forget a great deal. Except for the stink in my nostrils and my head ringing with your cries. Is he dead? Is he...?

Once I tried to describe him. A blank sheet of paper to be filled with *him*. I failed, failed utterly. What was there to say? Eyes the color of pebbles. No color at all. A few strands of graying hair combed across his head. Tiny pits in his cheeks—acne or smallpox scars. He squinted often. Said little. Sometimes, sticking his head into your room, he had a matchstick gripped between his teeth, sometimes a toothpick. He stopped smoking for months at a time, then started again. Cigars and cigarettes. And that terrible cough of his would follow, terrible to hear, in the very early morning, in the bathroom downstairs, coughing as if he were about to bring up his lungs. How I hated him! Oh God, how I hated, hated him! ...Except, when I saw him lying there, he seemed so small, so harmless.

Death is an idea, a melody. *Dead* is stony and permanent.

He had put the farm up for sale already, had found a buyer already. So the deal went through. Momma was numb, Momma was never the same again, could hardly cry, brushing away flies with her slow uncertain hand even as they settled on her face. Momma do this, Momma please do that, I gave instructions, I was the man of the family now, sickish and stammering as I was. Would childhood never end? Would we never pack our things and move, escape?

I fly back and forth across the continent, traversing his death. A triumph, a queer kind of relief.... I fly over *your* house. Often. Memories arise, stray facts demand to be braided together into a story, a narrative. In one version I described our mother at great length, lovingly and yet critically. Photos of her show a heavyset woman with a dull, placid expression, hair braided about her head peasant-style, her breasts big, her house-dress plain and shapeless. I suppose the photos are fairly accurate. But I reject them, I don't remember her that way at all; I remember a frightened, rather delicate woman, with red-brown hair and a milky, clear complexion, a woman who was not terribly intelligent but who loved us very much. (Wasn't that true? Or am I imagining it? She must have loved us, don't you think, to marry *him,* to bring a man home with her to be *our father?)* I invented a scene in which she came upon you, the two of you, struggling red-faced and hideous together—she heard this strange groaning, gasping noise, yanked open a door—saw him straining above you, heaving and grunting, and then saw *you*—your small wet face turned toward her, your mouth twisted: I invented the scene, sick with despair, with longing, hardly able to write down the words one by one as they forced their way into my consciousness. Then I stopped, quit; I could do no more, not a word more; I reeled with exhaustion.

I invented another scene, years later. A sketch for a scene. Mother has been drinking, you've been married now almost a year, she sits in your tiny kitchen in Yewville, nursing a beer, blowsy now and decidedly fat, muttering to herself. You want her to leave: you want to start supper. You want her gone before your husband gets home from work. But she sits there, grinning and muttering to herself. She isn't quite "right," is she? Everyone whispers, everyone knows. Not quite "right in the head." Her legs are lardish, the veins distended and broken. Mother. Our mother. Out of her body we came, far from her body we flee, fascinated, repulsed. She is muttering about the old times, the farm, her first husband's death and her second husband's death, how unfair it is, how unjust, the world is an ugly place for a person like her, who meant no one any harm—her own children betrayed her, turned against her, destroyed her chances for happiness. She does not look at you. You turn away, your face burning; you are very upset. But she does not look at you. She will not. Grotesque sentimental tears spill down across her slack cheeks; she is dreaming of *him* again, yearning for *him;* she loved him, we were told, far more than she had loved our father.... But why, why? My God, why? *Him?*

She loved him. He died; he was buried; the farm was sold and we all moved to town. Her life was over. Is over. In this scene she does not reproach you for anything—not a thing! If she did come upon you, the two of you, a scrawny twelve-year-old squirming in the arms of a ruddy-faced gasping man, she will never say a word.

I must erase all this.

I must begin again.

Fiction is not lies, not a clever tissue of lies; it is the desperate invention of a form of truth, less terrible than truth itself, but more inventive. If, in reality, our stepfather sought you out innumerable times, and if you offered no resistance, if you were stupidly passive, like a stunned animal, meekly submitting to fate, I could not bring myself to write of *that:* I would select one or two instances, I would dramatize them, so far as I was capable of dramatizing them, and, in the interests of art, I would pretend that the experiences, which covered a period of years, took place within a very restricted time-span, and totally obliterated all other concerns. If I had to admit that for the most part, day after day after relentless day, we were a quite ordinary farm family, and even *he* was a quite ordinary man—I could not bring myself to write at all. And if I had to deal with your hysteria after his death—which, too, went on and on and on, subsiding and surfacing for years, and no doubt continuing into your marriage at the age of eighteen to a man to whom I never spoke more than a dozen words (that contemptible ox!), if I had to deal with your grief, your frantic guilt, I could not invent a single sentence, so overwhelming would my disgust be.

You imagined that you had actually killed him, at last, after all the extravagant plans, you insisted—do you remember?—that it was you, and not me, who scrambled down the hill to the river-bed, to crouch over him, jeering, triumphant, your hands clasped together and gripped tight between your knees, your back hunched, neck craning, mouth twisted in exultation—you insisted it was you, and not me, who seized his head and brought it down hard, just once, very hard, on the edge of a rock....

You insisted you had killed him.

You insisted you were guilty.

At night I woke, grinding my teeth in my sleep, waking myself with the ugly jarring noise. I loved you, wasn't that enough? I saw your haggard face, your deep-set staring eyes. I wanted to run to your room, wanted to shake you, to smother you, anything to shut you up....It was nothing but babbling, crazy babbling, you must have known no one had killed him: he had been out there alone, had lost his balance and fallen some thirty feet, had died, alone, no one else near. *No one else near.* He had been missing for an hour when Momma sent me out to look for him. I found him and he was dead. Dead. It was over, he was dead. And it was a natural death: coronary thrombosis.

The farm was sold, people helped us pack, one of our neighbors drove the rented van to Yewville, you and I rode together in the front seat, absolutely silent, mute, staring ahead at the road. Why did nothing look familiar? Field after field of corn...wheat...barley...corn again, stalks seven or eight feet tall...the wind rustling through the leaves, that dry rasping unnerving sound...the dirt road giving way to a blacktop road...the heat of August, heat-waves writhing above the pavement...in the distance...wavy, watery, unfathomable ...disappearing as we drew closer, then reappearing farther off....

Mr. Breslow, someone is saying, politely, urgently, Mr. Breslow, we should be starting to the hall now, it's almost seven o'clock.

Would you be so kind as to...? they say smiling, crowding near. And this one also, this book, it's for my niece...if you would be so kind as to inscribe it, to Linda...? *Linda.* Yes.

Slowly, dully, I take someone's offered arm, I am careful of the unfamiliar stairs, careful to reply to every question that is asked, no matter if I understand it or not. What is this place? Who are these people, their radiant faces surrounding me? Why am I here tonight, being hurried politely along? Perhaps it is my day of trial, perhaps it is my execution. I mirror the alert interested faces, I ape them. It's a technique like any other. What begins as talent ends as technique. Later, they will say I was exquisitely polite, a true gentleman, with a quiet sense of humor, modest, thoughtful, slow-speaking—after all, I am not exactly in my prime now—and rather easily distracted.

I scan the rows for you, the dim bobbing faces. Who are they, all these people? What have they come to discover? I can't see you. I can't see you. So cruel! Never once did you come to hear me, never, though I gave a reading one day in Iowa City, not fifteen miles from your home. Cruel! Selfish! Unforgiving bitch!…But tonight, is it possible you have made the journey? In that case…

Mr. Breslow…?

Yes…? What…?

I am scanning the audience for you, I am looking for your small pale empty face. You are in the audience somewhere? Tonight? Here? Now?

Acclaim For the Work of JOYCE CAROL OATES!

"Few writers better illuminate the mind's most disturbing corners."

—*Seattle Times*

"I love her writing…Oates is simply the most consistently inventive, brilliant, curious, and creative writer going, as far as I'm concerned."

—*Gillian Flynn*

"Dread, in fiction, can be a magnificent thing…Oates isn't writing horror fiction, but she might as well be. Her stories pack the same kind of visceral wallop."

—*Los Angeles Times*

"Oates is a mind-reader who writes psychological horror stories about seriously disturbed minds, and it's hard to tear your eyes away."

—*New York Times Book Review*

"Wrenching…a grim examination of how humans cope with unspeakable physical and psychological pain. She illuminates the darkest corners and shows us the startled, troubled creatures hiding there, nursing their wounds, staring back at us, their kin."

—*Cleveland Plain-Dealer*

"Brilliant…A shattered spirit, furious, violent, confused, a creature of the gothic underbelly where Oates's sympathies most often lie…breathtaking."

—*Washington Post*

"Grimly compelling...terrifyingly hallucinatory."
—*Wall Street Journal*

"Sinister, edgy, delectably creepy."
—*San Francisco Chronicle*

"A graceful and excruciating story."
—*USA Today*

"Powerful...feverish..."
—*The New Yorker*

"Immensely moving."
—*People*

"An urgently compelling and drastically revealing study of evil, habitual terror, and survival."
—*Booklist*

"This unsettling tale showcases Oates's masterful storytelling."
—*Publishers Weekly*

"A raw and earnest mix of fiery drama and...bone-cold truths."
—*NPR, All Things Considered*

"A disturbing psychological thriller."
—*New York Post*

"Haunting, terrifying, disturbing."
—*Atlantic Wire*

"Oates veers between strikingly precise images and feelings recounted in eloquent prose and bluntly direct incomplete sentences that jab at the reader with knifelike edges."
—*Boston Globe*

"[Oates is] a superb storyteller…unsurpassed."

—*Atlanta Journal-Constitution*

"One of America's most accomplished writers."

—*St. Louis Post-Dispatch*

"Joyce Carol Oates, author of dozens of grim novels, knows the dark side of life better than most and explores it here in a lean and disturbing tale that reverberates after its ending."

—*Columbus Dispatch*

"Oates makes us squirm as she forces us to see some of the action through [a] twisted and warped perspective."

—*Kirkus*

"Joyce Carol Oates's latest book is a horror. As in horror story, frightening, alarmingly realistic. The monsters…are people, not fantastical creatures from the deep or outer space. They are human."

—*PopMatters*

"Ambitious, complex, and powerful."

—*Greensboro News and Record*

"A torrentially imaginative, compulsively readable tour de force."

—*Sunday Telegraph*

"A book of irresistible and terrible locomotion."

—*Commercial Appeal*

"Overwhelmingly vivid and powerful."

—*New York Review of Books*

"She is a genius."

—*Independent*

"A writer of extraordinary strengths."

—*Guardian*

"A phenomenon."

—*Daily Mail*

"A chilling thriller…Gothic in its paranoia, but thoroughly modern in its observations."

—*Bustle*

"Dark, bloody, and unforgiving."

—*Barnes & Noble Review*

"Oates creates characters that make you think about the potential madness in others, something that, in the end, turns out to be more than a little scary."

—*Missourian*

"Makes your skin crawl even as it also seems completely believable, like something you heard once, from where, you can't remember."

—*Minneapolis Star Tribune*

"A book not to be taken lightly…[it] pushes us to confront what lurks behind the front door."

—*New York Journal of Books*

The murdered man had been identified as "William Raymond Cobb of Elton, California." His wallet and rented car, a new-model Infiniti, were missing, and Nevada State police were searching for a female companion with whom he'd registered in the motel as "Mr. & Mrs. Elton Flynn of Los Angeles."

The desk clerk at the Paradise Motel told police that it had been obvious to him that "Mr. & Mrs. Flynn" hadn't been married. The man had behaved nervously and guiltily, making awkward jokes; must've been twenty years older than the woman; the woman was beautiful, glamorous; looked like a supermodel, or an actress, or a hooker—"but a high-class hooker." Another witness, staying at the motel, claimed she'd seen the woman swimming in the pool, wearing a tiny yellow bikini; the woman and Cobb were swimming and splashing in the pool, drunk; later, in the cocktail lounge, the couple had been observed quarreling by several persons, including the bartender. The desk clerk described the missing woman suspect as platinum blond, approximately twenty-three years old, stylishly dressed; about five foot five, weighing maybe one hundred pounds. Other witnesses recalled her seeming drugged, or drunk; as friendly and smiling; as not friendly at all but stiff, icy-cold—"Looking at you like she'd like to slit your throat..."

HARD CASE CRIME BOOKS BY JOYCE CAROL OATES:

DOUBLE TROUBLE
THE TRIUMPH OF THE SPIDER MONKEY

SOME OTHER HARD CASE CRIME BOOKS YOU WILL ENJOY:

JOYLAND *by Stephen King*
THE COCKTAIL WAITRESS *by James M. Cain*
THIEVES FALL OUT *by Gore Vidal*
CUT ME IN *by Ed McBain*
QUARRY *by Max Allan Collins*
THE KNIFE SLIPPED *by Erle Stanley Gardner*
THE LAST STAND *by Mickey Spillane*
BLOOD SUGAR *by Daniel Kraus*
LEMONS NEVER LIE *by Donald E. Westlake writing as Richard Stark*
ARE SNAKES NECESSARY? *by Brian De Palma and Susan Lehman*
KILLER, COME BACK TO ME *by Ray Bradbury*
FIVE DECEMBERS *by James Kestrel*
THE HOT BEAT *by Robert Silverberg*
LOWDOWN ROAD *by Scott Von Doviak*
SEED ON THE WIND *by Rex Stout*
FAST CHARLIE *by Victor Gischler*
NOBODY'S ANGEL *by Jack Clark*
DEATH COMES TOO LATE *by Charles Ardai*
INTO THE NIGHT *by Cornell Woolrich and Lawrence Block*
THE GET OFF *by Christa Faust*
SUPERMAX *by Ken Bruen and Jason Starr*